DATE DUE

DEMCO, INC. 38-2931

THE DRUMS OF CHAOS

BY

RICHARD L. TIERNEY

THE DRUMS OF CHAOS

RICHARD L. TIERNEY

MYTHOS BOOKS LLC

POPLAR BLUFF

MISSOURI

2008

Mythos Books LLC
351 Lake Ridge Road,
Poplar Bluff,
MO 63901
United States of America

www.mythosbooks.com

Published by Mythos Books LLC 2008

FIRST EDITION

ISBN 0-9789911-6-8

Set in *Rusticana* & *Adobe Jenson Pro.*

Rusticana by Linotype Hell AG.
www.linotypecom

Adobe Jenson Pro by Adobe Systems Incorporated.
www.adobe.com

Typesetting, layout and design by PAW.

OTHER WORKS BY RICHARD L. TIERNEY

Collected Poems: Nightmares & Visions
Arkham House

The House of the Toad
Fedogan & Bremer

The Scroll of Thoth
Chaosium Inc.

WITH DAVID C. SMITH

The Ring of Ikribu
Demon Night
When Hell Laughs
Endithor's Daughter
Against the Prince of Hell
Star of Doom

For the Witch of the Mists: Ban Mak Morn

WITH ROBERT E. HOWARD

Hawks of Outremer

CONTENTS

INTRODUCTION

The only reason I can think of not to call *The Drums of Chaos* Richard Tierney's masterpiece is that it might imply he will never reach its heights again, and there is certainly no reason to think that. But it is his finest prose so far, and that is saying something extraordinary, since Tierney is the obvious heir to Robert E. Howard's muse, as his many tales of Simon of Gitta and Red Sonja have amply proven. *The Drums of Chaos* illustrates like no previous Tierney opus what a wizard he is at synthesizing the *Weird Tales* cosmology (i.e., Howard's Hyborian Age *plus* Lovecraft's Cthulhu Mythos *plus* Clark Ashton Smith's Commoriom Myth Cycle *plus* the Bierce-Chambers-Derleth Mythology of Hastur) with *Star Wars,* Roman history, the Bible, and Gnosticism. This time one can taste a significant pinch of M.R. James as well.

The Drums of Chaos is essentially a hybridizing of the Passion narrative of Jesus Christ with Lovecraft's "The Dunwich Horror." As such, it certainly invites the characterization "blasphemy" more than just about any previous Lovecraft-inspired work, despite the fact that the word is almost casually tossed about within the confines of that subgenre. Readers of "The Dunwich Horror" have not been slow to notice the parody of the gospel narrative in that tale. After all, the virgin-born Wilbur Whateley is the semi-human offspring of "heavenly" powers sent to earth on a mighty mission of redemption, even though it would appear that way to only a handful of "enlightened" followers. The precocious lad shows profound erudition and grows to an early apprehension of his destiny. Prematurely slain, he is essentially reincarnated/resurrected as his invisible Twin and goes on to experience a kind of crucifixion atop Sentinel Hill, calling on his Father as he is driven forth into the Void from which he had first emerged. Tierney's genius insight is to turn things right around, to put the cart before the horse. In *The Drums of Chaos* we discover that the original gospel events were already like those of "The Dunwich Horror," even that "The Dunwich Horror" implicitly chronicles the Second Coming of the Christ (a theme I have pursued in a minor salute to this great novel, in my short story "Acute Spiritual Fear"). Likewise, if you have ever felt sure that Howard fashioned the blasphemous name Gol-goroth (one of his Old Ones) from the New Testament Golgotha, the site of the crucifixion, Tierney will show you that you were righter than you knew.

Tierney is a longstanding student of that class of pious novels which seek to bring the gospel narrative to life by the twin processes of psychologizing and historicizing the Jesus story (much as many allegedly nonfiction biographies of Jesus unwittingly do). These novels (Frank

Yerby's *I, Judas,* Thomas B. Costain's *The Silver Chalice,* etc.) seek to provide plausible motivation for actions which meet us in the New Testament with the sacred arbitrariness of fulfilled prophecy and divine miracle. (One can already witness the same process in the gospels themselves, where Matthew and John, especially, posit this or that motive for events Mark just lays down by authorial fiat, the greatest example being the betrayal of Judas.) And they tend, like all life of Jesus books, to make the Christian mythology (the healings, exorcisms, death, and resurrection of God's Son) into historically plausible events, much as Plutarch did when he historicized Osiris and Isis as ancient royalty in Egypt. Tierney does the same, only his lexicon is that of the Cthulhu Mythos. Tellers of the Jesus story, whether admitted novelists or historical reconstructionists, are trying to reconnect the dots by imposing this or that favorite template. Eighteenth century Rationalists like Paulus and Venturini, for example, were committed to the idea that all gospel events actually happened as reported, but their connection and explanation were in every case purely naturalistic. For example, Jesus couldn't have walked on the water—unless he knew where the stepping stones were! He couldn't have miraculously multiplied loaves and fishes, but what if he was being supplied extra food by his Essene buddies in the cave behind him? He died and was seen alive afterward, but this is because he merely passed out on the cross and was later revived in the cool of the garden tomb. Tierney does the same, only his is admittedly fictive. Suppose the gospel events happened by means of sorcery and/or superscience? This premise is not far from that of UFO sects who assimilate Jesus and imagine him virgin born by means of artificial insemination, healing by means of advanced medicine, raised from the dead like Klaatu in *The Day the Earth Stood Still,* and ascended by being beamed up. Such cultists are writing fiction without knowing it, while Tierney knows it and does an infinitely better job at it.

Even so, reading *The Drums of Chaos,* one is reminded of certain lines of inquiry among reputable New Testament scholars. Morton Smith (*The Secret Gospel, Jesus the Magician*), for example, demonstrated extensive parallels between the gospel depictions of Jesus the miracle working Son of God and ancient Hellenistic magicians, whose mystic initiation into divine sonship and miraculous powers was marked by the descent of a divine familiar in the form of a bird. And Barbara Thiering (*The Qumran Origins of the Christian Church*; *Jesus and the Riddle of the Dead Sea Scrolls*; *Jesus of the Apocalypse*) has recently revived the old Essene hypothesis which decodes a number of miracle stories as accounts of sectarian intrigue among Jesus, John the Baptist, Simon Magus, and their sectarian rivals.

I have mentioned the tendency among Jesus-novelists to add motivation and plausibility to arbitrary events in the gospels. You will find that Tierney's attempts often ring truer precisely for their extravagance!

What, for instance, is the sober historian to make of Matthew's odd report (27:52-53) that, coincident with Jesus' death on the cross, a great number of the local deceased came to life again and appeared in Jerusalem? Well, Tierney knows what to make of it! And the fact that only fantasy makes sense of it demonstrates, here and elsewhere, that we are just not dealing with history in the first place, that it did not begin as historical narration and cannot plausibly be made into historical narrative.

Previous embellishers of the Jesus story have made some narrative decisions that Tierney accepts and then hijacks in his own new direction. Among them are the love relation between Jesus and Mary Magdalene (a very old idea, present in the Gospel of Philip and recurring in Mormonism, the Radio Church of God, and *Jesus Christ Superstar*), the identification of Mary Magdalene with Mary the sister of Martha of Bethany, and of Joseph of Arimathea as Jesus' uncle, to whom the savior vouchsafes the Holy Grail for safe disposition to England.

Again, Tierney manages to make narrative sense of several odd items that have baffled previous gospel novelizers, to say nothing of New Testament historians, including the widespread ancient report that Jews worshipped an ass' head in the Holy of Holies, or that the rediscovery of the Ark of the Covenant would herald the Last Days. The Sect of the Thirty, as well as Dositheus' bid for its leadership following the death of John the Baptizer, comes right from ancient Jewish-Christian lore (Jorges Luis Borges mentions the same group in his brief piece "The Thirty"). And whence the allegiance of Annas to the great serpent Set? Well, the Talmud somewhere refers to the "serpent's brood of the house of Annas." As for the general picture of Jews and Samaritans worshipping a raft of competing gods, albeit in secrecy, this late in history, it may seem strange to some, but Tierney's scenario will surprise no one who has perused Margaret Barker's *The Great Angel: A Study of Israel's Second God.* (There are glancing references to adjacent weird fiction as well, such as the titanic heartbeat tolling during the rampage of Wilbur's Twin in the 1970 film version of *The Dunwich Horror* and the note about a young Vanir fighting Golgoroth in the Howard-completion tale "Black Eons," *Fantasy Book,* # 16, 1985.)

The Drums of Chaos is the greatest adventure of Simon of Gitta, but it is also the culminating exploit of another, less known, Tierney hero (or anti -hero), the time-traveler John Taggart. Though he is explained sufficiently in the course of the book, you may appreciate his participation in the story a bit more if you know more about his background. Taggart is a narrative symbol of the bitter misanthropy occasionally evident in Tierney's work, especially his verse (see, for instance, his "To the Hydrogen Bomb" in his Arkham House *Collected Poems,* 1981). We meet Taggart first in the slightly tongue-in-cheek tale "Countdown for Kalara" (*Space and Time #*

56, 1980), where Taggart hates his life as a menial laborer in a meatpacking plant. With himself and his miserable state he pities yet despises the whole human race. Suddenly he is drawn into an intergalactic conflict by the interference of a fellow-misanthrope, Pitts, who has made his way into the confidence of an alliance of space conquerors who have determined to wipe out all human life in the universe, starting with Kalara, the planet formerly composed of the Asteroid field between Jupiter and Mars. It had been colonized by the last, most-evolved humanoids from earth, whom the Great Race of Yith retrojected through time onto that ancient world to preserve the human species, replanting them in the past. Taggart befriends a band of these rebels whose adopted home world is about to be destroyed by Pitts and his cohorts. Pitts, who has taken the alias Taaran, "The Hateful One" (actually the name of an old Celtic devil god), invites the hate-filled Taggart to join the fun, but the latter sympathizes with the noble Kalarans and helps the group of them to escape into space. He is not able to save their world. Pitts (Taaran) despises humanity for the endless suffering they have brought upon themselves. So does Taggart, but in the last resort he cannot bring himself to sign on for their entire obliteration.

The space-war scenario of "Countdown for Kalara" has a larger cosmological background, and this is spelled out in more detail in the novella "The Lords of Pain." Tierney has upended the Derlethian hierarchy of Elder Gods and Great Old Ones, with the result that Elder Gods are now understood as cosmic sadists who created life to supply them psychic nourishment. They are the Lords of Pain, and all suffering feeds them. The Great Old Ones oppose their interests and seek to wipe out all the life the Pain Lords created, defeating the Lords in the process. Serving the Great Old Ones are the interstellar race of the Zarrians, gigantic cyborgs or living machines. In particular, their master is Black Zathog, whose name suggests a form of Tsathoggua, but who seems rather to be an avatar of Yog-Sothoth. Serving the Lords of Pain, the creators of life, are the Galactics, a purely mechanical robot force built to police the galaxy by a since-perished organic race in ancient times. They still seek to preserve order and protect humanoid life. In this story, Taggart has seemingly come to share in the ultra-Schopenhauerian antipathy for all life, a sort of super-Buddhism with only one noble truth: "Life is suffering." And the only way to eliminate suffering is to put life out of its misery. "The Lords of Pain" tells of the ultimate fate of humankind: after a series of devastating nuclear wars between America, Russia, and China, the Zarrians moved in to mop up the remainder of the human race, recruiting for their own purposes a handful of humans, like Taaran and Taggart, whose abilities and sympathies were beyond those of the herd. Henceforth Taggart, Taaran, and others assist the Zarrians by a series of cross-time expeditions meant to prevent human suffering by crucial interventions in past history. Again, these expeditions seek to ameliorate suffering by eliminating the sufferers! In "The Lords of Pain," Taggart himself is trying to open a gate to the Old Ones, using the ancient magic gem, the Fire of Asshurbanipal (see Robert E. Howard's tale of that title). And the Lords of Pain play a key role in the mythic background of the Red Sonia novels of Tierney and David C. Smith.

The Winds of Zarr (Silver Scarab Press, 1975) has Taggart and Pitts as allies once again, working together amid the events of C.B. DeMille's Bible epic *The Ten Commandments* (the novella is dedicated to REH, CAS, HPL, and DeMille) to free Yog-Sothoth from his imprisonment within Mount Horeb/Sinai. Yahweh Sabaoth, you see, is one with Yog-Sothoth. Taggart so hates the inherent self-destructiveness of the human race that he wishes to put us out of our misery. There are other Taggart adventures including "The Howler in the Dark" (see my anthology, *The New Lovecraft Circle*, Fedogan & Bremer, 1996), where we hardly see either Taggart or Pitts. We only learn of some sadistic experiments performed upon hapless locals in this early tale reminiscent of Ramsey Campbell's "The Room in the Castle." Another Taggart tale is *Let There Be Darkness*, in which Taggart sets to rights the egregious injustices of Big Brother's regime in George Orwell's dystopian apocalypse *1984*, by provoking an invasion of earth by the Crustaceans of Yuggoth!

But we have background enough, I think, to see that, if *Winds of Zarr* is Tierney's Old Testament, *The Drums of Chaos* is his New Testament. If we think we may gauge some progression of religious thought from the less to the more humane between the two parts of the Bible, we see the same amelioration of the angry god of Tierney's imagination from one story to the other. This development can be traced not only through Taggart's particular utterances in *Drums of Chaos*, where he has rethought his rage against hapless humanity, but also in the fascinating discourses of Dositheus and Daramos. These Gnostic magi set forth the rudiments of a Higher Knowledge akin to that of Hindu-Buddhist Tantra, but also resembling the actual salvation mythology of historic Simonian Gnosticism. According to it, the soul of Simon, the Great Power of God, sought after the lost soul of his primordial soul mate the Ennoia, Sophia, the First Thought. She had been lost in the material world, her own creation, and her male counterpart sought her from one incarnation to another. Furthermore, all Gnostics possessing a fragment of the light of the two primordial entities shared this heavenly identity and destiny. This protological myth is set forth most completely and compactly in the pages of the Simon tale, "The Throne of Achamoth" (a collaboration between Tierney and yours truly, available in *The Azathoth Cycle*, (Chaosium, Inc, 1995). It represents an ingenious compilation of elements from the Cthulhu Mythos and from Valentinan, Simonian, and Manichean doctrines. Daramos must for the sake of the reader, demonstrate how the super-

Schopenhauerianism of Taggart can co-exist with the Gnostic Tantrism of Simon. The former tends to occupy the role of Lower Knowledge as measured against the Higher Knowledge of the latter. It is true as far as it goes, but Taggart is not yet the Gnostic initiate Simon is.

But in a larger sense, Tierney has reconciled the very different narrative worlds of Taggart and Simon by his fantastically imaginative employment of the old black magic of pulp fiction, making Sword-&-Sorcery blend seamlessly with Space Opera Scientifiction. Who would have guessed that the result would be far more than a work of entertainment, but in its own way a genuine gospel of the spiritual imagination?

Robert M. Price
Willow Springs,
North Carolina
March 2008
Hour of the Opening to Gol-goroth

Think not that I am come to destroy the law. . . . I am not come to destroy but to fulfil. For verily I say unto you, Till heaven and earth shall pass away, not one jot nor tittle shall pass from the law, until all be fulfilled.

Matthew, *v., 17-18*

PROLOG

The white-robed man sat motionless atop the barren hill, gazing southward. He sat in the southern quadrant of the circle drawn in the dust and divided into four parts. Before him ragged peaks extended into the wastelands, while behind him, far below, sprawled the surface of the wide Sea of the Arabah, its shimmering surface dimmed by a thin haze of dust. The sun, though bright in the near-cloudless sky, was losing some of its heat as it declined toward the western hills.

A breeze blew across the wide, flat top of the hill, fluttering the man's white robe and the loose ends of his white sash as he sat cross-legged and stared southward as if in a trance. The sun, edging lower, lined the features beneath the white headband—the large dark eyes, the prominent curved nose with flaring nostrils, the straggling beard that partly concealed a slightly receding chin. They were strange, rather striking features, somehow sheeplike or goatish in their overall cast.

There was a sound in the air, far off and high up. The man in white stirred slightly and looked toward the southwest. There, high above the hills, a faint black dot appeared against the glowing bronze of the late afternoon sky.

Closer it came, growing larger and larger, descending, while its strange high-pitched humming increased. It appeared flat and circular, oblong in silhouette, with something projecting upward in the middle. It approached rapidly, but slowed as it drew near.

Then it was at the lip of the hill's flat top, little more than twenty paces away, settling slowly down while its humming diminished. It was like a horizontal disk about twelve feet in diameter, gleaming a dark metallic blue, its edge surrounded by a solid wall or rail about three feet high. The upright object in it was a man.

The thing came to a complete halt and its humming ceased. Yet it continued to rest in midair about the length of a man's arm above the ground. Slowly the figure within it climbed over the rail, dropped to the sandy hilltop and walked forward.

The man in white rose. He was tall, perhaps half a head taller than average, and solidly built. His strange features remained expressionless.

The newcomer drew near and stopped. He was a man of medium height, on the slender side, and clad entirely in black. His shirt, long trousers and shoes were of a strange cut, and his face and hands seemed almost white in contrast to their blackness. He wore a wide belt, seemingly of woven strands of blue metal; its clasp glowed with a dim blue radiance. His brown hair and beard were short and neatly trimmed. Strangest of all, his intent brown eyes stared through transparent discs held before them by a dark framework that hooked behind his ears.

"I know you," the man in white said in Latin, "and I know why you come. You are one whom men of old called 'the wizard'."

The black-clad man scowled briefly as in puzzlement; then, hesitantly, in the same language, he said, "Your—father—must have sent you dreams. You see, I know you, also. You are called Bar Yosef, but your real father's name would be—"

"Peace! You shall not tempt me as you have come to do, adversary of mankind."

The one called "wizard" glanced about him at the rock-littered hilltop. "You have been here many days, Bar Yosef—longer than any mere human could have endured without food or water, I think. Yet you are partly human, and so you must be hungry. For you, the son of your father, I am prepared to do much. If you wish, I will make some of these stones about you turn into loaves of bread."

"No." The man in white abruptly shook his head so that his tangled brown locks whipped about his shoulders. "It is written that a man shall live not only by bread, but also by those things that come forth from Yahweh-Zava'ot."

"You know the old writings," said the wizard, "and you do not hesitate to speak the Name. And I am sure you know far older writings, and even the Name's original form. But as for mankind—they shall not live at all if you do as your father intends."

The white-clad one stood motionless, saying nothing.

"Will you not eat or drink, then?"

"My preparation must continue."

The wizard sighed. "Will you let me try to convince you otherwise? I think I can, if you will come with me for an hour."

The one called Bar Yosef stared at the other for a long moment. "I sense no treachery in you. I will come. But I will not be tempted."

"We shall see."

The white-clad man stepped out of the circle drawn in the dust and followed the wizard to the strange craft that hung motionless just above the ground. They climbed in over the side, and the wizard touched one of many glowing squares set into a sloping panel of dark metal. Immediately the craft began to hum and rise. The man in black touched more of the squares; the breeze of their passage became a wind as they sped northward. Then a shimmering dome of bluish light sprang into being about them, and though their speed increased they felt the wind of their passage no more. Below them the brown slopes dropped away until they were hurtling above the gray waters of the Sea of Arabah far below.

The man in white watched as the westward hills sped by, as the sinking sun was repeatedly hid by their peaks and exposed anew. His features remained impassive, but his large eyes widened even more with what seemed to be a touch of wonder.

"This is but the tiniest taste of the power you could have, Bar Yosef. Will you not reconsider?"

The white-clad man said nothing.

The sun set as they angled toward the northwest. The sky was the color of glowing bronze, the few clouds in it purple and bordered with fire. The sea passed behind them and they flew over ridges and hills shadowed with dusk. Then, as they angled downward, the form of a large walled city came into view, sprawling over two ridges and the shallow ravine between them. The pinpoint lights of many torches and cooking-fires gleamed in the gathering darkness.

"The holy city!" muttered Bar Yosef. "So quickly. . . ."

Slowly the craft settled down, down, until it was directly above a complex containing the largest buildings in the city—a magnificent columned structure in the midst of wide marble-paved courts, and a dark, battlemented fortress just to the north of it.

Then the craft was still, sorcerously suspended just over the highest tower of the columned structure. The shimmering blue glow vanished and a cool breeze was felt once more. Bar Yosef turned to the man in black.

"Enemy of mankind, why have you brought me here to this, the holiest of temples?"

For answer, the wizard handed him a blue-glowing belt like his own.

"Put it on," he said.

The man in white stood motionless, his dark eyes glowing with a mute inquiry.

The wizard touched his own belt-clasp. It suddenly gleamed like a fire-filled diamond. Immediately the man was surrounded by a bright, unnatural radiance that made his flesh and even his black clothing like sunlit alabaster. Bar Yosef shielded his eyes until they adjusted. When he looked again, he saw that the man had climbed from the craft and was standing in space a few feet away, gleaming with a blue-white radiance as bright as the morning star.

"Put on your belt," the wizard repeated. "Come down with me into the innermost temple. I would have you see what your father is preparing for you."

Bar Yosef shook his head and threw down the belt; it clattered metallically upon the floor of the sky-craft.

"You have not seen your father," said the wizard. "But once, long ago, I saw his shadow."

"You shall not tempt me!" Bar Yosef said firmly.

The wizard sighed, touched his belt-clasp and floated back to the craft. Once within, the radiance blinked out and he was again a man clad in black.

Below, from the darkening courts and streets, came the babble of many voices raised in excitement.

The wizard touched a glowing square on the panel. Again the dim blue glow arced above them as the craft sped northward, faster and faster; again the hills fell away, until the pair were speeding at an incredible velocity above the wide valley where the Jordan wound in deep shadow. West of the hills the fires of sunset were but a dimming red glow, and beneath them the far-off Great Sea lay like a band of dark gray. Neither man spoke; only the shrill humming of the strange sky-craft sounded in their ears.

They passed above a vast lake, then a smaller one. Ahead loomed the towering bulk of a three-peaked mountain, its snow-streaked summits dimly white against the night's deep purple.

"The mount of Baal-Hermon," muttered Bar Yosef. "Why do you bring me here, wizard?"

The man in black did not answer until at length the craft had come to rest upon the loftiest of the three peaks and the pair had clambered out.

"Look about you," he said.

Bar Yosef did so. The west was now shrouded in twilight, but still visible even to the horizon of the Great Sea. The lights of villages gleamed here and there amid the wooded foothills below. To the east the desert land was bathed in the eerie light of a newly-risen moon.

"All this could be yours to rule," said the wizard. "All this, and all that lies beyond. All this world from pole to pole, and all the people who now live so tragically upon it. Would not this be better for them—and for you—than what your father intends?"

The wind blew cold among the rocks and spires. Bar Yosef shook his head; a sadness gleamed in his large dark eyes.

"No, there must be an end," he said. "I will save them from their misery."

"You can! But there is another way than your father's."

"No!" said Bar Yosef with sudden passion. "Begone from me, adversary!"

"You call me man's adversary, yet you would—"

"I would end their misery." The man in white stood tall, rigid; his large eyes seemed almost luminous in the moonlight. "And, as for me, it is written: 'You shall serve only your lord Yahweh-Zava'ot.'"

The wizard sighed in resignation. His shoulders seemed to slump slightly. "Very well, then. Come. I will take you back."

There was silence between them as they sped southward beneath the glittering stars. Far below gleamed the faint lights of torchlit villages—small sparks of warmth lost in the midst of immense cold shadows.

When at last they came again to the level mountaintop in the southern wastelands, and the man called Bar Yosef stepped down from the craft, the wizard asked, "Must all their thousands of years of sufferings, then, be for nothing?"

Bar Yosef's strange features, limned in the moonlight and the dim blue glow of the wizard's craft, again showed sadness. "They shall know mercy."

"Yet you are partly human, even as they."

"And you are entirely of them, wizard—yet you speak as if you were not. So it is always with you. Go, adversary of your own kind, and leave me to my destiny."

"You could rule them! I could give you the power!"

Suddenly a far, shrill humming came from the southeastern sky. The two glanced up and saw a number of blue-gleaming lights moving among the stars, growing brighter.

"They come to minister to me," said Bar Yosef, "—and to see that I am unharmed. My time here is fulfilled. You must go now."

The wizard nodded. "I know. The dreams sent by your father reached minds other than yours. I will go, but you will see me again. You are human. I hope you will think on my words."

The wizard's craft sped off into the sky, vanishing silently amid the stars toward the north. Now no bluish glow shone from it.

Slowly the man in white turned and sat down once again in the southern quadrant of his dust-drawn circle, then waited with impassive features as the blue-white lights in the southeast grew steadily brighter.

THE BLACK SYNAGOGUE

CHAPTER I

Gray clouds moved across the sky. A chill wind stirred the dust amid the grassy mounds and the jagged remnants of old walls and foundations. Among these ruins a lean old man labored with shovel and grubbing-hoe while his white hair and beard fluttered in the wind.

There came a footfall. Then, "Ho, Dositheus—still at it, I see."

The old man stood erect, pulling his brown symbol-emblazoned cloak more closely about him, and stared at the newcomer. "Had you but helped with the work, Simon," he panted accusingly, "it would have gone faster."

The one called Simon shook his head. He was a young man in his mid-twenties, tall and well built. The wind fluttered the edges of his dark cloak and the straight black locks that hung nearly to his shoulders. There was something grim in the cast of his angular, clean-shaved features and his dark, deep-set eyes.

"You work is madness. It will lead to nothing. Have done with it, O mentor, and come back to the inn."

Dositheus glared at him, then threw down his spade; it clattered on the stony dirt. "It *was* here, I tell you! Did I not show you the passage in the ancient book of Mattan, Priest of Baal, which says—?"

"Madness," Simon repeated. "The author of that work was as crazy as the sorcerer who owned it. I still think you paid far too much for the purchase of that sorcerer's books."

"Prodikos was no ordinary sorcerer, as you well know. He was the greatest mage in Ephesus, a city renowned for its magic. When he—died—I bid for whatever I could afford of his library, for it would have been a crime to let his books fall into the hands of anyone less learned than I."

Simon shook his head again. "You are obsessed. Day after day, for nearly a week now, you have come up here to delve in the dirt. What do you expect to find on this bleak ridgetop? Treasure?"

Dositheus' eyes narrowed, glittered. "You know better than that, Simon."

"Aye. Always you seek for some hidden knowledge that will add to your sorcerous power. But here? Look!" He swept his left arm toward the wide expanse of the ruin-cluttered ridge; as he did so his cloak fell open, revealing a red-brown tunic and a wide belt from which hung a large knife and a Roman gladius, or short-sword. "Look—rocks, dry grass and the stubs of ruins, which are well over a thousand years old. Did you really hope that anything of value would remain here after—?"

"The ages have hidden much," hissed Dositheus. "Have you learned so little from me, and from the great mage Daramos under whom we studied for four years at Persepolis? There are secrets that have lain hidden in the earth a thousand times a thousand years—things of magic forged by sorcerers of bygone ages. What I seek is young by comparison—young on earth, that, is, for it was forged amid the stars aeons before it was brought to this ruin when it was yet the wizard-built Shrine of Hali."

Simon pulled his cloak about him again, shuddering from something more than the chill of the wind. He did not like the reminder that this was the site of Hali, that town destroyed by the Twelve Tribes under the leadership of Joshua so many centuries ago. Dositheus' old scrolls from the library of Prodikos, most of them more ancient than the Five Books of Moses, told of monstrous rites that had been practiced here by the land's ancient inhabitants, not all of whom had been human.

"I would think, Dositheus, that after what we experienced in Ephesus you would leave off these dark delvings. I never again want to come as close to an unearthly doom as we did while confronting the servitors of Assatur, the Star-God."

Dositheus laughed suddenly. "And, yet, Simon, it was your own delvings into dark things that got us into that peril. Your goal then was revenge upon Rome for Helen's death."

"Speak not of that!" growled Simon warningly.

"Very well. But now you seek the Romans who slew your parents eight years ago and sold you into the arena. I think that if my delvings turn up a source of power, you will use it readily enough."

"A sword will suffice for what I have to do. But, come—we should get on our way. It is a long way back to the inn."

Dositheus nodded reluctantly, stashed his tools in a rock cleft, then took up a long wooden staff and accompanied Simon from the ruins and down a path that hugged the slope of the hill. They walked briskly, and Simon once again marveled at his white-haired mentor who, although in his seventies, seemed spry as a goat. As they hastened on, the wind continued to blow, bending the dry grasses and rattling the leaves of the occasional oaks. Infrequently the westering sun peeked between the cloud layers, giving color to the gray slopes and ridges that undulated down before them to the distant shore of the Great Sea and the walled town of Ecdippa, anciently called Achzib.

"That is another reason I must soon go my own way," Simon said presently as they walked. "In addition to avoiding any more of your entanglements with dark magic, I must do what I came here to do."

"I see." Dositheus was quiet for some moments, then, "What about young Menander, and the girl, Ilione? You rescued her from the dark designs of her false father Prodikos; she is partly your responsibility."

"No. Prodikos' daughter decided to go with you and Menander back to Persepolis to study under the mage Daramos. You should have gone there as you originally intended instead of accompanying me here to the land of my birth.

"Perhaps. But that was before I purchased Prodikos' books and learned of what might lie hidden in the ruins of Hali."

"And what might that be, Dositheus?"

"Ha! So you are interested."

Simon sighed. "No. Forget I asked."

They strode on in silence. For nearly two hours they walked, ever downward toward the town beside the sea, by worn paths and shallow grassy valleys and low ridges, until at last they began to see other people—farmers, sheepherders, travelers afoot and on mule-back. The sun had set beyond the sea when at last they spied the inn amid a clutter of lowly dwellings just outside the city walls, but its rays still tinged the undersides of massed clouds with red fire.

"Have you told Menander and Ilione yet?" said Dositheus.

"That I'm leaving? No—not yet."

Menander will be disappointed. He looks up to you, you know."

"I will miss him, too."

"And Ilione will be disappointed as well."

Simon said nothing.

"She's a lovely girl," Dositheus went on, "—as lovely in her own way as her sister Helen was. She even looks a bit like her, as I'm sure you've noticed."

Simon had noticed. Ilione, though not as tall as her older sister, and blonde rather than dark-haired, yet reminded him of Helen every time he looked at her.

"Fool!" Simon spun on old Dositheus, scowling. "Don't you realize that's another reason I must go? Ilione *is* lovely, but she can never replace Helen—and every time I see her it's like a knife being twisted inside me. Speak no more of this!"

Silent once more, they walked the short distance to the inn, Simon scowling in dark introspection, Dositheus' eyes showing irritation and a trace of sadness.

As they entered the gate leading to a path around the side of the building to a small garden, a stout man hurried out the front door and ran after them.

"A word with you, good sirs."

Simon felt a slight annoyance as the paunchy, bearded innkeeper plucked at Dositheus' sleeve. "Well, what is it?"

"I have information, perhaps," said the man, grinning and glancing from one of them to the other while rubbing his fat-fingered hands together.

"Yes, Isaac?" Dositheus inquired mildly, laying a coin into one of those hands.

"Two soldiers came here not an hour ago, inquiring about three Samaritan travelers and a golden-haired girl with them."

"Soldiers!" exclaimed Simon, laying a hand on his sword-haft. "Were they Romans?"

"I think not. They wore dark armor and black cloaks. I don't believe I've ever seen their like before."

"What did they want?" asked Dositheus.

"They asked where to find you. When I said I did not know, they asked where you roomed." The innkeeper glanced up at the second story of the building.

"And I supposed you told them, for a consideration?" Simon growled.

The man shrugged and spread his palms. "No, no, of course not—yet, they may have learned. I saw them questioning the servants."

"Where did they go? Into the city?"

"No, young sir. They took the road toward the hills—the road upon which you have but now arrived."

Simon and Dositheus looked at one another, each one thinking the same thought.

"I thank you, Isaac," said Dositheus, laying another coin upon the innkeeper's palm. "If you see these men again, please let us know right away."

The man bowed. "I shall. Of course I shall." He turned and hastened away, his fixed grin flashing in his dark beard. Simon and Dositheus hurried up the outside stairway to the ledge that ran around the second story and strode rapidly to the suite they had rented. They tried the door, found it unlocked, and entered.

Two young people turned to face them from opposite corners of the room. One, a girl whose golden hair was done up in a loose coiffure, rose from a stool beside a fireplace where warm flames flickered. The other, a lad with eyes and hair as dark as Simon's own, rose also. A large black raven stood upon the table at which the boy had been seated, one claw resting upon a partly unrolled scroll.

"Menander, why isn't the door locked?" Simon demanded.

"Why should it be?" countered the lad. "Ilione and I are both here."

Simon and Dositheus closed the door behind them. Dositheus asked, "Did either of you, by any chance, happen to see two soldiers dressed in black?"

"I *told* you!" cried the girl, shooting an accusing glance at Menander. "I told you they were from my father, but you wouldn't listen—you said not to worry!" She ran forward and threw her arms around Simon. "Help me!" she cried. "My father—he's come back from the grave! He's sent his guards for me!"

Simon gripped her shoulders and shook her. "You've got to stop this, Ilione."

Dositheus laid a hand on the girl's brow, captured her gaze with his own and uttered a short prayer in a tongue she did not understand. She immediately relaxed a bit; her eyes, a delicate hazel in color, lost much of their anxiety.

"You are both such a comfort to me," she sighed, but with a quaver still in her voice. "Tell me, Simon, what did the old wizard say?"

Simon looked away uneasily, but Menander stepped forward a pace and said, "It is a benediction given to our people by the ancient prophet Moshe. It means: 'The Lord bless and keep you, the Lord make his face to shine upon—'"

"And you!" cried the girl, whirling. "You wouldn't listen to me—wouldn't lock the door, even—" She turned back to the others. "Simon, we saw them when we were coming back from shopping in town. We hid in the bushes until they left—Menander didn't want to, but I insisted. They questioned the servants."

"Did you hear what they said?" asked Dositheus.

"No—they were too far away. Why were they here, old mentor? What do they want?"

Simon and Dositheus glanced at one another.

"I knew it!" wailed the girl. "My father has come back—he has sent them for me!" She turned away and flung herself down upon a blanket-covered mat beside the fireplace, sobbing.

Menander advanced a step toward Dositheus. "Old mentor, is it true?"

Dositheus shook his head. "No, it is not possible. Prodikos is dead. Yet, those soldiers you saw were indeed asking about us. The innkeeper told us so."

"Gods!" The lad hurried to the girl's side. "Ilione, I'm sorry—I should have listened to you. But, please don't be frightened. They can't be your father's soldiers. You heard Dositheus—it's not possible!"

The girl continued to sob, ignoring him.

Simon went outside and made a quick circuit of the balcony surrounding the second floor. He saw no one that looked suspicious, though, of course, in the gathering shadows of twilight many forms could hide. To the west the walls of Ecdippa loomed against clouds tinged with the last vestige of sunset's glow; eastward, the sky was clearing and the pale stars of Virgo, with diamond-bright Spica in their midst, were rising above the hills.

Returning inside, he closed and barred the door. "Lock the outer door of the adjacent room, too, Menander," he said. Then, for Ilione's benefit, he added, "I've no doubt this is a false alarm, but for our own peace of mind we'll sleep with the inner doors open so that we can call to one another if need be."

Much later, after Ilione and Menander had retired to their separate chambers, Simon and Dositheus sat at the table in the main room and spoke in low whispers. The still flame of an oil lamp burned between them, and flames still flickered in the fireplace across the room. Above, amid the shadowy rafters, the raven perched in fitful sleep, stirring ever and anon with slight rustlings and croakings.

"What do you think, O mentor?" asked Simon.

"I do not know," said Dositheus. "The description of the soldiers fits those which Prodikos employed."

"He was indeed a sorcerer, one of the greatest and most foul. It is said that such often return from death, especially to avenge themselves upon those who were their undoing in life. Could he—?"

Dositheus shook his head. "No. The soul of Prodikos is surely bound in the hell of Harag-Kolath, together with the souls he held in thrall who died with him. Still, he did serve beings far mightier than he, and their minions may yet walk the earth. Is it possible that someone in their service took note of me at the auction in Ephesus when I purchased several of Prodikos' ancient books?" For several moments Dositheus scowled in silent thought; then, looking upward, he hissed, "Carbo—come down here!"

The raven stirred sleepily, fluttered its wings, croaked softly, then flapped down from the rafters to the table.

Dositheus pulled a small leather pouch from his robe, untied its drawstrings and poured from it perhaps a dozen white objects that rattled upon the table. Simon saw that they were carved of bone or ivory, faceted in a strange, irregular manner; each facet bore a graven symbol unfamiliar to him.

"Choose, Carbo," said Dositheus. "Tell us from where the men in black have come."

Again the raven croaked, as if in sleepy annoyance. Then, quickly, almost impatiently, it stooped and snapped up one of the white objects in its heavy bill. Dositheus took it from him.

"What nonsense is this?" asked Simon. "Do you seriously think that this raven can—?"

"Quiet, Simon! You have seen what Carbo can do. Did he not even save your life once? Watch, now."

Simon did, remembering with a slight prickle of gooseflesh that occasion when Carbo's judgment had proven better than Dositheus' own. Yes, the raven's intelligence was uncanny—yet, did Dositheus really believe in such a method of divination?

"Choose again, Carbo," muttered the old man. "Choose as many of the bones as you like."

Quickly the raven snatched up one more of them, dropped it in Dositheus' outstretched hand, then spread its wings and flapped heavily up to his rafter once more.

"No more?" said the old man, looking up. "Only two?"

The raven tucked its head under its wing.

"So much for that!" growled Simon, rising. "I'm for bed."

"Wait, Simon. This is curious. Carbo has picked the symbols for 'darkness" and "holy place'."

"And what does that mean?"

"I asked from where the men in black came."

Simon nodded. "I see. 'Black fane'—that sounds sinister enough, I grant. But I think you're just stirring up your fears for nothing, Dositheus. Anyway, your cryptic message tells us nothing concrete. Let's clear our minds with a good night's sleep."

Dositheus nodded, though doubt remained in his eyes.

They bedded down in their blankets on opposite sides of the hearth, and Dositheus was soon asleep. Simon, however, lay awake for some time, staring thoughtfully at the wavering light-pattern cast by the dying fire upon the ceiling.

His mind was made up. Today he had finished buying supplies in Ecdippa; tomorrow he would take what he needed of them and journey southward—alone.

He sighed and turned restlessly, gazing into the glowing coals. He would miss his three companions. For many weeks they had journeyed together, first by ship from Ephesus to Antioch, thence on foot southward to Byblos, Sidon, Tyre and finally Ecdippa. They had made their living as street magicians, Simon and Dositheus performing slight-of-hand wonders that made the crowd gape while Menander and Ilione acted as stage assistants or collected the spectators' donations. They were good at what they did and they worked well together.

It was during their stay in Antioch that Dositheus had announced his change of plans. Originally he had intended to journey with Menander and the orphaned Ilione to far Persepolis, where they would study mysterious arts under the tutelage of Daramos, greatest of mages. During the sea-passage from Ephesus, however, the old Samaritan scholar had time to read the ancient scrolls he purchased—and something he discovered in them made him decide to accompany Simon southward. Just what that discovery was he would not say, and Simon had not pressed him, his own dark goal being uppermost in his mind.

They had done well financially in the cities along their route, but once at Ecdippa Dositheus had lost interest in street-performing, leaving that to his three companions while he went forth during the day to delve in the ruins in the hills to the northeast.

The ruins of Hali, denounced in the *Book of Jasher,* which some said was older than the writings of the prophet Moshe.

Simon woke suddenly. He had heard a sound. The room was dark, the coals on the hearth barely glowing. There was a smell of smoke that was not of the fireplace, and he felt a draft. Then his skin prickled as he saw that the outside door stood open and two black forms stood in it, silhouetted against the starlit sky.

Simon moved slowly, holding his breath. His hands touched the handles of the sword and dagger that lay beside him.

The figures moved into the room. Bright metal glittered in their hands.

Simon leaped up, struck and slashed with all the skill and power of his gladiator-training. The blade of his sica ripped into the chest of one of the dark figures barely an instant before his Roman gladius shore through the neck-cords of the other. Instantly both of the men went down with a clatter.

"Dositheus!" yelled Simon. "Get up, quick! Bring light!"

But the old man was already on his feet, thrusting a torch into the heart coals. As the flame sprang up it revealed two black-cloaked forms sprawled on the floor. Highlights gleamed on helms and armor of black metal.

There was no blood.

"Simon!" Menander appeared in the doorway from the other apartment, clad only in a tunic, an unshaded oil lamp in his hand. "What happened?"

"Shut the door, Simon," urged Dositheus, bracketing his torch upon the wall. "Hurry! No one must know of this."

Simon did so, wondering at his old mentor's anxiety—and suddenly noticed that the door was curiously burned. A large semicircular chunk containing the lock and part of the crossbar had been neatly taken out of it and now lay on the floor; evidently the sound of its fall had been what had wakened him. The chunk and the place where it had been were charred black and smoldering at the edges.

"Baal!" gasped Simon. "Dositheus, what in the name of Hades—?"

Ilione, clad in a white shift, appeared in the doorway behind Menander. Her eyes widened. "Gods! My father's guards!" she gasped, turning pale and gripping the door frame for support.

"No," said Dositheus, stooping beside the still forms. "That is not possible. Yet they may well have been minions of the same dark cult which your father served. Look!" He rolled one of the bodies over and pointed to a black-and-yellow medallion upon its chest. "See those inset jewels? They form the sign of the Bull's Face, emblem of the Cult of Assatur!"

But Simon was looking at the gaping wound his sword had made in the man's neck. There was no blood, and even as he watched the wound seemed to be slowly closing, knitting.

"Dositheus—*look out!*"

The old man gasped as the fallen soldier's hand shot out and gripped him by the throat. Ilione screamed. Simon snarled and struck with the short sword, shearing through muscles and vertebrae so that the guardsman's head fell back and hung by a shred of flesh and tendon—but still the hand continued to squeeze Dositheus' throat. Simon cursed frantically and hacked at the arm; it slackened its grip and fell to the floor, severed at the elbow.

"Simon! The other one!" screamed Menander.

Simon whirled to see the other soldier rising, its chest wound knitting bloodlessly beneath its medallion. Bright metal glittered in its rising hand. Simon ducked instinctively—just as a pencil-thin lance of light crackled from the weapon. Yelling, he leaped and struck; the guard's black-helmed head spun from his shoulders and went clattering into a corner. For a moment the body stood upright, wobbling uncertainly, then crashed to the floor.

"Gods!" cried Menander.

Dositheus rose, coughing and clutching at his throat, staggered to a chair and sat down. Menander placed his lamp on the table, then rushed to Ilione, who had slid to her knees and was clutching the door frame in wide-eyed terror.

Simon knelt cautiously by the dead guardsmen, his blade ready. The bodies did not move—they seemed truly dead now. But still there was no blood. Slowly he walked back to his blankets, put on his sword belt over his tunic and sheathed his weapons, never once taking his eyes from the still forms.

They did not move.

Dositheus rose from his chair, stooped, lifted from the decapitated guard's right hand a small object of silvery metal and held it close to the lamp. Simon advanced and looked at it. It was a mirror-bright sphere somewhat large than a walnut with a tube of similar metal about the length of a man's finger protruding from it.

"What is it?" Simon demanded.

"A weapon," muttered Dositheus. "A strange weapon. I have never seen its like. It shot forth that crackling ray."

Simon glanced at the far wall, where a small blackened patch smoldered upon the plaster. "Sorcery!" he growled. "Had I not moved quickly, it would have slain me. Dositheus, you'd better explain how—"

"No!" shrieked Ilione suddenly, pointing.

Simon whirled—and gasped to see that from the neck of each corpse a viscid greenish mass was oozing, gathering upon the floor as a veined translucent blob, pulsing, swelling. Then both blobs, each grown to nearly the diameter of a man's head, began to move forward across the floorboards. One of them paused by the hand of one of the guards; a formless pseudopod grew from the thing, lifted a small silvery weapon from the dead fingers, began to point it.

Simon hurled the sword. It pierced the blob-thing and thudded solidly into the floor, pinning it; another brilliant lance of fire flashed, crackling briefly against the plaster of the ceiling, and then the silvery object went clattering across the floor. The blob flowed away from the sword blade, apparently unhurt, leaving the sword sticking in the planks, and moved toward the outside door. Simon leaped over it, snatched up a wide-bladed shovel from beside the hearth. The thing was hurrying along the wall toward the crack under the door. Quickly Simon ran forward and scooped it up, then deftly flipped it into the embers of the fireplace. It bubbled, hissed, tried to crawl out of the fire, but Simon shoveled it back. The embers sputtered. Sweat ran down Simon's face; though the thing made no sound he seemed to hear its pain keening within his mind, along his nerve fibers.

Ilione screamed again. Simon whirled to see the other blob-thing clutching her ankle with a long pseudopod, flowing into that pseudopod toward her. Then Menander dashed forward with the torch he had snatched from the wall and held flame against it. Ilione shrieked as if her own flesh were being burned. The thing released her and retreated. Simon ran forward, scooped it up on the shovel and hurled it, too, into the embers, Menander following with the torch.

In another minute the blobs were nothing but tarry fluid bubbling on the ashes. The room was filled with a foul stench.

Ilione was trembling in old Dositheus' arms as he tried to comfort her. "It wanted in!" she sobbed. "It wanted my mind, my soul! I couldn't move! I felt its thoughts, its pain when the fire touched it!"

Simon strode forward, his expression grim, somber. "Dositheus, what were they?"

The old man, stroking the girl's blonde hair, looked up with troubled eyes. "I don't know. I've never seen their like. But you can be sure they are indeed minions of Assatur."

"Stirred up by your delvings in those ruins, perhaps?"

"I fear so. We must leave here, Simon, before—"

The door suddenly crashed open and the dark-bearded innkeeper hurried into the room, brandishing an axe. Three stout churls with clubs in their hands followed him.

"Baal and Ashtoreth!" he swore. "What's all this commotion? And that stink! What's been burning?" He glanced down at the hacked forms of the two guardsmen. "Gods! Murder's been done here!"

"No!" Dositheus hurried to his bedroll, plucked forth a pouch that jingled and approached the innkeeper. "No, good Isaac, not murder. These men attacked us in the night."

The innkeeper eyed the purse, then turned to his three burlies. "I'll handle this," he said. "Go—and reassure anyone who was awakened that all's under control now."

The three nodded and then left, muttering among themselves. Simon closed the door after them and turned to the innkeeper. "Are these two the men who inquired about us yesterday?"

"I . . . I think so." Isaac glanced uneasily at a severed head, then at the heavy-bladed sica at Simon's side.

"They are not from hereabouts?"

"I never saw them before yesterday."

Dositheus laid several gold pieces in Isaac's hand. "This should pay you for any damages and problems of—disposal. I am truly sorry for this disturbance, and I promise you that we shall all be gone from here before dawn."

The innkeeper jingled the coins meditatively. "I must consider my three loyal helpers."

Dositheus added three more coins to the pile. Isaac nodded, grinned, then popped them into his own pouch. Then, stealing a last appreciative glance at Ilione, he bowed and left the room.

"Dress and pack, all of you," said Dositheus. "Hurry."

"We're not going out there, are we?" said Ilione, her voice quavering. "What if there are more of them—out there, in the night?"

"I doubt there are," said Dositheus, "but we must leave before others of their kind learn of their failure—and before the local authorities get wind of this."

Half an hour later they had packed all their gear and were leading their three burdened donkeys up the valley east of Ecdippa, toward the hilly skyline where the first hint of dawn was beginning to glow.

CHAPTER II

An hour after dawn they came to a crossroads. Here they called a halt and breakfasted beneath a pair of oaks. The few travelers who passed at this early hour paid little attention to them as they sat and ate in silence. Ilione was still rather pale, Simon noticed, and though the sunlight was comfortably warm, she kept her cloak drawn closely about her. Still, she seemed calm now. Here in the clear daylight the terror of the night was withdrawing, seeming less real.

When they had finished their meal, Simon asked, "Where are you bound from here, Dositheus?"

The old man glanced toward the eastward hills. "Capharnaum."

Simon rose to his feet. "Then I must leave you. My mission draws me southward."

The others rose also. Dositheus said, "Must you, Simon?"

"You know it well, old mentor. I will miss you, but before we ever left Ephesus I told you where my destiny lies."

Dositheus nodded, glanced toward the three pack animals. "At least take one of the donkeys with you."

"No. I take only what I can carry comfortably. I must travel light."

"Money—"

"I have a fourth of what we have earned. It is more than enough to see me to Sebaste. The three of you will need the rest of it more than I."

Ilione suddenly ran forward and threw her arms around him. "Please, Simon, please don't leave us!"

The young Samaritan gently pried himself free of the girl's clutches. "I must, Ilione."

"What will we do?" There was a touch of desperation in the girl's voice. "You are strong, and a skilled fighter. You can protect us against robbers and—and things in the night."

"Nonsense, Ilione. Dositheus is a powerful wizard, you know that. And Menander has studied the arts of magic and self-defense under the mage Daramos as long as I have, and under Dositheus even longer. They will protect you—"

"Menander is young. No man is your equal, Simon—my sister often told me so."

Simon's face grew pained. He pushed the girl from him rather abruptly and turned to Dositheus. "My advise to you, old mentor, is to pursue your original plan. Take Menander and Ilione to Parthia, where they will learn and grow under the tutelage of Daramos."

"And will you follow us there, Simon?"

"Someday—perhaps."

Dositheus nodded. "If you survive, you mean. Well, Simon, I have a quest also. I have struck a trail and I must follow it."

Simon scowled. "I know you. The trails you have followed in quest of dark knowledge have often proven treacherous."

"More so than yours for vengeance?"

Simon could think of no reply.

"We must each follow our own destiny."

"And what of Menander and Ilione?" asked Simon.

"I shall continue to tutor them, as I have thus far."

"I trust that your—quest—will not bring them into danger."

Dositheus smiled. "Did you not just say that I am a powerful wizard? After all, I've lived to see well over seventy summers."

"Very well." Simon nodded. "Good fortune to you. And to you, Ilione. And you, Menander." He shook the hand of each in turn. "And you, Carbo," he added, addressing the dark bird that perched upon Menander's shoulder. Then, abruptly, he turned and strode away down the road that led southward, not looking back.

He had walked for perhaps five minutes when he heard rapid footfalls behind him. Turning, he saw the youthful Menander hastening in his direction, the raven Carbo flapping along in the air beside him.

"Simon!" gasped Menander as he caught up. "I'm going with you."

Simon stopped and faced the youth sternly. "You are not!"

"Ita!" croaked the raven as it settled down to its accustomed perch on the lad's shoulder.

"No, nor you either, you crazy bird! Get back to the others, both of you."

"Please, Simon! Let me go with you. Let me help you kill the Romans who slew your family."

Simon shook his head, anger and sadness mingling in his eyes. "You don't know what you're saying, lad."

"But I do! Didn't the Romans kill my parents, too?"

"That was when you were too young to remember. You were only six when Dositheus bought you out of slavery. But I was sixteen—the age you are now—when it happened to me."

"Yet I *know,* Simon. I think of it often. I want to kill Romans as much as you do!"

"Now listen, damn it!" growled Simon. "You have a responsibility to Dositheus and Ilione."

Menander shook his head violently. "Dositheus needs no one, as you well know. And as for Ilione, she despises me."

"Ah, so that's it," said Simon. He laid his hands on the lad's shoulders and looked into his dark eyes, saw the hurt there. "Tell me about it,

Menander. You and Ilione seemed good friends during the voyage from Ephesus and in Antioch. What happened?"

Menander sighed. "It started when Dositheus said we were going with you, Simon, instead of to Parthia. I'd told her so much about Daramos, about his strange and fantastic powers and what a wonderful and kind teacher he is."

"He is indeed. I know she was looking forward to the journey with excitement—she seemed almost to have forgotten the dark shadow that had lain upon her in her father's house. I sensed she was disappointed—damn old Dositheus' perversity! But surely Ilione hasn't turned against you because of it?"

Menander hesitated. "Simon—she loves you."

Simon started. Again he could find nothing to say.

"It's true, Simon. Her sister Helen talked much of you while the two of them lived in the mansion of Senator Junius in Antium. And now I fear that Ilione, in her disappointment at not going to Parthia, has fixed all her hopes upon you—and she despises me for having given her promises that were broken. I can't blame her—I, too, wish we could return to Daramos in Parthia."

Instantly Simon realized the truth of what Menander had said. It explained Ilione's moodiness, her impulsive clinging.

"Listen, Menander," he said. "There is nothing between Ilione and me. What Helen and I shared was something that—that only the gods share. I can't speak more of it. But you and Ilione?"

Menander shook his head. "We were friends—close friends. I . . . I have dreamed that something more might come of it, but . . ."

Simon clapped a hand on the youth's shoulder. "Return to her," he said. "She needs you, depend on it—now more than ever, I'm sure. And so does Dositheus. Keep him out of trouble if you can. They both need you, Menander, whether they know it or not."

The lad nodded. "Very well, Simon. I'll go back to them—but only if you promise me that you'll come back to us again."

Simon hesitated. "I—I will if I can."

"You will if you want to, Simon."

"Aye." Simon impulsively reached out clasped the youth's arm, gazed into his serious dark eyes. "I promise I'll see you again, Menander—and not the entire empire of Romans shall keep me from it!"

"In Capharnaum, then?"

"Capharnaum—or anywhere else you may be."

Menander nodded, stoutly returning Simon's handshake, then turned abruptly and hurried off back down the road. Simon stared after him until he was gone, then shifted his pack to a more comfortable position and resumed his journey southward.

All that day the three of them journeyed southeastward through the hills, Ilione occasionally riding the donkey that was least burdened. Menander sympathized with her, knowing that her weariness was due in part to the shock of fear she had endured, but whenever he spoke to her she answered as shortly as possible, hugging her feelings to herself.

Once during the morning, they paused while Dositheus gazed back toward a wide ridge northeast of Ecdippa. Menander watched him closely.

"Why could I not find it?" he heard the old sage mumble. "Was it not there? If not, who found it? Where was it taken?"

"What was taken?" asked Menander.

"The Chalice of Byakh—" Dositheus suddenly cut himself short. "Damn you, Menander, must you probe my very thoughts unbidden?"

The lad wondered at his mentor's unaccustomed vehemence. "Are not those ridgetops the ruins of Hali? What did you fail to find there?"

Dositheus glanced at Ilione who stood listlessly beside the donkeys, apparently paying no attention. "I'll tell you in Capharnaum," he said. "Come—we must get to a town before nightfall."

They pushed on, stopping briefly twice more during the day. The sky was clear, and well before midmorning the terror of the night before seemed to Menander only a dimly-remembered nightmare. Even Ilione's spirits seemed brighter. Still, Dositheus seemed anxious to press on with an urgency that made Menander wonder. Was the old man afraid that dusk might catch them outside of an inn's protective walls?

They spent the night in a small, crowded inn at a village in the hills, and resumed their journey early in the morning. By midafternoon they had passed the crest of the hills and could gaze down across the beautiful fertile plain of Gennesaret. Beyond it sprawled the wide lake of the same name, the city of Capharnaum nestled on its shore. An hour before sunset they passed within the city's western limits and before nightfall were lodged at a comfortable inn.

Menander saw to it that the animals were taken to the stable and given plenty of straw, then returned to the inn. After the three of them had ascended by the outside stairway to their suite of three rooms, they supped lightly and drank an herb tea, following which Ilione immediately retired to her chamber, exhausted.

"She will sleep well," said Dositheus. "The potion I gave her will insure it."

"Indeed. Are we safe here, O mentor?"

"Yes, of course."

Menander leaned forward, elbows on the table. "You promised you would tell me all. Do not spare me. Have you stirred up things that are a danger to us? What is this Chalice of Byakh which you seek?"

The old man sighed. "You read of that in the *Book of Jasher,* of course."

"Aye, only last night—while pursuing the studies you had outlined for me. It is written that the servitors of Assatur once gathered in Hali to perform monstrous rites, and to drink the Golden Nectar of the Primal Gods from the Chalice of Byakh—and for this the men of Asher under Joshua destroyed the town and many others in the region. What does it all men, O mentor?"

"I will tell you." Dositheus filled a wine cup, sipped from it and set it down. "The *Book of Jasher* is perhaps over a thousand years old, but there are books far older—books which I have not yet allowed you to study."

"The books you bought from Prodikos's library?"

"Aye. They tell of this Shrine of Hali, which was named after a terrible and remote region of the cosmos whose nature you could not comprehend at your present stage of learning. Yet the town of the Shrine was but the last surviving outpost of an age-old kingdom that had vanished long before Joshua led the chosen folk of Yahweh to this land. That kingdom's capital was the ancient and fabled city of Karakossa, whose long-vanished ruins lie buried beneath the soil of the valley of Gennesaret. There were worshipped the most ancient god and goddess Assatur and Shupnikkurat, whose rites were known to the men of age-lost Elam, Shem and even primal Attluma—aye, and even to those who ruled this world before the Elohim breathed life into Adam. Do you understand what I am saying, Menander?"

The lad sat motionless for a moment, his eyes wide with awe and perhaps a touch of fear. Then he recited in a hushed voice:

"Iä, Assatur! Iä, Shupnikkurat!
Kumat Karakossa ut Arag-Kolat."

"Quiet!" Dositheus glanced around as if fearful that someone might have heard, then took a deep gulp of his wine. "Aye, you remember—the chant to the great Spawning Ones in the temple of Ephesus. Do not repeat it!"

"Dositheus!" hissed the lad. "What forces are you tampering with?"

"Forces that will bring us power, perhaps."

"Will they endanger Ilione? Those soldiers who came seeking us in Ecdippa—they did indeed resemble those who served her father. Were they truly sent from him?"

Dositheus shook his head. "Prodikos is destroyed. Yet, many other sorcerers sill flourish. And even as the center of worship for Shupnikkurat was the great temple in Ephesus, so is the central fane of her mate Assatur in a city of this very valley. But, enough." Dositheus gulped down the rest of his wine. "You must go to bed, Menander. I will tell you more another time, when we are both less exhausted."

"Tomorrow?"

"No. Tomorrow I must inquire at the local synagogue concerning certain matters."

"You mean, matters pertaining to what we have been discussing?"

"I will tell you in due time."

"Dositheus—what were those blob-things that came out of the men in black armor?"

The old man hesitated, then poured himself more wine. "Call them demons, if you will. I am sure they were servitors of Assatur. Whence they come I think I know, for the *Book of Eibon,* more ancient even than the forgotten nations of Hyborios, speaks of them. They can take over the bodies of humans or animals, living or dead."

"And . . . were Prodikos' guards so possessed?"

"Some of them—and even Prodikos himself. The thing that possessed him—known to the prophets as Sakkuth, King of Night—was a chief of many such beings as those you saw at the inn near Ecdippa. But these are matters that strain even my understanding. I will say no more until another time, Menander. Good night."

After Menander had retired to his chamber, Dositheus leisurely finished his second cup of wine. Then, glancing up to the ledge above the window, he mutter, "Carbo!"

The raven fluttered in the shadows, opening its eyes.

"Carbo, do you hear me?"

The bird nodded. "Ita!"

"Tomorrow you will fly forth and find Simon. He journeys southward toward Gitta, his birthplace. Find him, but do not let him know. Do you understand?"

The raven nodded again.

"Good. I will open the window for you at dawn, that you may go forth." So saying, the old Samaritan blew out the lamp and retired to his bed.

Outside, in the night, the cold stars glittered down.

Simon finished his warm gruel, set aide his bowl and stared into the flames of his dwindling campfire. The air was cool and still. The last of twilight had faded, the light of a waxing half-moon was gleaming down through the branches of the oaks amid where he was camped.

A brief gust of a breeze stirred the dried leaves. Simon echoed it with a sigh. He was weary, for he had journeyed far these last two days—south through the coastal plains to the river Kishon and into the hills beyond. His rests had been few and short, and he had avoided towns, sleeping in the wooded hills beneath the stars.

Samaria—his home province. He was within its borders even now. Tomorrow he would pass through Gitta, the town of his birth. It seemed strange. And the day after, he would enter the city of Sebaste, where the Romans had looted his home eight years ago, and slain his parents.

Romans.

He had fought them well, with the *gladius* his grandfather had taught him to use—his grandfather Simon, who had been a soldier under Marcus Antonius before the Romans had set up their puppet-king Herod to rule the land. He had fought well enough to wound one of the Romans, and slay one of their killer hounds and one of the assistants of the contemptible tax-gatherer who had led them there—had fought well enough, in fact, to cause the Roman officer in charge to order his capture, unharmed, that he might be sold to one of the gladiator-schools.

The Roman officer—Maxentius. Through eight years Simon's hatred had clung to that name, together with three others: Scribonius, the officer's sadistic underling; Jahath, the chief tax-gatherer of Samaria; and Akrab, Maxentius' brutal keeper of hounds.

Maxentius, who had ordered the slaying of Simon's parents; Scribonius and Akrab, who had carried out that order; and the short, grinning, rat-like Jahath, who had instigated the plot and led them there.

Simon shook his head, lips shut firmly over clenched teeth, and looked away from the dying fire in whose flames he had seemed to see the leering countenances of his foes. For a long moment he gazed upward to the night sky until his eyes adjusted to the darkness and he could discern the moon and the glitter of the cold stars. Then he rose and finished unrolling his blanket, removing his few possessions from it in preparation for the night.

And as he did so he found a small leather packet bound with a thong—a packet he did not recognize as his own.

Carefully he untied the thing and spread it open on the ground. It contained two objects: a black medallion inset with several yellow gems and one red one, and a silvery sphere from which a slim cylinder of the same metal protruded. Simon started as he recognized these as the possessions of one of the black-clad guards he had fought at Ecdippa. Then he saw that the inner surface of the leather was written over with Aramaic characters, betraying the handwriting of Dositheus:

> *"May these bring you luck, Simon. I am sure there is magic in them. Investigate them carefully. I have kept their twins."*

Simon scowled thoughtfully. Surely there *was* sorcery in these things. Yet he did not trust them, nor the curiosity that led Dositheus to so often investigate such things. He peered more closely at the medallion—a thick disc of black metal, a pendant attached to a fine chain of the same material.

One face bore a rough "V" of gems, several yellow and one red—gems that glowed softly in the dark.

He laid this object aside and examined the other, being careful to point the protruding cylinder away from himself. He was sure the beam of fire had come from that hollow protrusion. But how had it been induced? Save for the cylinder, the sphere was absolutely smooth, featureless, except for a tiny circular section, exactly opposite the protrusion, moved slightly inward under the pressure of his finger.

Flame crackled harshly in the night.

Simon dropped the thing and leaped to his feet. The thin lance of fire that shot from the cylinder was still a bright line across his eyesight, fading slowly. Then he saw that the trunk of a great oak just beyond his campfire bore a smoldering scar with glowing sparks at its center.

Slowly he advanced, examining the scar that had cut through the rough bark deep into the wood—the scar where the lance of fire had touched. Then, just as slowly, he retreated, stooped and cautiously picked up the silvery object, awe in his eyes.

For a long moment he studied it. Finally, very carefully, he pointed the cylinder at a nearby rock and gently pressed the back of the sphere with his thumb.

Again the lance of fire. There was a sharp crack. Instantly Simon released the pressure; the flame blinked out. Where it had touched the rock, chips had burst away; for a moment a crater glowed redly in the stone, then faded.

Simon looked again at the thing in his hand. Then, gingerly, he laid it aside, making sure that the cylinder pointed away from him.

"Baal!" he muttered. "A weapon of the gods."

For perhaps another hour he sat pondering. Did Dositheus know the nature of this thing? True, the old mage was versed in sorcery, but—*this?* Simon hoped that his former mentor would be careful investigating the similar weapon he had retained for himself.

Weapon. A weapon that might kill Romans.

Still pondering, Simon rolled out his blanket, wrapped himself in his hooded cloak and lay down to sleep. The firelight faded slowly.

Despite his weariness his sleep was fitful. Dreams came to him, dreams that were half memory, showing him the square and arrogant face of Maxentius, the lean and cruel face of Scribonius, the rat-like visage of Jahath. Several times he woke, sweating with anger and a touch of fear—fear that he had sensed monstrous, inhuman faces behind those of his foes, faces of non-human beings looming against the stars. On such occasions he noticed the gems of the medallion glowing dimly in the darkness.

Shortly before dawn he woke for the last time and saw, in the east, the dim stars of Aquarius and Pisces gleaming above the first faint glow of morning. He rose and ate a few dates, then packed his belongings. He was very careful, when wrapping the silvery sphere, to make sure that its cylinder pointed away from him. Once more he glanced at the faintly glowing medallion. That gem pattern seemed strangely familiar.

He glanced up again at the fading stars of Aquarius. Pisces had already vanished in dawn's glow. The sun would be entering Taurus.

Then it hit him. Aye, the V-shaped pattern of the Bull's Face, with a red gem gleaming from one branch of it like a baleful eye! The Hyades—

With trembling fingers Simon stashed the medallion in his bundle, silently vowing that nothing would ever make him wear it.

Menander woke in the night to hear the low, guttural voice of the raven in his ear.

"Cavé!"

"What?" The lad sat up in the darkness, rubbing his eyes. "Danger?"

He heard the bird rustling nearby in the gloom, saw its dim shape, beak pointed toward the shuttered window.

"Ibi!"

Softly he rose and stole toward the shutter. He could see starlight in the chinks between its boards. Surely no one could be lurking out there, for the west wall of the inn was sheer and this room was two stories up. Quickly Menander gripped the shutter and opened it.

Icy terror gripped him. A great owl sat on the window ledge not an arm's length away, staring at him with round eyes. On its breast hung a rectangular object of dark metal that hummed softly and pulsed with weird, many-colored lights.

Carbo squawked loudly and flapped toward the owl, which immediately turned and launched itself away from the ledge. For an instant Menander saw its silent form winging away in silhouette against the deep blue night; then it was gone.

"Gods!" Menander sank to his knees, trembling from the sudden shock. "Carbo—what was it?"

Dositheus entered, an oil lamp in his hand. He glanced to the open window where the raven was now perched, then helped the shaking lad to his feet.

"Bubo!" croaked the raven.

"An owl?" The old man turned to Menander. "What was it doing here?"

"It . . . it was lurking outside the window. There was something hung about its neck—a metal box with flashing lights. What does it mean, O mentor?"

Dositheus leaned out the window for a moment, then drew back and took up Carbo on his arm. "It is gone. Close the shutter, lad, then join me in the next room."

Menander did so. Dositheus was adding wood to the hearth and blowing up the coals. At the same time, Ilione appeared at the door of her room, wrapped in a mantle and rubbing sleep from her eyes.

"What happened? A sound woke me."

"Nothing, Ilione," said Menander. "There was an owl on my window-ledge. It startled Carbo. That's all."

Ilione saw the pair of them exchange a glance. "If that's all, Menander, then why are you so pale and trembling?"

"Ilione," said Dositheus, "there's nothing for you to worry about."

"Stop it!" The girl's eyes flashed with anger. "Stop keeping things from me. We're in this together. I have a right to know. It was another of my father's minions, wasn't it? I know that owls used to come to him—talk to him."

Dositheus nodded. "Very well. I'll be frank. I don't think we're in danger right now, but we must leave this inn and find another as soon as possible. That owl was sent to find us, I think, and it will soon report to others."

"Others? You mean—like those who came to us in Ecdippa?"

Again Dositheus nodded.

Menander asked, "Who sent the creature to search us out?"

"Who? The owl, the lynx and the bat are minions of Assatur. I fear his servitors have indeed guessed why I was delving amid the ruins of Hali." He strode to the window and opened it. "Come, Carbo, you must make your journey earlier than we had planned—in fact, at once!"

The bird again hopped up on the old man's sleeved arm.

"The moon has set," said Dositheus, "and soon the sun will rise. Fly forth, Carbo, and find Simon. He follows the southward road to Gitta and Sebaste. Find him, and see how he fares. Then bring word to me."

"Ubi?" queried the bird.

"Where? I shall plant a staff with a white cloth tied to it upon the roof of the inn where we elect to stay. Look for it."

The bird nodded, croaked slightly, then fluttered out into the cool darkness and was gone.

"Now," said Dositheus, "let us pack and have breakfast. You two will then take our belongings and seek out another inn."

"And what of you?" asked Ilione.

"I must see about finding certain people. When you two have found a suitable inn, leave word for me at the White Synagogue. The—rabbi—there is a friend of mine."

"But what of those who seek us?" said Menander. "Will they not find us again?"

Dositheus glanced at a small leather-bound bundle that lay on the table by the lamp. "I think I know what led them to us this time. You need not worry. I'll carry it with me, and discard it if I think there's danger."

"You mean the medallion," said Ilione, "and the thing that shoots flame. I wish you would throw them down a well!"

"One does not so acquire knowledge. But fear not—you'll be in no danger, and I've learned enough about sorcery to take very good care of myself."

"Sorcery like *this?"* asked Menander.

"No more talk, now. Let's pack our things."

The lad glanced at Ilione—and caught her looking at him with the same doubt he knew his own eyes held.

CHAPTER III

Dositheus, hurrying through the narrow streets in the light of mid-morning, came soon to the White Synagogue of Capharnaum. Passing between the elegant Corinthian columns of its portico, he briefly noted the finely-wrought but un-Jewish carvings above the entablature—bas-reliefs of grape-bearing vines and other fruit-bearing plants, and in the center of them a large deer-like animal. For a moment Dositheus felt regret that this edifice was surrounded by such narrow streets, so that its fine architecture and the carvings executed in its white limestone could not be better appreciated. But his regret was fleeting. He had come here to gain important information.

Inside there were only two attendants, extinguishing some of the lamps and torches that had burned throughout the night. Dositheus attracted no special attention, for he had changed from his Samaritan robes into Galilean ones. Striding through the columned hall to the back of the building, he came to a narrow curtained doorway and, hesitating only briefly, pushed the curtain aside and stepped through.

An old, balding man, seated at a table upon which rested an open scroll, looked up at the Samaritan with started eyes.

"Ho, Tolmai," said Dositheus. "I had hoped I would find you here."

The old man rose and peered closely at the newcomer. "It—it can't be! Dositheus?"

"The same. We have much to talk of, my friend."

Tolmai strode forward, smiling incredulously. The two clasped hands. Then Tolmai said, "Wait here." He went out the curtained doorway and called to the attendants, "That is sufficient. Leave the cleaning of the women's aisles until noon. Your wages will not be diminished."

When Tolmai returned, Dositheus said, "That was wise."

"I guessed you had not come here to speak of mundane things, Dositheus. I see I was right. Gods of Demhe! It has been nearly five years since you last passed this way—on your way to Persia with two young acolytes, as I remember."

"Aye—with Simon and Menander." Dositheus smiled slightly. "But how long has it been, good Rabbi Tolmai, since you last spoke openly to another of the gods of Demhe?"

Tolmai glanced down a trifle nervously at the rabbi's robes he wore. "I've spoken to several, actually. There are nearly a score of us now, and on the appropriate nights we hold conclaves here to the ancient Goddess for whom I had this temple built and secretly consecrated."

"To Yhtill, the White Doe," said Dositheus, nodding, "and to her two servitors, Kasilda and Kamila."

Tolmai paled slightly. "Speak more softly! You know what these rustic Galileans would do to me should they even suspect that I serve any god but their monstrous Yahweh!"

"Fear not," said the Samaritan in a lower tone. "Have I ever betrayed you either by intent or indiscretion? And as for these Galileans, there is more of what they abhor in their own nature than they would care to admit—and many of them do secretly know it! Have they not mingled for generations with the *Am-ha-arez*—the Earth-Folk? Aye, and also with the Deep-Denizens who long ago carved passageways into this Lake of Gennesaret from the Western Sea? And if these Galileans only knew what their god Yahweh is planning for them, they too would think him the most monstrous god of all!"

"Silence!" Tolmai's face had become ashen. "We simply must not speak aloud of such things in places where someone might listen. I have none of my trusted guards posted—they are here only during the ceremonies." He looked out the doorway again to make sure the temple was deserted, then said, "Come, we will walk in the streets and talk. It will be safer there."

Dositheus was nothing loath. When they had left the synagogue several streets behind them, he asked, "What do you know of the Chalice of Byakh?"

Tolmai stopped and faced the Samaritan. "What do *you* know of it?"

"The Chalice has possibly been removed from its age-old hiding place. I recently dug in the ruins of Hali, in the exact spot where it was supposed to be, and I found only a great stone block of an altar. The Chalice was not there."

Naked fear shone from Tolmai's eyes. "You could not have learned of its *exact* location unless you had seen a copy of the—the original book of—"

"Aye, the unexpurgated *El-Halal*, by the Greeks titled 'Lord of Chaos', written by Mattan, Priest of Baal nine centuries ago. I was able to purchase it in Ephesus from the library of the deceased arch-sorcerer Prodikos. Fortunately, the auctioneers of the estate knew nothing of the value of it."

"You amaze me, Dositheus! Come—the lakeside is this way, and there are open beaches where we may stroll and observe all within earshot. Not even these streets are safe for discussing the matters of which you speak."

Dositheus complied, and soon they were walking north along the shore of the wide sea of Gennesaret, with none nearby save occasionally raucous fishermen yelling and cursing hauling their boats up on the strand or shoving them out into the water. High in the east, beyond the vast blue-gray surface of the lake, the sun was bright over far-off hills.

"To think," said Dositheus, "that this entire region—this lake and its fertile shores and the hills beyond—was once the domain of kings who ruled in the ancient and famous city of Karakossa!"

"The city of Karakossa," echoed Tolmai, "whose ruins, not far from here, are as utterly vanished as those of Eibon's Hyperborea. And, yet, incredibly, some of her ancient worships linger on. Tell me, Dositheus, why did you seek the Chalice of Byakh?"

"For the same reasons you would have, Tolmai: knowledge and power. Did not Thale and Aldones and the other kings of the ancient Karakossan dynasty once drink the Golden Nectar from it and thereby gain strange wisdom?"

"So it is written." Tolmai stroked his thin beard thoughtfully. "But now, perhaps, there is one who knows."

"Knows what?" Dositheus looked at his companion sharply. "You suspect then, who removed the Chalice from its hiding place?"

"If it was indeed accomplished, it can only have been done by the sorcerer Izhar, Rabbi of Chorazin, who serves Assatur even as I serve Yhtill."

"I suspected as much, also. But how, then, did Izhar acquire a copy of Mattan's book in the original ancient Canaanite script?"

"He did not have to. The Black Synagogue has had a copy of it in its archives for many decades. Izhar once told me so."

"Yet the Chalice appears to have been removed from its hiding place only recently. The soil above the altar-slab appeared to have been disturbed only a few months ago at most."

Tolmai nodded. "Strange things are indeed happening of late. Izhar has changed, I hear—and so have others." He paused, pondering, then, "Do you remember that new cult-leader Johannen the Baptizer, whom you and your two pupils met during your visit here five years ago?"

"Aye, of course. He intrigued me with his talk of one who was soon to come and 'fufill the Law'—enough so that I went through his baptismal rigmarole, and induced Simon to do so as well, in order that I might learn such wisdom as he had. But for all his prophetic fury he was disappointing—he practiced no sorcery, and he ranted constantly about the Law-fulfiller who would soon follow him. What has this Johannen fellow to do with Izhar of Chorazin?"

"Nothing directly—and now he has nothing to do with anything, for the tetrarch Herod had him beheaded some time ago."

"Indeed! Why?"

"He took it upon himself to upbraid Herod in his very palace in Tiberas—to publicly point out that the Tetrarch's life style ran counter to the imminent fulfillment of the Law. The fulfillment of the Law—that was Johannen's constant theme, as you well know."

"Aye. But, what has this to do with—?"

"Listen, Dositheus: Some time after you and your pupils left for Parthia a new cult-leader appeared upon the scene—the very one whom Johannen claimed had come to 'fulfill the Law.' Have you heard of the miracle-worker Yeshua bar Yosef?"

Dositheus nodded. "Yes—there was some talk of him in Tyre. Something about him turning bread crusts into fishes, I believe."

"Unlike Johannen, the man is a true sorcerer indeed—and, incidentally, Johannen's own cousin, or so I am told. There are curious tales concerning the births of both of these men. Strange things are beginning to happen in this land, Dositheus. Strange forces are awakening."

"What do you know about this wonder-worker Bar Yosef? Have you seen him perform any of his sorcery?"

Tolmai nodded; there was sadness and anger in his eyes. "I learned of him from Nathaniel—my own son, Nathaniel, whom I had initiated into the rites of Yhtill in hopes that he would one day replace me in carrying on her secret lore and worship! He heard this man Yeshua speak, saw him work his sorcery—and then became one of his followers! He even persuaded me to let the fellow lecture here in this very synagogue—claimed that he had knowledge even deeper and older than that of the ancient dynasties of Karakossa."

"The man lectured in your temple?" Dositheus interrupted.

"Aye, and he made this town his center of operations for quite some time—working his sorceries and insinuating that he had come to fulfill the Law."

"And you have met him in person, listened to him, even watched him work his sorceries?"

"Indeed I have!" Tolmai's lips clamped shut for a moment in indignation. Then he went on, "At first I was impressed. His constant theme, after all, was that the Law which Yahweh gave to Moshe must be obeyed to the last jot and tittle. Also, he seemed to have such a kind and gentle mien—a compassionate mien."

Dositheus wondered what sort of man could inspire such contradictory feelings. His friend's voice had trailed off into silence; his eyes, now grown strangely soft, seemed fixed on the memory his words had awakened.

"Tolmai," said the Samaritan, "tell me more of this Yeshua bar Yosef. Tell me all you know."

"He is a tall man," said Tolmai, "and broad in proportion. Taller and broader than most, half a head taller than you or I—and yet, not a domineering man for all that. Very soft-spoken and gentle. And his features—I never saw the like! They were broad and flat, like those of a young sheep or goat. Which is strange, for once during his sermon he said he wished he could offer himself up as a 'lamb of God' in sacrifice for the salvation of all life, and again that he could be the 'goat of atonement' and so carry off all our burdens to Azazel. But for the most part he spoke of the fulfillment of the Law—urged that we all lay aside our petty strifes and worldly affairs and concentrate on worship and obedience in accordance with Yahweh's Law, because the purpose of the Law was soon to be consummated and we would then be freed from pain and fear, sin and anguish."

"A rather simple-minded outlook, hardly original."

"So I've often thought since—but then I remember the man's eyes, the tone of his voice. There was something behind his words, Dositheus, something I sensed behind his genuine compassion. Tell me, wise friend: How can compassion convey a *threat?* For in this man's words I indeed seemed to sense a monstrous threat—an impending judgment, even, against us all."

Dositheus scowled thoughtfully. "You say, Tolmai, that the features of this Rabbi Yeshua seemed somehow—goatish?"

"Aye. But it was what followed that made me shun him—the thing that happened in the synagogue during his lecture." Tolmai paused and glanced around, though no one was near them; they had followed the beach to the northeast outskirts of town. The old Samaritan, catching his mood, glanced around also. The sun, nearing the zenith and warm at this low elevation, seemed almost like a watching eye.

"None can overhear us in this place, old friend," said Dositheus. "Tell me all."

Ilione paced the floor of the small suite of rooms she and Menander had rented in the inn they had discovered near the north end of Capharnaum. Anger, consternation and anxiety mingled in her expression. Menander had asked her to begin unpacking, but she had ignored his request; her nervousness had increased intolerably and all she could do to relieve it was pace, pace, back and forth.

She thought back to the time when these mysterious Samaritans had rescued her from her father in Ephesus—had rescued her from being a human sacrifice to monstrous gods. At first, after the shock had worn off, she had been immensely relieved and grateful; then, as her new life had begun to open before her, she had even been happy in the excitement and adventure of it. Dositheus was a wizard—not a dark and evil one like her possessed father, but a benign seeker after knowledge, training his two pupils Simon and Menander in his accumulated wisdom. Ilione, too, would share in that wisdom. Already Dositheus had begun to tutor her; moreover, he promised that she would accompany the three of them back to Parthia where, for nearly four years, they had once studied under Daramos, greatest of mages. All of them had attested enthusiastically to Daramos' wisdom, benevolence and strange powers, and had promised Ilione that she would love him in spite of his strange appearance and idiosyncrasies.

Ilione sighed. *I already love another.*

She shook her head to clear her mind of the painful thought. Simon had left her—strange, somber Simon, who had vowed revenge against Rome. She could see why her sister, Helen, had loved him so. Poor Helen, forced into death by Romans! Why would not Simon let her, Ilione, soothe his bereaved heart as she so longed to do? But it seemed that Simon craved only revenge.

And Dositheus—it seemed that the hatred for Rome was deep within his aged heart also. He, too, hinted at having lost someone to Roman brutality long ago. Ilione wondered if this hatred was at the bottom of his decision to delay their journey to Parthia, to delve in the ancient ruins of this region, which had been his homeland—this land which was so strange to her.

Now, in her frustration, she almost wished she were back in Ephesus. After all, she had never been really unhappy there, not knowing the fate her father had planned for Helen and herself. They had had very little contact with him, actually, having been brought up in a sheltered environment by slave women, eunuchs and tutors. It had been a sad life in some ways, for almost as soon as they had begun to form an attachment for a guardian or teacher, that individual had been replaced. Still, there had been no fear, no sense of the danger than impended. They had been pampered, amused and educated beyond the good fortune of most. The only really rigid restriction had fallen upon them at puberty—they had been allowed no unsupervised contact with men.

Ilione shuddered, again shook her head to clear her mind of her new understanding. Her father had wanted them kept virgins, for only as such would they be worthy sacrifices to his monstrous gods. But now—what of Dositheus? What did *he* plan for her? Was she always doomed to be the plaything of plotting sorcerers?

"No!" She whirled in sudden resolution and dashed from the room, out onto the ledge that ran around the inn's second story. Quickly she found the steps leading to the roof and ascended them. As she gained the top, she saw Menander standing upon the flat expanse, planting a pole against a corner of the low parapet.

"What are you doing?" she asked, hurrying toward him.

Menander glanced at her, secretly glad that she had come up to join him, then looked up at the white rag fluttering from the pole. "That's to guide Carbo to this inn when he returns to us this evening."

"Carbo? Oh, of course—he's gone to find Simon." The girl smiled briefly, but then grew thoughtful. "Menander, just what sort of danger does Dositheus think we're in?"

Menander hesitated. He wanted to tell Ilione, but Dositheus had advised him against it.

The girl saw his hesitation. Tears welled in her eyes. "I hate you, Menander!" she cried out. "You and that awful Dositheus—always keeping secrets from me! You told me we were going to Parthia to learn wonderful things from the wise Daramos—but we're not. You've brought me to this awful land and you're planning to do something terrible to me, like my father was going to do. But I won't let you—I won't stay with you!"

She whirled and ran back toward the stairway. Menander ran after her, caught up to her by the parapet, grabbed her by the shoulders and spun her around.

"Ilione, that's not true. You *know* it's not!"

"It is! *It is!"* she screamed, beating his chest with her clenched hands. Then, abruptly, she stopped and covered her eyes. Her body shook with sobs. Menander wanted to gather her close—but held back for fear that she would find the action unwelcome.

"Ilione—" His hands were still gentle on her shoulders.

She looked up at him, her hazel eyes seeming dark in contrast to the pallor of her face. "I—I'm all right," she said with an obvious effort at self control. "I know you're not evil like my father—but I can no longer endure this secrecy. Dositheus won't answer my questions honestly, Menander, and I sense that he has asked you not to answer either. But I can't live like this any more. I must know where my life is going. If you and Dositheus won't be honest with me, I must go my own way."

"Ilione—"

"You can see that, can't you, Menander? Dositheus has fired my dreams, and so has Daramos—if he exists! I *want* him to exist—I want to sit at his feet as you say you have, to learn the things you say he has taught you, to become free through knowledge and wisdom. But this secrecy frightens me."

Menander made up his mind in an instant. "It's true that Dositheus asked me not to tell you all. He didn't think you were ready. But now I think he was wrong. Ask me any questions you want to, Ilione. I don't know all Dositheus knows, but I'll tell you what I can."

The girl relaxed slightly. "Why did Dositheus bring us to this land?"

"He seeks something—something he read about in the books he purchased from your father's library. I think it also has to do with something he learned when he passed through this land over four years ago. I remember that he questioned a seer named Johannen, who persuaded him and Simon to be immersed in the Jordan as an initiation into strange mysteries—but what they may have learned as a result of this I do not know."

Ilione glanced at the tall pole with the white rag fluttering from it. "And Carbo?"

"You heard Dositheus. He has sent him to keep track of Simon. The bird should return by sundown to report."

Menander did not miss the gladness in Ilione's eyes. He let his hand fall from her shoulder.

"That was thoughtful of Dositheus," said the girl. "I—I should not have spoken so ill of him."

"Simon is his friend," said the youth, turning to face the southwestern horizon, "as I am. We have all been through much together."

Ilione laid a hand lightly upon his shoulder. "And Carbo?"

"Aye—he is a friend also."

"I mean—who *is* Carbo? *What* is he? He is not an ordinary raven." Then, as Menander turned toward her, she added, "You told me you would be honest. Tell me all."

The lad's scowl was one of honest puzzlement. "I wish I could, Ilione. I've often pondered that question myself, and have asked it of my mentor more than once. He tells me Carbo is his familiar spirit—one such as many wizards possess. I doubt that's the whole story, but he will not tell me more."

"I believe you," said Ilione. "Tell me, then: Why are we in this land? What does Dositheus hope to find here?"

Menander gazed toward the northwest, then pointed. "Look—do you see that distant town in the valley debouching from the hills? That is Chorazin. Dositheus once told me that the Black Synagogue is there, presided over by the Rabbi Izhar, who is a secret worshipper of Assatur, the very god your—your father served. Moreover, he hinted that this synagogue is the earthly center of Assatur's worship, which has been secretly practiced in this region during the thousands of years since the fall of Karakossa."

Again Ilione paled. "Aye—my father once spoke of such things to some of his black-robed guards, when he thought Helen and I were not listening."

"Dositheus thinks that the thing he failed to find in the ruins of Hali may have been taken to the Black Synagogue." Menander pondered a moment, then said firmly, "Listen: When Dositheus returns, we'll both confront him. I want to go to Parthia just as much as you do. Daramos *does* exist and he's as wonderful as I've said he is. Can you doubt me? I've seen him, studied under him!"

"No, of course I don't doubt you," said Ilione, sensing the genuineness of the youth's enthusiasm.

"And we'll find Simon, and he'll go with us. I know how much you—love him—Ilione."

"Oh, Menander!" The girl rushed forward and embraced him. Suddenly Simon's absence seemed a bit less important to her than it had. The moments of honesty she had just shared with this youth had made her feel calmer—safer.

Menander returned the embrace awkwardly, happily.

Suddenly a dark-helmed head appeared at the top of the stairs. Then a dark-cloaked figure rose into view, followed by another—two dark soldiers, faces blank, expressionless, stepping up onto the roof, advancing. Upon the shoulder of one perched an owl.

Icy fear lanced through Ilione. "Gods! *My father's soldiers!*"

The owl stared at Menander, extended a wing towards him, then trilled eerily, *Eeee-lleee!"*

Terror clutched the girl as she seemed to hear the first syllables of her name in the bird's weird cry. The youth unsheathed his dagger as the black-clad soldiers strode toward them. Then he saw that the foremost clutched something in his right hand—a cylinder of glowing metal about as long and thick as a man's thumb. From it issued a shrill, vibrating hum.

"Ilione, get behind me—!" cried Menander.

The glowing object brightened, shrilling loudly. For an instant the young Samaritan felt a strange tingling infusing his every nerve—and then abruptly lost consciousness.

It was the ninth hour of the day and the sun was inching toward the west when Simon of Gitta topped a low rise and saw before him the place of his birth—the farm of his grandfather Simon, after whom he had been named. The place appeared to be deserted.

For a long moment he stood there, staff in hand, cloak belling in the cool wind. Behind him lay the town of Gitta, less than a mile distant, hugging the bank of a narrow river where it debouched from the hills and began its course across the plain toward the distant haze that marked the sea. Ahead, amid a few oaks beside a stream, stood a familiar house and its outbuildings; a flock of sheep grazed on the slope beyond.

Old emotions stirred in Simon's soul, but his face might have been hewn from granite for all the expression it showed.

He strode forward. The wind abated somewhat as he descended into the small valley. He hoped the place was as deserted as it seemed; he wanted no one to know of his presence. He had skirted Gitta to avoid the slight possibility of being recognized by anyone who had known him—though he realized that his appearance must have changed a great deal during the last eight years. He had been tempted to enter the town in disguise and perform as a wandering magician, but his curiosity was outweighed by his urge toward revenge.

Still, another urge had caused him to make this slight detour to what had been the happiest spot of his childhood. He remembered the sadness when his grandfather died. Simon had been only fourteen at the time; his grandmother had then come to live with him and his parents in their fine house in Sebaste, but had died within the year. Simon was glad of it now; his grandparents had not lived to see the disaster the Romans had inflicted on their family.

As he drew near he saw that the house was indeed in a grave state of disrepair. Much of the stucco was gone from the walls, exposing the underlying bricks, and many of the trees in the yard had been chopped down, perhaps for firewood. The edifice was built largely in the Roman style, old Simon having gained some admiration for Greco-Roman culture during his service in the armies of Marcus Antonius. During its prime, it and the surrounding grounds had been a parklike showplace of rural elegance, a modest villa of a sort once found only in Italy, but now prevalent throughout the Roman Empire. Simon wondered who was the usurping owner who had let it fall into such disrepair.

He advanced toward the cracked columns of the portico, intending to enter—but then noticed that the flock of sheep he had noticed earlier was being driven down the hill in his direction. Behind the bobbing mass of animals strode a single herdsman, while two very large dogs harried their flanks with loud barkings, keeping them in line. Simon stood and watched as the sheep were driven into a wooden pen; then the man secured the gate and advanced toward him, the two dogs at his side. As he drew near, Simon noted that he was tall, bearded and powerfully built, clad in a rough tunic and dark cloak. He bore an oaken staff longer and thicker that Simon's, and a Roman short-sword hung at his side.

The two dogs bristled, barked and snarled viciously, seemingly about to charge. Simon gripped his staff more tightly. The animals were huge, powerfully built, obviously not ordinary sheep dogs.

"Rex, Regulus—*hold!"* growled the herdsman.

The fierce canines held their places, but continued to glower and snarl.

Rex—Regulus . . .?

"What do you want here?" demanded the herdsman, advancing. His face was wide, heavy-featured, eyes scowling under tangled dark locks. Several scars and a broken nose enhanced the ugliness of an already gross countenance.

And Simon recognized him.

"I said, what are you doing here? Answer, or I'll let these dogs chew your bones as they're longing to do."

Simon fought down a sudden surge of rage. Yes, he knew this man—and his dogs.

"Whose property is this?" His voice was even, hard.

The herdsman stepped back a pace, sensing a menace in this steely-voiced, granite-faced stranger. The dogs growled louder.

"This place belongs to the tribune Maxentius of Sebaste. He wants no trespassers here. Begone."

"Perhaps I'm a prospective buyer."

The herdsman eyed Simon narrowly. "How do I know that?"

"How do I know you're the caretaker?"

The man laughed harshly. "Would I be tending the Roman's sheep if I weren't? I keep this place up for Maxentius."

"You don't do a very good job. Maxentius must not come here often or value this place very highly."

The herdsman spat on the ground. "I keep it up well enough to suit him. He lives in Sebaste and comes here only infrequently, to entertain his hunting-guests."

Simon nodded. "And his whores? And his torture-victims?"

The man stared suspiciously. "You've heard the stories about Maxentius, have you? Well, if you want someone done in you'll have to go to Sebaste and talk to him, or to Jahath, the tax-gatherer who administers this estate. Frankly, you don't look rich enough to pay what it'll cost—nor to buy this place, either."

"I didn't come here to buy, *Akrab*. I came to settle a debt."

The herdsman scowled more darkly. "Baal and Anath! How do you know my name?"

Simon laughed—a soft yet sinister laugh. "Can it be, Akrab, that you truly do not remember me? Well, perhaps not, for I was eight years younger when we met, and hate had not yet made my soul hard with dreams of death and vengeance. Does that hardness now show in my face, O Akrab?"

"Speak plainly, damn you, or I'll let these dogs—"

"Aye, those dogs. Let me tell you about those dogs, Akrab. Those dogs were with you one night eight years ago when you entered a house in Sebaste with your master Maxentius and his Roman underling Scribonius and the tax-gatherer Jahath. A man and his wife and their sixteen-year-old son were there, and they resisted you because you and your masters had come to take away all they had."

Akrab's eyes widened. "You!" he gasped. "Simon bar Antonius!"

"They resisted, and you—you, Akrab—turned your dogs loose upon them at Maxentius' order. There were three dogs then, remember? They mauled the man and his wife, whom you and the centurion Scribonius then sworded to death; but before you did so, the son slew one of the dogs with his grandfather's sword, and wounded Scribonius. You, Akrab, subdued that lad by striking him on the head from behind. Then, because he had fought so well, the lad was sold to the gladiator-trainers, and for two years he was trained for combat and slew many men and beasts in the arenas of Rome. Then he escaped and wandered to far lands, learning secrets of death from mighty sorcerers, vowing always to return one day to avenge himself upon those who slew his parents and sold him into slavery. And at last he did return, Akrab, and now he stands before you."

"Rex—Regulus!" shouted Akrab, fear in his eyes. *"Attack!"*

The two huge dogs leaped forward, snarling and barking. Simon let his pack slide from his left shoulder and hurled it into the face of the first dog, then whipped his staff about smartly. The hardwood pole cracked against the head of the second animal, tearing loose one side of its lower jaw and spattering blood and teeth upon the grass. With a dying yelp the creature rolled away, twitching, its eyeballs sprung from its skull and flopping loose on their nerve-stalks. Simon whirled with the skill of a trained fighter—just in time to meet the first dog's renewed charge and ram his staff straight down its snarling throat with such force that the blunt end punched out beneath the tail amid a spray of guts and offal. Then he dove aside—barely in time to avoid Akrab's whistling staff.

He rolled to his feet in a crouch and whipped out his sword just in time to meet the bellowing herdsman's charge. Simon snarled and swung; Akrab's oak staff parted beneath the blow. The herdsman leaped back, flung the sundered stave aside, whipped out his own sword and charged again. Then for a few short moments steel whirled and clashed furiously—until suddenly the herdsman, realizing that he was up against a foe more skilled than any he had ever faced, drew back and began to retreat toward the house.

Simon laughed harshly. "Are you no fighter after all, Akrab? I had heard that you were, but evidently you are nothing without your dogs."

Akrab snarled and snatched up a stone urn, hurled it. Simon sidestepped the missile easily and dashed forward. Again steel clashed in combat, a whirl of bright metal too swift for the eye to follow—and suddenly Akrab's sword went spinning and clattering to the flags of the portico.

Clattering to rest, his right hand still clutching it.

Akrab shrieked as blood spouted from his wrist. His left hand plucked a dagger from his girdle, drew back clumsily to throw it.

Simon's sword hurled through the air and thudded solidly into Akrab's guts. The herdsman sank to his knees, eyes and mouth gaping in pain; he dropped the dagger and plucked ineffectually at the sword hilt. Then his eyes rolled up and he sprawled forward; the sword drove into his stomach to the hilt, the blade standing out a foot beyond his backbone.

Simon approached the impaled carcass and nudged it with his toe. It did not move.

"You are only the first, Akrab," he muttered. "By the gods of Ebal and Seir, I promise it; you are only the first."

CHAPTER IV

"Tell me all, Tolmai!" Dositheus urged. "What has this Rabbi Yeshua bar Yosef to do with what you have told me of Izhar and Chorazin and the minions of Assatur?"

"I know little," said the bald old man, "but I can assure you that Izhar and this Yeshua are not friends. In fact, I think one of the Rabbi Yeshua's followers may have stolen from the Black Synagogue of Chorazin the very Chalice you seek."

Dositheus leaned forward, eyes agleam with curiosity.

"Izhar changed some time ago," continued Rabbi Tolmai, glancing nervously toward the northwest. "Few attend his synagogue any more."

Dositheus, following his glance, noted the distant hills—and the town, perhaps three Roman miles distant across the plain, nestled at their base. Chorazin.

"Changed? How?"

"He has surrounded himself with black-clad guardsmen—perhaps a score of them. They guard the synagogue at night. Some persons who formerly attended Izhar's services, and who now come all the way to Capharnaum to attend mine instead, tell me that the eyes of Izhar and his guards glow in the dark. Others tell me that Izhar has become a wizard and keeps an owl for his familiar."

"I see. And this Rabbi Yeshua?"

"Ah!" Tolmai shook his head sadly. "A sorcerer indeed! Let me tell you what happened the day I allowed him to speak in the synagogue of Capharnaum. His message from the start was strange, for he spoke not as a teacher merely, but as one who had authority from Yahweh himself, emphasizing that he had come to fulfill the Law. I was irritated by this, and was almost at the point of rising and remonstrating, when suddenly another man rose and cried out: 'What have you to do with us, Yeshua Nazarene? Think you to destroy us? I know you—you who are of *Uagio-tsotho*!'"

"He said *that*?" exclaimed Dositheus.

"Aye. Most misunderstood him, however, knowing nothing of these things, and thought he had said *'o agios tou Theou'*—'the Holy One of God'. But I was nearby and heard it well. He clearly pronounced the Karakossan name *Uagio-tsotho*— the same the ancient Hebrews called *Yahweh Zava'ot* and the Stygians *Yog-Sothoth*."

Dositheus shuddered. "Gods! Tell me, then, who was this man who spoke so?"

"He was one of the black-clad soldiers of Izhar!"

Dositheus nodded as if in understanding. "Go on, Tolmai, go on. Leave nothing out."

"Then followed a strange thing. Rabbi Yeshua took from beneath his robe a small cylinder of metal that hummed strangely and held it out in the direction of the man, then said, 'Be silent, and come out of him!' And then, Dositheus, the man fell down in a convulsion and—and *something came out of him!* It was like a greenish fluid, pouring from his mouth, his nostrils, the very pores of his face. In another moment it had left him and gathered itself into a greenish, pulsing ovoid shape perhaps a hand's length in diameter; then, while the congregation watched in horror, it extended itself up the wall and over a windowsill, vanishing like a serpent into the narrow alley outside."

Strange emotions played across Dositheus' face. "Go on, Tolmai," he urged again.

"Of course, my congregation went wild. Many cried out such things as, 'Who is this who commands unclean spirits and they obey him?' When the Rabbi Yeshua left the synagogue they all followed him, including my son Nathaniel, and before the day was over there was talk of nothing else in Capharnaum."

"And what of the demon-possessed man?"

"I spoke to him when all the others had left, for he was too weak to follow them. He was a Greek named Nessos, a soldier; he claimed that just after having been discharged from the legions in Ephesus, a demon had possessed him and caused him to serve a sorcerer named Prodikos for two years, along with many other demon-possessed men. When this Prodikos was at last slain by the magic of other sorcerers, all his surviving demon-soldiers had journeyed to Chorazin, the aeon-old center of Assatur's worship, to put themselves in the service of Izhar—who was also demon-possessed, or so Nessos told me. The Greek was grateful to his rescuer, the Rabbi Yeshua, and as soon as he had recovered some strength, hurried off to follow him."

"Gods!" breathed Dositheus. "Prodikos . . ."

"You mentioned this sorcerer, and his library of arcane lore."

"Aye. I was one of those 'other sorcerers' who caused his undoing—and perhaps thereby saved the world from the All-Night!"

"And did you indeed slay him?"

Dositheus scowled in thought. "I wish I knew. I believe that he and his familiar were carried off to the caverns of Harag-Kolath—where, if the book of Ostanes speaks truly, he must now lie bound for a thousand years. But these are complex matters, Tolmai—as you would know had you delved as deeply into the ancient writings as have I."

"You must allow me to do so, then. I must see those scrolls you bought from the library of Prodikos."

"And so you shall. But first, tell me what became of this sorcerer Yeshua bar Yosef."

"I heard that he cast out more demons—which sometimes then entered into animals, driving them mad with terror. He also cured many persons of diseases by strange techniques. Once I saw him cure a man of a crippled hand in my very synagogue; another time, he healed my chief elder's daughter, who had been given up for dead. After that I allowed him to preach there no more, for the Pharisaic scholars had heard of his doings and came often to dispute him, creating a dangerous situation. Some went so far as to demand that he be tried for his sorcery, even though he accomplished by it naught but benefit for others. As for Rabbi Yeshua himself, he claimed his sorcery was nothing—that it was but a sign that he was come to fulfill the Law. I later heard that he went to Chorazin to confront Izhar, but that Izhar and his black-robed guards would not come near him and denied him the synagogue—which now, strangely, was protected by Roman troops! He then went to Bethsaida and likewise confronted our old friend Rabbi Samezer, who secretly preserves the lore of Yhtill and Demhe, even as do I; Samezer denied him his synagogue also, and bar Yosef finally left this region—but not before cursing all three of our towns, warning of a day of wrath soon to come beside which the destruction of Sodom and Gomorrah would pale!"

"And where did this mad rabbi finally go?"

"Nathaniel's most recent letter to me states that the man and his followers are now working their sorceries south of the Decapolis and east of the Jordan. Nathaniel urges me to join them—*me!* Had I locks to spare I would tear them out and burn them in sorrow upon Yhtill's secret altar!"

"And yet, Tolmai, you say that this Yeshua has cured many of their ills or delivered them from Assatur's demons—and that he urges the fulfillment of the Law which you publicly uphold."

"The Law is perhaps good for the commoners," said Tolmai, "but this man urges it upon all. Yet I know that he has secret knowledge—that he knows better. I sense from his sermons that he knows of the old worships of Canaan and even the far older ones of Karakossa. Why, then, does he curse our towns because we will not take up again the harsh Law of Yahweh, as Joshua once imposed it upon my ancestors? Surely he must realize that the Romans would not permit it!"

"They would not." A bitter glint stole into Dositheus' eyes. "Yet, if I thought this Yeshua could indeed fulfill the Law, I would follow him to the end—for Yahweh once commanded his chosen ones to put all other peoples in this land to the edge of the sword. Would that his command might be fulfilled one day upon the Romans!"

Again Tolmai looked uneasily around the quiet beach as if fearful that they might be overheard. "I have talked enough, Dositheus. It is time for you to speak. Tell me what you know of all this."

Dositheus complied. He told Tolmai of his journey to Parthia, where he and Simon and Menander had studied under the strange magus Daramos; of their return to Ephesus and their encounter with the black-robed minions of Assatur; of their subsequent journey to Antioch, then southward to Ecdippa, whence Dositheus had made his solitary forays into the hills to dig amid the ruins of Hali.

The sun had declined well toward the west by the time he had brought Tolmai up to date.

"I envy you," said Tolmai when Dositheus finished. "Would that Nathaniel had accompanied you on your journeys and shared in your acquired knowledge and wisdom!"

"Perhaps he has gained wisdom of his own which we do not share. Tell me: Who besides Nathaniel follows this strange rabbi?"

Tolmai grimaced. "Alas, my son is in a reprobate company! Of the rabbi's twelve closest confidants, seven are lowly fisherman—mere strong-arm louts. Another is a fanatic zealot against Rome, while still another is a tax-gathering extortionist for the Romans—talk about courting disaster! My Nathaniel and his friend Philip, son of Samezer of Bethsaida, are the only two Galileans of his company with any education, and they are very young."

"These number eleven," said Dositheus. "You said there were twelve."

"Ah, the twelfth! He is not a Galilean like the others, but a red-haired Judean named Judah bar Simon, of Kerioth. And I was wrong to say that Nathaniel and Philip had the only education in the group, for I suspect this Judah of Kerioth has more dark knowledge than the rest of the rabbi's followers put together. I have heard that it may have been he who managed to steal the Chalice of Byakh from the Black Synagogue after his master was not allowed to enter there."

Dositheus started. "The Chalice was stolen?"

"So I was told by Nessos the Greek; also, Samezer of Bethsaida heard it from another of Izhar's soldiers from whom the Rabbi Yeshua cast out a demon. This Judah of Kerioth is evidently a skilled sorcerer; none could have gotten past the unhuman guards to steal such a closely-guarded thing."

"You are right, Tolmai," said Dositheus, "—strange things are afoot in this land. Look." He reached beneath his robe and drew out a small leather packet, laid it upon a flat rock and untied the thong that held it closed. "Tell me—have you ever seen objects such as these?"

Tolmai gasped as he beheld the two objects that lay on the unfolded square of leather. "Yhtill! That medallion—it depicts the Hyades, Assatur's seat of power. One like it was worn by Nessos. He claimed it enabled

Assatur's minions who wore it to find one another's whereabouts for a distance of many tens of miles; after his deliverance he cast it from him, and I hurled it into the Sea of Galilee before sundown. And the silvery sphere with its slim protuberance—Nessos had one such also, and it shared the medallion's watery fate. The Greek told me that these objects were evil beyond imagining—the one an instrument of enslavement, the other of death. I urge you to cast them away, Dositheus!"

Doubt showed in the old Samaritan's eyes; he glanced toward the waves lapping the nearby shore. "Perhaps you're right, old friend. I sense that these objects embody strange sorcery. And yet, how is knowledge to be gained if we avoid all strangeness, all dangers?"

"Dositheus—*look!*"

Terror shone in Tolmai's eyes. Dositheus whirled and saw four men approaching them upon the deserted beach, four men in black cloaks and black armor bearing a black-draped litter between them. The foremost had an owl upon his shoulder and held a small metal cylinder that hummed.

"No!" cried Tolmai. *"No!"*

Then the cylinder glowed, shrilled—and they knew no more.

Simon paused at the top of the low ridge and glanced back to the northwest. Dark billows of smoke rose against the sky. Beyond them, to the west, the sun was descending toward the low hills across the valley, touching the tops of the oaks.

He sighed. Shadows of evening were already surrounding his grandfather's burning villa. For him they would surround it always, for never would he go there again. He had stayed only long enough to inspect the interior of the house; it was filthy—evidently Maxentius had turned it into a hunting lodge. Simon found several large amphorae of lamp oil, had emptied them all upon the floor, then had opened all the door and windows and kindled a blaze. While the flames crackled, he had retrieved his sword and staff, washed them in the stream—then, as an afterthought, had returned to take one last item from the dead Akrab.

His last act before leaving had been to throw open the gate of the sheep pen, that the animals might roam freely upon the hills.

"So ends your ownership of this property, Maxentius," Simon muttered. "If your messengers are swift, you may even learn of it before your life ends as well."

He paused as a fluttering sounded near him. Glancing up, he saw a large owl perched on a branch just above him. The bird flew off noiselessly in the same instant, but not before Simon glimpsed what seemed to be a small metal box upon its breast—a box that glowed with tiny, blinking lights. Then it was gone in the direction of the shadowy valley. Simon tried to follow its flight—but saw instead, on the far rise, the black silhouettes of two men amid the sparse oaks.

Black-cloaked men in dark armor, striding in his direction?

No, he could not tell. At that distance, against the light of the declining sun, the trees and the hill-crests themselves looked black. And now the men had vanished—whether toward or away from him, Simon could not know. He glanced skyward; a lone bird circled high up, perhaps the owl.

He shuddered, then turned and strode rapidly southward. It would not do to be in this vicinity when the body of Akrab was discovered.

While he followed the path in the waning evening light he tried to picture what the superstitious townsfolk of Gitta would do when news of the corpse was brought to them. They would bring a heifer and sacrifice it, and let its blood run off into the stream, that the waters might bear away from them any sin attached to the murder—for so the holy book of the Law prescribed. Such a strange land this was in which he had grown up, so steeped in dark visions of sin and sorcery! And how fortunate, Simon thought, that his grandfather had seen so much of the outside world—enough to cause him to vow that neither his son nor his grandson would remain uneducated and thereby inherit this land's dark legacy of superstition.

Perhaps because he was wrapped in such thoughts, he walked into the forest clearing before being aware that half a dozen Roman soldiers already occupied it.

The Romans saw him only an instant after he saw them; it was too late to retreat. One was mounted on a mule, the other five afoot. In their midst stood a young girl in Samaritan garments, her dark eyes wide with fear. Instantly Simon realized he had stumbled upon a sordid scene all too common in this land—the conquerors, taking their sport with the conquered!

The mounted soldier—no more than a decurion in rank, judging by his armor—urged his mule a pace or two toward Simon. The mule was hardly a quality animal—probably stolen from some poor local farmer, Simon judged. Then the decurion shouted in Greek, "Ho, Samaritan—you must be on your way. As you can see, there's barely enough meat in this camp for me and my men!"

The other soldiers laughed. Simon glimpsed the frightened-bird eyes of the girl amid them. For an instant he considered attack, then decided against it. There were too many, and he had a mission.

"Wait!" The decurion's eyes narrowed as they focused on Simon's weapons—as they recognized in the stranger the build and mien of a fighting man. "Wait, you! Before you go, I want to see some identification."

"Why?"

"To make sure you're not one of these Zealots who are going up and down the land making trouble. Why are you traveling alone so far off the main road?"

"Not for the same reason *you* are, obviously."

The Roman scowled. "Don't be impudent. Whose servant are you? Unless you can account for your presence, it will go ill with you."

Simon sighed, gazed momentarily up at the sky to calm his soul as his Parthian mentors had taught him, then faced his enemies. He knew he was going to have to fight, small as his chances were against six of Rome's trained soldiers. Still, his gladiator-skills might enable him to slay two in the first surprise, his magus-skills perhaps two more.

Suddenly there came the sound of rapid footfalls on the path behind him.

The decurion's eyes widened in surprise and annoyance. Simon turned, saw two men enter the clearing and come to a halt.

Two soldiers, clad in black cloaks and armor, now standing motionless. Upon the shoulder of one perched a large owl.

"By Hades!" exclaimed the decurion. "What do *you* want?"

One of the newcomers raised an arm and pointed at Simon.

The Roman scowled, and three of his men stepped forward, hands on their sword hilts; the other two hung back, holding on to the wide-eyed girl.

"You want *him,* do you?" The decurion's voice was loud; he did not like the look of these silent men in black. "How do I know he isn't a Zealot? How do I know *you* aren't?"

One of the newcomers took something from his belt-pouch—a small glittering object. His features were rigid, expressionless. "Do not hinder us," he said in Greek, his voice strangely toneless.

The Roman whipped out his short-sword. "By Pollux, you'll not order me—"

Flame lanced the air with a shrill crackling; the decurion shrieked as his metal breastplate peeled open in a long molten scar. He pitched from his mule with a crash and the terrified beast whirled to gallop away. Quick as thought, Simon grabbed its mane and swung himself up on its back, clinging for dear life as the animal dashed through the clump of soldiers and out of the clearing, into the circle of concealing oaks.

Immediately he grabbed the reins, brought the mule to a halt, glanced behind him.

The five remaining Romans were running toward the dark-cloaked figures, swords out. Then came more shrill cracklings, more flashes of flame— and agonized shrieks rang out. Three of the soldiers fell, smoke rising from their twitching bodies; a fourth spun and fled, while the fifth snatched a bow from his shoulder and nocked an arrow. In that instant

Simon saw another darting figure—the Samaritan girl fleeing from the clearing directly toward him; the fourth Roman was just behind her.

The soldier's bow twanged; an arrow transfixed one of the black-cloaked men, and the owl on his shoulder flapped into the air. Then a thin lance of fire shot from the hand of the second dark-clad soldier, and the Roman bowman flopped shrieking to the grass, his face blackened and bubbling like pitch. Simon caught a whiff of burnt flesh. Then he saw the girl dashing past him, the fleeing Roman just behind her. He kneed his mount between them and struck; the heavy staff cracked sharply against bone and the soldier flopped twitching to the grass, his skull shattered.

"Up here!" Simon yelled to the girl as he galloped after her. "Jump—quick!"

The girl responded with surprising swiftness, gripping Simon's extended hand and leaping up behind him upon the mule. Simon glanced back into the clearing.

"Baal!" he exclaimed.

And in the same instant the girl shrieked—for the arrow-pierced soldier was still on his feet, facing forward with his black-clad companion, both of whom were leveling glittering objects toward her and her rescuer.

"Hyah!" Simon kicked his mount in the flanks, causing it to dash off through the oaks. Behind him he heard shrill cracklings, saw flashes of light, smelled burning branches, felt the girl clinging to him in terror as they rode frantically away from the strange, unearthly danger.

Menander returned to consciousness slowly, painfully; his face and limbs tingled with agonizing pricklings; the rest of his body seemed numb.

He opened his eyes. He seemed to be confined within a narrow space. The light was dim. He tried to rise, but could not; his muscles would not respond. Then he felt a swaying motion. He was lying on his back; the narrow space in which he lay was solid above, curtained at the sides.

A litter. He was being carried along in a litter.

He flexed his hands, the muscles in his calves. The tingling was moving up his limbs, slowly replacing the numbness. He was able to raise his right arm, cautiously push back the right curtain. He saw dusk—and, nearby, another curtained litter being borne by four black-clad guardsmen.

Menander let his hand fall back. The curtain closed. He moved his left arm, managed to turn his head slightly, felt the warmth and smoothness of human flesh, saw the sweeping curves of shapely legs in the dimness. With a great effort he raised his head slightly, saw that Ilione lay beside him in the litter, her sandaled feet touching his left cheek. She seemed unconscious. Thick ropes arched over both of them, holding them fast to the floor of the litter.

Menander flexed his limbs; feeling returned to them slowly. He thought of the ways his Parthian mentor Daramos had taught him to escape from bonds; yet, these ways proved unnecessary, for as his arms became movable he found he could disengage them easily from the ropes, which were evidently meant only to keep him and Ilione from falling out of the litter. Cautiously the youth extended his left hand over Ilione's legs and parted the curtain, saw the fiery afterglow of sunset beyond distant hills, then let the curtain fall back.

Sunset on his left. That meant that he and Ilione were being carried northward.

Northward—toward Chorazin.

Menander flexed his limbs more vigorously, knowing that he must regain feeling and mobility before those who bore him reached their goal. Somehow he knew that his plight was due to Dositheus' delvings into dark sorcery—the old fool had unearthed forbidden secrets, and now the black guardsmen had come to punish them all. Menander cursed himself. They must have been watching the first inn, waiting to follow him. Why had he not been more careful?

Ilione moaned slightly. Menander redoubled his efforts to slip out from under the ropes. Feeling was returning to his thighs and shoulders with agonizing tinglings; he clenched his teeth against the urge to cry out. In a few more minutes he was free of the ropes, his ability to move almost completely restored. Slowly, carefully, he reversed his position; his captors must not guess that he was free.

Ilione moaned again, moved her limbs slightly. She, too, was beginning to wake up.

"Lie still," Menander whispered in her ear.

The girl opened her eyes—wide, hazel eyes, full of fear. Menander hoped that her fear was not mirrored in his own.

"Lie still. Flex your muscles. You'll be able to move soon. Don't be afraid, and don't move violently or cry out."

Ilione closed her eyes, appeared to be obeying the youth's instructions. Again Menander stole a look from the left side of the litter. The sunset was no longer visible, only the dark brick faces of buildings, the cobbles of a street. Evidently they were already in Chorazin. He heard Ilione's breathing, turned to see her chest rising and falling rapidly beneath her tunic as she flexed her limbs. Evidently her fear was bringing her back to consciousness rapidly.

"Don't be afraid—don't make any noise."

"Menander, where are we?" she whispered. "What's happening?"

The youth stole another glance outside the curtain. He glimpsed a row of Roman guards ranged before a pillared portico of black stone—a portico whose pillars reflected the guardsmen's torches, and above which leered the graven bas-relief of a serpent-haired Medusa. Instantly he let the curtain fall back.

Roman soldiers. Why were *they* guarding this dark fane?

"What's happening, Menander?" repeated the girl urgently, catching the anxiety in Menander's eyes.

"We're at the synagogue of Chorazin," whispered the youth. "Dositheus has told me of it."

Panic showed in the girl's eyes. "The fane of Assatur?"

Menander clamped a hand over her mouth. "Quiet! We'll get away."

Ilione nodded. In a moment she had freed herself from the ropes also. Menander felt the litter tilting—evidently they were being carried up the steps into the temple—then leveling out again. A dozen paces more and the conveyance came to a halt.

Cautiously Menander drew the right curtain back a crack. The other litter was still beside his—the black-cloaked guardsmen were setting both gently upon the floor. In the next instant one of the guards flung open the other litter's curtains and Menander gasped as he saw the two roped figures within—bald-headed Tolmai, whom he remembered as a priest of the synagogue in Capharnaum, and the white-bearded form of his mentor Dositheus.

Then the curtain of Menander's own litter was whipped aside and a harshly resonant voice rang out, "Come forth!"

Menander and Ilione, still rubbing feeling back into their tingling limbs, crept hesitantly from the palanquin. There were no Romans here in the synagogue, only black-clad guards. Looking apprehensively toward the back of the temple, where stood the ark and the podium, Menander saw a tall, dark-cloaked figure with glowing yellow eyes—and beside him a short, cowled figure with no visible eyes at all.

"Come forth," repeated the tall one, "and come here."

The two advanced slowly, cautiously—and as they did so, Menander recognized the taller figure as a man he had met four years earlier. Square-faced, dark-bearded, heavy browed . . . aye, it was Izhar, Rabbi of Chorazin, keeper of the ancient secrets of Karakossa—and yet, a *changed* Izhar with erect, rigid mien and menacing yellow eyes.

"Menander!" gasped Ilione, clutching his arm. "Who are they?"

The taller of the two figures strode forward, descended the few steps from the podium and leered down at them. Menander could not help cringing slightly before the eerie yellow glow of those eyes.

"This one is called Izhar," it said slowly, pointing to itself. "Its brain remembers you, youth—you are called Menander. It met you some years ago—you, and this white-haired one in the other litter."

Menander felt his flesh crawl. There was something inhuman—something *wrong*—about he way Izhar was talking to him.

Suddenly there came a groan from the other palanquin. Menander and Ilione turned, saw that Dositheus and Tolmai were both stirring and groping at the ropes that held them down. Their eyes fluttered and slowly opened.

"Gods!" moaned Dositheus. "Are we in the hells—?"

Izhar's eyes gleamed even more brightly, as if with a supernatural menace. "Good," he muttered. "Good. You are all awake. Now, if you would die painlessly, you will tell me all concerning how you have aided those who plot against us."

They had camped, Simon and the girl, amid the oaks upon the gentle slope of a hill, well off any trail. The mule, relieved of its saddle and packs, stood tethered nearby; it had been well laden with supplies, and from these Simon had prepared their supper over a small fire. The sun had not quite reached the horizon, but Simon wanted the fire to be extinguished before darkness, when its flame might be seen between the trees. Already the shadows were deepening.

They ate in silence. Simon was ravenous and to him the simple stew of lentils and dried beef seemed delicious. The girl ate lightly, hesitantly, casting nervous glances at him from time to time. Much of the fear had left her eyes, but there was still a haunted look in them—and something of puzzlement, of curiosity, as well. Simon could not fathom her.

"You need not fear me, you know," he said. "I am no Roman. Tell me, where were you bound when those soldiers accosted you? I will see you safely there."

"I was leading this mule to one of my master's estates."

"Ah! So we're consuming your master's supplies, not the Romans'. I'll see that he's paid for whatever's missing, so you won't get punished—though I can't imagine him begrudging me a good meal or two after what I've saved him. But, by Mot!—whatever possessed your master to let you, a young girl, journey into this countryside alone?"

Anxiety entered the girl's eyes. "It is not as you think. My master is a Roman—those soldiers were under his command. I fear they were sent to abduct me secretly, so that my mistress would not learn of it. My master was very angry with me." The girl shuddered. "His soldiers said they wanted me to . . . to entertain them . . . before they killed me."

Simon scowled darkly. "Romans," he muttered.

The girl set aside her bowl of stew and rose. "I must go. I will tell no one of this. I do not know you—I will not describe you. I will say that we were attacked by Zealots. Please, help me get the supplies back on the mule. If I am too late with them Akrab will beat me, no matter what my excuse."

"Akrab!" Simon was on his feet instantly. "You were taking these supplies to Akrab, servant of the Roman Maxentius?"

The girl, cringing back from the Samaritan's black, scowling gaze, nodded dumbly.

"Akrab shall not beat you," said Simon. "He is dead. I slew him not two hours ago."

"It—it can't be. No man could slay Akrab."

"Look, then!" Simon stooped, drew a leather-wrapped object from his pack and held it up. "Look upon his face!"

The leather fell away. The girl cringed back still father from the severed head that dangled by its hair in Simon's grip, its face white and its eyes rolled horribly upward, blood clotted about the severed neck.

"Look, girl! I bear it to your master, Maxentius. He shall see it also—before he dies!"

The girl sank to her knees, trembling. "Oh, Simon, no! You must not—you will be killed."

Simon's expression softened. He laid the head aside, strode forward a pace, scowling in perplexity. "Tell me, girl—how do you know my name?"

She looked up at him. "Do you not know me, then, Simon bar Antonius? I am Lotis. My mother was servant to your parents. You helped teach me to read. Do you not remember?"

"Lotis?" Simon bent closer, saw a familiarity in the girl's white, upturned features. "It is true! You were only eight when—when the Romans came to my home."

"Simon!" The girl leaped up and rushed into his arms. "Oh, Simon, you were so good to me!"

Simon returned her embrace, felt her beginning to sob. "Lotis—"

"Cavé!"

They released one another, startled by the harsh avian screech. A large raven was alighting upon an oak branch with a noisy flutter.

"Cavé!"

"Carbo!" Simon exclaimed. "*What* danger? What are you squawking about?"

"Cavé bubo! Cavé negrum!"

"The owl? The dark one? What—?"

"Negrum venit!" screeched the bird, flapping into the air.

"What! Come back! Where are you going?"

"Caphar!" squawked the raven, flying upward. *"Caphar!"*

Then it was above the trees, flying away northeastward, a black feathery blot against the yellow of the late afternoon sky. In another moment it was gone.

CHAPTER V

"You talked to it!" gasped Lotis. "It spoke to you! Did I hear it say to beware an owl and . . . a 'dark one'?"

"I think so. The bird speaks little but Latin, and not very well at that."

"Little but Latin?" The girl laughed nervously. "How many birds can converse in any language? Have you become a sorcerer, Simon?"

"No, only a wandering trickster. If anyone's a true sorcerer, it's my mentor Dositheus. I'm sure he sent Carbo to spy on me, and now the bird's on its way back to Capharnaum to report."

"It warned you of a 'dark one'." Lotis glanced amid the trees where thick shadows were gathering. "Could it have meant one of those black-garbed soldiers who slew the Romans?"

"I don't see how they could have traveled this far on foot so quickly. Sit down, Lotis, and calm yourself. We'll finish our supper. Then, just to be safe, we'll pack up and continue on while the moon is still high."

They resumed eating in silence while the sun set and the fire burned low. Simon's mind was working. Surely it was a stroke of luck, meeting this girl. Doubtless she knew Maxentius' habits and could help Simon gain access to him.

A sound broke Simon's thoughts—the sound of a nearby footfall. He glanced up. Someone was coming down the slope of the hill, through the forest.

Then Lotis gasped in sudden fear—for in the shadows beneath the nearest oaks appeared the form of a man clad in black—a man whose great glassy eyes eerily reflected the dying firelight.

Menander cringed before the yellow-glowing eyes of the Rabbi Izhar—and yet, what made the lad cringe even more was the hollow, black cowl of the squat being behind the rabbi—the being from whose dark sleeves protruded what seemed the fingerless palps of a squid. For a panicky instant he thought of bolting—but thought better of it upon seeming several of the dark guards, yellow-eyed like Izhar, standing near him with glittering metal objects in their hands.

"Tolmai!" cried Izhar. "Dositheus! Rise, both of you, and stand before us."

Menander watched as the two old men groped free of the ropes that had held them to the floor of the litter. Awkwardly they rose, then stepped forward hesitantly, fear in their eyes.

"Izhar!" gasped Tolmai. "What have you *become?*"

The yellow-eyed rabbi raised his hand. "Silence, and listen. I have become what you, too, are privileged to become. The thing for which we have all waited so long has come to pass. Those who aeons ago came to earth from the cloudy depths of Demhe have at last awakened. Those whom men call *Am-ha-arez*—the Earth Folk—have risen at last to possess our bodies, that we may serve them in their great purpose."

Tolmai trembled; the fear in his eyes was suddenly mingled with a mystical longing. "Can it be—?"

"No!" cried Dositheus. "Beware, Tolmai—they will use your body to the detriment of your soul!"

Izhar stepped forward a pace, scorn in his glowing eyes. "Do I look used, Tolmai? Look closely at me. We are the same age, are we not? Have I not changed since last we met?"

"Gods, it's true!" gasped Tolmai. "Look, Dositheus—his beard is darker, his face less wrinkled."

Dositheus scowled. "He seems unchanged to me."

Izhar grinned rigidly. "But remember, good Dositheus—you haven't seen me for about *five years!"*

"It's true," Tolmai muttered. "Dositheus, I saw him less than two months ago. He was older then, I swear! Older . . ."

Menander shuddered. He felt Ilione clinging to his arm, trembling, but was too frightened himself to take any satisfaction from the fact.

"You see truly, Tolmai," said Izhar. "Now, step forward."

The old man did so, slowly, hesitantly, yet with awe in his eyes—awe mixed with longing.

"Beware!" cried Dositheus.

"Listen not to our enemies. Come forward, Tolmai. Come."

"Enemies? Izhar, don't you know me? Or Menander?"

Izhar ignored Dositheus. "Come, Tolmai."

As the old man advanced, almost as if hypnotized, the squat, robed form in the shadows drew from beneath its robes a copper-colored hemisphere nearly the length of a man's forearm in diameter and held it out. Menander gasped to see the being's tentacle-arms extend farther from its sleeves than a man's arms ever could. Quickly it deposited the hemisphere on the floor beside Izhar, flat side up, then withdrew its weird appendages into its sleeves. Izhar drew a small, silvery cylinder from his robe and pointed it at the hemisphere.

"Now, Tolmai, kneel."

The old rabbi did so. There was rapture strangely mingled with the fear in his eyes. "So long I have waited for this—so long . . ."

The cylinder shrilled briefly, abruptly—and in that instant the hemisphere's flat side snapped open oddly, like the iris of an eye, withdrawing nearly to the rim. Now the hemisphere resembled an open bowl—a bowl within which a greenish jelly pulsed and scintillated.

Ilione screamed.

Menander felt a surge of horror as he beheld the pulsing mass of jelly flow over the rim of the bowl and go crawling toward the kneeling Tolmai across the stone tiles. The old man was trembling, muttering inaudible prayers, his eyes tightly closed; then the creeping fluid touched his left knee, spread up and over the fabric covering his thigh.

"Gods!" hissed Dositheus.

For now the greenish blob was dwindling in size—dwindling as it slowly soaked through the fabric of Tolmai's garment and into his flesh. Menander felt Ilione trembling violently as she clung to him, knew that she was remembering the two similar horrors they had seen at Ecdippa. He gripped her wrist in case she should suddenly try to bolt, for the black-cloaked guardsmen were standing by watching, small silvery objects in their hands.

In another moment the green blob had vanished entirely. Tolmai still trembled, though apparently he was in no pain. His trembling ceased; then his eyes slowly opened.

"Rise, brother," said Izhar.

Tolmai did so, then turned to face Dositheus. His eyes now reflected the torchlight brilliantly, eerily, as did Izhar's.

"It is well," he said in a level, emotionless voice. "It is good to dwell in flesh and blood once more, after having lain bodiless for so many thousands of sun-circlings. Now, Izhar—how shall we cause these other beings to talk? By pain, or by the privilege of possession?"

"Gods!" cried Dositheus. "Tolmai—you have become *Am-ha-arez!"*

"I am no longer merely Tolmai. I am him, yet I am more. You are a wise man, Dositheus, and so we offer you a choice. Submit your will to the lords of Demhe, even as have I—or resist, and suffer torments beyond all enduring."

"But *why?"* cried Menander suddenly. "Tolmai—Izhar—don't you remember us? When have we done you ill?"

Four gleaming eyes turned in the lad's direction.

"We must know why your mentor delved in the ruins of Hali," said Izhar. "We must know what part he played in the theft of the Chalice of Byakh."

"I stole nothing," Dositheus protested. "I found nothing!"

The eyes swung back in his direction. Then the cowled being made a deep, hollow sound, utterly unlike anything Menander had ever heard before. His skin crawled to hear it.

"Yes," said Izhar without turning. "Bring forth three more of the brothers."

The unhuman being moved away to the altar, stooped and reached behind it, brought forth in its tentacles another gleaming coppery hemisphere, then another and yet another, depositing the three of them in a row upon the tiled floor.

"No!" cried Dositheus. "You wouldn't!"

"Submit!" intoned Izhar. "Submit voluntarily and there will be no pain. Now must the three of you be brought into the Domain of Demhe—and then we shall know the truth, and you shall be enhanced beyond all human understanding."

Simon jumped to his feet, his sharp-bladed sica instantly in hand, and faced the black-clad intruder who stood in the shadows at the edge of the small clearing. In the same instant, the stranger touched the glowing clasp of his belt—and instantly a dim, deep blue radiance sprang into being around him.

"Who are you?" demanded Simon, feeling the hair prickling on the back of his neck. "Answer, or I'll—"

The man stepped forward a pace. "I—I understand very little of the Greek language," he said in faltering Latin. "You—need not fear me."

Simon stared. He felt relief as he realized that only a human being confronted him. Yet—what else had he expected? He heard Lotis rising, moving closer to him.

"Who—are you?" she asked hesitantly.

"My name is Taggart," said the man in his oddly-accented Latin. "I mean you no harm. I must speak with you."

Simon now saw that the stranger, fully revealed in the dim firelight, was indeed human. Yet his appearance was strange. He was clad in black—not in cloak and armor like the mysterious guardsmen, but in shirt, trousers and shoes of a cut Simon had never seen before. About his waist was a wide belt of what seemed to be evenly woven strands of deep blue metal, its clasp glowing with a dim violet light, and now Simon saw that this belt was the center of the dim blue radiance that surrounded the man. A small pouch of what seemed to be black leather hung upon his left hip, a larger pouch of the same material on his right, and from the latter protruded part of an object which Simon instinctively felt must be a weapon. In his right hand the man clutched a small silvery cylinder. It hummed softly.

"Simon!" breathed Lotis. "He speaks the language of the Romans."

"Don't be afraid," Simon muttered. Then, in Latin, "Stranger, if that's a weapon in your hand, I'll gut you before you can raise it."

"This?" The man called Taggart lowered his hand; the object in it ceased to hum. "It is not a weapon. I used it merely to find you. It has guided me down from the hilltop through these trees."

"*What?* Speak plainly, stranger. Are you saying that you are a wizard?"

The man smiled slightly. "Perhaps I must seem so to you. But I repeat, I mean you no harm. May I join you by your fire? I must explain something to you."

Simon regarded the man more closely. His brown hair was cropped short, though not so closely as a Roman's, and no Roman would have worn that sort of trimmed beard and mustache. And— what human ever wore such a grotesque device as that upon man's face?—a dark framework that rested upon the bridge of his nose and hooked behind his ears, supporting two transparent discs through which his brown eyes peered distortedly.

Taking Simon's silence for assent, the man stepped forward. Simon raised his knife menacingly. Its tip encountered the fringe of the blue glow surrounding the stranger—and slid aside as if upon a hard, frictionless surface.

"You see," said the man called Taggart, "you cannot harm me. Nor do I wish you harm. On the contrary. But you must listen to me. You are both in danger."

Simon drew back a pace. "You *are* a sorcerer."

"No." The stranger shook his head. "Nothing I do is magical. Yet, there are forces about you which you might not understand in any other terms. Have you sensed that you are being followed?"

"Sensed?" Simon abruptly threw back his head and laughed. Then, just as abruptly, he sobered, sheathed his sica and gestured toward the campfire. "Seat yourself then, stranger. And will you have food?"

"No food, thank you," said the man as he sat down on the ground. "But, please—call me Taggart."

Simon, sitting down opposite the man, decided that he did look fully human. "I am Simon of Gitta—Taggart. A strange name, that. You must be from a far western province."

"Why do you think so?"

"Because you don't speak Greek, and your Latin is strangely accented."

"You are right, I am from the . . . west. Farther west than you could imagine."

"You mean Hibernia, perhaps? Once, during my years as a gladiator, I met a man named Arawn MacSamthainn—a captive from the Hibernian Isle. Your name even has a Hibernian ring."

"No." Taggart shook his head. "The land I originally come from is far west of that. But these are things I haven't time to discuss." He raised the small cylinder in his right hand, and it began to hum again; he leveled it at Simon's pack, which rested beside the fire, and the humming grew louder. "Open that bedroll, please, and let me see what is in it."

Simon scowled. "Why should I?"

He felt Lotis close to him, clutching the sleeve of his tunic, heard her whisper tensely in his ear, "Obey him, Simon. Then, perhaps he will go away—return to the darkness."

Simon felt that the girl was trembling. "Don't be afraid, Lotis." Then, sternly facing the man in black, "Be brief, wizard. What do you want of us?"

"You have two objects in your pack. You must give them to me—otherwise, you cannot hope to throw off those who are on your trail."

Simon glared at him. "The black-robed guardsmen? Tell me, then, Taggart: Who are they?"

"The newly-awakened servants of . . . Hastur. But I have no time to explain. Open your pack."

Simon, sensing urgency rather than a threat in the stranger's tone, did so. Knowing instinctively what the man wanted, he plucked forth the silvery object and the medallion inset with the glowing gem-pattern of the Hyades, and handed them over.

"Here—and welcome to the sorcerous damned things!"

"Good." Taggart placed the small metal cylinder in his belt pouch, then touched the belt's clasp. The blue glow about him vanished. Quickly he grabbed the two objects from Simon and placed them in the pouch also. In that instant Simon and Lotis realized with complete certainty that the man was as human as they.

But then he touched his belt clasp again; the blue glow sprang into being around him once more.

"I must go now," he said. "The sooner I leave, the safer you will be."

"Wait!" said Simon. "You can't just go without telling us what brought you here."

"It was merely good luck. I was cruising around, hoping to detect some sign of . . . Hastur's servants. I located two of them, then realized they were following you."

A sudden shrill hum sounded from the man's pouch. Quickly he reached in and withdrew the small cylinder; it ceased its humming.

"Be quiet, both of you!" he hissed. "Your pursuers come!"

As he spoke, he rose, and in another moment he had slipped away amid the oaks, the dim bluish glow surrounding him fading quickly from sight into the darkness.

"Baal!" swore Simon, rising. *"Wait!"* He strode forward a pace, as if to follow the man—when suddenly a slight gasp from Lotis caught his attention.

"Simon—look!"

He glanced up to where she was pointing, saw a large owl perched on a low branch, its eyes unblinking as it gazed downward. About its neck hung a medallion with the gleaming "V" of starts upon it. In the next instant,

Simon heard another sound—slow, deliberate footsteps. Someone was approaching the small clearing, this time from the downhill side.

Lotis, rose, trembling, staring toward the approaching footfalls. "Demons?" she muttered tremulously.

Simon drew his blades. "Get back of me—hide among the trees."

The owl hooted shrilly, then extended a wing like a pointing hand. The girl stood rooted to the spot, petrified. Simon stepped around the fire, shoved her toward the trees, turned back—and saw two men entering the clearing from the shadows.

Two men wearing black cloaks and helmets, their eyes glowing yellow in the firelight. The breast of one of them was transfixed by an arrow.

Simon crouched facing them, waiting. The black-clad figures stopped and faced him, their eyes as unblinking as the owl's. On the breast of each hung the medallion glittering with the starry "V" of the Hyades. Behind him, Simon could hear Lotis' teeth chattering.

Then, deliberately, each of the cloaked men drew from a pouch at his side a small, silvery object and leveled it. Simon tensed to spring, knowing he was doomed—he could never leap the fire and reach his foes in time to forestall the twin lances of sorcerous flame that he knew would sear his flesh.

Suddenly a piercing metallic shrill sounded from the uphill side of the clearing. Instantly the black-cloaked pair dropped their weapons and staggered back, shrieking, hands pressed to their ears—then collapsed. In the same instant, the owl screeched and fell fluttering from its branch. The shrilling sound increased. Simon turned and saw that the man Taggart stood at the clearing's edge; the shrilling sound came from the small glittering cylinder he held in his hand. The two cloaked soldiers and the owl were threshing about on the grass as if in agony. As Simon watched, their threshings quieted to spasms of shuddering. Then—

"Gods!" Simon gasped.

Behind him he heard Lotis moan in terror—for, as he watched, there emerged from the mouth of each of the soldiers a large greenish blob of quivering matter, and from the beak of the owl, a smaller one. As soon as the things had separated completely from their hosts, the cylinder in Taggart's hand ceased to shrill. Immediately the blobs began to extend themselves toward the edge of the clearing, undulating like great translucent worms.

Simon sheathed his blades, leaped forward and snatched up a flaming brand from the fire. As he did so, he saw that the two largest things had reached the clearing's edge and were extending themselves upward along the trunks of two oaks—and then, incredibly, their substance dwindled rapidly as if they were soaking into the bark. Simon muttered a curse and ran forward.

"Let them go!" cried Taggart in his strangely-accented Latin. "They can do no harm in there."

Simon had no choice in the matter, for the things had vanished before he could reach them. Somehow they had penetrated the very substance of the bark, leaving not even a trace of moisture behind them.

The mule, tethered just within the first screen of trees, suddenly whickered shrilly. Simon ran to its side, grabbed its tether and spoke gently to it. Abruptly the animal grew quiet. For a moment Simon stroked it and spoke soothingly, then returned to the fire. Lotis ran to meet him, then turned to stare fearfully at the man called Taggart.

"Simon, he commands the demons—surely he is a demon himself!"

"No," said Simon. "I think he is as human as we."

Suddenly the owl which had fallen in the clearing struggled to its feet with a flutter. Uttering a shrill hoot, it flapped frantically upward and vanished into the night, leaving the medallion it had worn lying upon the ground. Simon remembered the small blob that had emerged from it—that must have been what had frightened the mule.

Then he saw that one of the fallen guards was stirring, struggling to rise. The man's eyes no longer glowed in the firelight.

"Gods—I'm free!" he gasped. *"Free!"*

Instantly he snatched the medallion from around his neck and cast it to the ground. As he stood up, he glanced from Simon to Lotis, then to Taggart. "Sorcerer, you have freed me."

"You'd better leave this area before I do," said Taggart, "or the thing may try to repossess you. Go quickly."

With a yell of terror, the man turned and dashed off in the direction from which he had come, vanishing into the woods. For a moment Simon heard him blundering away amid the shrubs and trees; then silence returned.

"You two must leave also. Pack your things. I'll watch until you're ready to go, to make sure the beings do not try and come for you."

Lotis had begun that task before the man called Taggart had even finished speaking. Simon glanced at the arrow-transfixed soldier who remained lying motionless upon the grass, then back to Taggart. "Why did not the Roman's arrow slay the man instantly? Baal! Can those demons animate corpses as well as possess the living?"

"They can, if the corpse is not too long dead. Hurry."

As Simon packed, he kept one eye on the black-clad Taggart, who quickly went around the clearing picking up the three medallions and the two silvery weapons the soldiers and the owl had borne. These he placed in the pouch at his belt. Simon noticed that he threw frequent glances at the two trees into which the blob-beings had vanished, all the while keeping the small metal cylinder ready in his left hand.

Lotis led the mule close to the fire and in another moment they had loaded their few possessions upon it. Immediately Taggart turned and set off up the slope, beckoning them to follow.

"No, Simon," Lotis whispered. "We can get on the mule and ride away. The sorcerer is afoot—we can escape him."

Simon shook his head. "If he'd meant us harm he would have slain us before now. Don't be afraid, Lotis. Come along—I mean to ask the man a few questions."

After a few minutes of uphill walking, the forest thinned out enough that they could draw abreast of the wizard. The weird glow surrounding him was even more apparent amid the moon-cast shadows.

"Where are you leading us?" Simon demanded.

The man paused and faced him. "Nowhere. You may go your way now—we are safely distant from the . . . things. They cannot follow you. In fact, you will be safer away from me."

"Why?"

"Because I have the weapons and medallions now. If there are any other . . . Hastur minions . . . still following you, they will seek me instead."

Simon felt a chill that was not of the night air. "Dositheus!" he muttered. "He carries such a weapon and medallion also—and Menander and Ilione are with him."

"What?" exclaimed Taggart. "These are friends of yours?"

"Aye. Tell me, wizard—are they in danger?"

"They may well be. You'd better tell me where they are."

"In Capharnaum, I think."

"Where is that?"

"Northeast of here, on the shore of the Sea of Galilee—but it's a two day's journey.

Taggart abruptly resumed striding up the hill; Simon followed, and Lotis came behind him, leading the mule. In another moment they had emerged from the last of the trees and stood upon a bare hilltop under the light of the half-moon.

Upon the summit rested a large, low object silhouetted against the rising eastern stars of Libra and glowing faintly with the same sort of blue radiance that seemed to surround Taggart. Lotis gasped at the sight, and held back; but Simon, spurred by the concern of his friends, kept pace with the enigmatic stranger and asked:

"What are these beings who endanger Dositheus and the others? Are these indeed the slaves of Assatur, who once served Prodikos in Ephesus?"

Taggart paused beside the large glowing object, which, as Simon could now see, was flat and circular and surrounded by a raised rim of dark metal. Somehow he sensed that it was a craft of some strange sort. Faintly glowing, yet of dark metal, its round interior blinked with dim, enigmatic lights.

"Prodikos?" Taggart eyed Simon narrowly. "The being inhabiting a human named Prodikos recently lost its hold on this world and fell into another . . . region . . . known as Harag-Kolath. How do you come to know of it?"

Simon barked a laugh. "I fought the demon! Ask my mentor Dositheus, and his young wards Menander and Ilione, if you would know more. Dositheus studies arcane things. But these blob-demons—I've never heard him speak of them."

"I have little time to explain it all." Taggart looked up at the stars. "The pertinent constellations are not visible—they will not rise until after dawn. But you must know them—the Hyades, the Pleiades and the Twins."

Simon recognized the names. "What have those star-groups to do with the fate of my friends?"

"The beings you call 'demons' come originally from those stars," said Taggart hurriedly. "The green blobs. But they are not all from the same stars, and they are not all enemies of humans. I have no time to explain more—I must go, if I'm to be in time to save your friends."

"I'm going with you!" yelled Simon, dashing forward—but immediately he encountered an invisible barrier, smoother than glass, frictionless. The glows surrounding Taggart and his strange craft had merged to include one another, as might have two bubbles."

"No," said Taggart. "I'm sorry. I must go now." His voice was faint, as if it had come from behind a thin wall. He turned and clambered within the craftlike object, bent and touched a small glowing square. A humming sound arose, began to swell.

"Simon," cried Lotis, "come away! It's sorcery!"

He backed slowly away, the hair on his neck prickling as he saw that the object was rising slowly into the air. Never had he seen magic like this!

"Don't worry," yelled Taggart from the ascending craft. "If your friends still carry the weapon and the medallion, I will find them."

"Damn you, wizard, *come back!"*

There drifted back a rushing sound, like windy thunder echoing from the distant hills—then, silence.

Simon felt a light touch on his arm. He turned and faced Lotis. Her face was white; she was trembling, yet there was awe mingled with the fear in her eyes.

"We—we should go, Simon—leave this place."

Simon gazed back to where the craft had vanished into the dark sky. "He said my friends were in danger."

"He also said he would find them and save them, did he not? Come, Simon, we must leave this place also, lest the demons should return."

Simon nodded, his mind benumbed, then followed obediently as the girl led the mule southward along the slope of a descending ridge. But often he glanced back, and the flesh on his neck continued to prickle at the sight of the glittering stars—strange stars, no longer familiar, seeming to symbolize unearthly mysteries.

"Submit!" cried Izhar, his yellow eyes seemingly ablaze. "Only if you resist will there be pain. If you comply willingly, there will be release, healing—and understanding beyond anything you have hitherto known."

The squat cowled being had placed the three coppery bowls upon the tiles, then had withdrawn to the shadows. Menander watched those bowls rock slightly, winking with soft highlights from the many torches. Then the flat lids opened like the irises of eyes, revealing the pulsing green blobs within.

"No!" gasped Ilione. She turned away as if to flee; immediately a black-cloaked guardsman blocked her way, grabbed her, turned her about. The three greenish blobs were spilling out onto the floor, probing forward like monstrous semi-fluid worms.

Menander tensed, terror and rage vying within him. He wanted to spring upon the guard that held Ilione, to flee this place of madness with her, yet knew that the guards would overpower him also. And then, to his horror, he saw old Dositheus, his trusted mentor, kneel upon the tiles and extend his arms, an almost mystical longing in his eyes.

"I will trust you, Izhar—Tolmai. Long have I studied the ancient writings, and long have I hoped for such understandings as you now promise. Do not fail me, friends—let me be a servitor of Demhe, even as are you!"

"Receive—exult—be born into Knowledge!" intoned Izhar and Tolmai together.

The foremost blob-being lapped against Dositheus' knee, began to vanish through the fabric of his robe. Horrified, Menander watched as the thing dwindled and vanished. Dositheus shuddered, bowed his head almost to the tiles—then suddenly snapped erect and stared about himself as if in amazement. His eyes began to glow in the torchlight, like those of an owl or a lynx.

"Gods!" he cried suddenly. "I see! *I see!*"

Menander continued to stare in horror as the two other blobs approached him and Ilione. Then, as the girl screamed again, he cast aside restraint and sprang at the guard that held her, howling his hate, striking with his bare fists. The man staggered back a pace, but did not release the girl. Immediately two other black-cloaked guards grabbed him, held him motionless despite his utmost efforts, while the two blobs came on toward him and the girl.

"Submit! Submit!" cried Izhar and Tolmai—and then, to Menander's horror, he saw Dositheus turn toward him and heard him also cry out, "Menander—submit!"

"No!" he screamed, struggling madly. He heard Ilione shrieking with a terror akin to his own. The demons were upon them—he felt the viscous substance of one of them touching him, enclosing the flesh of his ankle. He kicked frantically, shrieked in pain and fear as he sensed the being invading him.

Suddenly there was a thundering crash as the west wall of the synagogue burst and crashed inward and all within the building were hurled sprawling to the tiles.

CHAPTER VI

Menander rolled frantically upon the tiles, choking on the dust that had suddenly filled the air. Even the mighty concussion and the confusion following it had not driven from his mind the thought of the horrible being that had been about to seep into his flesh.

His rollings brought him up against the base of a pillar. He scrambled to his feet and looked about. The dust was settling and he saw many others rising also. He coughed, sneezed, groped forward a pace. Before him a white -clad form stirred, struggled to rise. He recognized Ilione, bent to help her up. Izhar, Tolmai and many of the black-cloaked guards were also on their feet, glaring in his direction with yellow eyes. But Dositheus and others of the guards were staring in the opposite direction, and beyond them—

"Gods!" cried Menander.

Through the clearing dust he saw a great hole gaping in the synagogue's west wall, and in the middle of it stood a black-garbed man whose form was surrounded by a faint blue glow. In his right hand he clutched a bulky object of dark metal, in his left a small silvery cylinder. Weapons?

Several of the cloaked guards groped amid the settling dust, retrieved the little glittering spheres they had dropped, raised them—

The silvery cylinder in the man's left hand glowed, emitting an eerie thrill. Instantly everyone in the chamber, save Menander and Ilione, shrieked wildly and collapsed upon the floor, writhing as if in terrible pain. And then, to Menander's astonishment, from each of those fallen and shrieking men there began to emerge a greenish blob. Ilione shrieked also, not in pain but at sight of those hideous things issuing from mouths and nostrils or oozing from the exposed flesh of hands and shanks, hunching like huge slugs across the rubble-strewn tiles in all directions.

The black-garbed man advanced into the synagogue. Menander saw that he had a trimmed brown beard and mustache, that he wore a curious lens-frame before his dark eyes. Then those eyes fell upon Menander and Ilione standing there petrified. The fallen men had ceased to shriek, but continued to lie shuddering in spasms; an eerie silence settled over the chamber as the blob-beings slithered hurriedly away into the shadows.

"A sorcerer!" Ilione whispered tensely, clutching Menander's tunic-sleeve.

"Get out of this place!" the man suddenly cried out to them in Latin, motioning toward the gaping hole in the wall behind him. "Hurry. Those things won't stay away for long—they'll be back with more!"

Menander suddenly realized that, incredible as it seemed, the sorcerer had come to aid them. And in that instant he saw something stirring in the shadows beyond the podium—a squat form in a hooded cloak, raising and leveling a large and intricate silvery object in its twin tentacles, aiming it like a weapon—

"Look out!" Menander screamed.

The stranger spun around in a crouch even as a beam of brilliant yellow flashed from the end of the hooded being's device, barely missing him; a frieze exploded in a shower of stone and part of the lintel above the front entryway came crashing down.

In the same instant a violet beam shot from the bulky dark weapon in the stranger's right hand, blasting the base of a pillar just beside the hooded being. The pillar cracked, leaned, then came toppling down with a thundering crash, hiding the being from view; again the chamber filled with billowing dust.

"You—you killed it?" gasped Menander, staggering forward a pace. Ilione clung to him, her blue eyes wide and dark-seeming in contrast to the whiteness of her face.

"Don't count on it!" yelled the stranger. "Out—quickly!"

"Wait—" Ilione tugged at Menander's arm, pointed to one of the fallen forms. "Dositheus—we've got to save him!"

Menander nodded, quickly knelt with her beside the old wizard, who was feebly struggling to rise. They helped him up, one under each arm, then half-carried him toward the hole in the west wall, stumbling often on the rubble.

"Hurry," said the stranger, motioning them on. "Turn right when you get outside, then follow the wall."

They obeyed, the stranger following them closely as they emerged into a narrow alley. Near the synagogue's northwest corner they came to the foot of a stone stairway built against the wall.

"Up those stairs, quickly!"

They obeyed automatically and were halfway up the stairway before Menander suddenly realized that they would now be trapped unless there were some way of escape across the rooftops. He paused, turned to face the stranger, saw that the man was covering their retreat as if expecting pursuit.

"We'll be trapped."

"No, we won't. Go up. Hurry."

In that moment there came the sound of many shod feet, the clank of armor and steel weapons. Then at the far end of the alley appeared a large group of soldiers. Not black-cloaked guardsmen, Menander realized, but the Roman troops who had been watching the front of the synagogue.

"Halt, you on the stairs!" yelled the centurion in charge as the group clattered into the alley. "Halt, or die!"

"Up, up!" the stranger urged Menander. Then, turning, he called out in his strangely-accented Latin, "Go back! There is . . . sorcery here. You're in danger."

The centurion raised his hand, brought his group to a halt. Menander heard the typical sneer of Roman arrogance in the man's derisive bark of laughter and, sensing what was coming, urged Ilione and Dositheus on.

"You dare threaten us with sorcery? Soldiers!" The centurion pointed forward without turning around. "Spear these insolent troublemakers!"

A dozen soldiers raised their javelins for a cast. Menander cringed. They would never make it around the corner of the wall in time.

The stranger snarled what sounded like a curse in an unknown language, shoved forward a knob on the side of his weapon, leveled it—

No lance of light came forth this time, but a violet burst of roaring power that filled the alley nearly from side to side. More than a dozen Romans burst into instant flame, filling the narrow way briefly with fire and thunder. Menander felt the building tremble, cried out with awe and terror, but could not hear his own voice.

Then silence descended. Smoke billowed in the alley below. Slowly it cleared, revealing the charred skeletons of the Roman soldiers, their armor and weapons lying half-molten amid their smoldering bones.

"Gods!" breathed Dositheus. "The power of the gods!"

"Up—up!" urged the stranger once more. "There will soon be Pursuers more dangerous than Romans—enemies from whom I cannot protect you."

They rounded the corner, crossed a short balcony upon which opened a narrow door—Izhar's quarters, Menander guessed—and climbed another short stairway. The three of them gasped in astonishment as they emerged upon the flat roof, for before them they beheld a strange flattish structure of dark metal, which hung motionless without support perhaps a foot or more above the roof tiles and glowed with a dim blue light. The stranger hurried past them, and Menander saw the glow surrounding the man merge with that of the craft.

"Quickly," the man called back as he climbed over the low rim to the interior, "—follow me."

Menander and Ilione hesitated, but Dositheus wheezed, "Do as he says—quickly!"

The bluish glow vanished, but the craft continued to hang there, humming strangely. Again the man beckoned, impatiently this time. Menander and Ilione helped their old mentor forward, boosted him over the rim as the stranger helped him in, then clambered inside also. The black-garbed man fingered the colored lights of a sloping metal panel just within the rim and part of it; the humming sound rose, increased in volume. Then fear clutched Menander's heart as he felt the upward motion.

"Hera!" cried Ilione. "We're *rising!*"

Menander and the girl rushed to the rim of the craft and peered down. Too late to leap out onto the roof—they were rising into the sky, higher and higher, faster—

"Don't be afraid!" shouted the man. "We won't fall, I promise you."

The craft shot forward, speeding past the moonlit roofs of the town below. Dositheus asked, "Sorcerer, where are you taking us?"

"To a safe place. Where are you staying?"

"What?"

"Point out to me where you are lodged. I'll take you there. You must gather your belongings, then I'll take you wherever you wish. You must not stay here in Capharnaum."

"But this is Chorazin, not Capharnaum," said Menander. "Capharnaum is more than two Roman miles southeast of here."

The man nodded. "I see. Hang on, then."

Menander felt the craft veer southward. Wind whipped his hair as the speed increased. He glanced back, saw the synagogue dwindling rapidly in the distance, black against the lighter moonlit walls of the buildings around it. And then—was that a squat, robed form emerging onto its roof?

Then he could see it no more, for the whole town of Chorazin was receding rapidly to the north. Hundreds of feet below, the moonlit landscape was rushing by at an alarming rate. The wind was so strong now that Menander gasped for breath, gripped the craft's edge for fear of being blown off.

Suddenly the wind ceased; the dim blue glow had sprung into being around them. Yet their speed had not lessened, for the ground still hurtled by beneath. Menander turned, saw that the town of Capharnaum was already closer, the pale walls of Tolmai's synagogue visible in its midst, the vast Lake of Gennesaret gleaming beyond under the moon. Dositheus was leaning on the forward rim, gazing at the scene, more awe than fear in his eyes.

"Tell me where your lodgings are," said the stranger.

Dositheus squinted ahead. Menander and Ilione joined him, looking for the small inn they had chosen on the town's northern edge. Things looked unfamiliar under the waxing half-moon, especially from this height. Then Menander spotted the white ribbon of the road leading into town from the north, and a moment later the inn itself, its flat-roofed bulk rising above the surrounding houses.

"I see it!" cried Ilione in the same instant. "There—the large building not far from this side of the road."

The craft slowed, veered and descended as the strange man guiding it followed Ilione's directions.

"Great sorcerer," said Dositheus, "who are you? What do you call yourself?"

"I am Taggart," said the man, keeping his eyes on the approaching town, his fingers dancing on the weirdly-lit panel before him. "But I am not a—"

"And whom do you serve? Surely not Assatur, Lord of Demhe and the Air Elementals, whose minions you have just thwarted in order to rescue us. Do you serve the Primal Gods, then? Or—?"

The man called Taggart glanced sharply at Dositheus. "I have a few things to ask you, too, old man."

Then he was silent as he guided the craft down, slowly and smoothly, until finally it settled to rest just above the flat roof of the inn. Menander could hardly contain his wonderment. They had traversed the distance between Chorazin and Capharnaum in only a few moments!

Once more the blue glow vanished.

"Gather your belongings," said Taggart. "I must get you out of this region altogether."

"Surely they can't catch us now!" exclaimed Menander.

Taggart glanced skyward. "Don't be so sure. They are probably signaling to others already."

"Others—up there?" said Dositheus. "Among the stars?"

"Yes. Circling the earth, waiting for signals. Hurry and get your things."

Dositheus turned to the two youngsters. "Do as he says."

Menander and Ilione clambered down to the roof. As they did so, they glimpsed the banner they had set upon a pole, a signal for the raven, waving whitely in the moonlight. They looked at one another.

"Carbo?" they both said at the same instant.

"Hurry," repeated Taggart, leaning over the rim while holding a glowing metallic object in his hand. "And, take this—it will save you the effort of kindling a light."

Ilione took the thing, wonderment in her eyes. It was a metallic cylinder as long as her hand; a cone of light shone from one of its ends. Then, turning, she led the way to the edge of the roof and started down the wooden stairway that hugged the side of the building, the light-device in her hand showing her where to step better than any lantern or lamp could have done.

While she held the light, Menander unlocked the door of their rooms. As they hurried inside, the first thing they saw was a dark form upon the table, the glitter of a beady eye. Both gasped—but in the same instant realized that it was only the raven. Evidently Carbo had found the flag on the roof, then had entered the open window and, recognizing their belongings, had remained waiting for them. Menander felt a great relief. The bird was an old friend, too good a friend to be abandoned.

"Carbo!" he cried. "Dositheus is on the roof. Go up and join him. We'll be along in a few minutes."

The raven croaked in acknowledgment, then flapped out of the window into the night. Menander and Ilione gathered up their possessions, including the pouch containing Dositheus' arcane scrolls. It did not take long, for they had not had time to unpack much before their capture by the black-cloaked guardsmen.

They managed to carry everything to the roof in one trip. Taggart and Dositheus stood within the craft, silhouetted against the moonlit sky, the raven perching on the latter's shoulder as if taking all this strange madness for granted. Quickly Menander and Ilione handed up the bundles, then climbed in after them. Again the craft began to drone more loudly and shrilly, then to rise into the air.

"Now, tell me—where shall I take you?" said Taggart. "And don't pick someplace nearby."

Dositheus scowled in thought for a moment, then said, "Can you convey us as far as Aenon?"

"Where is that?"

"South—a two-day journey afoot, at least."

Taggart nodded. "You should be safe there, since you're no longer carrying any of those weapons or medallions." He looked closely at Dositheus. "You're not, are you?"

"No, no. But how did you learn—?"

"Good. Hang on to the rail, then—here we go."

The craft sped southward. Dositheus' white beard whipped in the wind and the bird on his shoulder cawed in alarm, its feathers fluttering. Then the blue glow was suddenly about them once more; the wind ceased and the strange conveyance bore them southward ever more swiftly.

Simon gazed somberly into the firelight, flames flickering in his brooding dark eyes. Occasionally he lifted his face and stared toward the northeast where hills were darkly silhouetted beneath the moonlit sky. The thoughts in his mind flickered nearly as often as the flames of the campfire. Lotis, sitting opposite him, guessed at those thoughts.

"What now, Simon?" she said softly. "Will you seek your endangered friends—or your vengeance?"

He looked at her face, pale in the firelight and showing lines of weariness. The fear was gone from her eyes—perhaps the exertion of the last few hours had helped her forget the previous evening's terrors. They had traveled several miles along moonlit ridges and grassy valleys until Lotis' exhaustion had forced them to call a halt. Simon had kindled a small fire and cooked a meal while she rested.

"Friendship or vengeance," muttered Simon. "You have read my thoughts truly, Lotis. I have come so far to find my enemies, and now they are so near!" He gazed southeastward, down the slope toward the wide valley where, just beyond the lower slope of Mount Ebal, a few lights glowed in the darkness, showing the location of the city of Sebaste. Beyond, above distant Mount Gerizim and the lesser rises flanking it, a band of black cloud hung low beneath the stars, slowly advancing.

"They are there," Simon continued, fingering the haft of his sword as he gazed down at the lights of the city. "And yet, vengeance has already waited six years—perhaps it can wait a few days more. I feel I must journey north to Capharnaum—find out what became of my friends."

"Simon!" Fear again entered Lotis' eyes. "Would you leave me? Surely you can do nothing for them that the wizard Taggart cannot—he has great powers, he promised he would aid them!"

"Of course, I will not leave you, Lotis." Simon smiled a trifle sadly at the girl's apprehensiveness. "I would take you with me if I should go to Capharnaum. Yet—I'm afraid you are right. My only hope is that the wizard will do as he said."

"No—no, Simon, I think we—you—*should* go north—to try to find and aid your friends."

Simon scowled in brief puzzlement, then smiled again. "Ah, Lotis! You are so afraid of Maxentius, then, that you will not return—" Suddenly he looked at her closely, sternly yet with concern. "Tell me, Lotis—before you set out for Akrab's house, were you—punished?"

The girl's face paled. A fear near to panic shone in her eyes. "No—no punishment. I remember nothing like that—"

"No?" Simon's eyes held hers. "I sense that you fear Maxentius greatly."

Her face paled still more; she turned her eyes away from him. "Simon, he will kill you! He has power such as not even the Roman procurator Pilatus can withstand. When he learns that you have slain Akrab, he will use that power."

"What power, Lotis?"

The girl shuddered. "He consorts with sorcerers—the mightiest in the land. I know whereof I speak, for they have visited Maxentius in the night, and I once heard their conversation when none knew I listened."

"What sorcerers, Lotis? What did they speak of?"

"No, no! I must not say more—their curse will fall upon me. I wish I had never seen them—never listened to them!"

Simon could not get another word out of her, and her fear was so pronounced that he soon ceased trying. He moved around the fire and sat by the girl, stroked her gently and spoke to her as would a protective brother. As he did so he intoned his words in a subtle hypnotic rhythm he had learned from his mentor Daramos, the Parthian mage, and so effective was it that in a short time Lotis lay wrapped in her cloak by the fire in peaceful sleep.

Simon rose and strode a few paces down the hillside. He stopped and pondered the distant black hump of Mount Ebal, from whose summit the curse of Yahweh was said to brood over the land, then down to the lights of Sebaste in the valley below. The far-off band of black cloud seemed closer. A cool wind was blowing from the southeast.

Vengeance.

Menander and Ilione gazed out in awe over the moonlit waters of the Lake of Gennesaret drifting by far below, at the distant hills beyond and at the stars of Virgo rising above them. Upon the southeast horizon a band of dark cloud had formed.

"You have saved our lives, perhaps our very souls, great wizard," Dositheus was saying. "What can we do to repay you?"

"You can start," said Taggart, keeping his eyes ahead on the southern landscape, "by telling me the whole story of how you came by that medallion and energy-weapon. I understand that you had an encounter with—Hastur's—minions in Ephesus."

Dositheus started. "How did you know?"

"I've talked with your friend Simon of Gitta."

"Simon!" cried Menander and Ilione. They stepped forward, and Ilione impulsively clutched the wizard's arm—then drew back, frightened at her temerity. Yet the man's flesh had felt completely human beneath his black sleeve.

"You saw Simon?" Menander asked. "Where? Is he well?"

"He seemed so." Taggart quickly related the encounter. Ilione felt a pang of jealousy upon learning that an unknown girl accompanied Simon, then a breathless fear at the description of the beings that had come out of the dark in pursuit of him, and finally a great relief at the outcome.

"Good, good," said Dositheus when the man had finished the narration in his halting Latin. "Simon is safe, and is no doubt by this time close to the gates of Sebaste. You are indeed a mighty wizard, O Taggart."

The man nodded a trifle impatiently. "Now, *your* story."

Dositheus told briefly of their encounter with Assatur's minions in Ephesus and their journey to Antioch and Tyre, then in more detail of their encounter with the black guardsmen at Ecdippa and their subsequent wanderings and perils. Taggart interrupted him frequently, asking for clarification or elaboration on one point or another. Menander and Ilione listened silently as their aged mentor talked on for some time.

Amazingly, the strange craft seemed to be guiding itself on a straight, level course, for Taggart was no longer paying the slightest attention to the moonlit landscape. Once, looking over the rail, Menander saw what appeared to be a fairly large town gliding past far below. Now they were moving south of it.

Suddenly a high-pitched buzzing sounded. Taggart turned and touched two or three of the glowing squares on the panel beside him; immediately the buzzing ceased and the motion of the craft slowed.

"We are about a two-day foot-journey south of where I picked you up," said Taggart. "Do you recognize the landscape?"

Dositheus leaned over the rail. "That town back there must be Scythopolis." He hurried around to the other side and peered southward. "Aenon will be ahead, about five Roman miles."

Slowly the craft slanted downward until, after several minutes, it came gently to rest just above the top of a low hill. The dim blue glow surrounding them blinked out; the sound of the craft diminished to a barely audible hum. Menander felt a cool night breeze, saw the grass of the hilltop waving beneath it. A few scattered oaks stood blackly beneath the descending half-moon.

"There is the village of Salim," said Dositheus, pointing eastward. "Near the bottom of the hill. I know the innkeeper there."

"Good. It looks like an easy walk to your destination from here," said Taggart. "But before you go, Dositheus, I must ask you a favor. Those ruins you were digging in before you were first attacked by the—Hastur minions: Can you draw me a map showing exactly where they are?"

Dositheus hesitated.

"I can," said Menander. "The ruins of Hali are not far from—"

He stopped suddenly as he realized that Dositheus was glowering at him and shaking his grizzled head. The gaze of the stranger was now upon him.

"So," Taggart said quietly. "The ruins are called 'Hali'. That is most interesting." He glanced up at the stars, then turned back to Dositheus. "It happens that that is the name of the . . . region . . . where Hastur dwells—as I'm sure you know, old man. And now I think I understand why you were delving in those ruins. You sought the *Byakhtron*."

"Aye—the Chalice of Byakh," muttered Dositheus, trembling. "You have guessed truly. But I did not find it, great wizard."

Taggart scowled—in puzzlement rather than anger, Menander sensed. "How did you learn of its existence at all?"

Menander thought his old mentor seemed surprised at the question. Dositheus asked, "Have you never read the book of Mattan, then, great wizard?"

"I never heard of it—but I did suspect that there must be some sort of written tradition concerning the ancient Carcosan civilization. Tell me, what does this book say about the ruins of Hali and the . . . Chalice?"

"That it was once a town, and the site of the greatest shrine to Assatur, him you call Hastur. Every year, it is written, the lords of the kingdom walked from the great and ancient city of Karakossa—which you call Carcosa—to the Shrine of Hali, that they might drink the Golden Nectar from the Chalice and then summon the bat-winged *Byakhim* from the skies to do their bidding."

Taggart nodded. He stooped and opened a flat, rectangular box of black metal that lay near the rail in the shadows. From it he took a sheet of what appeared to be very flexible papyrus and handed it to Menander, together with a thin, pointed cylinder made of some smooth dark substance. "Here, young man, you can draw me a map with these. The young lady can hold the light for you."

Menander complied, placing the papyrus-like sheet upon the smooth metal of the craft's inward-sloping rim and drawing the coastline and the locations of Ecdippa and Hali in relation to Scythopolis and the Lake of Gennesaret as best he could remember them, while Ilione held the strange source of cold light near him. The material upon which he worked was not papyrus, he now realized, but something thinner and smoother; the thing with which he drew was no stylus or reed, but something which magically produced a thin line of dark blue ink from its pointed tip without going dry. Such a strange wizard this man was—and yet, how strangely ignorant of some things which a wizard, or even an ordinary man, might be expected to know! Obviously he must be from a far land indeed.

"Now, Dositheus," he said after Menander had finished the map and explained it, "I must have that scroll you mentioned—the book of Mattan, wasn't it?"

"*El-Halal*—the 'Lord of Chaos'?" The old man glanced uneasily at his bundle. "It is very valuable."

"Don't worry. I will get it back to you tomorrow night. But I must leave now. I have only a few hours until daylight."

Menander glanced eastward to where the faint stars of Capricorn were rising above the distant hills beyond the Jordan River. A chill crept over him, for he had heard of dark beings who could not abide the advent of dawn.

"Do the sun's ray . . . affect you badly, O Taggart?" he asked hesitantly.

"No, no." The man laughed briefly. "Nothing like that. But this is a populated area, and I must not be seen. Rumors spread fast and might get to the wrong ears—and there are those who would come searching for me should they hear of a craft like this flying about. Promise me that you will not mention my existence to anyone."

"I see," said Dositheus. "You have enemies. I could guess at their nature, but—" He glanced at Menander and Ilione. "I will not. We shall speak of you to no one." He stooped and rummaged in his bundle a moment, then stood up clutching a large yellow-tinged scroll. Menander saw that the papyrus, despite its tint, was new; also, he noticed a slight, sly smile on the old man's face.

"Here is the 'Lord of Chaos', the book of the ancient Baal-priest Mattan. The description you seek begins in the forty-seventh column from the beginning. I would not lend this to just anyone, great wizard, but since you saved our lives—"

"If you're worried about getting it back," said Taggart, "you may come along with me. I'm sure you could help me find the place of concealment of the Byakhtron more quickly that I could find it on my own."

"No, no," said Dositheus hastily. "I trust you fully, and—and I must see to some urgent business in Aenon."

"Very well." Taggart touched a few more of the glowing squares. "There. The craft will now remember the exact location of this hilltop. Come here before dawn after tomorrow and I'll return the scroll to you."

"You are going to the ruins of Hali, wizard?"

"Yes, but first I'm going to hide this craft in the hills and get a long, much-needed sleep. I'll locate the ruins tonight, when no one can see me, then try to extract the Byakhtron from them tomorrow night."

"The Chalice may no longer be there," said Dositheus. "The demon-possessed Rabbi Izhar of Chorazin seemed to think that it had been stolen from his own synagogue by one Judah of Kerioth, a sorcerer working for a wandering Galilean prophet. Which would imply that Assatur's minions, whom Izhar aids, had already taken it from Hali's ruins."

Taggart scowled in thought. "That would be bad—very bad. I had hoped to forestall that. Still, I doubt that any human—or even any earth-trapped Karakossan—could have removed the Byakhtron, even with exact directions. Unless he had help."

"How can you know that? asked Dositheus. "Have you, too, delved into ancient sorcerous writings after all?"

"No. Let's just say that I know from . . . experience . . . that such things as the Byakhtron would be concealed within solid rock, not merely buried. Probably that is why you did not find it, Dositheus. But, that's enough talk! You three must go now. But be here before dawn day after tomorrow. Even if the worst has happened, there may be a clue at the ruins, in which case I will have more questions to ask you."

Menander and Ilione had already hurriedly bundled their possessions over the side of the craft, and now hastened to help Dositheus down also. They had all walked away only a few paces when they heard the craft's low hum rapidly rise to a shrill whine and, turning, saw it hurtle past above them and dwindle with incredible speed into the sky, wheeling around and vanishing northward toward the hills—and the ruins of Hali far beyond them.

EYES IN THE NIGHT

CHAPTER VII

Elissa, more formally known as Elizabeth of Sychar, daughter of Rohan, knew the instant she saw the curtained palanquin outside in the damp roadway that it was no common visitor that had come to her house. The litter's plainness did not deceive her, for once before she had seen its dark-curtained form and the black-cloaked guardsmen who bore it.

The woman shuddered slightly. That had been the day that her little slave-girl, Lotis, had vanished.

Elissa pulled the shutter closed and latched it. The lamplit interior of her sumptuous room seemed brighter than the cold, drizzly day outside. For a moment she stood, indecisive, then turned and hurried with a purposeful, almost masculine stride from her room and down the tiled corridor to the stairway.

She met Maxentius at the foot of the stair as he was crossing the columned portico. Evidently the servants had informed him of the visitor's arrival.

"Maxentius—"

He faced her, and for an instant appreciation gleamed in his eyes and a slight smile flickered upon his hard Roman features. Elissa felt a brief satisfaction; though in her late thirties, she was still an unusually fine figure of a woman, dark-eyed and without a trace of gray in her black coiffure bound with strings of pearls, almost regal in her Roman-style *stola* of red and gold silk. But her satisfaction faded as Maxentius' features resumed their accustomed hardness.

"Not now, Elissa. I'm in a hurry."

"It's that horrible old man again, isn't it?—the one who first came here about four months ago. What does he want with you?"

The Roman paused; the hardness in his eyes became almost a glare of menace. "The house is large. If my guest offends you, you can avoid him easily."

"But I want to know who he is. Wasn't he here only two days ago—?"

"No questions, Elissa. Go to your chambers."

She knew better than to argue when that steely tone entered his voice. With a glance of resentment she turned and ascended the stairway. Maxentius strode away toward the front of the house to receive his guest in the vestibule.

Instead of going to her suite, however, Elissa hid herself in the shadows at the top of the stairs and watched. In a moment Maxentius returned and strode across the atrium below, accompanied by a lean, white-haired old man wearing a dark robe and curious mitre. They were closely followed by

Cratos, Maxentius' hulking bodyguard, who had once been a gladiator. In a moment the three of them had vanished between the columns at the far end of the atrium.

Elissa stole around the balcony that was supported by the atrium's columns and peered cautiously through the door to a similar balcony surrounding the peristyle. Again she felt the cool, damp air of outdoors, saw the damp foliage of the garden below gleaming dully in the drizzle. Toward the back she glimpsed Maxentius and the old man entering a room beyond the columns; then the door closed behind them and Cratos stationed his massive frame before it and stood motionless in the shadows, arms folded across his mighty chest.

Slowly Elissa closed the door to the balcony. Curiosity vied with a slight fear within her. She wanted to find out what Maxentius was up to, yet—would it be safe, even for her?

For the man had changed since she had come to live with him nearly two years ago. True, there had always been about him that hardness, that Roman arrogance, that dangerousness, even—but all that had made their relationship seem to her the more exciting. She knew he had sought her for her wealth as much as for her beauty, but then his position of power had allured her as well, and if there was a streak of cruelty in him—well, was there not that in all men? There had been an understanding between the two of them, and an excitement—the first such excitement Elissa had felt with a man for many years.

But during the last few months, Maxentius had changed. . . .

Elissa shook her head abruptly as if to cast off her fears. Her lips tightened with determination. She *would* find out what was going on here. Quickly she walked to the room at the south end of the balcony and entered it.

The four rooms overlooking the south side of the peristyle—servants' quarters—were connected by doorways, deserted now, their occupants busy about the house or on shopping errands. Elissa hurried through them, then cautiously opened the outer door of the last. Good—the eastern balcony overlooking the peristyle now hid her from sight of the gladiator. Softly she stole across it to the chamber above the one where she knew Maxentius and the old man were in conference, carefully opened the door and slipped inside.

The place was a small storeroom, cluttered with wooden boxes, rolls of fabric, old plaster statues and other impedimenta. Slowly the woman stole across the bare wooden floor, taking care not to bump against anything in the gloom. She could hear voices coming up faintly from below, and found that they became more distinct as she approached the northeast corner, near the outer wall. With infinite caution she knelt, saw the glimmer of lamplight through a narrow crack between the planks—and found that she could now hear the voices from beneath very distinctly.

". . . but, that's not possible!" Maxentius was saying, his voice harsh with tension. "A dozen men wiped out instantly, in a burst of flame—?"

"Aye, and with them their officer Marius, one of our most trusted men among those you command. It happened only last evening."

"But, then, how could you know? Chorazin is a three-day journey from here, even by swift messenger."

The old man chuckled. "Do you so soon forget whom we serve, Maxentius? One of Assatur's owls appeared on my window sill just after dawn, bearing the message."

There was silence for a space. Then: "I see why you came here in person rather than entrust this news to a messenger. You are indeed a great sorcerer, Annas."

Elissa gasped. Annas—that was the name of the man who was rumored to be the power behind the high priesthood of the temple in Jerusalem. Years ago he had himself been high priest until the Roman procurator Quintilius Varus had deposed him—for practicing sorcery, according to some gossips. Annas was old, far older than any man could remember. In the years since being deposed, his sons had held the high priesthood; the current high priest was Caiaphas, his son-in-law. But surely the sinister old man talking with Maxentius in the room below could not be the same Annas. . . .

"The wizard who slew your troops," the old man continued, "fled southward in a magical craft with three prisoners who were being questioned about the disappearance of the Chalice of Byakh from its ancient hiding-place beneath the ruins of Hali. You must alert all your troops to watch the roads, apprehend them—"

"By Pallas!" growled Maxentius. "Cannot you and all your Judean priests and wizards locate these fugitives? And if not, how can my soldiers?"

"The owl tells me the fleeing craft was lost track of south of Gennesaret. Evidently the wizard has cast a cloak of invisibility about it. Therefore, he and those he rescued must be sought by more mundane means. Here is the description Izhar gave the owl: The wizard himself wears black garments of a strange cut, rather close fitting—very impractical garb, and easy to recognize. He also wears, I am told, glass discs before his eyes—no doubt a hypnotic device, so take care to warn your men to avert their gaze from him as they would from the mythical Medusa. The three he rescued from Chorazin are a white-beared old man named Dositheus, a dark-haired lad named Menander and a girl with long blonde hair. Watch out for this Dositheus especially—I have heard of him before. He is something of a wizard himself, full of wiles and learned in the arts of illusion."

"Wizards," muttered the Roman. "These eastern provinces are evidently crawling with them. Well, I'll set my troops to watching the roads for the fugitives. But what if this black-clad wizard is with them? I want no more of my men burned with fire!"

"Take the fugitives if you can, but do not try to fight the wizard. If he is with them, report to me. There are—others—who can deal with him. He serves no power, having evidently defected from those servitors of *Yahveh-Zava'ot* who oppose us."

Elissa gasped slightly. Annas had spoken the Name of the One, the Name sacred to Samaritans and Judeans alike, not to be profaned in public speech. Moreover, the old man had just dropped that Name in casual conversation with an unbelieving Roman!

"Very well," said Maxentius. "I'll send word to the Jerusalem garrison immediately."

"You will do more than that, O Tribune. I came here not as a mere messenger. You will go to Jerusalem yourself, this very day."

"By Hercules, you vex me! No Judean sorcerer, no matter how powerful, shall order me about!"

The old man laughed—a low, sinister cackle. "Roman pride! Very well, then, Tribune, I *request* your presence at Jerusalem. And the reason may soften your resentment. The power that shall make you Emperor of Rome, and me the Monarch of the East, is now within our grasp—for another owl came to me last evening with the news that your underling Scribonius and his troops are even now returning from across the Jordan—bearing that which they sought."

Maxentius was silent again for a space. Then: "You mean—Caiaphas was successful in leading them to the hidden cave on Mount Nebo, where your ancient Judaean prophet hid the Ark?"

"Silence!" hissed Annas. "Do you not remember the last time we spoke of that matter in this very chamber? That slave girl, hiding in the room above, was listening to our every word—"

"Lotis?" Maxentius barked a laugh. "She's not there *now*, I can tell you! I gave her to Scribonius to use as he pleased; then, when he was done with her, I sent her to Akrab, who watches over one of my remote country estates. The message I sent the soldiers who accompanied her was clear: After they and Akrab had had such sport with her as they desired, they were to twist off her head. No doubt they have finished their sport by this time."

Elissa cringed in the darkness, fear clutching her heart. Now she knew why her young and trusted handmaid had not returned. . . .

"Good," said the old man. "Now I must go. You and your men will follow me in an hour on the road to Jerusalem. No doubt your horses will pass me and my guards well before you reach the city. Make no sign of recognition, for none must know that I have met with you here in the city of the hated Samaritans. Then ride all night—the moon waxes and will give light enough— and tomorrow we will meet Scribonius in the Tower of Set."

"I will remember. Hail, Monarch of the East!"

"Hail, Emperor of Rome!"

Elissa heard the men open the door and stride from the room; their footfalls faded away across the tiles of the peristyle. She shuddered, rose from her cramped position and stole from the small room, careful not to make a sound. A new fear of Maxentius possessed her; evidently his cruelty and lust for power went even deeper than she had supposed. . . .

Suddenly her fear intensified to a shock of terror—for, as she crept from the room she saw, only a few feet from her, a large owl perched on the rail of the balustrade overlooking the peristyle. The bird's large eyes were fixed directly upon her, and on its breast hung a strange medallion glittering with gems that resembled a V-shaped cluster of stars.

Without a sound the owl turned from her, spread its wings and swooped down into the darkness of the pillared and rain-dripping peristyle.

Elissa hurried away, back through the rooms and halls by which she had approached the chamber of her eavesdropping. Her legs felt weak beneath her and the shock of terror lingered. Why should the sight of an owl frighten her so? What had that dreadful old man in the room below said about an owl that had spoken to him? And what had her lover, Maxentius, said of her handmaid Lotis, who had been eavesdropping in that very room—Lotis, who had now been missing for two days . . .?

The house felt empty now, dark and full of fear.

She returned to her room, stood silently in the center of the floor and listened, waiting. There was a sound outside in the street. Elissa crossed to the shutters, cautiously opened them a crack, saw the old man climbing into his dark-curtained litter. Immediately the cloaked guardsmen carried it away into the gray gloom.

She closed the shutters, stood silently for a few minutes more, nervously clasping and unclasping her hands. Then she heard the sound she had expected—footsteps approaching down the corridor.

Maxentius entered. His eyes were hard, stern, his features rigid as if in cold anger.

"You were listening," he said.

"Listening? Maxentius, what do you mean—?"

"You needn't deny it. You were seen. How much did you hear? No—don't bother to answer. I'll listen to no more of your lies. I must assume that you heard all, and act accordingly."

Elissa felt a cold fear. "What are you going to do?"

"I must leave for Jerusalem this afternoon. I shall be gone for several days. During that time you must not leave this house or see visitors; I shall leave guards with you to see that you do not. They shall attend you; the servants have been dismissed."

Her fear subsided a bit. She wanted to ask him about Lotis, but dared not. "Maxentius, what is this dark sorcery you are involved in? What does that old Judean wizard want with you? He is dangerous—he will try to use you. I have heard tales—"

Maxentius flashed a hard grin and strode forward a pace; cupping one hand under Elissa's chin, he tilted her head back and glared down into her eyes. "The old Jew shall not use me—nor shall you. I will share my power with no one. You are an attractive woman, Elissa—you excite me as has no other. I would have you live on, that you may continue to excite me. Obey my orders and you shall. But do not give me advice or ask questions."

He released her and she stepped back, fear in her eyes. "What is this power you will not share, Maxentius? What has the sorcerer promised you in return for your aid—?"

The Roman slapped her in the face with such force that she fell sprawling to the tiles. Ears ringing, she groped to a sitting position and stared up at the man, tears of pain blurring her visions.

Maxentius grinned down at her. There was more admiration than anger in his eyes. Her dark hair, partly loosened from it coiffure, spilled in disorder over her shoulders, framing her startled, frightened face.

"I told you, Elissa—no questions. Come, now, get up."

She did so, hesitantly, never taking her eyes from him. He had been rough with her before, but not like this.

Maxentius slowly drew a dagger from his girdle, fingered it thoughtfully while holding the woman's gaze with his own. "How becoming you are, proud woman, with fear in your eyes!" Then, abruptly, he turned and struck a copper gong twice with the knife blade, then re-sheathed the weapon.

"I have summoned the guards," he said, grinning. "I must make preparations to go to Jerusalem. But before I leave, I shall return here to your chamber. I must say, your appearance at this moment excites me tremendously!"

There were approaching footfalls in the corridor and in another moment two guardsmen had entered. Elissa gasped. These were not Romans but black-clad soldiers such as had borne old Annas' litter. Their faces were wooden, expressionless under their dark iron helms, and their eyes seemed to glow with a faint yellow light.

"These are your new servants, Elissa. They will attend you in the coming days. But right now, they will prepare you for our parting pleasures." Maxentius turned to the guards and snapped: "Strip this woman and bind her. Give her a few lashes, but don't mar her skin. Then leave her here."

"Maxentius!" screamed Elissa. *"No!"*

"I'll return in less than an hour, my love, I promise it. By Hercules, but I intend to enjoy you before I leave! Such pride, such bearing—you could pass for a patrician's wife in Rome!"

He turned and strode from the room. Elissa shrieked as the expressionless black-clad guardsmen advanced and laid hold of her.

Dositheus opened his eyes, moved them, then remembered where he was—in the small upper room of the Inn of Peace where he had procured lodging before dawn. He had slept several hours without moving; he still lay supine, hands folded upon his breast. It was a technique he had learned from Persian adepts decades ago—the shutting off of thoughts that rested one even when natural sleep would not come.

He sat up, glanced into the far corner of the room where the lad and the maid slept close to one another, almost in one another's arms. Dositheus smiled. Theirs was a natural sleep. They had lain down in their bedrolls far apart, in agitation after the day's perils, and only a mixed potion had helped them to slumber; but as the potion wore off they had evidently drawn closer to one another, unconsciously, for comfort.

Dositheus' smile faded. He rose and donned his star-emblazoned robe over his faded tunic, then strode to the window and opened the shutters. A draught of cool air blew in. He looked out over the flat roofs of the village of Salim, looked up at the scudding clouds. The air felt damp, but the rain had stopped—the rain that had begun to fall in drizzling drops on him and Menander and Ilione by the time they had reached the village, possessions on their back, and had knocked on the door of this inn which he knew so well. . . .

He heard Menander stirring, muttering in a dream. Hurriedly the old man knelt, shook the youth's shoulder and whispered: "Menander, wake up!"

The youth's eyes opened, blurred with sleep, questioning. He glanced at the girl who slumbered at his side, her blonde hair streaming over his arm. "Master . . . what . . .?"

"Shhh! Get up. Don't wake Ilione. Follow me."

Outside in the hallway, with the door closed behind them, Dositheus told the puzzled youth, "I must leave you. The afternoon wanes, and the Thirty are gathering. My friend Botos, the innkeeper, has sent for them. They gather by the waters of Aenon even now."

Menander nodded. He remembered the Thirty—the followers of that wild-eyed prophet Johannen the Baptizer, among whom he and Simon and

Dositheus had sat four years ago, before their journey to Persia. His eyes became awake, alert.

"What do you want me to do, Mentor? Accompany you?"

"No. I want you to go and purchase an ass to carry our belongings. Botos can no doubt tell you where to find one. If I have not returned by the time you have accomplished this, bring Ilione and come to the meeting of the Thirty. You know the spot."

So saying, Dositheus immediately turned and left, descending the outside stairway. Menander went back into the room, looked down at the slumbering Ilione, then knelt beside her. She seemed incredibly beautiful to him in that moment, her blonde hair framing her face in tumbled waves and spilling out over one white outstretched arm.

"Ilione," he said gently. "Ilione, wake up."

She stirred. A slight rapture seemed to steal over her features. She muttered, "Simon . . .?"

Menander felt again the pang of jealousy. "Wake up, Ilione. I have to go out and purchase an ass. Do you want to go along, or stay her and sleep some more?"

The girl opened her eyes, sat up and shook her head a trifle petulantly; the blonde hair spilled loosely over her bare shoulders. "Menander! You woke me to tell me that I could sleep? Or . . . help you buy a donkey—?"

"Maybe I shouldn't have bothered. I just didn't want you to wake up and wonder where everyone had gone. Go back to sleep. I can tell that you were enjoying your dreams."

"No, I shall accompany you—I'll die of boredom otherwise." The girl looked around, blinking the last of the sleep from her eyes. "Where is Dositheus?"

"He has gone to join the Thirty by the waters of Aenon. He wants us to meet him there."

"The Thirty? Oh—that foolish cult you and he nearly joined once." Again Ilione shook her head. "Why do you two delay our journey to Persia for such foolishness—?"

"I've told you over and over, Ilione, it's not my choice. And don't call the Thirty a 'foolish cult'. I fear they are involved in very dark magic indeed. Their leader Johannen used to rant of a being who was soon to come and overthrow the order of the world. Johannen's dead now, I hear—beheaded on the orders of Herod the Tetrarch for his sorceries and seditious tongue—and I'm afraid Dositheus now has some hopes of leading the Thirty himself. He's a wise man, yet he can be foolish in his lust to acquire dark knowledge." Menander's eyes grew introspective. "The trouble he's gotten us into sometimes. . . . Ilione, I wish with all my heart that we were on our way to Persia to study under the wise Daramos. I do not trust the Thirty—they delve too much into evil, secret prophecies and seem too avid for their fulfillment. Nor do I wish to meet again that strange wizard of last night, even though he saved our lives—"

"The wizard Taggart." Ilione in turn grew thoughtful. "I can hardly believe I did not dream what happened last night. Menander, does even the great Daramos have such sorcerous power?"

"I don't know. I've seen Daramos do strange things—cast his insubstantial shape and voice into places far from his body, and even lift heavy objects by the power of his mind alone. Yet—no. Never have I seen him or any other perform such sorcery as we saw last night."

Ilione seemed downcast for a moment, then brightened. "Still, this Taggart said he was no true wizard, and I think he spoke the truth. Did you not sense it? He commands sorcerous devices, yet he has not the mien of one who holds true knowledge. I suspect he is but a server of masters who possess secrets of which he comprehends little. Did he not say so much in his halting Latin? And, think, Menander—would not a great sorcerer know at least Greek, not to mention the tongues of Persia and ancient Egypt?"

Menander nodded eagerly. The wise Daramos was his hero, and his enthusiastic descriptions of the mage had made him Ilione's hero also, causing the homeless girl to put all her future hopes in him. It was unacceptable to either of them that any wizard should be greater.

"And consider this, Menander," Ilione went on excitedly. "Dositheus loaned the man a copy of the *El-Halal*—and thereby tricked him."

"Tricked? I don't see—"

"You don't? And you hope someday to be an adept of arcane wisdom? Think, Menander—this Taggart speaks only Latin, and that not too well. He did not look at the scroll Dositheus gave him. It is the Greek translation he has been working on these last few months. The man cannot read it. So you see, he is stupid and easily deceived. Surely Daramos would not have been."

Menander felt a slight irritation, partly because Ilione had seen what he had not, but partly at his mentor's devious tactics. "What is Dositheus up to, then? Why did he deceive the man?"

"Perhaps to sound the true depths of the wizard's power."

Menander's irritation increased. "That rings true. Dositheus often uses wiles where honesty would serve better."

Ilione looked quizzically at the youth. "You question your mentor's wisdom in this matter?"

"I know him. He is no Daramos."

"And you trust the unknown wizard Taggart?"

"Why not? He saved all our lives, and in return asked nothing but the use of Mattan's old scroll. I'll wager he returns it, too, as he promised. But we're wasting time. Get up, if you're going with me, and let's prepare something to eat."

Ilione rose smiling, lovely in her sleeveless sky-blue tunic and tousled hair, and reached for her robe. "Maybe we've hope of getting to Persia yet, Menander—that is, if you continue to question your old mentor's wisdom."

Simon entered the small room bearing the lamp he had lighted at the inn's brazier downstairs. The lamp was necessary, for though it was more than an hour until sundown and the drizzling rain had stopped, the sky was still heavily overcast. Simon closed the door, bent over the still form of Lotis where she slumbered on her pallet next to the wall, then sat down at the rough table and lit a second lamp. The gloom lightened somewhat.

The girl's face was peaceful, her breathing regular. That was good. He would let her sleep on.

They had arrived at the western gate of Sebaste in drizzling rain, an hour after dawn. Simon had felt a few uneasy moments as they passed between the two massive round towers under the scrutiny of Roman guards, but nothing had happened; their ordinary Samaritan garb and the mule bearing their few possessions were not noteworthy, and they had not been challenged. But Lotis had not shared Simon's fears, appearing to be in a daze. By the time they had reached the small inn she seemed like a sleepwalker, staring blankly, responding to directions but not to questions. Evidently she had lapsed into a delayed state of shock as a result of her recent ordeal.

Simon had left her in the room, stabled the mule and paid the rat-faced innkeeper for a night's lodging. When he had returned to the room Lotis was sitting where he had left her, staring into space. He had removed her damp outer garments, then with the aid of a lamp-flame had hypnotized her, causing her to fall into a deep sleep, leaving her with the suggestion that she would remember all when she awoke.

He wondered now if that had been wise. The girl had evidently been through a terrible ordeal. Sometimes the mind could heal itself only by forgetting. . . .

Simon reached beneath his symbol-emblazoned magician's robe and took forth a pouch; it jingled softly as he placed it on the table.

After a few hours of sleep he rose quietly, opened the shutter a crack and peered out into the night. The rain had stopped. Turning to the pouch on the table, he opened it and began to count out the coins it contained. He had gone out and performed as a street-magician for a short time; that hour or so had brought in nearly twenty sestercii, many times the amount he had paid for the room.

He removed the ornamented robe, donned his plain Samaritan cloak, then moved again to the window and opened it wider. The air outside was breezy, chilly, but it dispelled some of the stuffiness of the small chamber.

Simon peered out. The clouds were beginning to break; westward, beyond the city wall, appeared faint streaks of afterglow from the vanished sun.

The girl stirred, moaned, mumbled. Simon turned, saw that she was tossing on the pallet, her eyes still closed, her face twisted in a grimace of pain or fear.

Suddenly she sat up, her eyes and mouth opening wide—and screamed.

CHAPTER VIII

Simon knelt at the girl's side. "Lotis, did you dream?"

She let out a long, shuddering breath; her dark eyes were wide with—terror? Pain? "Oh, gods. . . ."

He put an arm gently about her shoulder. "Tell me, Lotis."

Her eyes shut, her face twisted in a pained grimace; she groaned, clenched her fists before her mouth and slumped sobbing into Simon's arms. "Oh, gods, I remember it all now! I *remember!"*

Simon held her, stroked her hair, stared grimly while dark memories rose in his own mind. When after a few minutes the girl's violent sobbings diminished he asked again, softly: "Tell me. What do you remember?"

"When—Maxentius knew I had been listening, he—he . . ."

"Go on, Lotis. You must tell me. It will be better."

She looked up to him; tears streaked her pallid face. "I—I can't, Simon—"

"Maxentius. He hurt you, didn't he?"

"No. He—he gave me to one of his officers—a man I had feared for a long time—for over a year. I feared—because of the way the man always looked at me, the things he'd say to me when he found me alone. Maxentius gave me to him—he dragged me into a room, and forced me . . . Oh, gods, his face! His cruel face!"

Again she lapsed into sobs, and again Simon held her until she quieted, stroking her hair and rocking her gently.

"Then—then Maxentius ordered me to go to Akrab—and I know he told his soldiers to follow me and . . . and do what they wanted with me."

Simon nodded. "Cry, Lotis. You're safe now. Cry, and let the evil dissolve from your soul."

For a long time she sobbed in his arms. At last, quieting but still shuddering, she said, "Simon, Simon! Why do the gods permit such things—?"

"Blame not the gods for what men do," he answered. "Tell me, now: This man who violated you—what is his name?"

"Scribonius." Lotis again grimaced as if in pain. "He is in charge of the Roman guard at the Siloam Gate in Jerusalem."

Fire gleamed in Simon's deep-set eyes; his fingers, resting on the girl's shoulders, tensed. "Scribonius?"

She saw the pain in him, for a moment forgot her own. "Oh, Simon, I'm sorry. Yes, it was the same Scribonius who—who was with Maxentius when—"

Simon nodded; his grip on the girl's shoulders relaxed. "When my parents were slain and I was taken into slavery. Think no more of this, Lotis. Lie down and sleep some more. Sleep. When you waken again you will feel better. Sleep. . . ."

He repeated the words over and over, gently yet forcefully. The girl's eyes closed and in a moment she was again slumbering on the pallet. Simon covered her with a blanket, then rose and gazed down at her. Lotis' mind was very receptive to suggestion; evidently she was weary from her long terror, ready to obey the will of one she felt she could trust.

He closed the shutters, then lay down upon his own pallet under the window, leaving a lamp burning in case the girl should have nightmares. Breathing softly, he cleansed his mind of thoughts and set himself a command to wake in an hour, then lapsed into a sleep-like trance.

When he woke the lamp was still burning with a still, steady flame. He felt rested. As he rose he saw Lotis stir and open her eyes. There was no more pain or fear in them, only a sadness.

"Lotis, I must go out again—"

The fear sprang into her eyes. "You're . . . not going to leave me?"

"Of course not. I'll be gone for only a couple of hours. There is food in the pack, and a cooking-hearth downstairs. When I return, we'll get our things bundled up again, rest some more, then leave this city at dawn, as soon as the gates open."

Lotis relaxed slightly. "I'll be so glad! Yet, I am fearful for my mistress. She has been good to me. A year ago she intervened when Scribonius first accosted me, told him off roundly, even got Maxentius to order him not to bother me any more. Now she will be asking about me. If she should anger Maxentius—"

"I see. Tell me, Lotis, who is this woman whom the Roman has taken for a mistress within the house of my parents."

"Simon, believe me, she is not evil. You have heard of her—Elissa of Sychar, the woman who—"

Simon nodded. "The woman who was a favorite of the gossips even when we were children under the same roof. Aye, I remember. Her fifth aged husband had died, then. What possessed her to become a mistress to a Roman tribune? His wealth?"

"Partly. But there is a wild streak in her, Simon. She has confided much in me, has even told me some of her feelings for Maxentius. In a way, she loves him, I think. She says she has loved no man since her first husband, who died leaving her poor; since then she has married only men of wealth and advanced years, but now that she is wealthy she vows to wed no more—to have only lovers who challenge and excite her. She says Maxentius is one of the most exciting men she had ever met; she laughs at his bursts of anger, at his periods of dark broodings, and says that handling such a man but adds to the excitement. But I fear for her—she has not seen the depths of his cruelty."

"You are a good-hearted soul, Lotis," said Simon, "but do not trouble yourself about this woman. She sounds to me like one who can take care of herself."

"Yet she was good to me. And she will miss me, I think."

"She can hire a hundred maids. That house is not good for you to be in, Lotis. You have been there far too long. I must go now. Make yourself a good meal, cleanse yourself and your clothes. If the landlord wants more money in advance for his services, there is money in the pouch on the table."

"But . . . will you not tell me where you are going?"

"To pick up a few more food items, perhaps do a bit more street performing. It won't hurt to have a few extra sesterces when we leave here tomorrow."

He turned and left the room, his eyes avoiding hers, avoiding the sadness and fear he knew he would see there.

When he was gone, Lotis turned to the shuttered casement, opened it. Darkness had descended upon the streets below; stars gleamed amid the scattering clouds and the moon, just over half full, faintly illumined the dark flank of the southern slope of Ebal. There would be no shops open now, no street crowds to perform to.

She looked at the pouch on the table. He had left her all the money, she knew, in case he did not return. . . .

Simon descended the outer stairway, entered the small common-room on the ground floor and took a bracketed torch from its place near the hearth, then went forth again and made his way through the darkness to the rear of the inn. As he entered the small attached shed that served for a stable he saw the mule standing, eyes closed in slumber, near a pack that contained grain and a few utensils he had not taken up to the room. Kneeling, he groped in the pack and pulled out a large object wrapped in dark, bloodstained cloth.

"Akrab," he muttered to the bundle, "soon you shall meet your master in Hades."

Rising, he turned and strode back out the door, unaware that the mule had opened its eyes and was watching his departure—watching him with eyes that glowed strangely in the light of the torch, almost as if with a light of their own.

There were only eight of them. Dositheus stroked his white beard thoughtfully, fingered his long and newly-cut oaken staff. Only eight, standing in a semicircle before him on the bank of the wide pool. All were men, the youngest perhaps twenty, the oldest in his sixties. Each wore a brown robe like Dositheus', but without magical emblazonments. All gazed upon the old wizard expectantly, a touch of awe in the eyes of some of the younger.

"Brethren, where are the others?" Dositheus asked.

"We are all that remain in Salim, save the innkeeper Botos," said the eldest, a balding Greek with an iron-gray beard. "Four others reside in Scythopolis and Pella, too far from here to be summoned in one day. The rest now follow Yeshua bar Yosef, the Nazarene teacher, and two of them have become his very disciples."

"Two of our own Thirty? Who are they?"

"Nathaniel bar Tolmai and Simon Zelotes."

Dositheus nodded. "Zelotes was always impulsive, and as for Nathaniel—well, his father Tolmai has already told me much about that."

The graybeard shuffled nervously. "Tolmai opposes us. He would see the *Am-ha-arez* possess all and the land ruled again by Assatur, even as it was in the days before the Habiru came to conquer and impose their false worship. Has Tolmai also joined the Nazarene, then?"

Dositheus looked away, guiltily recalling the sight of his friend's body being invaded by something green and pulsing. . . .

"No, Isagoras. Tolmai opposed this Yeshua bar Yosef and resented him for stealing Nathaniel's allegiance, and now I fear that he has joined forces with Izhar of the Black Synagogue. . . . But, enough. You must all tell me all you know about this Nazarene wonder-worker, for I see that much has happened during the years that I have spent in Persia."

"Persia?" Isagoras nodded. "I remember. You and Simon and Menander were going there to seek Daramos, reputedly the greatest mage since Ostanes. Did you find him?"

"Aye—and studied the arts and the mysteries under him for nearly four years."

Several of the younger men gasped and the eyes of all shone with awe. Dositheus basked in that admiring glow, felt warmed by it.

"Is Daramos indeed only half human, as the rumors say?" asked a younger member, "or is he—?"

"I cannot tell you more at this time," said Dositheus. "Suffice it to say that I have brought back with me a copy of the Scroll of Mattan in the original Canaanite. I know of no Greek translation of it save for the one I am laboring to produce. Look—" The old man reached beneath his robe and drew forth a large yellowed scroll, then brandished it aloft. "Here is the *El-Halal,* and in it many of the lost secrets we have long sought."

"The others crowded close about him, peering at the scroll. Isagoras clutched at it. "Let me see!"

Dositheus unrolled it as far as his lean arms would allow. The old Greek peered closely at the archaic lettering, finally exclaiming, "It is ancient Canaanite indeed, and—gods!—this passage tells of the coming of the *Am-ha-arez* to this world—"

"Say no more," said Dositheus, hastily rolling up the scroll. "I will reveal all to you soon. But now, you must tell me of this rabbi Yeshua and how he came to draw so many away from our fold."

The others drew back reluctantly. Isagoras sighed. "You have no doubt heard that our former teacher Johannen bar Zachariah was slain some months ago by Herod the Tetrarch?"

"Aye—for baiting Herod concerning some domestic matters, I believe."

"You heard truly. Johannen preached violently against those who kept not the Law. He prophesied that it must now be kept more rigorously than ever, for soon there would come the One meant to fulfill it. We did not at that time realize that he meant his own cousin, Yeshua bar Yosef."

Dositheus gasped. "Johannen's *cousin?* I did not know—"

"Nor did we," said Isagoras. "Yet one day this Yeshua appeared among us—south of here, where Johannen was baptizing many in the waters of the Jordan. Johannen baptized him also, and when the man rose from the water and waded ashore we heard a faint rumbling like thunder, high and distant. I looked up and saw a thin white cloud extending itself across the sky, straight as a line parting the heavens. Many others saw it also. It faded and dissipated slowly, but before it had vanished a white dove suddenly flew to the man and alighted upon his shoulder, crying out in a curious trilling voice; I was close by, Dositheus, and heard it with my own ears. So did a few others, though none of us could understand the language in which the bird spoke, and it was soon rumored about that a voice from the sky itself had proclaimed this Yeshua to be its own favored son. What sort of sorcery can this be, Dositheus? What does it portend?"

"Much, I think. The stars are approaching a significant configuration, such as has not been seen for nearly fourteen centuries. Tell me, Isagoras, what was your impression of this Nazarene? What was his manner, his appearance?"

"His mien was one of solemnity, even sadness. I sensed strange power and yet compassion in him—I can believe the tales that he is a sorcerer and has healed many. His stature is above the average, and his face—it is hard to describe. A noble face, and yet with a touch of the sheep or the goat in its features. Do you find that hard to believe, Dositheus?"

The old wizard repressed a shudder, remembering what the rabbi Tolmai had told him in Capharnaum. "No, no," he muttered, more to himself than to his questioner. "It is one of the signs—the many signs. The time is indeed approaching, as I feared. . . ." He looked up. "Isagoras, have you heard of Those who beget their progeny upon mankind?"

A touch of fear glimmered in the old Greek's eyes. "Aye. Some whisper that this Yeshua is the spawn of the *Iao Sabaoth*. Can such a thing be true?"

Dositheus hesitated. "A Syrian blasphemy—"

"Do not hide your knowledge from us, old mage. Did you not just hint at such a possibility? You have learned much in your travels. Tell us all."

The old man affected a sigh. "Very well. In addition to this Book of Mattan, the scroll of Ostanes in the original Persian reveals much that is not in any Greek translation; moreover, I have acquired many other books from the library of the archimage Prodikos, whose dark fame is not unknown to you. As soon as we can arrange another meeting, with all members of the Thirty present, I will disclose the mysteries I have learned—and then you will see that these are portentous times indeed and that much must be done in order to prevent . . ."

"Prevent what, Dositheus?"

"I will tell you in due time."

"No!" cried the others. "Don't hold back!"

"Say it, Dositheus!"

"By Zeus, you will tell us," insisted Isagoras, irritated by the old Samaritan's portentous hesitation. "Don't lead us on so. What sort of disaster is this Nazarene about to bring upon the land? Just what is it that we must prevent?"

"Perhaps the doom of the world," said Dositheus. "Ask me no more. I will explain all I can when next we meet."

Many voices rose in protest, urging, begging for more information. But Dositheus remained adamant.

"When shall we next meet, then? asked Isagoras

"After I have met this Nazarene wizard. Where can I find him?"

"I heard today that he was but a day's journey south of here, in the town of Aphairema," said one of the younger members. "He preaches in the countryside not far from there. But they say he goes soon toward Jericho."

"Good. I shall return as quickly as I am able. And, should I encounter Nathaniel and Zelotes, I'll try to persuade them to return also. May I tell any I meet that I come in your name, Isagoras?"

The old Greek swallowed. "Why not in you own name, Dositheus? You are far ahead of us in arcane wisdom. Our band has fallen on evil days. We need a leader such as you, and new knowledge such as you have gleaned in your wanderings."

Dositheus suppressed a smile; this was what he had been secretly expecting and hoping for. "No, no. . . .," he said politely with a deprecatory wave of his hand.

"Yes!" urged the others. "Lead us, Dositheus. Lead us!"

"Very well, then. Send for the rest of the Thirty, as many as you can find. I shall return as soon as I am able and tell you all that I have learned.

Then the full membership shall decide whether I am to lead you. Let us disband now, for night approaches. I shall inform Botos of our proceedings, and leave at dawn."

They dispersed, and Dositheus walked slowly back to the village. As he arrived at the inn in the last glow of twilight he saw Menander waiting for him by the gate.

"Did the meeting go well, O Mentor?"

"It went very well, Menander. Did you purchase the ass?"

The lad nodded. "Botos helped us find a good one, though it took awhile. It's out back. Ilione is tending it. She has named it Dosiander—after us."

"She's not in a good mood, I take it?"

Menander sighed. "She is often very hard to live with. I'd cuff her good sometimes, I think, if I didn't love her so much."

Dositheus smiled gently. "I will tell you a secret, my lad. You are young and Ilione is an exceptionally beautiful girl, and so your feelings for her are running high, but you don't love her any more than she loves Simon."

"I—I don't? She—doesn't . . .?"

"Not in the way that I have told you of."

Menander remembered. "You mean, like Simon and Helen. And like you and—the one you've mentioned, whom the Romans slew long ago."

"Aye." Dositheus looked toward the east where Spica, blue-white gem of the Virgin, gleamed above the far hills amid the sky's darkening purple. "When it happens, Menander, you and the other will *both* know, and in that instant you will also know more of the universe and its ultimate nature than you could ever be told. But you must bide your time in patience, for this is a matter that will not be bidden nor hastened. Continue to treat Ilione as a friend and fellow pupil, and do not try to force her to be more, for that could lead to hatred. Friendship is better."

Menander nodded. "I'll try. Sometimes she irritates me even as she attracts me most. She is becoming more and more petulant in her frustration and takes it out on me. Part of the time she yearns for Simon, at other times she longs to journey to Persia and study under Daramos. When *are* we going to Persia, O Mentor?"

Dositheus hesitated. "Not for awhile. There are many things that I must do here. Urgent things."

Disappointment showed plainly in the youth's face. "Like what?"

"Menander, I have been asked to lead the Thirty."

"Ah."

"You can also become a member if you wish, for many have left the fold and I am sure that not all of them will return. Some are nearly as young as you. I may even be able to get them to accept Ilione as the first woman member, for they respect me greatly."

Menander sighed. "I knew you had been hoping for this."

"You are disappointed now, lad, but you shouldn't be. There are exciting times ahead. The Thirty is the most exclusive order of arcane wisdom in the eastern provinces. Under Johannen's leadership they became respected far and wide for their powers of healing and prophecy, and after my leadership has reunited them they shall become even more respected and sought after. You know what that means, Menander. Men bring gifts in return for healing and prophecy. Many gifts, often large gifts. We will become rich, and then you may journey to Persia—or anywhere else you choose. But first, there are urgent things to be done. The stars will soon be right for dark things; great events impend—events in which you must play a part."

"I don't understand."

"You will when I return and hold the next gathering of the Thirty. Until then, ask me no more."

"Return? Where are you going?"

"A day's journey south, to Aphairema—or perhaps two, to Jericho—to seek out this mysterious prophet Yeshua bar Yosef. If he is what I think he is, the world is in great danger. Pack my things now. I must sleep a few hours and leave while the moon is yet high."

"Tonight? But—will you not need my aid?"

"Botos will supply a sturdy lout to handle the donkey. I'll take Carbo, too, to be a messenger between us once each day. You must stay here and take care of Ilione. Reassure her that I shall return either tomorrow or the next day—or the next."

Menander felt a pang of anxiety. "You mean you don't know *when* you'll be back—?"

"Obey me, lad," said the old man sternly. "You are learned in magic and mystery, having studied under Daramos and me. But the maid is still new to this and must be reassured. Do not fail her—or me."

"But, when *will* you be back, Master?"

"In four or five days at the most, I trust. But even should it take longer, you must wait here and reassure Ilione. Keep her occupied with her studies. Don't let her slacken."

"I—I'll try. Is that all?"

"No. Tomorrow at dawn you must go to the hilltop where we last saw the wizard Taggart and see if he returns as he said he would."

Menander remembered, and was suddenly even more anxious. *"Me?* But surely I am not yet enough of an adept to deal with such a wizard!"

"Ah, but you are, and I am trusting you to do it well. In any case, the man is not as great a wizard as his powers make him seem, I'm sure. You see, I performed a certain test—"

Some of Menander's anxiety turned to irritation. "So Ilione was right! You deceived the man—after he saved our lives."

"Deceived? Call it a test. Remember the tale of the demon in the jar, Menander. When dealing with powerful beings it is well to learn the limits of their powers, just in case."

"I sensed no menace from the man. He could have destroyed us easily had he wished."

"And still, you are anxious about meeting him. You should know by now, Menander, that a wise man always tries to have something to bargain with. If this Taggart has not managed to translate the passage in Mattan's book, you will know that we still have something he needs—a knowledge of the Greek tongue. Use this advantage wisely, lad, and you may benefit us all greatly. We could use the aid of such a wizard."

Menander again felt a sinking feeling. "You will not come with me, then?"

"Would that I might! But I must pursue the more important matter immediately. Should this Yeshua bar Yosef be indeed the one foretold by Johannen and the olden prophets, the fate of the world may be at stake. I must learn as much as I can as soon as possible, before the Time is upon us."

"But the wizard—Taggart. Might he not also be important in these foretold events?"

"I know of none like him described in the ancient writings. Moreover, as I say, he seems to know little despite all his powers. Yet, learn from him whatever you can. You are of age now, Menander, and have for years studied the wisdom under two masters. Now is the time for you to use that wisdom. I am trusting you."

"But—"

"No more. And now, to supper, study and bed. Remember, not a word of this to Ilione until tomorrow, after I am gone."

They turned and entered the gate to the inn's courtyard, while Menander silently prayed to Baal to stop the flutterings in the pit of his stomach.

Hurrying through the deserted, shadowed streets, his dark cloak close about him, Simon felt a pang of guilt. He knew Lotis had not believed his stated reason for going out, knew that she must have seen his grim purpose in his face. He wanted to protect her, care for her—the gods knew she had suffered enough! Yet they also know, as she must, that the vengeance-thoughts that had burned in him these many years would not be denied. Their fire had kept him going during his darkest times, and now the hour of their fulfillment had come.

Maxentius—Scribonius. . . .

And then, there was Elissa of Sychar. Lotis had spoken well of her. Yet, how should he act toward this willful mistress of a Roman—this woman who had, during these last two years, lived shamelessly beneath his parents' roof, sporting carnally with the man who had slain them . . .?

He fingered the haft of the sharp-bladed sica beneath his cloak.

And now in the thick, torchless darkness the streets began to take on an uncanny familiarity to Simon. Though the moon was not bright enough to illuminate much of the narrow lanes, he hastened on without hesitation. This was the neighborhood where he had spent much of his youth, and even in the shadowed gloom he could tell that it had changed little.

Then, rounding a corner, he saw it at the end of the short lane—a high, familiar cornice silhouetted against the moonlit sky. The house was larger than those around it and built in the Classical style that his grandfather Simon had favored. The front was sheer and too high to climb. Carefully, making sure that the narrow alleys were indeed deserted, he stole around to the back. Here a lower flat-roofed structure—used as a stable, Simon remembered—abutted the main house.

He slung his bundle by a thong around his neck and one shoulder, so that it hung down behind, then unlooped a long cord from his belt. To one end of the cord was tied a small but stout hook with three prongs. Simon took a few deep breaths, let them out slowly, then began to whirl the hook about him in larger and larger loops. Suddenly he released the cord; the hook arched upward, clattered slightly upon the flat rooftop. Simon pulled on it gently until he felt it snag, then tugged. The cord held.

Slowly, with extreme care, Simon began to walk up the wall, pulling himself smoothly hand over hand, in a fashion taught him by his old Persian mentor. He knew he must make no sudden change in the pull on the cord, for if the hook were snagged on a mere irregularity to stone or stucco, the slightest change of pressure might dislodge it. For a moment as he neared the top he emerged into moonlight; then his left hand gripped the edge and he pulled himself up and over.

For several minutes he lay concealed behind the low parapet, slowly rewinding the cord while the tension drained from his muscles. The next stage would be easier: over the tiled roof and down to the balcony overlooking the open peristyle.

It was soon done, for he had accomplished it often as a child without the knowledge of his parents and the servants. The peristyle was shadowed, but he could see the pool within it shimmering softly beneath, reflecting the stars. His feet touched the balcony's tiles and he immediately eased away from the polished column down which he had slid, stealing deeper in the shadows.

He tried each door carefully until he found one unlocked and eased it open. For a moment he stood there, but caught no sound of breathing such as a sleeper would make. The room was for a servant, he remembered, but it felt empty. Slowly he eased within, closed the door and moved across the floor in pitch darkness, every sense acutely alert. This, too, was a technique his mentors had taught him well—how to find one's way through darkness without stumbling or upsetting things. One must not hurry—keep centered, explore gently ahead with one hand and toe. . . .

He found the remembered door to the balcony overlooking the atrium, eased it open a crack and saw light. A torch burned at the head of the stairs at the other end of the balcony. Cautiously opening it wider, he slipped through. No one was in sight. The atrium below was a well of shadow.

Slowly Simon crept to the right, past the main door to the peristyle balcony, and continued on until he had gained the corner of the quadrangle farthest from the torch. Still he heard no sound, saw no movement. Could the house be deserted? No, surely not with that torch burning. Yet, where were the servants . . .?

He moved westward along the north wall, tried both doors. Both opened at his touch, but standing silently within he could detect no other presence. A strange feeling came over him, for these two chambers had been his own. What would they look like now . . .?

Shadow-like, Simon stole to the western balcony. The first door there had been his father's room, the next his mother's; the two south chambers had been for guests. If all these were empty, he would have to check below. Strange, this utter silence. Carefully he tried the door to his father's room.

It opened.

Simon deliberately hesitated, composing himself. He gripped the haft of his sica. This would be the room most likely to have been chosen by Maxentius for his sleeping quarters.

Softly he crept inward, stood listening. A tinge of disappointment stole over him as he realized that here, too, he could detect the presence of no one.

"Baal!" he muttered inaudibly. "Where can—?"

"No!" a woman's voice sudden shrieked. *"Get out of here! Get out and leave me alone!"*

CHAPTER IX

Simon tensed, whipped out his sword—but realized instantly that the woman's frantic outburst could not be directed at him. It had come from the next room, muffled by the wall and a closed door. He could now see a faint line of light at the base of that door. His mother's room. . . .

"Leave me alone!" There was desperation in the voice. And then Simon heard a door open outside and crash against the wall, followed by hurrying footsteps upon the balcony tiles. Again the voice screamed, *"Get away from me!"*—this time from the balcony.

Quickly he pulled the door almost closed behind him, then peered out.

A tall, dark-haired woman had emerged from the next room, was hurrying away from him toward the stairway. She glanced back, and Simon glimpsed terror in the backlit profile of her face. Then two dark shapes emerged from the chamber and strode after her—black-cloaked guardsmen, silent and purposeful, their dark iron helms gleaming in the torchlight.

With a soundless snarl Simon glided from the room. A quick glance into the lamplit chamber from which the woman and her pursuers had come showed him that it was empty. He charged.

One guard whirled at the slight sound of rushing feet—just in time to meet Simon's broad-bladed gladius with his neck. His head shot whirling over the rail of the balcony and fell to the tiles below with a muted iron clatter; the body staggered, groping, then slipped and fell with a clangor of armor.

The woman screamed again.

The second soldier was advancing toward Simon, a dark silhouette, sword in hand. Simon hurled his wrapped bundle into the man's face, heard bone crack against bone. Instantly he charged in, slashed flesh with his sword and darted back out of reach of a counter stroke. The guard grunted, then strode forward with upraised sword. Simon swore, his hackles rising. The man did not drip blood, had not cried out, seemed unhurt. Another of those damned demon-possessed! Then blade rang on blade. Simon retreated slowly, warding off the mechanical repeated blows, seeking a place to strike the menacing silhouette—

A vase crashed against the guard's helmet, its shards clattering about Simon on the tiles. The guard half-turned to face the woman who had advanced and hurled it. In that instant Simon leaped forward and swung expertly; the blade of his short sword chopped precisely between the armor and the helmet's rim. The guardsman collapsed, head hanging to its carcass by a mere shred of flesh.

Simon leaped over the corpses, sheathed his blade. "Quick, woman, get away from them!" he snapped.

The woman stepped back warily, fear in her eyes. "Don't hurt me! I aided you—I'm glad you killed them."

"Don't be so sure I did." Simon pointed. "Look!"

Again the woman screamed—for from the severed neck of each corpse a thick green fluid was pouring along with the sudden gush of blood. Then the fluid streams formed into two viscous blobs that began to grope toward Simon across the tiles. He snatched the torch from it bracket and advanced, holding it low before him, and immediately the things retreated. Grimly Simon herded them between the posts of the balcony, saw them ooze over the edge and vanish—and heard, an instant later, their dull ploppings on the tiles below. Then he again faced the woman, who was leaning white-faced against the wall

"Anath!" she gasped. "Demons . . .?"

Simon strode forward and eyed her closely. "You are Elissa of Sychar?"

She looked at him, nodded. "Who are—?"

"What are you doing in my father's house, in my mother's room? Are you the paramour of the Roman?"

"Maxentius?" Her dark eyes sparked with sudden fury. "I *hate* him! He has humiliated me, beaten me—I, a daughter of the prophets of Gerizim! He as much as threatened me with torture and death when he returns—"

"He is not here? Are there more guards, then? Or servants?"

The woman hesitated. "Stay back! I'll call them if you dare to—"

Simon barked a brief laugh. "I see. We are alone, Elissa of Sychar, mistress of Romans."

The woman drew herself erect. There was pride and nobility in her, Simon saw, despite the pallor her fright had given her. "There is hate in your voice. What did you mean when you asked what I was doing in . . . your father's house?"

"Exactly that. I am Simon of Gitta. My parents were Antonius bar Simon and his wife Rachel, who were slain here eight years ago by Maxentius and his fellow extortionists. Surely you knew how he acquired this house."

"Then . . . the stories I've heard are true?" asked Elissa. "I had thought them the usual envy-inspired rumors that are often told concerning the wealthy and powerful."

Simon doubted that. All knew of what the Romans were capable. Still, he felt his anger subsiding. After all, the woman had helped him against the guards who had evidently been keeping her prisoner.

"Where did Maxentius come by such guardsmen?" he asked.

Elissa shuddered. "From Annas, the sorcerer who is the power behind the Jerusalem priesthood. Where he got them I know not. Lord of Gerizim!

They would not speak nor leave my side—they were with me when I lay down or rose, when I ate, even when I bathed or . . . Horrible! And always they would stare at me with expressionless faces and those evil yellow eyes of theirs until I thought I should go mad!"

Simon found that he could feel no anger toward the woman. "When did you first meet Maxentius?"

"Less than two years ago. I swear that I knew nothing about your parents. And now, are you going to slay me—after having saved me from Maxentius' guards?"

Simon shook his head. The woman seemed sincere in her new-found hate for Maxentius, and from all accounts she was wealthy and no doubt influential—potentially a valuable ally.

Besides, Simon had to admit, the woman was one of the most attractive he had ever seen.

"I'll spare you," he said, "for a girl named Lotis has spoken well of you, and I rate her opinion highly. She will probably be pleased to see you again."

"Lotis!" exclaimed Elissa, and there was no mistaking the genuine joy and relief in her eyes. "I feared Maxentius had—"

"He meant to have her slain, but those he appointed to the task died instead." Simon lighted another torch, plucked it from its bracket and handed it to the woman. "Go and collect what you can carry of your possessions. We must leave. Are there pack animals in the stable?"

"Just the guards' two horses. Maxentius took the rest when he and his troops followed Annas back to Jerusalem."

"Good. I'll bring them around to the vestibule. Wait for me there."

Elissa glanced nervously down into the darkened atrium. "The demons —?"

"If they approach you, use the torch. They can't stand fire. Don't let them touch you or they'll sink into your flesh. At a distance they are harmless."

Elissa hurried back to her room. Simon stooped and retrieved his bundle, strode past her door without glancing in and then entered his father's chamber. Somehow he was glad to see that none of the furnishings were the same. On the wall over the head of the bed hung a great square Roman shield and a pair of crossed pilums.

Maxentius. . . .

Slowly he advanced toward the great bed and, unwrapping the head of Akrab, placed it upon the pillow. It stared into the room with sunken, vacant eyes, pale in the light of Simon's torch, its blood staining the coverlet, mouth gaping as in a soundless scream.

"You shall give your master a message for me, Akrab," Simon muttered. "I shall write it for you.

He turned to a table where there were tablets and a stylus, parchments and papyrus. Taking up a pot of ink and a large writing brush, he returned to the head of the bed and wrote upon the plaster of the wall above it:

THE SON OF THE FATHER HAS RETURNED.

Then, hurrying from the room and its memories, he descended the stair and hastened to make ready the horses.

Menander had barely left the village when he heard the patter of feet on the path behind him. Quickly he ducked into the shadow of a palm tree, his hand on the dagger at his belt, and waited nervously as the cloaked figure following him approached. . . .

Then, seeing the flash of a white tunic as the robe of the hurrying figure fell open, he relaxed. It was Ilione.

He stepped from the shadow and confronted her. The dim starlight gleamed faintly upon the strands of hair escaping from her cowl and showed her face in the merest sketch of highlights, but even so Menander sensed fear in her wide eyes.

"Menander—?"

"Ilione! Why are you following me? I thought you were asleep."

"Menander, please don't leave me! I know I've been hard to live with. I've said angry things to you and Dositheus, but I didn't mean them. Please don't go away! If you do, how will I live? I don't know anyone in this land, I have nowhere to go, no one to protect me. I'll be robbed, taken away by slave-procurers—"

"Ilione, what are you talking about?"

"Dositheus is gone, and now you are stealing away to join him!" The girl was in tears. "I know you must both hate me for all the rude things I've said, but I didn't mean them. I'll make it up to you, Menander—I won't pout or be spiteful any more, and I'll do all the work—"

Menander laughed briefly. "Ilione, you're crazy! I'd never leave you. Don't you know how much I love you?"

The girl appeared startled. "You—you do?"

"Of course! How could I not?"

The girl rushed into his arms and clung to him almost desperately, shivering, nearly sobbing. "Oh, Menander, I'm so glad! I thought you hated me. You and Dositheus have been to me like the grandfather and the brother I never had, and in return I've been so spiteful—"

Menander gently stroked her hair where the cowl had fallen back. "You think of me as—a brother?"

"Yes, yes. Please don't think it presumptuous of me, Menander. You and Dositheus are all the family I have. I wouldn't have said so many spiteful things, only I was sad—disappointed that we're not going to Persia like Dositheus promised, that I'll never get to meet the wise and kind Daramos. . . ."

Menander swallowed, nodded. "I'm disappointed about that too, Ilione. But I'd never leave you. I promise I won't"

The girl wiped away her tears and looked at him with puzzled eyes. "But—where is Dositheus, then?"

"He left in the night for Aphairema—a long day's journey south of here. He has a notion that he must track down the mad Nazarene prophet who has been stirring up the populace recently. But he said he'd be back before many days, and he's left us plenty of provisions and money."

"I see. But, then, where are *you* going?"

"To meet the wizard."

"Ah." The girl nodded. "I had forgotten. He said he would return at this early hour. . . . Menander, I'm going with you."

"It might be dangerous—"

"Please don't deny me this. You and Dositheus are so close—I feel so left out sometimes. Please, let me share this with you. How can we grow close except by sharing our adventures, our misfortunes even?"

Menander sighed. "Grow close—like brother and sister. Very well, Ilione, come along. I won't deny that I'm glad to have your company. We'll meet this wizard together."

For some time they followed the path amid the scattered shrubs, saying little. The night air was cool and the stars glittered down coldly. Presently the trail faded out amid the many intersecting sheep paths of the slopes and they left the trees and shrubs behind, finally gaining the crest of the low, rounded hill. Here they paused, regarding the landscape as it lay all still under the faintly luminous blue of the night sky. Eastward gleamed the stars of Aquarius, dim amid the first faint, pearly glimmer of approaching dawn. A wind stirred the grass of the hilltop.

"This is where he said he'd meet us," said Menander uneasily.

Suddenly the raven on his shoulder fluttered, extended its beak and croaked, *"Qua!"*

"What? What do you sense, Carbo? Something near —?"

There was a shimmering in the air, a wavering close by like heat over the desert, though the air was quite cool. Menander stared at it intently, felt the prickle of gooseflesh. Did he seem to hear a faint, regular hum . . .?

In the next instant he and Ilione both cried out, startled—for directly in front of them the wizard's strange craft had abruptly materialized, hovering its usual foot or so above the ground, the dark form of the wizard standing upright within it. The faint blue light surrounded him, but then immediately blinked out.

"Gods!" Menander gasped. "Where did you come from?"

"I was here already," said the man as he clambered out of the craft. "I've been waiting for you for several minutes."

"But—how . . .?"

The man took a tiny black book from his pouch, shone his magic light upon it as he turned the pages. Then he sighed and replaced both objects in the pouch.

"This language has not the words to explain. Enough to say that light comes to us like waves, and that my craft has the power to bend those waves around itself and so become invisible. But this process drains much—strength—from the craft, so I do this only in areas where others might be—watching —and then only for short periods."

Ilione got the impression that by "others" he meant more than passing travelers or shepherds. "Do you have enemies, then, great wizard?"

"Let's say that there are those who would stop me if they knew what I was doing. But I haven't much time. Where is Dositheus?"

"I'm sorry," said Menander. "He had matters of great importance to attend to. But he charged me to meet you and see to your satisfaction."

Taggart scowled in irritation. "This is more important than he realizes. The survival of the human race is at stake."

"Why, that's what *he* said!" Menander exclaimed. "He told me that the time is approaching when the entire world may be destroyed if certain things are allowed to come about as foretold. For this reason he has gone to see the sorcerer Yeshua bar Yosef —"

"What? What does your old master know about all this?"

The two young people drew back a pace at the intensity in the man's voice. "I—I know little," said Menander. "My mentor has told me only that the stars are coming right, after some fourteen centuries, and that there are now some who gather to perform rituals that will cause the dark powers to stir."

"'Stars . . . rituals . . . powers'," muttered Taggart. "Of course—the ancient writings would put these things in such terms. Tell me, young man, do you read Greek?"

"Of course. So does Ilione. So does every educated person in the Empire—"

Menander stopped, embarrassed, feeling that he had perhaps offended the man. But Taggart only smiled slightly.

"I fear I'm not very educated by your standards. I come from far away. But, here—" The wizard turned, reached back over the rim of the craft and drew forth a scroll. "When you mentor gave me this I failed to look at it, and when I arrived at my destination I found I was unable to read it."

Menander noticed Ilione smiling slightly. He felt again a sense of shame and irritation, heightened by the stranger's obvious ingenuousness. "Was your journey to Hali for nothing, then, O Wizard?"

"Call me Taggart. No, not *entirely* for nothing, for I discovered that what I was looking for was indeed missing. Someone has taken it away."

"Dositheus told me someone else had delved there before him, yet he was not entirely sure that they had found the Chalice of Byakh."

"Well, they did find it, and much more. As I suspected, there are chambers not far beneath the excavated area which, though undisturbed, are now empty. Which means that the discoverers took forth what they wanted by means other than mere digging."

"How can that be?" cried Ilione. "How can one see through rock walls and take forth what is behind them, leaving them unbroken?"

"They no doubt saw as I did, by means of—" Taggart groped for a word—"of waves undetectable by the unaided senses. I suspect those chambers once housed, in addition to the—uh—chalice, those hemispheres of metal containing the beings you encountered in Chorazin. For thousands of years these beings have slept, but now they are being awakened. And to pluck them from beyond unbroken walls would have take far more—strength—than my sky-craft contains."

"Gods!" Ilione shuddered, remembering. "But, even my father Prodikos possessed not such sorcery—"

"He could have—or, rather, the being that lived in him could have—only he was isolated from his kind, stranded upon this world, always working to escape. Prodikos, I'm told, once found one of the smaller chambers beneath Sardis, wakened the beings in the hemispheres there—accidentally, no doubt—and was possessed by the chief of them."

Ilione clutched her face in her hands; when she again looked up she was white as death. "I knew my father was possessed, but—by one of *those?"*

Taggart nodded. "By the leader of those upon this world who serve the being you call Assatur. But, I'm sorry—I see this disturbs you."

"Gods! *Gods!* One of *those!"*

Menander took her in his arms, held her to him as she sobbed against his breast.

"It's all right, Ilione. He's dead—and you know he wasn't possessed until years after you were born." As her sobbings quieted, he turned to the man in black. "Damn you, wizard, how did you know about her father?"

Taggart shifted his stance awkwardly, uncomfortably. "I was once shown his—image—in the star-ship of the Zarrians. He was known of—was being kept track of—but was considered unimportant because of his isolation. I understand that later he acquired dangerous knowledge and was taken away by—others. I certainly did not know that he—the man possessed—was this girl's father."

Ilione raised her tear-streaked face. "Tell me, wizard, what happened to him? Do not spare me."

"No," said Menander. "Ilione, you don't want to relive any of that."

"Tell me, sorcerer! My father was taken away by demons in the great temple at Ephesus—he and his familiar, a weasel which was said to contain the soul of the dead empress Livia. It is said that they were taken to feed the monstrous Goddess of Nether Earth, consort of Assatur himself. Is this true? Tell me!"

Taggart sighed. "Your father was dead long before his body ceased to obey what was within it, for the minions of Assatur eventually destroy the minds of their—hosts. I know few of the particulars, save that the being inhabiting Prodikos was taken back to its master and destroyed, having become too human in its thinking after so many years in a human body. And, yet, I also heard that one who had earlier inhabited a Roman empress was subdued and—reduced—to serve in the body of a small animal."

"The weasel—Prodikos' familiar!" exclaimed Menander. "But, then, the Empress Livia was possessed also? We knew she was a great sorceress, but—"

"'Sorcery—possession'—sometime I may tell you the true meaning of these things," said Taggart. "But I haven't the time now. One of you must read to me the passage Dositheus indicated in this scroll."

Menander took it and the small magic cylinder; by the latter's light he could make out the Greek writing quite clearly. "You want me to render it into Latin, then?"

"No, I have a better way." Again the man reached into his craft, this time drawing forth two identical objects that gleamed with a faint blue sheen. One he placed on his head; it was a flexible band of what appeared to be woven metal, securing a wider disc of solid metal to his brow. Then he advanced, as if to place the other upon Menander's head. The lad drew back.

"Don't be afraid," said Taggart. "Here—*you* put it on."

Menander took the thing, gingerly donned it as he had seen the stranger do, so that the disc was over his brow. He felt nothing but the smooth coolness of the metal.

"Good," said Taggart. "Now, read the passage Dositheus indicated."

Menander gasped. He understood every word the wizard had said—even though those words were in *a language totally unfamiliar to him!*

"Gods —!"

"Don't be alarmed. These thought transmitters are devices of the Zarrians, not magic. They enable us to understand one another no matter what language we speak."

Menander's mind reeled. More than words were flooding into his mind. There were strange associations, connotations. For an instant he felt he vaguely understood why these "thought transmitters" were not truly magic, and when the strange word "Zarrians" was spoken he had a brief vision of monstrous blue beings, tall and powerful and sinister. His spine tingled. . . .

"Menander, what language is he speaking?"

"I—I don't know, Ilione, but—*I understand it!*"

"Please," said Taggart, "I haven't much time. Read the scroll."

Menander lifted it, held it awkwardly open, holding the small light on it with two fingers; it had been rolled to the passage Dositheus had indicated—the forty-seventh column. Slowly, carefully, he began to read it aloud, while the man called Taggart listened intently, apparently comprehending the spoken Greek:

> Now when the sons of Vanaheim conquered Stygia in the olden time, many fled therefrom under the leadership of the sorcerer Uhuot, settling at last far to the northeast where they founded a city. And this city they named *Karakossa* (which means "Soul of the Dark Sun") after that world amid the stars of the Bull's Face to which their great god, Set, had fled aeons before during the War between the Old Ones and the Primal Gods.
>
> Then Uhuot prayed to Set, saying: "*Ha-Set-ur* (that is, 'O Great Set'), aid us, we implore thee, against those who have conquered thine ancient nation of Stygia, and who even now gather to overthrow us, the last of thy worshippers!" Thereupon did Set send to them a number of cowled minions from that world beyond the Eye of the Bull—which minions are most terrible—and also many lesser ones from the Worlds of the Six Suns, which worlds are called *Ka'a-Set-ur* (meaning "Conquered of Great Set"). And these lesser minions, inhabiting the bodies of Stygian warriors, rendered those warriors exceeding hard to slay by blade or spear or arrow, so that all save the most severe of their wounds did heal even during battle. Thus were beaten back in slaughter and terror all of the Vanir horde who came up against them, and subsequently other foes also. And for many centuries thereafter the kingdom of Uhuot performed its dark worship and grew strong, none daring to wage war against it.
>
> Thus the city of Karakossa waxed great and famous, and westward of it was builded the Shrine of Hali, a day's journey into the hills. And it came to pass that each year processions marched from the city to the shrine, on which occasions the priests and kings would stand before the

> altars and quaff the golden nectar from the Chalice of Byakh in order to behold the Phantom of Truth. Then would the *Byakhtril* be blown, summoning the bat-winged *Byakhim* to come and bear the sacrificed ones skyward, even to the abode of Great Set amid the Hyades.

Menander paused. Strange visions had filled his mind as he read—visions of worlds and suns far-flung amid black immensities beyond the skies of Earth—of huge cylindrical ships of metal hurtling across those immensities from world to world—of cowled, tentacled beings filing in slow procession beside a black lake that rippled and roiled strangely beneath a dim sun. He felt awe and a tingling of fear as he realized that these strange concepts and flashes of wisdom were coming to him from the mind of Taggart.

"I—I'm sorry, sir—I can read no more."

Taggart nodded. "I understand. The device can exhaust one not practiced in its use. Take it off."

Menander did so. Immediately the vision fragments ceased to come. He heard the wizard say in Latin, "Ilione, would you please put on the headband and continue reading the passage?"

The girl hesitated. "Menander, you look so strange!"

"It's all right, Ilione," he assured her. "Do as he says."

She placed the band on her head, disc upon her brow. It was cool and dry, not the least warm from Menander's skin. She felt a slight tingling, sensed flashes of strange thought—

"Please, continue reading," Taggart urged.

The girl started, realizing that she now clearly understood words of the language unrelated to any she had ever known. Then, hastening to obey, she turned to the scroll and, as Menander held the light on it, read aloud:

> After Uhuot, Thale was king in Karakossa, and after him Naotalba, and after him Apop; and all of these lived far beyond the normal life span of mankind because of the beings that dwelt within them. And the kingdom grew great beneath their rule, and waxed mighty in conquest, until at the last Apop subdued even the land of Khem and sat upon the throne of the Pharaohs. Thus was Set's worship brought back into that land which had aforetime been Stygia, together with the worship of Gol-goroth, Yhtill, Shupnikkurat, and all the other dark Stygian gods, and for a hundred years and more the altars along the Nile drank human blood. And even the worship of Him who dwells in the cloudy depths of Demhe was revived, who

> was in olden Shem called *Yahweh Zava'ot,* in Karakossa *Uagio-tsotho* and in Stygia *Yog-Sothoth*—

Taggart gasped—and Ilione screamed as she sensed a terrible vision about to form in her mind. Frantically she tore the metal band from her head, threw it from her and stood trembling. She had seen nothing, yet the terrible name had evoked a wave of fear. . . .

Menander gripped her arm. "Ilione—?"

"I—I'm all right," she gasped.

"I'm sorry," said Taggart, who also seemed a bit shaken. "I didn't anticipate that—that name. And yet, I should have. I once had a very unpleasant experience—"

"How much more of this must we endure, wizard?" snapped Menander.

"No more than you wish. I'll not force you to help me. Yet, I repeat that the fate of the human race is at stake. If you could know what powers are gathering to possess this earth—"

On impulse Menander snatched up the band and replaced it on his head just in time to catch a vision vanishing from Taggart's mind—flame-clouds looming and boiling from horizon to horizon, huge alien shapes thundering through the skies, monstrous chasms opening, the very heavens themselves beginning to dissolve—

"Gods . . .!"

"Yes." Taggart's voice was somber as he again spoke in his own strange tongue. "That is what must be prevented."

Trembling slightly, Menander took up the scroll, found the place where Ilione had broken off, and continued to read aloud:

> But then came those minions of the Primal Gods from *Ka-Alantog,* which the Persians call *Glantok* and the Achaeans *Celaeno,* which star is in the Shoulder of the Bull. And in a single day perished the great and ancient city of Karakossa, which had flourished upon the plain of Gennesaret since the destruction of Stygia and all the lands of Hyborios. In that time, it is written, the Six Suns also threw off the rule of Set and regained their ancient freedom, and to this day they war against the Hyades and Him who rules there.
>
> But the Old Ones, rallying, drove forth the Primal Gods from Ka-Alantog, capturing thereby their mightiest libraries full of great and mighty secrets beyond the comprehension of men. And therein they plotted to expand their wars, together with their wicked allies from the Six Suns who had remained loyal to them.

But on Earth remained some of these wicked allies, who were sealed by the Old Ones in secret vaults to slumber until such time as Set and his minions should need them once more; and these are the Earth Folk, whom the olden Canaanites called *Am-ha-arez*.

Now when Karakossa perished, Ahmose raised up a rebellion and made himself Pharaoh of Khem, driving forth the sons of Apop. And those who fled were called Hyksos, or Shepherd Kings, because they worshipped Great Set, God of the Shepherds, and his consort Shupnikkurat, and even Him who dwells beyond Demhe—the features of those begotten by Them on mankind somewhat resembling the features of sheep, goats and asses. And the Hyksos founded the city that is now called Yeru-salem, and at its southern end they raised the Tower of Set, and at its western end the fane of Golgoroth. Yearly did they carry the Chalice of Byakh in grand procession from the Tower of Set to the fane of Golgoroth, and before the altar of the Old One their kings did drink therefrom, and then blow upon the *Byakhtril* that the Byakhim might come as of old to bear the screaming victims aloft to Great Set amid the Hyades; yet never did Yeru-salem attain the greatness of Karakossa.

Then came Yoshua leading the Habiru in conquest, and they took and burned Jericho and Ai and many other cities. And the Shepherd Kings grew afraid lest their city should fall also, and they hid the Chalice and the Byakhtril in crypts widely separated, so that should one of them be found, the Byakhim could not be summoned for lack of the other. Now the Chalice was hid beneath the olden shrine of Hali, which is near Achzib, and the Byakhtril beneath another shrine called *Beth-ananiah* (which is to say, "House of Pain", inasmuch as the Pain Lords were worshipped there), and it is near the road that goes from Yeru-salem down to Jericho.

So much have I, Mattan, learned from the writings of Hali, prophet of the Shepherd Kings, who took his name from the Shrine, which in turn took its name from that Lake beyond the skies wherein Great Set dwells.

Menander gasped and lifted the metal band from his head; his brain was swimming from the many fragmentary visions his reading had evoked from the wizard's mind.

"Is there more?" asked Taggart.

"No." Menander shook his head, blinked his eyes as if to clear them. "Dositheus' translation leaves off there."

The man took Menander's headband, then removed his own. "This place called 'House of Pain'—have you heard of it?"

"Beth-ananiah? No. . . . Wait! There is a town of similar name—Bethany —which I passed four years ago when I visited Jerusalem and Jericho in company with Dositheus. It is said to mean 'House of Ripe Dates', but perhaps its name was slightly changed long ago to hide its dark history—"

A buzzing sound suddenly came from the sky-craft. Taggart glanced eastward, then quickly climbed in and touched a glowing square; the buzzing stopped.

"I must go," said the wizard. "There will soon be too much light. Will you two meet me here again before dawn tomorrow?"

Menander and Ilione looked at one another, hesitating.

"Much depends on it," urged the man. "Read the first part of the scroll thoroughly—I'll no doubt have more to ask you after I've thought over what I've just learned. I think you have helped me greatly, but we can't stop now. Be here tomorrow at the same hour. Farewell."

"But—" Menander stepped forward. *"Wait!"*

The rising whine of the craft drowned his shout. Then the thing rose and shot away eastward with incredible speed, vanishing into the first gray light of dawn.

Slowly the young pair made their way down the hillside toward the distant village of Salim, saying nothing to one another, wondering. . .

CHAPTER X

The dark-robed man ceased his nervous pacing, strode to the stone-silled casement and peered out into the night. The moon had long ago vanished behind the westward hills. To the east, beyond an arid plain and distant rises, the light of approaching dawn was barely beginning to dim the stars; while northward, extending from just beneath the lofty window from which the man gazed, clustered the buildings of a large town, its lanes full of inky shadows.

"O Jericho, you are old, old," he muttered, stroking his full gray beard. "You have seen dark things, yet never in all your centuries have you seen the like of what is soon to occur—"

"O Caiaphas," said a voice within the room, "the one you summoned is here."

The graybeard turned and faced three men who had entered through the curtained doorway. Two were dark-cloaked guardsmen, and the man they escorted between them was tall and lean, clad in gray robes and a black skull cap. His hair and sparse beard were dark and scraggly, showing a tinge of russet in the torchlight, and his intensely gleaming black eyes seemed to project a strange mixture of sadness and fanaticism.

"Good. You may leave us."

The two guardsmen bowed low, then backed from the stone-walled room; their footfalls receded away down a tiled corridor. The graybeard hurried to the curtains, pulled shut the heavy wooden door; then, scowling, he turned and faced the newcomer.

"Those two are not possessed," the latter observed. "Their eyes do not glow in the torchlight. Can they be trusted not to creep back and listen to us?"

"They are loyal temple guards," said the graybeard. "Forget about them. You know much, Judah, but wise men keep their appointments more promptly than you. You are very late—it is nearly dawn."

"The tax gatherer, Zacchaeus, held a feast in honor of my master, and some guests did not leave or seek sleep until half an hour ago. We could have met sooner, Caiaphas, had we done so in the lane near Zacchaeus' house as I asked, rather than here in this Roman fortress."

Caiaphas shook his head. "This is best. I must not risk being seen, for many would wonder why the High Priest of the Temple is here secretly in the night. Your master is stirring up enough trouble already, Judah, with his speeches to the crowds about the coming fulfillment of the Law. No, better than I remain here in the fortress until—"

He broke off. The newcomer smiled darkly.

"You mean, until those who carried you here secretly from Jerusalem may leave with you just as secretly under the cover of night."

"You know much, Judah of Kerioth. I trust that your master does not also know this."

The man called Judah stared for a moment into space, his dark eyes glittering almost mystically. "Sometimes I think he may know everything."

"But—does he suspect you are here, then?"

Judah looked again at Caiaphas. "I told him nothing, and he said nothing to me."

The high priest sighed with relief. "Good. You are still with us, then?"

"I am. Have I not proved my worth? Did not your temple guards find the long-lost Ark of the Covenant in its secret cave on Mount Nebo, just where I told you they would?"

"They did, and it is here in this fortress even now. You have proven to be a most useful scholar of hidden lore, Judah. But now, concerning you request for this meeting—"

"Aye. To obtain the secret of the Ark I have had to spend all the money you advanced. If I am to continue to be useful to you, I will need more."

Caiaphas scowled. "How much?"

"At least thirty more days' wages of silver."

The priest nodded, turned to a table and wrote briefly upon a small scrap of parchment, then handed it to the man. "Here—present this to any temple scribe. Now, return to your master before you are missed."

"Just one more thing, O Priest. There is a man who may seek to prevent that which you and Annas are working to accomplish."

Caiaphas looked up sharply. "Who is this man?"

"A wizard of power. My master calls him 'The Adversary'. Be wary, for he may come at any time, as swiftly as lightning from heaven. He wears black garments of a strange cut and flies in a strange black craft."

"He *flies?*"

Judah said nothing more.

The high priest nodded. "Very well. I shall take more than the basic precautions. But you must go now, for I must leave for Jerusalem before dawn."

"In disguise, no doubt—and in the same covered litter in which you had the Romans and your temple guards bring you down from Jerusalem last night?"

"Forego these speculations, Judah, and repeat them to no one. Such would be dangerous for you. Serve me as you have and I will continue to pay you well."

"I think that I shall soon be in Jerusalem to collect your payment."

"Good. You are a clever man, Judah and a wise one. Continue to aid our cause and you will be rewarded with a high place in the New Kingdom. Now, go."

Judah let himself out of the room. Glancing back, he saw Caiaphas already turning to don his traveling cloak.

The two guardsmen escorted Judah down narrow stone stairways and let him out into a large courtyard, closing the iron grille behind him.

As he crossed the court, dimly lit by torches and the first faint gray of the expanding dawn, he saw a group of Roman soldiers and temple guards enter by way of a large arch in the fort's outer wall. Several of the latter carried something that resembled a palanquin, but it was covered with a single black drape, and the way the men strained at the gilded carrying-poles shown that the object was quite heavy.

Judah drew back into the shadows, staring at the thing, his dark eyes glittering with awe. He heard the centurion in charge bark an order to his men; the grille rose again, and several of the soldiers filed into the fortress. In a few minutes they returned bearing a heavily curtained litter.

"So, Caiaphas, you depart even now, and the Ark with you," muttered Judah. "You will not risk being seen here in the light of day. O El Shaddai! —that I should live to see the High Priest of thine own temple carried about this land even upon the shoulders of our hated enemies! But even as thou didst once smite Philistia, O Lord, soon shalt thou smite Rome—aye, and all such traitors as Caiaphas who aid her!"

Turning, he stole through a gate that led from the court into the town, then for a time threaded his way carefully along many narrow and unlit streets. As he approached the large house of Zacchaeus, surrounded by palms and gardens, he was surprised to see the tall, white-robed form of his master standing just outside the closed gate in the dawn's gray dimness.

"I have done as you wished, O Master," said Judah as he drew near.

"Did I tell you to do aught?"

As always, Judah was moved by the vibrant timbre of the voice, the sad but calm eyes, the lamb-like features that so poignantly suggested deep—compassion . . .?

"No, Master, There was no need. Caiaphas, having acted upon my earlier disclosures, has obtained the Ark. Now he shall cause it to be brought again into the temple, even as you wished and foretold."

"Caiaphas and Annas are traitors to the Covenant." The man raised his sad, sheeplike eyes toward the westward hills. "They would take power for themselves rather than obey my Father, and thereby they break His First Mandate. But it shall not be, for soon the Cherubim shall again spread their wings in my Father's house, and then shall His Kingdom come and all pain and suffering shall perish from this world."

And Judah, bowing low before his master, once more felt his soul exult with faith and a grand hope.

The three of them departed from Sebaste as soon as its eastern gate opened in the gray light of pre-dawn, Simon and Elissa wearing ordinary Samaritan garb and Lotis accompanying them as their slave. Though they left amid a crowd of others who had awaited the gate's opening, and though Elissa was veiled as well as commonly garbed, Simon was still uneasy as they passed between the flanking towers under the eyes of Roman guards. The mule in Lotis' charge looked common enough, but the black horses led by Elissa and Simon were beauties, perhaps a bit too conspicuous. . . .

"By Bacchus," a guard suddenly cried out in Syrian Greek, pointing, "—only a Samaritan or a Jew would use such fine beasts as pack animals!"

The other soldiers laughed. Simon felt their eyes upon him as he and his companions made their way down the road, but none made to pursue them, and in less than an hour the very walls and towers of the city had dwindled into the west.

All morning they continued eastward at an easy pace, pausing only once for a brief rest. To their left rose the slopes of Ebal, shadowy under high clouds, and to the right those of Mount Gerizim, holiest place in Samaria—or so, Simon reflected, he had been told often as a child. Upon Ebal had stood the pillar containing the curses of Yahweh Zava'ot, on Gerizim the one containing His blessings, both erected to comply with the Eleventh Commandment which He had given to Moses—or so the ancient writings said.

Now, Simon gazed upon these slopes with far less awe than he had felt in childhood. Many times during the agony of his captivity by the Romans he had desperately prayed to the God of Gerizim, had vowed a pilgrimage of sacrifice to its summit if ever he were released—but when after two years he was finally rescued by his mentor Dositheus, it was too late. By then he had seen too much horror and death; he could no longer believe in the blessings of Gerizim, only in the curse that brooded upon Ebal.

Since then, the things Simon had learned in his wanderings had confirmed in him the feeling that no gods could be relied upon. His mentors and his own experiences had taught him that supernatural forces were best avoided; failing that, one should know the art of controlling or escaping them. One should above all not seek their aid, for they were treacherous.

The three spoke little during the journey, for they were weary, having been unable to sleep for excitement since Elissa's rescue. During the remainder of the night Lotis and her mistress had traded experiences in detail, often pausing in their conversation to embrace one another in the sheer joy of having been reunited alive and unharmed. Simon had added less to the conversation, had descended frequently to inspect the stables or watchfully prowl the nearby alleys. Well before dawn the three of them had packed their belongings and left the inn.

It was late in the morning when they passed through the city of Shechem. Elissa noticed that Simon, though still silent, seemed no longer withdrawn into himself; his eyes held a hard glitter as he glanced about him amid the crowds of merchants, beggars and buyers, as if searching the crowds for a familiar face.

At length, as they approached a less crowded and more affluent neighborhood beyond the city's center, Simon remarked, "I have heard that Jahath, chief tax gatherer of Samaria, lives near this place."

"Aye." Lotis pointed to a house on a slope not far from the road, a large mansion surrounded by a wall overtopped by trees within. "It is there—"

She ceased speaking as her mistress shot her a sharp, worried look. Simon lapsed back into silence, his face hard, his eyes once more brooding and introspective.

About noon they arrived at the town of Sychar, a suburb of Shechem, where Elissa owned a house—left to her, she explained, by her second husband. Simon saw, as they approached the residence, that it was large as that of his parents, though built in an Eastern style rather than the Hellenistic or Roman. As they entered through the archway into a small garden, a grizzled and bent slave limped hurriedly from the house and came toward them brandishing a wooden staff.

"What do you want, strangers?" he demanded. "This is not a public thoroughfare—"

Elissa laughed, then whipped off her veil. "What, Gelon, don't you recognize your mistress? And if you'd repair that gate, you wouldn't have strangers wandering in!"

The oldster paused, wide-eyed. "My Lady, the street children broke it down, stole most of the vegetables . . ., but why did you not send word of your coming? Why are you dressed so? What has happened—?"

"I'll answer your questions soon," said Elissa, smiling at Gelon's bewilderment, "but first we must eat. Rouse the servants and have them prepare a meal. Then return here and attend our friend Simon of Gitta."

The grizzled majordomo ushered the three inside, then hastened away. Elissa said, "Wait here, Simon. Gelon will see to all your needs." So saying, she and Lotis ascended a stair to the upper chambers.

In a few moments the old man returned and ushered Simon into a small room where servants were depositing large earthenware jars of water beside a wide basin, and when they had all left him he enjoyed the luxury of doffing his trail-worn garments and bathing—a luxury he had not had since leaving Ecdippa. Finally a servant returned with a clean plain tunic and sandals and, when Simon had donned these, the majordomo reappeared and beckoned. Simon followed him out of the room and up the stairs, noting the questioning scowl in the old man's eyes.

They emerged upon a flat roof surrounded by a low parapet. Gelon motioned Simon to sit upon a couch before a low table which servants were loading with a variety of fruits, fish and wine. In a few moments Elissa, followed by Lotis, appeared on the roof also and joined him. The woman now looked as beautiful as when Simon had first seen her; her dark hair, confined now only by a golden band about her brow, spilled freely over her smooth olive shoulders and the pale yellow fabric of her Grecian-style gown.

Simon rose involuntarily. "My Lady, you are very beautiful."

She smiled, waved him back to his seat, sat down herself and began to eat. Simon followed suit, found that he was very hungry and attacked the food with gusto. He noticed that Elissa waved Lotis to the table also and that the slave girl, after a momentary hesitation at the unaccustomed favor, joined them and ate heartily.

Though very hungry, Simon sensed that Elissa wished to speak with him, and when his appetite was somewhat assuaged he looked up and found her dark eyes fixed on him. She had touched little of the food.

Feeling a bit like a glutton, Simon wiped his mouth with a napkin and asked, "What is it Elissa? Tell me."

She poured herself a goblet of wine, but did not touch it. "Lotis has told me that you are a great wizard, and now I see that you have some aptitude for reading minds. Perhaps you can explain a thing that happened to me about four months ago."

Simon noticed Lotis' sudden attentiveness. He arched his brows and sipped from his wine cup. "Does this have to do with Maxentius?"

"I would not bring it up otherwise, knowing that that Roman is your main concern."

Simon thought he detected a note of reproach in the woman's tone, but chose to ignore it. "Tell me."

"I met a man who claimed that he was the *Mashiah.*"

Simon, about to sip his wine again, saw the seriousness in the woman's eyes and set down his cup. He resisted an impulse to laugh.

"But, Elissa, many have claimed to be the Mashiah—the promised rescuer of our land. I remember several from my childhood—"

"This man was different." The woman's eyes sparked with a trace of irritation. "Don't imagine that I'm crazy, Simon. Lotis was with me when I met him, and many others in this town will vouch for the fact that he was—well, unusual."

Simon glanced at Lotis, but she lowered her eyes and seemed totally absorbed in her meal. "Go on, Elissa," he said.

"I had come to this house for a few days while Maxentius was in Jerusalem. There was little water, so I instructed Lotis and Gelon to go to the Pool of the Patriarch and fill several pitchers; I accompanied them, as it is a beautiful place where the water spills down into a rock basin surrounded by greenery, and I have loved it since childhood.

"While my servants were drawing water, a tall man approached and asked me for a drink. By his robes I knew him for a Judean, and I wondered at his temerity."

Simon nodded with understanding. Samaritans and Judeans had long vied strenuously as to which despised the other the most, and this in spite of their shared dislike of the Romans and their similar religious beliefs.

"Yet I took no offense," Elissa went on, "for there was something about this man—something strange and serious—that told me that he was not as others. I only asked him, 'Why do you, a Judean, ask a drink of me, a Samaritan woman?' The man replied, 'Had you knowledge of the Aeon of Tsotho, and who it is that asks a drink of you, you would have asked him instead, and he would have given you the Living Water.' I asked him, rather sarcastically I'm afraid, what he meant by 'Living Water' and where he got it, and he replied, 'Drink it and you will never again thirst, but shall become as a spring welling up to eternal life.' Again I asked him to produce this 'Water'—you see, Simon, it was thus far a game to me, bantering with this foreign man whom for some reason I found fascinating—when suddenly he changed his tactics and said, 'Go, call your husband, and return here with him.' I felt indignant, and answered, 'I have no husband.' To my surprise, the man said, 'I know, for you have had five husbands and the man you now live with is not your husband at all.' I was shocked, for the Judean had truly read my mind."

Simon raised his eyebrow skeptically. "Didn't it cross your mind that the man might have had Maxentius spied upon?"

"Not for a moment. Simon, I could *feel* that man's mind probing into mine. Moreover, I noticed at the same time a disc of faintly glowing metal upon his brow, barely visible beneath his dark locks, and somehow knew that it was the source of his power. In that moment I felt that he must be a prophet and told him so, yet reminded him that my people worshipped on Gerizim rather than in Jerusalem. He replied, 'Woman, believe me, the hour comes when neither upon this mountain nor in Jerusalem shall the Father be worshipped.' He said much else, but I paid little attention, for I was shocked. When he had finished, I said, 'Only the Mashiah who is to come can manifest such things.' Then the man said, 'I who speak to you am he.'"

"And you believed him?" asked Simon.

Elissa nodded. "At the time I did—and, maybe I *still* do. You weren't there, Simon, and you didn't see his eyes, nor sense the power of the disc on his brow. Nor did you feel the *compassion* in his tone, his gaze. . . ."

Simon turned to Lotis. "Is this true?"

"Yes, Simon. I, too, saw the glowing disc, and I sensed the power of the man's eyes, even though they were not turned upon me."

Simon nodded. "Go on, Elissa. What did the man do next?"

"Nothing, for at that point his disciples—a dozen or so rough-looking Galilean louts—returned from Shechem where they had been purchasing supplies. They also said nothing, yet I could see that they despised me as a Samaritan woman, so I left Gelon and his mule to bring back the water and departed with Lotis to this house.

"The man stayed in this town for two days, hinting to the people that he was the Mashiah. Many believed him—partly, I know, because of my testimony that he had read my mind. During this time I learned that he was called the Master Yeshua bar Yosef. He preached much, but would not take any food offered to him, saying 'I have food to eat of which you know not.' I also learned that he told many others of their most secret thoughts. Finally he departed for Galilee and I was disappointed, for I had sensed great wisdom in him and had even hoped that his claim of being the Mashiah might be true."

"What has all this to do with Maxentius?" asked Simon

"Maxentius, when I returned to Sebaste and told him of it, was at first very angry and suspicious. He felt that this Yeshua bar Yosef might be a Zealot who had come to spy him out—"

"Yeshua—'savior'," muttered Simon. "Of course. What other name would one claiming to be the Mashiah use?"

"—but when I finally convinced Maxentius that the man had truly read my thoughts, he became morose and would speak no more on the subject. Three or four days later old Annas made the first of his secret visits to the house. Does all this shed any light on your quest, Simon?"

"I don't know." Simon shook his head wearily. "Another strand in this tangled skein. . . ." He finished his meal in silence, then rose. "I cannot think on it now, Elissa; I must rest—I haven't slept since yesterday morning. Perhaps when I rise things will seem clearer."

"Aye." Elissa nodded. "We all need rest, Simon."

She instructed Gelon, who had been hovering in the background near the stair, to take Simon to his sleeping chamber, then departed with Lotis to her own rooms.

When the servant had left Simon alone, the Samaritan lay down upon the narrow bed, closed his eyes and breathed evenly. Slowly his breathing grew more shallow as he passed into a dreamless trance-state of deep rest by means of a technique taught him by his Persian mentor Daramos the Mage.

His last thought was the willed message to this body that he should waken just as the sun touched the slopes of Gerizim to the west, and his last vision was the ratlike face of Jahath, tax-gatherer of Samaria—Jahath, who had led the Romans to his parents' house eight years ago. . . .

Old Gelon wheezed as he deposited a heavy sack of feed on the stable floor, then bracketed his torch on one of the mud-brick walls. Turning, he saw that the two black horses were standing quietly in their stalls looking at him.

"A fine pair of beasts you are indeed," he muttered, breathing a bit heavily. "I wonder who my mistress bought you from?"

The torchlight reflected from the horses' eyes—more brightly than it should, Gelon thought uneasily. A horse's eyes should not glow like those of a lynx. . . . Shaking off the feeling with a snort and a shrug, he advanced and opened one of the stalls, then turned and stooped to the feed sack. "Time for your feeding, my dark beauties—"

The horse stepped forward, reared slightly and lashed out with one forefoot. The hoof caught Gelon squarely in the back of the neck; there was a sharp cracking of vertebrae. The old man hurtled forward over the feed sack, smacked his head first into the wall, then flopped to the straw-littered floor and lay still.

The horse tossed its black mane, then turned to the other stall and lifted the latch with its teeth. A moment later both beasts walked out into the sunlit yard, stood and looked about them, then at one another. Presently one of them pointed its head toward the south, extended one hoof slightly and scratched in the dirt the letters.

M A X

The other horse nodded, in turn extended its own forefoot and wrote:

J A T H

Immediately the first horse wheeled, galloped toward the broken gate and through the archway into the street, then raced away southward on the road to Jerusalem, scattering startled wayfarers.

The second beast, following closely, whirled to the right and galloped along the road to the northwest, back toward Shechem. The surprised foot travelers drew back to right and left as the animal hurtled past them; many made signs in the air or muttered protective prayers before continuing uneasily on their way.

In less than half an hour the black horse came to a halt before a large house—a mansion surrounded by a wall overtopped by the foliage of trees within. It walked to a wooden gate in the wall, raised a hoof and knocked heavily several times. Presently the gate opened and a dark-bearded man in a servant's tunic peered out, scowling.

"What do you want . . .? Ah!" The servant's eyes lit up. "What a magnificent beast you are. Wait here, nice horse, until I get a rope from the stable—"

The horse whickered, pointed its nose at the ground and quickly scratched a perfectly symmetrical "V" in the dust with the edge of his hoof.

The servant's dark face suddenly paled. "Baal and Anath!" he gasped. "The sign! But, surely, *you* couldn't be—"

The animal shouldered its way through the gate and into the shady garden, shoving the servant aside as it did so. Again it scratched a "V" in the ground. The servant, eyes and mouth agape, quickly shut and barred the gate, then turned and raced into the mansion. In a few moments he returned to the garden, followed by a short, stubble-faced man wearing a food-stained kaftan and a sloppily-arranged striped turban.

"What do you mean, a messenger?" barked the short man in a petulant whine. "I see only a horse."

"Yet it is true, Mater Jahath. Look—there in front of the beast in the dirt!"

The man looked down at the "V" in the ground. As he did so, the horse tapped its hoof beside the symbol.

"You see, Master?"

Jahath looked closer, wrinkling his great curved nose. That and his beady dark eyes gave him an uncanny resemblance to a rat. The breath hissed in through his clenched teeth, which were displayed behind fat lips in a fixed, mirthless grin; his jaw muscles worked beneath the sparse hairs of his coarse, graying stubble.

"By Ashima, it is so!" he gasped. "I had hoped that we would hear from *them* no more." Then, looking up at the black horse, "Has Maxentius need of me, then?"

The horse nodded, pointed its nose at Jahath, then turned and extended its head toward the south.

"I don't understand. You want me to go in that direction? Why?"

The animal shook its head, snorted as if in impatience, then scratched a word in the dirt. Jahath bent forward and read:

O W L

The man's rat-face paled. He turned to his servant and hissed, "Go to the upper window facing the grove and blow the goat-horn thrice."

"But, Master, it is still daylight—"

"It matters not. The sleeping owl will hear and come."

When the servant had left, Jahath turned again to the horse. Somehow his fixed grin now expressed a touch of fear, even as it had formerly expressed anger.

"The owl will soon be here; then we can talk," he said. "But tell me now—yes or no—if there is danger."

The beast nodded its head.

"For—me . . .?"

The black mane tossed in a more vigorous nod.

"From *what?*" shrieked Jahath, forgetting himself. "Tell me at once, mad beast!"

The horse scratched in the dirt and wrote the word:

SIMON

With a gasp the tax gatherer sank to his knees, his face whiter than ever, his eyes rolling wide in terror. "Surely not . . . Bar Antonius? It is said that last year he escaped from the Roman arena —"

The black-maned head nodded, inexorably as doom.

Then from a high window of the house came three shrill blasts from a goat-horn, ringing, echoing. . . .

Caiaphas climbed from his litter and wearily stretched his limbs. A breeze sighed among the scattered trees along the low ridge. It had been a long day's journey.

The high priest turned to his motionless bearers and told them, "Leave me, now. Return to the city. Come here for me again the second hour after tomorrow's dawn."

The soldiers set down the litter and moved off down the path that dipped westward into the Kidron Valley. Caiaphas watched them go. Beyond the Kidron the slopes rose to the mighty walls and terraces of the Great Temple, beyond which in turn sprawled the city of Jerusalem, its walls and towers blue-shadowed under the westering sun. The sky above it was slightly grayed by a smoke-haze from the many late-afternoon cooking fires just being kindled.

"Like a shroud," muttered the priest, his eyes troubled. "Does it indeed foreshadow your doom, O Jerusalem?"

He turned and walked from among the trees, passed through an open arch in a high wall, between the two silent, black-cloaked soldiers who guarded it. Inside, a path led through a small courtyard to the portico of a house—the largest and most luxurious on this entire Mount of Olives, as

Caiaphas well knew. Old Annas had planned cleverly in purchasing this place, for it was not only secluded and easily guarded, but also very close to the necessary location. . . .

The priest suddenly stopped, started. That tall figure standing amid the columns of the portico was not Annas. It was a Roman officer, plumed helmet held under his left arm, right hand hooked in his sword belt; behind him, dimly seen in the shadows, were half a dozen spear-bearing legionaries. Then the officer strode forward and Caiaphas saw that it was Centurion Scribonius, commander of the Siloam Tower. At sight of the man Caiaphas felt his usual dislike and uneasiness; there was a cocky arrogance in Scribonius' walk, a hint of dark cruelty behind his narrow eyes and lopsided smile.

"Greetings, High Priest," said the officer as he drew near.

Caiaphas scowled. "What are you doing here? You belong at your post in the Tower of Set—"

The Roman barked a laugh. "Easy, priest. I thought you were the one who told me never to use that name in conversation."

"The Tower of Siloam, then." Caiaphas realized that his weariness had caused him to make a mistake, but he drew himself up with dignity. "Your soldiers are too far away to hear. Answer my question.

"Annas sent me a packet by a—winged messenger," said Scribonius, some of his cockiness gone. "He and Maxentius are returning from the north, but they may be delayed. I was ordered to await your return here, and to give you this."

He handed Caiaphas a small sealed packet of parchment. The priest fingered it, but made no move to open it. "Good, Centurion. You may go now."

Scribonius nodded casually, motioned to his men, then strode past Caiaphas and out the archway; the soldiers followed after him briskly.

When they had gone, Caiaphas walked out through the arch and stood quietly, watching the legionaries recede down the path until they had vanished beneath the western slope of the ridge. The sun was nearing the horizon; the shadows cast by the city and the temple silhouetted on the opposite rise were longer, filling the Kidron Valley with deepening gloom. Southward along that rise extended the city's wall, a line of sinister blue shadow broken by occasional square, crenelated towers. Caiaphas' gaze fastened and lingered upon the southernmost tower, which was slightly taller and sturdier that the others.

"The Tower of Set," he muttered. "Roman, yet built on foundations older than Rome, older than Judea. O Jerusalem, what secrets your old stones hide!"

A cool wind sprang up. Caiaphas shivered slightly. He returned to the courtyard, then broke the seal of the packet. The inner surface of the parchment bore writing; it was a letter to him, and he began to read its Aramaic characters in the waning light.

> Izhar, with the aid of that which inhabits him, has managed to recall, word for word, those portions of Mattan's *El-Halal* which most concern us. He now journeys to Jerusalem via Jericho in hopes of locating that which lies buried east of Bethany, but we cannot wait for him; you must act swiftly, for the rabbi Yeshua is in Jericho already, as you know, and may come up to Bethany at any time.
>
> Izhar has sent me these parchments by winged messenger, and in like manner I send them on to you. Study them immediately and learn of the hiding place of that which is called the *Byakhtril.* It is not far east of Bethany. When you have done this, send Scribonius and some of his soldiers under cover of darkness to obtain it. Instruct them to disguise themselves well. When you have the Byakhtril in hand, go to the Tower of Set and hide it with that which is already there. I am proceeding with all haste to Jerusalem and will come to the Tower during the second night following this. Await me there.

The note was unsigned and undated. Caiaphas sighed wearily, fingered the tightly folded packet of parchment, then slowly ascended the steps of the portico. Tomorrow he must attend to many Temple duties, including plausibly explaining to many of his fellow priests his day-long absence. He needed rest, yet he knew there would be little of that for him this night. . .

CHAPTER XI

Simon awoke exactly at sundown. His sleep had been dreamless, save for a moment toward the last when he seemed to see the greenish-gray features of his former mentors Daramos—the pointed ears and wide, lipless mouth; the flattened nose; the sad, slanted eyes that yet had crinkles of laughter and wisdom about their corners. The mouth opened, as if about to speak. . . .

Simon started awake, sitting upright. "Daramos—?"

Then he rose, smiling at his folly. Almost he had expected a message from his dream image, felt a slight disappointment that there had been none forthcoming.

He washed his hands and face, then donned a plain brown Samaritan robe. Stepping through the curtained doorway in the hall, he found a single torch burning and carried it into his room, bracketing it in a sconce beside the door. The sky beyond his open casement was still bright, but the sun was behind the slope of Gerizim and did little to illuminate his chamber.

By the torchlight Simon extracted several items from his pack. Peering into a smooth bronze mirror, he began to apply a false dark beard to his face. During his late teens, while a captive of Rome he had acquired the habit of shaving his face, and in subsequent years he had kept the habit; it gave him more options for disguise, from aged graybeard to smooth-faced Roman, as the situation required.

He had finished applying the beard and was donning a typical Samaritan head cloth when he heard footsteps in the corridor. A moment later outside the curtained doorway he heard the rich, womanly voice of Elissa softly call his name.

"Come in."

She entered—then drew back, startled. "Simon—is that you?"

"Yes." He grinned at her. "I thank you."

"For—for what?"

"Your compliment to my skill."

She laughed, then came close to him. "I know you now, Simon. And there is humor in your eyes. I knew there was humor in you—and other feelings."

Simon felt her nearness. "Other . . .?"

"Feelings other than hate. Desires other than for vengeance."

His eyes grew hard at her words. Instantly her own eyes grew sad, contrite. "Oh, Simon, I'm sorry. You have felt the hate for too long—you should feel other things, happier things. I should not have reminded you."

Simon took her hand in his own, removed it from his breast—but her touch had awakened in him feelings that he had half forgotten. She was beautiful—one of the most beautiful women he had ever encountered. His left hand was on her shoulder—the feel of her smooth skin beneath the sheer fabric of her gown was a delight, a demand. . . .

"Simon—"

They were in one another's arms; her body was a warm fire against him, writhing, passionate. The fire became a burning flame as their lips met, held, melded. Elissa moaned, gasped, drew back her head.

"Simon, oh Simon! I'm so lonely, too—like you. . . ."

Again her words caused him to remember. Something within his breast tightened, hardened. Gently he pushed her back, his hands still holding her softly by her shoulders.

"Simon?" Her dark eyes held a sadness.

"I—I cannot. Not now."

A sob caught in her throat. She turned away. "It's Jahath, isn't it?"

He nodded. "I must go away for awhile. But it won't be for long. I will come back to you—later."

The woman faced him; her eyes, though damp, confronted his gaze levelly. "You don't have to. I know what you must feel toward me—a woman who shared your parents' house with the Roman who slew them."

"You are not wicked, Elissa. You are beautiful. Whatever Maxentius did to blind you to his true nature, I know that it was not your fault."

"Simon, I want to help you."

He sensed that she meant it. "You shall. Wait for me here. I will return before dawn." He kissed her again—not passionately, but gently, affectionately. Then he turned and, with a backward glance, glided through the door and was gone with scarcely a sound of sandals on the tiles.

Elissa stood there for awhile, motionless. *Simon, strange magician—you come like a ghost into my life, into my heart. . . .*

And Simon, hurrying away from her mansion into the dusk, wondered at the strange fate that had suddenly made this woman—the subject of so much glamorous and tantalizing rumor in this region when he was but a growing and curious youth—a part of his life.

Elissa, I'll come back to you. . . .

Then, hurrying down the dark road, he deliberately closed his thoughts to her and cast them ahead—to vengeance.

Dositheus swayed wearily astride the ass he rode, clinging to its mane. Ahead, he saw the lights of a town gleaming as torches were kindled in the dusk.

"Gods, old man!" exclaimed the youth who led the beast. "Must we continue until my legs are worn to nubbins? Surely you will allow us to rest in . . . what is that town ahead?"

"Doubtless that is Shiloh," said the old Samaritan wizard. "I had hoped to make it to the outskirts of Aphairema this evening, but if your weariness is too great—"

"My weariness? Old man, you'll kill yourself if you push it any more!"

Dositheus reined his animal to a halt, slid to the ground and stood tall, frowning sternly. "Take my place, then Eupatos," he said. "I will lead. But first, let us make a supper and allow your muscles to rest. There will be a good moon this evening."

The stout youth shook his head. "Very well—but I think you're crazy, old man."

While Eupatos gathered wood, Dositheus deftly kindled a fire with flint and steel, feeling a secret pride. He knew the stout young man was impressed. Not many men over seventy could have alternately walked and ridden over hill and vale for half a night and a day without showing fatigue. But, then, not many men had been trained by Daramos, master of mages. . . .

And yet, he was also slightly disappointed. Though he had come far, and was now several miles south of the town of Sychar in the hills near the boundary of Judea and Samaria, he was still many miles short of his goal. And somehow, he knew not why, he sensed that it was important that he continue southward as rapidly as possible.

But the fire they kindled behind sheltering rocks was warm, the broth they cooked over it was filling and good, and soon Dositheus felt his muscles relaxing. His bones were old and stiff. It was good to sit here, reclining against a smooth boulder, feeling drowsy. The sturdy Eupatos had already eaten his fill and was sound asleep, snoring. No doubt they should spend the night here; the boulders would shield them from sight of any passing bandits, once the fire was quenched, while the sky was clear and starry, promising no rain.

Suddenly there was a sound to the north—the sound of distant hoofbeats.

Dositheus rose stiffly, smothered the fire with sand, then peered out between boulders toward the roadway. The waxing gibbous moon shone high over the distant eastward hills. The hoofbeats grew louder.

Then Dositheus gasped as a great black horse rounded the bend to the north and came into full view, galloping southward, its eyes gleaming in the moonlight like those of a lynx.

In a moment it had vanished southward around another bend, dust hanging dimly above the roadway where it had passed.

For a moment Dositheus crouched silent, shaken. Then, after the sound of the horse's hoofbeats had faded away into silence, he hurried over to the snoring youth and prodded him with his toe.

"Eupatos!" he hissed. "Wake up, lout! We must hurry on to Shiloh and get the walls of a stout inn about us. There are demons abroad this night!"

Simon hurried quietly through the dark streets of Shechem, meeting few wayfarers, for most townspeople were indoors by nightfall. The lanes were pitch black despite the fact that the waxing moon was already high.

He hid in the shadows and waited while at least a score of cloaked men hurried by, led by a man on a black horse. In their midst they carried a curtained litter. The clank of metal and the glint of moonlight on steel indicated that they were armored and armed. When they had gone by, Simon hurried on, giving them little thought. Obviously they were not a city patrol, for they carried no lit torches. Possibly some nobleman with his armed guard on a clandestine visit to some other noble's wife. . . .

Within an hour of leaving Sychar he was at the house of Jahath, listening quietly at the gate in the high wall. There was no sound within, but there would surely be a guard. A tax gatherer had many enemies. Slowly Simon walked for a distance alongside the wall, nearly to its corner, then leaped lightly and gripped the top. It was but the work of a moment for his trained muscles to pull him up. He lay prone for a moment, listening; then, silent as a serpent, he let himself down into the garden by means of a nearby tree trunk and glided forward in the wall's shadow.

As he neared the gate he heard a slight stirring and in the same moment smelled strong wine. Someone burped; the sound was followed by a sloshing noise. Crouching, Simon could dimly make out the form of the guard, only a few feet away, raising a wine skin to his lips. The fellow was obviously half drunk, judging from the way he sat slumped against the wall. Simon grinned. Jahath's wages were ill spent this night—fatally ill spent.

Not a leaf rustled as Simon crept around the guard through the foliage and advanced toward the mansion. No light showed from within, which was strange at this hour. Softly he stole into the portico and gingerly tried the door. It was unlocked. This was almost too easy.

Could it be a trap?

Simon pushed open the door, but did not enter. He stood to one side and waited a moment. Inside was silence and darkness. No, not complete darkness, for now he could see, far within the house, the dim glow of a hidden light source.

Drawing his sharp-bladed sica, he crouched and slid inside, then closed the door noiselessly behind him. A long moment of motionless silence convinced him that the antechamber was empty. Slowly he crept toward the light, keeping his weight centered, feeling before him with fingers and toes before taking each step.

The house seemed deserted. If *felt* deserted.

After crossing a wide room, probably an atrium, Simon entered a kitchen area where he found the light source—a single small oil lamp burning within a wall niche. On a table beneath it were several other such lamps. Selecting one, he lit it and stole away from the kitchen to explore further.

After nearly an hour of slow and cautious prowling he had searched the entire house, upstairs and down. As he had thought, it was empty. That was strange. Jahath, with all his wealth, would surely keep more servants than a single guard at the gate. Where were they?

No matter. Jahath would return later in the night, perhaps from a carousal and full of drink. And when he did, there would be death awaiting him in the shadows.

Simon crept back down to the kitchen, doused his oil lamp and put it back on the table, then withdrew to the shadows of the stairway. Now he would wait.

Another hour or more passed while he sat in silence at the top of the stair, where Jahath would have to pass on the way to his bedchamber. Then, suddenly, he heard a sound from the garden outside. A man's voice. Then came the clatter of the wooden bolt in the gate outside, followed by the voices of two men in conversation. The gate closed; footsteps came up the gravel of the front walkway. Slowly Simon stood up, listening, scarcely breathing.

The front door crashed open, then slammed closed; heavy footfalls sounded, followed by coarse laughter.

"See that light, Phaidros?" growled one of the men. "Bring the wench in there. Follow me."

Simon heard more bumbling footsteps, the sounds of furniture being bumped into, curses and harsh laughter. He peered down the stairs and saw two men emerge from the shadows into the dim glow from the kitchen entryway. The first was a burly, florid-faced man of about forty who wore a sword, a brown cloak and a breastplate; he staggered slightly, clutching a half-empty wineskin in his left hand. The other was young, blondish and clean-shaven like a Roman, his form beneath his brief yellow linen tunic lean and muscular; in his belt was thrust a long, sheathed dagger, and he dragged a large and heavy sack along the floor behind him.

The two vanished into the kitchen. Slowly Simon crept down the stairs.

"Hurry up," he heard the older man growl. "Let's have a look at her."

"Take it easy, Kyros, just let me untie this sack—ah, there! Now I ask you, old man, is she a beauty or not?"

"By Bacchus, you've outdone yourself this time, lad! But—I've seen her before. She lives on this very street, probably no more than three or four houses away. She'll make good sport, but we can't let her go free to tell tales afterwards. Jahath doesn't mind what I do here when he's gone, but he'd hate a scandal."

"Oh, gods, *no!*" cried a feminine voice. "Don't kill me! Please—I'll do anything—"

Simon crept down the stairs, slowly, soundlessly.

"You hear her?" growled Kyros. "She says she'll do anything."

"Damn right she will," said Phaidros. "And she'll do it over and over and over."

Laughter. Simon reached the foot of the stair, peered into the kitchen. Between the two men knelt a young girl, pale and trembling, dark-haired and dark eyes, upon the heavy fabric of the sack in which she had been carried here—a white flower amid coarse leaves. She was younger than Ilione or Lotis—fourteen at the most. . . .

The lean youth clenched his fist in her hair, yanked her upright. "Stand up, bitch. Let's see those legs of yours."

She cried out in pain, then stood trembling in her brief tunic, clutching herself with pale arms. "Please—don't kill me—"

"We have no choice, darling," said the youth, his face taut in a gleeful, sadistic grin. "But if you cooperate you'll live for a few more days, until Kyros' master returns from Jerusalem. And during those few days this body of mine will be yours, all yours, over and over again. You'll die happy, I assure you!"

Kyros guffawed, took a swig of his wine. Simon stepped forward and stood in the doorway.

"Excuse me," he said.

The older man spewed out his mouthful of wine explosively; the younger whirled and crouched, glaring balefully. Both drew their blades.

"I'm sorry," said Simon, grinning, "but I couldn't help overhearing. I understand that you've captured this young woman and mean to enjoy her while your master's away—in Jerusalem, did you say?"

"Who in Hades are you?" snarled Kyros, his gladius trembling in his tense grip.

"Relax, old man," drawled the youth, chuckling. "Can't you see that this fellow just wants in on the fun?"

"No, Phaidros, I've never seen him before. He doesn't belong here—"

"Oh, but I think I do, Kyros." Simon strode a pace into the room and stared more closely at the guardsman. "And I believe I remember you. You've been Jahath's servant for quite a few years, haven't you? I believe you were with him one night eight years ago when he led two Roman officers to a certain house in Sebaste."

"Damn you!" roared Kyros. "Who *are* you—?"

Simon's grin tightened mirthlessly. He ripped away the false beard and cast it on the floor. "I am Simon bar Antonius. Do you recognize me now, Kyros?"

"Die!" screamed the guardsman, charging with outthrust sword.

Simon sidestepped easily and brought the edge of his hand down in a lightning chop; vertebrae popped loudly and Kyros sprawled clattering through the doorway and lay twitching, neck broken.

Phaidros howled and leaped at Simon, thrusting with his dagger—then howled louder still as his foe slipped under the thrust and caught his wrist with a grip of iron. The youth's arm bent back and cracked loudly. He whirled, shrieking, left fist clenched—and the edge of Simon's right hand chopped down to crisply break the bridge of his nose; in the next instant his shrieks were cut short as the Samaritan's left palm smashed savagely upward, driving the broken nose bones back through Phaidros' face and into his brain.

For a moment Simon glared down at his slain foes, his face still rigid in a tight grin, then turned to the girl, who was now crouching away from him in a far corner of the kitchen, eyes wide in terror.

"They died more quickly than they deserved," he said. "Don't be afraid of me, girl. Here—" He took the dwindling lamp from its niche, lit a bracketed torch, lifted it from its sconce and handed it to her. "Go to your own house, now—hurry. If anyone else accosts you in the street, cry out, and I will come and slay them also."

The girl took the torch, then edged around him, fear still in her eyes. She ran from the kitchen, and a moment later Simon heard the front door open, then the gate. For several minutes more Simon stood listening, but heard nothing.

"Good," he muttered finally, setting down the lamp. Then, kneeling, he drew his sica once more and slid its keen edge across the dead Kyros' throat. Blood oozed slowly out and puddled upon the tiles.

"You shall not escape me in Jerusalem, Jahath," he muttered. "I will find you. But if my message reaches you first, so much the better. You deserve to know fear."

So saying, he dipped his finger in the blood, then wrote on the wall above the corpse:

THE SON OF THE FATHER HAS RETURNED

Then, rising, he stepped over the body of Kyros and strode forth into the night.

Caiaphas felt a tremor of excitement as he squinted more closely at the tiny, crabbed lettering on the parchment scraps. Yes, it was here—the thing he sought. Old Annas had been right! His heart beat faster and his lips moved unconsciously, inaudibly, as he read the archaic script:

> Now the Chalice was hid beneath the ruined olden shrine of Hali, which is near Achzib . . . and the Byakhtril beneath another shrine called Beth-ananiah, which means "House of Pain" . . . near the road that goes from Yeru-salem down to Jericho. . . .

Caiaphas leaned back in his padded cedar-wood chair, gazing at the shelves that held Annas' numerous scrolls. Beth-ananiah—that was no doubt Bethany, which many thought meant "House of Ripe Dates"—a village little more than one Roman mile from this very spot! Doubtless its current name had evolved to mask its sinister original one.

The high priest turned again to the documents, but was disappointed to find no more on the subject. Caiaphas sighed and leaned back again, rubbing his weary eyes. Those eyes, he knew, were not as good as they used to be, and the writing was very small, crabbed and in the ancient Canaanite alphabet. Moreover, the subject matter of the centuried Baal-priest Mattan was dark and disturbing, pertaining to dark gods who had once ruled the world and would return to rule again—from the sea, from vast cavern-worlds, from the black starry spaces beyond the earth. Annas had told him often of such things, but here in these actual fragments of Mattan's writings were even more frightening hints. Caiaphas was especially disturbed to learn of the original meaning of *Am-ha-arez*, and by the knowledge that the pre-Davidic Jebusites of Jerusalem were the heirs not only of the Hyksos but also of dark Stygia, and had brought the worship of that ancient sorcery-riddled land to the very site of Jerusalem and its environs. . . .

Quelling his unease, he turned again to the parchments. What he sought must be elsewhere in their closely-written lines, for so Izhar had told Annas—and Annas would be displeased if he, Caiaphas, did not find and act upon it.

Another hour passed. Caiaphas' eyes watered as he read on under the light of the oil lamps; his soul cringed at some of the things that were revealed to him. Neither the earth nor the humans that dwelt upon it were at all what he had always believed them to be, and there were things beyond this world that were monstrous, impossible to conceive. . . .

Suddenly he found it—the information Annas had mentioned. He gasped, then peered more closely at the crabbed script.

> Seven stadia east of Beth-ananiah, where the road to Jericho begins to descend sharply, stands the ruined shrine to the Primal Gods. Men think it but a common tomb in the cliffside, but within it yet lies the byakhtril, with whose aid the mages of ancient Karakossa once summoned the Byakhim from the skies.

Again Caiaphas leaned back, rubbing his eyes, feeling a strange mixture of relief and apprehension. He must sleep. And tomorrow night he must send a gang of disguised Romans and temple guards east of Bethany to find the thing called the Byakhtril.

He rose, walked to the back of the house and went out into the garden. The air had a chill in it. He opened the back gate and passed between two black-cloaked temple guards who flanked it; somehow he was thankful to see that they were human and not glowing-eyed hosts of the *Am-ha-arez.* Then he continued southward between the trees. The moon, just beginning to wax past the half phase, was touching the western horizon; the vague constellation which the Greeks called Aquarius was rising in the east. They would be followed by the Fishes, the Ram and the sun-obscured Hyades and Pleiades, in turn followed by the Twins. . . .

The Twin Stars, one of which was *Ka'a-Set-ur* where circled the Worlds of the Six Suns, which the Greeks and Romans unwittingly called Castor—the worlds that had rebelled against Assatur, the One True God once worshipped by the Jebusite Shepherd-kings on the very spot where now stood the Temple to Yahweh Zava'ot. . . .

And the Pleiades, around one of whose suns circled the world of *Ka-Alantog,* source of the *Am-ha-arez* who served Assatur and upon which had been built the inconceivably vast Archives of the Old Ones. Ka-Alantog— "Conquered of the Serpent"—, which the Persians called Glantok and the Hellenes had innocently named Celaeno. . . .

And the Hyades, now home of ancient Set himself, and of those unnamed, black-cowled beings who served him most directly. . . .

Caiaphas stopped walking. South of him was a low rise, inky in the night—the hill that marked the end of the ridge. The hill called the Mount of Offense, where anciently Solomon had sacrificed to monstrous gods at the behest of his alien wives.

Jebusite wives . . .?

"Here you will soon come," he muttered. "Soon, O Great Lord, when the stars are right. Then shall your true worship be reestablished as of old. Come swiftly, then, O Great One, that they faithful may serve thee upon this world forever, ruling over all men in thy Name!"

A cold breeze sprang up. Caiaphas turned and walked back along the moonlit ridge, wondering why the impending fulfillment of his heartfelt desire should mingle a chill with the exultation he felt in his soul.

It was midnight and the waxing moon was setting when Simon returned to Sychar and approached the house of Elissa. The house was entirely dark and the night was still.

Too still. . . .

He slowed his pace and hugged the shadowed wall, then climbed silently over it as he had the wall of Jahath's mansion. For a moment he stood listening, then stole silently toward the broken gate, keeping to the shadows of trees and shrubs as much as possible.

His instinct had been right. Just within the archway stood the dim forms of three cloaked men, not drunken like the guard at Jahath's place, but erect, alert, obviously waiting. . . .

He stole away and made his way to the portico of the house. The door stood open; within, all was blackness. Could there be more of them in there, waiting for him? For long moments he listened, mind calm but with senses exquisitely alert, in the manner that his mentor Daramos had taught him; he sensed no presence beyond the door. One of the guards by the gate coughed softly. From the shadow of the portico Simon could just see the three of them, partly visible in the vanishing moonlight. At least they were human, for their eyes did not reflect the dim glow.

He crept inside, remembering the way, yet still occasionally touching unremembered objects in the dark. Evidently furniture had been overturned. A hearth still glowed in the kitchen area; Simon lit a torch in its coals, then proceeded to carefully explore the rear rooms and the upper floor, taking care that no light should be cast through outer windows. The place was a wreck; evidently it had been violently ransacked and looted. Then his light fell upon a crumpled body whose blood stained the tiles—a young, dark-haired girl in the tunic of maidservant.

Simon bent closer, relieved to find that the girl was not Lotis. The body lay across the threshold of Elissa's room—evidently the girl had put up a fight and had been slain there. Simon stepped inside and saw more evidence of ransacking—broken chests and furniture, scattered garments and bedding—, but no sign of any person. Elissa and Lotis had evidently been abducted and carried into the night, and now three of those abductors waited silently at the gate. . . .

Then Simon remembered the curtained litter and the troop of armed men he had avoided in the street; they had been heading this way. And Jahath's house, nearly deserted—

Jahath, on his way to Jerusalem!

Carefully the Samaritan stole to his own room, packed his few belongings, then left the house by the back door, shielding the torch's light with his spread cloak as much as possible. He entered the stable, closed the door and bracketed his torch—and in the same instant saw a crumpled form lying against the wall opposite the stalls. The form of a man—dead, surely, for no one would sleep in such an awkward position.

Simon advanced and turned the body over. It was the old servant Gelon, his neck broken, eyes bulging glassily from his grizzled face.

There was a noise from the stalls. Simon turned, saw that the mule was standing in one of them, head turned nonchalantly away. But the two fine black horses were gone—no doubt taken away by Jahath's looters.

He opened the mule's stall, led it out upon the straw-littered floor and quickly secured his light pack across its back. There was half a sack of feed near the dead Gelon; he tied it shut and secured it on the mule also. "Well, friend," he muttered to the animal, "I think we must now go to Jerusalem, and without delay—"

Suddenly the stable door burst open and three men rushed in, swords in hand. "Aha - I *knew* I glimpsed a light!" yelled one.

Simon whirled, whipped out his gladius and sica as the three charged. The men paused, startled by the Samaritan's quick reaction, then spread out in a wide semicircle. Evidently they were trained fighters, intending to rush him all at once from different directions. . . .

"Now!"

The three charged. Simon leaped at the man on his right, dodged his stroke with the adeptness of arena-training, dove under it and slashed; the man shrieked as the sica's keen steel spilled his guts. Without pausing Simon rolled, barely avoiding a blow from a second assailant, then thrust upward, piercing his foe's groin with the broad-bladed shortsword. But the third man was upon him, his own blade thrusting in too rapidly for Simon to evade—

A stomping of hooves, a loud crack—and Simon's last foe went flying over him to crash against the wall, his blade clattering on the floor.

Simon stood up, incredulous. His three foes lay dead or dying, the last one lying against the wall alongside the corpse of old Gelon—lying where he had been flung after being savagely kicked in the head by the forefoot of the mule!

And now the animal stood there quietly, calmly—with eyes that gleamed like those of a cat in the torchlight.

Simon felt his hackles rising. He gripped his weapons more tightly. "Sorcery," he muttered.

The mule shook its head, shoved some straw away with its nose, then began to scratch the dirt with one hoof. Simon watched closely, unbelieving. The scratchings became crude Greek letters, spelling out the word:

FRIEND

"Who—what are you . . .?"

This time the animal scratched the word:

OWL

Simon's flesh tingled still more as he suddenly remembered the fallen owl in the clearing two nights ago—the small blob-being emerging from it and crawling into the brush—the mule suddenly neighing in that brush where it was tethered. . . .

"Gods!" breathed Simon. "Then, you're a—"

The mule tapped the word FRIEND, then beside it added: I HELP.

Simon was suspicious. "But you aided the black-cloaked servitors of Assatur when—when you were the owl."

The mule snorted. It scratched: SLAVE. FREE NOW.

"What do you mean—?"

More scratching: NOW IN BIG BODY. I GROW. I REMEMBER.

Simon could make no sense of this. Slowly he backed away and sheathed his weapons. Again the mule tapped the words it had written: I HELP.

"Very well. I can certainly use your help. My friends are in peril and have been taken away—to Jerusalem, I think. Demon or not, you saved my life just now, and you're already carrying my pack. So, follow me. But, by all the gods, I'll not mount and ride you!"

Simon turned and left the stable, strode across the yard and through the archway in the wall, then set out southward at an easy jog. The mule followed after him down the deserted midnight road.

When they were out of sight an owl rose on noiseless wings from the trees beside the broken gate, wheeled for a moment against the stars, then sped away silently toward the south.

CHAPTER XII

Menander shivered slightly at the touch of a cool breeze and pulled his cloak more closely about him; Ilione, similarly cloaked, drew near to him as if for warmth. Above, the stars glittered down coldly. The moon had long since set in the west, while just above the distant eastern hills the sky ware barely beginning to pale.

"The wizard seems to be nowhere about," whispered Ilione. "Could he have made himself invisible again?"

"Perhaps. Wait here." Menander moved away from her and carefully walked across the gentle curve of the hilltop, one hand out in front of him; but although he thus crossed and recrossed the summit several times, and from several directions, he encountered no unseen obstacle.

"The wizard's not here," he said as he returned to the girl, "for if he were, surely he would have revealed himself by now."

"Perhaps something has happened to him. Menander, do you suppose his enemies found him—those whom he feared might be watching for him?"

Menander shrugged. "It's not quite dawn. We'll wait a few minutes more."

"And, then—?"

"Then we'll go back to the village, and come here again before dawn tomorrow."

They stood in silence while the sky slowly brightened beyond the black eastward hills. Then, suddenly, both gasped in astonishment. From beyond the hills, curving up from the northeast in a shallow arc, sped a gleaming object, brighter than Venus at its brightest. Then it arced down into the southeast, finally vanishing beyond the far hills.

"Gods!" muttered the youth. "Surely I'm dreaming. Did you see it too, Ilione?"

"Yes." The girl shivered, drew closer to him. "I saw it."

They stood in silence for a space, watching the eastern sky. Then the object appeared again, this time at a point slightly south of its first point of appearance. Slowly it arced south, crossing the dimming stars of Andromeda and Pisces, and vanished once more. Several times it repeated this while the sky slowly paled; it seemed to be circling in a series of vast arcs beyond the trans-Jordanian hills.

"It must be *huge!"* said Menander. "Those farthest hilltops are almost twenty Roman miles away."

Ilione clutched his arm. "Do you suppose, Menander, that it could be the—the wizard's enemies—searching for him?"

The object made a final arc to the southeast, then vanished behind the hills and did not return.

"You may be right, Ilione. If so, I hope they don't find him. Come on—let's get down off this hill and return to Salim."

They started down and in a few minutes were off the exposed slope and among the trees, feeling grateful for the concealing shadows. The night sky with its glittering stars, though paling steadily before the advancing dawn, seemed somehow more sinister than before, as if it were full of coldly watching eyes.

Dositheus woke suddenly from a long and much needed sleep. The dim gray light of early dawn was stealing into the small upper chamber in which he and the servant of Botos had spent the night. Slowly the old wizard rose, donned some plain Judean garments in place of his Samaritan ones, then leaned over and shook the sleeping serpent.

"Wake up, Eupatos. Dawn is breaking. We must be on our way."

The youth grumbled but rose stiffly and began to pack. In half an hour they had breakfasted at the inn's kitchen, reclaimed the ass from the stable and were proceeding through Shiloh's narrow and shadowy streets.

Just as the sun rose they arrived at the city's southern gate, where they were lucky enough to attach themselves to a party setting forth to Jerusalem—a group of devout worshippers intent on sacrificing at the great Temple and participating in the impending Passover feast.

During the journey Dositheus, claiming to be a pious pilgrim from Salim, talked with several of the men and made casual inquiry about the town of Aphairema, which they would reach before midday. One elderly and learned Levite named Aggaeus—a Galilean who had been visiting relatives in Shiloh—proved to be very informative on the subject.

"I know the place well," he said, "for my brother teaches in a synagogue there. He will join our party when we arrive."

"I've heard that a prophet was speaking there recently," said Dositheus. "I wonder if he is still there.

"Not likely. Your news is old. He left nearly two weeks ago for Jericho, and is now preaching beyond the Jordan near Bethramphtha—or so I heard but yesterday. You should see the mobs that follow him! When he was in Aphairema one would have sworn that the Temple Passover sacrifices were to be held there rather than in Jerusalem."

"You were there?"

"Aye. And I listened to him speak, and conversed with several who said they had been following him about the countryside these last few months."

"What was he like?" Dositheus could not keep a trace of eagerness out of his voice. "What did he say?"

"He seems a strange one," said Aggaeus. "What he *said* did not seem so important to me, for it was mostly old parables, or homilies drawn from Hillel and the Essene sages, or passages from the Law—such things as are well known to a scholar such as your speech indicates you to be."

"Thank you, Aggaeus; I *have* made some effort to study the ancient writings. But, tell me: If the substance of this rabbi Yeshua's discourses are so unremarkable, why does he draw such a huge following?"

The old Levite snorted disdainfully. "The unlearned mob is far more easily swayed than are the people of knowledge such as you and I. They will follow anyone who pretends to speak with authority. And this Yeshua bar Yosef certainly does that! There is something in his manner, in his eyes and the timbre of his voice that commands respect, even belief—I have felt it, and had he spoken of reasonable things I would not doubt his sincerity. But he is not the first to tell us that the time is soon coming when this evil world shall be destroyed and created anew."

Dositheus sensed a bitterness in the man—a bitterness he could sympathize with. He asked shrewdly: "Did he say, then that he was the promised Mashiah who would overthrow the rule of the Romans?"

The old Levite nodded. "Not in so many words, Dositheus, but his import was clear." He sighed wearily. "How many such false prophets have come and gone!—shamefully executed on crosses by the Romans, or stoned by the disappointed people when the promises failed."

"And yet, my friend, I sense that you wish it could be so—as do I and all others who must endure the tyranny of Rome. But, come, tell me more—for I also sense that this rabbi affected you more than your disdain for his message would indicate."

"And I sense, Dositheus of Salim, that you are very interested in this man! Well, when you hear him speak to a crowd you will know why he casts such a spell." The old Levite's eyes became almost mystical as he stared ahead, remembering; a shudder seemed to pass through him. "Especially when he talks of that day when all shall flee in terror from the fields and the housetops, and that then there shall be no place to hide, and that finally there shall come an end to all suffering and all things on this earth will be destroyed and re-created in a new manner. I feared him greatly when I heard him speak thusly, even though I sensed great compassion in his face—or, did I fear him *because* of that compassion . . .?"

Dositheus asked: "Was there anything else you noticed about his face? His cast of features, perhaps?"

Aggaeus looked at the old man sharply. "You mean the sheeplike or goatish aspect? Yes, and others have noted it also. But do not imagine the man to be grotesque on that account. When you've heard him speak, when you've seen his eyes, you'll know better."

Dositheus shuddered slightly, remembering the words of Mattan: *"The features of those whom They have begotten upon mankind. . . ."*

"What's that?" said Aggaeus. "I don't understand—"

"Nothing—just an old quotation I was reminded of. Tell me, my friend—you say you talked to some of this rabbi's followers. What did they tell you of him?"

"Many strange things. They say he has healed many by laying his hands upon them. I did not see this happen, but some months ago I heard that he raised a widow's dead son in Nain, my own city. And my brother tells me of two in Aphairema who were cured during the rabbi's recent visit—a man and a woman with wasting diseases of many years; these two told my brother that it felt as though a spirit had come into them from the man's hands to cleanse them, then had withdrawn into him again, so that when at last he lifted his hands from them they were cured. Many in the crowd testified that he had done the same thing elsewhere, and also that he had sometimes driven demons from the bodies of afflicted ones."

"Were these—demons—ever described?" Dositheus asked.

"Some claimed to have seen them come forth as a vile crawling fluid, hiding themselves from the light of day by seeping into crevices or trees, or even into the bodies of animals. On one occasion, at Gadara beyond the Jordan, some of these cast-out demons got among a large herd of swine who immediately panicked and stampeded over an embankment into a lake. But who can say what exaggerations are in such tales, passed among the mob by rumor as they are?"

"The *Am-ha-arez,*" muttered Dositheus.

The Levite looked at him. "That is what the Galilean commoners are often called—"

"Aye, though the term has an older and darker meaning. But please go on, Aggaeus. Tell me more of these—rumors."

"They are numerous, for this Yeshua has wandered through many regions during the last several months, even as far as Tyre in the north, and to those southern regions of Perea beyond the Jordan, always working his healing magic upon the crowds, then capturing their minds with his riddles and parables. Meanwhile, some of his disciples go through the throngs hinting of secret meanings behind these stories—meanings that only the inner circle of initiates may know."

Dositheus nodded. "A technique known to all skillful magicians who seek a gang of followers: Gain attention, hold attention, then excite curiosity to know more. But tell me, Aggaeus, what did you think was this rabbi Yeshua's chief message to the mob? What does he seem to want most from them?"

"That they should all follow the Law, which he says he has come to fulfill—every jot and tittle of it. He exhorts them to cease in their slackening, to return to the Law which Moses received many centuries ago from Him whose name must not be spoken, in order that its purpose may be soon accomplished. And that is very curious, for this Yeshua himself often publicly breaks the very Law he advocates, which greatly angers many scribes and scholars—including myself, I must admit. Moreover, some of his closest disciples are known to have flouted the Law grievously—Matthew the tax gatherer, for one, and also his brother Yakov, both of whom were notorious in Capharnaum for extortion and usury against their fellow Galileans. And then there is Judah of Kerioth, whom some think a sorcerer."

"A sorcerer?" Dositheus' eyes glittered with interest.

"A strange, dark man, at any rate, and a scholar learned in ancient lore and languages. Some say he is Rabbi Yeshua's closest confidant, though outwardly the rabbi favors one Kepha, a great lout of a Galilean fisherman. Then there is Zelotes, who is said to be good with the *sica*—"

"Did you talk with any of these men?"

"No, but I did talk with one disciple named Nathaniel bar Tolmai—"

"Ah! I know him. His father is a rabbi at the synagogue in Capharnaum. But, pardon me, good Aggaeus—please continue."

"This Nathaniel told me a most interesting tale to counter my skepticism concerning his master's powers. Once while in Capharnaum the rabbi Yeshua found himself in need of money, so he sent his fisherman disciple Kepha down to the Sea of Galilee to summon a fish-being who would bring them gold. The being came up from beneath the water; it was somewhat like a man with gills and scales, and it gave Kepha a strange gold coin worth about a shekel. Nathaniel swore that he got this tale from Kepha himself. He also said that the natives of that area know of the being and call it the *Proto-ichthon*—the 'First Fish'—believing it to be the ruler of many such beings who dwell in that vast lake."

The Denizens of the Deep, thought Dositheus, but managed to hide his agitation. "I've heard such tales," he said evenly, "but did not think that the beings were still believed in. The legends of them go back to ancient times, before Joshua conquered the land. No doubt this rabbi Yeshua and his disciples Kepha made use of these legends to impress the ignorant populace, and poor Nathaniel was taken in by them."

The old Levite shrugged. "No doubt. But there are too many strange things going on these days. Why does this rabbi urge rigid obedience to the Law, yet flout it by his behavior?—not to mention agitating the Romans by implying that he might be the Mashiah—the King which will rule Israel? Is he trying to get himself killed?"

Perhaps he is, thought Dositheus uneasily. He nodded and said aloud: "These are indeed strange times, my friend."

"And another thing," Aggaeus went on. "Why did this mysterious rabbi and his dark disciple Judah of Kerioth visit that old sorcerer Yosef bar Heli at his mansion in Aphairema?"

"Sorcerer?" Dositheus looked intently at his companion.

"So he is sometimes called, though of course not to his face. Yosef is the richest man in the region of Aphairema, a member of the Jerusalem Sanhedrin, and old—some say he is as old as the Temple priest Annas, whose youth no man remembers. During the rabbi's visit to Aphairema, my brother went one evening to old Yosef's house to discuss some matters pertaining to the impending Passover, and when he had finished and was leaving after nightfall he saw two newcomers being admitted to the mansion and recognized them."

"The rabbi Yeshua and his disciple Judah?"

"Aye."

Dositheus scowled at dim memories which his companion's words had stirred. "This Yosef bar Heli—how long ago did he come to Aphairema?"

"About ten years ago—from Jerusalem, it is said. I understand he has property in that city, as well as influence in the Temple. But there are rumors that he once practiced sorcery in Galilee and gained his wealth there by dark means."

Dositheus suppressed a shudder as he thought of fish-beings rising from moonlit waters, bearing gold in their webbed hands. "One more question, friend: Do you know if this old Yosef ever had—a son?"

"I know nothing of his family, but they may live in Jerusalem. It is said that a striking young woman sometimes comes from there to visit him. Possibly his granddaughter, or a niece. A beauty, from all accounts. I've heard that she is even now visiting in Aphairema."

"Hold on, there!"

It was a man's voice, loud and authoritative. Dositheus halted and turned with the rest of the group, irritated by the interruption. He saw a group of soldiers rapidly overtaking the party of travelers, and heading this troop was a man riding a large black horse—

A horse, Dositheus realized uneasily, as large and black as the one he had seen galloping riderless down a moonlit road the night before.

Yosef of Aphairema peered northward from the topmost window of his mansion, which stood just south of the village that lay between the gentle, greening hills. His old eyes, squinting against the midday sun, were still sharp for distance-viewing; they could just make out, beyond the trees of his estate and the flat-roofed houses of the town, the road that wound down from the hills, and on its farthest visible stretch what appeared to be a troop of soldiers stopping a caravan of pilgrims—a sight long familiar in this his native land. Despite the warm air he pulled his dark cloak more closely about him as if to ward off a chill. His lean right hand clutched absently at his white beard as he watched the distant drama upon the roadway; his dark eyes glittered angrily above his strong aquiline nose—an eagle's eyes above its proud beak.

"Cursed be the Romans," he muttered, "—they and their temple-toadies and tax collectors. They bully all the land now, but soon black doom shall be their lot. Soon. . . ."

Suddenly he was interrupted as a large dove, snowy-white, glided down from the blue sky and fluttered to a landing on his window sill. Old Yosef's eyes glittered more intently as he bent close to the bird; his voice rasped with intense emotion as he asked:

"What news, Parakleitos? I have waited long. Speak!"

The dove, its eyes gleaming with an uncanny intelligence, began to coo and trill rapidly. The old man listened intently for many long minutes, head inclined toward the bird as toward a human speaker whose slightest word he would not miss.

"You have done well," he said finally as the dove ceased its bobbing and cooing. "Return now to your mater. Tell him that Miriam and Martha send this message: 'Lord, he whom you love is ill.' He will understand."

The bird uttered a final trill, flapped its wings and fluttered up from the casement, wheeling away into the blue sky toward the southeast.

The old man turned to a scroll-littered table and sounded a small brazen gong that stood upon it. In a few moments a young, short-bearded man entered the chamber; his features were expressionless save for his dark eyes, which gleamed with intelligent awareness.

"The time has come, Zethos," said old Yosef. "Go and tell Miriam to come here to my chamber. Then, make preparations for our departure. We set out for Bethany this very night."

The young man bowed in acknowledgment, his eyes gleaming even more intensely, then turned and left the room.

Perhaps five minutes later Yosef heard a soft footfall in the corridor, and the next moment a stately young woman entered his chamber. She was tall, black-haired and clad in russet-brown robes of a sort worn by high-born Judean maidens. A slender, silver coronet, set with gems of many colors, rested lightly on the raven locks above her brow. Her features, uncommonly beautiful and delicate, reflected intelligence and determination—firm chin and mouth, high cheekbones, level gray eyes with a tint of feline green in them.

"Zethos tells me it is the Time, O Wizard," she said, the trace of a subdued excitement in her firm, richly feminine voice.

Yosef admired her, as any man would have been obliged to, though sexual fires no longer burned in his aged frame. "It is. The Bridegroom makes ready even now to journey to Bethany, and the Bride must be there to greet him. And then the raising of *El-ha-Zarria* shall be accomplished and the rite of the Golden King performed." He turned to a small cupboard of dark wood, opened its topmost door and drew forth a small bottle which he handled almost reverently. "Take it, beloved daughter-in-law, and cherish it, for tomorrow its contents must anoint the Mashiah."

The young woman stared in fascination at the ancient Canaanite characters engraved deeply upon the dark, green-tinted glass. "The anointing oil! But, this vessel appears to be many centuries old—"

"As it is indeed. Not for many a generation has a Golden King been anointed in this stricken land. But now he is here—the long-foretold, the long-awaited—and tomorrow his Bride shall anoint him and the Rite of Rising shall be performed. And soon after, he shall perform the great sacrifice that will usher in his Kingdom, one which shall overshadow all kingdoms that have gone before, and not even the might of Rome shall stand for an instant against it."

A slight hardness crept into the woman's eyes; she moved to the casement and gazed out over the land; her face, beauteous but stern, was like that of a judging goddess. "The Bride will perform her part well."

"The Groom must die, as you well know, but you shall provide the living vessel for his return into the New Kingdom, after the earth has been stripped of all life and made over. Then shall we few who have been faithful dwell in glory thereon, ruled forever by Him and His Father."

She nodded. "It shall be so. The world will be better without mankind and all its cruelties. Let the Time come swiftly!" She turned and with a stately, almost imperial gesture, drew shut the curtain, blotting out the sight of the landscape. "Away with this world—it no longer amuses me. I will have a new one." A slight smile played upon her beautiful lips; a whimsical twinkle banished the sternness from her cool gray-green eyes. "Let the Father try his hand anew at creating one worthy of me."

"Hold on there!" yelled the soldier who rode the black horse. "Clear the road, rabble! Move aside, all of you!"

Most of the group of pilgrims immediately obeyed, but old Aggaeus turned and stood his ground, bristling with indignation. "You are not a Roman, Captain. Why do you ape their arrogance and insult an unarmed band of holy pilgrims?"

The soldier kneed his horse forward. Dositheus snatched Aggaeus' sleeve and jerked him out of the way barely in time. A litter borne by eight dark-robed soldiers immediately followed. Suddenly the curtains of this litter parted and a stubbled, ratlike face peered out, dark eyes darting wildly—and rather fearfully, Dositheus thought.

"Hold up, soldiers!" yelled the man from the litter. Then, as the column stopped, he turned to Aggaeus and said: "A thousand pardons, revered elder, but we bear urgent news for the Tribune Maxentius." His glance darted back down the dusty road. "You have not seen a Samaritan traveling alone, have you? A young man, dark-bearded and leading a mule—?"

"We travel with no unbelieving Samaritans," shouted Aggaeus, trembling with anger, "nor with heathen Romans—nor their kowtowing tax gatherers such as you, Jahath of Shechem!"

"The Samaritan is a dangerous man," said Jahath, ignoring the outburst, "—a thief and a murderer. His name is Simon. If you encounter such a man, report him to the authorities immediately."

He barked an order to the soldiers, then made to close the curtains of his litter. A vagrant breeze chose that moment to stir aside one of those curtains, and Dositheus was startled to glimpse eyes gleaming within the shadowy interior—round eyes framed by the beak and feathered ears of a great owl.

Then the drapes closed and the soldiers tramped by. Jahath's litter was followed by an even larger one carried by twelve men; its richly-dyed curtains were sewn shut.

When the score or so of dark-cloaked soldiers had passed, the pilgrims reassembled and slowly continued on their way. Dositheus walked for a while in thoughtful silence, watching Jahath's column as it hurried down the dusty road toward Aphairema. He scarcely heard the continuous mutterings of Aggaeus against unbelieving Romans, Greeks, Samaritans and tax gatherers.

Simon.... Could it indeed be he?

Yes, Dositheus concluded, for he had often heard from Simon's own lips the names of Jahath and his Roman master Maxentius....

His thoughts were interrupted by the sound of a loud, harsh croak. Looking up, he saw a raven sitting amid the branches of a great oak not far from the road.

"I must stop and rest here, Aggaeus," he said. "You and your companions go on ahead—I will rejoin you in the village soon."

After a few protests concerning Dositheus' safety, Aggaeus and the other pilgrims did as he had suggested. After all, it was midday, travelers were frequent and the town was already in sight.

"Tend to the donkey, Eupatos," said the old wizard when the party had gone on its way. "Find him good fodder. I shall rest in the shadow of yonder oak."

The servant did as he was told, but upon glancing back noticed that the raven did not fly away at the old man's approach. *The wizard's familiar,* he realized with a slight shiver.

Dositheus sat down under the oak upon a flat-topped stone. "Well, Carbo," he said when the servant was out of hearing, "come down now and give me this day's news."

The bird fluttered from the branches and settled atop a low boulder, then uttered a long series of elaborate croakings. Dositheus listened intently to the halting Latin phrases interspersed with occasional Greek words; he nodded occasionally, sometimes interrupting to ask a question. Finally he said:

"Events are moving swiftly. I will not have time to return to the Thirty as I had hoped. You must go to Menander, Carbo, and tell him to bid them come to Jerusalem with all haste. And if you should see Simon on the road, warn him that he is in danger—"

"Vid!" croaked the bird, pointing with his beak northward up the road. *"Venit!"*

"What!" Dositheus rose quickly. "You saw him? He comes—?"

Even as he spoke he noticed a man coming into view around a far bend of the road—a man leading a mule. As the stranger approached, Dositheus saw that it was a tall, dark-bearded man wearing Samaritan garments.

"Ho, Simon," Dositheus called out as the man came abreast. "Come up here and join me."

The man hesitated briefly, then turned aside from the road and led his mule up the slope between the boulders. "I never would have recognized you but for your voice, Dositheus. You look like some pious old Judean pilgrim. How did you find me?"

"I didn't. It was Carbo who spied you. I see that you, too, came well disguised—yet you couldn't fool our friend's sharp eye. Nor those of certain night-watchers, evidently! Listen: you are in danger; Jahath and his soldiers are even now spreading the word that a dark-bearded Samaritan named Simon is to be apprehended for thievery and murder."

"Indeed? Then I must change my disguise." Simon carefully peeled off the false beard, rubbed his shaven chin, then sat down at the base of the oak. "News travels strangely fast to Jahath, it seems. One might almost suspect him of—sorcery?"

Dositheus nodded, sitting down again on the rock. "When Jahath passed us on the road I glimpsed an owl within his litter. You should know by now what *that* means! There was also another litter in his column—quite a large one, and with the curtains sewn shut."

"So!" Simon muttered a curse. "I've no doubt Elissa and Lotis were in it—probably bound and drugged."

"Lotis? Elissa?"

"Maxentius' former mistress and her handmaid." Simon rose and, walking over to his mule, untied a sack of provisions and let it fall to the ground. "Jahath kidnapped them last night. It's a long story. I'll tell you about it while we eat; then, I must press on. Here—I'd better feed the mule first. Get off the feed-sack, Carbo—"

The raven, which had fluttered up atop the sack to peck at its bindings, hopped obediently down to the back of the mule. For a second it stood there, eyeing Simon a bit indignantly—then suddenly squawked and flapped frantically into the air.

"In ibi!" it screeched as it fluttered up amid the branches of the oak. *"In ibi!"*

"Inside—what?" Dositheus glared in puzzlement at the mule, then up at the raven who was now perched upon a high limb. "Carbo, what's gotten into you?"

"I'm afraid it's what's gotten into the mule," said Simon. "Carbo must have sensed its presence."

Dositheus turned to the beast, which was now pointing its snout upward at the squawking raven. For a moment it stood thus, then lowered its head and began to scratch with a front hoof in the dust. To Dositheus' astonishment the scratchings took the form of crude Greek letters, which read:

RAVEN OTHER LIKE ME

"I see," said Dositheus slowly. "Evidently you knew, Simon, that this beast was so possessed.

"Yes. And it's friendly, for last night it saved my hide from one of Jahath's swordsmen. But, what has it written here, Dositheus? Is our old friend Carbo really another such being as this mule and ... those owls?"

The old wizard nodded. "I suspect so. Come, Simon, let us lunch in the shade while we share what we have newly learned."

Simon left the feed sack open on the ground for the mule, then joined the wizard under the big oak. While they snacked on bread and dates they told one another of their wanderings and adventures since parting.

"This is a time of strange happenings," said Dositheus at last. "As for your question concerning Carbo, I have long suspected that he might be something like this. Years before I met you I bought him from a Roman soldier stationed in Galilee, who had in turn gotten him from a fisherman of that country. Strange things have happened of old in that land, and many who dwell there still remember such things. I fear, Simon, that your mule and our friend Carbo are both *Am-ha-arez*, those beings from which the present-day Galileans take their name."

Simon noticed that the mule had finished eating and now stood only a few paces from them, while Carbo was perched upon the lowest branch of the oak. Both seemed to be listening to the conversation attentively.

"Do you remember, Simon," the wizard continued, "how the ancient mage Ostanes wrote of the flight of Great Set from earth to the Hyades after the war between the Primal Gods and the Old Ones? Set found new and terrible minions there, and in time even made a pact with Black Zathog, who is said to be Prince of the Powers of the Air, King and Lord of a race from beyond the stars. With these allies he fought anew against the Primal Gods and conquered many worlds and suns, including even Celaeno amid the Pleiades whereon the Old Ones established their greatest archives and filled them with monstrous lore. And also he conquered the Six Suns, which the Greeks name Castor, and around which circle the worlds from which originally came those we call *Am-ha-arez.*

"Set's minions took such of these Castor-beings as were congenial to his rule and sent them to serve him on the archive-world of Celaeno, or to be his servitors upon other conquered worlds. And powerful servitors they proved to be, for they were able to inhabit the bodies of many different sorts of beings, controlling their actions and even to some extent their thoughts."

Simon shivered slightly despite the afternoon heat. He glanced up at the raven and asked: "Is this true, Carbo? Are you and this mule truly of that race which in Galilee are called the 'Earth Folk'?"

"Ita!" The bird nodded. *"Am-ha-arez!"*

"Gods!" Simon turned to Dositheus. "Can this truly be?"

Before the wizard could reply the mule began again to scratch in the dirt. This time the words so formed read: TRUE. WE SIX-SUNS. ENEMIES OF SET. AID YOU.

Dositheus nodded knowingly. "Carbo, come down. Eat your fill of the grain, then return to Salim and inform Menander and the Thirty that they must join us as quickly as possible in Jerusalem."

The bird attacked the grain, and while he ate Simon asked his old mentor: "And where do you go now?"

"Yonder, to Aphairema. Tonight I shall visit the mansion of the sorcerer Yosef bar Heli and hopefully learn more of these matters. Will you aid me, Simon?"

"No. I follow Jahath. If he and his soldiers camp for the night I shall creep among them like a serpent, and those soldiers shall wake in the dawn to find their master headless. Then, I'll pursue Maxentius."

"I see. You still pursue the vengeance you have craved these many years. Well, I blame you not. But I sense that you also plan to rescue these two women-friends of yours, which may prove more difficult. Go carefully, Simon—and, if I may suggest it, discard that Samaritan garb along with your beard. Judean or even Syrian garments would serve you better from here on."

"I have no time to acquire such garments," said Simon, "but don't worry. I'll circle this village and be on my way. Samaritan garb will serve me well enough unless I try to enter Jerusalem. Hopefully I won't have to."

The mule tossed its head, then scratched in the dirt: I GO, TOO. HELP YOU.

Simon brushed sweaty dark bangs back from his forehead. "Well, mule, your help has been genuine so far—"

"I think, Simon, that your 'mule' needs a name," suggested Dositheus. "Why not call him—Balaam?"

The young Samaritan nodded. "Aye, why not? He cannot speak, as could the legendary she-ass of Balaam, but he can certainly write, and that's an even more marvelous thing! Come along, then,—Balaam. I'll turn down no honest offer of aid, whether from man or demon-spirit, in this my time of vengeance."

But Dositheus only repeated: "Go carefully, Simon—carefully."

THE TOWER OF SET

CHAPTER XIII

The sun had set when Caiaphas' litter was borne through the Siloam Gate and deposited by its dark-cloaked bearers before the door of the tower that guarded it. As he stepped out he glanced up at the looming Roman stonework, gray and ominous in the dusk, then beckoned to two of his robed and armored attendants. The three of them strode silently into the tower, two Roman guardsmen standing aside to make room for them.

Inside was a wide, windowless room, heavily beamed and columned, that evidently extended the whole width of the tower. A dozen or more Roman soldiers lounged informally about in the torchlight, gambling with dice, chewing on rations or muttering curses and bawdy jokes. No wine was in evidence, however.

Scribonius rose from the rough wooden table at which had been dining. "Well, priest, you're just in time to interrupt our meal. Look, then—these are the men who will accompany me. Do they pass your inspection?"

"They'll pass as road-ruffians quite plausibly—as will you also, my good Scribonius. Now, to make sure you understand your orders: You will leave the city openly as a Roman patrol, but when you have passed beyond the Kidron Valley you will hide your shields and spears and disguise yourselves as plain bandits. Beyond Bethany you will dig in the exact location that I have marked on your map; it is the ruin of an ancient shrine that used to stand at the base of a steep hill. You may have to shatter stone in order to enter the small chamber within where the *Byakhtril* is concealed. Deliver it immediately to Annas at his villa. With any luck you will complete your task by dawn and return here by midmorning, again openly as Roman soldiers."

"Jupiter!" spat Scribonius, irritated as always at having to take orders from this ornately-robed Judean priest. "Why should we go like sneaking thieves? Why not openly?"

"There are many—watchers—abroad lately," said Caiaphas. "I would go with you myself did I not suspect that I am especially under surveillance. But I will send these two Temple guards with you to advise and guide. They will recognize the shrine and that which it contains."

Scribonius did not like the way the eyes of those guardsmen gleamed in the torchlight. "Why couldn't they do the job alone?"

"The Byakhtril is too valuable to lose. We must not take the slightest risk of that. Thus, your large force of fighting men."

"Hades!" The Roman spat on the floor. "I'll do what you say, as Maxentius has ordered—but why he should cater this way to your Judean superstitions is beyond me."

"Your attitude, Centurion, is not good," said Caiaphas sternly. "It is very important that you take your mission seriously. Come—I will show you a thing the like of which you have not seen before. Have your men raise the stone."

"What, again? Oh, very well. You—Lucius—round up four men and get that damned trapdoor lifted up!"

The decurion hastened to do as he was ordered, and in another few minutes a great slab of stone had been lifted from the center of the floor by means of iron rings. Scribonius uneasily regarded the stone steps that led downward into darkness.

"Come—follow me," said Caiaphas.

One of the priest's own black-cloaked guardsmen was already descending into the pit, torch held aloft. Caiaphas went in after him. Scribonius followed as directed, noting with increased uneasiness that the second dark-cloaked guard followed in turn.

"Note how the Roman stonework changes to a more massive sort, following by living rock," said the priest as they descended. "These were once the foundations of the Tower of Set, which was overthrown by that King David who overthrew the Jebusites who built it more than a thousand years ago. Those Jebusites were descendants of the Hyksos, who were in turn descended from Karakossa and age-lost Stygia."

"So?" Scribonius tried to force scorn into his voice despite an oppression he felt from the surrounding gloom. "You have told me all this before—"

"Yet I have not shown you what lies beneath the tower. Look, now—here is the innermost chamber."

As he spoke they emerged from the narrow stairwell into a small circular room. In its center stood a low altar of dark stone; otherwise, the place was quite bare and featureless.

"Strange rites were performed here in olden times," said Caiaphas. Then, motioning to his two guardsmen, "Remove the stone."

The dark-cloaked pair, without setting down their torches, gripped two corners of the altar and slid it back easily. It grated heavily against the stone floor, and Scribonius gasped slightly. The altar, though not large, should yet have been too heavy for two men to move.

Then his amazement grew even greater as he beheld a faint red light streaming up from a small pit which the altar's removal had uncovered.

"Look in, Scribonius, and tell me what you see."

The Roman advanced slowly and peered into the pit. It was shallow, and the glow that filled it revealed—

"Gods!" hissed Scribonius. "The golden ass-head! Then . . . those old stories were indeed true—?"

"Aye. It is indeed the very eidolon which King Antiochus the Mad installed in the inmost shrine of the Temple when he conquered Jerusalem two centuries ago. It is the Abomination of Desolation."

The centurion stared at it, unbelieving. The thing was about two feet high, apparently of the purest gold and shaped somewhat like the head of an onager, or wild ass—yet with a disturbing suggestion of humanness in its features. About its base wound the golden coils of a serpent, widening as they rose until they formed the neck from which the grotesque head arose. The expression on the thing's face was sinister, disturbing, as were the lifelike details of the pointed ears and flaring nostrils, but most disturbing of all was the eerie crimson light that streamed from the thing's eyes and illumined the shallow pit with a steady glow.

Scribonius drew back, shuddering.

"It is the Eidolon of Set," Caiaphas intoned. "Some say it was carved by Thoth-Ammon himself during those dark times when Stygia ruled the land now called Egypt. The Jebusites worshipped it with blood-rites, and before them the Hyksos and the Karakossans. King Antiochus took it from this place and caused it to be worshipped in the Temple, but that act led to his doom. Afterwards, Set's secret worshippers recovered it and returned it here, to its ancient place of concealment. Tomorrow, Scribonius, when you return with the Byakhtril, the Eidolon shall be removed again to the Temple, to rejoin the Ark, which has already been placed there. Then shall the stage be set for that new Rising of which the stars foretell."

"Cover it up," growled Scribonius, shielding his eyes from the evil magical glow. "I believe you. Let's get out of this pit of Hades!"

The guards replaced the stone altar. The four of them returned to the upper chamber, and the slab covering the steps leading downward was quickly replaced.

"So you see, Scribonius, you serve great powers," said Caiaphas. "See to it that you serve them well."

Without another word the priest motioned to his two guardsmen and led them forth from the tower, feeling a dark satisfaction in knowing that he had impressed the hard-natured Scribonius. Yet this satisfaction was tempered by a slight chill—the chill he always felt after gazing upon the Eidolon of Set.

As he approached his litter he became aware of several guardsmen besides his own in the dim torchlight. Then a short, rat-faced figure came hurrying toward him from the shadows.

"Jahath!" exclaimed the priest. "Why are you in the city—?"

"I came with all speed." The tax gatherer's dark eyes, round with fear, glanced about him as if to anticipate a danger from the darkness. "I have journeyed night and day without rest. I must find Maxentius. They tell me that he has not yet returned to Jerusalem, so I hastened here to consult with Scribonius."

"Maxentius and his troop have doubtless gone on to Annas' villa upon the Mount of Olives. I sent him a—messenger—to advise him to do so. But why this haste on your part? What do you fear?"

"I, too, have heard from 'messengers', Caiaphas. Strange things have recently happened in Samaria. Maxentius must be warned—I must go to him."

Caiaphas noticed the two litters that rested upon the shoulders of Jahath's silent guardsmen. "Who accompanies you?"

"I bring—guests. A woman and her slave-girl, both of whom know much concerning the dark happenings of late. Maxentius will want to question them, good Caiaphas—and so, I'm sure, will you."

The priest nodded curtly. "Follow me to the villa, then. Maxentius is surely on his way there even now."

As the high priest was borne in his litter out the Siloam Gate into the night, he felt again the nervous chill. *Dark happenings,* he mused, *so many dark happenings of late. . . .*

Simon woke suddenly and sat up. The moon was high in the west. He must have slept several hours—longer than he had intended. Nearby, he saw the silhouette of the mule among the trees of the grove in which he had camped; its eyes gleamed faintly in the moonlight.

He took a swig from the water skin, then rose from the hard ground, muttering a curse. Maxentius and Jahath would be far ahead by now, perhaps even within the walls of Jerusalem. Inquiries along the road had gained him the information that a Roman officer and his troop had preceded him by less than a day, while according to Dositheus, Jahath had gone by only an hour or so before Simon, evidently in a great hurry.

How, Simon wondered, had Jahath learned that he was following him? Did Maxentius know as well? Surely there was sorcery involved. He must continue to proceed with caution despite his impatience.

He packed his few belongings, carried them to the mule and strapped them on. "Well, Balaam, are you full of grass? Yes? Then, let's get a move on."

The animal began to scratch on a patch of bare ground illuminated by the moonlight. Simon bent forward and made out the words: YOU RIDE ME. FASTER.

Simon shook his head, feeling his spine prickle. The suggestion made sense, but he could not yet bring himself to do it. Probably he could trust the beast—after all, it had saved his life the night before and had not attacked him while he slept. Yet the remembrance of what lived within it—

the greenish-gray blob that could seep into the flesh of any living thing—made him mentally unable to consider prolonged contact with it.

"Thank you, Balaam, but I'll not so burden you. I'm well refreshed after my nap, and we still have a long road to walk."

The mule snorted, nodded silently, then turned and began to lead the way out of the grove, back toward the moonlit road.

It was nearly midnight. Dositheus walked silently but openly down the flagged pathway that led between dark-boled oaks and sycamores toward the looming bulk of the mansion of Yosef of Aphairema, black under the moon.

He had rented a room in the town, along with stable-space for Eupatos and the donkey, and had spent several hours in slumber. Thus, his mind and senses were now fully alert, as he glided through the darkness toward the mansion. Though he knew not what to expect, he did know that the wizard Yosef and two women of his household had departed toward Jerusalem late that afternoon, together with many armed attendants; so much the roadside beggars had told him. Strange indeed, that departure. Why should the old sorcerer choose the secrecy of night travel over the comparative safety of day . . .?

"Halt! Who comes?"

Dositheus stopped, folded his arms and levelly regarded the young man who stood just behind the metal grille of the archway in the mansion's surrounding wall. "I am the mage Dositheus. Open the gate. Your master is expecting me."

"That is not possible, for my master has departed for Jerusalem this very evening. Moreover, he told me nothing of your visit, old man. How is it that you come here alone at midnight, with no retinue?"

"I am a wizard as mighty as your master," said Dositheus, "and therefore I fear no perils of the night. Moreover, your master told me that, in the event of his unforeseen departure, I should be admitted to his house and given access to his library. And, in case you doubt my word I am bidden by your master to show you—this."

During this speech, delivered in tones of calm but emphatic self-confidence, Dositheus had accentuated the words "your master" only slightly, meanwhile moving closer to the gate. Now he drew from beneath his robe a round bronze mirror, highly polished, and held it up before the young man's face. The youth peered closely, saw his own dark eyes starting back at him in the torchlight. . . .

"Look closely, and see that it is *your master* who commands this."

The young man squinted at the metal disc. No, surely it was *not* his own face reflected therein, but that of his venerable and white-haired master Yosef of Aphairema. . . .

"Open the gate, lad, and let your master's guest enter."

To the youth it seemed that it was not Dositheus who spoke, but, rather, the venerable face in the mirror. Slowly he nodded; then, with all the deliberation of a sleepwalker, he took a key from his belt and unlocked the metal gate.

Dositheus stepped through. "That's a good lad," he said in a kindly voice. "Now, lock the gate again. Good. And now, lead me to your master's library."

The young man nodded, turned and led the way into the interior of the house, through a short atrium and into a large columned space. A few servants lay dozing on mats between the columns; one or two looked up, then lapsed back into their slumbers, suspecting nothing. Dositheus smiled; his intuition had proven correct. The young gatekeeper was indeed hypnotically suggestible as one could have hoped.

They ascended a wide flight of stairs, then a narrower one, and passed down a short corridor to an archway in which was set a sturdy door of oak. The servant unlocked this door and stood aside.

"Good," said Dositheus, taking the torch from the youth's hand. "You may return now to your post and sleep . . . sleep."

The young servant nodded, his eyes blank, then turned and walked slowly away down the corridor.

Dositheus entered the unlocked room. It was fairly large, with a drape-concealed window at one end and many scroll-filled shelves along the walls. In its center was large table cluttered with bronze instruments, bottles and vial full of liquids and powders, and a reading-stand for unrolling scrolls. The old Samaritan's practiced eye recognized the place instantly as a sorcerer's den.

Bracketing his torch upon the wall, he found several oil lamps and lit them in its flame, setting them in sconces and niches about the room. Two he put upon the table, then turned his attention to the shelves.

Most of old Yosef's library was what one might expect of a learned elder of the Jerusalem priesthood, though in addition to the Judean scriptures in both Hebrew and Greek, were also quite a number of ancient Hellenic philosophers—Thales, Heracleitos, Anaximenes and Pythagoras, among others, and even such half-forgotten mystics as Pherecydes of Syros, who maintained that the universe was but "a vast robe upon which Zeus embroidered earth and sea and the sea's inhabitants." Dositheus felt a slight prickle of gooseflesh, for he recalled seeing a sculpture of one of these "inhabitants" made by a Greek artisan at Rome during Augustus' reign—an artisan named Batrachos whose fanciful creation, half human and half frog, had seemed nevertheless disturbingly lifelike. His uneasiness deepened as he discovered equally ancient works in Hebrew, supposedly long-lost, such as the *Chronicles of Hozai,* the *Book of Jasher* and even the *Scroll of Asherah* penned by the mad Queen Athaliah of Judah. But more disturbing still were the scrolls he discovered in a small cupboard in one corner of the room—a locked cupboard which Dositheus' skills managed to open quickly. Here were not only a complete Greek copy of Ostanes' dark works, but even fragments of many earlier and darker works upon which that mysterious Persian magus had drawn, including the *Scroll of Thoth* in an archaic hieratic Egyptian script, and an even more ancient Naacal rendering of the *Scroll of Eibon.* Most shocking of all were two fragmentary manuscripts labeled in Greek characters as *Pnakotikon* and *Kelaenon,* for he had heard that these legendary works were pre-human in origin; never had he seen copies of them before, and upon glancing through them found that he could not read a single one of their outlandish hieroglyphics.

Dositheus felt a brief pang of jealousy. Surely this mysterious Yosef of Aphairema must be one of the most learned sorcerers of this age!

Stifling his chagrin, he continued to rummage within the cabinet until, upon the bottom shelf, he discovered a small roll of new papyrus. Upon unrolling it he found written , in fresh Hebrew characters, a message:

> Yosef of Aphairema to Ormus of Lugdunum, peace. By now, honored and ancient friend, you will have removed from Egypt to Gaul, as we agreed long ago. Soon the Word shall come to me on white wings from the sky, and then I shall journey to Beth-ananiah to aid in the Rite of the Rising and the other things of which I have told you. With me shall go the Mother and the Bride.
>
> I must inform you, brother in arcana, that the Mother, who was herself once the Bride, has not yet regained her rightful mind after all these years, and this may cause problems despite the fact that the stars are nigh unto their long-awaited propitious alignment. This was no doubt to be expected—for, as the prophet Moses has written, no mortal may endure the sight of *Yahweh Zava'ot* and remain unaffected. Though more than thirty years have gone by since she gave birth, Miriam's mind remains addled to this day. Therefore I see to it that she remains near me always, that she may speak to no stranger.
>
> As for her young namesake, whom I briefly mentioned to you in my last missive, know that she had become the Betrothed of the Son, as I had hoped. She is a High One, but has suffered greatly at the hands of the Romans, having

lost all her family, and is of one mind with us that all suffering should be brought to an end. While seeking for sorcerous means to avenge herself she discovered, not far from her native town of Magdala in Galilee, one of those underground chambers wherein sleep Am-ha-arez. Seven of them awoke and possessed her, causing her to do their will, until He who is considered the son, perceiving her plight, drove them from her. She remains devoted to him to this day, and he to her also.

Therefore has she consented to become the Bride, the vessel for the new body of the Son, that He may return to earth after his great sacrifice; and also in order that the Seed might be transmitted down the ages should aught go awry at the sacrifice, which is to take place at this coming full moon. For though we anticipate no accidents, the Powers are not always predictable, as you well know. Therefore, should the Gate fail to open as planned, I shall send you another letter by winged messenger and, later, join you in Gaul myself, together with the Bride.

Yet I trust that naught shall go awry. All is ready and the stars are propitious. Even Caiaphas and old Annas appear ready to unwittingly do their part, thinking that godlike power over all men shall be their lot. For a thousand years and more the rites have been howled through the seasons and the blood of countless sacrifices have reddened the flags before the altar of Yahweh Zava'ot in Jerusalem; the sufferings of countless living beings have been as a sweet savor to His nostrils, bringing Him strength to burst the Gate and accomplish His great return. Soon that Gate shall open, and then all suffering shall be brought to an end and this world made again as it once was ages ago beneath His rule.

I hope you are watching the skies, arcane brother, and continuing to chant the spells. Soon, if we are successful, you shall see those skies roll back as a scroll and behold the advent of Him beneath whose congeries of lights no shadow may turn. Peace, and farewell.

Dositheus blinked, wiped stinging perspiration from his eyes; his forehead was rilling sweat. He knew full well what was implied by the statement that "all suffering shall be brought to an end" and what the advent of Yahweh Zava'ot upon the earth must portend. Suppressing a shudder, he rolled up the copy of the letter and replaced it in the cabinet, then began to examine several of the ancient scrolls of dark lore.

An hour later he left the mansion, unopposed by the sleeping attendant, and walked hurriedly back toward the town. Lines of worry creased his aged face as he glanced up toward the waxing gibbous moon.

"The time grows short," he muttered. "At tomorrow's dawn I must hurry on—to Jerusalem."

Simon paused and stood utterly still, listening. Had he heard the sound of tramping feet ahead of him on the moonlit road?

"Did you hear it?" he asked the mule, who also stood motionless.

The animal tapped the ground once with its right front hoof—the signal they had earlier agreed upon to indicate "yes".

Now he heard it again—the faint sound of many feet upon the roadway, perhaps a dozen men. Perhaps he should hide amid the rocks of the slope—it would not do to meet a Roman patrol, especially one that might have been instructed to watch for a lone Samaritan with a mule. . . .

But, no, the sound was getting fainter. Simon relaxed. No doubt he was overtaking a small party proceeding toward Jerusalem, a group whose holy zeal gave them the audacity to journey by night.

"Come on," Simon urged his four-footed companion. "But go carefully. It still might be a patrol."

A few minutes later they rounded a bend and came within sight of the group. Now Simon could make out three litters being borne by twelve bearers. Two other servants went ahead and behind, bearing lit torches. How foolish—so small a group abroad at this hour of the night! Simon felt an irritation. Jerusalem was still two or three Roman miles southward and he wanted to get there before daylight. That meant that he would have to hurry around this slow-moving party in their plain view. More tongues that might possibly wag—

Suddenly a number of shadows leaped from the rocks on either side of the road and rushed the litter-bearers. Simon heard yells, saw the flash of blades. Bandits—eight or ten of them! The bearers roughly set down the litters and drew blades of their own, but not before two of them were down on the road, butchered by the attackers.

Simon hesitated. Surely it was no duty of his to aid those pious fools. His revenge was too important to jeopardize—

A woman's cry rang out. Simon dashed forward, both blades out, heart leaping—for something in that cry had instantly awakened an uncanny excitement deep within his soul.

"At them soldiers!" he yelled in Latin at the top of his lungs, clashing the blades of his sword and sica together. *"Cut the brigands down! Don't let a man of them live!"*

Behind him he heard the mule clattering along, pounding the road loudly with all four hooves, as if it had immediately caught on to his stratagem and was trying to sound like a whole troop of horses.

The bandits turned and scattered, yelling terror as they fled away in several different directions among the rocks.

"After them—that way!" yelled Simon, motioning to the mule.

The beast clattered off among the rocks on the east side of the road, while Simon took the west side, occasionally yelling orders, clashing his blades or pausing to throw rocks after the fleeing outlaws. He heard the mule neighing and stomping not far away, playing its part to perfection. Uncanny, its intelligence. . . .

After a few minutes of this, Simon paused and listened. The sounds of the fleeing bandits had faded; the mule was still clattering amid the rocks of the eastern slope. Simon grinned. Once again his illusion-making arts had served him well. The scum would no doubt flee their separate ways until dawn.

He turned and made his way slowly down the slope toward the small caravan, his heart pounding with something more than the excitement of danger and the chase. A strange anticipation. . . .

As he drew near he confronted a tall old man in a dark robe standing beside an overturned litter. In the light of several torches, which had just been lit by the swarming, blade-brandishing bearers, Simon could see the old man's striking features—the full white beard, the noble aquiline nose, the keen dark eyes that were fixed on him.

Then one of the torchbearers—a young, short-bearded man—spied Simon also. "Halt, bandit!" he yelled, brandishing a Roman short sword.

"Bandit!" exclaimed Simon. "By Baal, I've just saved your hides!"

"Peace, Zethos," said the old man in the same instant. "This man has indeed saved us by quick wit or—more likely, I think—by the trained art of an illusion-master. My thanks, young magician—" he bowed very slightly to Simon "—for, though my practiced ears detected only two of you, the bandits evidently thought there was a squad of ten legionaries charging them."

"But—*wasn't there?"* said the bewildered Zethos.

The old man smiled. "You have learned only the rudiments of these arts, Zethos. When you have studied them as long as I have, you will sense their presence easily in other young adepts." He face Simon again and said, "Tell me, young Samaritan, who is your master?"

"I—I'd rather not say." Simon felt somewhat disconcerted facing the old man's dark gaze.

"Very well. Who, then, is your companion on horseback who did such a masterful imitation of a mounted company?"

Simon grinned, feeling a bit easier to know that the old man's powers of divination were not complete. "A most helpful and accomplished companion, I can assure you."

"As I noticed. What is your name, young adept?"

"Simon of Gitta."

The old man nodded slightly as if in recognition. "Know, then, that I am Yosef of Aphairema, priest of the Sanhedrin in Jerusalem. Accept my thanks, young Samaritan, and know that the animosity of our races for one another does not diminish my gratitude in the slightest. I sense, young magus, that more than good fortune was involved in your being here just at our moment of need—that some watchful Power has sent you to protect Her most high destiny—" The old man's brow suddenly creased with care as memory interrupted his thoughts; he turned toward the two litters, which rested upright upon the ground behind his own overturned one. "Miriam? Miriam—?"

"We are here."

Simon's whole being thrilled at the sound of that soft, richly feminine voice. And now he saw, advancing from the shadows of several mighty boulders of the eastern hill slope, two figures—one tall and slender and dark-robed, the other white-haired, bent and hobbling; two women, hands clasped, the tall one leading the other.

"Praise be to El Shaddai that you are not harmed!" said old Yosef.

"How could mere bandits thwart His will?" said the tall woman in accents that again thrilled Simon's soul. Then, turning her level gray-green eyes upon him, she said, "Simon of Gitta, I add my thanks to those of my venerable father-in-law. Surely the powers that govern Destiny have indeed sent you to protect us this night."

Simon could only stare at her in awe. "Gods! *Helen* . . . is it truly *you*—"

The woman started, seemed slightly taken aback. Simon gazed into her eyes; they seemed suddenly like deep pools, innocent yet filled with knowledge. He remembered his own Helen, slain by the Romans years ago. How he had mourned her passing, longed for her return! And now, here before him, stood one who seemed her very self. . . .

"No!" Old Yosef gripped the young man's arm. "She is not the one you evidently think she is. O Mistress Asherah!" The stern lines of his face softened, his eyes grew misty with compassion. "I sense, Simon, that you are a True Spirit who once lost your soul-companion to death—"

Simon faced him, eyes glaring. "The Romans slew her—she shall be avenged! Yet, how can it be that . . .?" He turned again toward the tall, calm young woman who faced him with compassion in her level eyes—compassion, and something more. . . .

"We know one another, Simon of Gitta," said the woman. Then, turning to old Yosef, she asked, "How is it, old mentor, that this young man and I should know one another . . . wait! Is it the Phantom of Truth that you have told us of—?"

"It is indeed." Old Yosef nodded gravely, sadly. "The Pain-Lords who decreed the laws of this cosmos ordained that the God and Goddess entrapped in it should remain unaware of one another. Yet this decree cannot be fully upheld, for the higher affinities must by their nature often break through the illusions of materiality."

The old man turned again to Simon and said, "You, young mage, are obviously an incarnation of the Highest One, even as she who stands here is a manifestation of—"

"Ennoia," breathed Simon, gazing at the woman's calm, beautiful face. "Helen. . . ."

Yet even as he said it he noticed subtle differences. The dark tresses framing the oval, delicate-featured face—the sadness of the eyes combined with a touch of humor about the mouth, all suggesting a deep awareness of life in which intelligence and compassion were profoundly combined—all this added up to his remembrance of Helen. Yet the eyes of her before him had a greenish tint in the torchlight, whereas Helen's had been as midnight pools that reflected starlight. More, there was an alienness about this woman, a difference not merely of race but of something having to do with purpose, with Destiny. . . .

At that moment the other woman came forward—a woman slightly stooped and white-haired. Simon guessed her to be in her fifties, for despite her aspect of age, her face was still fairly smooth-skinned. Her eyes, wide and frightened, were pink, proclaiming her an albino.

"My son, is it you?" she cried, rushing up to Simon and clutching the sleeve of his robe. Then, gazing into his eyes, "No, no, it is not. Yet I sense something of him in you. Peace to you, young man! Soon my son shall bring rest to you and all other suffering beings upon the earth!"

So saying, she stepped back, tittering, and buried her face in her hands. Simon gazed at her, astonished.

"She is mad," whispered old Yosef to him in a voice of compassion. "She has borne much. Yet her pain, together with that of all other living things, shall soon be justified. Simon, we go to Bethany. Will you accompany us thither?"

Simon hesitated. He recalled his mission of vengeance.

Maxentius. . . .

"Let him go, my father," said the tall woman. "Do you not sense that he is on a path of destiny? We, the Dark Miriam and the White Miriam, bid him go and do that which he must."

"Aye . . . he must do what he must," said the albino woman in a thin, absent voice.

At that moment there was a clopping of hooves and the mule emerged from the darkness. The litter-bearers drew back from it, afraid of the gleam its eyes threw back from their torches.

Old Yosef nodded. "I see now the nature of your companion, Simon of Gitta. You are a greater mage than I thought."

Simon nodded back, respectfully, then turned and bowed to the tall young woman of the dark locks and level, gray-green eyes.

"Peace to you, Dark Miriam. Almost, in this glamour of moon and torchlight, I thought you to be that Helen whom I once loved and then lost to the powers of darkness. I must go now, as you sensed; yet if you ever again need my aid, inquire for me in Jerusalem. Farewell."

So saying, he grabbed the mule's bridle and, turning toward Jerusalem, strode swiftly away into the night, wondering at his impulsive offer and his strange surge of reawakened feelings.

CHAPTER XIV

Once again Menander and Ilione ascended the ridge west of Aenon in the pre-dawn darkness. The gibbous moon was settling upon the western horizon as they neared the crest of the hill.

"Qua!" croaked the raven perched upon Menander's shoulder, trusting its beak forward. Immediately the pair stopped and stood motionless, hearts pounding.

"Does Carbo sense something?" Ilione whispered. "The invisible presence of the wizard, perhaps . . .?"

"Perhaps." Menander nodded, reflecting that the bird had been in an excited state ever since it had returned late that afternoon, bursting with a half-intelligible account of having contacted a kindred spirit within the body of a mule. "Or, perhaps he's gone mad! Did you ever see a diurnal bird so unable to sleep at night—?"

In that instant there was a low humming, a shimmering of the air—and suddenly the wizard-craft blinked into visibility before them, hovering motionless a foot or two above the ground. Upon it the wizard himself stood upright, blackly silhouetted against the yellow moon.

"Taggart!" cried Menander, running forward. "Why did we not find you here yesterday?" Then, sensing incomprehension on the wizard's part, he repeated his question slowly in Latin.

"There was a . . . watcher," replied the man. "It was in the sky for many hours, but now it is gone. No doubt it was from—" He glanced upward at the stars. "But no matter. Events are moving rapidly and I need your help. Have you studied the scroll of Mattan?"

"Most thoroughly, O Taggart—"

"Just Taggart, please! And did you gain any more clues as to just where the . . . the object called 'Byakhtril' is located?"

"Yes. The exact spot is—"

"Good. Climb aboard quickly, then. We have no time to lose."

Menander obeyed automatically; Ilione hesitated, then followed, even accepting the wizard's outstretched hand to aid her in clambering aboard. She was reassured by the fact that his flesh felt entirely human—but in the next instant felt dismay as the craft began moving rapidly upward and then toward the south.

"I've set a course for Beth-ananiah, just east of Jerusalem," said the wizard to Menander. "You can tell me what you know as we proceed."

"Gods!" Menander shook the raven from his shoulder and yelled, "Fly, Carbo! Tell the Thirty that we go to Bethany, then find Simon and tell him also!"

The bird flapped away into the night. Menander and Ilione faced the wizard, feeling some apprehension.

"Don't worry," said Taggart. "I'll return you here safely as soon as possible. But right now it's crucial that I find the Byakhtril before others get hold of it. What have you learned, Menander?"

"Mattan says that the shrine in which it is hidden lies exactly three stadia east of Beth-ananiah, on the left side of the road that goes down toward Jericho. In his time it was sealed and half buried by a rock-slope at the base of a cliff. He himself discovered the shrine nearly eight centuries ago; but though a great sorcerer himself, he feared to open it."

"He may have been wise." There was a grimness in Taggart's voice. "The Byakhtril was designed to produce vibrations that would open . . . gates . . . under the right conditions. Humans should not fool with it."

The three of them were silent for a time while the land sped by beneath them, shadowy and no longer illumined by the vanishing moon. After some time had passed the faint prophecy of dawn began to lighten the eastern sky, and Menander saw the ramparts of a large city far to the southwest—undoubtedly Jerusalem. Again he marveled at the speed of which the wizard's craft was capable. For a few more minutes they sped south by southeast, gradually descending toward unwooded hills—barren hills, beyond which the faint shimmer of a vast body of water could be seen under the first pale gray of dawn.

"The Sea of Salt," Menander muttered. "And—that village, just to our right, must be Bethany. I was there years ago with Dositheus when he journeyed up from Jericho to Jerusalem. When the light increases, look for the road that leads eastward from it—"

"No need to wait." Taggart donned a strange helmet, pulled it opaque visor down over his eyes, poke at a few of the glowing light-squares on the panel before him, then peered downward over the craft's rim. "I see it." He poked a few more of the squares; the craft veered slightly leftward. "There. We should cross it exactly three stadia east of the village."

Menander watched, fascinated, as the land passed beneath. A short distance east of Bethany it fell away abruptly, the level ground giving way to steep ridges and draws. The young man remembered how rugged that country had seemed to him years ago when he had traveled the cliff-flanked road that wound up through it from Jericho. . . . Then, abruptly, the craft crossed a ravine and settled to rest upon a steep slope strewn with boulders and sparse clumps of grass.

"Now, a concealing ledge—ah, there's one."

The craft skimmed gently around the curve of the slope and case to rest well back within the shadow of an outwardly-projecting cliff.

Taggart scanned the panel of glowing light-squares. "There is no watcher in the sky just now—but no sense taking chances." He laid aside his strange helmet, climbed over the side of the craft and beckoned the two youngsters. "Come—follow me."

They did so, feeling some relief to feel genuine ground beneath their feet, however steep and rocky. Then Menander's relief was somewhat dampened as he recalled how bandit-infested this region was reputed to be at night. . . .

As they began to descend the slope, Menander saw a dim blue sphere of light spring into being around Taggart, surrounding him with an eerie glow, and realized that the wizard had activated the protective forces of his magical belt of woven metal.

In a few minutes they had descended to the roadway and crossed it. Beyond rose a high cliff, a broad talus slope spreading out within the deep shadow of is base.

"I remember this place," said Menander suddenly. "Dositheus told me there was some old legend connected it. He must have been referring to the things mentioned in the writings of the Persian mage Ostanes. And—yet, I recall that he pointed *there*, to that steep draw where the edge of the rock-slope curls around the cliff's base. Gods!—that must be the place of which Mattan writes. . . ."

"We'll see."

As they advanced toward the ravine Taggart slung a light packsack from his shoulder, rummaged in it and drew forth a complex object of blue metal about a foot long and bearing a silvery disc at one end. Before long they reached the foot of the talus-slope and halted. Taggart held out the strange object toward the cliff like a wand; it began to hum, and the metallic disc glowed eerily.

"Yes," said the wizard after several moments, "there's a hollow space just within the base of the cliff, but the entrance to it is blocked by those boulders at the edge of the rock pile. Stand back, you two, and shield your eyes."

Menander and Ilione, seeing Taggart drawing the energy-weapon from its holster, drew back and turned away, covering their faces. Despite this they could see, when a fierce crackling noise ensued, a faint blue light flickering between their fingers. There followed a great crash, a rending and cracking of stone being blown asunder, accompanied by a slight tremor of the ground and a smell like burning rock-dust—then, silence.

Menander turned slowly around—and gasped. The wizard was sheathing his magic weapon, and beyond him, amid swirling smoke-tendrils and the blackened fragments of shattered boulders, a dark hole gaped in the base of the cliff.

Taggart hurried forward, stooped and peered within the low, square hole. Then, taking his small magic light from his belt, he set down his pack and stooped to enter.

"Wait here," he called back; then, dropping to his hands and knees, he began to crawl inside. Immediately he stopped and muttered something in a low voice; Menander took it to be a curse of frustration and noticed that the diameter of the faint blue light surrounding the wizard was slightly larger than the low doorway through which he sought to crawl. Then Taggart fumbled at his metallic belt clasp; the faint light blinked out and the wizard quickly vanished inside the narrow passage.

For many long minutes the young pair stood silently amid the boulders. The wizard did not reappear. Menander felt a growing unease. Despite the growing dawnlight, the ravine in which they stood was full of deep shadow; above, the pale stars gleamed down like watching eyes. Ilione was shivering slightly and Menander guessed that she felt the same uneasiness.

"Do you think the wizard encountered any—danger?" she asked presently.

"I hope not. That would leave us in a fix." Menander stole forward and stooped, peering into the black entrance of the passage. He could not see or hear anything within. He sensed Ilione joining him, stooping to peer within also. Softly he called out, "Taggart—?"

Ilione's feet scuffled on gravel; she emitted a high-pitched, stifled whimper. In the same instant Menander felt a heavy hand clamped over his mouth, another gripping the back of his neck. He struggled, but instantly another pair of hands gripped his arms.

"Get them away from here!" growled a man's voice. "Don't let them make a sound. Two of you—wait for that wizard and bash him when he comes out. Don't give him a chance to use his magic!"

Menander struggled futilely as he was hauled back amid the shadows of boulders. Three men now held his limbs; the fourth held his mouth and lower jaw so tightly that he could not breathe. Near him he sensed several shadow-shapes bearing Ilione's white and struggling form. Then he was thrown to the ground and held there, immovable.

With sick fear he saw that one of his cloaked captors had eyes that gleamed in the dim dawnlight, like those of an owl or lynx. . . .

"Hold still, or you die," hissed the man holding Menander's mouth.

Ilione, similarly restrained, whimpered again. Menander's lungs were bursting. By straining his eyes rightward he could see the clump of men holding the girl down—and, beyond them, the low, square aperture at the cliff's base, flanked on each side by a man who stood, back against the rock, with club upraised. Then, even as he watched, the wizard's head appeared in the opening.

"Menander—Ilione—I found it! Where are you—?"

The clubs descended. Menander heard them crack against the man's back and skull. The wizard sprawled forward and his attackers leaped upon him, striking again. Then Menander's captor released his mouth; the lad gasp, drew in great gulps of air, heard Ilione gasping also.

Immediately more men ran forward and began to strike at the fallen wizard with clubs and knives. Menander and Ilione were hauled to their feet and dragged forward.

"Enough!" yelled the lad's captor. "Bring up a torch. The wizard's done for. Strip him of all his magical devices."

For a few moments Menander heard only the ripping of fabric accompanied by the curses of men—the rough Greek and Latin swearing of Roman soldiers. His fear deepened. What were legionaries doing here in the pre-dawn darkness, dressed like common bandits?

Then the men drew back from the fallen wizard and the youth cringed at sight of the battered, bloody body. The man's very garments had been ripped from him, save for the wide metal-mesh belt and a few strips of black cloth depending from it.

"Get that belt off of him, too!"

"We can't, Scribonius," snarled a stocky, scar-faced Roman. "Not without cutting him in half. It's locked fast."

"You frightened fools! Here, let me try." The centurion knelt and fumbled with the strange glowing buckle. After a moment something moved under his fingers and one end of the metallic belt released and fell away. Triumphantly the Roman stood up and snapped it into place about his own waist. "Ha! Ha! The sorcerer's shield—I own it now. You—" He turned to the two black-cloaked guardsmen. "Show me how it works."

The guards remained silent, their yellow eyes unblinking.

"No matter, I'll find out later," growled Scribonius. "You men—did you find what we're after?"

One of the lynx-eyed soldiers strode forward a pace from the knot of men and silently held up a small metallic object. Menander could not see it clearly, but shuddered when a moment later the man announced in low intonations, *"The Byakhtril."*

"Good. Give it to me. And you—Fulvius—bind these two apprentices of the wizard. They'll bring a good price on the slave-block, I'm sure."

While the soldiers bound Menander's arms tightly behind his back he got his first clear look at their commander. The indignant question that was on his lips died at sight of the sadistic, clean-shaven, cold-eyed face. Those eyes glittered as they swept over him and Ilione; the thin-lipped mouth parted in a lopsided grin.

"Yes, a good price," he chuckled. "Maybe I'll keep them awhile for myself. . . ." The cold hardness abruptly returned to his face. "But, enough! Gather up the damned wizard's belongings—and let's get away from this road before dawn breaks."

"Mistress, I hear footsteps approaching," said Lotis tensely.

Elissa stopped pacing the marble-tiled floor of the opulent chamber and faced the locked, gilded door of polished cedar. The richness of her surroundings had done nothing to allay her fear; it was but a silk-draped prison provided by captors with unknown intentions.

A key rattled in the lock, the door opened and four men entered. She recognized three of them: the sinister priest Annas, lean and aged, bent but spry, his dark eyes unblinking like those of a spider upon its prey; Jahath the tax gatherer, ratlike, grizzled and gloating, who with his lackeys had broken into her house, bound her and Lotis and forced them to swallow a drugged potion; and, most terrifying of all, the Roman tribune Maxentius, his shaven face hard and haughty as that of an offended Olympian god. The fourth man, a graybeard with anxious eyes, wore priestly Judean robes similar to those of old Annas. His hand, still holding the key that had evidently unlocked the door, trembled slightly.

"Obviously you're resourceful, Elissa," said Maxentius. "Now that you've recovered from the drug Jahath was obliged to administer in order to counteract your perverse and rebellious nature, you can tell me who helped you escape from my house. Obviously you could not have slain the watchers I set to guard you—"

"Your house!" Elissa felt rage welling up, ousting her fear. "You gained it by illegal means, by a foul deed of cruelty and treachery. Don't deny it—I know all!"

"Mistress, don't!" hissed Lotis, terror in her dark eyes as she clutched at Elissa's sleeve.

Maxentius strode forward, fists clenched, his face lowering like a thunder cloud. "Just what do you know, woman? And from whom did you learn it?"

"Peace, Tribune," said old Annas, laying a claw-like hand upon Maxentius' forearm. "Do not let the woman bait you into pointless games of spite. We must learn a most important thing from her."

The Roman relaxed slightly. "Indeed? *What* thing, then?"

Annas fixed his spider-like eyes more intently on Elissa and asked, "Tell me, woman, of this 'living water' which the rabbi Yeshua, who claims to be the Mashiah, offered to you when you met him by the well in Sychar."

Elissa cringed involuntarily before the intensity of the priest's dark eyes, the pupils of which now gleamed an eerie yellow in the lamplight. "I—I don't know what he meant by it—"

"But he did use the phrase," Annas persisted. "Tell me, woman: *Did he offer you the living water?"*

Elissa shrank back still farther, appalled at the unnatural glare in the eyes of the ancient priest. Surely he was mad, perhaps even demon-possessed! "I—I do not know," she stammered. "He said that all who would drink of this water would know the spring of eternal life . . . or something of that sort. He looked into my heart and told me my own inmost thoughts, and in that moment I believed him to be the Mashiah—"

"He offered her the *Water!"* snarled Annas. "Maxentius, you did well to tell me of this tale of hers. She must not leave here, for if allowed to go abroad she could jeopardize the outcome of the Rite."

"I'm not sure what you mean," said the Roman, "but she'll stay here with you and Caiaphas if you wish it—much as I'd like to take her back just to teach her what it means to flout my will!"

"Aye, and there's another thing—she did not escape without aid. Our—messengers—" The old priest nodded toward the door, beyond which Elissa could see no one. "—have told us that the one who aided her was extremely adept in skills of stealth and combat. I suspect that he may have been an agent of this Yeshua Mashiah, who no doubt has plans for her. No, she must be kept here and guarded closely until the Rite has been performed. And now, I shall question her."

"Tell me your questions," said Maxentius, "and let me be her interrogator. I know a few tricks—"

"No." The priest waved his bony hand. "None of your crude Roman methods. I shall bend her mind to my will." He drew a small vial of blue glass from beneath his robe. "Do but hold her motionless, Tribune Maxentius—so. Good. Now you, Jahath—take this vial and force its contents between her lips."

"No!" Elissa struggled, but was helpless in the Roman's powerful grip. She felt her head being forced back, saw the leering Jahath advancing with the vial. *"No!"*

"Let her go!" shrieked Lotis tearfully, dashing forward and striking the tall Roman's muscular frame with her small fists. "Please—*don't!"*

Jahath grabbed the girl by the hair, yanked her back from the tribune and flung her savagely to the floor. Again he advanced with the vial. Elissa clenched her teeth, then felt Maxentius' strong fingers working at the base of her jaw, forcing her mouth open—

Suddenly there were hurried footsteps in the corridor outside. An instant later a Roman centurion burst into the room and saluted. "Commander, I have news—"

"Hades!" Maxentius relaxed his grip slightly. "Can't it wait?"

"It's urgent, Commander. I've ridden most of the night. There is death in your house in Sebaste."

"I know that, Cornelius." The tribune released Elissa and scowled darkly at his messenger. "The two I set to guard this woman were slain."

The centurion seemed taken aback. "How did you—?"

Maxentius laughed, glanced at old Annas. "There are swifter messengers than you. And now, if you have no more news—

"But I do. There was writing in blood upon the wall of your bedroom, Commander, over the head of your bed."

The tribune scowled more darkly still. "What writing?"

"I made a copy." The centurion took a small piece of parchment from his belt and unfolded it. "It reads: '*Bar abbas—*'"

"No, no, Cornelius, in Greek. You know I don't speak that damned Aramaic."

"Very well, sir. It reads: '*The Son of the father has returned!*.'"

Maxentius paled. *Bar abbas—the son of the father. . . .*

"Aiii!" shrieked Jahath, sudden terror in his dark eyes. "It is even as the demon-horse told us—"

"Shut up! Is there more, Cornelius?"

"No, Commander, but there was an object on your pillow." The soldier took a bundle from under his left arm, unwrapped it and held it up. "This."

Elissa gasped. The thing that lay nestled in its wrappings was a bloodstained human head with gaping mouth and idiotically upturned eyes.

"By Cerberus, that's *Akrab!"* snarled Maxentius. "I sent him to watch over the villa at Gitta—"

"Simon has returned! wailed Jahath. "Baal save us! He's come back to *kill us all—!"*

Maxentius' fist lashed out and smashed into the tax gatherer's face, sending him sprawling to the floor. *"Shut up,* you fool!"

"Silence, all of you!" hissed Annas. "It seems that you have a formidable enemy on your track, Tribune. If he is indeed an agent of this Yeshua bar Yosef, we must take all precautions as swiftly as possible. I want you and Caiaphas to return immediately to the Tower of Set and take forth the thing that lies hidden beneath it. Bear it, concealed in a litter and under heavy guard, to the Antonian Fortress; there, Caiaphas shall carry it via the secret tunnel into the Temple and conceal it with that which is already within the Holy of Holies. Then, this evening, you and he shall return to the tower and await my further instructions."

"Watch your tone of voice," growled Maxentius. "You're my advisor, not my commander, and don't forget it."

"Then follow my advice, and don't let your Roman pride make a fool of you. Take all the troops—the Eidolon of Set must be well guarded. Jahath and I will wait here in my villa for the return of Scribonius and his patrol. Upon their arrival, I'll send them and Jahath on to you at the tower."

Maxentius almost felt an impulse to salute in acknowledgment, so confident and imperious was the ancient priest's manner. Suppressing his irritation, he nodded at the anxious-eyed Caiaphas. "Come on, then, graybeard. You too, Cornelius. Round up the men—quickly."

When the three had left the room, Annas fixed his hypnotic eyes upon the rat-faced tax gatherer, who was rising shakily from the floor.

"Good," he muttered calmly. "Now, Jahath, you can tell me all you know about this man Simon, whose name so terrifies you. And after that, these women shall tell us all they know of him as well."

Dawn was breaking, filling the narrow gorge with gray light. Menander, sitting upon the ground with his back to the rock cliff, struggled futilely against his bonds. Though trained in elementary escape-artistry by Daramos, the cords about his wrists, upper arms and shoulders were beyond his ability to slip; in addition, his own cloak was wrapped like a sack about his upper torso and secured by still more cords.

He glanced at Ilione who sat beside him, similarly bound. She had long since ceased to struggle; her eyes were closed, her brows knit in fear, her breath coming in short, trembling gasps from between parted lips. Gods—if only he could help her—help himself! If only he had studied escape-artistry more assiduously. . . .

He glanced at the Romans who sat in a group a short distance away, munching silently on their rations. In place of ragged bandits' cloaks they now wore the bronze and leather of imperial legionaries. *Why*, he wondered again, *why* had they hidden their soldiers' garb here and ventured upon the Jericho road as common thieves?

They had slain the wizard called Taggart, had stolen his possessions and that small metal object—the Byakhtril—, which he had brought forth from the centuries-buried shrine in the cliffside. Then they had hurriedly re -crossed the Jericho road, as if fearful of being sighted by early travelers, and has hastened southwestward into the arid draws and ridge-spurs, dragging him and Ilione along with them. After an hour or so they had entered this narrow cleft and paused for rest, reclaiming their soldiers' garb from the crevices where they had hidden it. Evidently they were on a mission of secrecy.

Now they sat and ate, occasionally cracking jokes, save for the two dark -cloaked Temple guards who stood silently nearby, faces expressionless and eyes eerily lambent in the shadows.

Menander struggled again. The cords about his wrists seemed slightly looser, but not encouragingly so. The men who had bound him had taken more care than the average slave procurer would have. . . .

Then the chief of the Romans—the man called Scribonius—glanced in his direction and grinned. "Still fighting it, eh, boy? Go ahead. Fulvius here has bound more slaves than you've lived days. And even if you should get loose, I'll have the pleasure of bashing you back into your place." He chuckled and turned back to his companions. "They'll bring a good price, those two."

"I hope so," growled a scar-faced soldier. "But what about these possessions of the wizard? No jewels, but lots of intricate metalwork. I can't guess the purpose or worth of any of these things. And what about *this*—the thing we saw him use to blast open the rock? Evidently it's a sorcerous wand of some kind. How do you suppose he made it work? There must be some kind of spell—"

Menander tensed. The man was fumbling with the dark metallic object while pointing its stubby cylindrical end randomly about him. "Get down, Ilione!" he hissed; then, when the girl did not respond, he lurched sidewise against her, sending them both sprawling down on the rough gravelly surface of the draw.

"Be careful, Phocus—" Then, hearing the clatter of pebbles, Scribonius turned and rose to his feet. "Hey, those two are trying to get away. Finish up your breakfast, boys, while I slap them about a bit. Then, we'll be on our way."

"No!" cried Menander, struggling to rise. "You don't understand—"

The Roman drew a short, many-stranded whip from his belt and his eyes glared with a hard, sadistic humor. "A few strokes of this across your fine young calves—"

Suddenly an intense blue-white glare flashed briefly, banishing for an instant the shadows of the ravine. A sizzling crackle sounded, followed by the shrill cries of men in mortal agony. Then the dimness of the narrow draw returned.

Scribonius spun about, snarling. "Gods of Hades!" he hissed.

The scar-faced Roman lay writhing on the ground, his breastplate sundered and steaming, its edges red and glowing—and between those edges bubbled smoking flesh, rilling blackly before crisping upon the hot metal. Behind the dying legionary lay the two Temple guardsmen, also writhing in their death throes, armor and flesh smoking. Near the stricken trio lay the oddly-shaped wand of the wizard, a thin wisp of smoke or steam ascending from the tip of its elongated cylindrical portion.

A Roman strode forward, tentatively extended his hand toward the wand. . . .

"No!" cried out another legionary. "There is a death-demon in it!"

Even as he spoke the rest of the men also began to cry out, to curse and draw back. Scribonius hissed in awe as he saw that which had unnerved them—several, small, pulsing greenish blobs emerging from each of the twitching bodies of the Temple guards, inching their way across the gravel like crippled slugs.

"Back—get away!" shouted Scribonius to his men. "Leave those demon-slain corpses where they lie—and the wizard's lightning-wand with them. Hurry—up the draw! We'll deliver to Annas what he wanted—but, by Hades, he'll pay us twice what he offered!"

"Ho, beggar, wake up," growled Simon, nudging the huddled pile of rags with his toe. "There's money in it for you."

The sleeping vagrant, hitherto unresponsive, stirred and raised his head, staring up attentively.

"Did a Roman troop pass this way in the night?" demanded Simon.

"Aye, not long before dawn." The man sat up, then rose stiffly. "And I wondered at the time: 'Why do Roman soldiers pass through Bethany in the dark?'"

"How many were there?"

"At least a dozen, perhaps a score. It was dark—"

"And was there a commander of rank leading them?"

"Yes . . . I think so. Did you say—money . . .?"

Simon flung down two bright, new-minted denarii, then remounted the mule and rode eastward from the still-sleeping village, along the road that led toward Jericho. Weariness had finally convinced him to trust the animal, and he had found his trust justified. Now dawn was just graying the eastern skies, but the sun had not yet risen.

He felt a certain uneasiness, an intuition that he might be on a false trail. He had asked the same questions earlier of pilgrims encamped near Jerusalem's northern gates. Most, despising him as a heathen Samaritan, had refused to answer, but the few who had had been emphatic that a fairly large troop of Romans had passed the night before without entering the city, proceeding eastward on the road toward Bethany. One beggar, recalling a shouted exchange between the troop's commander and the guards on the city's walls, had even remembered the name "Maxentius".

But there had been several side roads between there and Bethany, especially the roads to Anathoth, the Kidron Valley and the Mount of Olives. Moreover, the troop just described to Simon by the beggar at Bethany's eastern gate sounded to him to be smaller than the one he had been pursuing. Still, how could it not be the same one . . .?

Abruptly Simon was startled to see several men come into view—not bandits, apparently, for they were approaching openly in file on the road. The first few were mounted and wore dark cloaks and armor; those following were bearded and bore long staves—Galilean pilgrims, judging by their garb. In their midst several more black-cloaked figures bore a large litter whose drawn curtains displayed the emblem of the Jerusalem Temple.

"Make way!" cried the foremost guardsman. "Make way for Izhar, priest of the Temple of the Holy One!"

Simon dismounted, stood aside and watched as the procession passed, wondering why a Jerusalem priest would be surrounded by Galileans. Several of the men scowled darkly at him—or at his Samaritan garb—as they passed. Then, for an instant, he glimpsed a dark-bearded face glaring in his direction from between the litter's curtains. Immediately the face was withdrawn from view, but not before Simon felt a shock of recognition.

Izhar of Chorazin!

Simon recalled meeting with the sinister rabbi years ago at a conclave of the Thirty in company with Dositheus. Why was the man impersonating a priest? Or, was he *truly* a priest, acting as rabbi at the Black Synagogue most of the year, save for high feast-days? And if so, why . . .?

The procession passed, and Simon saw a similar one no great distance behind. He stood where he was and watched it approach.

"Make way!" shouted the leading guard unnecessarily. "Make way for the priest's Levite!"

Again Simon watched as a line of staff-bearing Galileans passed, bearing a litter in their midst. Only such a formidable force as these two companies could have braved by night the bandit-infested miles between here and Jericho, he realized—but *why* had they? Did Izhar wish to avoid the public eye as much as possible . . .?

The litter bore a Levitical emblem indicating a priest's high attendant. Again Simon saw the drawn curtains part—and felt an even greater shock than before.

For the figure within was squat, shapeless, and wore a dark cowled cloak not at all like a Levite's typically white garb, and within the hollow of that cowl was naught but a deep, yawning blackness.

CHAPTER XV

The mule shied away from the roadside, and instinctively Simon backed away a pace also. Already the litter curtain had whipped back into place, concealing the cowled figure within. Simon shuddered. The hand he had glimpsed on that curtain had seemed to be mittened with a dark, slick substance, like the skin of a squid-palp.

In less than a minute the procession of Galileans and swart-robed guards had passed by, bearing the litter of the strange Levite with them. In another few minutes they had vanished up the road to Bethany, concealed by the foot of a steep ridge-slope.

"If that was a Levite," muttered Simon, "then I'm a Judean!"

The mule snorted, then scratched in the dirt. Simon looked down and read the word: MESSENGER.

"To whom? Izhar? Well, I guess that *is* the function of a Levite to his priest—"

Snorting again, the mule shook its head, then scratched again: FACULA.

This time it was Simon who shook his head. The word made no sense. 'Facula' was the red Eye of the Bull—the brightest star of the Hyades. . . . But then Simon remembered the strange star-emblem he had taken from the slain guardsman in the forest, and shivered slightly.

"Come on, Balaam," he said, remounting the mule. "We're wasting time."

The light of the dawn was brightening beyond the far hills. In the growing daylight Simon intently examined the surface of the road as he proceeded. There were a great many prints in the dust, probably of pilgrims and their mounts, but nowhere did he see any indication that a Roman troop might have passed this way in the night. The way grew steeper, with rugged cliffs and ridge-slopes looming on either side.

"Damn the luck!" Simon muttered. "I should have asked one of those Galileans if they'd seen—"

He stopped, the mule having abruptly come to a halt. At the base of a rocky talus slope, several yards back from the road, lay the body of a man. Not an unprecedented sight along this road where robbers often preyed upon ill-protected travelers—and yet, Simon thought, there was something unusual about this victim.

Dismounting, he hurried over to the man, saw that he was naked save for a few tatters of black cloth about his loins. There was something familiar about that fabric. . . . Yes, of course—the black-clad man in the forest!

Simon knelt beside the man and examined his face. The features, though bruised and bloodied as from many blows, were recognizable.

"Taggart!" he muttered incredulously. "The wizard—"

The man stirred slightly and his eyelids fluttered, half opening; his eyes were bloodshot, unfocused.

"Menander?" he gasped. "Is that you? Where's . . . Ilione . . .?"

"What are you saying, man?" hissed Simon. "Were they with you? Where are they now? *Tell me!*"

The man's head lolled to one side as he again lapsed into complete unconsciousness. Simon cursed softly. He repeated Taggart's name, but there was no response. Blood oozed from several knife-wounds in the man's pale flesh. The wizard was obviously in a bad way, probably dying—yet, if Menander and Ilione had been taken captive, the man must be nursed back to consciousness; he was their only hope.

The mule trotted up, lowered his head and nuzzled the body of the unconscious man.

"Hold still, Balaam," said Simon. "We've got to get him to shelter, then find a physician." Quickly he tore a couple of strips of linen from the hem of his tunic, gave them a soaking from his wineskin and used them to bind up two of the man's deeper stab wounds. Then he gently lifted the wizard and placed him face-down over the mule's back, wincing to see the wounds begin to bleed more profusely. The animal held very still as Simon hurriedly tied the stricken man into position. "Good," said the Samaritan finally. "Now, let's get him back to Bethany and find an inn—"

A sound distracted him—the sound of sandaled feet scuffling pebbles and gravel. Simon turned and saw three men hurrying up the road from the direction of Jericho. In the same instant they saw him also. Abruptly they stopped and looked over at him from the edge of the road. Two of them, Simon saw, were typical staff-bearing Galilean louts; the third—

"Ho, Samaritan, what are you doing in this spot? What has happened here?"

The speaker was a tall, lean man wearing a gray robe and a black skull cap—a Judean pilgrim, Simon guessed. His ragged hair and short, scraggly beard had a russet tinge in the dawnlight. Though the man's tone was not exactly unfriendly, Simon sensed a tense edge in this voice, saw a gleam of strange excitement in his large dark eyes.

"This man has been injured by bandits. Do you know of a physician in—?"

"Look, Judah!" interrupted one of the Galileans, pointing. "Is that not a hole in the cliffside?"

"Yaiii!" shrieked the russet-haired man. "It is!" He ran a few paces off the road, peered briefly into the black aperture, then wheeled and dashed back to his companions, his eyes glaring madly.

"Surely demons have preceded us there," muttered the other Galilean.

"Samaritan, what do you know of *that?*" demanded the man called Judah, pointing to the hole in the cliff.

"Nothing, by Baal!" retorted Simon. "Nor do I care about it. This injured man needs help—"

The Judean snorted in impatience, turned to his companions and gestured violently. "Come—we must tell the Master. Hurry!"

In another moment they had vanished back down the road, running hard. Simon listened to their footfalls dying rapidly away, then shook his head.

"Mad as moonstruck jackals, by the gods!" he muttered.

He led the mule to the roadway and saw that a distant band of Galileans was approaching from the direction of Jericho. This one was larger than the two he had met earlier, numbering at least ninety or a hundred people, all on foot, and in their midst was a strikingly tall man robed all in white. The three men he had just met were hurrying down the road toward them.

Simon started up the road at a fast pace, thankful that the approaching crowd had not arrived in time to delay him. The mule followed him closely, not needing to be led by the rope that hung slack between its neck and Simon's hand.

In less than half an hour they had emerged from the gullied terrain and were approaching the village of Bethany. As they drew near it, Simon saw small groups of people milling about in the early light of dawn—beggars, shopkeepers, laborers heading for the fields, encamped pilgrims preparing to continue on to Jerusalem. A few stared curiously at the injured man slung over the mule, or scowled suspiciously at Simon's Samaritan garments.

A short distance into the town he arrived at a large inn whose front wall was flush with the roadside. Carefully he untied the unconscious man from the mule and lifted him down. To his surprise, the man's wounds seemed to have completely stopped bleeding; the only blood he saw was caked and dried. He hoped that this did not mean a massive blood loss already . . . but, no, for the man was not dead; he stilled breathed.

A Judean woman emerged from the inn, followed by two young male attendants; though she was young, her figure was dumpy and her face rather sour.

"Why do you pause here, Samaritan?" she demanded. "Move on."

"I need a room for—"

"We don't rent to Samaritans," snapped the woman.

"Baal!" Simon growled. "I don't need your damned room, but this man does. He needs a physician, too. Robbers attacked him on the Jericho road, left him for dead—"

"Is he a Samaritan?"

"I don't know what he is!" yelled Simon. "Gods, woman, are you going to let him die? Who do you think you—?"

"I am Martha, mistress of this inn." Righteous indignation hardened the dumpy woman's face. "We allow no impious Samaritans here, especially during this holy season—"

"Wait, sister," said a rich feminine voice from the doorway. "Let the man enter, and give him his room. He has well earned it."

The sour-faced woman whirled and confronted the tall, graceful figure that now stood on the inn's stoop. "Miriam! What *can* you mean by that? We cannot accommodate the unclean here, especially during the sacred Passover time."

The tall woman smiled with a touch of sadness. "We must, sister. Is it not written: 'You shall not wrong or oppress a stranger, for you were strangers in the land of Egypt'? Besides, Martha, this is the man I told you of—the one who saved old Yosef and me from bandits only a few hours ago."

Simon stared at her, astonished. It was indeed the woman he had met on the midnight road, and her delicate features seemed even more beautiful in the early morning light than they had under the mystic night and the glow of torches; her eyes, which had gleamed like dark emeralds under that flickering torchlight, had now softened to melded tones of gray and jade, though the same mysterious wisdom or humor still underlay their hint of sadness. In this fuller illumination Simon could see that she bore less resemblance to his lost Helen than he had at first thought, though he still felt the same mystical attraction toward her.

"Oh, very well, Miriam," said the inn mistress crossly, "—though why I always let you have your way I'll never know. Leave the man here, Samaritan—you may bear him up this outside stairway to the farthest room in the back. Then go fetch a physician if you will. But do not think to stay overnight yourself. I'll have no Samaritans sleeping under my roof!"

Suppressing his irritation, Simon quickly carried the unconscious man up the stairs and around the high balcony to the back. The door of the last room was ajar; entering, Simon saw that it was a tiny place whose only furnishings were a footstool and a low cot. Gently he laid the man on the latter, then examined him closely. To his surprise he saw that the wizard had indeed stopped bleeding entirely; moreover, his breathing was more regular and less feeble than before, and . . . was it his imagination, or had the shade of the man's multiple bruises actually lightened a bit? Simon shivered slightly, remembering tales he had heard concerning the unnatural vitality of wizards.

"Taggart," he muttered, "can you hear me?"

The man did not move or open his eyes. His soft breathing continued, regular but shallow.

Simon stood up, left the room and returned the way he had come. At the foot of the stair the mistress of the inn confronted him, her black eyes still hard and suspicious. The other woman was no longer there.

"I'm going for a physician," said Simon.

"Wait!" snapped the woman. "That room will cost you a denarius for each day."

Simon did not argue about the exorbitant charge but immediately opened his pouch and counted out coins into the woman's palm. "There. One denarius. Now—"

"No. You must give me *two*—one for each day."

Simon clenched his teeth for an instant to hold his temper in check. "What in Baal's name are you talking about? I've hardly been here two minutes!"

The woman pointed to the east, where the rim of the sun was just beginning to shine between the summits of the far hills. "The rules of this inn are that each guest-day begins at sunrise. When you arrived the sun was not yet in view. That means you owe me for *two* days."

For an instant Simon considered how easily one quick, sharp blow of his fist would obliterate the woman's spiteful face. Instead, he rummaged in his pouch and counted out a second denarius.

"There. Take care of the man. And if that costs any more money, don't worry, I'll pay you when I come back."

As he turned to leave, a lad of about fourteen rushed up to them and gestured excitedly. The dust of the road muted the colors of his Galilean garments.

"Mistress Martha," he gasped excitedly, "come quickly! The Teacher approaches on the Jericho road—he sent me ahead to inform you—"

"The Teacher!" cried the woman, and Simon was amazed to see her stupid, vindictive face instantly transformed to an expression of rapt delight, of almost mystical happiness. He sensed that she had in that moment forgotten not only her bitter feelings toward him, but his very presence.

"He asked that you and Mistress Miriam come out and meet him upon the eastern road—"

"Oh, I shall, I shall!" exclaimed the dumpy woman, dancing almost like a child in her excitement. "How long we have waited! *Joel—Reuben,*" she called in through the doorway, "come out and accompany me. The Teacher approaches upon the road—he comes at last to perform the Rite of the Rising!"

The two young servants hurried out of the house. Without more ado they and their mistress, led by the young Galilean, set out rapidly eastward, leaving Simon standing before the open door of the inn.

Simon scratched his head. Why had not the woman informed her sister as requested, rather than setting out by herself in such haste? Had he detected a brief spark of resentment in her eyes when the lad had mentioned "Mistress Miriam"? Surely the women were not really sisters in literal fact, for they could hardly be more unlike! He peered within the door and found himself disappointed when he saw no sign of the stately, beautiful woman. No doubt she had retired to rest after her long and stressful journey.

"Well, come on, Balaam," he said, turning to the mule, who was cropping a tuft of grass near the stoop. "I've got to find a physician as soon as possible."

The mule continued to munch grass, unheeding.

"Come on!" Simon tugged at the beast's rope. "Didn't you hear me?"

Balaam looked up at him with mulish, uncomprehending eyes.

"What's wrong with you? Hurry up! Unless we find a physician for the wizard, he may not live long enough to tell us what happened to Menander and Ilione."

After repeated tuggings the animal followed, but at its own leisurely pace, and Simon realized that something had changed. The mule, for whatever obscure reason, was once again merely—a mule.

Menander felt the bonds about his wrists slacken. He was free. His efforts, though prolonged and exacting, were successful; the techniques of escape artistry, taught to him by Daramos the Mage, had finally borne fruit.

But he still had to be very careful. His Roman captors sat nearby in a rough circle, facing one another, chewing on fruits and strips of dried meat while exchanging ribald jokes. Slowly Menander eased his hands out from beneath his robe and loosened the bonds that pinioned his arms to his side. In another moment they fell slack also.

Ilione lay between him and the Romans. For a moment he considered freeing her also, but decided against it. She appeared to be in a stupor—probably withdrawn from the situation in a pall of fear. Untrained as she was in escape artistry, she would be of no help. Reluctantly Menander decided that he must go from this place alone, determining to return and aid the girl later in circumstances more to his advantage.

Silently as a lizard he slid from his bonds and crawled into a narrow crevice in the rock. The cleft ended abruptly; near-vertical walls rose on either side of him. Menander slowly drew a few deep breaths and let them out slowly, stilling his mind; then, continuing to imagine himself a lizard, he began to crawl upward upon one of the rock faces, taking advantage of every minute crevice and projection, never permitting himself to look down. . . .

A few minutes later—though it seemed more like an hour—he lay flat upon a narrow ledge, gasping for breath, gathering his strength for a further ascent. Glancing upward, he saw that the incline was far less steep—

"Hades!" yelled a legionary in the gorge below. "The brat has escaped. He can't be far—"

"Then find him!" roared a voice Menander recognized as that of the brutal Scribonius. "And do it quickly. Fulvius, how did he slip your bonds? You told me you were once a slave procurer, but by the gods!—you're nothing but an incompetent."

"I'm not!" growled a voice in protest. "By Pollux, the kid must have been a wizard to have escaped those cords!"

"Shut up. Just see to it that this girl doesn't escape as well. Get her on her feet, and don't take your eyes off her till we get to the villa of Annas. And you, Labanus—take three men and hurry back down the gully as fast as you can. Maybe you can recapture that slippery youth if he isn't already halfway to Jericho."

Menander hugged the ledge, not daring to peer over. He heard men running off down the ravine, their footfalls and the clanking of their armor fading swiftly away. Below him he heard many feet scuffling as the rest of the soldiers continued up the draw. He heard Ilione whimper slightly and gritted his teeth.

Don't let them hurt her, he thought—a prayer to no god in particular.

Then, after all the sounds had faded away, he resumed his laborious climb up the steep slope, determined to follow Ilione's captors. They would not expect that, and his mentor Daramos had trained him well in the art of concealment. And later he would find an opportunity to free Ilione. Yes, he would follow these furtive Romans even to the "villa of Annas", whatever or wherever that might be.

Annas stood on the portico of his mansion and silently watched the large band of Galileans that had gathered in the courtyard. In their midst they bore two heavily curtained litters, from the foremost of which a robed, priestly figure was emerging.

"Greeting, Izhar of Chorazin. You travel swiftly."

"Greeting, O Annas." The dark-robed priest bowed slightly. "I bring important news. But first, my . . . Levite . . . should have the special accommodations that he needs."

"Of course. Tell your Galileans that their job is now finished and that they may go complete their holy pilgrimage to Jerusalem. In addition, for their loyalty and continued silence, I shall pay them the same amount they have already received from you. My steward shall dispense the silver to them outside the courtyard gate."

When the Galileans had all departed back out the northern gate, Izhar nodded to his black-cloaked guards, who immediately lifted up the Levite's palanquin by its carrying-poles. "We must hurry," he said to Annas. "The sun is already up; soon it will rise above the wall and the trees."

The old priest descended from the portico. "Come, then—follow me."

He led them around the east side of the mansion, in the shadow of the inclosing garden wall, along an obscure path that wound among the boles of leafy oaks and terebinths. Behind the house and a short distance to the south of it, in a small clearing, stood a low flat-roofed hut of dark stone. It was windowless and had no entrance save for a single arched door of stout oak.

"This will be to your attendant's liking, I'm sure," said Annas, unlocking the door with a large iron key. "Now, bring the litter up and place it against the doorway—so. Good."

They watched in silence as the litter's curtains rippled. Evidently its occupant was sliding out the other side, into the blackness of the stone structure. Then the oaken door slowly swung shut and latched.

"Good," said Annas again, rubbing his bony hands together. "Now, Izhar, leave one of your guardsmen to see that no one approaches this place. And tell me of your news."

"Dositheus has returned," said Izhar as they walked to the house. "He is reorganizing the Thirty under his own leadership."

"Ah. I suspected something of the sort, for recently I learned that his pupil, Simon of Gitta, has returned to Samaria also. Tell me, do you think that Dositheus will work for the rabbi Yeshua as did his predecessor Johannen the Baptizer?"

"I think not. Dositheus has not the knowledge, for he has been gone from this land for several years. Moreover, he is the sort who works for himself only."

"Good. A house divided shall not stand—as that rabbi Yeshua himself once said when he tried to deny that he dealt with demons. But continue, Izhar."

"Dositheus sought the Chalice of Life in the ruins of Hali, but of course failed to find it. Nevertheless, his action convinced me that he knew enough to be a possible danger to us. I managed to capture him and two of his young assistants, plus the rabbi Tolmai of Capharnaum, and was about to cause them to be—inhabited—that they might be compelled to reveal all they knew. But Dositheus and his apprentices were rescued, though Tolmai was not and now has seen the Phantom of Truth, even as have we—"

"Dositheus was *rescued?"*

"Aye—by an unknown wizard of great power, a man all clad in black and bearing weapons such as only the Outside Ones possess."

"Interesting." Annas scowled in thought. "Didn't your most recent winged messenger tell me that just such a wizard—the same one, perhaps?

—evidently stole the Byakhtron from its supposedly impregnable hiding place in your synagogue?"

"Indeed he did!" As they entered the house Izhar's dark eyes gleamed yellowly for an instant in the light of a lamp. "And he also stole the synagogue's copy of Mattan's *El-Halal*."

Annas smiled slightly. "You made up for that very well, Izhar, for your . . . inner companion . . . recovered from your memory more than we needed of the scroll. Because of the parchments you sent ahead on swift wings, the Byakhtril will soon be in our hands. Things are going well. Even the Ark has been recovered from its cave on Mount Nebo and restored to its place in the Temple; the secret of its location was sold to us by a close disciple of the rabbi Yeshua, one Judah of Kerioth, who is now our paid spy."

"Judah of Kerioth!" exclaimed Izhar, his beard bristling. "Why, it was he who distracted my guardsmen while the black wizard stole the Chalice and the scroll! I'm sure it was no coincidence. And you and I, Annas, can guess by what sort of . . . magic . . . those items were detected within the vault of the Black Synagogue and plucked forth without piercing the walls!"

"But Judah has told Caiaphas that the Teacher has no copy of Mattan's scroll, nor the Chalice—"

"I'm sure he lies. Evidently this Judah is a tricky and dangerous double-dealer. I would advise you not to use him again until you are sure of his motives. I've heard that he is a learned man, perhaps even a sorcerer himself. It might be safest merely to slay him outright."

Again Annas scowled in thought. "Interesting, this suspicion of yours. Yes, Judah has been extremely helpful to us so far. What could be his motive? And who else do you think might be working for this subtle and ambitious rabbi?"

"Do you have any suspects of your own in mind, Annas?"

"Aye. Nicodemus for one, I'm sure, and old Yosef bar Heli for another. In fact, I would not be surprised if old Yosef proved to have played a great part in the coming of this . . . Teacher. I have learned some things about his past. Yosef will be coming down from Aphairema soon to participate with us in the Passover, and then I expect to see him and Nicodemus make their move."

"That is not good," said Izhar. "The Sanhedrin should be united if its bid for dominion is to be certain of success. Should two of our very members be working against us—"

At that moment a tramping of many feet sounded from the back of the garden outside. Annas and Izhar went back through the door and saw a band of Roman legionaries emerging from the trees. There were about a dozen of them, and in their midst stumbled a young blond woman bound with cords, fear in her eyes.

"Scribonius!" snapped old Annas as the troop approached. "Were you successful? Did you bring back the Byakhtril?"

"I did." The hard-faced centurion drew a small metallic object from his pouch and held it up. "Though why you wanted this trinket so badly is beyond me."

Annas peered closely at the thing Scribonius held between his thumb and forefinger, though he did not venture to touch it. In shape it was like a small pipe or whistle and its surface gleamed like highly polished bronze.

"Yes! Yes!" chuckled the old priest, rubbing his hands together. "Now we can summon even though we cannot perceive—even as the Teacher, if he does indeed possess the Byakhtron, can perceive though not summon. We have the advantage."

"What in Hades are you talking about?" growled Scribonius.

"Never mind, Centurion. Put that thing away again and keep it out of sight. Above all, do not blow upon it, for if you do something not at all to your liking may come to you. I want you and all your men to take it immediately to the Tower of Siloam and conceal it in that chamber where the eidolon of Set used to be enshrined."

"Used to be—?"

"Maxentius and Caiaphas have taken it to the Temple. Tonight they shall come to the Tower and take the Byakhtril thence also. Do not worry about these matters, Scribonius. Tell me: Did you lose some men? Your ranks seem a bit depleted."

"Aye. We slew a powerful wizard who was also after your magic whistle, and captured two of his young apprentices. But on our way here the wizard's death wand blazed with lightning and killed three men, including your yellow-eyed Temple guards. We left the wand where it lay and hurried on, but on the way one of the apprentices escaped. He must have been a wizard himself to have slipped those bonds. I sent four men in pursuit of him."

"I see," said Annas impatiently. "You should have brought the wizard's wand to me. Still, the Byakhtril is the main thing. Is this girl the other apprentice?"

"Aye. And I'm keeping her as a compensation for the loss of one of my legionaries and the hazard of confronting sorcery—"

"Ah. Then the escaped lad must be the other. Scribonius, was the wizard you slew an old man in Samaritan garb??

"No. He was a man perhaps in his thirties wearing black garments of a very strange cut."

Annas scowled thoughtfully. "It is obvious that many are seeking the Byakhtril. Scribonius, I want you and your soldiers to take it to the Tower of Siloam immediately. Take this girl along also, if you wish, but do not harm her; I may want to question her later. If your men show up here with the other apprentice, I'll send them along also."

When the Romans had tramped forth from the garden, taking their frightened captive with them, Izhar asked, "Why do we not accompany them even now?"

"Because Jahath and I are questioning two other prisoners," replied Annas, "and we are learning some very interesting things. Come with me. It may be that your particular skills with the Outside Ones may be of help to us. In any case—" The old priest glanced back at the windowless stone hut where one black-cloaked soldier now stood on guard. "—your Levite companion won't be able to accompany us to the Tower until after nightfall."

"Excuse me, good sir," said Simon, "I seek a physician—"

"Get away from me, Samaritan!" snarled the Judean merchant. "I'll have nothing to do with you. Such audacity!—that one of your kind would linger here in Bethany during this most holy of seasons. Get you gone!"

Simon cursed under his breath as the merchant indignantly stalked away. He had already approached nearly a dozen people; most of them had shunned him wordlessly, a few had offered insults, two had threatened violence. He realized that he must shed his Samaritan garb before he could make any progress.

"Alms, kind sir," whined a voice from a nearby alley. "Alms for the needy!"

Simon glanced down at the hand clutching at the hem of his robe. It protruded from a shapeless gray cloak huddled in a heap at the alley's mouth. From within the cloak's hood peered a lean, dark-eyed face hideously scabbed and blotched with white patches. A leper.

"Alms, good sir!"

Simon smiled, then dug into his pouch and dropped a shining silver denarius into the whining beggar's upraised up. The leper stared at the coin in astonishment. "My—my thanks. . . .," he stammered.

"Don't thank me. I'll give you two more of those if you'll trade me your cloak for my robe."

"Of course. But—" The beggar made an obvious effort to hold his eagerness in check. "But why would you want to purchase the garment of a poor leper?"

Simon chuckled. "You're no more a leper than I am. No, don't bother to deny it. I'm a trained magician and I know a disguise when I see one. Not that it isn't a good one. No doubt you make a good living at this trade—especially at this season when the streets are thronged with pious pilgrims."

The beggar grinned. "Well, a man must make a living. You must be very anxious to shed your Samaritan aspect—"

"No, don't dicker with me. My offer's more than a good one and you know it. If you don't like it, I'll seek out another panhandler."

The man nodded, rose and beckoned to Simon to follow him. When they were well concealed within the shadows of the alley he shed his cloak and handed it over. The brown tunic beneath it was clean and of good quality. Simon made to remove his travel-stained robe.

"No, no," said the beggar. "What would I want with a Samaritan garment? Just give me the money and I'll be on my way.

Simon nodded. "Just one more thing. I'll need some of your make-up. I plan to be a leper from here on."

"Done." The man passed a small pouch to Simon. "Here, take it all. Now, the other two denarii—"

Simon handed them to him, and without another word the man turned and hurried away into the shadows.

A few minutes later Simon emerged from the alley and retrieved his mule. Scabs of pliable tallow and blotches of white chalk made his face pitifully hideous, while his rolled-up Samaritan robe gave his cloaked shoulders a bent and hunched appearance. Though he sought no alms, several pilgrims flung coins to him as he proceeded through the narrow streets; on such occasions he was careful to gather them up and mumble thanks through a twisted grin.

Thenceforth he was given a wide berth, but received no abuse. But his luck proved no better than before. Several people offered directions when he asked about a physician, but in every case that physician proved too busy to spare any of his time. Evidently the influx of pilgrims, many of them wealthy, was causing business to boom.

"Damn their greed!" muttered Simon to himself after a particularly insulting rebuff from a fat leech. "If only I knew someone of influence in this town—"

At the thought he recalled the woman Miriam at the inn. Perhaps she would know someone. . . . And then a second thought struck him: Surely her guardian, old Yosef of Aphairema, must be at the inn also. The priestly patriarch might himself have medical knowledge—certainly he seemed a man of wisdom. . . .

Immediately Simon set out through the streets, leading the reluctant mule. What a fool he had been not to think of this possibility earlier!

Within a few minutes he arrived at the inn. As he was tying the mule to a post he saw the woman Miriam appear in the open doorway. Then, to his surprise, she said to him:

"Greeting, Simon of Gitta."

"What?" Simon felt suddenly flustered. "How did you know me?"

"I think I would know you anywhere, Simon." Her gray eyes now glimmered with greenish flecks—and a touch of humor—in the sunlight. "Your disguise is good, but old Yosef has trained me to recognize True Spirits—and you are one of the truest, Simon of—"

"Hush!" hissed the Samaritan nervously. "Call me Simon the Leper. And, speaking of old Yosef: Does he have physician's skills? If so, I'd like to ask a favor of him."

"Alas, Simon, he parted from me at Jerusalem, for he is obligated to join the priestly Sanhedrin there. Only his poor demented wife came on with me to this place. But do not despair. Yosef does indeed have healing skills, and he has imparted many of them to me."

"I should have guessed it, Lady Miriam, for there is an aura of assurance about you such as I have rarely sensed. Will you come with me to the room I have rented and—"

"I have already done so, for I sensed your concern for the man you brought here. But he needs no aid of mine. He sleeps peacefully and seems well on the road to recovery. His injuries were apparently not great. It is my judgment that he will awaken in a few hours. So let your heart be at rest concerning him, Simon."

But Simon, remembering the wizard's many severe contusions and stab -wounds, could only mutter anxiously, "Are you sure?"

"Believe it." The woman's face became serious, concerned. "I can see that the man means a great deal to you. Is he a brother? A friend?"

Simon shook his head. "I hardly know him. But I fear that the men who injured him have kidnapped two dear friends of mine—a lad and a young girl."

"I see." Compassion mingled with a touch of anger in the woman's eyes. "Stay here as long as you like, Simon . . . the Leper. I will see to it that my sister Martha does not object—"

At that instant a young lad rushed up—the same Galilean the lad Simon had seen earlier. Behind him, at a more leisurely pace, came the dumpy inn-mistress, Martha.

"Sister Miriam," she said quietly, ignoring Simon, "the Teacher is here and wishes you to come to him."

The tall woman's face was transformed with a sudden radiance. Simon had never seen its like. Her uncommon beauty seemed in this moment enhanced to a state of transcendence, and Simon felt a sudden pang of jealousy.

"He comes?" Miriam's voice held a flutter, like that of a dove waking to the first rays of dawn. Then, more matter-of-factly, "How is it, Martha, that you knew of this before I?"

The dumpy woman lowered her eyes, then raised them sullenly. "I thought that you should rest after your long journey, Sister. But the Teacher insists that you come nevertheless—"

"And so I shall!" cried Miriam exultantly. Then, her eye again catching Simon's, "But before I go, Sister, I want to stress that you must not interfere with this man. His name is Simon, and he shares the room with the injured man who was brought here earlier."

Martha recoiled with horror. "This *leper—?*"

"Have no fear. It is only a disguise."

The dumpy woman peered closer; her sharp dark eyes lit up with suspicion. "The Samaritan—?"

"That was but another disguise," Simon lied.

"I will explain all later," said Miriam. "Goodbye, Sister."

So saying, she set off at a rapid pace toward the edge of town with the Galilean youth. In a moment they had vanished eastward down the narrow street.

"Good day, Lady," said Simon to the inn-mistress, then turned and began to climb the outer stairway to the second floor balcony. As he ascended he sensed the woman's vindictive dark eyes fixed upon his back.

Entering the small room he had rented, he saw the wizard Taggart lying on the cot where he had left him. The woman Miriam had spoken the truth: nothing had changed, save that the injured man seemed to be breathing more deeply and comfortably than before. Simon peered closely and saw that his wounds had healed uncannily. Even the deepest of them were not scabbed; they seemed overlain with a thin film of something like glue or dry slime. The many bruises had vanished; there were no longer any bumps or discolorations.

"Taggart . . .?"

There was no response. The wizard continued to breathe deeply, evenly.

Simon sighed. He removed his cloak and robe, then lay down on the floor and wrapped himself in them. He was exhausted; his great weariness overwhelmed even his anxiety for Menander and Ilione. . . .

He slept.

CHAPTER XVI

Far above the earth the dark bird wheeled, searching the ground with sharp eyes like beads of polished onyx. Through its dim semi-avian brain droned a single thought:

Simon. Find Simon.

Below lay the village of Bethany, which Menander had mentioned, and which the bird remembered from a visit there some years ago. But the place was swarming with people and their donkeys and mules, while more were arriving all the time via the roads from Jericho and the north. The town's borders were crowded with pitched tents.

The bird rode the air currents, veering to the west. Here the road below was crowded with pilgrims, all heading toward the distant walled city around which countless more tents were pitched. How could even the sharpest-eyed raven pick out, in that seething mass, one man or his mount . . .?

For one uneasy moment the bird remembered landing upon the back of that mount—the mule beneath whose skin his own clawed toes had sensed something sentient, something *like himself*. . .

Then the impression—the memory—left him. It was easier not to think—easier to glide upon the gently surging currents of air. Now the bird was winging southward, randomly, following a divergent stream of pilgrims winding down a gentle valley like a sluggish caterpillar—an open, grassy valley bounded by the city wall to the west, dotted with leafy oaks and terebinths to the east. *The Valley of Kidron,* the bird remembered. From it the pilgrims were filing into the city through a gate near the wall's southern end—a gate overshadowed by a tall, massive tower of dark stone. Upon that tower several shining objects gripped the raven's attention: the iron helmets of Roman soldiers, gleaming under the midday sun. With an effort the bird looked away, denying the instinct that attracted it to shiny objects; it had a job to do, a specific person to find.

Simon. Find Simon. . . .

Then it spied more such shiny objects, perhaps a dozen of them. Below, upon a trail that wound down from the low eastward ridge, moved a small troop of legionaries; in their midst shone a gleam even more arresting that that which reflected from their helms—a golden gleam, somehow familiar. In spite of its inner promptings, the bird wheeled lower, curious. . . .

On the ground, the Roman leader hung back and let the first few members of his troop pass him. The captive blonde girl still trudged wearily along with her guards, her head bent low; a rope, cinched about her waist at one end, was held at the other by a grim-faced soldier.

"The tower's not far now, girl," said Scribonius as he walked beside her. "You'll have rest and a soft bed there—and food and drink also, if you prove sufficiently grateful to me. I might even make you my own handmaid rather than sell you to some rich old lecher. What do you say to that?"

The girl, head bowed as if in apathy, made no response.

"On the other hand," growled the Roman, clutching her shoulder, "I could enjoy you just as much *without* doing you any favors—"

"Ilione!"

Both the Roman and the girl abruptly looked up. Upon the lowest branch of a nearby oak perched a great black raven.

"What in Vulcan's fires—?" snarled Scribonius, reaching for his sword.

"Carbo!" cried Ilione, a desperate hope springing into her eyes. "Find Simon! Tell him the Roman Scribonius holds me in the Tower of Siloam—"

"Shut up, witch!" Scribonius' sword-pommel cracked against Ilione's temple, sending her half-stunned to the ground. "Fulvius—your bow, quickly!"

The legionary addressed dropped the girl's rope and snatched a stout bow from his shoulder, an arrow from its quiver—but already the raven was flapping into the sky, croaking, out of reach.

"By Pollux!" growled Scribonius, sheathing his sword. "Evidently Hermes, god of magic, fights against us. Old Annas evidently knew what he was talking about when he bade us to watch this girl closely. Guards! Bind her legs also, and carry her the rest of the way. I want her imprisoned in the highest and stoutest room of the tower!"

Above, the dark bird ascended into the sky, higher and higher, its jet-bead eyes scanning the terrain, searching. . . .

Menander felt grateful for the trees and shrubbery that grew more plentifully toward the top of the low ridge, for he had felt horribly exposed on the barren spur that led up to it. Now, warily, he followed the westward trail that he had intersected at the head of the gully. Upon it, plain in the dust, were the imprints of many Roman boots and, among them, the smaller outline of Ilione's sandals.

He slowed, redoubling his caution, as he saw the gleam of a white wall ahead amid the shrubs and tree-trunks. In a moment he stood near the base of its southeastern corner, crouching behind concealing bushes, watching. Some distance away, two motionless black-robed guards flanked a doorway in the southern face of the wall. The trail Menander followed led directly toward that doorway; doubtless Ilione was inside and this was the wall surrounding the "villa of Annas" of which his captors had spoken. He glanced southward; the trees were sparse in that direction, and beyond their dark trunks he saw that the ridge ended in a low rise topped with the silhouettes of jagged boulders—perhaps the ruins of an ancient shrine. Somehow the prospect stirred a vague uneasiness within. . . . Then, suddenly, he remembered: This was the Mount of Offense, which old Dositheus had pointed out to him years ago from the Kidron valley, which he now realized must lie just westward of here—the Mount whereon King Solomon had once worshipped monstrous gods, as had the ancient Jebusites before him.

The Jebusites, descendants of the Hyksos-Stygians who, driven forth from Khem, had founded Jerusalem. . . .

Menander shook his head, then began to steal northward along the eastern wall. Ancient legendry did not concern him now. He must somehow find Ilione and help her to escape.

Finding a fairly wide space clear of trees and shrubs, he backed away from the wall a few paces, then closed his eyes and breathed shallowly for several moments, stilling his mind in the way his mentor Daramos had taught him. For an instant he felt a twinge of fear at the risk he was about to take; he let it fade out like a dying spark. Then, when the moment was right he opened his eyes, let his Samaritan cloak fall from his shoulders to the ground—and ran to the wall.

At the last instant he leaped up toward the vertical surface, running upward a few paces upon the rough stones. His hands barely caught the top of the wall, and for a moment he hung there. Then, with a final effort, he hauled himself up and lay prone along the top, warily scanning the trees and shrubs of the garden below. The two-story villa of Annas bulked close by. Feeling exposed, Menander let himself down the wall's inner side, dropped to the ground and hurried into the concealing shrubbery.

The noonday quiet endured. Apparently no one had seen him.

Cautiously he made his way among the tree trunks and bushes, taking care to screen himself from the house and the gate in the back garden wall. He saw no one. The villa bulked high—a large place to have to search in stealth and broad daylight. But first, how to enter . . .?

Suddenly he came upon an open space in which squatted a small square hut of dark stone. Keeping to the trees, he stole around to where he could view its western side. Here a black-robe guardsman stood before a stout wooden door—the hut's only feature. Menander scowled in puzzlement. Why should a gardener's hut be warded by an armed soldier? Could Ilione be held within? If so, it could make his task easier.

Slowly he crept through the foliage until he was just west of the guard, then carefully climbed a tree. Now he could see the south wall of the villa. Again he closed his eyes and stilled his mind for a few moments; then, cupping his hands like a trumpet to his mouth, he faced the house and uttered a muted cry from far back in his throat:

"Guard!"

The dark-cloaked soldier turned and faced in the direction of the villa.

"Guard—you by the hut. Come quickly!"

The soldier strode rapidly northward and vanished among the trees. Instantly Menander climbed to the ground and ran across the clearing toward the hut. Ventriloquism had served him well, but now he must work fast. He had no weapon—his captors had taken all but his robe, tunic and sandals—yet there was a long bronze bodkin concealed in the sole of one sandal; he could pick the lock if need be. . . .

But the door was not locked. The latch yielded to his touch. Cautiously Menander pulled; the portal swung outward, creaking on rusty hinges. Within, all was blackness.

"Ilione—?" he called softly, peering inward.

Something stirred in the darkness. At the same time he caught a strange, foul odor, something like tomb-dankness commingled with sea-stench. . . .

Barely in time he leaped back as a squat, cowled form lurched at him; his heel struck a stone and he went sprawling. Frantically he rolled away, came to his feet crouched in a fighting stance—and saw the door of the hut swinging shut, gripped by something like a slug's body that glinted slimily in the daylight. Then the slug-palp vanished inward behind the jamb and the door slammed to.

Menander dashed back into the trees, shaken. He had recognized the thing in the hut as the monstrous, faceless being who had attended upon Izhar in the Black Synagogue of Chorazin. Izhar must be in the villa—and with him, perhaps, was Ilione. . . .

And now he could hear the footfalls and calls of several guardsmen, hurrying from the direction of the mansion toward the hut.

"Wait here, Tribune," cautioned Caiaphas. "From this point I must go on to the Temple alone. *Bearers*—set it down!"

The two slaves placed the curtained litter gently on the stone floor of the corridor. The high priest reached in and carefully took forth the large bronze-colored object that had rested within. Mirrored torchlight danced in the golden gleams upon its polished surface, while a deep ruby gleam shone steadily from its eyes. The two slaves turned away from the glow of those eyes, shuddering slightly, but Maxentius and his giant bodyguard gazed intently upon the thing.

"So that's the magic idol," growled Cratos. "What makes its eyes shine like that? A lamp inside—?"

"Those eyes have gleamed in darkness for ten times ten thousand years," the high priest responded. "It is old, this 'idol'—older than ancient Stygia, older than Valusia and primal Attluma. The beings who fashioned it were not human, but the Stygians who later came to worship it fashioned the hollow form of the ass-headed serpent that now encloses it."

Maxentius, who had seen the thing before, was yet impressed in spite of his outward impassiveness. "Are you sure I can't accompany you, priest? I'd like to see it in the place where it will work its magic—"

"No!" snapped Caiaphas nervously. "No Gentile may enter the Temple, and none but myself may enter the Holy of Holies. Any hint of such a scandal would cause a riot that would topple Jerusalem. Give me a torch—good. Now, return to the Antonian Fortress and await my return—alone."

He was careful to put special emphasis on the last word. He saw Maxentius and his giant gladiator glance briefly, understandingly, at one another. Then he turned and continued on down the narrow stone corridor, straining at the heady eidolon he bore under his right arm.

After perhaps fifty paces he came to a stairway that went upward into deep gloom. Here he rested the eidolon upon the lowest step and stood in the silent darkness, breathing in gasps, recovering strength for the ascent. Fortunately the climb would not a long one. That was good, as the Eidolon of Set was heavy and he was getting old. . . .

Suddenly a medley of shrieks rang out down the dark tunnel—shrieks of terror and agony. Caiaphas nodded somberly. That would be the two slaves being dispatched by the blade of Cratos. They had witnessed the Eidolon being placed in its litter at the Tower of Set, then being removed here in this secret underground passageway that led from the Antonian Fortress to the Temple; therefore, they could not be allowed to live and carry gossip abroad.

When he had rested Caiaphas laboriously carried the Eidolon up the short, narrow flight of stairs. The trap door at its top was open; he had made sure of that the day before. Setting down the image, he bracketed his torch on the southern wall of the chamber into which he had emerged, then paused to rest again.

The room in which he stood was cubical, perhaps thirty feet on a side, its eastern wall consisting of dark wood paneling in the center of which were high double doors; the other walls were of fine white marble. Against the center of the western wall stood a massive block of stone, before which rested a large object resembling a gilded chest surmounted by two golden, winged beings facing one another. Caiaphas gazed upon this object reverently, as if admiring its superb workmanship. He had only once laid eyes on it since it had been brought here two days ago from its hidden cave on Mount Nebo across the Jordan; since then, he knew, the slaves who had borne it hither from the Tower of Set in the dead of night had all been dispatched to Sheol, and their bodies were even now being consumed by rats and vultures in the Vale of Hinnom beyond the city's southern wall.

The Ark—the fabled Ark of the Covenant—hidden for centuries in the cave on Mount Nebo until the days when the stars should come right. Hidden until the time when it might be brought forth to serve as a Gate for that which would open the Greater Gate—that servitor of Yahweh Zava'ot, Father of the All, who would soon enable his Master to return and rule the world from which He had long ago been banished. . . .

Caiaphas shuddered slightly at these thoughts, then turned and reverently lifted the Head of Set once more. Slowly he carried it forward and placed it upon the massive stone block, so that its red eyes gazed eastward between the golden wings of the twin dragon-like beings atop the Ark. Then walking around directly in front of it, he bowed slightly and intoned an ancient formula—a Stygian chant whose words had not been spoken in this place since Antiochus the Mad had invoked the Abomination some two hundred years earlier:

"Setukh no inkon tho iramus. Ka nokomis ro Uagio-tsotho."

Suddenly, eerily, the eyes of the Eidolon seemed to glow more brightly, while from within the Ark came a faint, rhythmic, booming sound, like muffled drums.

Again Caiaphas shuddered. The sacred books told of how the Ark's exterior had been fashioned, supposedly at the direction of Yahweh; they also told of the things which supposedly lay within—the jar of manna and the living staff of Aarom, the First Levite. But the equally ancient writings of Mattan, Priest of Baal—based on vastly older writing still—told of what that jar and that staff really symbolized: the Power and the Sword of those from beyond the stars who would one day aid Yahweh Zava'ot in his Great Return. . . .

The slow, pulsing, booming sound continued. Caiaphas stared in fascination at the great gilded box. Once before, in this very chamber, he had lifted its lid and peered within, had seen neither jar nor staff but a bewilderingly complex arrangement of metallic planes and angles, faintly glowing crystals and filaments, all displayed in odd, even dizzying geometric patterns. In that moment the priest had realized that the Ark, like the Eidolon of Set, was an ancient and un-human thing, its alien interior having long ago been enclosed by worshipful humans within its present gilded and fine-crafted form.

Now once again Caiaphas felt the urge to peer within. Slowly, reverently, he moved forward and gently placed his hands upon the edge of the lid. A faint vibration trembled up his fingertips. Uneasily he recalled the ancient legend of Uzzah, who had been smitten dead upon merely touching the thing. What could be happening in the Ark's alien interior to cause that strange, muted pulsing . . .? Slowly, cautiously, he gripped the edge of the lid, raised it up a few inches, gazed within—and saw blackness.

Not the blackness of a pit or a tomb, but a seething, pulsing blackness powdered with gleaming, swirling clouds of stars that seemed to stretch away into infinity. And from the black, illimitable, churning space surged the deep pulsings he had sensed before—less muffled now, and accompanied by thin, distant whines, eerily harmonizing, like monstrous flutes. Chaos, whirling and churning to the beat of drums. . . .

With a gasp Caiaphas whirled away, allowing the lid of the Ark to thud back into place. Immediately the sounds were reduced again to a muted, menacing throb, barely audible.

"Have mercy, O Great Set!" muttered the high priest, his voice trembling. "Remember my loyalty in the day of thy Great Return."

Then hurrying to the southern wall, he snatched up his torch and descended the narrow stairway, letting the trapdoor fall shut behind him.

In the shadowed silence of the deserted chamber the eyes of the Eidolon of Set continued to gleam like the sinister dawning of twin crimson suns.

Menander crept silently through the trees. Behind him, in the back garden, he could faintly hear guards moving about. They did not seem to be actively hunting him yet; perhaps they were still unaware of his presence. But if the being in the stone hut should somehow communicate with them. . . .

Carefully he skirted the western side of the house. Most of that wall was blank, but there were three second-story windows, one of them open, but all of them too high to reach.

In front of the villa a wide courtyard extended north to the surrounding wall of the estate. From his vantage point amid the concealing shrubbery Menander could see several dark-robed guards standing hear the wide archway of the main gate; two or three more lounged upon the mansion's pillared front portico. In the courtyard itself a variety of people idled here and there—petitioners awaiting audience, old women selling fruits or flowers, young men dressed in the white robes of Levitical attendants. Obviously there was no access for him to the mansion here.

He returned to the open window and gazed up at it. A thick oak stood not far away, one of its branches extending in the right direction. There was just a chance. . . .

Quickly he shinned up the trunk and crept out upon the branch, again feeling dangerously exposed, until it began to bend under his weight. The window ledge was still above him, and a long leap away; should he miss, he would have a long fall.

Quieting his mind again, he waited for a moment when his will and instincts would merge as one—

It came. Almost without volition he sprang upward, outward, in a long graceful leap worthy of a trapeze artist.

Even so, his fingers barely caught the window ledge, and for an instant he feared he would lose his grip. Then friction against the wall stopped his wild swing. For a few seconds he hung, gathering strength, then slowly hauled himself up over the sill, silently grateful for the months of muscle-control training Daramos had put him through.

The space inside was dim and fortunately empty. It was a short corridor opening into a wider area. Menander could hear voices; their dim, echoing quality suggested that they came from a large open space. Stealing forward, he found that the area at the end of the passage was a balustraded quadrangle overlooking the floor below. As he had suspected, the interior of the house of Annas was built along Greco-Roman designs rather than Eastern.

Stealing cautiously to the balustrade, he peered over. As in the courtyard outside, guards and servants stood about the wide quadrangle, while an occasional white-robed Levite youth crossed the tiled floor, no doubt on the business of some priest. . . .

Suddenly footsteps sounded upon the steps of a nearby stair—perhaps guards ascending on patrol. Menander stepped back into the passageway, tried the nearest door. It was unlocked; the room it opened into was dark. He slipped within and closed the door, heard it latch softly. He sensed that the chamber in which he stood was small and deserted.

When the guards had passed he opened the door enough to let in a bit of daylight. Drapes and curtains hung from many racks, while pegs along the walls held many garments—cloaks, robes, tunics, stolas and shifts. That was a bit of luck—he would be able to disguise himself. . . .

Then he heard a low sound like the voice of a girl sobbing, pleading.

Instantly he closed the door again. Now he could see a dim outline of light coming from beneath a door in the far wall. The sound seemed to come from beyond that. Had he been lucky enough to find Ilione this quickly? He stole carefully forward, moving silently, avoiding objects in the darkness as Daramos had trained him to, using his fingers and toes like delicate antennae. Again came the pleading feminine voice, and then the rasping voice of an old man. Menander felt his hackles rise; there was something familiar about that rasping voice. Then he was at the door. Very gently he tried its latch. It would not budge.

"Please don't!" cried the girl. "I can tell you no more!"

"So you say." The man's voice was menacing. "I don't believe you, and neither does Annas."

"My mistress and I have told all we know. Have we not endured enough? My mistress still sleeps—I pray that the priest's drugs have not killed her—"

"She will awaken soon. Annas' drug was a hypnotic; under its influence she has told him all she knows. Or so he believes. But I have a surer way—and Annas has authorized me to try it on you."

"What is that copper bowl you bear—?"

The girl's voice was strained, apprehensive. Menander realized now that she was not Ilione, but the man's voice had that strangely familiar ring. The mention of a "copper bowl" jolted the lad's memory. The man was Izhar, sinister rabbi of the Black Synagogue!

Quickly Menander groped in the darkness, found a bolt and drew it softly back, then tried the latch. This time the door yielded. Opening it the merest crack, he peered out. The lean Izhar, now clad in priestly robes, stood on the tiled floor of an elegantly-furnished room; facing him was a young dark-haired woman with fear in her eyes. The coppery bowl clutched in the man's spidery hands was all too familiar to Menander.

"Submit, my pretty one," cackled Izhar, "and there will be no pain—"

Menander pushed the door open and raced across the tiles, dashing the metallic hemisphere from the priest's hands. As the old man whirled to face him, snarling, the lad struck a short, sharp blow to the temple, as Simon had taught him to do. Instantly Izhar went down with a cry. The bowl skidded across the tiles with a muted clatter.

"Thank the gods he had not yet opened it," Menander gasped.

The girl gazed at him wide-eyed, dumbfounded, then glanced at the bowl. "What's in it—?"

"You wouldn't want to know."

She glanced down at the old man who lay like a crumpled pile of blankets upon the tiles. "I sensed that he intended something horrible. Is he dead?"

"No, and I doubt he'll be unconscious for long. Look, you must help me—"

"But who *are* you? And how did you get in here?"

I am Menander, a Samaritan wizard. My skills enable me to go where I please."

The girl seemed impressed, which pleased him. "My name is Lotis and I, too, am a Samaritan. You seem very young to be a wizard. Yet, your symbol-emblazoned tunic is very similar to that of another wizard I once knew. His name was Simon and—"

"Simon!" gasped Menander. "Was he a Samaritan also?

"You know him, then?"

"I certainly do! Where and when did you see him last?"

"In Sychar . . . I think it was only two or three days ago. It seems so long since I was captured and brought here."

"Where did he go?"

"To Shechem, I think, and then perhaps on to Jerusalem, in search of revenge for old wrongs. I hope no harm has come to him."

Menander saw sadness and concern in the girl's dark eyes. He sighed. Here was another attractive young woman concerned with Simon's well-being. . . .

"Lotis, tell me: Is there another woman being held captive within this house?"

"Yes. Truly, you *are* a wizard —"

"Can you tell me where?"

"She lies in the next room, sleeping. That horrible old high priest, Annas, gave her a drug. Come."

Menander followed the girl into what proved to be a bedchamber, but to his great disappointment he saw that the sleeping woman on the bed was not Ilione. She was quite beautiful; her hair was nearly as dark as that of Lotis, and she was fully mature.

"Who is she?"

"Elissa, my mistress." The girl seemed puzzled. "I thought you knew—"

"Alas!—I'm not such a great wizard as you thought, Lotis. I was looking for another woman—a young golden-haired one named Ilione." He bent over the girl's sleeping mistress, saw that she was breathing regularly. He shook her gently by the shoulder, but she did not stir.

"She's been that way for hours," said Lotis worriedly.

Menander saw a small vial of blue glass sitting on a stand beside the bed. He unstoppered it and sniffed at its contents. "Is this the drug the high priest game her?"

"Yes."

"Your mistress will wake up soon, I think. I recognize this—it's a potion which Persian sorcerers use on those they wish to interrogate. It makes the user willing to tell the truth, after which it induces a deep sleep. But it causes no physical harm."

"Thank the Lord of Gerizim! Annas seemed mad to learn from her about another wizard, one from Galilee who had promised her something called 'the Living Water'—but she knew little. That made Annas angry. Then, old Izhar offered to question me in some more horrible way—"

"I know." Menander took up the vial. "There's still some of this potion left. Let's see how it effects Izhar."

The bearded priest was beginning to stir and mutter slightly when they returned to the furnished room. Menander lifted the old man's head slightly and poured the fluid between slack lips. Izhar coughed, gagged slightly and swallowed.

"What happened?" he gasped, glancing about with unfocused eyes. "My head—it pounds like the drums of Achamoth!"

Menander shuddered slightly at the blasphemous utterance. Surely this old priest or rabbi—whichever he was—had indeed delved into some very dark and ancient sorceries.

"Lie still, old man. I've given you a medicine. You'll feel better very soon."

"Ah." The priest closed his eyes for several moments; when he reopened them they were focused and bright. "O kind young man, you are right—the pain is gone. Bliss enfolds me! Where am I?"

"You are in your synagogue at Chorazin, sir."

The old man looked around. "Why, so I am! But why am I lying upon the tiled floor?"

"You hit your head. You must lie still and rest awhile."

"Of course. Whatever you say, good lad. Such a good lad. . . ."

Menander glanced up and winked at Lotis, who was staring at him in amazement. Despite their danger, he felt gratified that he was so obviously impressing her. She was, he noticed again, a most attractive girl.

"Izhar," he said, turning back to the priest, "I am looking for a golden-haired girl named Ilione, who was brought to the house of Annas. Where is she?"

"She is no longer there."

Menander started. "She isn't? Then where *is* she?"

"The Romans have taken her to the Tower of Set. I think their officer has conceived a liking for her."

Menander gritted his teeth. "I never heard of such a tower. Where is it?"

"It guards the Siloam Gate at the southern end of Jerusalem's east wall."

"Oh—the Tower of Siloam. Why didn't you say so—?"

"Its foundation are old, old. They were laid down before the coming of Joshua by the Set-worshipping Jebusites, who were the descendants of the Shepherd-Kings of Khem, who were in turn the descendants of—"

"Never mind that! How can I gain entry to this tower?"

"You cannot. It is impregnable. Moreover, it is guarded by a score of Roman Legionaries at all times."

"Baal! Is there no secret passage, no nearby buildings—?"

"No. It is a fastness that cannot be assailed."

Menander shook his head grimly. "We'll see. Tell me, Izhar: How might I slip unseen from the house of Annas?"

"Very easily," chuckled the priest groggily. "Annas' house is open all day to petitioners, and his courtyard to vendors of flowers and doves. Leave openly and boldly, and no one will notice. Only, cover up that wizard's tunic of yours before you do."

"I will. Thank you, Izhar. You will sleep now. You are already sleeping. This has been a dream. You will not remember it when you wake up."

The old man nodded slightly, then immediately dozed off. Menander let his head down easily, then stood up and faced the girl. "Good. He'll sleep for several hours, hopefully. Let's wake up your mistress and get out of here."

"Oh, Menander! Do you think we dare just walk out of here openly, like he said?"

They hurried to the garment-room and rummaged about, leaving the door open for light. It seemed to be a storage place for bedding and clothing of all sorts, including some of the most elaborate priestly robes and ceremonial altar-cloths. Menander selected a plain white Levitical robe of the sort he had seen being worn by several youths in the courtyard; Lotis in turn selected garb she felt was suitable for a Judean matron and her daughter.

When they returned to the furnished room they saw Lotis' mistress standing in the doorway of the bedchamber. She was leaning against the jamb while rubbing her eyes with both hands.

"Mistress Elissa," cried Lotis, running forward, "are you well?"

"Yes, Lotis." The woman smiled at her servant—a bit sadly, Menander thought, as if trying to show a bravery she did not feel. "But I am slow in awakening. Have I slept long?"

"Several hours, Mistress."

"Elissa glanced at the supine and snoring form of Izhar, then at Menander. "Who are these . . .?"

"The sleeping priest is a henchman of Annas. This young man is Menander, a Samaritan like ourselves; he is also a wizard, and has caused this wicked priest to slumber even as Annas caused you to. He knows Simon of Gitta, and he is going to help us escape!"

"You know . . . Simon?" Elissa's eyes were still sleep-glazed.

"Trust me," said Menander. "Put on the garment Lotis has brought you. And you, Lotis, pluck some of those flowers from the window boxes; you're a flower-girl now, and Elissa is your mother who has come to fetch you and take you home."

"And you, Menander?"

"I'm a Levite youth, attendant to some priest—call him Dositheus. I've found you wandering lost in the corridors of this mansion, in case anyone asks, and I'm escorting you to the gate. Can you play those parts if we're accosted?"

Elissa drew herself upright, shaking her head vigorously as if to banish sleep. "I certainly can, young man. I'd do anything to escape from this place. I only hope you're the wizard Lotis says you are."

"He is, Mistress—know it. I trust him."

The two women retired to the bedchamber to don their Judean garb, and again Menander felt a warm gratification at the girl's trust. She was, indeed, very pretty—possibly as much so as Ilione. . . .

Then squaring his shoulders and breathing deeply, he began again to still his mind in the way that Daramos had taught him. It was very important now, he felt, that he live up to Lotis' trust. . . .

CHAPTER XVII

Nicodemus, priest of the Sanhedrin, descending the steps from the Temple precincts into the vast, many-columned Court of the Gentiles, was startled to see the approach of an aged Judean who bowed piously and said:

"Greeting, O Defender of the Law. May we talk privately?"

Deciding that the oldster meant no harm, Nicodemus motioned to his two white-robed Levitical attendants and said to them, "Go on ahead. Wait for me near the Hall of Gazzith, and inquire as to whether Yosef of Aphairema has arrived." Then, when they were gone, "Speak, supplicant."

The old man winked irreligiously and said, "Do you not recognize me, good Nicodemus?"

The priest bent forward and peered closely into the old man's face for a moment, then drew back. "By El Shaddai!" he hissed. "Dositheus—"

"Aye. Your eyes are still sharp, old comrade."

The priest drew himself up indignantly. "I'm not of *your* circle any more, Dositheus. What do you here, disguised in Judean robes, in these sacred precincts—?"

"In these *gentile* precincts," said Dositheus hastily.

Nicodemus nodded. "Yet I wouldn't put it past you to try to attend the sacred ceremonies beyond these limits established to bar gentiles. . . ."

"And risk death? Why should I? I know already of the sacrifices that have been performed there for the last thousand years—the rites of blood and pain designed to prepare the way for the return of Yah—"

"Cease!" The indignation in the priest's face turned to horror; his hands groped at his robe, as if to tear it in grief. "How dare you, an outsider, think to speak the Name!"

"Peace, Nicodemus. You were once an aspirant to the ranks of the Thirty. You know very well that all names are mere sounds save under very extraordinary circumstances—"

"I abjure the Thirty!" hissed the priest. "Moreover, you know that it is death to be heard speaking the Name. Only the High Priest may speak it, and that but once a year."

"Aye, at the Passover—and therefore he shall speak it soon. But *this* time it shall be different, shall it not? I know from certain writings of your friend, Yosef of Aphairema, that this year is the Culmination—that when the Name of the Nameless One is pronounced in the suitable place, the Gate shall be opened and the earth shall be cleansed—"

"Silence!" hissed Nicodemus. Then, after glancing sharply about, he continued in a tense whisper, "Get out of here, Dositheus. You are meddling in matters of which you know little. Would you die—?"

"What would it matter? Will not all earthly life perish when the Gate is opened?"

Nicodemus' face paled. Sweat appeared upon his lofty brow; his lean, pallid fingers clutched nervously at his beard. "How *did* you learn of this? Did Yosef indeed write to you—?"

"Actually, I've only recently deduced it from the books and papers in his library—and from some other things I've read. I know now of the many years he spent in Galilee, living in obscurity while raising a son who was not truly his own—and I know what that son of will do, if we do not prevent him—"

"And why *should* we prevent him?" grated Nicodemus, his face suddenly as stern and dark as a thundercloud. "Is this earth such a paradise that we should preserve it? No, it is a vale of torment, worthy only of destruction—and it *shall* be destroyed, Dositheus! For a thousand ages the Primal Gods have worked their torment upon all life, feeding upon the pain thus generated; the agony of countless victims has fed them—"

"And so you would destroy it all?" Dositheus shook his head sadly. "How do you know that your god will then establish a better world? Does not Him Who is not to be Named demand countless animal sacrifices here before his Temple? And have they not been thus demanded for more than a thousand years?"

"Aye, in order that His energies might be built up for His Return!" Nicodemus' face, now lifted skyward, shone as with a radiant glory. "In that day the skies shall roll up as a scroll, the thunders of judgment shall descend like a sea-wave upon all the lands, and all suffering shall cease!"

Dositheus cringed back from the fanaticism in the priest's eyes. "Nicodemus, you do realize what you are saying—?"

"I know full well." Nicodemus seemed almost to grow in stature, towering over the old Samaritan like a prophet inspired with a vision of judgment. "Yosef has told me all. This world, and countless others like it, are vales of pain—chambers of torment for countless beings whose sufferings generate the energies which ascend aloft to pleasure the Primal Gods. But now, at last, the Nameless One has sent his Son to overthrow the rule of those monstrous gods. Will you oppose His advent, Dositheus? —you, who once lost a loved one during the reign of the monstrous King Herod? No! You, Dositheus, like all who have become aware of the enormity of the suffering this world bears, know that it is better that all beings should perish and that a new dawn should supersede the long darkness!"

Dositheus swallowed. "There is some truth in what you say, Nicodemus. Yet, is there not also a redeeming flavor in this life? Do you not enjoy a good meal, the drawing of a full breath, the glance of a loved one—?"

"Do these things outweigh the misery of those who are denied them?" snarled Nicodemus. "Does the absence of leprosy in many men outweigh the sufferings of those who are afflicted with it? Count each of your blessings, Dositheus, and know that for every disease you have not yet contracted, many thousands of others *have*—else you would not know of that disease at all! Have no loved ones of yours been slain by Romans recently, or sold into slavery? If you feel lucky on that account, it is because you know of many others who have! Have no friends of yours been slain by bandits, accidents, avalanches—?"

"Peace, Nicodemus. I have experienced sorrow, as you well know. Yet, life is—"?

"Speak not to me of life!" hissed the priest, his face rigid. "I am sick of all life! I seek that which is beyond it. Life is suffering. I seek relief from life, and so I follow the One who shall overthrow life and bring Joy to this world. Go, now, Dositheus, and keep silent about these things—unless you would taste death even before True Life begins to reign upon this world."

Dositheus, seeing the mad light in the priest's eyes, bowed respectfully and backed away. "I once felt as you, but I *have* learned to respect true life, Nicodemus. May it never perish."

Then, turning, he hurried away and vanished into the crowd as quickly as he was able.

Nicodemus scowled in consternation, regretting now that he had sent his attendants away. They could have detained the wily old Samaritan and taken him for questioning to Yosef of Aphairema. The ancient sorcerer must be warned.

He turned and made his way through the crowd, arriving in a few minutes at the southwest corner of the enormous, column-surrounded quadrangle. Here, at the entrance to the Hall of Gazzith where the Sanhedrin was wont to meet in council, he found his two attendants awaiting him.

"Has old Yosef arrived yet?" Nicodemus demanded.

"He arrived even as we did. He awaits you within."

The priest entered. Torches dimly illumined the narrow, columned hall. In the shadow of a nearby pillar Nicodemus spied a tall, slightly bent form clad in priestly robes. As always, he marveled at the vigor in the spare form, in the alertness of the dark eyes in that hook-nosed, white-bearded face. Though he had known old Yosef for two decades and more, the aged mage's aspect never seemed to change.

"Greeting, Nicodemus. I see that you received my message."

"Aye. Zethos delivered it but an hour ago. It read, as we had beforehand agreed: 'He whom you love is ill'."

Old Yosef nodded. "The notice of the imminence of the Healing of the World." He lifted one busy eyebrow quizzically. "But, good Nicodemus, why do you repeat it to me word for word? I detect an uneasiness in your voice?"

"I wanted you to confirm that the message had not been altered. Do you think Zethos was followed when he came to me?"

"Why these suspicions? Tell me what has made you so wary."

Nicodemus glanced toward the doorway. "I just met Dositheus the Samaritan—out there, in the Court of the Gentiles. He was dressed in Judean garb. And he as much as admitted to me that he had recently been in your house at Aphairema."

Old Yosef scowled slightly. "Ah! That is curious indeed, for last night I met his pupil, Simon of Gitta, upon the roadway."

"There! You see? There is a conspiracy afoot. You know how wily Dositheus is, and how learned in magical lore. He knows that the Great Return is about to occur, and what it means concerning the fate of all flesh, and he does not like it. Are you sure he did not intercept and read your message to me?"

"That is not likely, for I have taught Zethos to recognize trained mages, to see through illusions, to resist hypnosis and other such magical ploys. In any case, Dositheus could not know the meaning of our code-message. No, I suspect he was but trying to gain information from you—for, were you not once a companion of his, back when Johannen was performing magical rites at Aenon?"

"I have abjured all that," said Nicodemus, "and you may be sure that I gave him no information. I do not trust him. I have just heard him attempt to speak the Name aloud, and I would not put it past him to try to enter the very Temple itself to spy out our secrets."

Old Yosef smiled darkly. "You know that the Name is harmless unless it should be spoken at the Time and in the right place. Moreover, if Dositheus seeks to enter the Temple after tonight, it will definitely mean his doom. Concern not yourself with him."

"But if he should tell what he knows to Annas or Caiaphas, what then? They anticipate their achievement of absolute power, not the destruction of all flesh—"

"They have always been enemies of the Thirty. Dositheus will not trust them. Besides, they and all others would doubtless think him a madman."

"And what of his pupil—Simon of Gitta?"

"I sense that his coming here was a coincidence, for he seems to be on some mission of his own—"

"You sense? He seems?" Nicodemus waved his arms in exasperation. "How do you *know*? Did he claim it? And if so, can you believe him?"

"Simon would not name Dositheus even when I asked him the name of his mentor, but—"

"Ha! There you have it," said Nicodemus triumphantly. "He has something to hide."

"—but my intuition tells me that it was out of loyalty rather than from an ulterior motive. When a man lives as long as I have, my friend, he develops a sense of such motives. No, Simon was not the least bit interested in me, though I'm quite sure he became interested in my—daughter—very quickly. Do you know that he aided Miriam and me against bandits on the road last night? Aye, and offered us his further aid in case of need, then rode away without even attempting to question us. I somehow sense the hand of Fate in this, Nicodemus. As the stars come right, all things are subtly bent to our purpose."

The old priest bowed again to the older. "I hope you are right, Yosef."

"Trust me. Now, come—we must attend the meeting of the Council before night falls."

Simon woke in darkness and sat up rubbing his eyes, sensing that he had slept many hours, remembering that he was in the inn at Bethany. He rose and found the door latch, opened the portal and blinked as daylight flooded into the small room. The man called Taggart still lay on the cot, breathing evenly, just as before. Bending closely, Simon found that he could now find not the slightest trace of the man's wounds. He shook Taggart's shoulder vigorously, but the wizard did not respond.

"Baal!" he breathed in wonderment. "Will he sleep forever . . .?"

Simon girded on his weapon belt, donned his gray beggar's cloak, then let himself out on to the balcony and closed the door behind him. The sun was westering; it was mid-afternoon.

Hurrying around the balcony and descending to the street, Simon found the mule where he had tethered it.

"Balaam?" he said tentatively. "Balaam, can you understand me?"

The beast looked at him, but with no more intelligence than might be expected from a normally alert animal. He tried again, "Balaam—"

"Are you crazy, Samaritan?"

Simon turned and saw the sour-faced woman, Martha, standing in the door of the inn. "I was just—"

"Were you trying to sneak away? If so, you'd best take your heathen friend with you. The day will be over at sundown."

Simon felt his irritation rising. "So you've changed the rules? And now you'd cast out a wounded man for lack of a day's rent?"

"My sister Miriam, who has physicians' skills, tells me that he is not ill—that he sleeps peacefully."

Simon could think of no rebuttal. He looked within his pouch, saw that his coins—despite the morning's intake—were getting low. He would have to do some begging.

"If you could give me until tomorrow—"

"No, Simon, you bogus leper! Maybe you did aid my sister and her guardian, but that carries little weight with me. Miriam's not very practical, and old Yosef has always been half crazy. I don't know what you're up to, but you won't fool me as easily as you did them."

Simon stifled his anger. "Then take this mule as collateral. You can see he's a good beast, worth a few nights' lodging, I'd hope. And in the name of Baal, take him into the stable and give him some fodder! Why did you let him stand out here all day in—"

"I touch nothing which is not mine to touch—and I trust you'll do the same while you're here, Samaritan. Moreover, I'll expect you and your unclean friend to be gone from here before Passover."

So saying she untied the mule and led it away into the walled quadrangle surrounding the sides and back of the inn. Simon cursed under his breath. Obviously the woman had not believed the story about being a Samaritan only in disguise. He hoped she would not gossip about his presence here; that could lead to ugly incidents, especially during the impending religious holiday, or even prove fatal if it came to the ears of certain Romans. . . .

When Martha had gone, Simon suddenly became aware of another woman standing within the shadows of the inn doorway. Instantly he knew her.

"Miriam—?"

"Greeting, Simon of Gitta." She emerged from the doorway and the light of the westering sun illumined her regal and gently smiling face. "I hope you rested as well as I did."

Simon nodded. Again he wondered how she and the sour Martha could possibly be sisters.

"I must leave for awhile, My Lady, and earn a bit of money. Your sister will have me and my—friend—out on the street otherwise."

The smile vanished; sparks of irritation glittered in the woman's gray-green eyes. "Martha overreaches herself. She is jealous of the Teacher's fondness for me and of my destiny with him as his betrothed. But she will not cast you out, Simon; I owe you too much. Moreover, if you need money—"

"That's not necessary. I'm grateful to you for checking on my . . . my friend while I was gone earlier."

"Ah, your friend." The woman smiled again. "The Teacher told me of how you found him injured alongside the Jericho road and brought him here; he and several of his Galilean disciples saw you take him up the road ahead of them—after the man had been passed by an indifferent priest and his attendant Levite."

Simon remembered. "My Lady, do you know anything about that priest and Levite? Did they pass this way?"

"I'm told they did, and that they continued on toward Jerusalem. Had they stayed here they would have been shamed indeed, for this very afternoon the Teacher told a crowd here of your exploit—of how a priest and a Levite passed by a robbed and wounded man and left him to die, but then a Samaritan took him up and brought him to an inn and left money that he might be cared for. It was a most touching story, Simon, and many in the crowd were moved despite their scorn for Samaritans."

Simon guessed that the 'Teacher' must be the tall, white-robed figure he had seen coming up the road from Jericho with his band of followers. However, save for a slight irritation at Miriam's obvious adoration of the man, he was uninterested in the subject.

"I must go on to Jerusalem, then," he said. "That priest and his—Levite—may know who kidnapped my two young friends. He is no true priest, incidentally, but a rabbi named Izhar from the Galilean town of Chorazin—"

"Chorazin? Then he *must* be Izhar!" said Miriam. "I know of him; he is an enemy of the Teacher and a sorcerer of great power. Strange, how fate weaves the strands of destiny together. But before you go in pursuit of this dark rabbi, Simon, will you not sup here? You must be famished after your night-long journey and day-long sleep."

"I have no time."

"Then at least take a loaf and a skin of wine with you." Miriam went into the inn, returned a moment later with a bundle which she passed to Simon. "Go, then, Simon, and may the blessing of the Highest One go with you. Beware of Izhar, and even more of his so-called 'Levite'. I have heard strange stories told of them."

"Thank you, Miriam. Watch over the sleeping wizard upstairs; if he wakes, don't let him leave. With luck I'll be back by dawn. Peace be with you."

He hurried away into the crowd, wondering again at this woman whose mystical gray-green eyes could sense the presence of "true spirits" even through disguises, whose beauty and demeanor hinted at something regal, even supermundane, within her. And then he remembered that she had wished him well in the name of the 'Highest One'—the Being of whom only initiates of the Secret Wisdom knew—the One Who Stands Eternally, above and beyond all worlds and creator-gods.

"Mot and Baal!" he muttered, wondering. "Who *is* she . . ."?"

Dositheus hastened from the Golden Gate of the Temple quadrangle and descended the wide stone stairway, glad to be gone from Jerusalem and its stench of congested humanity. Still, the Kidron Valley into which he was descending was hardly less congested. Flocks of pilgrims jostled him upon the stairway, hoping to gain access to the holy city before its gates closed at sundown.

At the bottom of the stairs he found the stolid Eupatos holding the reins of their donkey. Beyond him, and the mob surging up from the Kidron, the eastern slope rose, green and golden under the rays of the westering sun, its low crest clad with the oaks and terebinths of the Garden of Gethsemene.

"Hurry, Eupatos," he growled. "We must put many miles between us and this city."

The sturdy slave followed his master without question; if he felt any amazement at the seventy-year-old Dositheus' ability to set a rapid pace and sustain it, he did not say so.

Dositheus, for his part, berated himself for having dared to contact Nicodemus. "Damn Fortuna!" he muttered under his breath as he breasted the flow of the mob. "And damn Nicodemus, too, for a weak-headed fool! Now I have shown my hand to no advantage. Well, I'll try to finding lodgings in or near Bethany, then rest there until the Thirty come."

About an hour later, when they had left the Kidron behind them and Jerusalem was no longer in view, Dositheus and his servant paused to rest. Bethany was less than an hour's walk to the east; hopefully it would be less crowded than Jerusalem. Here, at least, the crowd thinned appreciably, though pilgrims still passed frequently. Some had begun to pitch tents alongside the road and on the gentle hill slopes as the sun declined toward the west.

Not far away, a man in a ragged gray cloak sat on a boulder and munched on a loaf of bread. Dositheus looked away as the man rose to his feet and began to advance with a lame gait. Another damned beggar! Wayfarers were plagued by them during holiday seasons, and most of them were frauds. He prepared a curt rebuff as the man drew near—but then was surprised to hear, instead of the typical importuning whines, a firm and youthful voice saying:

"Well, Dositheus, this is a stroke of luck. Don't you recognize the pupil you instructed in the art of disguise?"

The old man peered closely at the beggar. "Simon! You are indeed a tribute to my skills. Yet, I would have recognized you had my thoughts not been elsewhere."

"'A master's thoughts do not depart from the immediacy of reality,'" quoted Simon, smiling.

"Wise, those words of Daramos," Dositheus acknowledged, a slight irritation in his voice. "Well, I admit that I have not yet attained to the level of that accomplished archimage; after all, I am fully human. Moreover, I am preoccupied with heavy matters of late. Listen—"

He proceeded to tell Simon of his visit to the house of Yosef of Aphairema and his recent encounter with Nicodemus the priest. "It is as bad as I feared," he concluded. "Those two mean to aid this rabbi Yeshua in the destruction of the world by means of opening a Gate to the greatest of the Old Ones!"

Simon wondered about that, knowing his mentor's occasional tendency to self-dramatization; still, there was certainly strange magic afoot, these days. "Can you be sure of this—?"

"I have no time to argue, Simon. Quickly, tell me all that has happened to you since last we met."

Simon did so in a few minutes while the old man listened intently and the dull Eupatos stood close by in silence, comprehending little more than did the donkey he tended. When Dositheus heard of the kidnapping of Menander and Ilione his eyes grew pained, and he clutched at his robes, Hebrew fashion, as if to rend them; but he made no interruption.

"You must find them," he said evenly when Simon had finished. "But if that priest-robed Izhar had anything to do with their abduction, I am almost certain that you will find him at the house of Annas rather than in Jerusalem. I have long suspected the two of them of dark collusions. You will find Annas' villa by taking the southward trail at the next fork; it stand upon the ridge overlooking the Kedron Valley and Jerusalem, not far beyond the Garden of Gethsemene and just before the Mount of Offense where Solomon once sacrificed to demons. Go carefully, Simon, for Izhar knows much wizardry and Annas knows even more."

"And you—?"

"I would only delay you if I tried to accompany you. Instead I will go to Bethany, perchance to room in the very inn you have told me of. I would meet this Miriam, ward of old Yosef, and the mysterious Teacher to whom she is evidently espoused. And perhaps my arts can awaken this strange wizard, Taggart, with whom I am most anxious to talk further."

"Good. When you speak to Martha, the—lady—who keeps the inn, tell her that 'Simon the Leper' sent you. And she'll probably want more money."

Dositheus nodded, embraced his pupil briefly, then beckoned to Eupatos. "Farewell, Simon. Return soon and tell me what you have learned."

Simon waved in return, then grimly set out down the dusty road in search of the house of Annas.

Elissa, hurrying northward along the ridgetop path, suddenly stumbled and went to her knees. She rose shakily, helped by Menander and her handmaid Lotis.

"I'm so tired!" she gasped. "Can't we . . . rest just a moment?"

Menander looked at her anxiously. Evidently the woman had not yet fully recovered from the drug old Annas had forced her to drink.

"Very well. Here, sit on this boulder—but just for a minute. We must be on our way as quickly as possible."

Lotis glanced nervously back the way they had come. The path was deserted in that direction; the house of Annas was no longer visible, hidden now by a sparsely-treed swell of the ridge to the south. "Do you think they are in pursuit of us already?"

"I don't know. It depends on whether they've discovered your absence." Menander sat down on the ground. He, too, was dreadfully weary; he could use the rest. He wished there were more people about. Save for a few distant pilgrims to the north, they were alone. There were trees and shrubs here and there, too sparse to offer effective concealment. Just west of the dusty roadway was a high wall bordering an extensive tree-filled garden, but there was no nearby gate in it, while bends in the road to the north and south blocked a view of the nearer terrain. It was not a good place.

"I can continue now," Elissa said presently. "How much farther must we go?"

"I recognize this spot," said Menander. "The Garden of Gethsemene is beyond that wall. The road to Bethany from Jerusalem is not far north of here. When we get there we an lose ourselves amid the crowds of pilgrims and—"

Suddenly a group of men came into sight around the southward bend. They were but a short distance away and approaching at a rapid trot—four Roman soldiers in light armor led by a short, rat-faced man with a stubbly beard.

"It's Jahath!" gasped Elissa. "Lord of Gerizim! He'll recognize—"

"Put up your veils—quick!" Menander snapped.

But it was too late. The rat-faced man pointed at them and yelled, and the soldiers dashed around him at a full run. By the time Menander and the two women were on their feet the Romans were nearly upon them. Then one soldier stopped, nocked an arrow to his bow and drew back the string.

"Don't try to bolt, lad," he shouted, "unless you'd like steel for supper."

The other three hurried forward and surrounded them. Menander silently cursed himself for a fool. If only he had forced the woman to go on a little farther—perhaps they would have found a gate in the garden wall. . . .

"Ha! It's the Samaritan woman, all right," exclaimed Jahath as he joined the soldiers. For a moment he stood panting, catching his breath, a gloating grin frozen on his rat-face.

"Aye, and this lad's another prize," said one of the Romans. "He's the one Scribonius sent us to find after he escaped us. Evidently he doubled back and eluded our pursuit, then entered the mansion and helped these women escape also. A slippery kid indeed—I'd have thought only a wizard could have escaped the bonds we put on him!"

"The gall!" laughed Jahath. "Look how he's disguised himself in a Levite robe, and these women in Judean garb. You slipped up in one matter, though, boy: that girl's wearing the garment of a Temple virgin." He laughed more loudly, raucously. "You couldn't have picked a more conspicuous disguise. Several people along this road noted it and so were able to point us on our way. Annas will be pleased that we were able to catch you so quickly."

Lotis clenched her hands, obviously feeling guilty and chagrined. She had picked out the elegantly emblazoned garment herself, not guessing its significance. Despite his fear, Menander's heart went out to her in that instant.

"Enough talk, Jahath," growled one of the Romans, drawing a stout length of cord from his belt. "Get out your knife. We'll hold him while you make a cut behind each of his wrist-tendons, then I'll loop this through the cuts and knot it. I'd like to see him wiggle out of *that!"*

"Labanus, you Romans are ingenious!" Jahath drew a short curved dagger from beneath his robe and advanced, grinning. Menander's fear turned to terror as two of the soldiers laid rough hands on him and held him tightly, twisting his arms behind him.

"No!" screamed Lotis, grabbing at one of the soldiers and trying futilely to drag him away. *"Don't—!"*

The third Roman grabbed her roughly by the shoulder and hurled her to the ground, then turned to help the other two hold the struggling lad. Jahath and Labanus advanced, knife and rope ready—

"Alms good sirs," whined a quavering voice. "In the name of the Most High, alms for the wretched and needy.

All heads turned as one toward the ragged beggar who was tottering toward them, left hand extended, palm up and quivering, from beneath his tattered gray cloak.

"Hades!" growled Labanus, wondering how this wretch had managed to approach them so closely unawares. "Alms, is it? Get you gone, maggot, or you'll get steel instead!"

"Have mercy on the needy," said the beggar, continuing to advance as if he had not heard. He was hunched and bent, his face twisted, his eyes rolling and unfocussed as if he were demented or half blind. "Mercy, O generous ones."

"All right, insect." Labanus advanced, sneering, and planted himself before the beggar. Deliberately he measured the distance, then drew back his fist for a killing blow. *"Here's* an alm for you—"

There was a flash of steel, the *whick* of a blade cutting the air—and flesh. Labanus jerked backwards and sprawled heavily to the ground without a cry, his head half severed, neck-arteries spurting blood.

The beggar leaped forward with a wild yell, throwing aside his cloak, a gladiatorial Thracian blade in his right hand and a Roman gladius in his left. The two Romans holding Menander released him and clutched for their own short-swords. One died instantly as the beggar's curve-bladed sica slashed through his side and up into his heart; the other, lunging, found his hand suddenly lopped from his wrist by an unorthodox left-handed swing and chop of his opponent's sword; he staggered back, howling and cursing while clutching his severed stump. In the next instant he, too, slumped down dead, his neck slashed open by the sica.

The remaining Roman, who had drawn back, nocked an arrow to his bow and took aim—then suddenly staggered forward as Elissa smacked him hard across the back with a large stick she had snatched up from the roadside. His arrow ploughed harmlessly into the dirt. Snarling, he spun about—to receive another sharp crack of the stick across his face. Then the beggar's sword plunged into his back and stood out several inches from his breast; his eyes rolled up and he pitched forward without a sound.

"I hate Romans!" screamed Elissa, her dark eyes wild with fury.

Jahath was dashing down the road, squealing like a terrified pig. The beggar caught up with him in a few swift bounds and, throwing down his gladius, grabbed him by the back of the neck and spun him around. The tax -gatherer sank to his knees, terrified and trembling.

"Enslaver of children, look at me," snarled the demonic beggar. "Look, Jahath—look, and know your doom!"

"Gods of Sheol!" gasped Jahath, his rat-face blanching. *"Simon of Gitta!* Spare me, spare me—I am a rich man. All my wealth can be yours, O Simon—"

"Jackal! You stole that wealth from my parents, and from many others. Did you spare *them?"*

Jahath lunged desperately with the curved dagger in his right hand. Simon caught his wrist easily and twisted; there was a loud snapping of bone, a howl of agony and terror. That howl was abruptly silenced as Simon clutched the tax gatherer by the throat and lifted him into the air. For a moment the man's feet kicked feebly; his hands clawed at the steely arm that held him off the ground, while his ratlike face grew dark, puffy and bulge-eyed.

"Die!" Simon drove his curved blade into the tax gatherer's round paunch and ripped savagely, then contemptuously hurled the body away.

For a moment Jahath lay gurgling and twitching in the dust, blood and entrails spilling from him; then his heels kicked the dust in a final tremor and he lay still.

Simon retrieved his short-sword, wiped his blades clean on the dead Romans' garments, then rose and sheathed them.

"It's . . . really you, Simon?" said Menander, hesitantly advancing a pace.

"It *is!*" exclaimed Elissa. "Thank the Lord of Gerizim! Simon, you came just in time to save us from this scum, this torturer of children—" She strode forward and savagely kicked the gory remains of Jahath. "—this *pig* who called himself a Samaritan—"

"My Lady, please!" Lotis grabbed her mistress by the arm and turned imploring, frightened eyes on Simon. "She was drugged—she is not herself."

"You did well, Elissa," said Simon. "You have courage."

The woman laughed. "Thank you, gladiator. Gods, Simon, what a master of disguise you are! Seeing you standing so tall and grim at this moment, I can hardly believe that you were that decrepit, bent beggar. And that fire of rage in your eyes—I've never seen you like this!"

At her words his expression relaxed a bit, became more sober. "I'm so very glad to see all of you. But how do you happen to be together on this road?"

"Menander rescued us," said Lotis. "We would have escaped altogether but . . . but for my ignorance in choosing a Temple maid's garment for a disguise. On the road I opened my cloak because of the heat, and several people noticed us."

"Yes—I see. Don't leave that cloak open again!"

"It was my ignorance also," said Menander, and proceeded rapidly to explain all that had happened to him since their parting. Within a few minutes the three of them had given him a full picture of the last two days and Simon had reciprocated with a hurried account of his own experiences.

"But, enough," Simon concluded. "You must hurry on now to Bethany. Here, Menander, take the rest of this bread and wine—you look famished. And take this pouch of money also. When you get there, inquire for the place of the innkeeper Martha and tell her that you are guests of 'Simon the Leper'. I'll guard this road until you're safely gone, and if any more Romans pursue you I'll slay them also."

"But what of you, Simon?" asked Menander. "Will you follow?"

"Not right away. I'm going on to Jerusalem to see if I can rescue Ilione from this 'Tower of Siloam' which Izhar told you of. Wait for me in Bethany. With luck I'll be back by dawn."

Menander shook his head sadly. "Please, Simon, don't go. It pains me that Ilione is gone, but it would pain me doubly to lose you also. Perhaps we can rescue her later, when they bring her forth, but it is impossible to do so now. Izhar says that the Tower is impregnable; moreover, it is garrisoned by the centurion Scribonius and a score of his legionaries—"

"Scribonius!" hissed Simon, the dark fires returning to glitter in his shadowed eyes.

"Yes—the Roman who led the band that kidnapped Ilione and me."

"No stronghold is impregnable to an adept trained by the Magi," said Simon grimly. "I must go now."

"Then let me come with you—"

"No. You have done well, Menander—extremely well. But you are tired. Also, you must see these women safely to Bethany. Hurry, now—go!"

The three embraced him briefly and bid him farewell, then turned and continued northward along the road. Simon watched until they were out of sight. A slight breeze had begun to blow, herald of approaching dusk; the sun, already out of sight behind the trees and the high garden wall, was casting long shadows.

"The hound is on your trail, Scribonius," he muttered.

He picked up a stick, strode over to the rent carcass of Jahath and, bending, wrote in the dust beside it the Aramaic words:

B A R A B B A S

"A message for you, Maxentius, that you may again be reminded that the 'son of the father' has returned!"

So saying, Simon donned his beggar's cloak once more, then hurried away, his shadow merging with the greater shadow of the impending dusk.

CHAPTER XVIII

Dositheus and his servant entered the place they had been told was the house of the innkeeper Martha. The main room was deserted save for a young Judean lout who was tending the fire in the large stone hearth built into the east wall.

"I am Dositheus, a physician," the old man announced. "My servant and I require lodging."

"There is no room," said the Judean youth without looking up.

"I am to lodge with one Simon the Leper."

The youth rose and faced the newcomers. Dositheus sensed from his expression that he was slightly retarded.

"I know that one. Martha says no one is to go to his room. A sick man sleeps there."

"I am a physician. I was sent here to treat that man."

"No." The lout shook his head. "Martha says to allow no one in. The rooms are full."

"I shall speak with your mistress, then. Call her."

Again the youth shook his head. "She is not here. She has gone to attend the Master."

"Ah." Dositheus recalled a large crowd he had seen on the west edge of town, some distance south of the road. "Could that 'Master' be the rabbi Yeshua bar Yosef, whom so many are recently flocking to see and hear?"

"He is." The lad's eyes lost some of their hard suspicion. "I have heard him speak. He is a Great One, it is said."

"Indeed? I must hear him also. Listen, young fellow, do you not at least have space in your stable where we may feed our pack-ass and catch up on some sleep?"

"Aye." The lout nodded. You may share the space where the mule of the 'leper' is already stabled. It will cost you three sestercii."

"What?" Dositheus momentarily lost his stately dignity. "But—that's robbery!"

The youth shrugged. "It's the Passover season. Take it or leave it."

Dositheus, scowling, counted out the coins, then followed the lout outside and around back to the stables, Eupatos following in turn with the donkey in tow. The stables consisted of a large rectangular area abutting the inn, all four sides inclosed by roofed stalls full of straw and animals. Quite a few people were already rooming there also.

The youth left them at one of the stalls and went away. While Eupatos tethered and fed the donkey, Dositheus examined the mule which was already tethered there. For a moment he examined its eyes closely, but could detect no sign of intelligence save that of a normal animal. He waved his hand before the beast's face and spoke to it softly, but there was no response.

"Curious," he muttered.

"What are you doing, Master?"

"Nothing, Eupatos. Here, break out the rations, then I'm going to lie down on this straw and rest a bit."

After eating lightly, Dositheus slept for perhaps an hour. He was then startled awake at the sound of other people entering the stall. Quickly he sat up and rubbed his eyes. A young lad and two women stood before him, their forms outlined against the golden glow of the evening sky.

"Eupatos, wake up!" he growled testily at his snoring servant. "How dare that inn-lout send others to share our meager—"

"Dositheus!" exclaimed the lad. "Don't you recognize me?"

The old man peered closely at him. "Menander? Simon found you then. Thank the gods! But who are these two with you?"

"Elizabeth of Sychar and her maid, Lotis."

"Ah." Dositheus rose to his feet, brushed straw from his robe and bowed slightly. "I have heard of you, Lady—"

"And I of you, Dositheus," said the woman. "Menander was just telling us, during our walk to Bethany, that he and Simon both studied the arts of the Magi under you. You may be proud of both of your pupils, for by their skills they have just rescued me and my handmaid from the most dire straits. But tell me, venerable countryman—why are you here in a Judean village disguised in Judean robes and passing yourself off as a Judean physician?"

"You've been talking to the young lout in charge of the inn, I see," said Dositheus. "We have much to discuss. Sit down, all of you. This humble straw is all I have to offer for cushions, but it is soft enough. Eupatos—get up and break out the rations."

For the next half hour they told one another all the things that had happened to them severally, while the gold of the western sky slowly dimmed to the dark blue of dusk. When at last they had finished, Dositheus shook his head, then gazed silently out at the newly-kindled torches by the well in the center of the courtyard.

"Such strange things are happening," he muttered. "Well, Menander, I know that you and the others are exhausted and must rest. But now, I must go forth and see if I can learn what this mysterious rabbi Yeshua is up to. Come, Eupatos—hurry. We haven't must time before dusk fades to night."

The old man and his servant hastened out into the twilight. They had barely entered the street before the inn, however, when they saw a large number of people approaching from the west. Many of them were singing and chanting, and in their midst strode an unusually tall, white-robed figure. In another minute they had reached the inn and began to file and jostle in through the door.

Dositheus, beckoning to Eupatos to follow, walked forward confidently and entered with the foremost of them. The room within was large and furnished with many rough wooden tables and benches; savory odors of cooking pervaded it, emanating from pots and grills arranged within a broad fireplace set into the east wall.

The guests, who fell silent as they entered, began to seat themselves at the tables while servants hastened to serve them bread and porridge. Dositheus, moving among them with the confidence of one who belonged, found himself a place in a shadowy corner whence he could watch and listen inconspicuously; he pulled a stool up to the table and sat down, motioning to Eupatos to sit on the floor next to him.

When the white-robed man entered, Dositheus eyed him closely. He was unusually tall, his head almost touching the low-beamed ceiling, and his bearing was calm, assured, even regal. There was a sadness, even a weariness, in his noble features—features which nevertheless possessed, even as Aggaeus had said, a strange, almost goatish cast. But it was the eyes that most gripped Dositheus—the dark, large, limpid eyes that reflected the oil lamps like still pools. In their depths he sensed empathy, compassion and a boundless mystery, and in that moment felt an impulse to reach out in warm friendship, to confide old sorrows. . . .

But he restrained the impulse and turned his attention to the tall and stately woman who walked beside the noble rabbi. Her face and gray-green eyes reflected the same mystical strangeness and compassion as his, though without the alien touch of goatishness. Dositheus felt his heart constrict; she was one of the loveliest women he had ever see. Dim, half-lost memories of an ancient love were suddenly reawakened vividly in his mind, and a voice seemed to whisper to him: *O Thou, Desire of Memories, Mistress of Infinity. . . .*

Then the pair passed by and vanished through a doorway, ascending the stairs leading to the inner and upper chambers.

Dositheus, realizing that he had forgotten to breathe, inhaled deeply. "Gods!" he muttered, shaken. "Can it truly be *her . . .?*"

"Her?" said a young man who had moved close to the old mage's table. "Do you know our master's bride?" Then, bending closer, he suddenly hissed in astonishment, "By El Shaddai! Is that truly you, Dositheus?"

The old wizard scowled up at the youthful, bearded face, irritation and a slight apprehension in his eyes. The youth drew back, made an apologetic gesture and began to move away.

"No, Nathaniel, don't go," said Dositheus, recovering quickly. "You startled me. Come, sit down. I was in Capharnaum a few days ago and talked with your father. He would be joyed to hear news of you, if—" He paused guiltily, remembering that Tolmai had not escaped from he Black Synagogue and was now probably in thrall to Izhar.

The young man obeyed, shaking his head sadly. "Would that my father might see the light and join me on the path I must follow."

"You mean the path of the rabbi Yeshua? That was him and his bride who passed through this room but now, I gather. A most impressive pair, I must say, but with an air of great weariness about them."

"And no wonder," said Nathaniel. "Both traveled all night to reach Bethany; since then, the rabbi has spent most of the day preaching to the crowds, she constantly at his side. Then this evening, just after the sun went down, he performed the Rite of the Rising. . . ." The young man turned abruptly away, as if suddenly realizing that he had spoken out of turn. "Martha!" he called out to a dour-faced woman who had just entered. "Bring us bread, porridge and wine."

While the woman served them, Dositheus, learning that she was the proprietress, informed her that he was a friend of Simon the Leper and a renter of some of her stable space. She answered him curtly and somewhat impolitely, then left to serve other guests.

"What's wrong with her?" asked Dositheus when she had gone.

"Martha's always a bit like that," said Nathaniel, "and now in addition she's preoccupied with the Master and his doings. Just between you and me, I sense that she's a bit jealous of her sister Miriam, the Master's bride."

"Ah, yes." The old man nodded. "As any ordinary woman might well be. When this Miriam entered the room, I felt something—I think I am sure I have not felt since. . . ." His voice trailed off, and for a moment his face grew tranquil; his eyes, touched with awe, seemed to gaze through the far wall of the inn as into lost times. Then, recovering himself, his eyes again grew shrewd as he said, "Tell me, friend Nathaniel, what you know of this—bride."

"Only that she is the ward and great-niece of old Yosef of Aphairema, and that she comes originally from a town called Magdala on the shore of the Sea of Gennesaret. The Master, who once rescued her from possessing demons, says that she is the incarnation of . . . of that Mistress of Wisdom who existed with the Highest One in the eternities before the worlds were created."

"Sophia," muttered Dositheus, staring at the intricate grain of the table's dark planks. "Luna, Selene, Helen—Her for whose sake that creation was performed."

"You do not scoff," said Nathaniel, wondering. "You *know!*"

"Aye. I sensed it. And so did Simon when he met her—"

"Simon?"

Dositheus shook his head as if to clear it, then chuckled. "Simon the Leper, a friend of mine whose quarters I share. Of course, he's not really a leper—"

"I see. One of those charlatans who work the crowds during holiday times."

"Exactly. But now, Nathaniel, concerning this Rite of the Rising—"

The young man paled. "Do not speak of it," he whispered, glancing nervously about at the men seated at the other tables. "Kepha and the others would be angry to find me discussing it with you, for the Master has often enjoined us to silence concerning his miracles."

To ensure their widespread telling, Dositheus thought cynically. Aloud, he said, "You know your secrets are safe with me. Have I ever betrayed to outsiders the hidden doctrines of Johannen, of whose sect you and Kepha were once initiates? Besides, I already know much of this matter. Listen: The Eye of the Bull now sets with the sun; what, therefore, shall rise when the sun sets?"

"What, then, Dositheus?" said Nathaniel with a slight shudder.

"The great Dragon of Babylon, whose heart is the red fire of Antares, and not until another moon has passed shall his pursuing enemy the Centaur gain the ascendant at that hour of propitious tension. The stars are right, Nathaniel, and when the moon is full the Gate shall open to its widest. Who shall then pass through it? And who has but now risen to aid in that passage?"

"You know much indeed, Dositheus." Nathaniel gulped his wine. "As you have guessed, it is the Twin who has risen—the brother of the Master. No human eye may behold him, and he is named *El-ha-Zarria.*"

"*El-ha-Zarria*—'Lord of the Zarrians'," muttered Dositheus, taking wine in his turn. "It is indeed as I feared. Eibon and Thoth-Ammon have both written of it. When the stars are right, two brothers are born into the world—one like man's truest eidolon, one like Those who are without visibility or earthly substance and who command the star-demons. . . ."

"*What?* Dositheus, what are you talking—?"

"Never mind." Again the old men shook his head. "Pay no heed to an old man's ramblings. Tell me, Nathaniel: How does this *rising* come about? I saw a crowd near the town's west edge just before sunset. Was the . . . rite . . . taking place there?"

The young man nodded. "Actually it began some days ago, when we were yet with the Master in Perea beyond the Jordan. A message came to the Master from the Bride and her sister, saying: 'Lord, he whom you love is ill.' When we asked what this meant, the Master replied: 'This illness is not unto death. No, rather shall Yahweh Zava'ot and his son now be glorified. El-ha-Zarria now sleeps, but I go to awaken him.' This I did not understand, but later the disciple Judah of Kerioth, who is privy to more of the Master's secrets than any of the rest of us, explained to me that the Twin was stirring in its crypt and must soon arise to aid in the return of the Father. Our Master had often spoken to us of his Twin, sometimes as if that being were present among us and directly speaking to his mind.

"A day or two later the Master said to us: 'El-ha-Zarria is dead, yet he waits dreaming; soon you shall see him rise, and then shall you believe all I have told you. Come, let us go to him.' I saw Judah smile as if with understanding, but the rest of us were puzzled. Then the Master's eyes grew wide and dreamy, as they were wont to do when he received a message from spirits or demons; we had witnessed it often. A moment later he turned to us and said: 'The Twin bids us to come and die with him.'"

"By which he meant 'die to this world', no doubt," muttered Dositheus. "Ostanes has written: 'Some things from death may rise; the Old One's spawn ne'er dies.'"

"You indeed know many strange things, Dositheus, but none stranger than what I witnessed but an hour ago. Listen." Nathaniel lowered his voice still more and leaned forward. "When we arrived here in Bethany this morning, the sister of the Bride came to greet us. She was angry and scolded the Master for tarrying overlong, but I heard him say to her: 'The Brother shall rise again.' Later, after he had spent the day preaching to the crowds, admonishing them to obey the Law with renewed vigor in order to prepare for the Father's return, he led us finally to the grotto at Bethany's edge as the sun sank toward Jerusalem across the distant valley. Not a few of the townsfolk continued with us. We passed among many tombs and at length came to one greater than all the rest; actually it was a cave opening from the hillside and blocked by a great stone. As the sun set the Master commanded us: 'Remove the stone.' We did so, though not without much labor, for it was huge and firmly set in place—and immediately a dreadful stench welled forth. 'Surely he has been dead for many days!' Martha shrieked accusingly—but then we all heard a strange sloshing and saw movement within. The crowd shrieked and ran off, and I almost followed them, feeling a strange terror. Within the cave I glimpsed something formless—like huge grave-garments, it seemed to me, billowing from the entrance; it was as if a white curtain of misty substance were being pushed aside by something monstrous and invisible, something that pulsed and lapped fluidly. I saw the Master standing before it, crying out to us: 'Believe now in the glory of Yahweh Zava'ot!' But we all continued to back away in fear, save for Judah and a disciple who is called Thomas the Twin-keeper. 'Father, I thank thee,' intoned the Master; then, after a few more short incantations, he cried out: 'El-ha-Zarria, come forth!" The thing brushed the mist-curtain aside and surged out into the twilight, and I turned and fled, together with most of the rest. I saw nothing, Dositheus, yet I sensed a presence of something more awful than I had ever before—"

"So, Nathaniel," rumbled a deep voice, "this is how you keep the Master's trust, is it?"

Nathaniel ceased speaking, cringed as a broad shadow fell across him. Dositheus looked up and recognized the craggy face of a burly Galilean—Kepha the fisherman.

"Babbling to strangers, eh?" growled the dark-bearded giant.

Nathaniel trembled, tried to reply but could not.

"Strangers?" said Dositheus. "Am I a stranger to you, Kepha? Were we not brothers in the cult of Johannen the Baptizer not so long ago?"

"Johannen is dead, Samaritan," said Kepha, "—slain by the Tetrarch Herod, whose sins against the Law he denounced. He died well and in good time, after announcing the advent of his cousin, our Master."

"Did he indeed?" said Dositheus mildly. "Johannen said nothing of this to me—nor, as far as I know, to the rest of the Thirty—the band of which you were once a member and of which I am now leader."

The dark-bearded giant clenched his fists. "Get up, Dositheus," he snarled, glowering, "and leave this place. You are not welcome here."

The old wizard, sensing the imminence of violence, rose hurriedly, gestured placatingly, then beckoned to Eupatos and hastened out the door and into the night.

Once outside, he and his servant hurried westward through the dark narrow streets until at last they came to the edge of town. Twilight had given way to moonlit night, but despite that fact Dositheus was surprised to see how utterly deserted the streets were. Not a soul was abroad. The moon, now well over half full, gleamed wanly in the eastern sky.

At length he came to the grotto of the tombs—the place just beyond the town's edge where he had earlier seen the crowd gathered, no doubt to hear the Master speak. Silently he and his servant circled the area until they were on the downward slope and could see upward into the gentle, tomb-studded swale. No one was about now, though one torch still flickered dimly from a bracket set into the rock wall of the hollow's eastern end. Far back in that narrowing draw gaped the mouth of what appeared to be a natural cave, and beside it lay a huge round boulder, evidently recently rolled away. From this black, yawning aperture rolled a stench which made Dositheus gasp.

"Wait here for me, Eupatos," he commanded.

Then, cautiously, he stole forward, holding his hand over his nose and mouth, and peered within the cave entrance. The dim torchlight revealed a spacious cavern whose walls and floor glistened with slime, and from its entrance led a trail of prints, each as round as the widest part of a large amphora, suggesting a trail such as a monstrous caterpillar might make.

"Gods!" hissed Dositheus. "How many years was the thing confined in this place, until—"

He ceased speaking as, suddenly, he heard voices. Gazing upward, he spied two dark figures standing atop the low cliff, apparently engaged in conversation as they stared up at the sky. Carefully, silently, Dositheus stole forward and began to creep up the flanking slope, straining to hear what the pair were saying.

The first words he heard were: ". . . to wait here until the Dark One comes, Thomas. Such were the Master's instructions."

Thomas—the "Twin-keeper". Dositheus wondered why a man would bear such a name. These, then, must be the two whom Nathaniel said had not fled from . . . from whatever had emerged from the "tomb". The old mage wished he could see the features of the pair rather than just their silhouettes against the night sky.

"I know, Judah," muttered the other, confirming Dositheus' suspicion, "but I wish this night were over. I sense an evil impending."

"Surely *you* do not fear the newly-risen Brother—you, who have been his keeper during this last decade?"

"No, no." The one called the "Twin-keeper" shook his head. "The Brother knows his part in this. Tonight he has had his Second Birth, has come forth from his Second Womb; he is full of knowledge and purpose. He will abide in the Vale of Hinnom awhile, hiding by day, ranging and feeding by night, gathering strength toward the Time of the Aligned Stars."

Dositheus, crouching behind a concealing boulder, shuddered. His dark readings had prepared him for some understanding of these things.

"Tell me then, Twin-keeper," said Judah, "what *do* you fear?"

"The man you call Taaran—the Dark One. I have seen sorcery, but never any like unto his!"

"You fear sorcery?" Judah laughed briefly. "You, for twenty years the apprentice of Yosef of Aphairema, who was the Keeper of the Twin before you—?"

"It's not just the Dark One's magic. There's something about him—a hatred, an evil. Why does the Master associate with him?"

"Because the masses need miracles and Taaran can supply them."

Dositheus felt the prickle of gooseflesh. The name *Taaran* was that of one of the most ancient and evil gods know to mankind, a being to whom ancient writers attributed the destruction of Attluma, Atlantis and the Hyborian lands, and who was still worshipped by the forest-dwelling Druids as a god of storm and thunder. Taaran, God of Evil, hater and destroyer of mankind. . . . What sort of man would go by such a name?

"You fear most what you know least," Judah continued, "as do we all. The Dark One is only human, despite the legends that center about him; I have spoken with him many times at the Master's request. But you, Thomas—you have for years aided the Master and old Yosef in raising, nurturing and instructing the Brother—a being whose form I could not see even in torchlight, but whose presence this night filled me with dread. Though the Master has thoroughly instructed me, I was yet not prepared for what I sensed coming forth from this unsealed grotto. I can scarcely believe even now that the Master and his Twin share the same origin—"

"Quiet!" hissed Thomas suddenly. "The Dark One comes."

Dositheus started, but managed to remain silent. A third figure was suddenly silhouetted, tall and stark, against the moonlit sky. Dositheus had not seen the man approach, but there he was—black-clad, standing on a dark circular platform with high-raised edges—a platform which hung motionless above the ground to about the height of a man's knees. Glassy discs were held before his eyes by a dark frame, while upon his brow a larger blue disc glowed dimly. An even dimmer blue nimbus of light surrounded the man.

"Gods!" muttered Dositheus beneath his breath. "The wizard Taggart—"

But in the same instant he saw that he was mistaken. This man was taller, leaner and clean-shaven, rigid-featured, and his eyes under the blue disc glared with a light of— hatred? Madness?

"Ally of the Master!" cried Thomas, dropping to his knees. "Maker of miracles for our cause! We await your commands."

Then, to Dositheus' surprise, the man called Judah immediately translated Thomas' words into Latin, his tone of voice conveying none of the latter's superstitious awe.

"No need for that." The stranger's Latin, like Taggart's, was halting and ill-accented. He tossed to Judah a metallic headband upon which another blue disc glowed. "Put this on."

Judah did so, then said in Aramaic, "The Master bade us await you here, O Taaran. The rites were performed this evening, and El-ha-Zarria has risen."

Again Dositheus started. El-ha-Zarria—God of the Zarrians—was a monstrous being reputedly served by a race of demons from beyond the stars. How had this Judah learned of such things, which were known only to those mages most learned in age-lost arcane writings?

Then the stranger answered in a language Dositheus had never heard despite his wide learning and many travels. Only one word of the answer—*Byakhtril*—was intelligible to the old Samaritan.

"You have found it?" cried Judah excitedly. "Then did you, with your magic, draw it forth without shattering the rock, even as you did with the *Byakhtron* at Chorazin?"

Again the black-clad man answered in his strange tongue.

"Too much intervening rock? Aye, the foundations of the Tower of Set were carved into the living stone of Ophel. But can you not blast your way in with your lightnings, O Dark One?"

The tone of the stranger's reply was harsh, abrupt. Judah glanced uneasily upward at the stars.

"I understand. Our enemies must not sense our presence here. What, then, shall I tell the Master?"

The stranger pointed at the man called Thomas and again spoke unintelligibly. Dositheus recognized only the words *El-ha-Zarria.*

"Of course!" Judah exclaimed. "The Brother! He has now risen in power and burns to do the will of his Father. Thomas—" He snatched the blue disc-band from his head and handed it to his companion. "Thomas, make all haste after the Twin and given him *this.*" He turned again to the stranger. "I go now, Dark One, to inform the Master of your discovery and convey to him your counsel—and he, in turn, shall inform the Brother."

"It is well," said the stranger in awkward Latin.

Then the man in black was gone.

Dositheus blinked. There had been no warning. The man and his craft had simply vanished. Then, briefly, there came a faint windy sound as of something rushing upward through the air.

"Make haste, Thomas," Judah repeated.

The pair separated and hurried away into the night, Thomas toward the Gethsemene road, Judah back into town. Dositheus remained hidden for several minutes, breathing slowly, allowing the pounding of his heart and the tingling of his nerves to subside. Then, slowly, he stole from the shadow of the boulder and cautiously returned to the spot where his servant waited.

The lout was already asleep on the ground, snoring.

"Get up, Eupatos!" Dositheus prodded his servant awake. "Up, lazy fool! Dark powers are astir. We must get back to the inn at once."

The voice came to him as he drowsed upon his high throne above the blue empyrean: *Awake, Lord Mazda! Whom do you seek in dreams?*

It was true. He had slept and dreamed strangely. Now, awake, he had already forgotten most of those tangled slumber-wanderings through innumerable worlds of his own creation. About him now, crystal-pure and infinite, extended the boundless potential of his creative power, empty yet pregnant with endless possibilities. He was alone—there was none other, nor could there be. And yet, the voice lingered in his mind, lovely and soft and womanly. Was it a being other than himself? No, it was more. It was the reason for his own being, the cause that alone could stir his infinite creative powers into play, the sole purpose that could motivate them.

Ennoia, he thought, remembering. *Sophia, all-knowing. Selene, bright and unfading, seen easily by those who love her, found by those who seek her.*

The cerulean infinities about him deepened to a violet hue; a sadness, like the twilight herald of impending Night, fell over him. There had been a vast loss—and infinity ago, an instant ago. *She* was gone—and yet he felt her presence, nearby and yet concealed by veils of cosmic immensity.

She seeks those who are worthy of her, said the Voice, *and at her whim She appears to them in their wanderings, meets them in their inmost thoughts.*

He rose from his throne, as Zeus upon cloud-robed Olympus, and the infinite crystalline power about him sang and surged. The dreams he had dreamed began to return—the worlds Her fancy had envisioned and which, for Her sake, His creative power invoked and sustained. Once again Her many names stirred in his mind: *Ennoia, Sophia, Selene, Astarte, Aphrodite. . . .*

I shall trace Her out from the beginning of creation, he declared, *and have clear knowledge of Her. I shall not bypass Truth. . . .*

Menander started into wakefulness, his eyes instantly open. Or had they ever closed? Had he dreamed, or . . .?

He was in darkness. No, not completely, for through the stable's ill-patched roof streamed the moon's rays, faintly illuminating the face of the girl who slumbered next to him.

Slowly he faced her, wondering and a bit afraid. Her arm was beneath his head; her dark-lashed face, beautiful in innocent slumber, was turned toward him; the fingers of her left hand entwined with his right. She breathed softly, easily.

For long moments he lay gazing at her, wondering at her incredible beauty, yet feeling a strange familiarity, a naturalness, about her nearness—as if the world itself might revolve about that nearness.

She stirred slightly; the soft straw rustled beneath their cloaks. Then her delicate lips parted and she murmured dreamily, "Mazda. . . ."

"I called, and the spirit of Sophia came to me," whispered Menander. "I preferred her to scepters and thrones, and found no wealth comparable to her, no precious stone her equal."

Her eyes opened, dark and lovely and full of mystic knowing. "It has been long, My Lord, but the wait has been worth it. . . ." Then puzzlement disturbed the calm of her features. "Menander—is that you? What are you doing here?"

"That's what I was about to ask *you,* Sophia—I mean. . . ."

"That name! You—someone—called me that in my dream."

"And you, Lotis, called me—Mazda."

"Aye." The girl sat up, dark hair tumbling over her pale shoulders. Nearby across the narrow stall lay her mistress, gently breathing in slumber, her form faintly illumined by reddish torchlight from the court. "It—it looks like I came over to you, Menander."

He sat up beside her. "You come unbidden, and in that way only. How could it be otherwise?"

She looked at him strangely. "Did I dream that also? It has such a familiar ring! And those words you said—about the spirit of Sophia. . . ."

He remembered. "They are from Sirach's *Book of Wisdom*—but when I said them, they seemed my own."

"This is a strange night," said Lotis. "Menander—who are we?"

Something Dositheus had once told him came into his mind, but he found himself reluctant to say it to her. In silence he put aside his covering cloak and donned his sandals, then stood up. She followed suit, and for a moment they stood shivering slightly in their light tunics. The night air felt cool upon them in contrast to the warmth of their recent slumbering embrace.

He donned his dark robe. "I need some air," he muttered, "and—I must think."

"And I." She donned her cloak also and they stole out the doorway, softly, so as not to wake the girl's sleeping mistress. Outside, the wide courtyard was dimly illumined by two torches, one by the stone-walled well near its center, the other bracketed upon the inn wall. Above the stars and the pale moon, over half-full, gleamed from the deep blue vault of night.

"Do not turn from me, Menander," said the girl softly. "Did you not tell me that you would not . . . bypass Truth?"

"Gods," breathed Menander, gazing at her unbelievable loveliness. How could she have seemed but a humanly pretty girl yesterday? "Lotis, you asked me who we are. Who do you *think* we are?"

"I don't know, but I think we are not just . . . ordinary people. Our dream has told us that, and I know I shall never forget it. Never have I had such a dream before!" She laid her small white hands upon the well's stone coping and gazed pensively up at the moon. "Selene," she murmured. "To mankind it symbolizes Her—the one *I* was in our dream. And the blue night that enfolds Her must symbolize Mazda. Is it not so?"

To Menander the girl's words seemed almost to echo from another world, for the flavor of the dream was still upon him. "It is so." He swallowed, for his voice was husky, and laid a hand gently on her shoulder. "Listen, Lotis, Dositheus once told me that some people are True Spirits—fragments of the great God-soul that was sundered and trapped within matter at the creation of the worlds."

She turned to him, wonder and fascination in her eyes. Then, suddenly, those eyes widened like a startled doe's. She pointed over Menander's shoulder and whispered tersely, "Look—that man on the balcony!"

Menander whirled and looked to where she pointed. A man was indeed standing upon the walkway that ran around the inn's second story, leaning on its stuccoed parapet and gazing upward at the sky. He appeared naked save for a tattered black garment about his loins, and his pale features were faintly limned by the moonlight.

"Gods!" hissed Menander. "It's the wizard Taggart—"

Then the man faced them, and Menander started—for within the wizard's eyes a faint, eerie yellowness appeared to gleam.

CHAPTER XIX

Simon crouched in the shadow of the alley's mouth and stared up at the looming square bulk of the tower. There were two dark windows on this western face, both far too high to reach with his scaling rope. He wondered if Ilione was imprisoned behind either of them.

Before the tower's door several Roman soldiers loitered, leaning against the rough wall or sitting upon the stone steps.

"Baal plague them!" Simon muttered in frustration. Until now he had had good luck, managing to gain the city's Siloam Gate at dusk and joining the last crowd to enter just before the ponderous doors were pulled shut for the night. He had mingled with the throngs who bought and sold in the great square of the Siloam Pool, disguised in his great dark cloak, and had passed the time begging for alms while he checked the area of the tower carefully. He had even taken in several sestercii from those who pitied his crippled and diseased condition. But now night had fallen, the crowds had thinned almost to nothing, and only the torches flanking the tower door faintly illuminated the area. The tower seemed impregnable. Worse, Simon occasionally saw legionaries prowling about the square and urging stragglers on their way.

Suddenly he heard a footfall down the alley behind him and, simultaneously, saw the flicker of a torch. Turning, he glimpsed the glimmer of metal and oiled leather. Too late to flee—the approaching Roman had already spied him.

"Alms for the afflicted!" Simon wheezed, holding out a trembling hand.

"Another damned beggar," growled the soldier. "Afflicted by the gods—and justly, no doubt. Get up and begone. Quickly!"

"Help me up—"

"What! And touch your god-cursed flesh?" The soldier spat on the ground. "I'll help you get up—with *this!*"

Simon adroitly avoided the spear-point prodding at his side and leaped erect. His right fist crashed full into the Roman's face, precisely between the eyes, and the man's knees buckled. Simon caught his unconscious body and quietly lowered it to the ground, then snuffed the flame of the fallen torch in the dirt.

"Sweet dreams, lad," he muttered. "I'd guess you'll sleep a few hours, at least."

Casting aside his cloak and the other trappings of his disguise, Simon quickly stripped the legionary of his armor and sword-belt, donning them himself. Hardly had he finished doing so when he heard the clatter of many more soldiers approaching the tower from a street to the north. Cautiously he peered out of the alley and saw that there were perhaps a dozen of them, many bearing torches. At their head marched a tall officer wearing a crested helmet, and by his side an even taller, heavily-muscled man—a gladiator.

The guards by the door of the tower stood smartly to attention.

"Open!" yelled the officer as he stopped at the foot of the steps. "Tell your centurion that Tribute Maxentius has come."

Simon gripped his spear tightly; his lips drew back in a silent snarl. He had recognized the voice of his hated enemy even before the man had announced his name.

The guards opened the tower door and hurried inside. Simon inched forward amid the shadows. Presently a Roman centurion appeared in the stone archway, and again Simon felt a surge of hate, for beneath the light of the torches he recognized the sadistic face of Scribonius. Immediately Maxentius mounted the stairway and the pair stood there in the doorway, exchanging salutes. Simon gripped his spear firmly and drew it back for a cast. The range was easy, the spear heavy and sharp—he could pin them together like a pair of insects, then vanish into the night. . . .

Yet Ilione was a prisoner in the tower. If he cast the shaft and fled, would the gods ever grant him another chance to rescue her? And if he did not, would they ever give him another such cast at his enemies?

Then, in that moment of indecision, Maxentius and Scribonius entered the tower—and the chance was gone. Immediately the huge gladiator and the soldiers began to follow them in through the archway.

Simon calmed himself with two deep breaths, then stepped deliberately from the shadows, walking briskly, but with no show of undue haste. He had but one chance now. As the last of the soldiers entered the tower he joined them; the final pair glanced at him, but gave him no particular notice.

Then the heavy door was closed behind him and he heard the massive wooden bolts go clattering into their stone slots. A moment later the group emerged from a short passage into a huge square chamber. Simon bore himself with the same military confidence as the rest; with any luck, each group of soldiers would assume him to be a member of the other.

"At ease, all of you," snapped Maxentius, "but don't open that door again until I'm ready to leave. Admit no one—not even if he claims to be a messenger of the Emperor. Understood?" He turned then to Scribonius. "Do you have the thing, as promised?"

The centurion nodded curtly. "Aye. It is hid in the same vault that formerly concealed the ass-god. You three—" He pointed to the soldiers nearest him. "Lift that stone trap."

"No. My personal bodyguard can do it more quickly and easily." Maxentius grinned at the huge gladiator and pointed to an iron ring set into the floor. "Lift it, Cratos."

The giant advanced, stooped and gripped the ring with his right hand. Enormous muscles bulged along his arm and down his back while his brutal features grimaced and strained. A slight crackle of mighty muscles was briefly heard; then, smoothly and ponderously, the stone was lifted up and set down with a reverberant thud beside the hole it had blocked.

"By Pallas," gasped a soldier, "what a Hercules of a man!"

Cratos laughed gutturally and flexed his arms. "Who will fight me?" he challenged the legionaries amiably.

"Any six of you would be mad to try it," said Scribonius with as much pride as if the gladiator were his own, "even were he unarmed. Such strength! I've seen him, with only one hand, squeeze the head of a rebellious woman and crush it like an egg."

"Enough," snapped Maxentius. "Go on down, Scribonius, and get the thing."

Simon thought the centurion hesitated for an instant, but then he grabbed a torch from one of his men and descended the narrow steps into the hole. In a very short time he reemerged, his forehead slightly beaded with sweat, and handed Maxentius a small bronze-colored object which looked to Simon like a child's whistle. The tribune hastily put the object into his belt-pouch and pulled the drawstrings tight.

"Good. And now, Scribonius, I understand you have something more to show me."

"I—I do?"

"Another of Annas' winged messengers came to me at dusk. What of the other items you took from the slain magician?"

"Oh, of course. I have been examining them—"

"To see if you could discover their magic, no doubt. Bring them to me."

"I—I wanted to see if they might be dangerous, like the object that killed three of our men. I wouldn't want you to handle anything that might be dangerous before I'd examined—"

"Bring them."

Scribonius nodded, hurried to a rough table across the room and groped about under it, then returned with a large bundle of rough brown cloth. To Simon it appeared to be a packsack with heavy woven straps, its material resembling that used for tents or sails. On one side was some sort of lettering, large and even, but faded.

"What does it say?" demanded Maxentius. "Most of the characters are Latin ones, but they make no sense. Can anyone here read them?"

The nearest soldiers shook their heads. Simon edged a bit closer until he could make them out. They were arranged thus:

U. S. ARMY
ISSUE

616

He shook his head in turn. Despite his knowledge of several written languages, he could make no sense of these characters.

"No doubt some numerological spell," remarked Scribonius, dumping a number of strange objects from the bag onto the table. "Look at this, Sir." He held up a silvery, cylindrical object a bit longer than his hand. "This gives out a beam of light when you press this little projection forward—thus."

The soldiers gasped in amazement to see the circle of light that sprang into being upon the stone wall of the chamber. Again Scribonius flicked his finger, and the light vanished.

"So!" Maxentius raised both his eyebrows, impressed. He picked up a more complex object with a movable disc on one end. "And what does this do?"

"I don't know—but I think the wizard used it to find the Byakhtril."

Simon held in his surprise with an effort. It was now clear to him that the "wizard" they were talking about was the man called Taggart.

"And these objects?" Maxentius held up a small rectangular box of dark metal and another of unknown black substance with glassy insets.

"One makes a hissing sound when a projection is turned, the other makes clicking sounds. I don't know what they are."

"And what of that belt you're wearing? I've never seen one like it before. Was it the wizard's also?"

"Yes, Sir. It—it does a strange thing."

"I see. There is a dim bluish glow about its clasp. Why is that?"

"I don't know, but—"

"Never mind. Take it off and put it in with the rest of the wizard's things," said Maxentius. "I'll take them with me when I return to the Antonian Fortress; no doubt Annas and Caiaphas will be able to divine their use. Right now, though, we have matters to discuss."

"Yes, Sir?" said Scribonius. He made no move to take off the belt. Simon wondered if the man had divined its secret already. If so, he could be a formidable opponent indeed.

"Annas' winged messenger has also informed me," Maxentius went on, "that Jahath, the Samaritan tax gatherer, has just been found dead on the ridgetop road near Gethsemene. He had been slain with a knife or sword, and in the dust beside him was written a message identical to the ones left in his house in Sychar, and in mine in Sebaste."

"Hades!" For once there was no trace of Scribonius' set smirk. "'The son of the father'! And of course that can only be—"

"So, look to yourself, centurion! Stay within this tower as much as you can, and never venture out without at least a decan of your men along.

Above all, no more night forays after wenches until this matter is settled—which brings us to the last matter we must discuss."

"What's that, Sir?"

"The maid you are keeping here. Annas has consulted his 'spirits' since he met her, and now he thinks that she may be what he calls a 'true spirit' and therefore a perfect victim for the Rite. If so, he would not like it if her spirit were broken beforehand, Scribonius—and neither would I."

"By that," said Scribonius glumly, "I suppose you mean she must remain a virgin."

Maxentius laughed. "Not at all, good Scribonius. Forget that old nonsense. I said her spirit must not be broken. But should you do anything to rouse her hate, her fear, her loathing—why that would be all to the good. It's high emotion that makes the Rite effective, or so Annas tells me. Hate, fear—that's what They feed upon. . . .

During this conversation, which most of the soldiers were listening to avidly, Simon had edged closer to the doorway that opened to the tower stairs. Now, slipping within, he laid aside his spear and began to climb the steps as quickly as silence would allow. Ilione must be confined in one of the chambers above; he would have to release her, then hurry on to the top of the tower. From there, dangerous though it would be, they must climb down by means of his cord to the top of the battlemented wall, then find a place low enough to descend to the ground. It was the girl's only chance—.

"Eee-yeeh!" The tower reverberated to the shrill hooted scream. *"Eee-lee-yeeh!"*

Simon cursed as, too late, he spied the glowing-eyed owl perched upon a window ledge. As the bird spread its wings and flapped up the stairway in screeching flight, he caught sight of the gleaming "V" of stars upon the medallion dangling from its neck. In the same instant he heard shouts and the clattering of soldiers' boots from below—and above.

Snarling with rage, Simon whirled and raced back down the stairs. Hopefully he could slash a path through his enemies and escape into the night; if not, he could at least try to take his two hated enemies down to death with him.

A legionary dashed through the doorway at the base of the steps and Simon met him full tilt, burying the blade of his gladius in the man's guts. He short-sword was twisted from his grasp as the dying soldier gripped its hilt with both hands and sank down; a second legionary, charging in, met unexpected doom as the keen sica in Simon's left hand slashed his neck.

The soldiers drew back a pace, and Simon, roaring with fury, snatched up his spear from the floor and hurled it through the chest of the nearest of them. Then he charged like a lion into their midst, slashing; the gladiator-blade gashed the neck of a second legionary, spilled the guts of a third.

Straight before him he saw the centurion Scribonius, face twisted in terror, right hand fumbling frantically at his belt clasp.

"Die, Roman!" yelled Simon, leaping and slashing.

At the same instant a blue veil seemed to spring into being between him and Scribonius. Incredibly, his knife blade was deflected as if by an invisible frictionless shield and he bumped hard into what felt like an invisible wall, convex and resilient. He lost his balance and fell to one knee; Scribonius, too, lost footing and rolled howling toward the wall, pin-wheeling just above the floor as if held up by magic, surrounded by a dim sphere of bluish light.

"Cratos!" yelled Maxentius. *"Take him—alive!"*

Simon leaped up, slashing, but the charging giant gladiator nimbly avoided the blade; then a sharp blow on the Samaritan's left shoulder half numbed his arm. He whirled to lash out at the soldier who had struck him with a spear-shaft, but the man managed to parry the wicked sica, knocking it from his weakened grip—and then Simon felt himself caught from behind in a powerful choke hold. Frantically he stomped down on the gladiator's left foot, elbowed him savagely in the ribs; the giant, ignoring the blows, growled a harsh laugh and applied pressure more tightly. The blood pounded in Simon's head; his face felt like a balloon about to burst. . . .

The last thing he saw before lapsing into unconsciousness was the hateful face of Maxentius grinning down at him.

"Taggart!" exclaimed Menander in astonishment.

The man looked down at him for a moment, then turned and moved away along the balcony and around the corner of the inn.

Menander turned to the girl beside him. "The man seems dazed, Lotis. I must go after him—"

"Be careful, Menander! Did you not see the glow in his eyes? Surely he is a wizard.

"He is, but I think not an evil one. Stay here, Lotis."

The young man hurried out of the courtyard and around the corner of the inn toward the street. Lotis, suppressing her fears, followed him. As they emerged from the alley they saw the wizard descending the stairway. He reached the street and stood there a moment, hesitant, then turned eastward and passed a few feet in front of where the young pair stood concealed in the shadows, walking toward the edge of town.

"Go back, Lotis," whispered Menander urgently. "I'm going after him. I'll be back soon."

He slipped from the alley and silently followed the wizard. To his consternation he heard Lotis following him again. At the same moment the man in the ragged black loincloth turned around and confronted them with eerie yellow eyes.

"Menander?" he said. Then in halting Latin, "But who is this young lady with you? And where is Ilione?"

The pain of remembrance that stabbed through the youth was followed immediately by a surge of guilt. He had completely forgotten Ilione until now!

"The Romans have captured Ilione, O Wizard. They kidnapped us after leaving you for dead on the road to Jericho. I escaped, but they have taken her to the Tower of Set—"

"And my possessions?" said Taggart, fumbling absently where his belt should be. "Do these Romans have them also?"

"Aye."

The wizard nodded briefly. "Come with me then. You must guide me to this 'Tower of Set'."

Lotis gripped the edge of Menander's robe. "What is he saying?"

Menander quickly exclaimed in Greek. "I must go with him, Lotis. He can save Ilione if I guide him to where she is. And Simon may need help also."

"Simon." Lotis, for her part, realized that Simon now meant much less to her than he had before this night. Immediately she, too, felt a pang of guilt. "Menander, I must go with you."

"No! It might be very dangerous, Lotis. I must know that you are safe, no matter what happens to me—"

"And how do you think I will feel, Menander, knowing that you are in danger?"

"Your mistress needs you. You cannot abandon her now."

The girl sighed, knowing that it was true. Elissa was the one person who had sustained her more than any other.

"Come, lad," said Taggart. "We must return to my craft—and I hope that no one has discovered it."

A thought struck Menander. "How do you know that you are on the right road? You were left unconscious—"

"Your friend guides me—the one called Balaam."

The lad stared at him, uncomprehending.

"He was living inside the mule who carried me here. Now he is inside me. He has explained much—by writing in Latin upon the inner surfaces of my eyes. Don't be bothered by the way he makes my eyes reflect the light; he's our friend, and the enemy of Assatur's minions who reduced him to servitude in the body of an owl. He has healed me of wounds that would have otherwise killed me, and he will continued to aid us."

Menander stood nonplused. Taggart had, in effect, admitted to being possessed by a demon. Yet he seemed in command of himself. . . .

"I must go with him, Lotis," he said finally. "If I do not return soon, you and your mistress must stay with old Dositheus. Tell him where I have gone. He and Simon are trained in the ways of arcane lore, and so am I. I shall rejoin you as soon as I can."

Lotis said nothing as they embraced, briefly and tenderly. Then Menander turned and said, "Lead on, Wizard."

She watched until the two of them were out of sight, then turned back, her heart heavy and yet, at the same time, strangely buoyant in a deep part of her being. There was something within her that she had not know before, something she could never henceforth lose—a Knowledge of the tension that existed between the ephemeral, material world in which she lived and the supernal Realm to which she, by virtue of her inmost nature, belonged.

They walked for nearly an hour in silence, and Menander noticed that the wizard's pace, hardly brisk to begin with, grew slower and slower. Occasionally he stumbled.

"Taggart—are you ill?" the lad asked finally.

"No." The man paused as if to catch his breath. "Just . . . very tired. And so is—Balaam. He has used up much of his—strength—to heal my wounds. I . . . I think we are both very hungry. Do you have any food with you, Menander?"

The youth dug into his pouch, came up with part of a small bread roll and two meager scraps of jerked meat. "Just these, O Wizard. But they're not nearly enough for a meal, I fear."

You're right." Taggart smiled wanly. "I won't eat them yet. Wait until we get to the craft."

Shortly after this they reached the bottom of a rocky slope which Menander recognized as the place where they had been assaulted by Romans disguised as bandits. Taggart made a feeble attempt to climb it, but could not; after a few moments of effort he slid back to the dusty roadbed, exhausted. Menander helped him to his feet.

"You must rest," he urged the man, "then try again." A vague fear nagged at him. What if some of the real bandits known to prowl this moonlit gorge should suddenly appear?

"No," said the wizard, "I have a better method." He cupped his hands and, facing up the slope, shouted three clearly enunciated syllables in his strange language.

"Be careful," urged Menander. "Bandits are known to lurk hereabouts at night. If they should hear us—"

Even as he spoke, his heart sank. There came a sound of many feet upon the pebbles, followed by a harsh cry in Aramaic, *"Look*—two wayfarers! Escaped slaves, by the look of them."

Shadows emerged from the narrow gorge across the road. "Praise Baal!" chuckled a second voice. "They'll bring in quite a few sestercii on the slave-block in Jericho."

Three were at least six of them. Menander cringed as they advanced, knife blades gleaming in the moonlight. In the same instant he sensed a broad, circular shadow moving upon the roadway, realized that something was descending from above.

The bandits halted as they, too, sensed its approach.

Then Taggart, gripping Menander's arm, drew him close to his side and yelled a single, sharp word.

Searing shafts of flame lanced the night. For an instant the youth saw the forms of eight bearded, blade-clutching bandits outline in fire, eyes wide in terror; their shrieks were brief, intense.

Menander rubbed his eyes, opened them. A stench as of burnt meat filled his nostrils. His vision returned slowly, and when it did he saw a number of charred forms upon the road, steaming and smoldering—and, descending from the sky to settle gently beside them, the black, circular sky-craft of the wizard.

"It obeys my spoken commands, you see," said Taggart. "Now, lad, help me into it, then give me that bread and meat."

Menander did so and immediately the craft lifted them up above the gorge and settled down upon a lofty outcropping.

Taggart, his hands trembling, pressed a glowing square on one of the panels; immediately a squat, domed cylinder about a foot in diameter rose up from the center of the craft, an enormous blunt peg of dark metal. The wizard opened a square door in its side, revealing a cubical, blue-glowing chamber, and thrust the bread and meat within.

"Now, Menander, do you have any material items with which you don't mind parting?"

The youth suddenly realized that he still held two hefty stones, one in each hand, which he had instinctively snatched up when the bandits had approached. He held them out.

"Good! Good!" Taggart snatched the stones, then opened a circular door just beneath the square one. Menander saw that the space within was red-litten. The wizard thrust in the stones, then closed both apertures. For a few moments thereafter Menander heard a rising whine from within the domed cylinder, as if intense magical powers were at work inside. Then, as the whine subsided and tapered off to silence, Taggart pressed another glowing square; immediately the hemispherical top of the cylinder swung away, revealing an equally hemispherical concavity.

Menander gasped. Within that metallic hollow, revealed by a dim silvery glow, were several half-rolls of bread and twice as many strips of dried meat—exact duplicates of the ones he had given to the wizard!

Taggart grabbed them and began to eat voraciously. In a few minutes he had consumed all the items, then for several minutes more he lay motionless on the floor of the craft. Menander wondered anxiously if the man had fallen into a trance, but presently was relieved to see him open his eyes and then sit upright, apparently fully alert.

"Good. We're restored," he said. "Now we must be off." He rose and, opening a small square hatch in the floor, drew forth a flat, square bundle of dark cloth. Discarding his tattered loin cloth, he unfolded what proved to be a new set of garments, identical to his former ones, and donned them. Then he punched a number of the glowing squares with his nimble fingers and the craft rose into the air.

"Unfortunately I don't have duplicates of the metal objects that the Roman stole from me," he remarked. "Did you say, Menander, that they were taken to this 'Tower of Set'?"

"Aye—all but the lightning-wand, which they abandoned in a gorge after it slew three of their number."

"I see!" Taggart grinned, and his eyes gleamed yellowly as they caught the moonlight. "We'll fly low and slow, then, while you guide me to that gorge. My craft's scanners will detect the weapon's presence."

Menander nodded, wondering what "scanners" were, then pointed to the southwest. Then, as they floated up and off over the crests of the dark hills, his skin prickled with gooseflesh as he again contemplated this strange wizard who could be injured unto death yet recover in a matter of hours, and who apparently commanded demonic forces beyond even those of the mages of old.

When Dositheus arrived back at the inn he found it dark. No sound or light came from behind its sturdy wooden door. He tried it cautiously, but, as expected, found it to be bolted from within.

"Evidently they want no visitors this night," he muttered. "Come, Eupatos—into the alley. Perhaps I can find another way in from the courtyard out back."

There proved to be none. Standing beside the central well in the dim torchlight, however, Dositheus thought he could see an open door behind the stuccoed face of the second-story balcony. As he shaded his eyes from the torch on the inn's wall, straining to see better, a light footfall sounded behind him. Whirling, he saw with relief that it was only Elissa's young maidservant advancing from the stable.

"Dositheus . . .?"

"What is it, Lotis?" The old Samaritan sensed that something was amiss. "Why are you up at this hour?"

"Menander is gone."

"Gone? Where?"

"With a wizard called Taggart." The girl looked worried. "Menander said I should wait here for you. They have gone to rescue Ilione—"

"Eupatos, you may retire," said Dositheus. Then, after the stout servant had vanished within the stable, "Tell me all, Lotis."

The girl hurriedly told the old mage what had transpired during his absence, omitting only the strange dream she and Menander had shared. "I am frightened for him, Dositheus," she concluded. "I fear he may be in great danger."

The old man pulled thoughtfully at his beard. Despite her fear, there seemed a firmness of character about this girl, an inner strength, that he had not sensed earlier. He decided to be frank with her.

"He may indeed. Yet Menander is resourceful, for I have taught him many subtle arts. Moreover, the wizard Taggart has proven friendly to us, and has shown himself to be as adept in the practice of magic as I." The old mage glanced up at the open door beyond the balcony. "You say he emerged from there?"

"Yes."

"Then that must be the room Simon rented. I shall sleep there. Go now, Lotis—rejoin your mistress and get as much sleep as you can. I'll give you a sleeping-potion if you wish."

The girl shook her head. "I will sleep, but lightly. Please wake me if—if anything happens."

"I will, Lotis."

"And whatever happens, Dositheus, I know that Menander *will* return to me—if not his present guise, then in another."

After she had gone the old mage pondered her parting statement. But not for long. Glancing up at the black doorway beyond the balcony, he remembered that he had work to do. Snatching an expired torch from his bracket beside the well, he rekindled it at the flame of a still burning one, then hurried around to the front of the inn and up the stairs to the second story.

Entering the small room Simon had rented, he found it to be bare save for a cot, a stool and a small table.

Bracketing the torch, he went back outside and closed the door behind him, then continued on to the stairs leading up to the third story and the roof. Perhaps he might be able to force an entry through the roof-hatch, then steal down into the inn and spy upon Judah of Kerioth, his fellow disciples and their mysterious Master. . . .

Suddenly, while ascending the last flight, he heard voices. He had been preceded; evidently many men were emerging from the interior onto the roof. Then he heard the resonant voice of the Master—deep, almost inhuman in its vibrant timbre:

"Come forth, O Brother, from the Vale of Hinnom. Come forth, and do that which I have begged you to do."

Then came the voice of Judah, firm but almost hushed by comparison, "Did he hear you this time, O Master?"

And another voice, "Perhaps Thomas has not yet reached him."

Dositheus recognized the third voice as that of Kepha. Slowly, carefully, he inched his cowled head above the rim of the roof-wall and saw that several robed figures stood there, clustered at the southwest corner, gazing out over the moonlit town and the hills beyond. In their midst stood a white-robed man who towered over them all by a head, and as the man turned toward the disciple at his right Dositheus saw that a glowing disc rested upon his lofty brow, its faint bluish light limning his strangely goatish yet noble features.

"And what do you think, Beloved Disciple?"

"I think he will answer you. Call him again."

Dositheus started. The voice was that of a woman, and in that moment he recognized her as the almost inhumanly beautiful woman he knew as Miriam, ward of the ancient wizard Yosef of Aphairema.

"Aye," said Judah. "Try again, Master."

The tall man again faced southwestward. *"Come, then, O Twin, come! it is your brother who calls. Smash that place which I have named, even the Tower of Set, and bring forth from it that which we need to open the Gate. In our Father's name I ask it: IA-HE, VAU-HE!"*

Dositheus shuddered, not merely at the unhuman timbre of the voice, but also at that which he recognized as the Symbol of the Unspeakable Name.

"Perhaps," said Judah after a long pause, "your brother ignores you, preferring to revel in his new freedom—"

"No. He knows his duty, and . . . ah! I hear him!" Then, after another long pause: *"I have heard your answer, O Brother. The blessing of our Father be upon you. Tomorrow night I shall come to Hinnom and receive from you the gift which you shall have won for us. Yet I ask you to spare as many as you may in the acquisition of it, for this world has suffered far too much. Soon, with your aid, that suffering shall end and the reign of our Father shall begin."*

Trembling, Dositheus silently crept down the stairs, retired to his room and bolted the door. He realized now that he might already be too late, too ill-prepared. Monstrous forces had already been loosed upon the world this night and he could do nothing about it. Best now to say indoors, protected by such spells as he could concoct within the boundaries of a pentagram.

Yet he still had perhaps four days before the full moon would reinforce the baleful influence of the impending stars. Perhaps, with luck, that would be time enough to somehow prevent the opening of the Gate. . . .

CHAPTER XX

The raven started awake upon his branch and stared nervously southward down the valley. Human cries rang out distantly from that direction—screams of terror—and they were moving closer, becoming clearer. Then, faintly, at the very edge of awareness, came the pulse of a slow throbbing upon the air, like the beat of a giant heart or a deep, muffled drum.

The dark bird's feathers bristled. With a low croak he spread his wings and flew from his high perch, westward under the moon, across the Kidron Valley toward the dark walls of Jerusalem.

Something was abroad this night, he sensed, something monstrous and evil, and it was moving this way. He must warn Ilione, the golden-haired girl who was imprisoned in the tower.

As he approached the tower's looming, crenellated bulk he saw a large owl launch itself from one of its high windows. He veered, but the predaceous bird ignored him and went winging northward, swiftly and silently. It, too, could evidently sense the approach of doom.

Veering around to the west wall of the tower, which faced inward toward the city, the dark bird fluttered finally to rest upon the stone casement of a narrow window. Craning its head forward into the darkness within, it croaked softly, *"Ilione!"*

The girl's face, wan and haggard, appeared at the embrasure. "Carbo! Thank the gods! Did . . . did you find Simon?"

The bird shook his head slowly, then pointed his beak southward. *"Cavé!"* it croaked urgently. *"Cavé!"*

"Danger?" The girl's eyes widened in terror. "Gods, Carbo! How can I get out of here? The door's locked—"

But the bird only cocked its head, as if listening to something afar off, then flapped from the casement and vanished into the darkness.

"Pour me another goblet, Fulvius," growled Scribonius. "It's late and the wine jug's still half full.

"Aye, it's late," replied the legionary as he complied. "Perhaps we should call it a night, sir. Tribune Maxentius will want us to be alert tomorrow."

Scribonius made an obscene gesture. "That for Maxentius! He made me give up the wizard's belt of invulnerability, so I'll have my bit of fun tonight. And maybe I'll figure out how these other items work."

"I think you already have, sir," said Fulvius wearily. "The little flat silvery object offers a small flame when you flick the projection on it—very handy for lighting torches and lamps. The metal cylinder makes a beam of light, the other little cylinders and the black boxes make clicks or crackling—"

"Damn Maxentius!" The centurion drained his goblet with one quaff.

"At least he let you keep these things in exchange for the belt."

Scribonius slammed the goblet down on the rough boards of the table. "Toys! Maxentius wanted me to take the risk of fiddling with them to find out how they work. I wouldn't have minded if they'd turned out to be weapons, but they're junk—wizards' trinkets!"

"Useful, though, some of them," ventured Fulvius placatingly.

"Toys!" Scribonius pounded the table, causing the weird objects to jump. "We should have kept that lightning-wand instead of leaving it to lie there in the gorge.

The legionary paled slightly. "That . . . might not have proved wise."

"Tomorrow I'm going back after it."

"Look, sir, you don't need protection from Simon of Gitta anymore. He's locked up in the deepest dungeon of the Antonian Fortress by now. His wizard's skills won't help him get free—his chains will be riveted, not held by padlocks he could pick, and he'll be searched thoroughly. Maxentius explained all that. There's no need to be afraid—"

"Maxentius!" The centurion rose, scowling. "He made me give up the belt, but I'll have the lightning-wand. In the morning. But before then—" He scooped the wizard's items off the table into the packsack, all save the cylindrical light-projector, which he kept in his right hand. Then, slinging the pack over one shoulder, he turned and lurched toward the stairway.

"Where are you going, sir?"

"To see the little blonde witch. She was the wizard's apprentice, no doubt, and probably his plaything, too. I'll make her tell me how to use these trinkets, and the lightning-wand as well. Then I'll have a bit of fun with her.

He left the torchlit chamber and began to ascend the stairs, flicking on the cylinder. Immediately the light-beam flashed out, cold and steady. Scribonius chuckled. Some of these wizard-devices were indeed useful and clever; this one beat a torch or an oil lamp any day.

As he passed the first barred window, which looked eastward over the Kidron Valley, he heard the sound of many human voices to the south. They were approaching, growing louder, and there was a note of terror in them. Scribonius peered out into the night, but could see little down in the dark valley. Something was evidently frightening the multitudes of pilgrims who were camped there, stirring them up. . . .

The centurion shrugged, turned away and continued his ascent. No need to worry, for no mob could possibly penetrate Jerusalem's strong walls or the towers that guarded it.

Presently he came to a stout wooden door and unlocked it with a large iron key. Shining his beam of light into the small room beyond, he saw the girl huddled upon the stone floor against the far wall. She was staring at him, blue eyes wide in terror.

"Well, well!" Scribonius licked his lips, then groped in the pack and brought forth the small, flat silvery object, flicked its steady flame into being and lit a torch that was bracketed on the wall. "You look like you've seen Hades gaping, girl. I like that. Fear is very becoming to a female." He replaced the silvery thing in the pack, switched off the light-cylinder and placed it in the knapsack also. "Now—*get up!*"

Ilione rose, trembling, clenching her small hands together in front of her. "S-sir, there is great danger abroad this night. Do you not sense it?"

The centurion scowled at her, puzzled—then suddenly laughed. "You feel fear, do you? Ha! *I'm* the one you fear, and I like that. And there's good cause for your fear, girl—but only if you defy me. I am your master; you must do everything I command." He held out the packsack and opened it before the girl's face. "First, you must tell me the uses to which these wizard -trinkets may be put."

Ilione stared at the strange, glittering objects within the pack. "I—I do not understand those things. The wizard Taggart is a strange man, unlike any I have ever met before."

"Is that so?" Scribonius threw the pack aside and it went clattering into a corner. "What, then, of his lightning-wand? Tell me the secret of *that* and I'll let you off with just a little fun. Otherwise, girl, you'll soon know that *I'm* a man unlike any you've met before—and after that, you won't be fit even for the blood-sacrifice Annas and Maxentius have planned."

"Gods!" cried Ilione, more terrified of this brutal Roman than even the formless horror she had sensed approaching outside in the night. "No, please—I know nothing about what you ask!"

Scribonius smirked with pleasure. The fingers of his left hand dug cruelly into the girl's right shoulder, squeezing, bruising the white flesh; his right hand drew slowly back—then suddenly struck, openhanded, with savage force. Pain seared the whole left side of Ilione's face; stars sparked in her brain. She would have fallen had not the centurion's left hand, gripping her shoulder, held her upright; his right hand drew back for another blow—

Suddenly a black bundle of feathers, cawing furiously, launched itself from the window ledge straight into the Roman's face—and Scribonius shrieked in pain as a heavy dark beak thrust itself into his right eye-socket and clamped firmly upon the eyeball. He released the girl and fell to the floor, clutching madly at the demon-thing that assailed him.

"Carbo—don't!" screamed Ilione. "He'll kill—"

The centurion's right hand clutched the bird and pulled it from his face. Bones cracked. Then the Roman hurled the feathery bundle against the wall and rose up, one eye bloodied and half-popped from its socket, the other glaring with mad fury.

"Witch!" he yelled, advancing with hands clutching at the girl's throat. "You die *now!*"

Ilione, cringing back in terror, suddenly sensed a black shadow moving in the open doorway behind the Roman. It moved closer, entered the room, and she saw that it was a man clad in black, his face pale in the dim torchlight, a bulky, intricate object of dark metal clutched in his right hand.

"Taggart!" screamed the girl.

Scribonius whirled, whipping out his short-sword—and saw the lightning-wand in the hand of a wizard he had supposedly slain. In that instant the terror of doom gripped his heart, but his warrior's instinct caused him to draw back the sword for a desperate throw.

"Dead wizard," he yelled shrilly, *"die again!"*

Then a searing blast of flame filled the room with blinding light, fusing the Roman's blade and charring to ash the hand and arm that held it.

For an instant Ilione beheld that awful light and felt its heat upon her face. Then all was darkness, punctuated horribly by mad shrieks of pain from the fallen Scribonius. A stench of burnt flesh pervaded the air.

Gradually the girl's vision cleared and she peered up into the pale, scowling face of Taggart.

"Ilione . . . are you . . . well?"

She laughed hysterically at the sound of the man's faltering Latin—then, abruptly, found her laughter dissolving into sobs. She sank to her knees, felt the wizard's hand gently gripping her right shoulder, holding her upright.

"Ilione!" It was Menander's voice. "Don't cry—you're safe now."

She looked up, saw the youth bending toward her over the wizard's shoulder, concern in his face. The sight gave her new strength. She rose, trembling. "Menander . . .?"

"Hurry, Ilione—follow me. The wizard's sky-craft is on the tower's roof—"

"The roof? But . . . there are always guards up there!"

"There were. They're charred meat now. Hurry!"

"No, Menander. Carbo is hurt. Look!"

Menander saw the dark bundle of feathers against the wall where Ilione pointed, hurried over to it. The bird fluttered feebly, and the youth felt grief well up with him.

"He attacked the Roman," wailed Ilione. "He tried to save my life—"

Tenderly Menander gathered up the stricken, quivering bird in his cupped hands. Then he sensed the wizard Taggart kneeling beside him.

"Your friend can be saved," said Taggart. "Take him and Ilione up to the craft—quickly."

"But, aren't you coming—?"

"I'll rejoin you soon." The wizard rose, snatched up his pack and worked his arm through one strap; then, reaching back, he pulled from it a device Menander had seen before—and object of blue metal with a disc at one end. "I'm going down to find the Byakhtril. Go now—hurry!"

Menander and Ilione nodded, then hastened from the room to the stairs, the youth cupping the stricken raven in his hands. For a moment they paused, saw Taggart striding after them out the doorway—

Suddenly a voice within the room hissed painfully, "Wizard, I swear by Mars that I'll live to kill you—"

Taggart's eyes hardened. He turned and confronted the white-faced centurion who writhed on the stone floor, features tensed in agony and hatred, charred right arm crumbling and staining black the stone flags beside him. Slowly the wizard raised the lightning-wand, aimed it. . . .

In the same instant the air began to vibrate as if to the pulse of a giant drum, low and barely audible, yet powerful. . . .

Taggart lowered his weapon. "No, Roman," he said in carefully enunciated Latin. "Were I a kindly man, I'd burn the rest of you to ash. Instead, I leave you to—"

Abruptly, without finishing his sentence, he turned and hurried from the chamber. "Get up to the craft!" he snapped at the young pair, then hurried off down the dark stairway.

Menander and Ilione obeyed, shortly gained the top of the stairs and emerged into the cool night air. Sprawled against the battlements were two dark forms—legionaries, their charred flesh mingled with their molten breastplates. In the center of the stone floor, and suspended about two feet above it, was the wizard's craft. Quickly Menander helped Ilione up into it, then handed the raven to her and climbed in himself. There, huddled in darkness, they listened to the sounds that began to well up from the Kidron Valley—terrified human voices and, mingled with them, the measured pulsing as of a monstrous drum, advancing. . . .

"Gods!" muttered the youth, his hackles rising. "Let the wizard not delay overlong—"

Suddenly the tower vibrated as if a great blow had been delivered to its base. In the same instant Menander heard a liquid, lapping sound from below, almost like ocean waves, but more viscous.

"It's attacking the foundation!" cried Ilione. "Oh, Menander, what is it? What's keeping the wizard?"

The tower vibrated again, as if to the impact of a giant battering-ram.

In the same instant a fierce crackle of energy, accompanied by a flickering blue glow, emerged from the stairwell. Men screamed in brief agony within the tower. A few seconds later the wizard Taggart dashed up out of the stairwell, nimbly sprang into the craft and began to frantically poke at the glowing, colored squares upon the panel.

The tower shuddered a third time.

"Wizard—?" ventured Menander anxiously.

"The Byakhtril's not here," snarled Taggart. "I had to blast a few more Romans. Don't ask any more—"

Again the tower shuddered and Menander actually saw it sway slightly beneath the supernaturally hovering craft. Then the craft began to rise slantingly eastward—and, abruptly, stopped. Taggart snarled a curse in his strange tongue. Ilione, in the same instant, screamed frantically and lurched against the craft's raised edge, right arm outstretched rigidly. Menander grabbed her and, with a shock, felt something rubbery and *invisible* wrapped around her right arm.

Taggart yelled out the sharp syllable Menander had heard before—and, again, searing beams of flame lanced the night, far more intense than before. Below, bathed in the crackling glare of those beams, a monstrous *being* was suddenly outlined—a gargantuan, pulsing thing like a mass of churning ropes—like a giant slug plastered against the tower's base. Thick, writhing tentacles streamed up from its sides, slithering against the massive wall, groping into every window, straining at the stones and causing the mortar between them to crumble. A thick, conelike protuberance, writhing atop the sluglike body, sported a dimly-glowing bluish disc near its apex, held in place by a metallic band—and then Menander screamed as he beheld the *half-face* on the front of that cone.

In the same instant an even more terrible scream rang out from one of the topmost windows into which groped, serpent-like, a monstrous tentacle—the frantic scream of Scribonius, expending his last energies in a bellow of mad terror.

Then the thin tentacle-tip about Ilione's arm fell away, as did other tendrils which had been clutching the craft. Taggart jabbed at the glowing squares; the craft rose rapidly into the night sky, and Menander and Ilione felt the wind whipping about them as they sped upward and eastward at a fantastic speed.

"Hang on!" cried the wizard.

They barely heard him—for, glancing back, they saw the great square bulk of the Tower of Siloam reeling and swaying against the moonlit west. And then, with a great grinding and rumbling of stone, it toppled and crashed inward upon the city, its fall accompanied by an enormous cry of horror from the hundreds encamped in the Kidron Valley below.

The sky-craft gathered still more speed and hurtled eastward.

Tribune Maxentius, descending the stairs to the dungeons beneath the Antonian Fortress, suddenly felt the stones tremble beneath his feet.

"By Pluto!" exclaimed the hulking, torch-bearing gladiator who preceded him. "Earthquake! Sir, we'd better get out of here."

Maxentius paused, scowling. He ached to begin the "interrogation" of the Samaritan imprisoned and chained below—to hear the man shriek as the gladiator, Cratos, slowly broke his limbs one by one. Yet, if the walls should suddenly fall in upon them all—what good, then, would vengeance be?

"Very well, then," snarled the Tribune. "Hurry—back the way we came. If there's an earthquake coming, we'll have to get the troops out of the fort and into the Kidron Valley."

When they regained the main floor of the Antonia they found many soldiers milling about. Maxentius called one of his officers to him.

"What's going on, Lentulus?"

"The sound came from the south, sir. I think part of the city wall may have collapsed."

"Well, round up a couple of decans. Hurry! I'll go with you."

In a very few minutes Maxentius and his burly bodyguard were marching double-step at the head of a score of armed and armored legionaries—southward between the high columns of the paved portico that flanked the western edge of the mighty enclosure surrounding the Temple of Yahweh.

As they approached the Hall of Gazzith, at the southwest corner of the temple-complex, they were met by a group of robed and bearded Judean priests; Maxentius recognized Caiaphas and several others among them. At their head was a Roman soldier without armor, a half-dazed expression on his face.

"C-commander Maxentius. . . ." he stammered.

"What in Hades is wrong with you, soldier? Speak!"

"I was . . . someone knocked me unconscious near the Tower of Siloam," said the legionary. "When I came to, my armor was gone. Then I heard screams and saw a flash of lightning. The tower fell. Something came out of the night—something that pulsed like a giant heart—and began to scatter the fallen stones. I could not see it, but I smelled its awful stench. Gods! Poseidon has shaken the earth and sent demons to despoil it!"

"Calm down, soldier!" snapped Maxentius. "I think I know who stole your armor. Report back to the Antonia; I'll talk to you more later."

When the man had gone, the tribune confronted Caiaphas. "What's this all about? Did the Tower of Siloam indeed fall?"

"I fear so," said the priest, "and I also fear that it was not a natural thing. Something that should not exist may be abroad this night."

"I'll talk to *you* later, too. For now, come with me—all of you."

The soldiers and priests continued southward, skirting the eastern edge of the squalid Valley of Cheesemakers by means of various pillared porticos, bridges and walkways, until at last they arrived at the foot of Ophel where the Tower of Siloam had stood. Here a large crowd had gathered and many torches had been lit. A multitude of onlookers were conversing in excited yet subdued voices.

Maxentius and his soldiers, followed by the priests, pushed through the crowd to where the tower had been, and the tribune felt the flesh prickle all down his spine. There was a great gap in the city's wall; the smell of stone dust still hung in the air, and together with it a heavy alien stench such as he had never smelled before.

"Start clearing that rubble," yelled Maxentius. "Lentulus, go back to the fort and bring a whole cohort down here. Hurry!"

When the decurion had gone, Maxentius drew Caiaphas away from his troop of toiling soldiers and demanded, "What could have done this thing?"

"I ... I do not know. It is not yet the Time. I wonder, though, if this rabbi Yeshua may have employed some dark magic against us. Whatever destroyed this tower was evidently in quest of the Byakhtril."

"Go immediately to the villa of Annas, then," snarled the tribune, "and consult him. He knows more about dark magic than anyone. Make haste!

Annas, however, had a busy evening: First, the discovery of the drugged Izhar and the fact that their prisoners had escaped, then the later discovery that Jahath and the Roman soldiers sent to pursue the escaped prisoners had been slain. At dusk the old sorcerer had sent an owl to the Tower of Set to inform Caiaphas and the others of all the details concerning these developments.

Shortly after sunset Izhar was completely recovered from the drug he had imbibed—a dose that would have incapacitated a normal man for many more hours at least. Annas, in his arcane wisdom, knew why: The thing inhabiting Izhar was as capable of inhibiting diseases and adverse chemical influences as it was of hastening the healing of injuries.

Now the old priest chafed with impatience as he was borne westward down the steep trail by his litter-bearers, for the rite to Set should have been performed in the Temple an hour ago. Not that it mattered greatly, save that appearances should be kept up for the morale of Caiaphas and others of the lesser grades of knowledge. . . .

Behind him, similarly borne in their own litters, came the graybeard Izhar and his cowled "Levite" attendant. . . .

Suddenly he felt his palanquin jerk to stop, and in the same instant heard his leading torchbearer cry out, "By El Shaddai, what is *that?*"

Annas thrust out his balding head from between the litter curtains and peered ahead. "What perversity is this?" he demanded. "Why do we not proceed?"

"Something evil has passed this way," said the servant, an odd quaver in his voice.

Annas, active and agile despite his great age, slipped out of his conveyance and strode forward. A strange, somehow disquieting smell immediately assailed his nostrils, a stench suggestive of slugs and serpents and less identifiable things. Then he saw that his bearer stood at the edge of a wide swath of crushed weeds, shrubs and grass whose flattened leaves and stems gleamed as with a tarry slime. In the midst of this swath, illumined by the torches of his trembling bearers, were many round indentations in the earth, each as large in diameter as a gladiator's chest, their smooth concavities showing the imprint of intricate striations or veinings.

"Gods, Master Annas!" breathed the chief servant. "What has passed this way?"

The old priest, ignoring his servant's impiety, gazed southward and saw, under the light of the waxing gibbous moon, that the weird trail continued on indefinitely in that direction. Judging from the way the vegetation was flattened, that was the way the thing had proceeded. The trail came down from the northeast, curving from the direction of the crest of the Mount of Olives.

Then he saw Izhar at his side, eyes gleaming yellowly in the torchlight.

"I see," said the rabbi of Chorazin, nodding, "that something is abroad this night—something we had not counted on."

"Aye." Annas tugged nervously at his long, square-trimmed beard. "Izhar, I want you and your—companion—to follow this trail northward and discover whence it originates. Meanwhile, I will take the more dangerous course and attempt to follow it to its destination."

"But what of the Rite to Set in the Temple?"

"That can be made up later this night. This matter, I sense, is far more important. Leave the litters here. Speed is essential."

Izhar nodded again, and a moment later he and his dark-cloaked companion were hurrying northward into the night.

Annas beckoned his chief torchbearer and two others to accompany him, then strode out south along the ridge-slope, leaving the rest of the servants to watch the three palanquins. They had not gone far before the three noticed that the ancient priest's eyes were glimmering back the torchlight even as old Izhar's had done. Evidently Annas, in order to see better in the dark, was letting his—demon—peep forth from his eyes, something he permitted only around his most trusted servants.

The chief torchbearer shivered slightly. No matter how often he had seen those lynx-eyes glowing—whether from his master's face or another's—he found that the light always somewhat unnerved him.

The noisome odor persisted as they walked parallel to the wide slime-trail, and in the old priest's mind echoed a disquieting line he had once read in the centuried book of Ostanes: *"As a foulness shall They be known unto you. . . ."*

Below the slope of that ridge-bulge known as the "Mount of Offence" the slime-trail turned slightly upward, as if the thing that had made it had been attracted toward that eminence; but then it resumed its southward course. Annas and his servants followed it for some distance farther, until at last it turned abruptly downhill at the end of the ridge and its destination became unmistakably apparent: the deep Valley of Hinnom south of Jerusalem, the place where all things corrupt and unclean were cast out from the city and where only the most vile and vicious dregs of humanity dared to prowl and forage by night.

Annas stared down for several long moments into that deep, dark valley where a few dim red fires gleamed in the blackness. Then, turning to his servants, he muttered, "Come, we must return swiftly."

The servants, nothing loath, led the way back more quickly than they had followed their master. Upon arriving at the litters, they had to wait for some time until Izhar and his dark companion finally arrived also. The latter, as usual, quickly concealed himself by crawling into his palanquin and drawing shut the curtains.

"What did you find, Izhar?" demanded Annas, unable to conceal his commingled eagerness and anxiety.

"The thing came from a grotto near Bethany," said the grizzled rabbi. "The entrance to it had apparently been sealed with a great round boulder, evidently to disguise it as a tomb, but within it was a tunnel leading down to a vaster cavern, and other tunnels leading still farther downward from it. And in the rock above the entrance to that cavern was inscribed the Sign of Koth. You know what that means, Annas."

Annas gasped. Gooseflesh pimpled on his neck and arms.

"Are you sure?" His query was a barely audible hiss.

"How could I mistake such a thing? My companion and I explored the place thoroughly. We found a hole in the cavern roof where food had evidently been let down for many years. The floor was littered with the bones of sheep, cows—other things. Moreover, we found other tunnels leading down to depths we dared not take the time to explore. Apparently this was a place discovered and prepared long ago for the incubation of—"

"Aye. I know. Ostanes has hinted of such things. For each true eidolon begotten by the Old Ones upon mankind, there is begotten at the same time a—a *brother*. Evidently this rabbi Yeshua is, as I have long suspected, far more than a mere sorcerer. Come, Izhar, we must make haste and warn—"

Suddenly a scream from hundreds of throats rose up from the Kidron Valley below, and with it came a strange, slowly intensifying sound: the slow *boom . . . boom . . . boom . . .* as of the pulsing of a giant heart or the beating of a monstrous drum.

"By Set!" hissed Annas, forgetting himself. "What is *that*—?"

The booming sound grew louder, louder, accompanied by the intensifying shrieks of terrified multitudes . . . and then came a thunderous grinding and grating of stone on stone—a strange lapping, sucking sound as if a viscid sea had hurled itself against a rocky shore—

And finally, cataclysmically, a burst of unnatural lightning—an intense blue-white light that for a moment illuminated something hideous, something utterly monstrous that clung with multiple viscid tendrils and tentacles to the side of the Jerusalem wall across the valley, rocking the massive bulk of the Tower of Siloam.

Annas and Izhar screamed aloud in involuntary horror, but in the next moment their screams were drowned out as the Kidron Valley was filled with a vast reverberating thunder—the awesome thunder of the Tower of Set reeling against the stars and then, ponderously, crumbling and crashing down in titanic ruin.

During the rest of the night the legionaries, together with many of the city's inhabitants who had come to gawk and found themselves impressed into service, labored to clear away the stones of the fallen tower. Maxentius noticed, with great uneasiness, that those stones were not arranged naturally; rather, they were scattered as if some gigantic ant-lion had dug down through them, arranging them in a huge cone-shaped pit. At the nether apex of this pit was the entrance to the underground chamber where the Byakhtril had been hidden; moreover, the pit was coated with a tarry slime which gave off that pungent alien stench the tribune had noted from the outset. Even more disturbing was the fact that several of the bodies discovered within the ruins were charred and blackened as if by the lightnings of Jupiter, while others were covered with strange, oozing, circular wounds.

When at last the pallid dawn came it was discovered that a trail of monstrous ovoid tracks, veined line palm-fronds and filled with stinking slime, extended to and from the ruined tower. Something had come up from the south in the night, had wrecked one of the city's most massive fortifications, then had gone back the way it came. A large number of terrified campers in the Kidron Valley even claimed to have glimpsed it during that brief flash of unnatural lightning, but their descriptions were garbled and unbelievable.

Hours after sunrise the last of the rubble had been cleared enough to show that eighteen Roman soldiers had perished in the tower's fall, a few of them mysteriously burned black as if by intense heat.

And toward the end of that search, Maxentius shuddered as he gazed upon the pale, bloodless features of Scribonius.

"By all the gods!" muttered the tribune. "What could have done *that* to him?"

The legionary Lentulus, unable to speak, merely shook his head and fingered a good luck charm while prickling gooseflesh crawled over his neck and arms. For the dead face of Centurion Scribonius was tensed in an expression of stark terror, his right arm was charred to a crisp and his body was covered with raw, circular marks that suggested the suction discs of a monstrous octopus.

THE GOAT OF AZAZEL

CHAPTER XXI

Menander sat quietly in the darkness, feeling fear. His fear was partly due to the tenseness he sensed in the wizard Taggart, who stood hunched over the panel of dimly glowing colored squares by means of which he evidently controlled the speed and direction of his sky craft. For all Menander could now tell, however, the craft was not moving at all; at least, he could detect no motion.

Beside him, huddled against the craft's rim, Ilione lay in an apparently peaceful sleep. At first, as the wizard's craft had sped at an incredible speed eastward following the destruction of the Tower of Siloam, she had screamed hysterically about the invisible tentacle that had briefly gripped her arm; then, as Menander had held her and spoken to her gently, Taggart had pressed a small cylinder to her shoulder. The object had hissed briefly, like a serpent, yet more mechanically, and immediately Ilione had become tranquil, then lapsed into a deep slumber.

Next to her squatted the raven Carbo, eyes closed and outthrust beak just touching the sky craft's floor. Alive, evidently, yet for how long?

"Wizard," Menander made bold to ask, "will the raven live?"

"The raven?" Taggart made an effort to focus his attention on something other than the colored squares. "Oh, yes. I checked on him awhile ago. His bones are set and are mending well, even though he's a very old raven indeed. He should be able to fly again in a few days."

Menander found that incredible. "Are you sure?"

"Of course. Your friend Carbo is an excellent practitioner of internal medicine, despite the limitations of his reduced state. He will have that old bird patched up in no time at all. Still, I would recommend that he be provided with a new and larger body soon, for the raven is about worn out and will not last much longer."

Menander could make no sense of this. He asked, "What of Ilione?"

"She has had a great shock—contact with the flesh of an Outside One. But I think she will wake up soon and be none the worse for her experience."

Menander stood up. "Your words comfort me, wizard, and yet—where are we? When we fled the destruction of the Tower of Siloam, I sensed great speed; yet now we seem embedded in a darkness devoid even of stars. . . ."

"I have shut down the entry of all light so that we won't be detected by . . . by watchers. Though it feels to you that we are motionless in darkness, we have been traveling steadily eastward at the rate of a hundred Roman miles per hour. I don't dare go faster, or watchers in the sky would take note of it." Taggart glanced at his panel of glowing squares. "It has been some two hours since we left Jerusalem. The watchers will not be scanning this far eastward. We can have light now."

So saying, he touched one of the squares.

Menander gasped at the sight of the vast sunlit panorama of landscape that sprang into being around them. For a few minutes he had to close his eyes to shut out what seemed a blinding glare, but when they had adjusted to the daylight he stared about him with awe. The wizard's craft was still hurtling eastward, straight into the sun which was blazing above far hills. Several hundred feet below them was the desert, rocky and lifeless, extending in tumbled browns and yellows all around them to vast horizons.

"That looks like an oasis ahead," said Taggart. "We might as well rest there and decide what to do next. We certainly can't go back to Jerusalem now."

"We can't?" Menander felt his fear deepen. "Why not?"

"That last burst of energy from my craft will have alerted any sky watchers in Earth's vicinity, both Zarrians and Galactics. We'll have to stay away from the Judean area for awhile."

Menander asked no more questions. He did not fully understand, yet for some reason he feared clarification more than ignorance.

Taggart proved to be right; the green patch at the base of the eastward hills turned out to be a small oasis surrounded by grass, shrubs and a few shady palms, all huddled at the mouth of a rocky and narrow wadi. Dusty trails intersected there, but as the craft settled slowly groundward Menander saw that the place was at present deserted.

Ilione stood up shakily just as the floating platform came to rest beneath the palms. "Menander . . . where are we . . .?"

"In a safe place, Ilione, far from all perils. Come—I'll help you out of the craft."

They walked together to the pond and drank deeply, then sat on the grass in the shade of the palms. Ilione seemed somewhat dreamy, as if still partly under the influence of some soporific drug.

Presently Taggart joined them, bearing an armload of fragments of dry bread and bits of jerked meat. To Menander' surprise, all the bread fragments were absolutely identical, as were the meat bits.

"You magic is amazing, Taggart! Have you again duplicated the food I gave you on the Jericho road? Is there no limit to the number of times you can do this?"

"Not as long as the . . . magical power lasts," said Taggart. He smiled slightly as if at some private thought. "I could multiply them several thousand times if the need arose. . . ."

They ate in silence. After the meal Menander felt his spirits rising and decided that he had been foolish in hesitating to question the wizard. "Does you sky craft have infinite power, then, Taggart?"

"Hardly." Taggart's scowl conveyed a touch of worry. "I need to tap into a power source soon, or—" He paused and gazed skyward, then went on, "This craft no doubt seems very advanced to you, but actually it is very primitive. It's close to a million years old and getting to be something of a museum piece."

Menander thought of the temple of the muses in Alexandria where scholars studied the writings and relics of antiquity. Taggart sometimes had a very odd way of putting things. . . .

"You see," the wizard went on, "this conveyance is a relic from the remote time when the Zarrians ruled only their home sun-system and roamed about as individuals on a limited number of worlds, sometimes engaging in one-to-one combat. At that time they were of a greater variety of temperament than they are today, and were even of two sexes, just as we humans are. That was before Zathog, the Great Old One, fled from our galaxy to theirs after the Primal War and made them his minions."

Menander understood the word *galaxy*—the great "milky" band of stars that traversed the night sky—but could make no sense of the way in which Taggart used the word. Was the wizard insane . . .?

"I'm afraid that all this makes little sense to you, Menander," said Taggart, sighing. "It's all very strange and complicated, I know, but somehow I must explain it to you. With your help, there's still a small chance that I may be able to avert the world's destruction."

Menander felt suddenly cold. "With *my* help? But I'm only a—"

"What is he saying?" cried Ilione suddenly. "Menander, I don't understand Latin very well, but—did he say that the world is going to be *destroyed?*"

"Ilione, don't be frightened—"

"Oh, gods! Where are we, Menander? What's happening to us? I can't stand any more of this madness. Why did we ever come to the accursed lands of Samaria and Judea? Why didn't Dositheus take us to Persia as he promised, to study under the wise and kind mage Daramos—?"

"Daramos!" Taggart suddenly exclaimed. "Do you know a Persian mage of that name?"

Ilione could only stare openmouthed at the wizard, shocked mute by his intensity. It was Menander who replied:

"Daramos was my mentor in Persepolis for a time. Dositheus and Simon have studied under him also. He is very old and wise."

"Old, you say! How old?"

"No man knows. Some say he has lived for centuries. Have you heard of him, Taggart? You seem to be very inter—"

"What does he look like? Tell me."

"Why, he is very short and broad-faced, his skin has a greenish cast, and his ears—"

"Ha!" Taggart smacked his right fist into his left palm; his eyes were alight with glee. "It's *him!* It has to be!"

"You know Daramos?" said Ilione, awe replacing the sadness in her face. *You know him?"*

"Yes, but . . . *alive!* Who would have thought it? I haven't seen him since the night the Persians stormed and sacked Babylon! But, then, he once told me that his ancestors were long-lived, very long-lived indeed. . . ." Taggart stood up and brushed bread crumbs from the front of his black shirt, then strode rapidly to his sky craft and climbed in. "Hurry up," he called back to the young pair.

Menander and Ilione hastily joined him, and immediately the sky craft began to speed upward and eastward once more, coasting above the slope of the barren hills.

"Persepolis, did you say?"

Menander nodded. Taggart punched at the colored squares and his craft rose higher and sped eastward more rapidly. There was a strange excitement in the wizard's eyes, and somehow that excitement caused hope to rise in Menander's breast. The man was obviously very anxious to find Daramos, and though Persepolis was a thousand miles or more east of Judea, the wizard's craft was evidently capable of covering at least a hundred of those miles in a mere hour.

Ilione felt that hope also, Menander noted. Her wide blue eyes, formerly sad and apathetic, were now fixed with fascination on the vast desert horizon which stretched endlessly ahead.

But in Menander's secret thoughts that hope was mingled with a strange uneasiness connected with what Taggart had said concerning the Persian invasion of Babylon. For that invasion, he recalled, had taken place more than five centuries ago.

Annas rose much later than was his custom, for the previous night had been an exhausting one. He had spent much of it questioning witnesses to the collapse of the Tower of Siloam; then, rather than return to his villa, he had retired to the mansion of Caiaphas in the southwestern quarter of Jerusalem.

As he rose from his bed he felt—despite that within him which had sustained him in vitality beyond the years of ordinary men—a certain weariness. He shook off the feeling quickly, for he also felt the new excitement, the anticipation of the event that was soon to fulfill all his long-held ambitions.

"The world!" he muttered as if to someone else within the room, though it was empty. "Let but two more dawns pass, and then you and I shall rule it all."

For a fleeting moment his eyes gleamed yellowly in the dim lamplight.

Half an hour later, while the servants were dressing him, he heard a commotion as of a distant multitude. When his attendants had finished and withdrawn, the old priest stepped from his chamber onto a wide balcony which gave him an eastward view across Jerusalem. Even from this distance he could see part of the great gap in the city's wall where the fallen tower had stood. The shouting multitude, though he could not see them beyond the many intervening buildings, were evidently between that wall and the shallow Valley of the Cheesemakers which divided the southern half of the city into eastern and western portions; no doubt they were clustering about the lower courtyards of the extensive Temple complex. It was obvious that huge crowds were surging into Jerusalem, as had been the case for several days, but this morning they seemed much noisier than usual. Annas hoped that there was not another insurrection brewing; if that were the case, Maxentius and his legionaries would have their work cut out for them.

"Nothing must interfere now," he muttered. "We are too close—so very close!"

A servant entered the room behind him and announced Caiaphas. As Annas reentered his chamber he saw that the High Priest was accompanied by a thin, balding, white-haired old man clad in the robes of a rabbi.

"This is Tolmai, teacher in the synagogue at Capharnaum," said Caiaphas. "He is one of us now."

"Izhar told me to come to you as soon as I arrived in Jerusalem," said Tolmai. "I am happy to serve Assatur, O Annas, for I no longer live in darkness. My inner companion has told me all and has opened my eyes to the Phantom of Truth."

Caiaphas shivered slightly. Though learned in arcane lore, and very loyal to his father-in-law Annas, he had somehow never been able to bring himself to accept an "inner companion".

"Good, Tolmai." Annas grinned and rubbed his lean hands together. "Izhar tells me that you are hereditary guardian of the Mysteries of Yhtill, handed down from those forgotten times when Gennesaret was still known as the earthly Lake of Hali. Such ancient lore could be very useful to us. But, Tolmai, why did you not come here to Judea with Izhar?"

"I went first to Bethsaida, bearing another 'companion', to see if I could recruit the rabbi Samezer to our cause; for he, too, knows much of ancient Karakossa and the prophecy concerning the Last King. But he had already journeyed south toward Jerusalem—no doubt seeking his son Philip, who has joined the rabbi Yeshua's band of followers."

"That is unfortunate," said Annas. "Still, we may recruit him yet if he shows up in the city. But tell me, Tolmai, did you not say that you have just arrived in Jerusalem?"

"Aye, by the Siloam Gate. What happened to the tower that used to stand there? They say it collapsed only last night—"

"I'll tell you about it later. Did you pass through the crowd that is now making so much commotion in that part of the city?"

"I entered with that crowd," said Tolmai. "Most of them are followers of the rabbi Yeshua, who this morning came into the city mounted on a young ass in the manner of the Karakossan and Jebusite kings of old."

"The ass!" gasped Caiaphas. "The symbol of Set! Then Yeshua bar Yosef must be—"

"No!" snapped Annas, "—though obviously he's trying to *pass himself off* as the prophesied Last King. Tell us all you know, Tolmai."

"I was passing through Bethany this morning," said the white-haired old rabbi, "when I caught up with a crowd and learned that they were Rabbi Yeshua's followers. I immediately ordered my group of servants to join them—for, like my friend rabbi Samezer, I seek a son whose enthusiasm led him to join the Nazorene's cult. But though I looked for Nathaniel I could not find him in the throng, which grew ever larger.

"Before long, the crowd paused on the road near the village of Bethphage and a small group of men led the young ass out from there. Then I saw the rabbi Yeshua, very tall and conspicuous in his white robes, mount the beast and continue on his way toward Jerusalem; and as he did so, the mob grew ever larger, casting before him leafy branches and even their very cloaks for his beast to tread upon."

"Aye, it is the Rite of the Coming!" hissed Annas. "Later he will exchange his white robes for the tattered yellow garment of the Golden King . . . but go on, Tolmai. Go on!"

"I stayed with the ever-growing throng as it wound southward down the Kidron Valley and finally surged in the city via the Siloam Gate, but so great was the press that never was I able to approach my son Nathaniel, though I glimpsed him from time to time. In the city it was even worse, and at last I abandoned the effort and came here. The last I saw of the rabbi Yeshua, he was preaching to the mob from one of the outer porticos of the Temple-grounds."

"Indeed!" Annas turned to the High Priest. "Caiaphas, summon an escort of guards. I think that we should hear what this very popular rabbi is telling the mob. If he's urging insurrection, we'll have Tribune Maxentius nip it in the bud."

"Yet this Yeshua may not be an enemy," said Caiaphas hopefully. "After all, he seems to be reviving the ancient homage of Assatur, and he obviously knows much of the Karakossan traditions—"

"*Too* much!" snarled Annas. "And the man's not just reviving tradition, he's claiming to *be* the Last King—the *Mashiah*—just as our spy Judah has hinted. Get going, Caiaphas—and after you summon your escort, send messengers to as many members of the Sanhedrin as you can locate, and announce a meeting in the Hall of Gazzith at sundown. We dare take no chances now, not with our plans so near to completion!"

Dositheus and the two women in his charge woke very late in the day despite their various worries, for exhaustion had contrived to prolong their slumbers. They arose well after noon and, inquiring at the inn, found that meals were not to be served there for the rest of the "holy season" save to the well-connected.

"You must pay up now and depart," the belligerent Martha had informed them, "for henceforth only the Holy One and his followers may dwell here."

Dositheus, who had thought he was already "paid up", nevertheless gave the woman the two extra denarii she demanded, then took Elissa, Lotis and the servant Eupatos with him and passed eastward through Bethany on the road to Jerusalem. This was a worrisome development, for now he would have to find new lodgings or camp out in the countryside—the first nearly impossible at this season, the second uncomfortable and dangerous. Moreover, unless one of their party kept watch at Martha's inn at all times, Menander would have no way of finding them upon his return. . . .

His gloomy reverie was suddenly interrupted at sight of a young man of about twenty hurrying along the road toward them—a man whom Dositheus recognized as the youngest member of the Thirty.

"Parmenion!" the old wizard cried out. "Well met, lad!"

The man paused, glanced without recognition at Dositheus and the two women, then at the servant leading the donkey. "Eupatos . . .? But, then—" He looked again at the old man. *"Dositheus!* Why are you dressed in Judean robes? And who are these Judean women with you?"

"Actually they're Samaritans," chuckled Dositheus. "How lucky we are to have met you! Menander told me, Parmenion, that he had sent Carbo to bid you and the rest of the Thirty to come and join us at Bethany, but I hardly expected you so soon. Where are you lodged?"

"There are no lodgings to be found. We are encamped half a mile north of here on the road to Anathoth. I will guide you there."

"No, no." Dositheus opened his purse and pressed silver coils into Parmenion's hand. "We will find your camp unaided. I want you to continue on to Bethany and find the Inn of Martha. Wait there for the arrival of Menander. When he comes, bring him to us."

"But I have news which I must convey to Isagoras."

"Tell it to me, then, and I will convey it to him."

The young man took a deep breath. "Very well. This morning all of us went into Jerusalem, save for Isagoras, who stayed in camp with the servants and pack-beasts. We mingled with the mob, learning all we could about this rabbi Yeshua bar Yosef. I suppose you know that he rode into the city this morning upon a young ass and clad all in white—"

"Gods, no!" said Dositheus. "Yet, I suspected this might happen. Evidently he is enacting the ancient Karakossa rite of the Coming of the King."

Parmenion regarded the old man questioningly. "You know much, wise mage, for the mob is treating him as a king indeed. He spent the morning preaching to them, exhorting them to follow the Law in whose service they had grown lax, expounding many parables—and finally, about midday, he led them in an attack on the Temple precincts! The few priest who opposed him were swept aside by the popular furor; the money changers and beast sellers were driven forth into the streets, and the beasts were given freely to all who had come to sacrifice at the altar of the Temple. I was on the outskirts of the crowd and could barely hear the rabbi Yeshua above the tumult, yet once I head him cry out in his great bleating voice, 'No den of robbers shall deny my father his due!'"

Dositheus suppressed a twinge of fear. "So the blood sacrifices are increasing then! What else did you learn, Parmenion?"

"The Tower of Siloam collapsed in the night. Something came up out of the Valley of Hinnom and destroyed it. There were great round tracks left by some monstrous being that came and then departed, but no one saw it, though at least eighteen guardsmen perished in the tower's collapse—"

Dositheus listened in growing fear as Parmenion continued his detailed description of what he had heard. Then his fear was augmented by a more personal anxiety when the young man said, "We fear that Simon has been captured by the Romans. Some of us were talking in a tavern with a few legionaries stationed at the Antonian Fortress, and they told us of a man who, attempting to avenge his murdered parents, had managed to penetrate the Tower of Siloam disguised as a legionary; the man was captured, but not before slaying several Romans and a tax-gatherer—"

"Simon?" interrupted Dositheus. "How can you know that the man you describe is indeed he?"

"The legionaries we spoke with were on duty in the Antonia when Simon was brought there a prisoner, and they heard the tale from his own lips. They were not without admiration for Simon, for they expressed a certain resentment for their commander, the tribute Maxentius—and even more for his flunky, the centurion Scribonius, who perished in the fall of the tower."

"So Scribonius is dead then! I know that Simon had sworn revenge on him and Maxentius—"

"And on many another, evidently," said Parmenion enthusiastically. "Street talk has it that he has slain a score of Roman officials, tax-gatherers and extortionists who have slain the virtuous, stolen their money and possessions and sold them into slavery. How much of this is true I know not, but it seems that Simon is fast becoming a hero to the mob, lower-class Judeans and Syrians alike. Even one of the Roman officers spoke well of him—a centurion named Cornelius, whom I heard exclaim that no man had ever done the world a better favor than Simon when he gutted the corrupt tax-gatherer Jahath. Aye, he said that, and the tavern crowd cheered him for it!"

"I'm glad to hear that," said Dositheus, touched by the young man's obvious admiration for Simon. "It offers hope that we may be able to set our brave comrade free. I shall study how I may turn my arts to the task. But for now, good Parmenion, hurry on to Bethany and watch for Menander. I shall find Isagoras and tell him all I know."

When the young man had vanished away eastward, Dositheus motioned to Eupatos, who was in charge of the donkey, then led the way toward the northward road to Anathoth. Elissa, who had kept silent only with great effort, now hurried to the old wizard's side and burst out, "Simon a prisoner in Antonia? Dositheus, we've got to get him out! Accompany me to Jerusalem—I know a banker there. He can arrange any ransom those Roman extortionists want, payable against my estate."

The old mage saw the true concern in her eyes. "Alas, it would do no good. Simon's enemy is Maxentius."

Elissa felt the truth of it and it chilled her soul. "But, then, what *can* we do?"

"We can hurry on to the camp of the Thirty and consult with them. They are all learned and resourceful men. If Simon's plight has indeed caught the attention and sympathy of the Jerusalem mob, I think I may be able to contrive his release. But let us not get our hopes up until we know more. Look—there's the crossroads ahead. No more talk. We must press northward and find the camp of Isagoras with all speed."

Menander and Ilione gazed ahead in awe at a landscape of rising hills, ridges and ravines, beyond which rose the distant snowcapped peaks of mighty mountains.

For many hours they had thus gazed as vast panoramas of desert landscape had sped beneath the wizard's craft, eventually giving way to equally vast plains of rich green through which mighty rivers flowed. This last region, Menander realized, was the Plain of Shinar where mankind's civilization was said to have had its origins. He had felt doubly awed when Taggart pointed to a dark region to the north and announced that it was Babylon, a city Menander had once visited years before in company with Simon and Dositheus. And now, at last, the plains had given way to the hills and mountains of Elam. Beyond those distant eastern peaks, Menander knew, brooded the ancient and semi-ruined city of Persepolis, which had held such fond memories for him. Evidently the wizard Taggart was keeping his word.

"Taggart," he said, "apparently your sky-craft can bear you anywhere on this earth. How far away is this western land from which you once told us you came?"

The wizard's gaze grew introspective and troubled. "In miles alone it is many thousands, in years nearly two thousand . . . but I have not the words. That land was . . . or, rather, it *will be* destroyed. I can never go back there."

Menander perceived a hardness in the wizard's voice and features—the mask, he sensed, of a great sadness. "You come from a country that *will be* destroyed? How can you know that—?"

"I know."

"I don't understand."

"Hopefully you and your descendants never will. My world . . . was . . . one in which mankind had conquered most of the problems of disease and famine and, had its leaders been kind and sensible, might have conquered poverty, ignorance and cruelty as well. Instead, those leaders bent their efforts to acquiring more and more power, encouraging the world's populations to multiply in order to breed more and more slaves and purchasers. In time, as a result, disease and famine returned on a far greater scale than the world had ever known before, and humanity seethed and swelled and rotted like yeast in a sealed vat. Humans died by hundreds of millions, many of them perishing in wars ignited by the unrest of deprivation—wars fought with weapons too terrible for men of this primitive age of Rome to understand. Then, in the aftermath of that ruin of nations, new governments rose to power—terrible despotisms based upon terror and torture, ruling over all men by means of . . . of techniques which people of this age would call 'sorcery'."

Menander kept silent, sensing an intensity of feeling in the man called Taggart beyond anything he had sensed in him before.

"But then," continued the wizard, "the Zarrians came from space and shattered the power of Earth's rulers utterly, destroying human civilization and blasting the few survivors back into the darkness of savagery. I was one of the few who were glad to see it, and I laughed even when I felt that I was about to perish—as I watched the towering black wind-clouds stretching from horizon to horizon, advancing with titanic thunderings, flattening and shattering the last remnants of mankind's cities. . . ."

Menander again felt fear, for now he sensed that the intensity in the man's eyes and voice was born of hate—perhaps a hate for all things human.

"The Zarrians 'adopted' me," Taggart went on, "as they did Taaran and perhaps half a dozen other humans whose mind-waves, as measured on their instruments, indicated them to be so different from common humanity as to be useful in administering this planet. Thus, I have been their tool for centuries, visiting Earth's history to probe for what the Zarrians consider weak points—loci where their ruler Zathog and others of the Old Ones may one day break through. *This* time point—Jerusalem at just this time in its history—is the weakest that Taaran and I have yet discovered . . . but I sense, Menander, that you do not understand me."

Menander's fear increased, for he felt that he *did* understand. Behind Taggart's formal yet faltering and involved Latin he discerned the message that he wizard was in some sort of alliance with mighty and monstrous demons who plotted to destroy the world. He glanced at Ilione, saw that her eyes were wide and questioning. She, too, sensed the menace—perhaps more from Taggart's tone than from his actual words.

"Don't be afraid," said the wizard in answer to their mute expressions. "I've decided that I'd rather live than see justice done, so now I'm working against the Zarrians and their Master. It seems they were mistaken about my 'mind waves'—I'm just as corrupt and selfish as all the rest of you." The man laughed briefly, harshly. "Cheer up, Menander. Look—we're crossing the mountains. Soon we'll all be with our wise old friend Daramos, and if I know him he'll have some advice for us."

For the next hour they proceeded in silence while the sky craft, following the upward slope of the terrain, rose constantly. Menander and Ilione sensed that the wizard was wrapped in his own dark thoughts and strange, bitter memories. Yet the gloom his last remarks had induced in them did not long persist, for momentarily the landscape about the craft grew more and more enthralling to behold. The rising ridges swelled into the shoulders of mighty mountains whose peaks and flanks were white with the unmelted snows of spring, and whose steep rocky escarpments fell away into vast valleys and deep shadowy canyons. The air, despite the craft's invisible magical shield, felt ever cooler and fresher, while often the ears of the young pair felt congested to the point of deafness, only to release abruptly into full hearing once again. Never had Ilione seen such enormous and ragged mountain panoramas, even in the vicinity of Olympus and its environing peaks; while Menander, who had seen some of this region from the ground during his earlier visit some years ago, could not help but gasp in awe as the wizard's craft carried him between those titan precipices, offering him views of them hitherto known only to kites and eagles.

Then, as they passed between two enormous snowy crags and began to descend, Menander beheld a vista familiar to him, though from a lofty and unprecedented vantage—the wide plain of the Araxes River, beyond which more foothills and ridges rose up to incredible snowy peaks. And far to the east, at the very base of those foothills, sprawled a geometrical maze that Menander recognized—the tumbled, many-columned ruins of what had once been an enormous city.

"God!" breathed Ilione, awed. "Menander, what is it—"?

"It's Persepolis, Ilione. Persepolis, the home of Daramos. . . ."

The girl clasped her hands in front of her face, peering over them with wide blue eyes. Menander easily read the emotions in those eyes—awe, fear, anticipation and, above all, hope. In that moment he felt that he shared it all with her, and a sudden anxiety pierced him—a fear that the girl might have built up unrealistic expectations, that she might be about to experience a great disappointment.

"Ilione," he said, "I've told you that Daramos is not as other men. He is wise and kind and old, but his appearance is—well, unusual, to say the least. . . ."

"You have described him to me often," said Ilione. "I shall love him. I know I shall. . . ." Her voice trailed off faintly.

Taggart's craft dipped lower, floated over the sun-silvered Araxes toward the distant ruins, continued to descend. Again Menander felt his ears congest, swallowed energetically and felt them clear. The columned ruins of Persepolis were rapidly expanding, becoming more and more distinct in detail. Now their tallest columns were standing up against the deepening blue of the eastern sky, lofty in their splendor—and then the sky craft settled to rest amid them, humming with subdued power, hovering a mere foot or so above the stone flags of a vast courtyard.

The power-whine of the craft subsided to near-silence. A few human figures darted away like fleeting shadows between the columns and then were gone—peasants from nearby shops and villages, Menander realized, come to sell their wares to the monkish community, but now undoubtedly frightened away by the sight of the wizard's sky craft.

Taggart climbed out and helped the young pair to descend to the stone pavement after him. Menander, despite his past familiarity with the many-columned immensity of the ruined palace, felt anew a great awe at sight of it, and sensed that Ilione's awe was even greater. Then he glimpsed a squat shape moving within the dusky shadow of one of the columns—a shape that emerged into the full light of the declining sun and began to move toward them.

Ilione gasped.

"Gods—that's *him!"* muttered Menander. "He must have sensed our approach. Don't be afraid, Ilione."

The figure that slowly advanced to meet them seemed at first to Ilione to be that of a very fat child clad in a brown robe emblazoned ornately with mystical symbols, but as it drew nearer she saw that it was not a child at all, but a very strange being indeed. Its head was extremely wide and flat, spanned by a long lipless mouth and bracketed by two high, sharp-pointed ears. Its arms were as stubby as those of a child's toy animal, its nose so short and blunt that it was hardly a facial feature at all, and the hue of its skin was a strange grayish-green. But all of its grotesquerie was counterbalanced and overcome by its large, almond-shaped eyes—eyes in which, paradoxically, all the human and tragedy of sentient life seemed to lie dormant yet ready at any moment to be expressed.

"Daramos!" exclaimed Taggart. "It's really you? Who would have expected you to be yet alive, after all these centuries!"

Daramos slowly blinked his large heavy-lidded eyes. "Taggart?" he said in a deep, vibrant yet gentle voice. "I sensed the approach of friends, but never did I suspect that you were among them. It has been more than five centuries since we undid the despots of Babylon and you caused the Black Hand to write its warning of doom upon the wall of Belshazzar's feast!"

"You sensed our approach?" said Taggart. "But how—?"

"And Menander!" said the dwarf, turning toward the youth. "You were but a boy when you and Simon and Dositheus studied under me years ago. I see that you are now a fine young man, fit for all the responsibilities of the world."

Menander bowed respectfully, then said, "Revered Mentor, this young woman is Ilione, who desires to be your pupil. Her father was a dark sorcerer who sought to use her for his evil purposes, yet she has cast off his influence and desires to be a disciple of the Light."

Daramos waved a stubby paw deprecatingly. "You need not defend her, good pupil. I sense that she is a True Spirit, and that spirit of hers speaks for itself to all who can perceive."

Then, to Menander's surprise, Ilione rushed forward and, falling to her knees in front of the dwarfish being, said in a trembling voice, "O Daramos, I have longed to know you ever since I first heard of you! You are good and kind. Please let me stay with you and learn from you."

The eyes of the kneeling girl, wide and blue and hopeful, were exactly on a level with the dark almond eyes of the strange dwarf. For a long moment those two pairs of eyes stared quietly, each into the other, like the blue-golden dawn confronting the dark and starry west. Then, like night yielding to the influence of morning, the face of Daramos seemed to brighten; his wide mouth curled slightly in a calm smile, barely perceptible, but the crinkles about the outer corners of his eyes deepened—and somehow Menander sensed, in that slight change of expression, an acceptance,—a joy, even—born of deep perception and great love.

"Welcome, True Spirit," said the great mage quietly, taking each of the girl's trembling hands in one of his small, stubby paws. "I sense that yours has been a hard lot, but that stage of your journey is over. You are safe now—as you have always been safe, had you but known it. For, are you not the reason for the creation of the worlds? Come—I will show you to the women's quadrangle, where you shall meet new friends, then eat and rest and sleep. And tomorrow you shall awaken to the beginning of a new life and a new awareness."

Menander, seeing the tears of joy and relief that sprang into Ilione's eyes, and recalling his own first encounter with the kindly old mage, turned away to hide his own tears. And in doing so he glimpsed, in the hard features of Taggart, a working of jaw muscles and a tightening of the mouth, and sensed that the wizard was uncomfortable, perhaps even embarrassed, in the presence of a mystery he did not understand.

CHAPTER XXII

Parmenion, letting himself out the door of the inn, saw that he was being watched closely by the two burly Galileans who stood guard there. They made no move to stop or questions him, however, no doubt still assuming him to be one of the group of inconsequential servants with whom he had contrived to enter earlier.

Outside the dusk was gathering and a single torch was burning beside the inn door. Before that door could close Parmenion saw a short man in the robes of a rabbi hurry forward and attempt to enter. His whiskers bristled laterally and stiffly in a manner that made Parmenion think of a cat, and his brow was knit in a scowl of determination.

"Stand aside, Boanerges!" he shouted to the pair of tall Galileans. "My son, Philip, is in there and I mean to see him."

"Begone," growled one of the men through his thick brown beard, "or this time we'll pitch you *all* the way across the street. And this time you'll land on your head, not your rump."

"Louts! Kidnappers! I *will* see my son—"

"Peace, shrimp. Philip joined us of his own choosing. As for you, false rabbi, did not the Master shake dust from his sandals after you refused him leave to speak in the synagogue in Bethsaida? You shall not now disturb this feast in his honor. Begone."

So saying, the Galilean shoved the little old man in the chest and sent him sprawling in the dust, then withdrew and slammed the door.

Parmenion stepped forward and helped the little rabbi to his feet.

"Thank you, young man," said Samezer, brushing the dust from himself with his short arms. "Ah, would that all young men were as helpful as you! My son has been tricked into joining the accursed cult of Yeshua the Nazarene, and he is no longer allowed to see or speak with me. . . . But did I not see you leaving this very inn but a moment ago?"

"You did. I contrived to enter with the servants of the rabbi Yeshua and his disciples, and have just been witness to a most interesting ceremony. My name is Parmenion and I am a member of the Thirty—a group to which you once belonged, good sir."

"What?" The old man stepped back a pace. "How do you know that?"

"I gather that you are Rabbi Samezer of Bethsaida. Dositheus has told me that you and Rabbi Tolmai were once members."

"Yes." Rabbi Samezer scowled briefly toward the inn door. "You must have seen my son Philip inside. Do you know him?"

"I met him there briefly. He seems well, and so does Rabbi Tolmai's son Nathaniel."

"I am joyed to hear it. But why are you here, Parmenion? Spying for Dositheus, perhaps?"

"Actually, Dositheus has instructed me to watch for his apprentice Menander, but the young lad seems to be greatly delayed. Too bad, for I have news which I'm sure Dositheus would be interested in hearing."

"Indeed? Listen, young man, I'd like to talk to Dositheus myself. Tell me where I can find him and I'll convey your news to him in person."

Parmenion nodded. "I'd appreciate that, sir. And when you go to him, please ask him to send someone to relieve me at my watch." He glanced at the inn door, then down the street to a group of young men gathered around a pair of heavily laden donkeys. "Are those men your servants?"

"Aye."

"Then let's join them and move away from this inn a bit."

When they were all settled in the shadow of a building which gave them a good view of the torchlit door while being well out of earshot of it, Parmenion continued, "This is what I want you to tell Dositheus, sir. Tonight I witnessed a ritual whose significance I am sure he will understand better than do I."

"A ritual!" said Samezer with obviously keen interest. "I fear that I know what it may have been, for at this time of year the ancient kings once conducted their . . . but I interrupt. Please go on, Parmenion, and leave nothing out."

Parmenion looked at him curiously. "There's little to tell. After the rabbi Yeshua and his followers were seated at table, and we 'servants' had sat down along the walls and in the corners, a beautiful dark-haired woman, regally clad in a robe of gold tissue and wearing upon her head a diadem of stars, came into the room bearing a small white jar apparently filled with alabaster. From this she took forth a vial of dark green glass and, without a word, poured out its contents upon the rabbi's head; I could smell its spicy odor immediately pervading the room and knew that it was some pungent ointment. Then a lean, dark man with reddish hair and intense black eyes rose up at the other end of the table and intoned, as nearly as I can recall: 'Why pour ye forth this precious oil of anointing? For could it not have been sold for the relief of the poor?' Then the Master answered in a ritual monotone: 'Leave her be and trouble her not, for she has served me well, preparing me for my down-going. The poor suffer always among you, but would you aid them in their suffering forever? Soon I go forth to bury all suffering, and she who has anointed me shall be eternally remembered with gratitude for it.' Then the rest of the company murmured together: 'She has anointed him, and he shall now go down for burial.' Then all fell to the feast and I, after appeasing my hunger and conversing a bit with some of the servants, stole away and slipped out the door."

Old Samezer made a sign in the air before him. "It is as I feared. The Betrothal of the King has been sealed, and tonight it shall be consummated. Parmenion, give me the directions to your camp. I must tell Dositheus of this."

Parmenion obeyed, then asked, "But what is this rite of 'The Betrothal of the King' which I have witnessed?"

"These are matters beyond your grade of understanding, young man. Suffice it to say that in ancient Karakossa each 'Last King' vowed to end all suffering, but all failed to do so. Yet the Betrothal of the King is meant to ensure that the King's seed will continue down the generations in order that one of his descendants may someday attempt to . . . but enough. I go now to consult with Dositheus. I thank you, Parmenion. If we all work together and pool our knowledge, perhaps my son Philip—and all others in this world—may be spared the fate planned by this cult of madness."

Menander, after supping with the acolytes and napping in the small cubicle assigned to him, woke and rose. Despite his weariness, he knew he could not sleep now, not with so many questions unanswered.

Still hardly believing he was truly here, he threaded the well-remembered maze of corridors beneath the abandoned palaces of Persepolis until he came to the modest chambers of his old mentor Daramos. No guard stood by the curtained entrance to those chambers, and as Menander approached he could hear the voices of two men within—Taggart and old Daramos himself. As he drew nearer, Menander realized that they were speaking in a language he could not understand, for Dositheus had once taught him some of its elements. It was an ancient form of Egyptian, unused by men for centuries.

Parting the curtains, Menander saw that both the speakers were sitting upon floor mats, facing one another, in the center of a chamber cluttered with scrolls and many of Daramos' varied instruments of divination.

"Pardon, most excellent Daramos, but I beg leave to speak to you."

The venerable dwarf bowed slightly from the waist in acknowledgment, then waved the lad toward another floor mat. "It is well that you came, Menander, for we have much to discuss."

As Menander seated himself he saw that the raven was nestled quietly upon a cushion in the corner of the room, apparently sleeping. "Have you examined Carbo, O Mentor?"

"I have. The bird is healing extremely well. But it is a very old bird and so will not sustain our friend much longer. This is but one of the things you must learn about, Menander, in order that you may make wise decisions concerning your role in the mighty events that are impending."

Menander noticed that Daramos was now speaking in a carefully enunciated Latin, doubtless for the benefit of Taggart. "Taggart has told me something about mighty events, but I fear that my ignorance still far outweighs my knowledge. What role am I to play?"

"Taggart has asked that you be allowed to accompany him back to Judea tomorrow and accomplish a thing he cannot do himself. But before we go into that, I must ask you about this scroll." Daramos held up a cylinder of papyrus which Menander recognized. "I have just finished reading Dositheus' partial translation into Greek of Mattan's *El-Halah*, a book of which I have heard but never before seen. Tell me, Menander, does Dositheus indeed have a complete copy of it in the original Canaanite language, as Taggart believes?"

"He does." Menander quickly told all he knew of the manuscript and how Dositheus had acquired it. "But I know little of what it contains," he concluded, "save that it evidently prophesies ill for humankind."

"More than that," said Daramos. "But I will let Taggart tell you of the things he has just told me."

Menander felt a subtle chill. Always before, his venerable mentor had been the confident expounder of knowledge and wisdom, but now it seemed that he had just learned of matters which had made him deeply concerned, even uncertain.

Taggart reached into a black carrying-case which rested beside him, drew forth a blue metal circlet and placed it upon his own head so that its faintly glowing disc rested upon his brow. Menander, recognizing the device, cringed inwardly.

"Don't worry," said Taggart, noticing the lad's discomfort. "You won't experience the vivid imagery you would if you also wore one of these. By wearing this device I'll be able to project and understand the nuances of our thoughts a bit more clearly than my ignorance of Latin would otherwise permit—and that is necessary, for what I must tell you is complicated as well as important. Listen carefully now.

"Many thousand upon thousands of years ago there was a great war between beings too vast and powerful for humans of this age to comprehend. Some of these beings had created life upon Earth and many other worlds in order that they might feed upon the psychic energies generated by the sufferings of that life; but they were opposed by other beings who, needing no such energies for their sustenance, sought to exterminate life that they might put the worlds to other purposes. Certain ancient human writers have called these beings 'Primal Gods' and 'Old Ones' respectively. I cannot now go into the details concerning their nature; suffice it to say that the Old Ones were defeated in this part of the galaxy and driven forth or imprisoned on various worlds."

Without a thought-disc on his own brow, Menander yet found that he understood the strange and unsettling concepts, even when Taggart happened to misuse a word or structure a sentence wrongly. The vivid visions were not coming to him as before; nevertheless he somehow had an understanding of a frighteningly vast universe in which the stars were innumerable suns gathered into pinwheeling clouds—called *galaxies*—where monstrous beings warred across unbelievable immensities of space and time. . . .

"Recently," Taggart continued, "—which is to say, some thousands of years ago—the ceaseless war flared up again in this star-region. One of the mightiest of the Old Ones, called Set or Hastur by some of the ancient human nations, took up its abode amid the stars of the Hyades and made the dominant race of that star-cluster its minions. You once encountered one of those minions, Menander—the cowled and tentacled being in the synagogue of Chorazin."

Menander's spine prickled. "It is there no longer, O Taggart, for I encountered it and the rabbi Izhar at the villa of the priest Annas, near Jerusalem." Quickly the lad told both of his listeners all he knew of the matter, then asked his mentor Daramos, "Have you ever encountered such a being as this, sir?"

"No," said the dwarfish sage," for I have never been out to the star-worlds, as Taggart has, and the few such beings on earth have until now lain hidden in deathless sleep. Yet I have read of such things in very ancient works handed down from the days of Valusia and Commoriom."

"Right now, that being is the only one of its kind on this planet," Taggart went on, "but many beings of another sort also serve Hastur—the green blob-things. Several hundred of them came to Earth and aided the Hastur-serving Karakossan nation to rise to the height of its power. Later, after Karakossa's destruction by other minions of the Primal Gods, the blob-beings hibernated in caverns beneath the Galilean hills, sealed within their coppery hemispheres, only a few of them emerging now and then over the centuries to check on human progress, occasionally inhabiting people or animals in order to accomplish their spying. Humans vaguely remember them as the Earth Folk, or as 'demons' who enter and possess.

"The Hastur-minions came to Earth from the star Celaeno in the Pleiades, where the Old Ones have established their greatest information center, but they are only a traitorous minority of a race which once ruled the Empire of the Six Suns—that light in the sky which the Greeks know as the star Castor. To this day a mighty celestial war is being waged to determine the fate of the Six Suns, the blob-beings there defending themselves against conquest by Hastur's Hyades-minions and the traitorous blob-faction of Celaeno."

"The gods battling for worlds!" exclaimed Menander, awed. "How can all this pertain to me? How could I possibly aid or play a part in—?"

Daramos lifted his right hand. "Listen attentively, Menander. It is your friend Carbo whom you must first aid, that you and he may work together in the impending trials and dangers."

"You see," said Taggart, "Carbo is one of the blob-beings from the Six Suns. He was captured decades ago by those of the Celaeno faction and . . . reduced . . . to be imprisoned in the body of the raven. Many such prisoners, in order that they might serve as slaves and messengers, were put into small Earth creatures—mostly owls and desert-cats, which can see at night, but sometimes diurnal birds or animals too. For, the . . . units . . . which make up these blobs are far smaller than those comprising humans and other earthly animals; this, plus their nearly structureless fluid nature, allows them to seep into—to inhabit—people and other creatures. It also means that they are not killed or maimed when part of their substance—or even most of it—is destroyed. They are like . . . *holograms* . . . in which a part implies the whole. But once reduced, they lose most of their memory and become susceptible to suggestive influence, like children obeying the orders of their owners. The only way to restore them to full intelligence is to allow them to live inside larger hosts and grow back to their original size. So, Menander, if you want to help your friend Carbo—"

The man hesitated. Menander felt a strange excitement, recalling how Dositheus had told of buying Carbo from a Roman legionary in Galilee many years ago. Dositheus' raven familiar, strangely intelligent for a bird—was he indeed one of those *Am-ha-arez* of Galilean legend? It was hard to imagine Carbo as something other than the raven itself—and yet, had not everyone heard that a wizard's familiar was possessed by a spirit being that lived within it . . .?

"A larger body for Carbo to grow in? You mean, like an ass or a goat?"

"Or, better," said Daramos quietly, "the body of an intelligent human, preferably one who knows him and has his trust."

Menander shuddered, though he had sensed the suggestion coming. It was true that he thought of Carbo as a friend during the many years they had lived together and aided one another. Yet the thought of one of those blob-things creeping into his own flesh. . . .

"There is no danger," said Taggart. "As I've said, there is one of Carbo's companions inside me even now. I owe my life to that fact. The beings of the Six Suns have a code of honor: their policy is to never possess or dominate other intelligent beings, but to inhabit them only in a spirit of mutual respect and voluntary cooperation—a policy quite opposite to that of the Celaeno faction, as you well know."

Menander shot an anxious glance toward his mentor. "Do you advise this course for me, O wise Mentor?"

"It must be of your own choosing, Menander. But not now. Listen first to the rest of what Taggart has to say."

"This planet—the Earth—is now in great danger," Taggart resumed, "—not so much from the minions of Hastur as from those of an even greater Old One which the Karakossans called Uagio-tsotho and Judeans still worship as Yahweh Zava'ot. These minions are the Zarrians, a mighty race who rule an entire galaxy in the constellation the Greeks call Andromeda, and who know this mighty Old One as *Ghod Zathog.*

"Tsotho, Zava'ot or Zathog is not a being such as we know, for it has more . . . extensions . . . than those of mere space and time. Therefore, in our cosmos it can exist in many places at once. It is one; yet, to beings such as us, it can appear to be many."

Menander's mind whirled. He had heard of such bizarre concepts from Dositheus, who had tried to describe certain ancient writings to him, yet even Taggart's thought-disc could make such a thing seem only vaguely intelligible.

"Zathog has 'gates' to and from many worlds, the greatest being the mighty black vortices that lie at the centers of all the galaxies. After the Primal Gods closed all his lesser gates in the vicinity of Earth and it neighboring worlds, Zathog induced the Zarrians, his mightiest minions, to invade this galaxy and conquer it for him. Yet their task was not easy, for this galaxy was already controlled by mighty metallic servitors of the Primal Gods. Thus began the latest phase of the cosmic war, a phase which has raged for thousands of years between the Zarrians and the Galactic Defenders.

"Earth, a remote outpost of the present Galactic Empire, has so far experienced little of this conflict, but it shall soon know more of it if Zathog succeeds in his newest purpose, which is to reopen a gate that will allow him access to this world. To that end he has caused two beings who share his nature to be born on Earth, that they may prepare the way. One of these beings appears to be almost completely human and he is known as Yeshua bar Yosef, Rabbi of Capharnaum."

"I suspected as much," said Daramos gravely. "He it is who was born under the 'star' a generation ago."

"The star?" asked Menander. "What do you mean, O Mentor?"

"It appeared in the heavens more than thirty years ago," explained the dwarfish mage, "arcing across the night sky from east to west—a great bright gleam, brighter even than Venus, moving among the constellations. For several nights it did this, traversing the sky every few hours, vanishing in the west only to eventually rise in the east again, until one night it was seen no more.

"Then, more than a year later, a band of magi who called themselves the Order of the High Guardians passed through Persepolis. Their leader, one

K'shasthra, told me that they were returning from a far journey to the west, a journey they had made in hopes of finding the place where the star had come to earth; for, K'shasthra claimed, the High Guardians were keepers of ancient secrets and suspected that the star was the fulfillment of a dark prophecy. In Judea, the astrologers of King Herod directed them to a village where the star was said to have paused and hovered one night, so near to the earth that the landscape was lit by it as if by many full moons. During that night many shepherds had come down from the hills to worship a newborn male child, intoning blessings upon him in the name of Assatur, God of Shepherds. At this news, K'shasthra and his fellow magi were very excited and sought out the child themselves. They found him still living in the town with his parents, a toddler now and quite large for his age. After certain examinations they satisfied themselves that the child was indeed one of the New Elohim, a son of the Most Ancient One, and in adoration gave rich gifts to his human parents, plus promises of future aid and service to his cosmic Father in the impending New Aeon. And now, Menander, I sense that that New Aeon is near to being accomplished, for only last evening I saw a new star in the heavens, similar to the star of old, yet much fainter and crossing the sky more slowly."

"It is the same 'star' indeed," said Taggart, "though circling the Earth at a much higher elevation than before. Actually it is a great metallic starship of the Zarrians, containing mighty magical . . . devices . . . of surveillance and destruction. There is even one Zarrian on board, and . . . and it was from that ship that Taaran and I came to Earth several months ago."

The black-clad wizard ceased speaking, and Menander sensed that the man was reluctant, perhaps even ashamed, to continue. "You and your companion aided the Zarrian demons?" the young man prompted.

"Yes. Ours was a minor and rather menial task—to provide 'miracles' with which the rabbi Yeshua might impress the mobs to whom he preached. To this end we located and awakened several of the hibernating blob-beings who serve Hastur, promising to return them to Celaeno in return for their aid. One of those beings inhabits the rabbi Yeshua even now and aids him in his healing through 'laying on of hands'. Thus the rabbi's followers grow in number and fervor, and unwittingly supply the psychic zeal which is being focused and directed to aid in the opening of the Gate."

"So, there are now *three* factions of the beings!" exclaimed Menander.

"Not exactly," said Daramos, again raising his hand. "Please pay attention, Menander. Listen with a quiet mind, as I have instructed you often. Afterwards you may think and question."

"By this time," Taggart continued, "I had realized that the advent of Ghod Zathog to Earth was to result in no mere destruction of corrupt human civilizations, with a few humans spared to start a new and higher civilization under the direction of the Zarrians. No, the opening of the Gate would mean the obliteration of *all earthly life,* not only at this time but for the last several million years, and Earth itself would be shunted into a distant region of space-time, to be ruled thenceforth by Zathog and his minions. In short, the human race would not merely be destroyed, *it would never have existed at all."*

In the ensuing silence Menander again glanced at his old mentor. The dark eyes of Daramos, though still calm, reflected the light of the oil lamps solemnly.

"And that means, Taggart," said the dwarfish mage quietly, "that you, too, would never have existed."

"Yes. I have long dreamed that somehow, in some timeline, despite all the horror and suffering, something worthwhile might eventually come of the human race. But *this—!"* The man clenched his fists in a sudden violent tension, as if at a loss for further words.

"So that is why you defected."

Taggart nodded. "But first, I went privately to the rabbi Yeshua while he was alone in the wilderness and tried to persuade him to change his plan, to show him that he could rule the human race to their betterment rather than destroy every possibility of their existence—and his own. He would not listen. To annul their sufferings, he will sacrifice even himself."

"And what of Taaran, your companion?" asked Daramos.

"He is of the same mind as the rabbi Yeshua—that the human race should be obliterated so thoroughly that no chance of its existence will be left open in any of the possible universes. His motive, however, is hatred rather than compassion."

"Are the two feelings so opposed," said Daramos, "that they cannot spring from the same source?"

For a moment Taggart looked puzzled; then he chuckled slightly. "You haven't changed at all, Daramos—even though, for you, it has been several centuries since we last met. For me, though, it has been only a couple of decades, yet I feel I've changed a great deal."

"Not in appearance. But please continue."

"There's little more to tell. Some time after my failure with the rabbi Yeshua, Taaran and I were again sent down to Earth to meet with him, this time upon a high mountain slope north of Bethsaida. With him were his three chief followers, whom we were to impress with their leader's supernatural power. The rabbi wore a Zarrian force-belt—an item I had once offered him, but which he had refused. He used it to surround himself with its spectacular white light, which of course impressed his three human followers greatly, as intended; I gather they felt their leader was a god and that Taaran and I were supernatural beings also.

"After this bit of chicanery I made the decision that I had already been considering, and when Taaran returned to the Zarrian craft that had brought us to Earth, I stayed behind on the pretext of recruiting more allies from the hibernating Am-ha-arez. I did not return. Since then I have worked to thwart the advent of Zathog to this world—with little success so far, I'm afraid. Taaran and the Zarrian *robot*-craft have searched for me a time or two, but not with great effort, for I have to admit I'm not very important in the Zarrian scheme of things."

"Then how, O Taggart, can you and I hope to prevent the impending destructions?" asked Menander.

"Actually we'll have a mighty ally, for the Zarrian ship is not the only one presently circling the Earth. Today a Galactic ship arrived and placed itself in a far higher *orbit*—an Earth-synchronized one which keeps it above and in view of Judea at all times. Undoubtedly it is watching the Zarrian ship. Tonight, when I return to my sky craft, I will send it a tightly-beamed message; at that time the Zarrian will be on the other side of the Earth and so will not detect it—nor will Taaran or any other ground scouts, who will be a thousand miles away from here in Judea. So, Menander, we do not fight the 'gods' alone. Will you help?"

Menander felt a deadly chill of fear. His participation would require that he take . . . Carbo . . . *into* himself, then go forth to face vaguely defined perils of incredible magnitude. No, it was impossible. More, it was unfair! How could this alien wizard Taggart, or even his respected mentor, Daramos, demand of him, a mere lad, that he go forth to battle monstrous gods?

He glanced at Daramos, saw that the face of the old mage was as calm and solemn as ever. Evidently nothing could disturb him in his deep wisdom, not even the impending annihilation of the world, of all humanity, of all life, of even himself. . . .

Then Menander felt a sudden relief. Had not Daramos often explained to him that innumerable worlds and souls have perished and will continue to perish countless times in the great cosmic cycle of birth and death? Had he not taught that one must not become attached to any time, place or condition, since these are illusions which generate fear and suffering? Perhaps it would be best that this Earth, so full of pointless pain and horror, should perish utterly like a monstrous nightmare dissolving in the rays of dawn. Perhaps the more-than-human being called Yeshua bar Yosef was right—perhaps the creating gods were the evil ones and the annihilating gods the harbingers of good. . . .

Yet had not Daramos also taught that good and evil, too, were but part of the Great Illusion? Menander had never felt that he understood that truth, if truth it was. . . .

Then, as a vision unbidden, unanticipated, he suddenly saw in his mind the face of Lotis—the face of a girl, yet more than that—a girl whose dark hair gleamed with brilliant highlights like countless stars, whose dark eyes seemed to reflect the infinite depths of the cosmos. And in that moment Menander remembered why that cosmos had come into being, and for Whom.

"Yes," he said, a bit surprised at the firmness of his own voice. "Yes, Taggart, I will help. Tell me what I must do."

"Good." Taggart rose stiffly from the mat, then picked up his carrying-case. "But not now. We must sleep and be fresh in the morning. Tomorrow I must instruct you in the use of some devices, especially one in particular. Until then, good night to you both."

When the man had gone, Daramos said quietly, "I see that you have recently learned a new truth, Menander."

"Yes, O Mentor. In Judea I met a girl named Lotis, and . . . and now I think I understand a thing which Dositheus once tried to tell me."

The mage closed his eyes for a moment, then reopened them. "It is well. You now understand what even Taggart does not, despite all his knowledge of sorceries unknown to the peoples of this age. He knows nothing of True Spirits, though he is one of them, for the wisdom of his time made—or will make—such knowledge impossible. He knows much concerning how the cosmos came to be, but nothing as to *why* it did. He knows that the churnings of the universe had produced Mind, but of its corollary—that Mind produces the universe—he knows nothing. And he knows much about the minions of those Old Ones whose purposes he hopes to thwart, but of the nature of those Old Ones themselves there is much that he does not understand."

"What does he not understand about them, O Mentor?"

"That the One is many, and the Many One." Daramos picked up a parchment scroll from the floor and unrolled it. "Do you remember this symbol, Menander, and the things I once told you about it?"

Menander recognized the drawing and shuddered slightly. It depicted the heads of seven ancient Egyptian gods whose necks were joined to a common body suggestive of a tangle of serpents and skulls.

"The original of this symbol adorns the door of an ancient buried tomb in Upper Egypt—the tomb of Anubis, Guardian of the Gate. It's meaning is that there is One who is of a higher level of Being and who may manifest Himself in many times and places and in many guises. Now I will tell you more: this Being, whose Name you were taught in writing as a youth but warned never to speak aloud—this One Who Is Not to Be Named—this Yahweh Zava'ot, or Iao Sabaoth, or Uagio-tsotho, or Yog-Sothoth or Ghod Zathog, as he is variously called depending on which race is symbolizing him—is the same entity as Set, Assatur, or Hastur, Lord of Celaeno and the Hyades."

For a moment Menander struggled to understand the significance of this. Then it struck him.

"But that means . . . the priestly Jerusalem faction and the faction of the rabbi Yeshua are serving the same Being! Do they know this, O Mentor?"

"I am sure that the rabbi Yeshua knows it full well. The sorcerer Annas and his fellow plotter do not, I am equally sure; they believe that they work to set themselves up as rulers over all the world. They do not realize that they are part of an even greater plot to destroy this world utterly."

"Gods!" Instantly Menander's exclamation struck him as totally inadequate, absurd. His mind was reeling from the glimpses he had had of cosmic immensities overshadowed by even vaster levels of sentient Power and Being. "How can I—or any of us—possibly play any meaningful part in all of this?"

"You are a part," said Daramos calmly. "You play the greatest part of all. There are still higher levels of Being in which even the Primal Gods and the Old Ones merge into Unity—into the Chaos of Azathoth, where even the primordial Light and Darkness swirl and merge to swallow up all possible worlds. And beyond that—"

"No!" cried Menander, leaping to his feet. "I cannot bear to hear more of this!"

"You need not, for already you know. You have made your decision from deep Knowledge, even though you are still less than fully conscious of it all. You know what is important to you, and you will act on it."

Menander thought of Lotis, and the thought was like an anchor to sanity, a tie to his world and race. What did it matter that gods and worlds might be swallowed up in cosmic wars? That was not important, save that if it happened he would never see *her* again, and he wanted to see her again very much. Without the world, *she* would never again exist—at least, not in just *that* way, the way in which she had captured his heart. And so, somehow, the world must be saved!

"You have journeyed far this day, Menander," said the ancient mage, "and not merely in miles. Go, now, and sleep well, for I sense that soon you will have even greater journeys ahead of you."

CHAPTER XXIII

Simon of Gitta awoke suddenly, hearing the clang of metal on metal. For many long hours he had lain on the cold, rough stones of his cell deep within the Antonian Fortress, sleeping as often as he was able, striving to calm his mind and conserve his energies during his hours of wakefulness. He had no idea as to how long he had been confined, whether for hours or days, but sensed that it had been the latter. Yet if so, why had his arch foe, Maxentius, delayed so long in coming to him in order to taunt, torture and slay . . .?

Rising up on one elbow, Simon saw Roman guards forcing two ragged, wild-eyed men into ankle-chains similar to his own, hammering the iron circlets shut with rivets. In a few more minutes, their task completed, the guards withdrew, vanishing away up the narrow stone staircase, bearing most of the light with them. When they had gone only one torch still burned within its wall bracket, a beacon too dim and smoky to inspire hope.

"What day is it?" Simon ventured to ask.

"Does it matter?" growled one of the prisoners. "Henceforth darkness is life; tomorrow's dawn will see us crucified."

"Silence, Gestas," said the other. "Why should we be surly on the point of death? Stranger, today is the day before the Passover. We are here because we opposed the Roman oppressors, having slain their tax gatherers and attacked their patrols."

"Then you are friends of mine," said Simon. "I am here because I slew certain Romans and tax gatherers who murdered my parents and stole my inheritance several years ago. The tributne Maxentius coveted the house and holdings of my parents, and so he—"

"Maxentius!" exclaimed the one called Gestas. "I know him well. Many are the Galileans, Syrians and Judeans he has dispossessed. I'd dedicated my knife for his throat . . . but, alas!—his demon Luck led him to me first."

"You must be the one called Bar abbas," said the other prisoner.

Simon started. "How did you know that?"

"Many people are telling your tale in the streets. They are even calling upon the mob to demand your release according to the custom of pardoning one prisoner of their choice at the Passover time, and the mob seems to be responding favorably to the suggestion. I heard them cry out: 'Would that there were more such "fathers' sons" to save us from oppression!' I heard even a Roman soldier or two speak out in approval of your acts, though not in favor of your release."

Simon sat up with interest. "Evidently those whom I slew were not popular. Yes, I recall now that the centurion in charge of bringing me here said to his soldiers that I had done well to kill the extortioner Jahath. But who can be spreading this tale and making this demand on my behalf?"

Gestas shrugged, shook his head violently so that his tangled locks whipped his bare shoulders. "Who knows? Would that Dysmas and I were as lucky as you, 'Father's Son'! Your chance of escape may not be great, but at least it would seem that you *have* a chance."

Simon settled back, feeling new hope and new anxiety. The only explanation was that Dositheus, with the aid of the Thirty, must be agitating the crowd on his pupil's behalf. No doubt the artful old mage was hiding the fact that he, Simon—"Bar abbas"—was a hated Samaritan, and if that fact did not come out there might indeed be cause for hope. If so, Simon knew that he must quiet his mind, conserve his strength for the hour in which he would need it.

"There has been great turmoil in the streets," Gestas went on, apparently wanting to talk, "—what with this agitator Yeshua bar Yosef claiming to be the Mashiah, and then the collapse of the Siloam tower—"

Again Simon sat up. "Evidently a lot has happened since I was brought here. Tell me all you've seen and heard, Gestas. If there's a revolution brewing, there may yet be hope for all of us. . . ."

Tribune Maxentius, marching westward through the noisy and noisome streets of Jerusalem, was glad to have the company of his giant bodyguard and the decan of legionaries who followed him. Behind him, in the direction of the Temple, he could hear the tumult of the unruly crowds, but here between the ruins of the Old Wall and the Palace of Antipas the rabble clustered less thickly and carried on less rowdily.

As he passed the columned northern portico of the Palace he noticed a number of black-cloaked Temple guardsmen. One of them beckoned to him, and he motioned his legionaries to a halt; then, accompanied only by the mighty-thewed Cratos, he followed the guardsman to the shadowed portico. Despite the brilliance of the noonday sun he could barely make out the lean, robed figure standing behind the pillars, yet instantly realized who it must be.

"Annas," he muttered as he entered the welcome shade, "what are you doing here? I'm on my way to—"

"To visit the prefect Pilatus. I know. I think that you should know a few things before you talk with him."

"What things?"

"Last night, in Bethany, the rabbi Yeshua was officially anointed in accordance with the ancient customs of Karakossa, Israel and Judea, and then proclaimed by his followers to be the Last King."

"By Pluto! That's the title *you* aspire to."

"Keep your voice down!" snapped the priest, glancing about the portico. Then in a near-whisper, "If I fail to gain that title, and the mighty sorcerous powers that go with it, neither of us will rule as we hope to."

Maxentius, too, glanced amid the shadows of the pillars uneasily. "What are we to do, then?"

"Tonight you must arrest the rabbi Yeshua and see that he is put to death."

"Gods! Must I do everything?" snarled the tribute. "I've already been run half ragged trying to keep these unruly mobs in check, not to mention organizing the repair of the breach in the city's wall at Siloam. And the arrival of the prefect Pilatus from Caesarea this morning has put even greater pressure on me. He wants to know why the tower fell last night, and why the crowds are now milling about in the Temple's outer precincts with such furor. I've slept barely four hours during the last two days! If Pilatus should find out that I'm involved in a plot against the Empire—"

"Silence!" hissed Annas. "Your voice is rising. There is nothing to fear if you do as I say. Last night, while we priests of the Sanhedrin held conclave in the Hall of Gazzith, our spy Judah of Kerioth came to us with the news of Rabbi Yeshua's anointing. He also told us that the rabbi and his followers are to meet this very night in the Garden of Gethsemene across the valley east of the city. Judah has agreed to lead us there under cover of darkness. It is there, Maxentius, that you must arrest Yeshua bar Yosef, and you must bring with you a cohort of legionaries to make sure that you accomplish that task."

"A *cohort!"* exclaimed Maxentius in spite of himself. Then in a lower voice, "Why in Hades should I take several hundred armed men in order to arrest the leader of a few ragged Galileans?"

"Forget not that the rabbi has evoked multitudes to his cause—pious zealots, haters of Romans, dreamers who believe that he has come to fulfill the Law and establish the New Kingdom. Even worse, he has undoubtedly drawn some of the unhuman *Am-ha-arez* to his cause, and you know what that means: he will be protected by great sorceries even if his human followers are too cowardly to stand up in his behalf."

Maxentius drew himself up firmly. "Don't worry, Annas, I'll do my part if you continue to do yours. Your magic and plottings won't gain you anything without the backing of my military expertise. After I see Pilatus I'll snatch a few more hours of sleep, then pluck your ambitious rabbi from the very midst of his followers."

"Good. Yet have a care when you go to see Pilatus. I fear that one or two members of the Sanhedrin may be plotting against us, and that they may even have influence with the Roman prefect. In particular I suspect old Yosef of Aphairema, who knows far more than he lets on concerning the mysteries of the Nameless One. I fear that he, too, aspires to become the Last King."

"Why not just have him done away with, then?"

"He is prominent in the Sanhedrin, and we have no proof against him as yet. Besides, he is working with us against the rabbi Yeshua. Yosef claims to have evidence against the prefect Pilatus concerning former dabblings in sorcery and the death of the previous prefect, plus the usual illegal plundering of the public till. He tells me that he has already suggested to Pilatus that Yeshua must die for aspiring to be King of Judea, and the prefect has agreed. Pilatus will therefore play his part, and he will not release the perverse rabbi even should the mob demand it."

"Curse of the gods!" snarled Maxentius. "I've heard many in the crowds demanding that Simon of Gitta, whom they call 'Bar-Abbas', be released at the Passover. I'll not permit *that,* by Hades! I have a score to settle—"

"No!" said Annas sternly. "However the matter develops, you must not let your personal grudge interfere with our plans. It is of the first importance that this Yeshua must die, for he aspires to the same power that we ourselves seek. When that power is ours, then you may deal with Simon of Gitta and I with Yosef of Aphairema. Until then, however, you must bend all of your energies toward eliminating the rabbi Yeshua. In fact, should it develop that an appreciable faction in the mob calls for Simon's release on the Passover, I want you to actively work for that release. Hire Syrians and Samaritans to clamor on his behalf; disguise legionaries as Judeans, even, if you have to. Do you understand?"

"By the gods of Tartarus!" Maxentius ground his teeth; his clenched fists trembled at his sides. "I had looked forward to torturing the Samaritan scum for hours—days—"

"Do not harm the man, for we may need him. Later you may do to him as you will, and the same to all others who have offended you. Now I must go. Do not forget to remind Pilatus of all that is required of him. *Vale, Imperator!"*

Maxentius stood proudly erect. "Hail, King of the East!"

Then, as the ancient priest and his black-robed guards departed beyond earshot from the portico, the tribune added under his breath, "Hail, old goat! Don't worry, all who plot against me shall indeed die—including you. I've no doubt you intend my doom when my usefulness is done, even as you intend the doom of old Yosef of Aphairema. Well, you're not the only one who has been studying sorcery lately. . . ."

Motioning to the nearby Cratos, Maxentius left the portico, snapped an order to his men, then led them on toward the old Herodian palace where the prefect Pilatus resided.

Menander, leaning against the rim of the wizard's motionless sky craft, gazed westward in awe across the wide valley of the Jordan. Above the Judean hills, perhaps twenty miles distant, the late afternoon sun was declining. A slight breeze, rustling the sparse grasses of the ridge upon which the craft had settled, brought a cool hint of approaching evening.

"This is as close as I dare approach to Jerusalem without using the screen of invisibility," said Taggart, "and I have too little power left for that. Now, do you remember all that I have told you?"

Menander nodded nervously.

"Good. Don't take the voice-capturing device out of its protective pouch until you are ready to use it; that will minimize the risk of detection. Now, stand exactly in the middle of this craft and keep your arms down at your sides. I'm going to . . . project . . .you up into the Galactic ship, which will immediately project you back down to Earth at a spot familiar to you; this craft remembers its location exactly. Do not move during the process. Tomorrow, after you have accomplished your mission, return to the same spot; the Galactic ship will then project you back to this craft, wherever it may then be. Do you have any questions about this or any of the other things we have discussed?"

Menander drew a deep breath, then stood stiffly in the craft's center with arms held rigidly at his sides. "No, O Wizard. I am ready."

Taggart turned to the panel and tapped a glowing square. Immediately Menander felt a tingling chill, then saw that the world around him seemed to be dissolving, fading, as if viewed through the haze of a sudden snowstorm. . . .

In the next instant the world was solid again—but it was a world far different than anything he had ever seen.

He stood upon a smooth, glowing disc of metal, one of several set into a dark and perfectly level floor. Beyond and above this area of the discs extended vast spaces where gigantic intricacies of metal towered in a dim silvery haze—awesome structures beyond his ability to name or comprehend. Far off among them, upon lofty catwalks and balustrades, he glimpsed vaguely humanoid giants walking slowly and standing motionless—beings that gleamed with the same metallic luster as the intricate planes, angles, balustrades and pillars around them. Colored lights pulsed here and there, and the entire vast and alien space was pervaded with a strange humming, low and even. . . .

Then, again, the cold prickling—the world-dissolving snowstorm—and Menander abruptly found himself standing atop a ridge not unlike the one he had just left. But this time he recognized the spot. It was the very hilltop overlooking the Jericho Road as it rose out of its ravine onto relatively level ground, and not far to the west lay the village of Bethany.

The sun which had been visible from beyond the Jordan was now hidden behind the nearest hills.

"Gods!" muttered Menander shaken. "Surely this is the greatest sorcery of all!"

Menander hurried down the slope and joined a late group of pilgrims, and by dusk he had entered into Bethany.

As he approached the inn of Martha he saw a young man running toward him and recognized the fellow as Parmenion, one of the youngest members of the Thirty.

"Menander! We had almost given you up for lost," said Parmenion as the lad drew close. "We've been watching this inn in shifts since yesterday—" He stopped speaking and peered closely at Menander. "What's wrong? You look like you've seen a demon."

"I have experienced sorceries beyond anything men dream of! But I have not time to talk, Parmenion. Where is Dositheus?"

"He is no longer at this inn, which has been taken over exclusively by the rabbi Yeshua and his followers. Come with me. I will show you to the camp of the Thirty, which is on the road to Anathoth."

As they walked northwestward out of Bethany, Parmenion told Menander all he knew of what had been transpiring during the last two days. Menander was relieved to learn that Lotis and her mistress were with Dositheus at the camp of the Thirty, but expressed concern that Simon was now a prisoner of the Romans.

"We're working on getting him released," said Parmenion. "Most of the Thirty, including Dositheus and Isagoras, were in Jerusalem today, stirring up the crowds on Simon's behalf. It seems that the Romans release one prisoner before the Passover as a concession to the mob, and we have seen to it that Simon's cause has become a popular one."

"Dositheus can do it if anyone can," said Menander hopefully.

At the crossroads they met others of the Thirty returning from Jerusalem in the twilight, and by the time they had reached the camp of the Thirty the round moon was well up in the east. Menander saw Dositheus and Isagoras seated upon rugs in front of the largest tent, together with several other members of the band, and hastened to join them.

"Menander!" exclaimed the old wizard. "Thank the Lord of Gerizim! Where have you been these last two days?"

"To Persepolis, O Mentor, conferring with the great mage Daramos. The wizard Taggart took Ilione and me there in his sky craft."

"Persepolis?" said Parmenion, looking closely into the lad's face. "Menander, are you feeling well?"

"Let him speak," said Dositheus. "Menander, come join us. I sense that we have much to tell one another. Parmenion, tell the women to bring us food. This has been a strenuous day."

Menander settled down cross-legged on a mat and began to tell all that had befallen him, while the members of the Thirty clustered around him, listening incredulously. While he told his tale he noticed that Lotis and her mistress Elissa had joined the group and were also listening in rapt attention, the light of the flickering campfire dim on their beautiful dark-eyed faces. The wives of some of the members served dates and bread to the gathering, but soon most had forgotten about eating as they listened in rapt attention to Menander's fantastic story. Some, watching the lad's face closely, noticed that his dark eyes seemed occasionally to gleam like those of a nocturnal beast as they reflected the firelight.

"So Ilione has remained with Daramos," said Dositheus when the lad had finished his account. "It is well, for she was not happy in this land, and I am glad for her. But—" the wizard leaned forward and looked his apprentice in the eye "—where is Carbo?"

"He . . . he is here with me, O Mentor. Last night, after much thought, I held the raven in my hands for a time, and . . ."

Dositheus nodded gravely. "I see. Carbo is with you indeed. Tell me, lad: have you felt any . . . effects?"

"None, O Mentor. I felt nothing at the time, nor have I felt anything since then, save a bit more hunger than usual. The wizard Taggart, who also carries within him a . . . companion . . . touched my arm, then assured me that Carbo was well and would rapidly grow in size and understanding—and that he would soon communicate with me."

A few of those present drew back from the lad uneasily, but old Dositheus merely sighed and then remarked, "I think I envy you, Menander. For a moment in the synagogue of Chorazin I, too, hosted a companion, and for that moment I seemed to feel a strange new understanding of things."

"I have felt nothing like that, O Mentor. Taggart says that only those *Am-ha-arez* who serve Assatur try to influence the minds of their hosts. Those of the Six Suns have a code of honor which forbids them to do so."

"Well, perhaps I am lucky, then," said Dositheus wistfully. "But now, Menander, I must tell you of all that has transpired here since you left."

When the two had finally finished sharing all their experiences the fire was burning low and the full moon had risen high in the east. Dositheus rose stiffly to his feet and said, "We must all retire now and sleep well, for tomorrow we shall have must to do. It is evident from what Menander has told us that the rabbi Yeshua intends to perform the Rite of Azazel and thereby open the Gate. We must prevent that or all is lost."

"How can you know such things?" demanded Isagoras. "And what is this 'Rite of Azazel'?"

"Mattan's *El-Halal* describes it as a sacrifice of self-immolation through extreme pain, performed to gratify the Outer Ones who feed on the psychic energies generated by suffering. The rabbi Yeshua, as you must surely know by now, is no mere human. Being partially an entity of a far higher order than humankind, he is capable of far greater sufferings than we, and that is why he is deliberately courting his doom. He intends, by offering himself up in sacrifice as the Goat of Azazel, to provide the final burst of psychic power that will open the Gate—and then, *Those of his own kind will come through it to avenge him and establish their rule upon this world."*

Menander nodded nervously. "Taggart has told me as much, O Mentor. But, listen: he has also instructed me how to prevent—"

At that moment a pair of young men came running into the circle of firelight and hurried to Isagoras.

"Master," gasped one of them after he had partially caught his breath, "we have followed . . . the rabbi Yeshua, as . . . we were instructed to do. . . ."

"Yes? Yes? Where is he, then?" demanded Isagoras. "Has he again returned to the inn at Bethany?"

"No," said the other young man. "He and a number of his followers stole forth from the city and have gone to the Garden of Gethsemene. They are gathered there even now, little more than a mile from here."

Menander quickly stepped to the speaker's side. "I know the place. Tell me, man, how many of them are there?"

"Perhaps a dozen, no more than a score. But—?"

Menander whirled and dashed away. As he hurriedly wove his way out of the small group he suddenly found his path barred by a slim, robed figure and brought himself to a halt barely in time to avoid a collision.

"Menander! Where are you going in such a—?"

"Lotis!" He took both her hands in his and gazed earnestly into her dark eyes. "I must go away again for awhile. There is something I must do."

"You have told us so many strange things this night, Menander! I can hardly believe that all this is really happening—that the entire world is in such peril."

"It is, but I may be able to change that. I have a device—a thing the wizard Taggart taught me how to use—"

"Can I help? I'll go with you if you wish."

"No. This task will require stealth, and I'll do it better alone. Please inform Dositheus that I'll be back before dawn. I'll tell you more when I return."

"May the Lord of Gerizim protect you, Menander."

They embraced briefly, and then Lotis watched her new-found friend again hurry off into the night toward unknown dangers. In another moment his white-robed form had vanished away like a ghost among the black, moon-cast shadows.

In little more than half an hour Menander came to the northeast corner of the stone wall surrounding the Garden of Gethsemene. Despite his feeling of urgency he turned aside from the road, hid himself amid the trees and shrubs and rested for several minutes, allowing his breathing and heartbeat to subside to normal. All his senses, he knew, must be calm and alert when he entered the garden, lest he blunder into human watchers.

At length he removed his conspicuous white Levite's robe, then his tunic, folding them carefully and hiding them under a leafy shrub. It would not do to wear flowing garments that might catch on branches or offer purchase to a pursuer's clutch. When he stole toward the road again he was clad only in a loin cloth of plain dark linen, and over one shoulder was looped a thong which crossed his chest and supported a small black pouch at his side. . . .

Suddenly he halted, sensing movement, and hung back amid the shadows of the trees. Someone was passing along the road toward the garden. As the figure drew nearer Menander saw that it was a tall but slightly bent old man wearing a dark cloak and carrying a long staff; his face was hidden by a cowl from which depended a long white beard that gleamed palely in the moonlight. In another minute the figure had passed southward—and then, abruptly turning right, it vanished through a narrow dark archway in the garden's wall.

Menander hesitated. The eastern face of the wall was bathed in moonlight; if he followed the black-cloaked figure through the archway he would be clearly visible to anyone waiting within. Better not to take the risk.

Following the north wall westward, he came soon to a place where a tall tree concealed it in shadow. It was but the work of a few moments to clamber over its mere eight feet of height and let himself down silently within. Here the trees and shrubbery clustered more thickly and he stole forward with extreme caution. He saw no sign of the cloaked figure or anyone else, nor could he hear anyone. Where, he wondered, was the rabbi Yeshua and his followers? Doubtless they would be near the western entrance to the Garden, the one in the wall closest to Jerusalem and overlooking the Kidron Valley. . . .

He came to a narrow path and hurried on a little faster, yet with undiminished caution. At each branching he took the path that bore most toward the southwest, the direction in which he felt the western entrance must lie—though he was far from sure, never having been close to the Garden of Gethsemene on that side. . . .

Abruptly he stopped, listening. Yes, he had *not* been mistaken—he had heard the low mutter of a man's voice not far ahead of him.

"Abba—"

The Aramaic word for "father"! Menander crouched tensely, peered through the stems of the shrubs—and saw, only a few paces ahead of him, a white-robed man kneeling on the ground in a pale patch of moonlight. Instantly Menander realized that he had blundered upon the very one he had come in search of—the rabbi Yeshua bar Yosef himself.

"Father," repeated the trembling voice, "all things have proven to be possible to you."

Menander fumbled at the pouch suspended from his shoulder-thong, wondering at the heavy sorrow, almost an agony, that seemed to radiate from the man's strange, goatish features and vibrate in his voice. That voice, though deep and resonant, was yet too low and distant, and Menander realized that he would have to creep still closer to the man in order to use the device Taggart had given him. . . .

"Take now this cup from me—"

Menander froze in fascination as the kneeling man drew forth from beneath his white robe an object that appeared to be a slender and delicate chalice. As he held it out in the moonlight the vessel seemed to glow softly with its own silvery-golden sheen.

"—O Father, that you may work your will. Ah, if only it could be otherwise!"

Menander's fascination suddenly turned to horror as he saw that the man's face was altering grotesquely, seeming to darken and flow downward. For a few moments it was as if a fluid veil, glistening in the moonlight, had emerged from his brow and cheeks like a sweat of blood. Menander bit his lip to keep from crying out, for he understood what was happening: the strange rabbi was giving up the "companion" which inhabited him!

Now the thing had flowed to the ground, where it lay motionless, one shadow among many, leaving the man's face and white robe as clean as before. In the same moment there was a movement in the shrubbery toward which the rabbi faced—and then Menander again bit his lip as a lean, black-robed form stole silently forth from the shadows. Quickly it stooped and took the gleaming chalice from the hands of the kneeling Yeshua, then turned and vanished silently away among the trees, the black blob-thing following after it like a great rapidly-flowing slug. In a moment they were gone, but not before Menander had glimpsed a flash of moonlight on the long white beard beneath the figure's dark cowl.

For several minutes more the white-robed man remained kneeling, his great dark eyes gazing up toward the moon while the anguish in his features slowly subsided. At length, his face composed and calm, yet still exhibiting a deep sadness, he rose to his feet, turned and walked away at a slow and steady pace, vanishing finally amid the inky shadows of the trees.

Menander, realizing that he had been holding his breath, let it out and inhaled deeply, then rose also. His first impulse urged him to follow the black-robed old man who had come and gone as silently as one of the night's own shadows, for his previous talks with Dositheus made him suspect who that man must be, and also the nature of that eerie luminescent "cup" he had just received into his hands. But, no, he must not deviate from the task with which Taggart and Daramos had entrusted him. There was too much at stake.

Menander turned and stole silently through the trees in the direction the white-robed rabbi had taken, his cautious progress necessarily slow. He had proceeded less than a stone's throw, however, when he began to hear men's voices and slowed his advance even more. Finally, crouching between two bushes, he carefully parted the leaves and peered out. Just ahead, the moonlight limned a small clearing and, beyond it, the garden's western wall in which gaped a large archway. In the clearing stood the rabbi Yeshua and three other men. The latter were rubbing their eyes and weaving awkwardly, as if just awakened from sleep.

"I ask your pardon, O Master," said one of them in a Galilean accent. "Again we have failed you at the watch. This day has been most wearisome and full of turmoil."

"Fret not, Kepha," said the rabbi gently. "It is now the Time, as I foretold. Come, let us be going, for he who was appointed to betray me is even now at hand."

Menander fumbled at his pouch, began to creep closer-but even as he did so he heard the clamor of many voices and the clatter of armor from beyond the garden wall. The sounds rapidly grew louder, and then a great crowd of soldiers began to surge through the archway. Many of them carried swords, staves and torches; most were Roman legionaries, but a few wore the black armor of Temple guardsmen, and Menander noticed with a pang of fear that the eyes of these latter gleamed strangely in the torchlight. At their head walked a lean, gray-robed man with darkly reddish hair whose tangled locks spilled in snaky cascades from beneath a black skullcap; his eyes gleamed with an intensity that seemed a combination of fanaticism and mystical rapture. At his side walked a tall and muscular Roman officer whose handsome face was set in an expression hard and grim.

"Which is the man, Judah Of Kerioth?" snapped the officer.

The lean Judah strode forward, his face taut in a strained grin that seemed to Menander to have something of agony in it, and embraced the rabbi Yeshua, crying out as he did so, "Greeting, O Teacher!" Then, in a low voice that only Menander was close enough to hear, "It is done now, Master, even as you wished."

"Seize that white-robed man!" barked the Roman officer.

The foremost soldiers surged forward. Judah immediately sprang away. But even as the Temple guardsman in the lead made to lay hands on the rabbi the burly Galilean called Kepha drew a short sword from beneath his robe and struck, yelling furiously. Menander heard the dull clang of metal glancing from bone, saw the black-armored guard go reeling back, his right ear dangling from his head by a mere shred of flesh.

"Hold!" shouted the rabbi in a mighty voice, thrusting out his hand as if to stop the charge of soldiers by the force of his will.

All halted in their tracks, startled at that inhumanly vibrant command. Even Kepha and the wounded guardsman stopped and stood motionless, while a number of the legionaries actually drew back a pace. For an instant all stood in frozen silence.

Then Menander barely heard the rabbi Yeshua mutter, "Peace, Kepha. Do not interfere."

And in the next instant Menander saw, to his horror, that the yellow-eyed guard's injured ear was not bleeding—that, in fact, it was slowly drawing back up into its natural position, held there at its cut edges by a glob of substance that was greenish and translucent. . . .

"Seize him, I said!" roared the Roman officer.

Kepha and the other Galileans whirled and dashed away southward among the trees. The soldiers, paying no attention to them, converged on the rabbi, the Romans shouting and cursing, the black-cloaked Temple guards strangely and grimly silent.

"Am I a mere thief that you come to arrest me thus?" boomed Yeshua suddenly in his inhumanly great voice.

Menander heard no more in the uproar, for he now realized that some of the soldiers, rushing to encircle the rabbi, had come dangerously close to his hiding place. As he turned to flee two Romans spied him and shouted an alarm; in another instant he felt himself seized by a third legionary whose approach he had not seen.

"I've got this one, lads! By Bacchus—it's that kid who escaped from us in the ravine!"

Menander twisted suddenly, freeing his left arm from the soldier's right hand, then dipped supplely in a crouch that freed him from his loin cloth which the man gripped tightly. Instantly the youth sprang up and dashed off amid the trees, leaving his only garment behind in the startled legionary's hand.

"Get the slippery brat, Lucius!" yelled the officer. "I want him for questioning!"

Menander doubled to the left, then headed northward as rapidly and silently as he could, ignoring the sting of shrubby twigs against his naked hide, silently thanking his mentor Daramos for his many painstaking lessons in escape-artistry. Before long the sounds of clumsy pursuit faded away, and after a few minutes more the youth had found the north wall and scaled it in the shadows as swiftly as before.

At length, moving cautiously among the sparser shrubbery of this area, he found the spot where he had concealed his clothes. Quickly he donned his dark tunic, then rolled up the white cloak into as small a bundle as possible. He heard no sounds of pursuit.

How fortunate that he didn't grab this thong, Menander thought, fingering the cord that held the dark pouch at his side. It would have ruined everything had he been forced to leave the wizard's device in the grip of the legionary. Nevertheless, Menander realized, he had failed this time. He would have to try again tomorrow. If only he could discover where the rabbi Yeshua was being taken. . . .

He hurried away northward, paralleling the road, but keeping away from it, avoiding patches of moonlight as much as possible. He must get back to camp, consult with Dositheus. . . .

Suddenly Menander froze as he glimpsed a figure moving to the north of him—a lean, tall, slightly stooped figure, robed and cowled, silhouetted briefly and blackly in a patch of moonlight upon the road.

CHAPTER XXIV

Dositheus, dozing upon his blankets just within the open flaps of his tent, woke suddenly at the sound of a soft footfall. Peering out, he saw a figure standing just beyond the fading glow of the campfire—a young man clad in a white robe and dark tunic, his eyes glowing in the light of the flickering flames.

"Menander?" The old man rose and hurried outside, clutching his dark brown robe closely about him. "I've been waiting for you—"

"And so have I, Menander."

The second voice was that of a young woman. Dositheus turned to see her slim, robed form emerge from the shadows and was not surprised when he recognized her.

"Dositheus? Lotis?" said Menander. "I thought all of you would be abed. It is the third watch of the night."

"I'm sure you have news," replied the old Samaritan, throwing a faggot upon the fire, "and I would hear it now. Join us, Lotis."

When the three of them had seated themselves around the rekindled campfire, Menander began to relate all that had happened to him in the Garden of Gethsemene. Lotis, glad that the old wizard had not ordered her away, listened without interruption, noticing uneasily the way Menander's eyes occasionally gleamed in the light of the flickering flames.

When the lad told of again spying the cloaked, white-bearded old man upon the moonlit road, Dositheus nodded knowingly. "That could be none other than the sorcerer Yosef of Aphairema. And the thing he received from the hands of his stepson, the rabbi Yeshua, was without doubt the Chalice of Byakh. You followed him, then, Menander?"

"Yes, O Mentor. He returned to the main road, then followed it in the direction of Bethany. Before he reached the town, however, he turned southward upon the path that leads to the grotto of the tombs."

"Ah. The grotto—yes. . . . Menander, the man is a most astute and practiced wizard. Are you sure he was not aware of you?"

"Yes, sir. I was very careful. The road was lined with the tents of campers for most of the way; one more figure moving among them could hardly have been noticed. And during the last, deserted stretch before we reached the grotto I was careful to practice all the arts of stealth which you and Daramos have taught me."

"Good." Dositheus nodded again. Go on."

"The sorcerer Yosef met a man there among the tombs—his servant and apprentice Zethos, as it turned out. I was able to steal quite close to them among the tombs and listen to much of their conversation."

"And what did they say?"

"You shall hear it for yourself, O Mentor." Menander opened the dark pouch at his side and pulled forth a black, rectangular object about as long and thick as a man's hand. Laying it upon the ground, he then pressed a small stud that projected slightly from one end of its upper surface. "Listen."

Dositheus and Lotis, curious, bent forward slightly. For a moment they heard only a smooth, barely audible hiss from the black object. Then—

". . . after which he passed round to the twelve of them the Chalice of Byakh, that they might all drink therefrom and see foreshadowed the Phantom of Truth. And, now, his purpose being accomplished, he has passed that cup on to me, his earthly father."

Lotis and Dositheus started, glancing about them. The voice, that of an old man, had intoned the words with a proud, almost ritualistic intensity; it had seemed to come from very close by, yet no one was visible in the light of the campfire.

"Who—?"

"Quiet!" Menander urged his old mentor, pointing to the black box. "Listen."

"Has he then no more need of us, O Master?"

This time the voice was that of a young man, and Dositheus felt his spine tingle as he realized that it was issuing from the black box which lay on the ground before them. This was sorcery indeed!

"Not if all goes as he intends, Zethos." It was the old man's voice again. *"Tomorrow they will take him to the mound of Gol-goroth and slay him by means of the Rite of Pain, which the Romans unwittingly inherited from Karakossa by way of Carthage. He shall die in the Agony of Azazel, whereupon Gol-goroth shall come through the Lesser Gate by means of the Ark in the Fane of the Nameless One. Then shall the Greater Gate in turn be opened by Gol-goroth and the Brother, and the Father shall come through it to cleanse this world and make it worthy of him."*

"That will be a great shock to Annas and the tribune Maxentius."

(Brief laughter.)

"But it is all very complicated. What if our plans should go awry?"

"You know well, Zethos. We must then convey the Bride to safety in a far land, that she may bear our Master's seed and pass it on down the generations. Is she now prepared to travel in that eventuality?"

"Aye. But she is no longer in Bethany. Tonight she resides in Jerusalem, in the house wherein our Master this day revealed to his disciples the Phantom of Truth, intending to be near him tomorrow in his hour of doom and triumph. At dawn she will go to pray in the Temple, then go forth to her Lord's sacrifice. Such action is worthy of her great spirit. Come, Zethos—we, too, must leave Bethany and go to Jerusalem this very night, for it may be that I shall have much to do there tomorrow. I must contrive

to purloin the Byakhtril from Annas, for we shall need it to summon the Byakhim to our aid should we fail."

"Yet surely we cannot fail, O Master, after all these many years of preparation."

"I trust not, and before tomorrow's sunset I hope to be upon the Mount of Offense, quaffing the Golden Nectar in order that I may see Selene rise ere the Nameless One and his cosmic legions come surging through the Gate. Still, we must prepare for any contingency. Come, Zethos—we must hurry on to the inn of Martha and rouse our servants."

The black box briefly emitted a sound like the scuffling of sandals on gravel, then fell silent with an abrupt click.

"That was most of the conversation I heard, O Mentor," explained Menander. "Evidently the rabbi Yeshua feasted in Jerusalem last night with some of his followers, then met the sorcerer Yosef in the Garden of Gethsemene in order to pass on the cup—"

"The cup—the Chalice of Byakh!" muttered Dositheus. "The rabbi has performed the Rite of Revelation to his followers—yet I am sure he has not revealed all to them, for they are but a part of his alternative plan should he fail. . . . Gods, Menander!—what sorcery is this of the wizard Taggart which captures men's voices in a box?"

"I don't know, but so far I have failed to use it as he instructed me to. He said that it is imperative that I capture in it the voice of the rabbi Yeshua."

"Very strange. Did he tell you why?"

"No. I am instructed to deliver the black box to him tomorrow, atop the knoll overlooking the Jericho Road east of Bethany. But I cannot, for I have failed. I must go into Jerusalem and try again."

Dositheus scowled silently into the campfire's embers for several minutes, then said, "They will slay him on 'the mound of Gol-goroth'—that would be the knoll of Golgotha, so named because folklore has it that the skull of Adam is buried there. But Mattan writes that it is the site of an ancient shrine to the Old One called Gol-goroth. An apt corruption—for, to the ignorant populace hereabouts, who is more of an 'old one' than Adam?" Dositheus rose stiffly to his feet. "Tomorrow promises to be a full and trying day for all of us. You are weary, Menander, and I will not tire you further with more questions. Go to bed. We will talk more in the morning."

"Thank you, O Mentor. I am weary indeed." Menander rose and, after embracing Lotis, bid them good night and retired into the tent. Lotis, her mind awhirl with the things she had just heard, turned and walked away toward the tent of her mistress—but then suddenly sensed Dositheus following close behind her in the dark.

"Wait, Lotis." His voice was quiet, yet urgent. "I must speak with you."

She turned to face him. Dositheus saw the mute question in her calm dark eyes and realized again how different was this young woman from the frightened, perplexed girl she had been the day he had first met her. And how beautiful she was, how radiant her face under the pale rays of Selene, the Moon-goddess. . . .

O Thou, Desire of Memories, Mistress of Infinity. . . .

"Lotis, I must ask a favor of you."

"You are Menander's mentor and friend, O Dositheus. Ask of me whatever you will."

"The favor I ask may be dangerous for you and your mistress to perform, so think well before you consent. I want the two of you to go into a place which I dare not enter—the eastern court of the Temple of Jerusalem, where the woman Miriam intends to go tomorrow morning. I dare not enter even the Temple's outer precincts now, for there are adept ones who watch for me and would see through any disguise."

"You mean the sorcerer Yosef of Aphairema?"

"Aye, and shrewd old Nicodemus, and probably acolytes of theirs who have now been alerted. Perhaps even the sorcerer Annas has learned by now of my presence in Jerusalem. But you, Lotis, in your garb of a Temple virgin, accompanied by Elissa claiming to be your mother—"

"I see." Lotis' face was grave. "This is indeed a dangerous thing that you ask, for I have heard that all non-Judeans who are caught within the inner Temple precincts are put to death. Yet if it will help you and Menander, I will do it, and I think my mistress will agree also. We have been of little help to you thus far, I'm afraid."

"Think on it carefully," said Dositheus. "At dawn I shall talk with you again, and with your mistress also. Should you decide to do it, I shall put all my arts to your aid, both as to instruction and disguise. For I suspect, Lotis, that you of all people may well be best qualified to resolve the enigma of this mysterious 'Bride' of the rabbi, and to discover her secret knowledge. Good night, now, and sleep well."

So saying, the old mage turned and made his way back to his tent, wondering again at his respect for and confidence in this young woman, Lotis, and in his assumption that she could speak not only for herself but for her mistress as well.

"How many of your avatars there are!" he muttered, glancing up at the round moon once more. "Yet how few of them become aware of their own nature. And how strange that there should now be, in just this time and place, *two* of them, conscious and in the process of meeting one another. O Great Goddess, it is a strange game that you play with yourself and with all the rest of us, and tomorrow we'll learn how the game plays out upon this world!"

Simon of Gitta awoke from a fitful, nightmarish slumber and sat up on the cold flagstones. Footsteps were approaching in the corridor outside. The nearby rattle of chains in the pitch darkness told him that his two fellow prisoners had awakened also.

There was a clattering of bolts and locks, then a glare of torches. Three men entered the prison cell—Roman soldiers clad in oiled leather, bronze and iron. Simon rubbed his eyes, then looked again, saw that one of the three was Maxentius.

"Bracket those torches," ordered the tribute, "then strike off the ankle chains of these prisoners."

The guardsmen obeyed, and as they fell to with hammers and iron chisels Simon's eyes became accustomed to the torchlight. Maxentius was pacing impatiently back and forth across the narrow cell, his face set in an angry scowl.

"It is dawn, then?" asked the man Simon knew as Dysmas. His voice seemed strangely calm.

"It is the hour of your doom." Maxentius turned to one of his soldiers. "Take these two up to the courtyard and prepare them for crucifixion."

"You idol-worshipping swine!" snarled the man Gestas. "Your dark sorceries have defended you from *my* blade, but ten thousand more blades still thirst for your blood. You shall not evade them all!"

Maxentius gestured, and the fist of a guardsman cracked sharply into Gestas' face, sending him sprawling. Maxentius sneered, then gestured impatiently.

"Get the two of them out of here."

"Yet it is a fact that you have practiced black sorceries, Tribune Maxentius," said Dysmas evenly, "and for this your doom now truly impends. I know, for this night I have dreamed a dream."

The guards hung back. Maxentius clenched his fists. Somehow he disliked this prisoner, who stood tall and calm in his chains, even less than the angrily defiant Gestas.

"A—dream?" he repeated in spite of himself.

"Woe to you, despoiler!" intoned Dysmas loudly, his dark eyes suddenly agleam with a mystical intensity. "To you who have slain our nations' fathers, dishonored their women, plundered their homes and sold their children into slavery—to you I say, Woe! For I have seen a vision of doom, and a spectacle of death in a dream. Your scheme of empire crumbles even now, O commander of cohorts, and your intended kingdom is fallen even before it has arisen. You have lusted to rule all men, O exalted Tribune, but even now the demons with whom you have allied yourself are rising to crush you, and soon your human allies shall flee from your side and leave you to face your doom alone. Not by the blades of your raging foes shall that doom come upon you, O prideful Roman, but from out of the black gulfs that lurk beyond the worlds. Aye—hark!" The man's voice rose; his mystical eyes stared intently ahead, as if he gazed through the stone walls at something fearful yet invisible to others. "I hear it coming from the outer blackness, O Maxentius! Your cup of iniquity is full, and even now your doom approaches, striding from out the night to the muffled beats of the drums of Chaos—a doom more terrible than any man has ever known before!"

Maxentius felt a towering rage rise up within him, but with a mighty effort he held back the angry outburst that surged for release.

"Get this lunatic out of here!" he snapped. "To the cross with him and his fellow rebel! Yet leave one torch behind when you go, for I would speak with this Simon alone."

"Sir, are you sure?" said one of the guards, uneasily regarding the tall, well-muscled Samaritan. Even with his hands still manacled in front of him the man appeared capable of being a dangerous foe.

"Do as I say, Marcus. Go. And close the cell door behind you."

When the guards and their prisoners had departed, Maxentius stood and gazed silently, broodingly at Simon, who stood tall before him with dark eyes glaring. Simon, for his part, warily held his hatred in check. His emotions urged him to spring upon his foe, strangle him with the chain of the wrist-manacles, snap his neck . . . yet he instinctively realized that the Roman would not have come here alone without protection, perhaps of a sorcerous kind. And in that moment he noticed the wide belt about Maxentius' waist—the same belt of glowing, blue-woven metal that he had seen worn by Scribonius in the tower of Siloam and, earlier still, by the wizard Taggart.

"You are wise," said the tribune. "You cannot harm me, for I am shielded by sorcery. And should you slip past me, my bodyguard Cratos is on guard just outside this cell. You've met him before."

Simon suppressed his fury. "What do you want then?"

"I have decided to release you, Samaritan. What do you think of that?"

Simon glared at the Roman suspiciously.

Maxentius laughed. "No, it's not a trick. I've decided to have some more fun with you. It would be too easy to just kill you now after all the trouble you've caused, so I'm going to prolong the game a bit. It seems you have become a popular man, 'Son-of-the-Father'—so popular that the mob spent much of yesterday afternoon howling for your release. You know, of course, that it is the custom to turn loose one prisoner at their whim each Passover season, so I'm going to indulge that whim. After all, since I am about to become their supreme ruler I might as well be popular with them. But don't get your hopes up, Samaritan, for I'll soon have you back in this place again, waiting for dawn and the cross. You can never escape that fate, for my power is enormous and soon it shall be absolute."

Simon sensed that the man was lying, but to what extent he did not know. He suddenly stepped forward a pace, hands out—and, as he had feared, encountered the firm, invisible barrier of force.

Maxentius laughed again. "So you see, Samaritan, my magic is great. You cannot harm me, and I can play cat-and-mouse with you as long as I wish. Later this morning, when the mob again demands your release, I shall send a guard to strike off the rest of your chains and free you. The governor Pilatus shall play his part in the little drama, as I have instructed him to do. Enjoy your day of freedom, Simon of Gitta, for it shall be short—as short as the favor of the fickle mob. Soon I shall be emperor over all men, and in that day you and all others who have offended me shall know a dreadful doom."

Simon could not resist saying, "Yet I have just now heard a doom pronounced upon *you.*"

Maxentius paled slightly; his jaw-muscles worked in anger. Then, abruptly, he touched the glowing clasp of his belt. Instantly the dungeon cell was flooded with a glare of white light. Simon gasped and staggered back, raising his arms before his eyes to shield them from the intolerable brilliance that surrounded the tribune's form. There was a faint but shrill humming in his ears.

"Aye, mortal—*cringe!*" thundered the Roman. *"Cringe before your master and your god!"*

Simon sensed the madness in the man's voice. Peering with watering eyes between his fingers, he saw Maxentius standing at the center of that intense radiance, his right hand pointing judgmentally, his armored form gleaming like that of an Olympian deity. Then, to his amazement and terror, Simon saw that the Roman's feet were not touching the floor—that he was standing unsupported at least a foot above it!

"Cringe, mortal, and know that you can never escape your doom!"

Simon crouched back against the wall, shielding his eyes, knowing that he must not provoke the tribune further in his present madness. He thought frantically, *Maxentius has mastered the wizard's sorcerous belt. I must not let him realize how much I know.*

The light faded abruptly. Simon heard receding footsteps, the clatter of an iron latch and the grating of hinges. . . .

Then the cell door clanged shut and he was alone once more, his eyes slowly beginning to readjust to the soothing darkness.

Maxentius, his strange belt once more glowing its usual dim blue in the gloom, hurried up the stone stairways that led from the dungeons of the Antonian fortress, his hulking bodyguard closely following him. In the inner courtyard he paused to bark a few curt orders to the soldiers there, then proceeded up more stone stairways to his chambers, leaving the burly Cratos outside to guard the door.

When he was alone he furiously banged his right fist down upon a tabletop, making decanters and goblets clatter.

"Damn old Annas to Tartarus!" he snarled. "But for him the Samaritan would have been nailed to a cross this very hour. Well, my threat wasn't idle—I'll have him back soon. And when I do, by the gods, Annas will no longer be around to interfere!"

He poured himself a flagon of wine, quaffed it down and poured another, then strode over to a bin full of papyrus scrolls. Selecting one of the bulkiest of these, he sat down at a table and began to unroll it. The scroll was written in Latin of a slightly archaic sort, and Maxentius felt his anger subside as he began to pore over it, for of all the books he had ever plundered from the libraries of his victims this was the one that most fascinated him. It had once belonged to an aged physician of Caesarea who was said to have translated it from the original Persian of Ostanes the Mage, and its perusal had led Maxentius to his interest in sorcery and, eventually, his alliance with Annas.

"Ha! ha! Annas, you old buzzard," chuckled the Roman to himself, "you'd be less cocksure if you knew that I've read *this.*"

For an hour or more he sat quietly, occasionally sipping wine while intently reading the scroll. Once he scowled as an allusion to dark gods made him uneasily recall the curse of the condemned rebel Gestas, but a few minutes later this was forgotten as he discovered a passage he had remembered from earlier readings—a passage he had been seeking:

> . . . for the sorcerer who would gain Assatur's favor, and his demons for servitors that he might rule over men, must sacrifice the living bodies of True Spirits by means of pain and torture and death. And this must be done nigh unto the equinox of springtime, when the sun is at the nadir in the Hyades and the moon aloft in the Scorpion, which constellation was of old called the Great Dragon of Chaos. Furthermore, this must be accomplished in a place which has been hallowed by many centuries of magic and sacrifice to the Old Ones, and of such places there are on Earth but few. Now, these are the rites and invocations. . . .

Maxentius rubbed his eyes, then read the passage again and yet again. Rites and invocations—Annas and Caiaphas had accomplished most of that. They had done little else for the last several weeks, both in the Temple and, at night, upon the knoll called the Mount of Offense just south of Annas' villa on the low ridge beyond the Kidron Valley. That knoll would be the "place . . . hallowed . . . to the Old Ones"—for had not Solomon, and the Jebusites before him, sacrificed to demons there for "many centuries"? And midnight tonight would be the Time, when the full moon would be at the zenith in the constellation of the Great Dragon of Babylon. Yet what of the "True Spirits" to be sacrificed? Annas had said that only a few of humankind were such—humans whose souls contained a larger than usual portion of the spirits of the primal God and Goddess, anciently sundered and trapped in matter—and claimed to be able to recognize them by magical means.

"Elissa!" The name was a vindictive hiss on Maxentius' tongue. "She and her servant-girl, Lotis—aye, and that young blonde who was sent to the tower of Siloam. . . ."

Yes—the old buzzard had mentioned to Scribonius and a few other legionaries that all three were True Spirits. Doubtless he had intended them all to be sacrifices. Yet all three of them had escaped, and now Roman soldiers and Temple guards alike were seeking them, while Annas was no doubt arranging to discover and kidnap alternative victims in case the others were not found.

"O gods, let it be my officers who capture them!" muttered the tribune fervently; then, at a knock on the door, he hastily rolled shut the scroll and yelled, *"Enter!"*

The centurion Marcus came into the chamber, accompanied by a sturdy, stubble-faced man clad in a metal-studded leather tunic and a weapon-harness that held both sword and dagger. There was something cruel and rapacious about the man's narrow and shifty eyes.

"This is Rabdos of Scythopolis," said Marcus, "—the man we hired to stir up the mob in favor of—ah—'Bar-Abbas'. He wants his money."

"My Syrians did a good job of it, most excellent Tribune," growled the man with a lopsided grin. "Governor Pilatus has had me to do work of this sort before, so you might say that I'm an expert. May I hope that the tribune's magnanimity will match my expertise?"

"His men indeed did well enough," said Marcus wryly, "—though some of them got confused and yelled for the release of 'Yeshua bar Abbas'. Many of the rabbi's followers were also shouting in the crowd, you see."

"Our men clubbed many of them down, though," said Rabdos, "so it came out our way alright."

"Pilatus has condemned this Yeshua to the cross, then?" said the tribune.

"Aye."

Maxentius nodded. "Good. Centurion Marcus will see that you are paid, Rabdos. First, though, I want you to do me one last favor—a rather distasteful one with which I'd rather not burden any honest legionary." He took a large key from his belt and handed it to Rabdos. "Go to the dungeons and release one Simon of Gitta from his cell, then take him up to the courtyard and strike off his manacles before the mob. Marcus will show you the way."

When the pair had gone, Maxentius rose and left his chambers. By means of several narrow corridors and stairways he descended to the ground floor of the fortress, avoiding the main courtyard from which he could hear the noise of the moiling mob, and emerged finally into the praetorium, a spacious but gloomy hall lit by only a few torches. The judgment seat at the far end was now empty, but near it stood a score or so of legionaries and, in their midst, a tall, white-robed prisoner bound with cords.

The troops snapped to attention as Maxentius strode toward them down the long hall.

"Centurion Longinus," said the tribune as he drew near the group, "is this prisoner the seditious rabbi I am told we are to scourge and crucify?"

"Aye, Tribune Maxentius." The officer smote his breastplate in salute, then held out a rolled parchment and a small board with writing upon it. "We are also ordered to robe him in kingly scarlet and purple, crown him with a plaited crown of thorns—and affix *this* to his cross."

"Kingly robes? Crown?" Maxentius snatched the parchment, glanced at the inscribed board. The stark black lettering read, in three languages:

KING OF THE JUDEANS

"Who ordered this rigmarole?" snapped the tribune.

"Governor Pilatus himself, sir," said Longinus. "It's all spelled out there in the parchment."

Maxentius scanned it quickly, saw that it was so. He could have bitten his tongue for displaying surprise and ignorance before his troops. No doubt this was another of those damned rituals devised by Annas, whose orders had probably been conveyed to Pilatus through that old extortioner Yosef of Aphairema. Well, best to carry out those orders for now. Annas was, after all, the expert regarding ritual preparations. . . .

"Good." Maxentius rolled up the parchment, thrust it under his belt. "But before we stage this comedy, Longinus, have the prisoner stripped for his scourging."

The legionaries, unbinding their tall charge, roughly whipped the white cloak from his shoulders, then removed his long tunic and his sandals. The man did not resist or protest; his large, sad eyes stared blankly into the far darkness of the hall, as if focused on other and unworldly realms.

When he had been stripped naked save for a tattered yellow rag about his loins, Maxentius barked, "Bind him again." Then, while the soldiers complied, the tribune stepped forward and glared directly into the prisoner's great dark eyes. "So you're the one who would have been the Last King," he growled. "Well, you've failed. Your seditions have caused me a lot of trouble, mad rabbi, but now you're about to become nothing but a scarecrow-king on a cross. As for the true Last King—*you're looking at him!"*

The prisoner slowly inclined his face downward and gazed directly into Maxentius' eyes. Involuntarily the tribune stepped back a pace. He hated having to look *up* when confronting any man; moreover, there was something very disconcerting about the rabbi's mystical dark eyes and slightly sheeplike features. . . .

"Insolent one!" Maxentius roared furiously, smiting the man in the face. "By the gods, I'll scourge you myself—just to see that it's done right!"

"Commander. . . .," said Centurion Longinus uneasily.

Maxentius got a grip on himself. The prisoner had staggered back a pace, but now stood impassive, expressionless; blood—strangely thin, pinkish blood—rilled from his wide, goatish nose and down his chest, staining the yellow cloth about his loins. Maxentius wondered vaguely about that tattered rag, so mean in quality compared to the man's finely spun outer garments. . . .

"Finish stripping him," snapped Maxentius. "Longinus, hand me your scourge."

The centurion nodded, then drew the many-stranded whip from his belt and handed it to his commander. Maxentius hefted it appraisingly, approvingly. One of the soldiers ripped the yellow tatters from the prisoner's loins. . . .

A sudden chorus of gasps and screams burst from all the soldiers. As one man they drew back, leaving the naked man standing alone at their center; a few sword blades rasped from scabbards.

Maxentius gazed in horror, suppressing a sudden urge to retch. Again he found himself regarded by eyes whose gaze he could not bear—eyes set amid monstrous mottlings and writhing, fleshy tubes and feelers. . . .

"Caves of Hades!" screamed a soldier hysterically. *"He's not human!"*

"Shut up!" Maxentius gestured with his whip at the legionary who held the tattered yellow loincloth. "Put that back on him—*now!"*

"Sir—" Longinus' voice trembled slightly "—what does this mean?"

"It means that the world is about to be rid of a most foul demon," snarled Maxentius, fingering the whip's heavy strands and the bits of sharp iron knotted into them, "and I intend to personally make sure that he doesn't last out the day on the cross. Longinus, if this creature is still alive after the ninth hour, I want you personally to dispatch him. He must not live until sundown."

"Of course not, sir, for sundown begins the Passover, and the Judeans would riot again were we to allow executions to take place during their feast. Yet, why hasten—?"

"I have my reasons. Just do as I say."

The centurion nodded, then again smote his breastplate in salute.

Maxentius gripped the scourge and moved toward the prisoner, eyeing him with anger and loathing. So you're Annas' new sacrifice, he thought grimly. *Well, I'll see that you don't live long enough to accomplish what he intends. And yet, by all the gods you will suffer!*

Then, he silently resolved, after this repulsive business was over he would join his troops in a redoubled search for Elissa and her handmaid. He would then have his own True Spirits to sacrifice, and that sacrifice would take place on the right day, in the right location and at the right hour. . . .

CHAPTER XXV

"Bar Abbas!" The crowd thundered its wild acclaim. *"Give to us Bar Abbas!"*

Simon of Gitta blinked in the morning sunlight as he stood before the southern portico of the fortress facing the exultant mob. He was unkempt and dirty, clad only in his torn and dungeon-stained loin cloth—but, thankfully, unchained at last.

"You're a lucky rascal," growled Rabdos with a harsh laugh. "Go to your admirers now and have fun. They seem ready to treat you to all the drinks and whores you'd like."

Simon, without acknowledging the jibe, moved down the steps toward the crowd. He did not trust this Rabdos of Scythopolis, who had a reputation as one of Pilatus' most brutal and unscrupulous agents. Doubtless many of his Syrian agitators were still in the crowd—some, possibly, with murderous instructions from Maxentius.

As he reached the foot of the wide stone stairway he began to see familiar faces in the forefront of the mob and recognized them all as members of the Thirty. Among them were Isagoras, Parmenion—and Dositheus.

"Hurry, Simon," urged the old mage. "We must get you out of here as quickly as possible."

The Thirty—actually only about half that number—surrounded him and began to push their way through the crowd, shouting as they went, "Make way for Bar Abbas!"

"Way for Bar Abbas!" responded the mob. *"Way for the hero, the new Samson, smiter of our Philistine enemies!"*

South of the wide courtyard they passed under the shadow of the long portico bordering the Temple precincts. Here, surrounded by his escort, Simon felt a cloak being thrown over his shoulders, then found himself being hurried through a small gate into the spacious marble-paved Court of the Gentiles. He glimpsed, beyond another long portico, the gleaming white bulk of Yahweh's temple, and for an instant he thought he caught the sound of muffled drums.

"Bar Abbas!" yelled the pursuing crowd. *"Where is Bar Abbas?"*

"Here, good friends!" shouted one of the Thirty—a dark-haired man whom Simon recognized as Yakov, a Judean. The man was wearing only his loin cloth. "I go to the Temple to give sacrifice in gratitude to the Nameless One, who has but now brought me forth from the Valley of the Shadow of Death. Come with me—"

"Quick, Simon," hissed Dositheus, "—down into this cleansing-pool!"

Simon descended the steps into the small stone-rimmed pit, felt the cloak lifted from his shoulders. Just before he ducked beneath the surface of the water he saw, between the shanks of his protectors, the man Yakov lifted up on the shoulders of the crowd and carried off with wild shouts of acclaim.

He held his breath as long as he could, enjoying the cool and cleansing touch of the water. When at last he cautiously rose and stood erect he saw that the courtyard in this area was nearly empty; the crowd was streaming eastward, bearing their hero toward the Portico of Solomon and around the corner to the main gate of the Temple's inner courtyards. Simon sighed with relief, then emerged dripping from the pool. Immediately his companions, crowding close to shield him from sight, removed his loin cloth and toweled him down, then hastily clad him in a clean tunic of dark linen.

"By the gods, I never needed a 'cleansing' more!" said Simon. "I hope Yakov comes to no harm on my account—"

"He'll be shown a royally good time, I suspect," said Isagoras, throwing the cloak over Simon's shoulders once more. "Anyone who tries to harm him now would be torn limb from limb. But come—we can't stay here."

They left the Temple precincts through a western gate and, after winding their way through several narrow streets, entered a small and unpretentious synagogue. The place was deserted, but in a back room a table was plenteously set with food, water and wine. With little ado Simon sat down with the rest of them and fell to gratefully and ravenously; he had been given nothing to eat in the Antonian dungeons.

"I am deeply indebted to you, Dositheus—Isagoras," said Simon between mouthfuls of bread and meat. "I heard that the mob was agitating on my behalf and I suspected that you might be behind it."

"We began the agitation," said Dositheus, "but the crowd took up the cause so readily that I suspect that others were also anxious for your release—not for your sake, but in order to insure the rabbi Yeshua's doom."

Simon took a long swallow of water, then a sip of wine. "That seems to worry you."

"It does, for even as we sit here the rabbi Yeshua is being led away to undergo the Pain of the Goat. And you can guess what that means, Simon. I'm afraid there's to be no rest for you today—nor for any of us. Directly after we finish eating, you must hurry back to Bethany and meet the wizard Taggart atop the knoll at the beginning of the descent of the Jericho Road. Once there, you must stand still with your arms at your side—such were Menander's instructions—"

"What insanity is this?" demanded Simon. "And—where *is* Menander?"

"He has gone on to the Mound of Gol-goroth, to accomplish a task the wizard set him. You must persuade Taggart to come here in person, Simon, for time grows short. Menander will meet us here also when he has accomplished his task."

"At this synagogue? How do you happen to have the use of it, by the way?"

"Rabbi Samezer conducts the ceremonies here each Passover. He has agreed to rejoin the Thirty and aid us for the sake of his son Philip, who has joined the cult of the rabbi Yeshua. Even now Samezer is at the Temple with Elissa and Lotis, hoping to gain more information concerning the Nazarene's monstrous plot—"

"Elissa and Lotis?" Simon glared at his mentor. "They're not Judeans—they could be put to death if discovered! Is this another of your audacious schemes, Dositheus? If you've put Elissa and Lotis in peril . . . Gods! I should wring your silly neck!"

"Peace, Simon. There is no danger, for Samezer is pretending to be Elissa's uncle, and Lotis his daughter, and I have seen to it that they have papers to prove it."

Simon felt a bit easier. His mentor, he knew, was qualified to count forgery among the many arts he had mastered to perfection.

"Now listen carefully, Simon," Dositheus went on, "for much has happened since you were captured, and you must know all. . . ."

Elissa of Sychar gazed about in awe at the great courtyard where square-bearded priests, white-robed Levites and other worshippers came and went, many of them bringing animals or birds to sacrifice. Even here, she noticed, men seemed to predominate in the traffic and transactions; the place was called the Women's Court only because women were not allowed beyond it into the holier westward court surrounding the altar of sacrifice and the Temple itself, and even within it they were confined to a raised, single-colonnaded gallery, which surrounded the area on three sides.

She felt less uneasy now about the risk they were taking than when they had first entered the Temple precincts. For one thing, no Roman soldiers were allowed into this area; for another, when old Samezer had paid all their offerings into the Temple, he had declared to the officiating scribe that the two women were his niece and great-niece, and no one had questioned it. Moreover, a loud and large crowd had just surged into the courtyard through its eastern gate—a crowd acclaiming one "Bar Abbas"—which would make it hard for the Temple guardsmen to take note of individuals.

Lotis, Elissa noted, seemed quite unworried. How the girl had changed in the last few days! Elissa was still a bit puzzled by the request Dositheus had made of both of them this morning, but Lotis had seemed to understand it immediately and intuitively. It was enough for Elissa that she could be of help to Simon and Menander, but she wished that she could make more sense out of the web of menace and dark magic in which her life had become entangled.

"The Temple virgins are instructed in *that* area," said Samezer, pointing toward the northwestern corner of the great court. "Follow me—and stay close to me, both of you. I will do the talking."

They ascended the few steps to the northern gallery and proceeded westward in the shadows of the colonnade. Presently they reached an area fenced off by a line of high folding screens, in a gap of which stood a woman whom Elissa recognized as the innkeeper Martha.

"What do you want here, false rabbi?" Martha demanded. "You will not find your son Philip among us, for he had fled with all the rest of the cowardly men who professed to be our Master's loyal followers. Only we women have remained truly loyal to him in this dreadful hour."

"I am sorry, Martha. I know that your Master was arrested only last night—"

"They will slay him!" wailed the woman. "I warned him, but he would not listen. It was as if he deliberately sought his doom. Oh, why are men so foolish! And why are we women so loyal to those we love whether or not they deserve it!" She shook her head angrily, wiped away a tear, then glared with sudden suspicion at Elissa and Lotis. "Who are these? Were they not among those who slept in my stables—?"

"My niece Elizabeth has come down from Galilee to dedicate her daughter Lotis to the service of the Temple," said Samezer smoothly. "They wish to gain instruction from the renowned and learned Lady Miriam."

Martha glanced at Lotis' garments. "They may enter," she said grudgingly, "but not you. Men are not allowed."

Samezer peered past her through the gap in the screens. "But do I not see a priest within? Ah, yes, I do. And if I can still trust my aging eyes it is none other that old Yosef of Aphairema."

"Yosef is initiated in . . . in certain mysteries."

"I see." Samezer smiled gently. "You mean in the mysteries of the Great Goddess."

"Shut up!" snapped Martha, glancing about nervously; then, seeing that no one was within close earshot, "You must go now."

"No, I am qualified to enter." Samezer made a swift, intricate gesture with his left hand. "Let me pass."

Martha bit her lip, scowling in consternation. "Wait here," she said, then hastened away behind the screens. In a moment she returned with the ancient white-haired priest at her side.

"Greeting and peace, Samezer," said old Yosef, "and welcome to our conclave. Martha tells me that you have given the Sign."

"Greeting and peace, Yosef." Samezer repeated the gesture. "We who serve Yhtill have always known her mysteries. By what name do *you* serve Her?"

"We call her Asherah, for under that name She was anciently worshipped in this very place. But does the name matter? Enter, my brother."

Martha stood sullenly aside as Samezer, followed by Elissa and Lotis, entered the screened place. It was wide and well shaded, partly open on the colonnaded side where several matrons stood guarding each point of access. Perhaps two dozen Temple virgins sat, on rugs that had been thrown down on the flagstones, facing the massive stone wall that separated the Women's Court from the Temple area.

"You are more hospitable to me today, Yosef, than were your son's disciples at the inn last night."

"My apologies, Samezer. The Anointing of the King could not be interrupted—as you, an initiate into the ancient Karakossan lore, will well appreciate. But now the Time is accomplished, and we need be at odds no more. As for your son, Philip, fear not, for he is safe—as safe as anyone can now be."

Samezer's brow furrowed as with sudden worry. "Then it is indeed the Time?"

Yosef bowed slightly in acknowledgment. "Soon the world shall know peace."

Elissa, listening to this interchange, felt a strange chill. She forgot herself so far as to say, "Do you know, O Priest, that Annas and the tribune Maxentius plot to rule the world between them and are employing dark magic toward that end?"

Samezer motioned to her to be silent, but Yosef said, "No, let her speak." The old priest bowed toward her, then to Lotis. "Annas and Maxentius are fools who are soon destined to become wise. They do not matter. But you, My Lady—ah, you are a person of high importance indeed! As soon as I beheld you and your . . . daughter . . . I sensed that I was again in the incarnated presence of Her Who Is Above All. There is a fate in this. Fortunate am I among men to have met you on this day!"

Elissa, shocked and confused that a Judean priest would show her and her handmaid such deference, was even more surprised to hear Lotis say, "You know, then, venerable sir, the mystery of how the One became Two, and how the Two now seek forever to find one another?"

The ancient priest nodded gravely. "I see that you, My Lady, are an Awakened One, even as is my ward the Lady Miriam."

"I have come to hear her, Venerable One," said Lotis.

"And so you shall, this very moment. Look—she is here."

Elissa looked toward the west end of the hall, saw that the beautiful black-haired young woman was standing there in front of the massive stone wall, not far from the columns, facing the group of Temple virgins and their matrons. Next to her, in a low chair, sat the old albino woman looking weak and frail, but with a faint smile on her lips and a distant look in her pale eyes.

"Rise, O acolytes of Asherah," said the young woman Miriam, raising her arms aloft, "and sing with me Her praises."

The Temple virgins all stood up and, after a moment of silence, began to chant in unison, led by the woman who stood before them:

"I, wise Asherah, came from the High Domain
And, like a mist, I covered all the world.
Once in the High Pleroma I abode,
My throne upon the pillars of the clouds.
Alone I spanned the vastness of the sky
And walked within the dark and deep Abyss.
Mine were the ocean waves, mine all the lands,
And every tribe and nation knew my sway."

Elissa shuddered, realizing that she was hearing blasphemies that, under Judean law, could bring down death by stoning upon everyone present. Then she heard Samezer, as if echoing her own fears, whispering to old Yosef, "Praise the Goddess! Yet, is this safe?—here in the Nameless One's very Temple precincts!"

"Fear not, brother," Yosef whispered back. "Last night all these virgins and their matrons partook in this very place of the Living Water, and therefore beheld the Phantom of Truth. Young Miriam herself administered to them the holy rite, and they have one and all pledged to her their loyalty and secrecy."

"Praise be!" muttered Samezer. "For who can more fittingly be worshipped here than Asherah, who was anciently revered in this very Temple as the Consort of the Nameless One?"

The young singers had paused, and now Miriam took up the chant alone, her voice clear and musical as ringing crystal:

"Then the Great Lord to me his message gave,
Bade me descend to Earth and spread my tent.
'Pitch your pavilion now in Jacob's Land,'
He said, 'and find your favored place in Israel.'
Before the dawn of worlds He visioned Me,
And I shall bide throughout eternity."

Elissa suddenly realized that the chant was a slightly distorted form of Yeshua ben Sirach's paean to Sophia, Goddess of Wisdom. This Miriam had great audacity, surely, to recite such a thing in the very Temple of the male and jealous Nameless God of the Judeans! She felt a sudden resentment toward the beautiful chanteuse, then realized why: Samezer and Dositheus obviously revered, even idolized her, and the latter had indicated to Elissa that Simon did also. Aye, *idolized* literally—for they seemed to regard the woman as a symbol, even a very incarnation, of some ancient Goddess! Moreover, Elissa's own handmaid Lotis, strangely mature and contemplative of late, seemed overly curious about the woman—and now, Elissa realized for the first time, there was a strong resemblance between Lotis and this strange prophetess Miriam. . . .

Prophetess? Like her namesake Miriam, the sister of Moses, who of old had gloated in song over the drowning of the Egyptian armies . . .?

Elissa must have voiced at least a part of her thought aloud, for she suddenly heard old Yosef whisper to her, "Aye. Prophetess and Goddess. For She comes and goes as She will, from this world to that, testing each to see whether it suits Her fancy. The Father and his compassionate Son know far more than humankind, but She knows more than all—as you will someday realize also, woman of Sychar, when you awaken fully."

Elissa was startled to realized that old Yosef knew her identity; yet, strangely, she felt no fear. She even liked the sound of what he had said—partially. But before she could think on it further she again heard the virgins chanting in unison with their instructress the Lady Miriam:

> "To whom has wise Asherah been revealed,
> And who has known Her deep and occult ways?
> Even the Nameless One who made the worlds
> Made them for Her own pleasure, that She might
> Inhabit them, and meet Him there in love."

"This is a strange paraphrase and rearrangement of Ben Sirach," whispered Elissa to the old priest, for whom she now felt a strange affinity, even a familiarity.

"Sirach is the paraphraser and rearranger. Miriam sings the original ancient chant, which the Judean priests later distorted in their vain attempt to dishonor the Goddess and suppress Her worship."

"But how does she dare to sing it here?"

"She dares nothing," said Yosef. "She lives and judges; it is Her Lord, the One who is above even the gods, who dares all. He creates worlds for Her pleasure, and it is Her judgment that determines His creation's failure or success."

The chant had ended. The woman Miriam, Elissa now saw, was standing fully within a broad beam of sunlight that streamed between two columns. She resembled Lotis even more in that light—resembled her not merely in the delicacy of facial features and the silky blackness of hair, but in poise and expression and bearing, unconsciously noble, regal, queenly.

Lotis, for her part all unaware of this, had advanced slowly forward through the group of virgins, fascinated, and now stood out in the forefront of them, confronting the Lady Miriam with wide-eyed awe. Nor was her awe totally for an admired *other*, for she now strongly felt an affinity toward one she sensed as being basically like herself.

"My Lady. . . . .," she ventured a bit hesitantly.

The level gray-green yes gazed into the dark, questioning ones—sunlit sapphires mirrored in dark pools. Then the woman smiled slightly, one corner of her mouth dimpling the merest bit—a smile of kindly amusement touched with wonder. . . .

"I seem to know you as my own self, young woman. Surely, despite the garment you wear, you must be the servant of the woman who stands yonder—the woman to whom at Sychar my Lord offered the Living Water. But I sense that *you*, at least, require no such draught of illumination. Was it while you slept at Martha's inn that you were awakened? I had a dream there on a certain night."

Lotis forgot the presence of the virgins and their matrons who were all listening in puzzlement, forgot the Temple and its crowds, forgot even the peril she and her mistress risked by being here. It was suddenly as if she and the woman Miriam stood along in the midst of that beam of sunlight, somehow above and beyond all worlds, twin bright presences upon an illuminated floor of Olympian flagstones, surrounded by the infinite glooms of uncreated Mysteries. . . .

"Lady of Light," said Lotis, her voice trembling slightly, "is it true that this world is now in danger of being plunged into darkness?"

"Has it not always been so endangered?" said Miriam. "Aye, and has not that danger given this world its highest zest? Can we love the imperishable?"

"I do indeed love one, and I would not that he should perish!"

"You love the One, as do I. He, like ourselves, has lived and perished in countless forms. Yet never do we lose one another."

"And, yet, I want him in just this form! O Lady of Wisdom, he and I have met so recently. Must I lose this greatest of all treasures even in the moment that it is found?"

The woman sighed, and Lotis seemed to see in her eyes an infinite sadness, a cosmic tragedy even. "They take my Lord away to crucify him even now, and I would that it could be otherwise, for he is the kindest and gentlest of all men who have ever been, and the bravest as well. Yet it is of his own will, and therefore how can I but approve it? He has dared all, and I must hope for his success, even though it means his doom in just *this* form. And having said that, there is yet a part of me that hopes for his failure, that I may continue to know and love him in just *this* form. Is this weakness?"

Lotis saw tears in the woman's eyes, tears that mirrored her own sadness and anxiety. The woman had asked the very question that Lotis herself had wanted to ask.

"How can you bear it?" the girl cried. "Should I lose Menander now, I know that I must perish also!"

"And so you shall—with him. And if that should come to pass, then shall we and all others perish also, and find one another anew in worlds yet to come."

"If?" Lotis grasped at the word desperately. "Then it is not certain—?"

"Nothing is certain, as you well know. My old mentor Yosef knows much, and my Lord much more, yet even they do not intuit the full wisdom of the Goddess—namely, the insight that ultimately all things must perish, and yet nothing perishes ultimately."

"Then you, too, have hope that—?"

"How can I hope for my Lord's failure? How can I not hope that this world will be set free from fear and pain, and from the even worse sufferings that will surely come to pass upon it should it endure?" Her eyes grew suddenly hard, her voice vibrant with a regal, even Olympian contempt. "This Roman empire—this entire human race, even—has become too petty, too little in its heroisms, and consequently too vast in its sufferings. Humankind is on a great downslide, and only its destruction can save it. No longer does it amuse me, and I would see it swept away that the stage of the world might be made free for new and better actors. For the Goddess can admire even tragedy, but for the sufferings of countless hopeless human insects She can feel only contempt! And yet—" again the woman's voice softened, her eyes grew sad "—yet, somehow, I *do* hope that the destruction may not come, for I love my Lord in just *this* form. Aye, and in addition I bear his seed, which I yearn to pass on down the generations. . . .

Lotis buried her face in her hands to hide her tears. She had found no answer, only a mirror of her own soul. And yet that had turned out to be the answer to the only question that mattered.

Elissa, meanwhile, too far from Lotis and Miriam to hear what was transpiring between them, asked old Yosef, "How, then, O venerable one, did you guess my identity?"

"I am gifted and trained to descry True Spirits," said the priest, "and, moreover, the Master had described both you and Lotis to me. He was much disappointed that you did not receive from him the Living Water which he offered, for he recognized in you and your handmaid veritable Sisters of his own Bride. Yet destiny works strangely, for lo!—you are here even now in this fateful hour."

"Living Water?" said Elissa musingly. "Yes, he did offer it to me. But what is it?"

"The Golden Nectar of the Primal Gods." The ancient sage drew from beneath his robes a slim, golden-gleaming and long-stemmed chalice, smooth and undecorated, which seemed to gleam softly with an illumination of its own. "Last night I received this cup from the hands of my son, together with his inner companion, his healing spirit; both were brought to Earth many centuries ago from the far Pleiades. This cup is the source of all the Living Water on this world, and one sip from it gives visions of worlds and Beings greater than any known to mankind. Here—I am honored to give to you of the Nectar in my Master's name." Yosef drew forth a small vial of clear crystal and unstoppered it, then pressed the stem of the chalice near its base. The chalice made a sound—a brief, delicate hum or chime—and then Yosef tilted it and poured a few drops of amber liquid from its lip into the tiny vial.

"That's . . . the Living Water?" said Elissa incredulously.

"Aye." Old Yosef again hid the goblet beneath his robes, then stoppered the crystal vial and handed it to Elissa. "Drink this and you shall see the Phantom of Truth, even as did the Master's disciples and the Temple virgins last evening. Then shall you know the will of the God and Goddess, and why the fate of the Last King must be one of suffering and horror and death. But after you drink it, gaze not into the cloudy depths of Demhe as the Gate is opened, or your soul may be drawn therein to perish amid ultimate horrors."

Elissa, wondering now if this strange old man might be insane, took the vial from him and marveled at the scintillating pure gleam of the amber liquid within it, yet resolved with an inward shudder never to taste it. "I thank you, Yosef of Aphairema," she said, putting the thing away within a pocket of her gown. "Perhaps later—"

"Aye, not now in this sad hour. Drink it tonight when the moon rises and before the Gate opens. For the moon is Her symbol and its rays will enhance the Nectar's effect."

Elissa turned uneasily, then to her surprise saw Lotis and the woman Miriam locked in what seemed an embrace of mutual consolation. The sight touched her strangely. A moment later the pair separated, looked in Elissa's direction, and then, hand in hand, moved across the flagstones toward her while the virgins and matrons parted to let them pass.

As they approached, Elissa became aware of an increased tumult outside the virgins' quadrangle, realized that a large portion of the crowd which had come to sacrifice were now surging away through the eastern gate of the Women's Court. Many of them were crying out, *"Bar Abbas! Bar Abbas!"*

"The 'Son of the Father' indeed!" muttered Yosef disdainfully when the tumult had died down. "They acclaim one of their seditious heroes of the moment, no doubt. Yet their words ring more truly than they know, for this is the day of the 'Son of the Father' indeed."

"We must leave now, good Yosef," said the dark-haired Miriam as she and Lotis drew near, "for it is almost the Time."

As she spoke Elissa became aware of a sound she had not been able to hear over the earlier tumult of the crowd—a deep, slow, rhythmic booming like that of a muffled drum. It puzzled her, for she could not recall having heard of such a thing as being part of the Judean Passover rites. Yet it seemed to be coming from the direction of the Temple. . . .

She sensed a slight dimming of the daylight, as if a cloud had passed in front of the sun; yet glancing skyward above the portico-columns, she saw no clouds, only the blue sky—a sky that seemed more deeply blue than normal, and a sun that seemed a shade too pale.

"It is the Time indeed," said old Yosef. "Martha—go call our litter-bearers. Miriam, fetch your mother and her servants and meet us at the middle gate in the north wall of this court."

As the old sage moved away after Martha, Lotis turned to Miriam and said, "My Lady, I will follow after you also."

They embraced again, wordlessly, and then Miriam hurried away as if reluctant or unable to speak more.

"Do you think that's wise, Lotis?" asked Elissa when the woman and the albino matron in her charge had left the quadrangle. She felt an irritation that the girl's loyalties had seemingly shifted so suddenly from her to this strange woman Miriam.

"Not wise at all," said Samezer decisively. "They are going to the place of execution, I am sure, and there will be a large and sordid crowd there. Besides, we must return to the synagogue and report what we have learned to Dositheus."

"Both of you go there, then. Perhaps I may learn more from the Lady Miriam. Besides, Menander will be there."

"Lotis, what's gotten into you?" said Elissa. "You can't help any of them, and you'd just subject yourself to a morbid spectacle. No, you can't go. As your mistress I forbid it!"

The sound of muffled drums issued more loudly from the direction of the Temple, and the sky seemed to darken a bit more.

"It has begun already," muttered Samezer. "Come, no more talk. We must report to Dositheus immediately."

At his urging they hastened out of the screened quadrangle and toward the westernmost gate of the court's north wall. Here the crowd had thinned out almost entirely. As they entered the gateway they could see down into the wide Court of Gentiles, where they glimpsed the palanquins of old Yosef and the two women moving westward through the crowd—

"Wait!" Samezer's voice was suddenly urgent as he laid a hand on Elissa's shoulder. "Don't go out there, either of you!"

In the same instant Elissa saw with a shock the reason for the little rabbi's warning, and laid a restraining hand on Lotis' arm. At the foot of the steps leading down from the wide portico beyond the gateway stood a line of Roman legionaries. They were paying little attention to the crowd in the Court of Gentiles, but were carefully watching the gates that led to the Women's Court. Then—

"Lord of Gerizim!" gasped Elissa. "There's Maxentius among them. Someone must have seen us enter—"

"Back!" Samezer muttered, pushing them away from the wide gateway. "The Romans are forbidden to enter these sacred precincts. Go—mingle with the crowd wherever it is thickest, just in case they send in Temple Guards to find you. None of them knows me—I shall slip out one of the southern gates, then inform Dositheus with all speed. Perhaps the Thirty can create another diversion. Don't leave this court, either of you!"

Then he hurried off into the crowd as Elissa and Lotis stared after him in dismay, realizing that they were trapped in this place. The drums from the Temple boomed deeper, louder, and the sky continued to darken. . . .

CHAPTER XXVI

Simon had to fight the press of the crowd streaming into Jerusalem, but once through the eastern gate he found the going easier. Even so, he had to leave the pilgrim-choked roads and avoid the clogged bridge over the river. He waded the Kidron just north of where the noisome Temple drains, dark with the blood of innumerable sacrifices, emptied into it, then set out at an energy-conserving jog across country, angling up the gentle slope of the Mount of Olives. It was good to be running free in the daylight after his cramped confinement in Antonia's dungeons.

And yet, he now noticed, that daylight seemed to be dimming very slightly. . . .

Suddenly he heard, from the south, the distant screams of many voices—muted wails of terror, shrill prayers and curses. Pausing, he looked southward and saw a large band of pilgrims surging from their encampments on the valley's eastern slope, pressing across the brook toward the walls of Jerusalem and the ruins of the Tower of Siloam. They seemed frantic to get into the city. Then glancing up above these refugees toward the ridgetop, Simon suddenly beheld a strange sight—a flattened band of vegetation extending diagonally up from the south toward the ridge-hump known as the Mount of Offense. Even as he watched, the flattening extended itself a bit farther up, as if a gigantic invisible slug were oozing its way up the slope from the Valley of Hinnom. . . .

Then, faintly, he heard a deep, rhythmic sound upon the air, like the beating of a distant muffled drum or the pulsing of a giant heart. And, yet—the light of day was indeed definitely dimming!

"Gods!" Simon resumed his running, this time at an increased pace, suddenly fearful of his own thoughts. Evidently the thing that had destroyed the Siloam Tower was again abroad, and this time by day. . . .

It was no longer day, however, when at length he approached the village of Bethany on the other side of the ridge. The sky, though still cloudless, had darkened first to a deep twilight blue, then to a dusky purple. Now it was nearly black, and yet the afternoon sun still shone it—a disc of deep and smoky red, fainter than the full moon at midnight. From the town and the campsites along the distant road to the north Simon could hear multitudes wailing in fear.

He paused again, this time to rest, and realized that the pounding he heard was not his own heart, but that same eerie boom as of a distant drum, louder than before. Gazing to the southwest, he found that he could just see the hump of the Mount of Offense silhouetted blackly against the last faint band of daylight. The deep drumming boomed on. It seemed to be coming from that hump, though Simon could see nothing atop it. The sky-blackness seemed to center over it, expanding outward as a hazy disc of darkness toward all the horizons. Soon it would obscure all the sky. . . .

"AZAG-THOTH!"

The distant crowds screamed and Simon froze in terror. The mighty reverberation that had rolled from the Mount of Offense was no natural thunder. It had been a *spoken word.*

"TASHMAD . . . TARTZAH . . . HALEL-EL. . . ."

More of those terrible words, thundering upon the air. Something—some Thing, monstrous and invisible—was uttering a cadenced *chant* atop the Mount of Offense!

Simon turned and ran toward the village as swiftly as the increasing darkness would allow, while behind him he continued to hear that thunderous Voice chanting on, slowly and ponderously, as if pronouncing a sentence of doom upon the world.

Nicodemus, leaving the torchlit Hall of Gazzith, shuddered as he gazed up into the unnaturally black sky. The sun seemed like a moon of blood, shedding scarcely any light. Next to it, uncannily, shone a cluster of stars—the dim "V" of the Hyades—while other stars were also faintly visible here and there against the inky vault of heaven.

"Lord of Zion!" gasped the young man at Nicodemus' side. "It is happening, even as my master Yosef said it would. Look—there are Castor and Pollux gleaming, and northward the Goat-star over the Temple, and the stars of Orion high in the south. What man ever before saw *those* stars at this time of years!"

"True, Zethos. But hurry, now, for we must join your master at the Mound of Gol-goroth. Call Parakleitos to us."

Zethos uttered a low, trilling whistle and a moment later a large white pigeon flew down from the shadows of the columned porch and fluttered to rest upon his right shoulder. Again Nicodemus shuddered slightly at the way the bird's eyes gleamed in the torchlight.

They hurried across the wide Court of Gentiles and made their way southward along the western colonnade of the Temple precincts. Here, too, torches had been lit upon many of the pillars, but the place was still dim and also strangely deserted; the few people they met hurried by them wordlessly save for muttered prayers, their faces white with terror. Behind them, from the direction of the Temple, came a rhythmic, muffled booming as if a giant drum were being sounded.

As Nicodemus and Zethos passed from the colonnade through the southwestern gate and descended the steps toward the great bridge spanning the Tyropean Valley, they found that the city appeared to be even more deserted than the Temple precincts. Evidently, during the hour in which the unnatural night had descended upon the land, the Jerusalemites had fled in terror to their homes and the pilgrims to their campsites. Several torches gleamed along the coping stones of the bridge, and a few others amid the distant streets and palace-grounds beyond, while a few red fires glowed up from the deep narrow valley below, but nowhere was a human figure to be seen.

"El Shaddai!" muttered Nicodemus. "To think that but an hour ago this place was filled with noisy throngs—"

"Sir—look!" Zethos interrupted suddenly. "Someone comes!"

The white dove cooed nervously. Nicodemus stopped and peered ahead. A man was running toward them across the wide Tyropean bridge, dark cloak streaming out behind him. In the silence his footfalls rang out sharply upon the stones. Then, as he drew nearer, the old priest recognized him and cried out, "Well met, Judah of Kerioth! Where are you going?"

The man stopped just abreast of a flaming torch and stared at the pair of them, breathing hard, too winded for the moment to answer. His teeth were bared in a white grimace and his dark eyes glittered with a wild, even fanatic excitement.

"Zethos and I are on our way to the Mount of Gol-goroth," Nicodemus continued, "to join Yosef of Aphairema and the Lady Miriam—aye, and to witness with them our Master's doom and triumph. Will you not come with us?"

"No, for I go to witness the final confounding of our Master's enemies." Judah glanced toward the looming wall beyond which lay the Temple courts and porticos. "Are they there, in the Hall of Gazzith?"

"They are," said Zethos. "We have just come from there. My master Yosef bade Nicodemus and me to remain there and keep watch on our enemies until the Time. An hour ago, as soon as the sky began to darken, Annas sent out a frantic command for the Sanhedrin to reconvene. Only a dozen or so have managed to come, however." The young apprentice chuckled. "No doubt the rest are cowering in their mansions or blundering about in the darkness of the streets!"

"Ha! ha!" Judah's laugh was shrill, exultant. "This morning they gathered to condemn our gentle and selfless Master to torture and death—*that* meeting was in darkness, too. They cringe in fear because they sense the Gate beginning to open *many hours before they expected it to!* Alas, that I had to play the traitor for them! But now, in this hour just before they and all other earthly beings find eternal peace, I mean to fling their accursed silver back in their faces and proclaim to them that their own vile actions have earned them naught but black doom!"

"Is that wise?" said Nicodemus. "Annas and some others there are possessed by Am-ha-arez, and Izhar is accompanied by his terrible black-cowled familiar. They will be furious if you tell them of your treachery."

Judah shrieked with wild mirth. "What does their fury matter now?" Then, the mirth suddenly gone from his eyes, though not the madness, "Listen, Nicodemus: Is not the Brother even now going up to the High Place from the Pit of Hinnom? Aye, he is, and soon his words shall open the great Gate of Fire and Terror. The drums of Chaos are sounding even now—do you not hear them? Hark—"

At that moment, uncannily, the air vibrated as if to a giant voice, thunderous yet muted with distance, *"AZAG-THOTH . . . KU-TULUGH . . . NA-YARLOG. . . ."*

"Ha! ha! Ha!" shrieked Judah insanely. *"Said I not so?"* Then, dashing away eastward up the steps and through the high archway, he vanished quickly among the black shadows of the Temple's columned porticos, howling, *"Annas—I bring you back your silver!"*

"Come, sir." Zethos pulled at the sleeve of Nicodemus' robe. "We'd better not stay here."

They hurried across the long bridge as swiftly as the old priest's faltering stride would permit, hearing as they went the distant cadenced booms as of monstrous drums accompanied by thunderous chanting. To Zethos, slowing his pace to match that of his companion, the transit seemed interminable. Nicodemus, for his part, refused to halt even after he began to wheeze and gasp with weariness. The darkness behind them, though relatively quiet now that Judah had gone, yet seemed replete with menace; the bridge, well over three hundred feet long and faintly illumined by torchlight, seemed too exposed to watching eyes.

Eyes—like those dim red fires far below in the inky Tyropean Valley, Jerusalem's most vile slum. . . .

"Judah was right," gasped Nicodemus suddenly. "Let us rest, Zethos—for why should we fear doom *now?"*

Zethos knew the answer instantly: *Some dooms are worse than others.* Aloud he said, "Don't worry, sir, we're almost across. When we get to the other side, we'll take a torch and go on to—"

Suddenly, from amid the black colonnades far behind them, they heard a wild scream, shrill and prolonged. Nicodemus felt a pang of terror. Without glancing back, the pair of them quickened their pace. The white pigeon spread its wings and, launching itself from Zethos' shoulder, flew on ahead.

In a few more seconds they had gained the far end of the bridge.

"Here, sir—into the shadow of the abutment. Get down and lie low. Don't move."

Nicodemus did not question the apprentice's order. No sooner had he settled himself in the black shadows than he again heard the wild scream of terror, closer this time. Then he saw the form of Judah of Kerioth emerge beneath the archway from the colonnades and come dashing out upon the wide bridge into the dim torchlight.

"Keep down!" whispered Zethos, quite unnecessarily. The white pigeon, now squatting on the ground beside him, cooed softly, nervously. . . .

As the man Judah raced toward them, cloak streaming out behind and sandals slapping frantically on the stone flags, Nicodemus saw another shape dart out of the dark archway in pursuit—a shape black, squat and cowled. It made no sound as it came on, undulating strangely beneath its cloak as it ran, closing the gap between itself and its quarry with unnatural swiftness. Then, less than a hundred feet from where the terrified pair lay hidden, it leaped forward upon its prey, laying hold of the man with twin squidlike tentacles—ropy arms that glistened blackly in the torchlight while extending unnaturally far forward from the sleeves of the thing's robe.

Nicodemus cringed inwardly at the sound of Judah's mad shriek. It was as if the inmost part of the man's soul were being twisted out of him. For a moment Judah struggled insanely; then one of the glistening black tentacles looped about his neck and squeezed tight, contracting like a coiled snake. Abruptly the scream stopped. For a few moments more the man continued to struggle, his eyes bulging in pain and horror—and the Nicodemus heard a distinct *crack* in the silence. Judah's head lolled acutely to one side, puffed tongue protruding from gaping and swollen lips, eyes popping from their sockets.

In the next instant the dark being lifted him high in both tentacles, held him aloft for a moment, then hurled his body over the stone coping of the bridge.

Nicodemus shut his eyes and trembled in the dark. He heard the faint, turgid thud of the body striking the ground nearly two hundred feet below. Then there was silence, save for the eerie, distant drumbeats. . . .

After many long moments Nicodemus, daring to open his eyes once more, perceived that the wide expanse of the bridge was again deserted. Fearfully he glanced over at his companion and saw that the young man had risen to a tense crouch, the white pigeon against perched upon his shoulder.

"The thing has gone back into the Temple precincts," whispered Zethos. "Come, sire, I'll help you up. We must leave this place."

"Aye." Nicodemus took the man's hand and stood up, trembling. "We must hurry on. El Shaddai, what horrors this earth has known! And praise be to the Nameless One, who shall soon bring all such horrors to an end!"

Zethos nodded vigorously, then snatched a nearby torch from its bracket. "Amen to that, sir! Now, come. Surely the others await us even now at the Mound of Gol-goroth."

Menander had thought that a cloud was passing in front of the sun, but then he heard the increasing babble of wonder and fear from the massed crowd in front of him. He glanced upward. There were no clouds, yet the sky was darkening. The position of the dimming sun indicated about noon.

"Gods, it's happening," he muttered to himself, "just as Dositheus said it might—"

"Dositheus knows much."

Menander gasped. He had not heard the words, he had *read* them. Their Latin letters, already fading, seemed to have been written on the sky. No, on his own vision, rather, for they moved with him as he turned his head. Then he remembered something the wizard Taggart had said the night he had awakened from his coma at the inn—and understanding hit him.

"Carbo?" he muttered, gazing again at the dimming sky. "Is that you?"

"Yes." Written words again formed across his field of vision, dark yet semitransparent. "I have grown much. I remember much. I know now what you must do."

Despite the eeriness of the experience Menander felt a sudden relief at not being alone. He pictured the raven, his friend and companion of many years. "You understand, then, what Daramos and Dositheus told me?"

"Yes, and much more. I remember about the Six Suns of the star you call Castor, and about those beings of Celaeno and Facula who enslaved me, and about the opening of Gates."

Menander stood on tiptoe, peered westward over the heads of the crowd toward the distant knoll upon which three grim objects stood silhouetted—crosses upon which hung condemned victims. "How am I to approach him, Carbo? The throng is too dense, and he is surrounded by Roman guards who fend off all who approach too closely."

There was no reply, and Menander now saw that the sky was darkening rapidly. The crowd crew hushed, then began to stir restlessly, hissing like grass in the wind as the people urgently whispered their fears to one another. And as they did so, Menander thought he could hear, just barely, the slow and muffled beating of a distant drum.

A drum, or a giant heart—like he had heard that night in the Tower of Siloam. . . .

The outer fringes of the throng were breaking up, beginning to form into streams of people hurrying east and south, back through the arched gates into the city. Menander pressed himself back into a corner formed by one of the wall's massive abutments and watched the people surge in. Most of them were men—Syrians, Edomites and other foreigners, by and large. Judeans seemed very much in the minority—not surprising, Menander thought, for most of them would now be preparing, in their homes and synagogues, to slaughter lambs for the impending Passover feast. The faces in the crowd displayed degrees of mounting apprehension as the sky continued to darken, and those of the few Judeans showed pious horror as well—outrage, no doubt, at the unholy and cruel Roman method of execution being inflicted on one who had been a spiritual leader among them.

For at least an hour the mob streamed back through the city's gates. By then the sky was pitch black save for a silvery band along the western horizon, and the dim red sun shed less light than a full moon. Whispers of apprehension had given way to numerous cries of outright terror, and many who fled were being trampled by the crowd as it surged through the constricting archways. Far away, several torches now gleamed upon the mound of crucifixion.

"The crowd thins. We must go forward now."

Menander gasped at sight of the bright yellow letters, almost like flame, etched against the black sky. "Carbo! How do you do that?"

"I stimulate the . . . color cells . . . in your eyes. Hurry. We must do as the man Taggart instructed you."

Menander nodded, then strode away from the wall and began to breast the thinning crowd in the direction of the distant torchlit knoll.

Maxentius strode rapidly through the darkened Court of the Gentiles, pausing to question the guards he had stationed at each gate leading into the Women's Court. Cratos and a decan of legionaries followed him closely, half of them carrying torches. At each post his soldiers reported that, although worshippers had been deserting the inner Temple courts ever since the strange darkness had fallen, none of the virgins nor their matrons had emerged.

"Don't let them slip out," Maxentius repeated at each post. "I know they're hiding in there. I saw them at one of the north gates."

They rounded the southeast corner of the wall surrounding the Women's Court and marched westward. The centurion Marcus glanced at the occasional signs announcing death for all non-Judeans daring to enter the inner courts, then said, "How are we to come at them, Commander? We don't dare go in—"

"Ha!" barked Maxentius derisively. "Don't we? Who's better at dealing death, Marcus? Judean priests or Roman legionaries?"

"But you know, sir, that some of the Temple guards are demon-possessed."

"Aye—hard to kill, but clumsy. The goo-blobs can't do much with a body whose head or limbs have been hacked off. Go for them with the edge, Marcus, not the point."

"Are you serious, Commander? If we invade the Temple's inner courts, we'll precipitate mass riots, and then not even the prefect Pilatus could shield us from Caesar's wrath!"

Maxentius chuckled. "Do you see any crowds to riot here? Look—the whole Temple area is deserted now. Everyone is fleeing the streets and courtyards, hiding in houses and synagogues. Even Pilatus is holed up in the Antonia—petitioning the protection of Bacchus, I'll wager. Don't worry about him, Marcus. He's a superstitious coward, and after today—tonight, rather—neither he nor anyone else will be a threat to us."

Marcus glanced uneasily at the black sky, suppressing a shudder at the unceasing sound of the great drum. Or, *was* it a drum? And did the sound come from the great Temple beyond the wall to their right, or from the ridge beyond the Kidron Valley east of the city, or from the entire sky? He knew that Maxentius had studied sorcery, and sensed the man's confidence even now, yet felt that it might nevertheless be wise to join Governor Pilatus behind the massive walls of the Antonian Fortress. After all, there had also been thunderous drumbeats in the air the night the Siloam Tower had been destroyed.

"Look!" Maxentius suddenly pointed ahead. "Priests and Temple-guards coming out. On the double, lads!"

They hurried forward at a trot, weapons and armor jangling. A small band of priests, accompanied by several dark-armored guardsmen, had just emerged through an archway from the Temple area. Maxentius had posted no soldiers at this particular gate, as it led to inner courts adjacent to the Temple where women were forbidden to go. The priest halted and looked uneasily toward the band of legionaries hurrying to intercept. them. As Maxentius drew near them he recognized the gray-bearded priest in the lead.

"Caiaphas! Where in Hades to you think you're going?"

The high priest grimaced, but otherwise ignored the blasphemy; his eyes expressed fear. "Allow us to proceed, Tribune. I have ordered the cessation of all Temple sacrifices until—" he glanced up at the black sky "—until I find out what has gone wrong."

Rats deserting the ship. Aloud, Maxentius said, "So old Annas has double-crossed you, too, eh?"

A look of angry reproof replaced the fear in Caiaphas' eyes. "Of course not! My father-in-law is a man of honor, and I am even now on my way to consult with him in the Hall of Gazzith. I am sure that it was the rabbi

Yeshua and sorcerous old Yosef of Aphairema, not Annas, who somehow contrived to precipitate events prematurely. What their purpose is I do not know, but I fear greatly."

Maxentius snorted in derision. He was about to reassure Caiaphas concerning the mad rabbi Yeshua, then suddenly thought better of it. "Good idea—go consult Annas," he snapped. "Hurry. I'll post more guards here, set up more torches, just in case of looters."

The high priest and his attendant priests and guards hastened on their way southward across the spacious Court of the Gentiles. In a few moments their forms had vanished in darkness, the light of their torches dimming rapidly away in the distance.

"Good," said Maxentius when they were gone. "Now, Marcus—Cratos— all of you, follow me."

He led his soldiers in rapid stride back eastward along the wall until they came to the first entrance into the Women's Court. Here a half dozen legionaries stood on guard, their armor and helmets gleaming in the light of bracketed torches. Maxentius recognized the decurion in charge of them.

"Lucius, you and your men fall in with us. We're going in."

Lucius blinked in surprise, glanced up through the forbidden archway. "In? You mean—in *there*, sir? But the penalty is death—"

"Legionaries *deal* death, soldier."

The decurion grinned and smote his breast in salute. "Yes, *sir!*"

The Romans, now numbering nearly a score, clattered up the few steps and through the column-flanked archway. Centurion Marcus admired his commander's confidence and the way he communicated it to the men, yet couldn't help wondering if Maxentius really knew what he was doing.

"Don't worry, Marcus," muttered the tribune as if he had read his subordinate's mind. "The mob is gone, the priests are gone. We have things all our own way now. No more fooling around with Caiaphas or that traitorous old sorcerer Annas. They thought to use us, but I'm well ahead of them. Just do as I say and it will all work out to our advantage. No, more than that—to our power and glory!"

Marcus hoped so, but his doubts persisted as they entered the spacious Women's Court. The sound of muffled drums was louder and now seemed to be coming primarily—though not entirely—from the direction of the Temple, whose pale facade could now be seen looming dimly beyond the wall to the west. The court, sparsely lit with scattered torches, was cluttered with numerous booths and tables, many of them overturned during the recent flight of the vanished crowds. Pillared porticos surrounded the place on three sides, while to the west a wide semicircular staircase of fifteen steps led up to the ornate gateway leading to the Court of Sacrifice. Near the base of this stairway, half hidden amid shadows of booths and pillars, stood a group of shadowy figures.

"There," hissed Maxentius, "—the women! Spread out in a line, soldiers, then close in. Don't let any of them escape. Elissa of Sychar and her maid are among them and I want them alive. A silver talent for the man who captures either! As for the rest, kill them—leave no witnesses!"

Marcus nodded, then waved his hand and barked, "Fan out, men!"

Armor jangled, boots clattered on the marble tiles of the court. Women screamed and, realizing that they were discovered and being attacked, began to mill about in terror, seeking exits or places to hide.

Beyond the wall, the muffled drums beat slowly, ponderously. . . .

Simon, having left the deserted streets of Bethany behind him, hurried eastward along the Jericho Road as swiftly as the darkness would allow. At the base of the knoll overlooking the beginning of the steep descent he paused a few minutes to catch his breath, then began to walk up the smooth slope. Behind him, far off, he could still hear the deep low booming of drums, the thunderous muttering of chanted words:

"HALEL-EL . . . TASHMAD . . . IÄ, ABBA SHADDAI!"

Simon stood atop the hill, hands at his sides, and calmed his breathing. Far to the east he could see a dim line of twilight above the Transjordanian hills. For a moment he felt a sense of futility. Dositheus' instructions now seemed foolish. Could Menander really have had the experiences he had reported—?

Suddenly he felt a brief tingling all over his body—and then, incredibly, he was in an utterly alien place, standing upon one of many softly glowing discs of light, surrounded by towering and intricate structures of humming metal among which moved distant, gleaming, vaguely humanoid forms. Forms of giants, or gods. . . .

Again the brief tingling. A blaze of sunlight blinded him. For a few moments he rubbed his eyes, then opened them. Through a mist of tears he beheld a hilly landscape, a ridge covered with boulders and sparse clumps of grass. To his amazement he was standing in the middle of a circular metal platform of dark metal, surrounded by a rim of similar metal about three feet high and inset with panels of many-colored squares. Instantly he recognized the thing as the sky-craft of the wizard Taggart. A few paces away stood the wizard himself, black-clad and somber of expression, and beside him a squat, greenish-skinned, brown-robed being with pointed ears and dark, almond eyes full of wisdom.

"Daramos!" Simon nimbly vaulted the craft's rim and strode over to the pair. "Menander did not tell me that *you* were with Taggart."

"I summoned him back to Parthia to fetch me," said the dwarf, "for in my meditations I realized that I am needed here at this time."

Taggart looked puzzled. "What do you mean, you 'summoned' me? I decided to fetch you on my own, Daramos."

The dwarf smiled blandly. "When two minds decide as one, they *are* one. You know much about the physical cosmos, Taggart, yet there are many mysteries which you still do not understand."

"So I've noticed. You—and some other beings I've met on various worlds—seem to have abilities that are . . . unusual. Well, that's why, on reflection, I decided to bring you here and—"

"Here?" Simon interrupted. "Where are we?"

"In the Transjordanian hills," Taggart pointed westward. "Look."

Simon turned, saw that the bright westering sun hung just above a vast lenticular cloud of blackness that hid the far-off hills beneath it. No—not a cloud, but a featureless inky region that appeared to absorb all the light that impinged on it. It stretched north and south nearly to both horizons, and beneath it most of the wide plain of the Jordan was shadowed in darkness. Simon felt his spine tingle.

"The darkness is spilling from one end of an . . . opening," explained Taggart. "Or, rather, the 'opening' absorbs much of the light in its vicinity. It's one end of what you might call a 'worm-tunnel' leading from one region of the cosmos to another; the other end lies somewhere amid the star cluster called the Hyades."

"The ancient writings call such openings 'Gates'," added Daramos. "But tell me, Simon, why are *you* here rather than Menander? Was he not able to accomplish the task which Taggart set him?"

"He wasn't, but he is still trying. He and Dositheus wanted me to tell you that, and to help you in any way I can."

"This is bad news, very bad." Taggart swept his hand toward the great band of darkness. "If the rabbi Yeshua accomplishes his own doom in the way he intends, then that—that Gate will expand to engulf the entire Earth and monstrous *things* will come through it. All life—all *possibility* of life, past and present—will become impossible on this world."

"And therefore," said Daramos, "this small part of the cosmos shall forever stand outside the awareness of the Mistress of Wisdom, the Mother of Being. For the sire of Yeshua—the Father, the One-Who-Is-Many—has no part in this cosmos save by intrusion. All which He manages to enfold is taken away *elsewhere* as if it had never been."

Taggart glanced briefly at the dwarf in what seemed to be puzzlement, but then turned back to the Samaritan. "I remember you, Simon. Menander told me how you saved my life. He also said that you were trained as a fighter, a gladiator. There is a chance that you may be able to help us delay the opening of the Gate."

"How? Tell me!"

"A lesser Gate is being opened in the Jerusalem Temple, powered by the psychic energies generated by the rabbi Yeshua's self-immolation upon the Mound of Gol-goroth. At the . . . rite's culmination, the being called Gol-goroth will itself surge through that opening and proceed to the Mount of Offense, there to aid in opening the Greater Gate. I don't pretend to understand all of this, but I know that the thing the ancients called Gol-goroth is a being composed only partially of natural matter and energy. If it could be defeated, its material portion killed and its mind-energies driven back into its own dimension, that would buy us time until Menander returns."

The prickling along Simon's spine intensified as he recalled what he had read in the ancient writings. Gol-goroth, one of the sinister black gods of the Stygians, tentacled, soul-devouring. . . .

"Gol-goroth is a major servitor of Uagio-Tsotho, Lord of Demhe," said Daramos, "yet part of him is indeed material and therefore temporarily mortal. Once, ten thousand years ago, a Vanir hero fought him in a Stygian temple and sent him back to his own dark dimension. It can be done again, Simon."

"By me? Gods! But how—?"

"With this." Taggart, clambering into his craft, slid back a long section of the metal floor and drew forth a great dark sword. "Here." He climbed back out and handed the weapon to Simon. "In very ancient times the Zarrians themselves used these in individual combat."

Simon took the thing, marveling at it. Never had he seen such a weapon. The blade, straight and smoothly tapered, was well over four feet long, and the handle, more than large enough for a two-handed grip, was wrapped round with what appeared to be smooth dark wire; the pommel was a smooth, polished ball, the crosspiece short for the sword's size and deeply inset with unknown glyphs or letters. The whole weapon gleamed a deep metallic blue and, despite its great length, was perfectly balanced and a pleasure to hold.

Both of Simon's companions stepped back a pace. "Now," Taggart said, "push that little inset near the crosspiece—and be sure not to let the sword's blade touch you or anything else you value!"

Simon obeyed—then gasped to see that a fine line of bluish-white light had sprung into being along both edges of the blade, outlining it like a silvery thread. A high whine of power, barely audible, sang in his ears.

"Good." Taggart pointed at a tall, narrow boulder that stood up sharply from the grass and gravel of the ridgetop. "Now strike that."

Simon hesitated, reluctant to damage the magnificent blade, but then obeyed, swinging the weapon with only a fraction of his strength, expecting to hear it clang against the stone. Instead, astonishingly, the blade bit deeply, almost effortlessly, more than two thirds of the way through the boulder! The high keening in Simon's ears became a shrill whine. Instinctively he pulled out the sword with both hands; the whining subsided and the top of the boulder, cracking, slid heavily to the ground, its sheared side smoking slightly and glowing a dull red. Simon caught the smell of hot stone. Again he pressed the small inset just behind the crosspiece and the silvery thread of power vanished.

"Lord of Gerizim!" he breathed, awed.

"Now you are armed," said Daramos. "Yet be warned, Simon, that Gol-goroth is a servant of Demhe and as such is a master of the Phantom of Truth. Therefore you must also be protected from his cloud of illusion."

"Right." Taggart removed his metallic headband, strode forward and handed it to Simon. "Wear this so that the blue disc is on your forehead and then you won't be deceived by . . . unreal projections. The device can also project illusions in its own right, but there's no time to teach you that technique; besides, it wouldn't work against a being like Gol-goroth. Quick, now—into the craft."

"Are you sure?" Simon felt suddenly like one being pushed into raging rapids upon a fragile raft. "Would not your death-wand serve better for this task, Taggart?"

"I don't dare carry high-energy weapons into the Temple area," said the wizard. "And I'm not skilled with swords. The Zarrian ship is above the horizon now and will be watching the Jerusalem location closely at this crucial time. If the Zarrians sense interference they will . . . eliminate it. Don't activate the blade until you're under the roof of the Temple, Simon, and then turn it off as soon as you are able. Understand?"

Simon nodded grimly.

"One more thing. We haven't many more hours left even should you succeed, so when Menander accomplishes his task, tell him to press the 'location' inset in the device I gave him. He'll know what I mean. But tell him also to wait until the last hour of the day to do it. By then the Zarrian ship will have dipped behind the Earth for awhile and only the Galactic ship will be aloft."

Simon glanced up at the steely blue heaven. "So the ships of monstrous powers even now sail our skies! Will they soon battle one another for the world, Taggart?"

"No, for they know that that would result in their mutual destruction. But many of the Zarrian minions are already on Earth in the Jerusalem area, as you know. With luck, and with your help and Menander's we may soon swing the scales the other way." Taggart climbed in and fingered one of the panels of colored squares. "Now, stand upright in the center and hold that sword so that it's parallel to your body. I'm going to put you down in the courtyard right in front of the Temple."

"Good fortune, Simon," said Daramos, lifting a stubby paw in salute.

Simon checked the impulse to wave back. Then, as Taggart's fingers moved rapidly over the glowing squares, he again felt the tingling. . . .

AGAINST THE GODS OF DOOM

CHAPTER XXVII

Too late, thought Menander as he slowly walked up the shallow slope toward the three condemned ones who hung from the crosses of execution.

The crowd had at last dwindled to almost nothing, but by now the smoky red disc of the sun, gleaming feebly from the inky sky, had descended halfway from the zenith toward the western horizon. Save for its dim glow, the only light was that of several torches atop tall poles spaced here and there upon the mound. In their flickering glare Menander could make out five or six Roman legionaries standing or sitting near the crosses and, a little down the slope from them, a small group of quiet spectators, mostly women.

Menander drew near the group, but stopped some distance away, not wishing to draw too much attention to himself, nervously aware that his white Levite's robe made him conspicuous even in the dark. He was thankful that the crowds had gone and their tumult and most of the Roman guards with them. It was now quiet enough for him to do what the wizard had asked of him—if that were still possible. The three condemned ones hung motionless; they had been upon the crosses for several hours already and might be unconscious if not dead.

He found a thin, pale stick lying on the ground—doubtless a walking stick someone in the throng had lost—and picked it up. It had given him an idea. Opening his pouch, he drew forth a slender cord of woven camel hair, then the small black device Taggart had given him, and carefully lashed the latter close to one end of the stick. If he could get close enough, he reasoned, he might yet capture the rabbi's voice, however feeble it might be. . . .

If, that is, the man were not already beyond speech forever.

"Menander—"

Startled, the lad turned to his right. No one was there, yet the voice had seemed like that of an insect buzzing directly into his right ear. He whispered, "Carbo! Are *you* doing that?"

"Yes," buzzed the voice, jerkily and hesitantly. "I am moving the bones of your ear."

Menander reflexively fingered his right earlobe. Since when had ears contained bones . . .?

"Listen!" the voice of Carbo went on. "If you can get close enough to the crucified man to lay hands on him, I may be able to stop his suffering and prevent his death. That would cut off the psychic power he is using to open the Gate."

"I don't know, Carbo. There are still a few soldiers. I doubt they would let me approach closely. Perhaps, though, if I claimed to be a Levite, come to utter a last rite of comfort—"

At that moment Menander heard footsteps approaching through the dark stillness and, turning, saw two men coming from the direction of the city's nearest gate. By the light of the torches they bore he could see that one of them was young and dark-bearded; upon his shoulder perched a large white pigeon whose eyes gleamed in the torchlight. The other man was an elderly priest. As they drew close to the group on the knoll Menander could see a bit more clearly the members of that group, recognizing among them two: the tall, white-beareded sorcerer Yosef of Aphairema and the dumpy innkeeper Martha.

"Nicodemus!" Yosef's voice was high yet calm as he hailed the approaching priest. "Peace, brother! What news do you bring?"

"Peace to you also! Zethos and I have just come from the Hall of Gazzith," answered the old priest in trembling tones, gasping for breath. "Judah has perished Yosef! He flung the silver of the Sanhedrin back into their treacherous faces and for this he was set upon by Izhar of Chorazin's demonic familiar. We saw his broken body flung into the Tryopean Valley less than an hour ago."

Zethos, thought Menander. Yes, he now recognized the young man—the servant and apprentice of the sorcerer Yosef. His face had not been so visible in the grotto of tombs near Bethany. Menander wondered how he was able to hear so clearly the present conversation, which was conducted in low tones. His right ear seemed especially acute and he suspected that Carbo was somehow enhancing its receptivity.

"It's sad, Nicodemus," said Yosef somberly, "that Judah, our Master's best friend, has died in fear and pain like the countless millions who have died before him. Yet he is now beyond all pain and fear and soon all creatures upon this world shall share his liberation. It is nearly the Time."

Nicodemus, sadness and even reverence in his eyes, looked up at the dimly-illumined figures hanging limply from their crosses. "Our Master still lives, then?"

"Aye. But he cannot live much longer."

"Has he spoken?"

"He . . . he forgave all those who tortured him and plotted his doom. He—" The ancient sorcerer's voice quavered, cracked; then, regaining his power of speech, he went on in a hard, even vindictive tone, "Today he frees from torture even those who inflict it upon him. They are not worthy of his sacrifice! Had I his power, they would die ten thousand deaths! And yet—" He looked up toward the three crosses, tears now streaming down his wrinkled face to mingle with the strands of his long white beard. "O my son, beloved though not of my flesh! My very anger proves that I am not more worthy than thine enemies. I would return hate for hate, pain for pain; but only *you,* who are more than human, would dissolve all evil with your love rather than punish it. Let you true Father come now and that swiftly! *Come, come, O Yahweh Zava'ot!"*

Menander trembled at the sound of the forbidden Name. He saw now that many of the others in the group were also weeping openly, their faces turned upward toward the crosses and the torches surrounding them. Among these faces was that of a curious old albino woman, and beside her a tall young woman of striking beauty whose features, form and long dark hair somehow reminded Menander—incredibly—of Lotis.

He was still reeling mentally from this realization when he heard the buzzing voice of Carbo saying, *"Look. The man moves."*

Menander shifted his attention toward the hilltop, saw that the man on the central cross was indeed writhing feebly. Instantly he pressed an inset on the black wizard-box, then raised aloft the thin staff to which it was lashed and began to boldly stride forward up the slope, hoping that the Romans would think he carried a priestly rod and not mistake it for a weapon. With this thought in mind he made his pace deliberately slow and sedate.

Behind him he heard, with his acute right ear, the voice of Zethos saying, "Who is that youth in the Levite robe—?"

Then he began to see more clearly in the torchlight the form of the crucified rabbi and all other things were suddenly driven from his awareness. The man was indeed stirring, his deep chest heaving as if for breath and his limbs knotting as if straining for freedom. In the dim and wavering light those limbs seemed strangely hairy and deformed, the torso strangely mottled as if with writhing shadows, the nail-pinioned feet curiously hard and blunt. About the man's hips hung a tattered yellow loin cloth whose folds seemed to hide abnormal contours, and Menander wondered at this, for the other two crucified men were naked. Dark bruises, cuts and whip-welts marred nearly every inch of the rabbi's body; for whatever reason, he had obviously been tortured far more than the usual crucifixion victims. Finally, and most ignominiously, a plaited pseudo-crown of thorny stems surmounted his dark locks, its sharp points pressing into his high forehead and causing thin pink rivulets of what seemed to be diluted blood mingled with sweat to rill down over his features. To Menander those tortured, writhing features seemed, in this hour of tension and torchlight, more sheeplike or goatish than they had ever seemed before, and he shuddered as he recalled things of which he had read in ancient scrolls concerning certain ancient and terrible rites:

The Goat of Azazel . . . The Pain of the Goat. . . .

But it was the *eyes* that most unsettled him—the great dark eyes full of life and compassion and suffering. They expressed, Menander sensed, a vitality surpassing anything earthly, a pity beyond human comprehension—and, therefore, a suffering far greater than anything terrestrial life could experience or identify with.

A suffering that knew and identified with every creature that had ever lived and died on the Earth—with every beast and bird that had been sacrificed in Yahweh's Temple since Solomon's building of it a thousand years ago—with the thousand lambs that were even now being butchered for the Passover feast in every house and synagogue in Jerusalem. . . .

"Halt!" cried out a Roman soldier, snapping Menander out of his dark fascination. "Come no closer."

Menander saw that the soldier was an officer. "Please permit me to approach, good centurion," he said, the tremor in his voice not at all feigned. "I am a Levite, come on a merciful errant of last rights—"

He said no more, for at that moment the man on the cross drew in an audible rasping breath. The centurion turned to face the crucified one, anger in his eyes, then strode back toward his soldiers. "Snap to, men! The creature's not yet dead. Watch his followers closely!"

Menander strode forward, his slim staff held aloft. The doomed rabbi was straining upon the cross as if hoping that his corded, strangely misshapen muscles might free him from the thick iron nails that pinned him there. Then his great glistening eyes rolled upward toward the heart of the darkness that lowered above Jerusalem; his wide mouth gaped, and from deep within his chest he cried out in a loud voice:

"Iä! Iä! Abba Yog-Sothoni!"

The sound of muffled drums, of which Menander had been but dimly aware, suddenly increased; it came from the east, from the direction of the distant Temple. Menander again shuddered as he realized the significance of the terrible cry, for he knew its Aramaic meaning: *"Hail! Hail, my Father, Yog-Sothoth!"*

Then his acute hearing picked up a question from someone in the group behind him on the hill slope, "What did he say? Did he call on the prophet Elijah . . .?"

And in the same moment he heard the man on the cross mutter, in a far more subdued voice, "I . . . thirst. . . ."

Menander saw a water bucket near the base of the cross. At the same instant the voice of Carbo buzzed, "I can guess what you are thinking, Menander. Do it—it's now or never."

He whipped a soiled rag from his girdle, wrapped it loosely about the top of the staff just above the wizard's box, knotted it firmly, then ran forward. Instantly the centurion ran to intercept him, the steel point of his heavy spear outthrust.

"Stop! Where do you think you're going?"

"Please, sir," whine Menander. "The man dies. His followers ask whether he calls on our revered prophet Elijah, but he can now barely speak. Let me dip this rag in that bucket and wet his lips, that he may give one last utterance to those who love him and whom he loves."

"That bucket?" The centurion relaxed, grinning. "Why, sure, lad. Go ahead."

Menander ran forward and dipped his rag in the bucket, then held it up on the stick to the lips of the dying man. He felt a tingling in the hand that held the staff, then suddenly realized that his right ear had lost its unnatural acuity. He saw thin, slick filaments flowing rapidly up the staff, into the rag. Carbo was leaving him!

The crucified rabbi's lips touched the rag, sucked at it—then, convulsively, drew back. Menander let the rag fall against the man's neck and chest, held it there. . . .

"Ha! ha!" bellowed the centurion, doubling over in convulsive mirth. "That's not water, Jew boy. It's *vinegar!"*

Menander felt a surge of hate at this last indignity, but in the next instant he heard the crucified man again cry out in a powerful voice, *"It is done!"*

And then Menander fell heavily to the ground as a mighty tremor shook the earth beneath his feet.

Elissa sensed at once the lethal intent of the charging soldiers. Maxentius, she knew, would not have led his pagan legionaries into these forbidden Temple precincts save as a last desperate measure.

"This way—follow me," she cried out to the half-dozen terrified matrons. "Quickly!"

They obeyed her imperative command, dashing after her into the shadows of the northern inner portico of the Women's Court, whimpering in fear as they blundered through the maze of booths and curtained-off cloisters. Fortunately they sensed the general plan of the area well enough to flounder onward in the darkness without excessive noise. Not a soul did they meet, and Elissa feared that they were indeed the only ones who had not already fled the Temple precincts, save for the dozen or so sacred virgins. . . .

Lotis, may the Lord of Gerizim protect you! Elissa's silent prayer was a flash of desperate hope. Her handmaid was with the virgins, who had gone up the fifteen steps to the wide semicircular platform before the Nicanor Gate, which led westward into the court of the Altar, there to pray in unison to the Nameless One for safety. With any luck, the Romans had not seen them there. . . .

Then she glimpsed flickering light ahead—the dim outline of a high archway. It was, she realized, the westernmost of the exits through the northern wall of the Women's Court.

"Stop!" she cautioned her companions. "There will be guards there, but they may not yet be alerted. If we go out in an unhurried manner they may let us pass. It's our only hope—"

But the matrons, frantic to be free of the darkness, pushed past her and surged in terror through the archway and down the steps into the wide Court of Gentiles. Elissa, covering her face with a veil, muttered another brief prayer and hurried after them.

"Halt, there!" yelled a legionary. "Men, don't let these women pass until I've had a good look at them. Bring torches."

Elissa's heart sank as she slowed her pace and descended the few steps to the court, for she recognized the officer in charge—Lentulus, one of Maxentius' most trusted centurions. His soldiers were detaining the women while he, torch in hand, was beginning to examine the faces of the captives one by one. Elissa half turned to retreat, but then heard the approaching clatter of more soldiers beyond the dark archway from which she had just emerged.

"Soldiers, let us go, we beg you," wailed one of the matrons. "There are demons within! They have surely devoured our daughters and now they pursue us."

Two or three of the legionaries laughed, loudly but rather nervously. Lentulus snorted in disgust. "Let these boobies go. The woman we seek is not among them." He turned and pointed to Elissa. "You, there—you in the veil. Come here."

Elissa hesitated. In that moment more than a dozen Roman troops came clattering out of the gateway behind her and leading them was Maxentius.

"That's her!" bellowed the tribune. "I'd know her bearing anywhere, veil or no veil. Grab her, Lentulus!"

Elissa raced to escape between the guards, but three of them grabbed her and held her securely. While she struggled in furious silence, the centurion Lentulus strode to her and ripped away her veil. "Aye, it's her. You were right, Tribune."

"Those other women . . . *Hades!"* Maxentius swore as he realized that the matrons had already fled away into the darkness of the western portion of the vast court. "Well, never mind them—this beauty is the only one who really matters."

Elissa, looking up into the man's grinning, gloating face, tried to work up enough saliva to spit. Her mouth was too dry. She tried to conceal the deep fear that had welled up within her. Maxentius' eyes were strange;

besides their usual display of anger and arrogance, she now detected in them a dark glare of madness.

"Search her and bind her, Lentulus," he order, "then gather up the men from all the gates and get ready to march. Marcus, you go back into the Women's Court and round up a couple of litters. We may have some plunder to carry away from here. Meet us at the east gate."

As Marcus and three torch-bearing legionaries hurried back up the steps and through the archway, Lentulus whipped Elissa's robe away and began to search her. She cursed and struggled fiercely as he began to paw her with deliberately lingering hands, then kicked him in the shins. Two other soldiers held her firmly while a third began to bind her arms behind her back.

Maxentius laughed. "That Judean matron's gown doesn't suit you at all, Elissa! But why so angry? You should thank me, woman. Had it been a priest or a Temple guard who saw through your disguise rather than I, you'd have been stoned like a harlot. An inglorious death—not at all like the one I have planned for you. Here, here, hold still! If you don't like Lentulus, I'll search you myself—you've felt *my* hands on you often enough!" He stepped forward, gripped the fabric of her gown near the throat, then tore it away savagely; the garment ripped open all down the front and fell from her shoulders, leaving her clad only in her brief white tunic.

"That *is* more becoming!" chuckled Lentulus. "A body fit for Aphrodite to inhabit, by the gods!"

Maxentius, wadding up the torn gown, suddenly felt a small, hard object under this fingers. Fumbling in the cloth folds, he pulled forth a small crystal vial whose contents reflected the torch flames with a clear amber light. "What is this?"

Elissa stood proudly tall and averted her face from his.

"Ah. So that's how it is." Maxentius held up the vial and looked at it more closely. "Since you won't tell me, it must be important. How clearly it shines!—almost with a gleam of its own. . . . By the gods! Can *this* be what old Annas was trying to find out about from you?"

Elissa remembered what the old sorcerer Yosef had told her. She made as if to speak, then deliberately turned away, her lips shut in firm determination.

"So." Maxentius stepped forward and gripped her chin with his left hand, forcing her to face him. "I can *make* you talk, you know. In fact, I'd rather enjoy that."

Elissa pretended definant resistance as long as she felt she dread. Then, as the Tribune's open right hand drew back for a blow, she said, "Very well. Since you've obviously guessed already, I'll tell you."

He released her and grinned widely. "So I was right." He held up the shining vial once more. "It's what Annas called the 'Golden Nectar', isn't it! Who gave it to you?"

"The old priest Yosef of Aphairema. He also called it the 'Living Water' and said that it would—"

Again she deliberately hesitated.

"Would what? Don't hold back from me, sweet Elissa."

"He said that tonight I should drink it, then gaze into the Gate—whatever that is— and I would see invisible beings and have power over them."

Maxentius scowled. "How strange. First the mad rabbi offers you this 'Living Water' at Sychar, then the old sorcerer Yosef gives you a vial of it here in Jerusalem. I think they planned to use you, Elissa—they were preparing you. Ostanes, too, says that the Golden Nectar enables one to see invisible beings—the bat-winged Byakhim—but that only the byakhtril enables the sorcerer to command them. . . ." The Roman stood silent for a moment, pondering, then carefully placed the vial in his belt pouch. "Just one more question, Elissa. Where is Lotis?"

Elissa glanced involuntarily toward the Women's Court, then bit her lip and cursed herself silently.

"So she's still in there," said Maxentius, grinning again. "Well, she's probably not important to me now, but it might be well to have a spare sacrifice, just in case." He turned to his giant bodyguard. "Cratos, you're good at creeping about in the dark. Go back in there and search the area where we first saw the women. See if you can flush the little bird out of hiding. You'll recognize her, won't you?"

"Aye," growled the gladiator. "Scribonius used to let me watch when he—"

"Good. Bring her to the eastern gate if you capture her. Otherwise, wait for me on that big stairway by the gate to the Temple court. I'll join you there soon."

Cratos bowed briefly from the waist, torchlight gleaming on his bald cranium, then strode up the steps to the forbidden area and vanished through the dark archway.

"And now, Lentulus, gather up all the men and bring them to the eastern gate. I'll accompany you that far; then you can go and round up the men on the south side and bring them there, too. As for this woman, tie a rope around her waist and bring her along. If she fights it, drag her over the flagstones a bit. Hurry—on the double, now."

A few moments later the troops were marching eastward down the wide Court of Gentiles, Elissa being forced to jog awkwardly after them in order to keep up with their long military strides. At each archway they passed, Lentulus barked an order to the guards on watch, who immediately fell into step behind the group. By the time they had rounded the northeast corner of the portico and joined the troops at the main eastern gate, the legionaries numbered more than a score.

Lentulus hurried off to gather up his troops stationed along the south wall, and at the same time Marcus and his men appeared, emerging from the wide, column-flanked eastern gate itself and bearing two curtained litters with them.

"Good, Marcus," said Maxentius. "Now gag this woman and tie her securely inside one of the litters. Then come with us. Pick six soldiers to follow us with the empty litter."

Marcus complied and soon he and his half dozen troops were accompanying their commander up the wide stairway and between the high, ornately-carven portals of the great eastern gate. Those portals gleamed back golden and jeweled light from the torch flames. Never had the centurion seen them this closely before and he now realized more fully than ever why this entrance to the Women's Court was called the 'Beautiful Gate'. Still, in this unnatural darkness it seemed, like the rest of the Temple precincts, more sinister than beautfiul.

"Commander," said Marcus as they passed through into the wide court beyond, "why do we again enter this forbidden area?"

"I told Cratos I'd meet him at the eastern stairway. More importantly, though, I'm going to visit the Temple itself and collect a few items Annas left there."

"What!" Marcus suddenly became conscious again of the eerie sound as of muffled drums—the sound that had never ceased since the onset of the strange darkness. "We're going in *there?*"

"Sure as Hades, Marcus! Annas has double-crossed us and now I'm doing everything *my* way. I'm going to move all his magical apparatus out of this priests' nest and up to the Mount of Offense before he—"

But at that instant Marcus heard a deep roaring and grinding noise, felt the flagstone floor lurch beneath his feet—and then he and all the others cried out in terror as great stone columns and lintels began to lean, crumble and come crashing thunderously down.

Lotis, peering cautiously down from the high stairway into the Women's Court, saw a giant figure emerging stealthily from the shadows of the northern portico, its bald cranium and muscular arms gleaming in the dim torchlight.

Cratos—Maxentius' bodyguard.

She turned and crawled back on hands and knees to the group of Temple virgins, who were kneeling on the wide semicircular stone platform, facing westward through the columned Gate of Nicanor toward the

Temple. They were still praying in silent terror to the Nameless One—begging him, no doubt, to save them from the strange darkness and the dangers that prowled in it.

"Up! Up!" she hissed. "The Romans are returning. We must get away from here."

The virgins recoiled in horror as they saw that Lotis was motioning them toward the Nicanor Gate. "We can't go that way," whine one of them. "Only priests or those who bring sacrifices are allowed in the inner court. The Lord of the Temple will slay us if we enter—"

"The Romans will slay us if we don't." Lotis sprang up and ran through the gateway, then paused amid the columns beyond and beckoned to the virgins. "Hurry!"

Her decisiveness impelled them to action. In a moment they were racing after Lotis, their sandals slapping on the tiles, terror in their hearts.

"Quiet! Go more slowly. The Romans mustn't hear—"

Suddenly the floor of the courtyard shook violently. Immediately half the virgins lost their footing and fell to the flags. Then, slowly, a column leaned and fell, crashing thunderously upon the stone floor.

"We are doomed!" shrieked one of the young women. "The Lord is angered—"

"This way!" Lotis yelled. "Out into the court—away from the columns."

They raced on, emerging from the porticoed area just as several more columns crashed down. Again the ground trembled and Lotis, looking back, saw the immense lintel above the Nicanor Gate crack in two and ponderously fall. The courtyard trembled with a booming thunder as the two halves of the great stone struck the pavement.

Then there was silence—an eerie silence punctuated rhythmically by the sound of what seemed to be deep drumbeats within the Temple.

Lotis glanced around the wide courtyard, which was better lit than the Women's Court had been. Despite the many torches, however, there were no priests or worshippers to be seen; evidently all had fled the place. Across the court to the west loomed the high white bulk of the Temple, its main door gaping wide, its interior illuminated with many lamps and torches, while not far to the southwest stood the enormous stone-built block of the altar of sacrifice, the great sacred bonfire still burning redly atop it. The smell of burnt meat hung in the air, while about the altar's base lay the abandoned carcasses of many half-butchered cattle, sheep and goats, their blood rilling sluggishly into dark puddles and rivulets that dripped into the courtyard drains. Then—

"Listen!" wailed a virgin. "It is the voice of *El Shaddai*—the angry Lord!"

Lotis heard it, too, and her spine prickled. The rhythmic booms from the Temple had grown louder and now seemed to be the voice of some monstrous Being uttering spoken *words*:

"DONE . . . DONE . . . IT IS DONE. . . ."

At that moment the air began to shimmer a few paces away from her, toward the center of the court—a vertical oblong, twinkling with a myriad of points of luminescence taking on what seemed to be a human form. . . . And then, incredibly, she saw standing before her a grim-faced young man holding a very long sword in his right hand. He wore a plain dark tunic and his dark hair was confined by a band of woven metal, which held a faintly glowing disc of blue metal to his brow. Immediately the virgins all cowered back in fear from this apparition.

"Heaven have mercy!" cried one of them. "An angel of the Lord has come to slay us for trespassing upon—"

But Lotis, running forward, gasped, *"Simon!* How did you get here? Where did you come—?"

"No time to explain," snapped the Samaritan. "I don't know why you're here, Lotis, but you and these others must get out right away." He turned to the trembling virgins and in a low voice to Lotis, "Lead them out through the court's northwestern gate, then find the synagogue of Samezer if you can. Take some torches when you go. Hurry!"

Spurred by the urgency in his voice, Lotis and the Temple virgins raced across the court, pausing at its northern colonnade only long enough to lift a few torches from their brackets. Then their white-clad forms vanished into the shadows and the sound of their slapping sandals faded rapidly away to silence.

Simon, gripping his dark sword grimly, strode westward across the courtyard and mounted the Temple stairs. From within he could hear the deep echoing voice booming, like a great vocal drum, the words:

"IT . . . IS . . . DONE. . . ."

Passing between the lofty portals and the parted curtains beyond, Simon entered the great hall, his long sword held out before him in both hands as he warily scanned the shadows. Ahead of him, about sixty feet away, stood a small gilded altar and beyond it was hung an elaborately embroidered drapery depicting a symmetrical pair of winged monsters—the curtain, he knew, that veiled the entrance to the Holy of Holies, the most sacred room in the Temple. Simon recognized this and other features of the place—the great, golden-gleaming seven-branched candelabrum on his left, the solid gold shew-bread table on the right— from the descriptions Dositheus had often given him of them; for was not this temple, magnificent though it was, but an impious copy made by evil King Herod of the one erected centuries ago by the Samaritans on holy Mount Gerizim . . .?

"DONE . . . DONE. . . ."

The monstrous voice was louder now, reminding him of those thunderous utterances he had earlier heard sounding from the Mount of Offense. Perhaps the two were somehow one and the same. It now emanated unmistakably from behind the veil at the end of the hall, and though Simon knew that the chamber concealed behind it was only a room about thirty feet on a side, yet the booming voice seemed to echo as from vast caverns or from mighty halls extending into other dimensions.

"DONE . . . HALAL-EL . . . AZAG-THOTH. . . ."

Simon's spine tingled, for as the sound increased so did the feeling of impending menace. He touched the small, blue-glowing inset just behind the sword's crosspiece, saw the thin silvery line of force spring into being along the blade's edge, then rounded the altar and approached the curtain that veiled the entrance into the Holy of Holies. That curtain now seemed to be stirring slightly—something was causing it to billow. Simon felt a cold draft about his feet and ankles.

Gol-goroth. . . .

Simon growled angrily—a deliberate attempt to override his fear—and sprang forward, slashing with the great sword. Instantly the billowing, Cherub-emblazoned veil parted and fell away, its sundered edges smoldering, revealing the doorway into the Holy of Holies.

"DONE. . . ."

Simon gasped. No lamp or torch burned within the chamber, yet the place was flooded with an eerie red light. The light streamed from what appeared to be two great red eyes set within a gigantic ass' head that loomed above a stone altar against the far wall—eyes that seemed to glare down straight into Simon's own. Before this altar rested a large chest of elaborate design, gilded and gleaming, and beside it lay what was apparently its lid, surmounted by twin images of golden winged monsters similar to those emblazoned on the sundered veil. Instantly Simon realized that the thing could be nothing other than the fabled Ark of the Covenant, said to have been hidden within Mount Nebo centuries ago by the prophet Jeremiah. The deep booming seemed to be coming from its hollow interior, accompanied by faint eerie whinings as of distant flutes. And now, in the air above it, an insubstantial swirling disc seemed to be forming, expanding, obscuring the gigantic golden ass-head save for the two burning eyes. The disc pin-wheeled, became rapidly larger and ever more visible; now it seemed to be a revolving, red-glowing tunnel that pulsed like a giant artery in rhythm to the echoing drumbeats and flute-tones. And then—

"DONE . . . ABBA YOG-SOTHONI. . . ."

Simon screamed with rage and fear as he saw, surging rapidly up that swirling tunnel toward him, a monstrous churning Thing of inky blackness whose myriad dark tentacles and pseudopods were extending toward him with unspeakable menace.

CHAPTER XVIII

Simon leaped backward as the great writhing wave of blackness surged at him. From a forest of inky palps and tentacles one member, python-thick, shot forth and slapped smartly against his left flank and thigh, clinging viscously. Simon screamed with rage and swung his blade; there was a hissing crackle, a vile stench as of burning bitumen and squid flesh, and the great tentacle fell severed to the floor, still writhing. A great booming bellow filled the temple like the angry roar of a god.

Simon spun about and vaulted the small altar, half deafened by that enormous bellow, then whirled to confront the thing anew. It was surging after him, merging with its severed member, flowing around the altar and engulfing it on both sides, swallowing it from sight in its vast looming blackness. Again Simon screamed as the flowing forest of ebon palps and tendrils surged forward to engulf him, then swung again. Half a dozen more writhing members hit the floor soggily, their severed ends smoldering, then wriggled like giant worms back into the heaving mass from which they had been shorn.

Just in time Simon whirled and dashed halfway down the wide hall, then turned to face the hellish being yet another time. It was rolling—or oozing—rapidly toward him, its thousand tendrils writhing like the feelers of a gigantic sea urchin, its palps and tentacles groping forward. Above its churning oblate mass spread several vast vanes resembling monstrous wings. The thing did not reflect the torchlight as a normal material object would have, seeming to swallow up all light that impinged upon it. Nowhere was there visible anything resembling the sense organs of any earthly creature, and Simon realized that the thing could only be some monstrous demon called up by sorcery from the black Outside.

He felt a burning in his left flank where the tentacle had struck him, saw blood rilling from half a dozen circular wounds on his leg beneath his torn tunic.

Gol-goroth—blood-feasting god of Stygia. . . .

Simon stood his ground as long as he could, then involuntarily turned to flee again. No human determination could hold firm in face of the viscid black wall of advancing doom. But this time he was not quick enough; the thing's speed was greater than he would have thought possible in view of its vast gelid bulk, and Simon suddenly found himself overwhelmed by a churning thicket of vile palps and tendrils. A third time he screamed in rage and loathing, then lashed out blindly and furiously with the great Zarrian sword.

Again came the booming bellow, deafening, as he lopped off the monster's appendages by the scores and the vile burning stench grew thick in his throat and nostrils. He staggered back, continuing to hack madly yet feeling himself about to be sucked into the surging blackness before him. His limbs burned with pain where groping tentacles had twined about his flesh before being slashed away, while his chest and face smarted from the touch of many darting tendrils whose tips needled into his skin like the envenomed stings of wasps. Worst of all, he felt waves of horror surging over him from *without* and realized that, despite the shielding disc on his brow, the thing was trying to overwhelm him with a deathly psychic attack.

"Die, demon!" he screamed, hacking and slashing.

The blade sheared deep into the thing's body beyond the flailing tentacles. Simon glimpsed the instantly cauterized edges of the yard-long wound trying to close as more fluid blackness welled viscously from within. Again came the booming bellow, which seemed to resound from all space rather than from any localized vocal organ, and then a dozen tentacles and pseudopods gripped Simon and began to haul him in toward the pulsing black monstrosity. He felt a flailing, whiplike tendril smack the left side of his head, heard the metallic band with its blue-glowing disc go clattering away across the floor—then cringed within himself as the waves of horror washed over his mind, their intensity increased tenfold.

"TASHMAD... TARTZAH... AZAG-THOTH...."

The thunderous words seemed to beat not so much on Simon's ears as on the very fibers of his entire nervous system. Frantically he slashed again at the wall of blackness, heedless of the myriad whipping tendrils, then held the Zarrian sword outthrust as, relentlessly, he was drawn forward into the tarry substance of the black amoeboid demon. The thing's flesh made little resistance, and Simon churned his burning blade within it, feeling suffocated by the vile stench of sizzling alien tissue. He saw a dull redness blossoming before him, wondered if his mind was going or if a Gate to the Hells might be opening to receive him....

Abruptly there was a roaring concussion, an explosion, greater than all the mighty boomings that had preceded it. Simon felt himself hurled violently back across the marble flags of the great hall, rolling and tumbling. He glimpsed the marble columns of the portico flash past him, lost his grip on the sword and heard it go clattering and keening down the marble stairs into the courtyard. Shaken, half dazed, he nevertheless rose instantly to his knees, desperate with the fear that the thing would abruptly be upon him again.

But, no—for to his astonishment—he saw within the Temple only a great black cloud, churning and boiling and filling up all the space of the great hall. Even as he watched it began to thin and dwindle, soon he saw that it was streaming rapidly back through the door of the Holy of Holies and into the pulsing Gate that yawned above the Ark. More, the rhythmic boomings that issued from that Gate were diminishing in volume, fading. . . .

"Baal!" gasped Simon, shaken to the core of his being. Never had he felt closer to doom—or, perhaps, worse than doom—than during that awful battle. Yet the wizard Taggart had been right—the being Gol-goroth had evidently had a material portion that could be destroyed. The great Zarrian sword had burned deep into its heart of darkness and now the thing was retreating back to the black Outside whence it had been summoned. Even as Simon realized these things, the last wisps of blackness vanished from the Temple; the Gate dwindled, then sank from sight within the Ark, and the drumlike pulsings faded altogether to silence—

A silence deep in contrast to what had gone before, complete save for the ringing left in Simon's ears from the thunders that had assailed them. And above him—was it his imagination or was the inky sky beginning to lighten to a deep twilight purple?

Slowly he got to his feet, every muscle aching, and looked down into the torchlit court. Blood seeped from dozens of small round wounds on his limbs and flanks, as if suckers like those of an octopus had rasped away skin, and he became aware of the burning pain of them. He wanted to shout out in agony—

Suddenly Simon's pain gave way to fear as he saw the great sword lying upon the flagstones, several yards out into the open courtyard. Its blade still gleamed with that silvery thread of power along its edges; smoke rose in a thin wisp from the spot where the point touched the stone. What had Taggart said . . .?

If the Zarrians sense interference, they will—

Simon hurried to the edge of the steps, knowing that it was imperative that he turn off the sword of power at once. It must not be left glowing under an open sky. . . .

In his haste his weakened legs buckled as he began his descent and he went tumbling down the short flight, again bruising his already battered and torn flesh. At the bottom he lay still for a moment, assuring himself that he had broken no bones, then rolled over and weakly strove to rise once more.

"By Hercules, Samaritan, you're a mess! I hardly recognized you."

Simon tensed as he recognized the giant gladiator Cratos standing only yards away from him, bald cranium and muscular limbs gleaming in the torchlight. The man's scarred, beefy face was split in a gloating grin—and directly at his feet lay the great Zarrian sword.

"So you got caught in the quake," continued Crator, "—trying to plunder the Judean god's temple, no doubt. It sounded like a thunderstorm in there—the place must be demolished! But what have we here—?"

"Don't touch it," gasped Simon as the gladiator stooped to grasp the Zarrian sword. "It is a weapon of the gods."

But Cratos had already picked up the thing and was hefting it appraisingly in both hands. A look of awe came into his eyes. "By Pallas, I believe you, Samaritan—never have I held a weapons such as this! Such balance—such beautiful dark steel! The mere touch of it makes me want to leap slashing into a band of foes! And that sheen of fire along its edges . . . did I not see its point burning into the very stone?" Suddenly he raised the blade, then swung it downward; its edge sliced keening through two tiles and part of another, spattering red sparks where it emerged. Cratos grinned with a mixture of awe and childish pleasure, then swung again, cutting the stone more deeply than before; sections of sundered flagstones flew upward, crackling and glowing redly.

"Ha! ha!" roared Cratos gleefully. "It is a sword of the gods indeed! Far too good, certainly, for a pig of Samaritan to own. Did you steal it from this barbarian fane, Simon of Gitta? Well, it looks like Fortuna has allowed it to pass to an owner more suited to it. Now, let's see how it works on human flesh."

Simon lay still save for deliberately feeble writhings, hoping the gladiator would think him completely helpless, knowing that his only hope lay in using his last reserves of strength in a sudden burst of speed and fighting skill. Little enough chance of victory or escape, he realized, but at least he would die fighting. Cratos took a step toward him—

Suddenly the air near the gladiator shimmered—a tall ovoid of bluish light, vaguely humanoid in outline and twinkling with a myriad pale sparks. Cratos whirled toward it—then bellowed in sudden terror at sight of the monstrous being that materialized out of the air beside him.

Simon gasped. Though Cratos was a far bigger man than most, the thing bulked hugely over him, glaring down at the gladiator with its two round, red-glowing eyes. Though somewhat humanoid in form, its proportions and musculature told Simon that it was not human, nor even anything earthly. It had no hips, its relatively short legs tapering abruptly downward from its massive torso, and its hairless skin was a very dark blue, almost black in the dim torchlight. Its head rose up as a great hump from its wide shoulders, with no trace of an intervening neck, and down the front of that head ran a ridge with many horizontal slits that might have been mouths or nostrils. The thing wore a skin-tight uniform of nearly the same hue as its flesh, and about its tapering waist was a wide belt of woven metal whose square clasp glowed with a dim blue phosphorescence.

"Devil from Tartarus!" roared Cratos, heaving the great sword aloft. "Die at the hands of Rome's greatest glad—"

Simon gasped again as the thing moved with a fluid, superhuman swiftness, gripping both of Cratos' wrists in one of its massive four-fingered hands. Bones cracked; the great sword went spinning away, clattering and keening in a shower of sparks on the flags. Cratos howled; his fingers swelled and split like cooked sausages under the pressure of the creature's grip, spurting blood. The thing's other hand swept around and clamped upon the gladiator's bald head as upon a doorknob. Cratos' howls rose in pitch, became an insane screech of agony—and then his entire skull caved inward with a loud grinding and crunching of bone and gristle.

Simon scarcely dared to breathe as he watched, between barely parted eyelids, the gladiator's body clatter to the flags, popped eyes dangling from their sockets by the optic nerves, puffed tongue protruding like a fat pickle.

For a moment the Zarrian stood motionless, human blood and brains dripping from the four thick digits of its right hand; then, in two long strides, it moved over to the sword and picked it up. Simon held his breath, hoping the thing would think him dead. Perhaps it did, for it was not advancing toward him, not even looking in his direction, merely standing straight and tall, sword held vertically in hand....

Then the thread of light vanished from the blade's edge, and in the next instant the great blue form of the being began to shimmer and sparkle, fading swiftly from sight. In another moment it was gone.

Simon sighed with relief, then rose shakily to his feet, casting wary glances all around. But the torchlit court was empty save for the body of Cratos, its pulped head staining the tiles with a dark and widening pool of gore. The sky, he now realized, was definitely taking on a lighter hue.

"Gods...." he muttered, awe and fear struggling within him.

He walked unsteadily over to the dead gladiator and removed the man's sword-belt, then strapped in on about his own waist. The sword was a good one, he noted, longer and heftier than the ones most Romans bore. Then, shuffling and hobbling as rapidly as his wounds and exhaustion would allow, he crossed the courtyard and hurried from it into the shadows of the northern colonnade, making for the outer gates that led to the safety of the dark streets beyond.

"Something has gone wrong," said Zethos, staring upward. "The sky is beginning to lighten. And the Master—he abides here still!"

Yosef of Aphairema made a mystic sign in the air with one gnarled forefinger. "Aye, it is no illusion. He abides indeed. What can have happened? Why does he not die?"

At these words the Roman centurion, who had been standing among the torches near the three crosses, strode a few paces down the mound toward the small group of watchers. "Not die, you say? Nonsense! Look at him—he's dead as butcher's meat. His soul would be across the Styx by now, save that I doubt he brought enough coin along to pay the boatman!"

Zethos thought he sensed an uneasiness behind the Roman's rough manner and tone of voice; certainly the events of these last few hours were enough to frighten even the most hardened veteran. He saw the centurion's face working angrily, noticed that his soldiers were pacing about nervously upon the mound, fingering their weapons almost as if they expected a surprise attack from some quarter. Zethos found that he could sympathize with them, for though he had served his old master and the rabbi Yeshua for over three years, he had never before seen such sorcery as he had seen this day.

This day? What day was it? Zethos wondered. For, though the sun was now declining toward the west, its return to brightness after the inky darkness gave it the aspect of the herald of a new dawn.

Then he heard the Lady Miriam saying, "It is true, O Father Yosef. The Master does not die. Apparently it is not yet his time, after all."

Her voice, low and even and calm, seemed to sting the centurion to a fury. "Not dead? *Not dead!"* He turned and strode back to the crest of the mound, then turned and pointed his spear at the drooping form of the man who hung limply from the central cross. "By Hades, my dark-haired beauty, I'll *show* you that he's dead! Watch. My commander bade me to make sure of it—like *this!"*

"No—!" gasped Zethos involuntarily.

The Roman turned and thrust his spear into the crucified man's flank just below the rib cage. The body did not quiver, but as the javelin was withdrawn Zethos saw that a fluid was gushing forth—not blood, but a thin pinkish ichor that trickled down rapidly. In the next instant the flow dwindled, and in the waxing sunlight he could see that the wound was diminishing, slowly drawing shut of its own accord.

"Vulcan's forge!" swore the officer, dropping his spear and quickly drawing back a pace. "Surely this man was the son of a god!"

"Centurion," said old Yosef sternly, striding forward, "your task is done. I must now ask that you have this man's body taken down, that I may give it a decent burial before sundown."

The Roman scowled down at him. "By whose authority?"

"That of Pilatus, Prefect of this province of Judea."

"Let me see the order."

"You know quite well," said the old priest sternly, "that Pilatus has given me authority in this matter."

"I know that you have some sorcerous influence over the prefect. Still, he has given me no direct order. I take my orders from Tribune Maxentius. If you want any of these bodies,"—he swept his hand toward the crucified trio, now darkly silhouetted against the brightening daylight—"you'll have to bring me the governor's written order."

Yosef turned and gazed toward the great Herodian palace, which loomed just beyond that portion of Jerusalem's wall, which lay immediately to the south of the mound. "I shall. Come, Zethos—Miriam—all of you. We must make haste."

For several minutes Zethos strode southward in silence beside his master, wondering as always at the ancient sage's energy and spryness. Behind him he could hear the centurion yelling to his solders to break the legs of the other two prisoners and thus hasten their demise, and it seemed to him again that the Roman's belligerent commands incompletely masked a tone of fear. Then he heard old Yosef saying in a low voice:

"There is a demon inside our Master, Zethos—one of those Castoran *Am-ha-erez*. It has cut off his pain and is keeping him alive."

Zethos nodded. "I suspected as much."

"That boy in the white Levite's robe brought it," continued the sorcerer. "Did you see what became of him?"

"Aye. He fled away toward the north immediately after the earthquake. No doubt he has by now entered the city through another gate, or hidden himself in the countryside."

Yosef pointed a lean, gnarled finger at the white dove that still perched on Zethos' shoulder. "Parakleitos, fly northward and search among the lanes and fields for the white-robed youth. If you find him, follow him; if not, await us amid the branches of the great terebinth-tree in the grove of the tombs. Go, now."

The bird cooed softly, bobbed its head, then flapped upward and sped rapidly away to the north.

When after a few more minutes the group had passed through an arched gateway into the city, Yosef halted his party near the wall and said, "Nicodemus, I want you to escort the Lady Miriam, her mother and these other ladies and their attendants back to the lodgings I have provided for them. See that your servants aid them in preparing for a journey."

"I take it, then," said Nicodemus, "that our plan has failed."

"Not quite yet, but time runs short. Should I indeed fail after all, then all these loyal followers of the Master must depart for Aphairema tomorrow morning as early as possible in order to avoid Annas' wrath. I shall send Zethos to you also, as soon as I may; he knows all the details concerning the arrangements I have made for the Bride and her entourage to journey to Caesarea and thence embark for Gaul. As for me, I shall join you when and if I am able, but do not wait for me." He turned to Zethos and muttered, "Send Joel and Reuben to purchase burial cloths as quickly as they can, then tell them to meet us back at this gate. Meanwhile, you and I shall visit the prefect Pilatus and remind him of his obligations."

While Zethos was conveying the burial-cloth order to the two young servants, Nicodemus said, "I shall do as you say, Yosef. After that, shall I return to the Hall of Gazzith and learn what I can concerning Annas' reaction to these events?"

"No, old friend." Yosef shook his head emphatically. "It would be too dangerous for you. Annas has surely guessed by now that it is we who have pre-empted him in his sorcerous schemes to gain power over all. No, you must go with these others to Aphairema also."

Nicodemus nodded—so readily, in fact, that Zethos realized that the old priest had already arrived at the same conclusion and was relieved to be disburdened of his dutiful offer.

"You seem nearly convinced, then, O My Father," said the Lady Miriam, "that my Lord's plan has failed and that Earth shall continue to abide."

Zethos' soul thrilled, as always, to the sound of that low, sweet voice. It was for her sake, even more than for that of his revered old mentor, that he had labored loyally these three years and more in the cause of this incomprehensible work of sorcery. Something deep within him had responded to her at their first meeting within the great old mansion at Aphairema—some affinity or affection that no other human, man or woman, had ever evoked in him before. It was not a sexual longing, nor a yearning for maternal love heretofore denied him, nor even a desire for the most profound sort of human friendship. It was, rather, the recognition—unlearned, instinctive, perceived—that he, the searching acolyte, had found the Goddess he had longed to serve and was destined to serve. And now, in this moment, his soul, vibrating in affinity with Hers, realized that She was not entirely displeased at the prospect of old Yosef's—and her Master's—failure.

"Rest assured, beloved daughter," said the old sorcerer, "that there is yet a good chance that your husband's will shall prevail, and that I shall do my best to see that it does. I am your servant and his, dedicated to the noble vision you both share—that all suffering upon this world should cease."

"Suffering—aye." The woman sighed. "There is far too much of it. I weary of it, and yet. . . ." She paused; then, "What would the Father bring in its place, should He conquer those evil Archons who first instituted it? Would He set as good a stage as this for us to play upon?"

Old Yosef drew himself up so that he seemed a foot above his usual height; he dark eyes glowered down upon the woman from beneath craggy white brows. "You know not what you say, daughter. Do you presume to counter the will of your husband and his . . . true Father?"

"Their will is to serve me," said Miriam calmly. "I thought that you had already learned that, beloved wise one."

Again Zethos thrilled to the woman's even, low voice. In that instant it seemed to him that they stood, he and Miriam and Yosef and all the rest of them, not in a gritty stone-flagged courtyard before one of Jerusalem's gates, but in a great hall of the cosmos-ruling gods. Then the thrill in his soul increased as he heard the voice of the queenly Miriam, enhanced as if by strange Olympian acoustics, continuing:

"I had a dream some nights ago, O my father, and today I met a young woman named Lotis who had shared my dream. I knew at once that she was in some sense *myself*—a True Spirit who has experienced the Goddess as fully as did I when the Master saved me from the possessing *Am-ha-arez*." She glanced up at the brightening sky, the ghost of a smile hovering at one corner of her lips. "That white-robed lad who gave my Lord to drink in his last agony—I think that *he*, too, recognized that Spirit, which manifests itself within the girl Lotis. And in myself."

Yosef's brows knotted, his craggy face glowering down upon Miriam like a storm cloud. "I do not know you, woman. Do you now declare, after all your pretense of support, that your deepest hopes are set against my will—and your Lord's?"

The woman laughed briefly, lightly. "You will is adamant, O my father. That I well know. Yet with all your wisdom, I think that you have not yet fathomed *his* deepest will, which is nothing less than to serve *me*. Did he not say that he had come to this world to destroy the things of the Female—the Goddess? Well, so he did, for at that time it was my will, also. I was ill with a vast melancholy, and it seemed to me that all the things of the Female—all Life, that is—were but a sick torture that must be done away with, as least as they manifested themselves upon such a flawed state as this Earth. Yet now, thanks to *him*, I am whole and wholesome once more. In addition, I carry *his* very life within me—a thing which even you approved, O my father, in case your first and most cherished plan, that of the Earth's destruction, should go awry."

"Fickle Spirit!" snapped Yosef. "You speak lightly, as though you had not been recently and most terribly bereaved. Have you no shame, no sense of duty—?"

"Fickle?" Miriam drew herself up with queenly pride, and Zethos thought he had never loved her more than in that moment. "Because my mind, my purpose, is not rock-hard like yours? You would kill all life, but I am She who judges whether any life is worth the living. My Lord, like Myself, has many forms; in his form upon the cross, he obeyed my will that life upon this world should cease from suffering; but now, in his form of the desperate young lad who would save his Lotis, he strives for life in spite of all suffering. In both cases, he works to please Me. For, what *is* there but mine own desire of the moment—ever changing, yet never truly changing—to give to life any meaning at all?"

"You are a harsh and cruel mistress," said Yosef, tears springing into his old eyes. "Yet I forgive you, for even though your Lord dies, you yet carry within your womb His renewed life."

"Forgive? You have power to forgive me only to the extent that you and my Lord are one and the same, as you well know. Yet this extent is greater than you may realize, O my father, and for this reason I gratefully accept your forgiveness. Without you and Him, my desire could never be embodied in Creation; without Me, that Creation would be without value or meaning."

Yosef waved his hand impatiently, as if to cast off invisible webs of illusion, then turned and strode off down a wide street, beckoning to his apprentice. "Come, Zethos. We must go to the palace of Pilatus. We haven't much time."

The young Greek followed his revered old mentor, his mind whirling from the things he had just heard.

And the aged priest, Nicodemus, weary to the point of exhaustion from the things he had experienced this day—or had it been a day and a night?—felt totally unable to untangle the cosmic web in which he had come to feel himself strangely entrapped. As he hurried through the narrow and twisting streets of Jerusalem, leading the troop of women and servants with whom he had been entrusted, he could feel only a growing anxiety, a foreboding as of monstrous and evil events impending.

Annas, together with a handful of his fellow priests who had not fled to their homes, gazed warily up into the twilit sky. The stars had faded and the sun was slowly resuming its wonted brightness. The small group stood in the southwest corner of the spacious Court of Gentiles, in front of the Hall of Gazzith from which they had recently fled during the earthquake, and from whose entrance a slight haze of dust still billowed. On a high ledge above the partially fractured portico perched a long row of owls, their yellow eyes blinking in the returning daylight.

"You did well, Caiaphas," said Annas, "to halt the rite of sacrifice and order the guards to clear the inner courts of the Temple. See, the darkness is now lifting and the drums of impending menace have ceased to beat."

"Yet something has gone very wrong," said Izhar of Chorazin, scowling from beneath his thick, iron-gray brows. "There was almost an opening of a Gate today, I think—and that many hours before the time you had planned for it."

"This is the doing of Yosef bar Hali and his fellow conspirator Nicodemus," growled Annas. "I know it. Yosef was not at the gathering today, and Nicodemus stole away early. Izhar, listen: as soon as night falls I want you to send forth your demon-familiar. Let the creature find and deal with that traitorous pair even as it has already dealt with Judah of Kerioth."

"No, Annas." Izhar glanced at a heavily curtained litter, which rested upon the flagstone of the courtyard, surrounded by several yellow-eyed guards in dark armor. "My . . . familiar . . . tells me that the premature opening of the Gate has caused certain stresses in the cosmic fabric, which make it dangerous for us to proceed with our plans. No one can now predict what might emerge during a reopening. I advise you to abandon this venture, Annas. For my part, I am going to depart for Chorazin this very moment, together with all my followers."

"You can't!" cried Annas angrily. "There is still a chance for us to succeed if we act before tomorrow's dawn. Consider the power we shall—"

"The risk is too great. Farewell, Annas bar Set, until such time as the stars shall come right again."

"That may not be for *centuries!* Listen, you fool, if we pass up this opportunity for unprecedented power—"

"Izhar is right, Annas," interrupted Tolmai of Capharnaum. "My inner companion has told me the same thing—that the Gate to the Hyades may now be slightly askew and that it would be dangerous to re-open it. What comes forth might not be that which we would summon."

"Traitors! *My* companion is not so cowardly. He was a mighty ruler once, until cast forth from the confederation of the Six Suns, and he would fain reclaim his power. In his view, the minions of Facula and Celaeno can still traverse the tunnel. At worst, the skewing of it may cause the other end to open upon mere emptiness, so that nothing comes forth. It is worth the chance."

Tolmai shook his head sadly. "You and your inner companion delude yourselves, I fear. No, I will accompany Izhar back to Galilee. Now that I know from your messengers that my son Nathanael is again safe and sane, having fled from the mad rabbi Yeshua, together with all the man's other disciples, I shall go back to Capharnaum and wait there for his return."

"And it would be well, Annas," said Izhar, "that we take back with us all those unopened coppery bowls, which you caused to be brought here from the vaults beneath Chorazin."

Annas started. "The bowls—the *Am-ha-arez*!" His face was suddenly white. "They were hidden within sealed tombs near the city. The earthquake—"

"What are you raving about? What damage can a few more of them do . . .?" Izhar suddenly scowled with suspicion. "Annas, just *how many* of the Earth Folk did you bring up to Jerusalem with you?"

"I . . . a hundred, perhaps. Or perhaps somewhat more. . . ."

"Idiot!" hissed the Rabbi of Chorazin. "And you call me traitor? You, who thought to form your own independent army of the Folk! And now, obviously, you fear that they may be bursting forth unbidden from their tomb-confinement." He turned and motioned to his black-cloaked guards. "Take up that litter, and bring mine around also. We depart for Chorazin immediately!"

Tolmai, too, called for his own attendants, who were waiting not far off in the gloomy courtyard. In a few minutes more, despite Annas' vociferous protests, the two Galilean rabbi-priests were being borne eastward in their litters, closely followed by the curtained palanquin in which was concealed the sinister cowled Faculan, toward the nearest gateway leading from the Temple precincts into Kidron Valley. More than half of the black-robed guardsmen marched away with them, and as they departed more than half of the owls perched above the portico of the Hall of Gazzith took wing and flew swiftly away toward the northeast.

"Fools!" Annas yelled after the group as they strode away amid the high, distant pillars of Solomon's Portico. "I will succeed! And when I have gained power over all things, you'll regret that you—"

"Let them go, O father," said Caiaphas, laying a hand on the old sorcerer's lean arm. "Perhaps Izhar is right. At least, let us proceed at this time with the greatest caution."

Annas nodded, his angry expression changing instantly to one of hard, even cold calculation. "You are right, my son, even though it is your cowardice speaking rather than your reason. I have long sensed that you have had doubts about this whole venture. Well, I will not ask that you continue to play any important part in it. Your task will now be a purely defensive one, just in case things should go awry. Take the rest of these priests who remain loyal to us and go back to our mansion in the southwest quarter of the city; see to it that the place is immediately fortified like a castle, with stout locks and planking ready to seal every door and window, and many guardsmen at the ready within."

"Fortified?" Caiaphas glanced about the wide courtyard nervously, peering into the pillared shadows even though the daylight had now increased considerably. "You mean—the *Am-ha-arez*?"

"If the earthquake has jarred some of them into wakefulness, they will surely wake others, then perhaps come into the city. And, of course, they will use whatever hosts they find available. . . ."

Caiaphas shuddered in spite of the rapidly returning warmth of the afternoon sunlight. "I see. I will do as you say, O father. But what of you?"

"I will take eight of these remaining guards and hasten right now to my villa upon the Mount of Olives. Send the rest forth, Caiaphas, and have them scour the city for Yosef of Aphairema; I shall order the owls to join in the search also. When the traitorous old plotter is captured, have him brought immediately to my villa. He must not be allowed to interfere further. Make haste."

Caiaphas bowed low in acknowledgment, then ordered the other priests and most of the Temple guards to follow him from the courtyard.

When they had gone, Annas gazed up at the pediment above his columned portico of the Hall of Gazzith, then uttered a few shrill syllables in an unknown tongue. Immediately a dozen large owls flew into the air, circled about uncertainly in the increasing daylight, then wheeled and flapped away in different directions toward the various quarters of Jerusalem.

CHAPTER XXIX

"Gods of Tartarus!" exclaimed the centurion, Marcus, gazing down in awe at the dead gladiator. "His head's been crushed like an egg! What could have done it?" He glanced nervously westward across the twilit courtyard toward the looming white mass of the Temple. "Perhaps we should leave this place, Commander."

Maxentius shook his head. "No," he said, gazing steadily into the Temple's high, torchlit entrance. "Cratos apparently ran afoul of whatever demon caused the disturbance we heard, but it seems the danger is now past. Listen—the drums have ceased their pounding utterly. I was right—Annas sought to preempt us all by sacrificing the mad rabbi on the mound to Gol-goroth, but now Centurion Longinus has thwarted that plot with a simple spear-thrust."

"I don't understand, sir."

"Never mind, Marcus." Maxentius turned to the six legionaries who bore the empty litter. "Come on, men. We're going into that temple."

The soldiers obediently followed him, though with some unvoiced trepidation, up the stairway and through the high, column-flanked portal. Marcus fingered his sword-haft nervously as he glanced about the great lamplit space, searching the shadows. A strange, foul odor pervaded the hall, while all down its center extended an irregular dark stain, rapidly evaporating as a fine dusky mist, as if something huge and slimy had crawled down its entire length. Here and there lamps, braziers and gilded furniture lay randomly upon the tiles, evidently having been violently knocked about.

Maxentius, suddenly spying a band of woven blue metal, stooped and picked it up. The small silvery disc it supported seemed to glow with a faint bluish light of its own.

"Aha! Look, Marcus—this metallic weave is of the same sort as the wizard's belt I wear. Yet its size would suggest that it should be worn as a headband rather than a belt. What do you think?"

"I think we should be careful of it, sir."

Maxentius, however, slipped the band over his head without hesitation. As he adjusted it so that the disc rested upon his brow he felt a sudden qualm of fear that seemed almost to come to him from *without*. Instantly he felt angry with himself for feeling it.

"I'm sorry, sir," said Marcus, "but why are you angry with me?"

"What? I'm not—" Suddenly it hit him and he laughed aloud. "Why, Marcus, it's *your* fear I feel, not mine! I mean . . . I felt your fear and now you sense my anger. How strange!"

"Fear?" The centurion shook his head. "Not I, sir—although I admit that I do have some qualms about our being in this place."

"Ha! It's fear, all right. And I can feel it from the rest of you men, too. But don't worry that I'll think you cowards, for I can sense your determination also. Good soldiers, all of you. But by Pallas!—this thing lets me sense your very feelings, and evidently projects some of mine to you as well."

"I'd suggest you take it off, sir. It could be dangerous."

"Of course—you don't want me reading your thoughts." Maxentius grinned as he took of the thing and put it away in his belt pouch. "Another wizard tool. It will aid me greatly when I perform the rites this night—I'll be able to sense the intentions of whatever beings come through the Gate. Come on, now, let's collect the rest of this wizard gear. Follow me."

Maxentius led the group of soldiers down the great hall, around the altar near its end and through the doorway that gaped beyond. Marcus glanced with some uneasiness at the charred edges of what appeared to be two halves of a curtain that had concealed the portal. Then they stepped into a cubical chamber about thirty feet on a side, and the centurion and his men gasped at sight of two gleaming red eyes hanging motionless in the gloom near the far wall.

"Don't worry, men," said Maxentius. "Bring a lamp here, one of you."

When the light was fetched, Marcus saw that the gleaming eyes were set in a golden, life-sized ass's head resting upon a cubical altar. On the floor directly before it rested what seemed an elaborately gilded chest fitted with golden loops for carrying-poles; beside it lay its lid, surmounted by two winged golden demons facing one another.

"You are privileged, men," said the tribune, laughing. "This is the Judean Holy of Holies, and we are the first Romans to stand within it since Pompeius Magnus conquered Jerusalem nearly a century ago. Look—before you lies the sacred Ark, by means of which the traitor Annas hoped to invoke demons to his aid, and beyond it rests the ass-headed Eidolon of Set."

"The thundering drums," said Marcus. "Are *these*, then, the things that caused them?"

"Aye. But they shall serve me now. They—and *this!"* Maxentius strode around the Ark and lifted a small gleaming object that lay upon the altar before the Eidolon of Set. "The *byakhtril,* which summons demons. With this, together with the elixir I took from the Samaritan woman, I can both perceive and command the things I shall call up to serve me." He quickly slipped the small metal cylinder into his pouch to join the bluish headband. "Now, Marcus, help me lift this lid and put it back on the Ark."

The centurion did so, and as they lifted the thing into place Marcus thought he glimpsed, within the Ark, a jumble of unearthly gleaming shapes suggestive of alien geometries. And did he, just before the concealing lid slid over those shapes, catch the faint sound of distant drumlike boomings from the Ark's interior . . .?

"Good! And now, men, get those carrying-poles from the corner. And put that ass-headed eidolon into the litter. Between the eight of us we can carry it and the Ark out of here. Hurry, now—the gloom is lifting outside. We want to be on our way across the Kidron Valley before Annas and Caiaphas discover that we've looted their priestly lair."

The men obeyed with alacrity. Yet, as they hurried with their burdens away from the Temple and across the twilit courtyard where lay the dead gladiator, his blood now mingling with that of the sacrificed bulls and goats lying near the great altar, Marcus again felt grim forebodings and wondered what monstrous events his commander's strange, un-Roman obsession was soon to bring about.

Menander crept out of the dense shrubbery from which he had been watching the Romans who paced nervously upon the knoll. Noting the increasing daylight, he stole farther away to the north and presently found himself within the tree-shaded boundaries of an old cemetery—a place where tombs, carved like caves into the very substance of rock outcroppings and sealed with great stone discs that resembled coins standing on edge, brooded within a grove of ancient oaks and terebinths. Glancing back toward the south, he noted that the three crucified men still hung motionless, their forms pale and stark, from his vantage, against the dark battlements of Jerusalem's wall.

"Carbo, old friend," he muttered to himself, "I won't leave here until I see what they do with the body in which I caused you to be trapped!"

He watched the Roman soldiers moving about upon the mound of Gol -goroth, saw that they were beginning to take down two of the crosses and remove the bodies from them. Yet the middle cross remained upright. Did that mean that the Romans realized that the rabbi Yeshua might still be alive . . .?"

Then he spied a group of four men approaching the Romans from the direction of the Herodian palace. They joined the Roman soldiers, and one of the group—the bent, black-robed old man whom Menander recognized as the sorcerer Yosef of Aphairema—handed the officer in charge a piece of parchment. Immediately after scanning it, the officer barked an order and the soldiers began to take down the cross. In a few minutes more the body on it had been unfastened, wrapped in shrouds by the group of four, then lifted by them and carried rapidly toward the graveyard in which Menander crouched concealed. As the group approached Menander drew back amid the trees, then turned and hurried away from the tombs. He knew he must find a new spot of concealment, watch the approaching group, find a way to liberate his friend Carbo if that were at all possible. . . .

Then, as he stole silently through the graveyard, he suddenly noticed a tomb whose stone disc had fallen outward from the entrance—evidently the result of the earlier earth tremor. Within the black entryway he caught the gleam of coppery metal and, pausing to look more closely, saw what seemed to be a large number of hemispherical bowls tumbled about within. A shock of fear jolted him, for these were not ordinary bowls, but metallic hemispheres such as he had seen within the synagogue of Chorazin. And—did he now detect a dark movement amid them, as if great sluggish worms crawled about in the gloom . . .?

Then Menander saw that the group of four were rapidly approaching the grove in which he was concealed, bearing with them the shroud-wrapped body of the crucified rabbi. Hastily he drew away and hid himself in the most shadowy part of the grove, then crouched and watched in tense silence.

"Here—here is the tomb," croaked Yosef of Aphairema, gasping for breath. "We are in time, for the sun is still well above the horizon. Joel—Reuben—wait here, outside; the eyes of the uninitiated must not witness the Passing of Azazel. Zethos, help me carry the Master within."

The young Greek regarded the open tomb with some uneasiness. In that moment its black mouth seemed, to his imagination, to gape like an entrance to Tartarus. To the left of it rose a great shady terebinth tree, its roots humping like thick serpent-coils from the earth and groping into crevices in the rock outcrop; to the right rested the heavy stone disc, poised on its edge, ready to be rolled down its stone trough to seal the tomb. Fortunately it had remained in place during the recent earthquake—but, thought Zethos, what if another tremor should cause it to roll down while he and old Yosef were inside . . .?

"Hurry, Zethos—help me," urged Yosef. "I cannot carry the Master by myself."

Overcoming his qualms, Zethos aided his old mentor in hauling the body inside. It was bulky and heavy—and, the young man thought, somewhat more soft and resilient than a human body should be. Within the tomb was a single shelf of rock whose surface was at about the height of a man's knees, and upon this the old sage and his assistant managed with some labor to lay the body of their former master.

"Now you may go, Zethos, if you wish," said Yosef, panting.

The young man nodded and turned away. At the entrance, however, curiosity overcame his uneasiness; he turned and saw that his old mentor was unwrapping the shroud that had concealed the body. In the gloom he could barely make out the bloodied, somewhat goatish features of the face. Strange how those great dark eyes, now open, still seemed to gleam with life. . . .

Then Zethos' spine tingled, for he realized that the Teacher was not quite dead after all. Incredibly, his body was beginning to twitch silently and spasmodically. Then his chest heaved as though he were trying to draw a deep breath. The lips writhed; the beard that straggled from the receding chin began to tremble; then, without turning or raising his head, the man began to mumble words of a language Zethos could not understand:

"N'gai, n'gha'ghaa, bugg-shoggog, y'hah: Yog-Sothoth. . . ."

"I hear, O Master," said Yosef. Then, standing erect and drawing back a pace, the old man drew forth an object from beneath his dark cloak. Zethos saw that it was a small silvery cylinder that seemed to glow very slightly in the gloom. Yosef held it out at arm's length, leveled it toward the man on the stone slab, then intoned in a loud voice, "Now, O demon of the Six Suns, *come out of him!*"

The small cylinder increased its glow and emitted a high, shrill keening; to Zethos it seemed more like a ringing in the ears than an external sound. He saw that the Master's chest abruptly ceased to heave; a deathly change came over the goatish face as the great dark eyes seemed almost to shrink inward, the light within them suddenly vanishing like a lamp-flame in the wind. In the next moment Zethos saw a dark shadow seeping from beneath the shroud—saw it slither down to the floor and writhe quickly toward the far end of the tomb, where it bunched itself into an oblate mass, pulsing like a giant slug.

The whining ceased, but old Yosef kept the cylinder trained threateningly upon the blob-thing, which did not try to venture from the corner where it huddled.

Then Zethos gasped, appalled to see that the body on the slab was rapidly shrinking and disintegrating. The face was no longer a face, but a melting white mass; the shroud was collapsing, and from beneath it oozed a whitish fluid that rilled down sluggishly from the stone slab in many streams, puddling upon the tomb floor. A frightful, alien stench suddenly choked the small chamber.

"Farewell, O Master," said old Yosef. "Now, truly it is done!"

Zethos turned and dashed from the tomb, terrified and sickened. He saw Reuben and Joel staring at him in dumb fright. Then, turning, he beheld his old mentor emerging from the dark doorway, his lined face expressing sadness combined with grim purpose.

"Close the tomb," the old man rasped. "Quickly, all three of you—put your shoulders to it!"

They obeyed, galvanized by the urgency in his voice. Beneath the force of their combined strength the great disc of stone slowly rocked forward, then ponderously rolled down its rocky slot and thundered into place, sealing the tomb.

"Good," said old Yosef, panting as if he, too, had taken part in the exertions. "The Passing of Azazel is accomplished, and still in time! Yet my work is not finished. Zethos, return now with Joel and Reuben to Jerusalem and rejoin your mistress and Nicodemus. If I do not return there tonight, be ready to depart for Aphairema with all the others at the first light of day."

"But what of you, O Mentor? Where do you—?"

Just then there came a flutter of wings overhead. Zethos glanced up, saw that the white dove had just settled upon the lowest branch of the great terebinth.

"Did you find the spying youth?" asked the old wizard.

The bird cooed and shook its head slightly.

"Well, no matter. All is accomplished here. Fly now, Paracleitos, to the villa of Annas. Observe all that is happening there. I will join you there before the sun sets."

The white dove cooed again, then flapped into the air and sped away eastward, vanishing finally behind the city's looming wall.

"You go to confront Annas, then?" said Zethos uneasily.

The old mage nodded. "I must go first to the Temple, then to the Mount of Offense, there to accomplish that which was to be the task of Gol-goroth."

"The task of aiding the Brother in the opening of the Greater Gate?" muttered Zethos. "Surely no mortal man could survive such a thing!"

Yosef shrugged. "What care I for that? If I succeed, all beings upon this world shall cease to know suffering, and if I do not—well, better then that I should perish! If you live to see tomorrow's dawn, Zethos, you will know that I have failed. In that event, you must consider yourself my successor and bend all your energies to ensuring that the Master's seed shall be passed on down the generations. Good luck to you, my loyal servant."

The embraced briefly, and then old Yosef turned and strode away eastward, following a winding path which led out of the grotto of tombs toward the nearest of Jerusalem's gates. Zethos, watching him go, experienced a sad, sinking feeling within his heart.

"I pray for your survival, old mentor," he muttered softly to himself. "But I find that I can no longer pray for your success. May our Mistress' will, not our Master's, be done!"

Beckoning to Joel and Reuben, he led them back southward, past the knoll of Gol-goroth and on toward where the Herodian palace loomed beyond Jerusalem's crenellated wall, thankful that the two young servants had not seen what he had seen within the tomb. For, though he had long known that the man he had called "Rabbi" was only partly human, he realized now that the really human portion, despite outward appearances, must have been very small indeed.

When the four had gone, Menander stole cautiously from the shadows of the trees and approached the sealed tomb. Placing one hand upon the edge of the great stone disc, he felt deftly with the other for any crevice, however slight, between it and the tomb. There was none.

"Carbo?" he called softly, bending close toward where the disc's edge touched the tomb's rock face. *"Carbo!"*

There was no sound from within. Menander turned and put his back to the disc's edge, then braced his feet against the thick trunk of the gnarled terebinth and pushed with all his strength. The great stone did not budge in the slightest. After several more such attempts he ceased, trembling from his efforts, his mind anxiously turning over other possibilities. Perhaps if he could find a fallen tree branch, use it for a lever. . . .

I'll get you out somehow, Carbo!

He turned back toward the shadowy grove, and suddenly saw movement there. A human figure, and behind it the gaping black doorway of an open tomb. The figure was lurching forward, occasionally half stumbling, and Menander decided that it must be one of the gardeners, no doubt under the influence of wine. He took a step forward and said, "Good sir, you must help me! My friend has been accidentally trapped living within this tomb—"

Then the figure lurched forth from the shadows—and Menander froze in horror. The thing had eyes like peeled onions, and flesh that was unnaturally pallid and covered with dark pustules of oozing rottenness. A corpse, clad in white tomb-cerements—and now, behind it in the shadows, other lurching and white-shrouded figures were becoming visible. . . .

Menander yelled, whirled and bounded away. Then, even as he ran, a memory struck him—a vision of bloblike things crawling amid coppery bowls within an opened tomb— and suddenly he understood. He stopped and looked back, saw the thing lurching stiffly after him down the path, arms outstretched and clutching, while behind it a number of similarly animated liches were emerging from the cemetery shadows. Despite the horror the things inspired in him, Menander stood his ground, fumbled within the black pouch that Taggart had given him and drew forth a small silvery cylinder. Leveling this item at the approaching corpse, he pressed its near end with his thumb as the wizard had instructed him. A high whine, barely audible, shrilled from the object—and instantly the lich collapsed upon the path, twitching and shuddering. Then it grew still as a greenish, melon-sized blob-thing flowed from its pores, elongated itself and crawled away in the shadow of a boulder.

But the other corpses still came on, arms outstretched and eyes hideously upturned, while behind them still more were emerging from the tomb- grove. . . .

Menander turned and ran, not looking back until he was well out of the cemetery and half way to the Jerusalem wall. Then, pausing, he shielded his eyes from the westering sun and scanned the grove anxiously. He could see no movement. His flesh crawled at the memory of the things he had just escaped from. Yet there were now a few people coming and going along the roadways in the renewed sunlight, and that made him feel a bit easier. Turning eastward, he strode rapidly to the nearest gate and entered the city, then made his way through Jerusalem's narrow and winding lanes as rapidly as the increasing the agitated crowds would allow.

After about half an hour he came to the familiar synagogue presided over by Samezer. Mounting the steps to its small pillared portico, he saw that its doors were closed. Then a young man stepped out of the shadows of the porch and demanded, "Who comes?"

"Is that you, Parmenion?" cried Menander. "Do you not know me?"

"Menander! We had nearly given you up for lost." The young man wrenched open the double doors, beckoned Menander to follow him within, then called out, "Master Samezer, Menander is here!"

Menander, following the youth into the dimly-lit synagogue, saw a short figure hurrying toward them, recognized the catlike features of the little rabbi. Samezer clutched Menander's hands in his own and said, "Thank the White Goddess that you are safe!"

"I fear I have little time, sir." Menander glanced about the lamplit gloom, saw that many other members of the Thirty were present also. Across the pillared hall, on the women's side of the synagogue, he noticed about a dozen young girls dressed in the gowns of Temple virgins, together with a number of matrons. The sight of them made him think of Lotis, but he did not see her or Elissa among them.

"Lotis is with Dositheus in one of the rear chambers," said Samezer in response to the young man's unspoken question. "They are attending to Simon, who has been grievously wounded."

"Simon wounded? What happened?"

"I and others of the Thirty were hastening through the dark streets to the Temple to rescue Elissa and Lotis. On the way we met a number of matrons who feared for their virgin charges who, they said, were in danger from Roman soldiers in the Temple—"

"Romans—*there?*"

"Aye. Evidently the sacrilegious audacity of Tribune Maxentius knows no bounds. Well, no sooner had we directed the matrons to this synagogue and continued on our way than we encountered their charges, the Temple virgins, who were hastening toward us in terror, claiming that they had encountered an angel with a fiery sword—only Lotis, who was with them, whispered to me that that 'angel' was Simon. And not long after that, we met Simon himself staggering through the dark streets, half fainting from many wounds, so we carried him here. Come, I will take you to him."

Menander followed the little rabbi to a room at the back of the synagogue. As he entered the lamplit chamber Lotis, who had been bending over a cot where Simon lay, set aside a basin of water and some towels and ran to embrace the youth. "Oh, Menander, you are safe! Did you accomplish what you hoped to?"

"I think so." He glanced toward the cot. "How is Simon?"

"In great pain. He has many wounds—"

"Yet he will recover," said Dositheus, who was bending close over Simon's reclining form. "He is conscious and his wounds are all shallow. As soon as we finish poulticing them I shall give him a draught to lessen the pain and allow him to sleep."

"No!" protested Simon, rising on one elbow. "Gol-goroth is repulsed for a time, yet a monstrous doom continues to threaten the world—you have said so yourself. I cannot rest until the threat is ended. Is that Menander who just entered?"

The young man stepped forward and stood beside the cot. "I am here, Simon."

Simon grinned up at him, but Menander could see the pain behind the grin. He was appalled to see the extent to which red welts, dark bruises and shallow cuts covered the man's limbs and chest.

"Good lad! Did you accomplish the wizard's task, then?"

"Yes, but . . . gods! What happened to you?"

"A little fight—one which I fear is not over yet. Listen, Menander, I have a message for you from the wizard Taggart. You are to wait until the last hour of the day, then press the 'location' inset on a device he gave you. Does that make sense?"

"I . . . yes. I remember. The wizard gave me four things and instructed me in their use. But the 'location' inset was to be pressed only in the event that I could not return to our agree-upon location, or in an emergency."

"Evidently it's an emergency, then." Simon strove to rise, then grimaced in pain and fell back. "Gods, I need a new skin! Dositheus, bring me wine. I can't just continue to lie here while—"

"Hold still," snapped Dositheus. "Let Lotis finish swabbing your wounds. This poultice will ease the pain." He glance dup at Menander. "What were those other things the wizard Taggart gave you, lad?"

Menander drew two tiny objects from his dark pouch. "He said these were medicine, O Mentor. The dark oblong capsule aids in healing wounds, the white circular one restores strength for a time."

"What are they called?"

"The wizard called the dark one *antibiotic*—"

"'Antilife'?" Dositheus eyed the capsule uncertainly.

"He said it heals inflamed wounds. And the other, he said, is a 'Rigellian' drug called *krax*, which is dangerous if used often. I was to take both if I became wounded or exhausted during my quest."

Dositheus nodded knowingly, though he was sure had had never heard of either medicine before. "Good. Give them to me, Menander, for as things have turned out, Simon has more need of them than do you. And now, the last hour of the day has come, so you had better go and finish doing the sky-wizard's bidding. Yet, stay—you mentioned a fourth object?"

"Aye, this." Menander pulled a small silvery cylinder from the pouch. "You recognize it, O Mentor, I am sure. It causes the blob-creatures to leave the bodies of those they inhabit."

Dositheus grimaced at unpleasant memories. "I remember. And have you had occasion to use it?"

"Indeed I have." Menander quickly told of the things he had seen in the cemetery outside the northwestern walls of the city, and of his narrow escape from the walking dead.

"Gods of doom!" exclaimed Dositheus. "And you say that you saw many of those coppery bowls within a tomb whose door had been shaken down? Surely Annas or Izhar had them brought here from Galilee, and doubtless they have hidden other such bowls in yet more tombs. Those *Am-ha-arez* who have escaped will no doubt try to free all the rest, and should they succeed and manage to enter the city. . . ." The old man rose. "Samezer, we had best see to sealing and fortifying this synagogue most thoroughly."

"Here, then," said Menander, placing the little cylinder in his mentor's wrinkled hand. "You may need this more than I. Look here's how it works: point *that* end of it toward the possessed one, then press *this* end with your thumb."

"I see. Do you have another such device, then, Menander?"

"No—but where I'm going, I won't need it."

"And where might that be, lad?" asked Simon.

Menander glanced toward the ceiling. "Up on the roof of this synagogue. Taggart said it would help if I were in an open place beneath the sky when I pressed the 'location' inset, though it wasn't absolutely necessary. Where is the stairway?"

"Come, I will show you," said old Samezer.

Moments after bidding farewell to his friends, Menander emerged from the stairway and stood upon the synagogue's flat roof. The sun had declined far toward the west, causing the great western wall to cast its broad shadow over much of the city. A chill breeze had sprung up, and Menander shuddered slightly—partly in memory of what had happened in the cemetery. But he could not see over the city's high wall to those tombs and the mound of Gol-goroth.

As he turned to bid Samezer farewell he was surprised to see Lotis emerge from the stairway and advance toward him across the rooftop.

"Menander, why have you come up here?"

They embraced again, and then he said quietly, "You must now stand well away from me, Lotis—and you, too, Samezer. I go now."

"By sorcery this time, Menander?" she asked.

He nodded. "As before. But I will return soon, Lotis, I promise it."

"Only the Goddess can know that."

"This bodes to be an evil night," said Samezer nervously. "Should we all survive it, I and the rest of the Thirty plan to leave this dark-fated city at dawn and return to Aenon. Therefore do not return here, Menander, but meet us east of Bethany at the knoll where the road begins its descent to Jericho."

"I shall." Menander drew the small black box from its pouch and pressed the inset as he had been bidden. "Farewell, Lotis, Samez—"

Then he again felt the strange tingling all over his body. For an instant he saw his two companions staring at him wide-eyed, Lotis with one hand raised to her open mouth in shocked surprise—

And then the world was gone.

Yosef of Aphairema, entering through the high portal of the Temple, was surprised to find the place as empty of life as the wide courtyard outside. Slowly he advanced, his footsteps ringing hollowly within the great hall. A strange, alien odor hung faintly on the air, while the golden tables and articles of ritual lay scattered randomly about on the marble flags as if a great struggle had taken place.

Rounding the altar at the hall's end, he peered through the door into the Holy of Holies, whose sundered and charred veil no longer protected it from unauthorized eyes—and gasped. The Ark was no longer there, nor the ass-headed Eidolon of Set that had stood upon the stone cube behind it.

"Annas, you fool!" he muttered to himself. "Have you then removed these things to your own villa?"

But, no, Annas would not have taken them there, for he was too well versed in the warnings contained in Mattan's *El-Halal*; he knew the danger of moving the things too close to the spot where the Great Gate would open. Could it be, then, that Dositheus and others of the Thirty had stolen the Ark and the Eidolon, hoping to hide them and thereby forestall the world's doom . . .?

Yosef smiled. It did not matter. The Gate *would* open this very night, for the Goat of Azazel had suffered mighty agonies and had finally passed through the portals of death. Nothing could reverse that. In a few hours, when the sky-axis that linked the Bull and the Dragon again aligned itself with the global location of Jerusalem, the Gate would again open, and this time with consequences more vast than even Annas could anticipate.

Returning to the courtyard, the old sorcerer saw that several dark-cloaked Temple guardsmen were standing there as if waiting for him. In the late afternoon daylight he could not make out the hue of their eyes, but sensed from their silence and motionlessness that they were possessed ones.

"Come with us, Yosef of Aphairema," said the leader of them stiltedly. "Annas summons you to his villa. Do not resist."

"Resist?" snorted Yosef contemptuously. "I go to the villa even now, to call Annas to account for his stupidities. Fetch me a litter at once, dogs, and carry me there with all speed!"

The guards stiffly nodded their assent, showing no annoyance, and went to do as the old man had bidden them. In a few minutes more they were bearing him out of the splendid eastern gateway from the Temple precincts and down the wide stone stairs that descended into the Kidron Valley.

After a half hour of rapid marching they attained the crest of the opposite ridge near the southern wall surrounding Annas' estate, and here they overtook another small group of Temple guards bearing a similar litter. Both parties stopped, and Yosef felt his palanquin being set down upon the ground. Slowly he got out and stood erect, then saw that Annas had emerged from his litter also.

"Traitor," said the ancient priest, "you have failed to thwart me, and now you shall interfere no more."

Yosef smiled slightly behind his white beard. "Did you bring the Ark and the Eidolon of Set up here, Annas?"

"What? I am no fool. Would I risk—?" He suddenly stopped speaking, scowled and then demanded, "Why do you ask such a thing?"

"Because those items are no longer in the Temple. I suspect that Dositheus and the Thirty may have carried them away. But it does not matter. At sundown the Drums of Chaos shall again begin their first faint pulsings, and before midnight the Gate shall again begin to open, this time to release the hounds of doom upon all the earth. Think not to stop the process, Annas, for it is inexorable and irreversible. The Goat of Azazel has suffered and died before sundown on this day of days; soon night shall come and the peace of death shall settle upon the world."

Annas glanced fearfully toward the sky, then westward toward the city whose walls and towers now cast long shadows beneath the declining sun. But then, turning again to Yosef, he laughed harshly. "Fool! Do you think to daunt me with your lies?" He beckoned to the black-armored Temple guardsmen. "Come—follow me, all of you, and bring this vile croaker along as well."

The entered through an archway into the grounds of the villa and hurried down a winding pathway among the trees, Yosef being ushered along roughly by two of the guards. In a moment they stood before a small stone cubicle of a hut in whose western side an oaken door stood ajar.

"Put him in there," said Annas. "Lock it securely and guard it well—he's full of wizard tricks. The rest of you, follow me."

"Fool!" cried Yosef, a touch of exultation in his voice. "You seek power, but doom shall be your lot—yours, and all others'. Rejoice, O all ye afflicted of the earth, for soon ye shall be blessed with mercy and know peace!"

"We shall see." Annas motioned to his guards, then strode on toward his mansion, grinning with angry satisfaction as he heard the hut's door slam solidly shut, cutting off the old sorcerer's ravings. "Lunatic!" he muttered to himself. "It's too bad Izhar's demon-familiar is no longer in there to keep you company. . . . *Aiee!* What is *this?*"

Soldiers were coming forth from the back portico of the mansion—Roman soldiers, perhaps a score of them, with Tribune Maxentius striding and grinning at their head.

"Greetings, old buzzard. I thought you'd soon be showing up here."

Annas clenched his fists in frustration and cursed under his breath. More complications! Would they never cease . . .?

CHAPTER XXX

Again Menander glimpsed the alien metallic vistas, felt for a second time the odd prickling sensation as those vistas faded—and then found himself standing in the middle of the wizard's sky craft. Around him stretched desert hills lit by the westering sun—and was it his imagination or did that sun seem a trifle closer to the horizon than it had a few seconds earlier . . .?

He heard a shout and turned eastward, saw trees and a pool, recognized the oasis at which he and Ilione and Taggart had earlier rested. Taggart was striding in his direction, while behind the man—

Menander gasped. The object which loomed beyond the wizard at the edge of the oasis was nothing that could have been made by man. It was huge, flattish and circular, at least a hundred feet in diameter and of a silvery grayish-green color. Its shape was that of a very flattened bell, its bottom side resting upon the sand; the smooth, graceful curve of its upper portion was split by a dark vertical aperture from which a finely corrugated ramp of dark metal descended to the ground.

"Menander!" said Taggart as he hurried up to his sky craft. "Were you successful?"

"I think so." The youth held out the black box he carried. "It was difficult, but—"

"Good. We still have time." Taggart snatched the box, turned and hastened toward the looming bell-dome structure. As he reached the foot of the ramp Menander gasped again, for a being emerged from the vertical aperture of the dome—an unhuman being. Though humanoid in general outline, it towered to at least nine feet and its "skin" gleamed with the same silvery-greenish luster as the surface of the structure from which it had emerged. Somehow Menander sensed that this entity, whose very movements suggested a godlike power and confidence, was something greater than a biological organism. Beneath a narrow, visor-like band across the front of its domed head gaped a rectangular cavity, but there were no other facial features. Within the blackness of that cavity burned two points of light like eyes of living flame.

Taggart ran up the ramp and handed the black box to the metallic giant, who then turned about and walked back through the aperture. The wizard followed.

Menander shuddered despite the desert heat, then climbed from Taggart's craft and stood on the pebbly ground. As he did so he saw a figure approaching him from the direction of the tree-shadowed oasis—the squat, brown-robed form of his old mentor Daramos.

"Gods!" exclaimed the youth, forgetting his usual respectful form of address. "Daramos, what *is* that bell-shaped thing?"

"A sky craft," said the dwarf, "one much superior to the one Taggart uses. It came down from the invisible ship which he told us of, and the tall being you just saw is one of those whom he calls 'Galactics', because they rule over every star of the Milky Way. They are minions of the Elder Gods, and Taggart now aids them in order that life upon this world may be spared."

"Gods!" repeated Menander, awed almost to numbness. "Is there no power of magic beyond the knowledge of this wizard, that he may summon such demons?"

Daramos blinked slowly, thoughtfully. "Taggart knows much indeed, yet there are things he knows not of—things which the knowledge of his homeland, great as that was—or, rather, will be—could not see or acknowledge. Come, Menander, and I will show you one of those things."

They walked to the shade of the oasis and stood near the clear pool. While the youth knelt and drank, Daramos opened a cloth-wrapped bundle and drew forth a wide bronze bowl engraven with ancient Persian characters. With this he scooped up water. Then he laid the bowl on the ground and stood quietly above it, calmly contemplating the subsiding ripples within.

Menander rose. "What are you doing, O Mentor?"

"I am regarding the essence of the One Who Manifests," said the mage. "Quiet your mind, Menander, in the way that I have taught you."

The youth closed his eyes for a few minutes, breathing evenly and ever more slowly, then knelt beside the venerable dwarf and gazed into the bowl. The water in it was now unruffled, still.

"What do you see there, Menander?"

"Sky . . . palm-fronds . . . our two faces. . . ."

"Regard the essence, O Acolyte—the essence of the One who transcends all transient forms."

Menander began to see it now—a faint silvery haze outlining and limning the reflection of his face and that of Daramos—and marveled. The silvery sheen grew brighter—a frame of light following the outlines of their bodies, the inner edge bright, the outer portion dimming to indistinctness.

"The aura of the True Spirit," said Daramos calmly. "We have it, you and I, and so do Simon, Dositheus and Ilione. So, too, I am sure, does the girl Lotis of whom you have told me—else, you and she would not have sensed the true nature of one another."

"Lotis . . . Dositheus. . . ." said Menander dreamily. "They are with Simon, who is badly hurt. . . ."

Even as he spoke he saw the reflection in the bowl fade and a new image take its place. He saw Simon lying abed in a lamplit room, face twisted in pain, while Lotis and Dositheus hovered over him, tending his wounds, concern in their faces. About the three of them glimmered silvery auras, the out outlining Simon's form a bit dimmer than the other two and pulsating faintly.

"He is hurt indeed," said Daramos, "but he will live. Yet, where is the other woman you told me of—the mistress of this Lotis? You have said that she, too, is very devoted to Simon."

"I do not know, O Mentor. I did not see her at Samezer's synagogue, and I had no time to inquire."

"Think of her," said the ancient mage. "Call up your remembrance of her. My heart tells me that it is very important."

Menander recalled Elissa's face and form, comely and shapely—and suddenly he saw her within the water's surface. She lay upon a floor of smooth tiles, bound hand and foot with cords, wearing but a brief tunic of white linen. Fear shone in her dark eyes, while near her stood two Roman soldiers, grim and hard-faced, leaning on their spears. Occasionally they looked at her, mouths moving as in speech and stretched in tight grins, and Menander, though he could hear no sound, sensed that they mouthed jests and taunts. The silvery aura around Elissa fluttered and pulsed, somehow suggesting fear. About the Romans hung only a dull yellowish glow—the aura, Menander sensed, of those who possessed no True Spirit, but only the common life force of all creatures.

"I sense something of their speech—of their very thoughts," said Daramos. "The woman lies captive with the villa of a mighty sorcerer who is also a powerful priest in Jerusalem. Her True Spirit is to be sacrificed to the Outside One this very night."

Menander's mind rebelled at the thought. Instantly the vision faded and was gone.

"Is this the thing that we must prevent, then, O Mentor?"

The dwarf blinked slowly, then calmly nodded.

A footstep sounded on the gravelly soil. Menander looked up, saw the black-clad form of Taggart approaching from the direction of the Galactic sky craft.

"The Galactic is doing what he can," said the wizard. "We still have perhaps half an hour." He glanced nervously toward the setting sun, then down at the water-filled bronze bowl. "What are you looking at, Daramos?"

The squat dwarf gestured toward the bowl. "Look within, and see."

Taggart bent over the mage's shoulder and peered down. In that moment Menander again saw the silvery auras outline the reflections of himself and his ancient mentor—and, to his amazement, a similar aura about the black-clad form of Taggart also.

"I don't see anything," said the wizard. "Just reflections. If you're reading our future, old friend, I hope it's a good one you see." He straightened, then strode away toward where his dark, metallic sky craft rested just above the desert sands. Menander sensed tension in the man's movements.

"You see," said the dwarf calmly, "for all his great knowledge there are things he does not know, things he cannot even perceive. He knows much about the material universe, yet nothing of its essence, its true nature. He needs our help as much as we need his. Yet, together we may prevail against those who would sacrifice the soul of the incarnate Goddess to the Outside One and thereby cause Her, and all life, to withdraw from this world."

So saying, Daramos again bent his broad head toward the bowl and began to concentrate his gaze upon the water's still surface.

Annas glowered at the grinning Roman tribune. "Why are you in my villa, Maxentius, rather than at the Antonian Fortress?"

"I've been waiting for you, old vulture. Where is Caiaphas?"

"In Jerusalem. He will not be joining us."

Maxentius shrugged. "It doesn't matter. You're the true expert, Annas. Together we can accomplish the Gate's opening this night, after which we will share all power over the world, as we agreed." The Roman grinned more widely still. "That's what you will have to settle for, old sorcerer—partial rather than total power. For, you see, your little plot against me has been thwarted."

"Plot?"

"Don't pretend ignorance." Maxentius' eyes suddenly blazed vindictively, all trace of humor gone. "You planned to sacrifice the Goat-man—the mad rabbi—in order to open the Gate this night. You even tried to use me as your instrument, but I have forestalled you. A Roman centurion's spear has cut short the Suffering of the Goat—and now, as you can see, the darkness has lifted. Doubtless you were wondering why your attempted treachery failed."

"Treachery?" Annas' eyes glared and his white, square-cut beard seemed actually to bristle. "Why, you fool! *I* had no hand in the manner and place of the mad rabbi's self-sacrifice. Aye, his self-sacrifice, for I now see that he must have planned it from the start. And as for treachery, it was the sorcerer Yosef of Aphairema who aided him, thereby using and betraying both of us. Nicodemus was in on this plot, too, I am certain."

Maxentius felt a slight doubt. "Don't think to lie to me any more, priest. I am here to supervise tonight's ritual myself, to see that you play your part loyally. You see, I studied the Dark Gnosis a bit more than you may have supposed. "The tribune drew forth a large scroll from beneath his military cloak. "This is a copy of the *Spientia Magorum* of the ancient Persian mage Ostanes, and you may be sure that I have read it closely from end to end."

Annas glanced contemptuously at the scroll. "An abridged Greek copy. You have just enough knowledge to be dangerous to yourself. To control what may come through the Gate you would need the knowledge contained in Mattan's *El-Halal* as well, plus the skill that comes only after long practice of the Dark Arts."

"Perhaps so, Annas, and perhaps not. But if we work together, what of it? We can still snatch the victory we crave despite the plots of old Yosef and his fellow traitors. I trust that you have had them all put to death."

"Judah of Kerioth has perished and old Yosef is even now imprisoned in the stone hut in my gardens. But Nicodemus has fled, and with him many of Yosef's other accomplices, I fear."

"Fled? Good. They will cause us no more trouble, then. Come with me, now, Annas. I want you to see the preparations that I have made."

"What preparations?"

"First, the sacrifice that I have secured. I believe that she is one who has already met your approval, Annas." The tribune turned to his soldiers. "Wait here, men."

Annas followed the Roman through the portico and into the mansion, leaving his own black-cloaked guards to wait outside also. After walking a short distance down a dim hallway, Maxentius paused at a doorway and softly drew back one of the curtains before it. Annas peered through the narrow gap, saw a lamplit room wherein were three figures—two Roman soldiers and, lying bound at their feet, a dark-haired woman clad in a white tunic.

"Do you recognize her?" muttered Maxentius softly.

The old priest bent forward and peered more closely through the crack between the curtains. "Aye, of course. Elissa of Sychar."

"And have you not divined by your magical arts that she is a True Spirit, a worthy sacrifice to the Old Ones?"

"Yes, but still . . . *wait!"* Annas suddenly stiffened, his indrawn breath an abrupt hiss. Then he whirled about and hastened back down the hall and out onto the pillared portico. Maxentius, startled, hurried after him, stifling an urge to swear aloud.

"Where do you think you're going?" he blurted when they stood once more in the back garden amid their waiting soldiers.

"I sensed a presence in that chamber," said Annas, "—someone in addition to the soldiers and the woman. A watching spirit, invisible and powerful. I fear that you have provoked sorcerous enemies, Maxentius, and that they are even now spying on you, perhaps plotting your downfall."

"Nonsense," said Maxentius, though feeling a slight unease. "But in any case, I'm sure your sorcery can counteract any such enemies. And now, come with me to the Mount of Offense and see whether I have arranged the Ark and the Eidolon of Set to their best advantage."

Annas gasped and actually paled. "You . . . you had those things moved *there?*"

"Aye." The Roman's sarcastic grin returned. "It seemed to me that there were too many priestly intrigues going on in the Temple. Besides, I'm sure that this move will concentrate our power greatly, focusing all our resources upon a single Gate rather than two."

"No doubt." Annas drew back, scowling in consternation, then motioned to his soldiers. "Come, guards—we return to Jerusalem immediately."

"Wait!" commanded Maxentius. Then, in a more moderate tone of voice, "Are you, too, deserting the cause, Annas? Or are you holding out for a better bargain? I've offered you rulership over this province plus all the East not yet in Roman hands, as we had already agreed—but, by the gods, I'll not offer you more!"

The priest shook his head in exasperation. "Izhar was right, after all—things have gone awry in too many ways. Farewell, Maxentius."

"Stop! You can't just walk away from me. My troops are picked fighters and they outnumber yours."

Annas smiled grimly. "Aye, but mine are uncommonly hard to slay, as you well know. Save your troops, Maxentius. You may need all of them if you persist in your folly."

Maxentius clenched his fists at his sides, then glanced briefly toward the stone hut. "Go, then traitor. If you won't help me, perhaps another skilled in magic shall."

"You mean Yosef of Aphairema? He's a madman whose goal is not power but, rather, the destruction of the world, and if he is let loose he may yet accomplish his goal. He's a tricky old wizard, and I advise you to leave him securely locked up where he is. I don't care if you bring about your own doom, Tribune, but I'd hate to have you thereby bring on a wider holocaust than necessary, for I would like to continue to live. Again, farewell."

Annas and his guards turned and strode away, past the stone hut and into the shadows of the trees. As they went, Maxentius saw a few large owls fly out of the foliage and go winging away over the western wall of the estate toward Jerusalem. For a minute or two he eyed the stone hut uncertainly, angry yet hesitant, and as he did so he saw a white dove flutter down from a cornice of the villa and perch upon the hut's flat roof. Evidently that meant all the owls were gone from the grove. The traitorous sorcerer, in going, had taken all his familiars with him.

Maxentius strode past the hut and followed the shadowy garden path southward to the archway in the estate's southern wall. Emerging from it, he saw Annas' litter already being borne rapidly downhill toward the Kidron Valley. In the distance the walls and towers of Jerusalem rose dark beneath the westering sun, casting long shadows across the far slope.

"Traitor!" he bellowed after the receding palanquin. "Coward! Go, then, for your lies shall not deter me. All the power shall be *mine!"*

A silent shadow flew past him and wheeled westward—a final owl, winging down from the low rise of the Mount of Offense to the south. Maxentius shivered slightly in spite of himself. Suddenly, for no reason he could fathom, he remembered the prophecy of the condemned criminal Dismas whom he had sent to the cross: *Woe to you, despoiler . . . the demons with whom you have allied yourself are rising to crush you, and soon your human allies shall flee and leave you to face your doom alone.*

"Lies!" howled Maxentius, shaking his fists. *"Lies!* Go, cowards, and leave all the power to me—to me, as the gods have ordained it from the beginning!" Again he drew forth the large scroll and waved it aloft in one hand like a thick scepter. *"Here* is the power, and by it my greatness shall be made manifest this night—the greatness that abides only in him who has persevered unto the final triumph—the greatness that is favored by the crown-bestowing gods!"

The declining sun, a blazing globe of white in the cloudless blue of the west, seemed to reflect a glare of madness from the Roman's eyes.

Taggart paused in his nervous pacing to glance at the sun, which hung above the western horizon a distance barely equal to its own diameter. Menander rose from where he had been sitting beside Daramos, vainly attempting to emulate his mentor's contemplative calm, and strode to the side of the black-clad wizard.

"O Taggart, how long do we have now?"

Taggart glanced at a small disc strapped to his left wrist by a black band. "Much less than an hour."

"And what will happen if we fail?"

The wizard stopped his pacing. "The Gate whose opening we stopped will open again, only this time in a different and more random manner. This noon it was aligned with a cosmic 'flow', you might say, that would have sucked the Earth into a 'worm tunnel'—which, in turn, would have drawn it into the star-cluster of the Hyades. But tonight, culminating at midnight, the 'flow' will appear reversed relative to this part of the Earth's surface, and the Gate centering above the Jerusalem area will have an *outward* flux."

Menander nodded, fearing that he understood. "I see. Tell me, O Taggart: What will emerge from that Gate?"

"I don't know." For the first time Menander sensed fear, not merely worry or concern, in the wizard's manner. "That 'Gate', as we call it, is what the scholars of my time called a 'naked singularity', and from such a rupture in the space-time fabric anything might emerge. Absolutely *anything!"*

Menander, burning with more questions yet fearful of asking them, suddenly heard a sound from the strange bell-shaped Galactic craft, which rested at the edge of the oasis. Instantly Taggart turned to face the ramp and the dark aperture in the side of the craft, his poise tense. Still, the sound that had issued therefrom was only that of a human voice, dim, muffled . . . but then, as it was more clearly repeated, Menander tensed also.

"Iä! Iä! Abba Yog-Sothoni!"

Menander felt his blood chill as he recognized the words he had heard at the foot of the cross. Frozen, listening in apprehension, he heard a garble of softer voices -- and then, loudly and belligerently, *"Ha! ha! That's not water, Jew boy. It's vinegar!"*

"Damn!" muttered Taggart. "Other voices have intruded. Still, I'm sure that the Galactic will be able to sort them all out and successfully reconstruct—"

Abruptly, before Menander could speculate upon Taggart's mutterings, a wild yell reverberated from the interior of the Galactic sky craft. The sound of a scuffle then came from within, together with more wild cries—and suddenly, to the youth's astonishment, a Roman soldier clad in full armor and brandishing a stout spear dashed out upon the level space at the top of the sky craft's ramp. Menander's astonishment redoubled as he recognized in the madly fleeing figure the centurion who had been in charge of the crucifixion of the rabbi Yeshua and the two other felons.

"Demons!" shrieked the Roman as he dashed down the ramp. "Fiends!" Then, feeling earthly sand beneath his feet, he regained some of his courage and turned about, brandishing his spear aloft. "My commander Maxentius warned me of your sorceries, mad rabbi—" Suddenly, catching sight of Menander, Daramos and Taggart, he crouched and turned his spear-point menacingly toward them. "Foul Wizards, I don't know how you brought me here, but now you shall die—!"

At that moment the towering Galactic emerged from its sky craft and stood at the top of the metallic ramp. Between its eyes—twin white stars glowing within a rectangle of blackness—a third and brighter star suddenly swelled, and from it there lanced down a pencil-thin beam of intense white light. That beam touched the Roman centurion's breastplate—and, instantly, a mad shriek of agony burst from the man. He dropped his spear; a pale, rapidly intensifying glow swelled into being about him; then, as he screamed wildly to his gods, his form began to blaze whitely and dissolve. In another moment he had faded from sight and was gone.

Gone, utterly gone.

Menander, after several minutes of fearful hesitation, finally shuffled forward to the spot where the Roman had stood. He found nothing there save the man's footprints in the sand. Glancing up the ramp, he saw that the Galactic's head was bowed as if in sad contemplation, its visor now closed.

Then, even as he watched, the gigantic being turned and slowly re-entered the craft.

"A failure," said Taggart, who had followed Menander and now stood beside him. "But don't fear, lad. The Galactic will soon succeed in separating the other voices you gathered from the rabbi Yeshua's."

"Gods!" Menander sensed, behind the matter-of-fact evenness in the wizard's tone, a desire to be comforting. "Taggart, was that brutal centurion captured merely to be tortured by demons?"

"No. He was a human like you and me, and if he was brutal it was by circumstance. Moreover, he was not captured, merely *duplicated*. . . . Listen!"

Tensing, Menander heard again that voice from the sky craft crying: *"Iä! Iä! Abba Yog-Sothoni!"* Then, after a few moments, quieter though just as distinctly audible: *"It is done!"* Then for long moments there followed a period of silence. Menander turned away, shuddering at the lifelike tones that had been captured by Taggart's recording device. *Why?* he wondered. *Why should the wizard wish to capture so vividly a man's dying agony . . .?*

Then, to his astonishment, he heard from the aperture of the Galactic craft: *"It is done—and yet, why do I not die?"*

Menander felt a strange horror. *That* had not been recorded on Taggart's device!

For several more long minutes Menander stood motionless upon the sand, gazing toward the Galactic sky craft, his mind whirling with questions he dared not ask. Then at last the great Galactic again appeared at the top of the ramp, bearing in its massive metallic arms the limp figure of a human male—the rabbi Yeshua, his many wounds still red yet unbleeding, his eyes closed, his limbs hanging as if in exhaustion, his loins still concealed by a tattered yellow rag stained with blood.

Taggart ran forward to meet the Galactic as it descended the ramp, and together the two of them strode to the wizard's sky craft. There the giant metallic figure, his attitude somehow expressing a sad concern despite his featureless face, gently placed the tall and limp figure within Taggart's dark-hued vehicle, then turned and strode back up the ramp and into his own craft. Immediately afterwards the ramp slid inward and the vertical aperture of the craft narrowed and hissed shut, leaving no trace upon the smooth metallic surface.

"The rabbi Yeshua lives again," said Taggart, gazing at the sun which hung barely above the western horizon. "We are just in time. Yet, to be certain we must return him as nearly as possible to the spot where he died."

"I can guide you there!" cried Menander.

"Yet the world's danger is not past," said Daramos, his voice as calm as ever. "Though it now no longer faces extinction, the Gate may open yet one more time this night, before the moon moves completely out of alignment with the sun—and if it does, it may spew forth abominations unpredictable. And I sense that there is at least one who aspires to call forth those abominations to do his will. If he succeeds, the world may know his savage and destructive rule for many years, after which will follow a long, demon-ruled All-Night unparalleled since the black millennia following the cataclysms which destroyed the ancient Hyborian lands."

"You 'sense' this?" said Taggart doubtfully. "Who is this 'one' you are speaking of?"

"Perhaps this old high priest Annas, of whom I used to hear tales long before Menander told me of him. Or perhaps another. Remember, friend Taggart, you once doubted my 'sensings' before, and which of us then proved to be right? Believe me, we have yet much to do to prevent a prolonged All-Night from falling upon the world."

"A future even more terrible than the one that must now follow in any case," said the wizard, a tone almost of regret in his voice. "Well, come, then—into my craft. We have a lot of desert to cross."

At that instant the great sky craft of the Galactic abruptly vanished. Menander gasped.

"Ah!—that means the Zarrian ship is again coming up over the horizon," said Taggart. "We'll have to travel invisibly, too, and slowly, in order to avoid detection. But at least my craft has plenty of power now; we should be back at Jerusalem in about two hours. Quick, get in, both of you."

Simon woke abruptly from a sound sleep and sat up. How long had he slept? Surely no more than an hour or two, he sensed, yet he felt himself a new man. His many wounds were already thinly scabbed over and had ceased to pain him. Dositheus' poultices and Taggart's capsules had apparently worked wonders.

Feeling a sudden sense of urgency, he rose and donned tunic, cloak and sandals, then strapped on the sword-belt of the gladiator Cratos. As he strode from the chamber into the pillared main hall of the synagogue he saw, in the dim lamplight, many whom he recognized as members of the Thirty. Some were clustered near the closed and bolted entrance as if guarding it; others sat on benches nervously fidgeting or talking together in low voices. Old Dositheus stood at the lectern poring over an opened scroll, while at the old wizard's side stood Lotis looking pale and anxious. Simon approached them.

"Where," he asked, "are the matrons and the Temple virgins who sought refuge here?"

Dositheus looked up. "They left before nightfall, seeing that there was no immediate danger in the streets. I hope they all arrived safely at their homes before the living dead began to prowl the streets."

Simon scowled at his old mentor questioningly.

"Aye, the walking dead," Dositheus went on, "clad in the holy cerements of the grave. Shortly after dark we began to see them passing down the streets from west to east, some carrying torches, others bearing armor and weapons. Sometimes we heard the screams of fleeing citizens, at other times a clamor and clatter as the walking liches clashed with Roman patrols. One such skirmish took place directly in front of this synagogue—we watched it from the roof. The Romans roared in anger and fear as they attacked, but the walking corpses kept on in silence in spite of receiving great wounds; they dragged down some of the soldiers, and the rest fled. That was about half an hour ago, and since then we have seen no more of the shuffling horrors. I am sure that they are possessed and animated by the demonic *Am-ha-arez*, released by the earthquake from the tombs where Annas and Izhar had hidden them, and now they are passing eastward through the city."

"Toward the Temple," mused Simon, "—or perhaps beyond it, to the villa of Annas himself."

"Annas' villa!" Lotis cried, and Simon saw distress and concern in her eyes. "Oh, Simon! I am dreadfully afraid that the Romans have again captured my mistress Elissa and taken her there."

Romans! Simon gripped his sword-hilt, felt anew the towering urge against the foes he had come here intending to slay. Abruptly he turned and strode down the central aisle of the synagogue, shouting, "Open the door!"

Dositheus and Lotis hurried after him anxiously. At the door the Samaritan confronted Isagoras and the little rabbi Samezer. The latter shook his head and placed a restraining hand against Simon's breast.

"No, Simon, please. It is too dangerous out there."

"The danger shall be from me to others. Stand aside."

Samezer and the rest obeyed, cowed by the sinister hard glitter in the Samaritan's deep-set eyes. Simon drew back the bolt, wrenched open the door and hurried out, vanishing into the darkness.

Lotis made as if to follow. "Simon—"

"Let him go." Dositheus laid a hand on her shoulder. "Evidently the wizard-drug *krax* has renewed his strength and determination. He will be well, I think. He goes to find his destiny, to accomplish his revenge against those who so cruelly wronged him. This is his hour."

Lotis wrung her hands. "I pray that his destiny is not also his doom."

"That is out of our hands," said the rabbi Samezer. "Quickly, bolt the door again. Good. And now, friends, let us perform the ritual to the White Goddess. In all the other synagogues of this city the rite of the Slaying of the Lamb has been enacted and the Feast of Flesh and Blood is even now in progress. We must do whatever we can to counteract that influence."

Outside, Simon sped eastward through the dark streets, feeling a strength and exuberance he had never experienced before. He realized that it must be due to the medicines that Taggart had left with Menander, yet he sensed no mind-clouding effects. Rather, his every sense seemed heightened, his body electrically alive, his mind concentrated with confident purpose. The streets were barely illumined by the moonlit sky, yet he picked his way among the inky shadows swiftly and with ease, almost preternaturally aware of every obstacle. Many of these obstacles, he realized, were the bodies of men, some clad in Roman armor, others in civilian robes , a few—severely gashed, even dismembered—in the pale cerements of the grave.

He met no living person until he entered the Temple area. Dashing through the shadowed forest of columns just within the wall surrounding it, he emerged into the wide and moonlit Court of Gentiles—and immediately confronted a band of about half a dozen Roman soldiers. Instantly one of them cried out, "You, there—halt!"

Simon dashed grimly on toward them; the blade of his great sword flashed forth in the moonlight.

"That's no animated corpse—look at him run!" yelled another soldier. *"Halt, felon—!"*

Then Simon was among them, slashing with incredible speed and power. Before the Romans knew what had hit them the helmed head of one and the sword-gripping arm of another spun into the air, spraying blood. For a few seconds more there was a mad tornado of action too rapid to follow—the clash of blades, the shrieks of men mortally wounded—

And then, incredibly, it was over and Simon stood, alone and exultant, amid the gashed bodies of all his foes. Wonder grew upon him as he gazed down at those twitching corpses. His sensations were no illusion; somehow the *krax* drug had actually speeded up his activity, enhanced his perceptions and reflexes beyond those of normal men. During that brief battle the motions of his foes had seemed to him strangely sluggish, their reactions pathetically slow. . . .

He laughed aloud, then turned and ran on eastward across the deserted courtyard, naked blade in hand. "That was for you, Dismas and Gestas," he muttered grimly, "and before this night's done I'll add a great many more to the tally of vengeance."

He saw the great pale bulk of the Temple looming beyond the wall to his right, and a slight doubt smote through his exultation. Why had not Taggart given him the *krax* drug before sending him to confront the demon Gol-goroth? Was he indeed feeling an overconfidence, a clouding of judgment . . .?

His doubt grew when, a few minutes later, he emerged from the great eastern gate of the Temple courts and gazed out over the Kidron Valley. To the north and south he could see torches and fires, could hear the excited voices of encamped pilgrims, but the center of the valley before him was as deserted as the city streets had been. Abandoned tents and expiring cook fires testified that something had recently caused the masses of campers to flee from that area. To the east hung the full moon, half way up the sky above the black ridge of the Mount of Olives, the ruby gleam of Antares close beside it; upon that ridge he could make out the location of the villa of Annas and, south of it, the sinister hump of the Mount of Offense.

Then his preternaturally keen eyes made out, just beyond the river, an irregular mass of white-shrouded figures advancing slowly and stumblingly up the far slope. He saw the pale gleam of more tombs on that slope, saw that some of the white figures were clustering around moonlit mausolea—and suddenly knew what had frightened away the pilgrims. The walking dead, seeking to liberate still more of their kind. . . .

Then he heard a new sound, realized that he had already been partly aware of it for some time—a familiar, far-off booming as of a gigantic but muffled drum. Peering in the direction from which it seemed to come, he saw a dim light glowing atop the Mount of Offense to the southeast. Slowly but steadily the pulsing booms grew louder; the scores of pale, shrouded figures across the valley seemed to be marching up the far slopes, lurching and shuffling in time to the eerie drumbeats. . . .

Suddenly a new light flooded the valley. A ringing peal vibrated the air—and Simon, glancing skyward, saw that a great new star, blazing with an intense blue-white radiance brighter than the moon, had sprung instantly and uncannily into being.

CHAPTER XXXI

Daramos, who had been squatting silent and motionless beneath his plain brown robe, suddenly opened his eyes and said, "We are nearing the ridge upon which rests the villa of Annas. I will get out there, friend Taggart."

The black-clad wizard glanced at the panel of glowing squares. "You're right, Daramos, though how you knew it is beyond me. Very well, I'll begin the descent. I'm sure you know your own purposes, and I know better than to argue with you. But it won't be safe to shut off the invisibility screen for more than a moment. When I do, you'll have to jump out immediately, and then you're on your own."

"Are we not all continually?" said the dwarfish mage blandly.

A few minutes later Menander was startled to see the dimness of the sky craft suddenly give way to the comparative brightness of a moonlit night. Stars twinkled above; he recognized the bright diamond of Spica west of the zenith, red Antares next to the full moon about half way up the eastern sky, and realized that it must be nearly the third hour past sunset. Rising to his knees, he saw that the craft now rested upon a deserted narrow road flanked by trees and recognized, not far off, the stone wall that surrounded the Garden of Gethsemene. Then he thought he heard, muffled and far away, the slow, pulsing sound of a gigantic drum.

Daramos scurried over the side of the sky craft, dropped to the roadway and hurried off southward into the moonlit night without a backward glance.

Instantly the night scene vanished and Menander could again see only the dim interior of Taggart's craft. A slight rise in the pitch of the craft's power drone told him that they were once more on their way. He glanced down at the sleeping rabbi, whose great body took up nearly half the floor space of the small craft; the man's chest was rising and falling evenly. Amazingly, his wounds were all but completely healed. The nail holes in his wrists and feet, as well as a few of the deeper whip cuts on his back and sides, still showed dark and conspicuous, his numerous lacerations had faded to mere white lines, unscabbed, and there was not even the sign of a bruise on him.

"We are almost there," said Taggart. "I think I detect the low mound you mentioned, Menander, and the cemetery grove just north of it. When we're just over the trees I'll drop the shield so that we can scan the area briefly."

Menander stood up and leaned tensely against the craft's rail, ready to peer outward. After another long minute or two the night sky again sprang suddenly into view. Looking down, Menander could see that they were actually level with the topmost branches of an oak grove. He saw the walls of Jerusalem to the east and south, black-shadowed beneath the rising moon, and a little to the south of the grove the low mound of Gol-goroth.

"Yes—this is the place!" he cried out.

"Good." Taggart touched a red-glowing square and immediately the craft was filled with and surrounded by a bright silvery radiance. "There—the power shield is up and we also have some illumination. Look down, Menander, and see if you can see the particular tomb you told me of."

Menander blinked, rubbed his eyes, then leaned over the rail. "It's . . . *there,* I think. I'm not sure from this angle. . . ."

"I'll bring us down, then."

No sooner had the craft begun to descend, however, than a chorus of frantic yells broke out from the darkness below. There followed a clattering of metal, a rapid scrambling of many booted feet, and in the next instant a number of helmed and armored men burst from the shadows of the grove and raced away toward Jerusalem's looming west wall, yelling in terror. In another minute they had dashed into its shadow and on through its nearest gate and were gone from sight, even the sound of their frantic cries fading rapidly away.

"A Roman patrol!" exclaimed Menander gleefully. "We frightened them thoroughly, Taggart. Surely they thought we were demons!"

The wizard grinned tautly. "No doubt. We must have been quite a sight to them, descending from the sky surrounded by light, visible to them only from the waist up. Well, they're not likely to return here tonight. You say this is the location of the tomb in which the rabbi Yeshua died?"

"Yes. I think it's the one over there, by the big terebinth."

"Good. We're near enough." Taggart brought the craft down into a small clearing in the grove. The power hum subsided. "Here we are, Menander. Now, if you will, take the man's feet and help me lift him out."

In a few moments the sleeping rabbi lay on the grass. Taggart, taking a small black box from a pouch at his belt, pressed an inset on one of its surfaces; instantly the sky-craft vanished, again surrounded by its cloak of invisibility. "Good," he said again. "And now, we must awaken the sleeper."

Taggart knelt beside the unconscious man, and Menander glimpsed in the wizard's hand a small, slender cylinder that glittered in the moonlight. This object Taggart placed against the rabbi's left shoulder. There followed a brief hissing sound, after which the wizard stood up and drew back a pace.

Then, to Menander's astonishment, the man on the grass opened his eyes, stirred and sat up, then rose shakily to his feet.

"What do you here, Adversary of Mankind?" he intoned in a deep and vibrant voice, his great dark eyes fixed on Taggart. "Are you again come down to Earth like a lightning-bolt from the skies? Get you behind me, for I will hear no more of your deceits and temptations."

Menander shivered. He had seen this man—this being—placed dead into a sealed crypt, within this very cemetery, yet now he stood before them, alive and speaking, amid the moonlit tombs.

"All that is past," said Taggart. "This world abides. Go your way in peace."

"No. No." The rabbi glanced up at the moon and the stars, and Menander sensed a look of confusion in his eyes, a yearning as for something lost and only partly remembered. "There is a great work to be done. I must go now even unto Galilee and gather my followers." He turned his mystical dark eyes upon Menander and said, "Tell me, young Levite, where is the road that will guide me there."

"Northward," said Menander, pointing. "That way, just beyond the northwest corner of the city's wall, lies the road to Samaria and Galilee."

The rabbi turned away and, without another word, walked slowly off into the night. In a few moments his tall, pale form had vanished away among the shadows of the trees.

"Gods!" muttered Menander. "Taggart, of all the wonders that you have performed this is surely the greatest—to thus restore an utterly destroyed man to life and to the world! And yet . . . is he truly and entirely as he was before his death?"

Taggart shook his head—sadly, it seemed to Menander. "No. His mind is partly gone, and his body will not endure much longer, either. The Galactics are masters at such restorations, but always there are slight flaws in the sound recordings, flaws which show up as defects in the restored individuals. The rabbi may live on for a few days, a few weeks, perhaps even a month or two, but then he will die and dissolve away as he did before. Fortunately, this time it will be painless. Come on—we had better get back into the craft before—"

At that instant Menander was startled to see the wizard's sky craft spring into visibility. But . . . no, it was *not* the wizard's, for it hovered just above a different part of the clearing and there was a man standing upright within it—a tall man dressed in black garments identical to Taggart's. Upon his brow a small disc glowed with a dim blue phosphorescence. Menander, sensing a tension in Taggart's manner as he turned to face this man, felt his scalp tingle; instinctively he drew back toward the shadows of the trees behind him.

"Taaran," said Taggart evenly, his expression grim.

The stranger climbed out of his sky craft and strode forward. Menander saw as he approached that his clean-shaven features were lean and pale, rigid with a grim intensity. Before his eyes he wore a lens-frame similar to the one Taggart had worn before the Romans disguised as bandits had attacked him. Those eyes seemed almost to glow under his scowling brows—not with the yellow glow of an inner demon, but as if with a cold, icy light of their own. Involuntarily, Menander drew back still farther until he felt the shadows of the oaks enfolding him.

"I suspected that you would bring the lesser son here," said the man called Taaran, "after you restored him. It wasn't really necessary, you know. The restoration alone was quite enough to undo all we have worked for."

Taggart's hand hung casually beside the bulky black pouch at his right hip. "Have you come to kill me, then?"

"What good would that do?" The stranger's grim expression did not change. "No, I have come to bid you farewell. We have roamed the worlds and the ages together for many centuries, but now we must part."

"I know you don't approve of what I have done, Pitts," said Taggart, "but, think: had I not done it, we would not now be here talking about it. Had the Zarrians succeeded in their purpose, as you wished them to, they would still exist now—but *we* would not."

"What of that?" The scowl in the stranger's eyes intensified. "Because of you this planet will continue to know monstrous sufferings for centuries to come. It may be as much as two thousand years before we can try again to open such a Gate. The Zarr could have cleansed this planet and taken it away to other regions for a higher race of beings to inhabit, but now it will fester on as it was, perhaps for thousands or even millions of years more. Think about that, Taggart, during the centuries remaining to you. Think about it while you serve your new masters, who seek prolongation of this sort of life that *their* masters may feed upon its sufferings."

Taggart stepped forward a pace. "Pitts—"

"Speak no more!" The stranger held up his right hand. "I came only to bid you farewell. I know why you did what you did, and so I can understand your motive and even wish you well. But I cannot approve."

"Pitts, I chose *life!"* cried Taggart. "Is that so—?"

The moonlight in the clearing suddenly seemed to double in intensity. Menander glanced up involuntarily, saw that a new star had come into being just east of the midheaven. It was brighter far than Sirius or even Venus, and its light was of a piercing blue-white quality that almost hurt his eyes to gaze at directly. In the same instant Menander heard increasingly that far-off beating of what seemed to be a monstrous, muffled drum.

"The Drums of Chaos," said the stranger, "sounding the opening of the Gate. But the opening comes too late to benefit this world. Farewell, Taggart."

"Wait!" cried the wizard. "You know more of the Zarrians than I. What do they think will come out of that Gate?"

The rigid-faced man paused and turned back. "You know as much about that as they or I, now that our work is undone. What emerges from a naked singularity is completely unpredictable. In this case it will probably not be enough to destroy this world—you have seen to that—but it might still change things drastically. Possibly it will increase suffering on this planet far beyond what would have normally been the case. But why should you care? You can embark from this world with the Galactics now, even as I am about to leave it with the Zarrians, and be far from the disaster when it happens."

"Why should I *care?*" Taggart glanced in Menander's direction. "I . . . I have made several friends here."

"That was always your worst fault," said the man called Taaran. "You were never able to keep from local entanglements." So saying, he turned abruptly, climbed back into his sky craft and hunched down behind the rim. There was a rising whine of power, and then the craft abruptly rose above the trees and sped away into the sky, vanishing rapidly amid the glittering stars of the north.

For a few moments Taggart stood there motionless, his right hand upraised in a frozen gesture. To Menander there seemed something sad in that poise, as though it were locked indecisively between a beckoning gesture and a wave of farewell.

Then the wizard lowered his arm, drew forth his black box and pressed one of its surfaces. Instantly the shield of invisibility vanished from about Taggart's sky craft.

Menander hesitantly advanced from the shadows into the clearing.

"I must go now," said Taggart, his voice strained.

Menander glanced around at the rock outcroppings that leaned here and there amid the trees. "But what of Carbo, O Taggart? He is still trapped within the tomb—"

"I doubt it. He could escape through the slightest crack. Stay here and search for him if you wish, Menander." The wizard glanced up at the zenith, where the strange new star seemed to be visibly swelling in brightness. "In any case, you must not accompany me. It would be too dangerous. Don't go into Jerusalem for the rest of the night, lad, and above all don't approach the villa of Annas or the Mount of Offense. If Daramos and I survive we'll meet you tomorrow at the place where Dositheus told you he and the Thirty would be."

"Taggart—no! Wait!"

But the wizard had already climbed into his craft. Again came the shrill hum of power, and then the strange vehicle shot into the sky and sped eastward in a graceful arc, a black disc against the moonlit sky and the gleaming stars of the Scorpion—the constellation which, Menander recalled, his ancient mentor had once referred to as the Dragon of Chaos.

Simon of Gitta, hastening up the slope toward Annas' villa, suddenly spied a torch-bearing procession upon that part of the ridge-crest to the southeast, which inclined upward toward the Mount of Offense. The procession was emerging from the grove just south of the villa, and by the light of those torches Simon could see that those who carried them were Roman legionaries. At their head strode an officer in plumed helmet and gleaming bronze dress-armor, and behind him followed a white-clad figure that appeared to be a woman. Atop the ridge-hump toward which the procession advanced was a low block of stone, black in silhouette against the eerily brightening sky, and Simon knew that this was the altar upon which Solomon had once sacrificed to the Old Ones. Upon it rested two objects gleaming with a witch-light of their own—the ass-headed Eidolon of Set and, in front of it and open to the heavens, the Ark of the Covenant. Strangest of all, from the interior of the Ark there streamed upward a dim and shimmering pillar of light, which, twining and twisting like a luminous serpent, rose to merge with that brilliant new star, which had so suddenly appeared north of the moon and Antares in the sign of the Dragon of Babylon. The light pulsed in rhythm to that eerie sound so like the distant booming of giant drums.

Pausing to catch his breath, Simon shielded his eyes from the unnatural brilliance of that star, whose blue-white light now illumined the landscape with the radiance of a dozen moons. Yes, he was sure of it now—the white, womanly figure, stumbling upon the slope as if her arms were bound, was Elissa, and the Roman officer leading the procession was none other than Maxentius! A growl of rage rose in Simon's throat and, gripping more firmly the hilt of the great sword of Cratos, he resumed his charge up the hillside.

Almost immediately he caught up with the rearmost of those demon-possessed corpses, which, climbing the slope ahead of him, seemed to be drawn by the drum-sounds. A few of these liches turned to confront him, mouths gaping slackly, eyes blank, pale claw-hands groping. Simon laughed, roared an oath to the Lord of Gerizim and leaped among them, his great sword slashing in silvery arcs. The corpses fell asunder before his sure and rapid blows, severed limbs twitching, severed heads rolling down the slope, while from enormous bloodless wounds flowed great greenish blobs—the fleeing spawn of Celaeno, servitors of Assatur, frantically oozing across the gravel and sward of an alien world in search of new hosts.

Leaping over the sundered corpses, Simon dashed on up the slope toward his Roman foes, laughing gleefully to feel the surge of the *krax* drug still strong within him. This was the moment for which he had lived during the last eight long years—the moment when his greatest enemy, who had slain his parents and sold him into the arena, should finally know pain and terror and death.

His feet seemed fitted with the winged shoes of Hermes, so rapidly did he ascend the slope; yet he was not in time to intercept the procession, for as he approached the altar of Solomon he saw that the Roman troops had already formed into a ring about it. In their midst stood Maxentius, clad in imperial regalia that included a laurel wreath and a purple cloak, his plumed helmet now cradled in the crook of his left arm. Two centurions lifted the bound, white-clad Elissa and laid her upon the altar, quickly tied her ankles with white cord, then stood aside at attention as if they were priestly acolytes. Maxentius, laying aside his helmet, drew forth a scroll and opened it, quickly mouthed something that sounded like a brief incantation; then, laying the scroll upon the ground beside his helmet, he advanced toward the frantically struggling Elissa, drawing his gleaming shortsword from its scabbard. The drum-sounds seemed to increase slightly. . . .

"Maxentius!" roared Simon at the top of his lungs. *"Maxentius, behold your doom!"*

Every Roman head on that hilltop turned in his direction—and then he was dashing among them, howling in savage glee as his great blade flashed, smiting and slaying in a rage of madness. Legionaries screamed as their limbs were lopped from their bodies, their bellies gashed open, their guts spilled by the inhumanly swift blade of this demon in the shape of a man.

"Elissa, I'm coming!" he yelled.

Surviving legionaries scattered frantically as he burst through their ranks and dashed on toward Maxentius. The tribune, his features contorted with fear at sight of the apparently superhuman figure hurtling toward him, cried out, "Lentulus, use your sword—slay her! The rite is done. I'll deal with this presumptuous Samaritan." He touched his wide belt clasp and an aura of pale blue light sprang into being around him.

Elissa, wailing in terror, strained against the pinioning cords as the centurion Lentulus drew his broad-bladed gladius and advanced toward her. Simon stooped, snatched up a fist-sized stone and, with the preternatural swiftness imparted to him by the *krax* drug, hurled it with uncanny force and accuracy. The missile caught Centurion Lentulus full in the throat just above his breastplate, crushing his trachea, and the Roman immediately dropped to the ground, coughing and strangling in his death throes.

"Maxentius, now *you* die!" roared Simon, dashing forward.

The tribune, despite his dimly glowing shield of invulnerability, felt a surge of primordial fear as he beheld his Samaritan enemy, brandishing the great blade of Cratos, charging toward him. Yet he stood his ground, back to the stone altar, and raised his own sword, yelling, *"Perish, Simon!"*

The blades of the Samaritan and Roman met—and instantly Simon felt himself hurled back as if he had collided with a rock wall.

Shakily, Simon rose to his feet, realizing that the shock had nearly rendered him unconscious for a moment. Maxentius, still protected by the impregnable Zarrian force belt, was advancing toward him, while from all sides were converging a score of Roman legionaries. He was trapped—doomed. The overconfidence of the *krax* drug had driven him into a position of deadly peril—and now he could feel it beginning to wear off!

Grimly, Simon crouched and prepared to engage his encircling foes and flight them to the death—his own death, as it now seemed likely. . . .

Daramos, master of wisdom, seldom encountered anything that caught him unawares, yet he was mildly surprised to find the villa of Annas unguarded either materially or magically.

Suspecting a trap, but encountering none, he slowly and carefully entered and searched the mansion. Before long he found a room which he recognized as the one in which the woman Elissa had been imprisoned, but she and her guards were gone. Ascending cautiously to the upper chambers of the mansion, he searched them as carefully and thoroughly as he had those below. He encountered no one, nor did his keen senses detect any hidden presences, human or otherwise. Evidently the sorcerer Annas had cleared his residence of even his most trusted servants. . . .

Then, in the rearmost chamber, Daramos caught the cadence of a voice that seemed to be raised in a chant. Traversing a small bedchamber, he peered out a narrow casement that opened to the south and found that it overlooked a vista of moonlit groves and gardens. In a large open space between the mansion and the nearest trees stood two or three dozen Roman soldiers, some bearing torches, all formally ranked and at attention. In front of them two centurions flanked a tall, dark-haired woman clad in a white tunic, holding her upright as she struggled against their grip and the white cords that bound her arms behind her, and Daramos instantly recognized her as the one he had seen in the vision of the bowl and whom Menander had called 'Elissa'. Facing her and the ranked legionaries stood a tall, proud-faced Roman officer in full ceremonial armor and purple cloak who sported a laurel wreath on his temples and a blue-glowing disc on his forehead. He was intoning a chant in classical Greek while holding before him in both hands a partly unrolled scroll.

"O Ancient Ones, awaken and devour
The sacrifice I offer in this hour,
And grant me in return the dark-starred Crown
That I may rule this world in boundless power. . . ."

Daramos eyes narrowed in curiosity. This was obviously not the great sorcerer Annas, but some presumptuous and incompetent Roman amateur. True, the man intoned the chant with vigor and concentrated will, which was far more important than knowing the original language and following it precisely but slavishly; yet, considering the nature of his sacrificial victim, his *timing* was off by precisely twelve hours. His sacrifice at this hour of the woman—an incarnated True Spirit—would offend the Great Goddess rather than gratifying the Most Ancient One. The *flow* was exactly wrong, a fact the Roman would have realized had he been able to read the complete original text in the ancient Persian of Ostanes. As it was, the man could only, at most, induce vengeful forces to surge through the Gate during this final night of propitious lunar-solar, planetary and stellar alignments; yet, his bumbling bid for power might succeed in bringing down an unprecedented horror upon the world—the fury of the Goddess in her darkest manifestation. . . .

Turning away from the casement, Daramos hastily resumed his search of the mansion's upper chambers.

He soon discovered the one which he knew must be the place where Annas had performed his most arcane sorceries. A spiritual miasma of menace seemed to hang about the windowless room, whose walls were adorned with dark tapestries in which antique scrolls protruded in great numbers from wooden cubbyholes while metallic instruments of bewildering intricacy littered the single broad wooden table.

The dwarf's dark eyes rapidly but calmly surveyed the array of scrolls, and presently he selected one and unrolled it upon the tiled floor. It was, as he had sensed from its sinister psychic aura, the *El-Halal* of Mattan.

"Aklo writing," he muttered. "Remarkable!"

Then, hunching over it, he began to read. Nearly half an hour passed as he rapidly scanned the archaic characters of the age-yellowed parchment, slowly rolling it from one of its wooden spindles to the other. And as he read, his broad and normally untroubled brow gradually acquired furrows of concentration and concern. . . .

A sudden high ringing in his ears—or was it in the sky?—roused him from his concentration.That ringing, rapidly subsiding to tones resembling the keening of eerie flutes, was mingling rhythmically with the sinister drum -beats, which had long been steadily resounding, with increasing volume, from the direction of the Mount of Offense. Setting aside the scroll, Daramos hurriedly began to open cupboards and draw forth vials of various powders and liquids, glancing at their labels and then mixing them together in his wide, shallow bowl whose rim was inscribed with ancient Persian symbols. Presently a thick smoke began to billow from the bowl, filling the chamber with fumes so thick and choking that Daramos was forced to withdraw for a time into the corridor. When at length he was able to return he found the bowl half full of a hard and pale encrustation. In a few minutes more he had reduced this substance, by means of a stone pestle from one of Annas' crucibles, to an extremely fine white powder.

Carefully bearing his powder-filled bowl to the ground floor of the mansion, Daramos became aware of a pallid light streaming in through the windows, a light so strong as to suggest a premature daybreak. Emerging from the back door of the villa, he saw that the light emanated from what appeared to be a gigantic new star approaching the zenith. Despite its uncanny brilliance the moon and ruddy Antares were quite visible not far to the south of it, while Spica and a few other bright stars could also be clearly seen. The star's light, though too intense to bear looking at directly for long, did not appreciably brighten the sky beyond a twilight hue, while the landscape revealed by it was one of gray shadings, white highlights and black shadows, having no trace of color. The treetops of Annas' grove looked inky in silhouette against this twilit sky, while beyond them shimmered a pale column of light, wavering upward toward the star like a misty rope, pulsing to the rhythm of unearthly drums and flutes.

Daramos hastened from the mansion and down the southward path through the groves and gardens, noting with some consternation that the Romans had already departed. Their commander had hurried through the preparatory ritual—his defective Greek translation of Ostanes had omitted part of it.

"Taggart, come rejoin me swiftly," he muttered.

Then, as he passed a small stone cubicle of a hut he suddenly felt the presence of a powerful observing mind—a mind, he intuitively realized, as versed in arcane lore as his own. Glancing at the windowless hut, he saw only a closed oaken door, but knew that the watching mind was behind it, at least as aware of him as he was of it; moreover, he sensed that mind was in a strange state that enabled it to see not only beyond physical barriers, but into *other* realms of being as well. Atop the hut perched a dove, its plumage pure white under the new star's unnatural brilliance—undoubtedly the familiar of the powerful wizard within. Could it be Annas, betrayed and imprisoned by his ambitious but inept Roman ally . . .?

No time, Daramos decided despite his intense curiosity; the rite the Roman was performing would soon climax. Gripping his bowl more tightly, he hastened on amid the trees toward the southern wall of the estate.

Emerging from the open and unguarded archway, he saw before him the stony slope rising gently up toward the Mount of Offense. Atop its rounded summit stood a massive, square-hewn altar, inky in silhouette against the eerily glowing sky, and upon it rested two faintly luminous objects which Daramos immediately recognized from his arcane studies as the sinister Eidolon of Set and the Ark of the Covenant, both of them extraterrestrial artifacts left on Earth by alien beings millennia ago for sinister purposes. From the latter streamed upward that glowing and pulsing column of light, which seemed to be merging with the new and uncannily brilliant star. A troop of Roman soldiers was arranged in a ring about this altar, while toward them surged a larger, closing ring of oddly lurching figures clad in the pallid shrouds of the grave. At one point between these converging rings a disturbance seemed to be occurring—a clash of rushing figures, a shimmer of many flashing swords, the cries and curses of wounded men—and all the while, as an eerie backdrop, the vague Ark-based pillar of light twining and pulsing upward toward the star in rhythm to the pounding of unseen drums and the keening of eerie flutes. . . .

Then Daramos sensed a strange low humming in the air near him and realized that he was in the immediate presence of some unseen being.

Simon, fighting desperately against the score of legionaries that were closing in around him, realized that he was doomed despite the superhuman speed and strength which the *krax* drug imparted to him. Roaring with rage, the blade of his great sword a whirling blur, he smote and clove in a mad fury, determined to take as many Romans as possible down in death with him.

Suddenly the press of his foes slackened as, from the troops who had moved downslope to encircle him, mad shrieks rang out. Walking corpses clad in grave-shrouds, some grotesquely sporting armor and clumsily brandishing weapons, were engaging the legionaries and rapidly closing with them in ever greater numbers.

Instantly Simon whirled and charged through the weak point of the menacing circle, his great blade sundering Romans and animated corpses alike. In another moment he had burst through and was dashing down the slope. Whirling, he saw that no one pursued him; the pale-shrouded liches were attacking the legionaries, who were no longer arranged in a circle about the hilltop, but were rapidly forming into a defensive clump, shields upraised in a ranked wall. Their shortswords drove like bobbins through the bodies of corpses, but without effect, and slowly they began to draw back up the slope. Simon crouched, gripped his sword tightly, then again sprang forward as if to rejoin the fray—

And Elissa, from her vantage atop the altar, saw the blue-glowing form of Maxentius hurrying back toward her from the direction of that strange combat. She made a frantic effort to roll off the stone block. Maxentius, switching off his force belt, gripped her by the hair and forced her back down; she felt the cold point of his sword against her throat.

"Hold still, my sweet," he snarled, grinning tautly, "and I'll let you live long enough to see my victory."

She obeyed, staring up fearfully into the man's glaring eyes. A blue disc glowed upon his brow, and from it Elissa fancied she could feel waves of hate emanating. Beyond him she could see the eerie new light in the sky, no longer a mere star, but an expanding disc, swelling and brightening. Already it was larger than the moon; its edges were hazy and swirling, like the mouth of a spinning tunnel, and within its bright core she thought she discerned movement—a brilliant congeries of spheres, churning and expanding in rhythm to the sounds of drums and flutes. . . .

Maxentius released her hair, though he continued to hold his sword ready. He glanced briefly at the line of embattled legionaries and animated corpses; then, with his left hand he groped in his pouch and drew forth two small objects, which he placed upon the edge of the altar. Elissa saw that they were a short bronze-colored tube and the vial of "Living Water", which old Yosef had given her.

"Annas has again betrayed me," snarled the Roman, "but my men will soon hack his clumsy walking liches into vulture-bait. As for you, fair Elissa—"

He paused as a new sound became audible over the clamor of combat—a strange lapping and pulsing as of sea waves, approaching rapidly. To Elissa the sound also strangely suggested the pulsing of a giant heart, or perhaps many hearts—a throbbing that kept time with the drumbeats resounding from the Ark and the high flute-keenings from the expanding sky-Gate. It seemed to be coming up the slope from the southwest, from the direction of the Valley of Hinnom, and as it drew ever closer a strange odor, foul and alien, began to pervade the air. Elissa, straining over on her side to peer in that direction, could see nothing despite the cold light, which now illuminated all the landscape.

"Hades!" roared Maxentius. "Annas has sent an invisible demon against me—but I'll thwart him!" Laying aside his sword, he picked up the small vial, unstoppered it and quickly quaffed its contents. Then he snatched up the scroll of Ostanes and hastily unrolled it. "Bring on your devils, Annas! The Golden Nectar will enable me to see them, the blue disc will let me sense their very thoughts, and with the aid of Ostanes and the *byakhtril* I'll now summon demons of my own to command."

He reached out for the small bronze whistle—and found it abruptly snatched away. A fluttering bundle of feathers had hurtled down from the sky, alighted briefly upon the altar, and was now frantically flapping away with the gleaming *byakhtril* firmly clamped in its beak.

"Devil bird!" Maxentius grabbed up a stone and hurled it after the rapidly vanishing white dove. The missile barely missed its mark. Whirling, he snatched up his sword, touched the clasp of his force belt and turned to face the oncoming sounds. Elissa still could not see the advancing being, though judging from the way the ground was beginning to tremble it must be of elephantine size. The sloshing sounds were louder, the stench was becoming overpowering, and just down the southwestward slope the bushes and grasses were being bent and flattened in a wide and slime-glistening path.

Maxentius, the blue disc glowing upon his forehead, held up his scroll and began to read it aloud, a note of urgency in his voice: *"Iä! Iä! Assatur! Assatur cf'ayak 'vulgtmm—"* Then his eyes bulged in sudden terror and, dropping the scroll, he bellowed, "Great Zeus—no! *No!*"

Elissa, still unable to see the advancing demon-thing, screamed out in horror as she sensed its enormous bulk bearing swiftly down on the both of them. Then her scream and the terrified bellows of Maxentius were alike drowned out amid the thunderings of a titanic Voice:

"TARTZAH . . . TASHMAD . . . ABBA YOG-SOTHONI!"

Daramos, recognizing the tone of the humming in the air near him, called out, "Taggart, show yourself."

Instantly the dark sky craft became visible, only a few yards away and no more than a foot off the ground. The wizard was standing upright in it, a black silhouette against the eerie glow of the sky. "I heard your call and came here as quickly as I could, Daramos," he said, touching the blue disc on his forehead. What's that commotion on the knoll to the south?"

"The man Roman is about to sacrifice to the Most Ancient One," said Daramos, "but he knows not what he does. The woman he intends to slay is a True Spirit, and her death at this time and place would enrage the Goddess and cause Her to devastate much of this portion of the Earth."

"Goddess?" Taggart glanced up at the whirling, brightening disc in the sky. "That's an interesting name for it." He raised a dark device to his eyes— an elaborate arrangement of two short tubes whose outer ends were formed of large glassy discs—and peered in the direction of the Mount of Offense. "I see the woman—she's lying on the altar, right by the Ark and the Eidolon. A fine looking woman indeed—it would be a shame if . . . *wait!* That Roman beside her is wearing a Zarrian belt—he just switched it on. He's impregnable!"

"Have you no weapons that can destroy him, friend Taggart?"

Taggart laid aside the viewing device, nervously fingered the bulky holster at his right hip. "Yes—only, the power required to overwhelm that force shield would blast the entire hilltop to atoms, and then the woman would perish in any case."

"Then we must go to her aid ourselves." Daramos thrust his bowl into the wizard's hands, then hurried scrambled into the craft.

"What *is* it?" said Taggart, eyeing the white powder doubtfully.

"The powder of Ben Ghazi, whose formula I just learned from Annas' copy of *El-Halal.* It will enable us to see the invisible enemy."

"Invisible . . .? Oh, I see—a micro-prism dust. A holo-scanner would work better, if only I had one aboard this craft. But what enemy? Do you mean that thing from the grotto—?"

"Aye. The Greater Son. I sense its approach even now. It is coming to avenge the thwarting of the mission which it and the Lesser Son were to have carried out with the aid of Gol-goroth. Hurry!"

The craft rose into the sky with a high whine. At the same instant a white dove streaked past it in the direction of the villa, a brazen object gleaming in its beak.

"The *byakhtril!"* exclaimed Taggart. "I've got to get it—"

"No time! Save the woman first, or abominations will infest the Earth."

Taggart glanced up at the swirling sky disc, then sent his craft hurtling toward the Mount of Offense. "Naked singularity," Daramos heard him mutter grimly. "Anything might come out of it."

"Aye, for it is the Gate to the Pleroma—the Fullness, from which all things come forth. And that bright congeries of churning spheres within it is the Pallid Mask, which hides the true aspect of the great Father-Mother, creator and destroyer of all things—"

"Worm tunnel—powered by a white hole near the galaxy's center," countered Taggart.

Then their interchange was abruptly terminated by a great Voice booming from the top of the Mount of Offense:

"TARTZAH . . . TASHMAD . . . ABBA YOG-SOTHONI!"

CHAPTER XXXII

"... ABBA YOG-SOTHONI!"

Simon, racing around the north flank of the embattled knot of legionaries and animated corpses, fell to his knees in shock at the sound of the monstrous intonations. At the same time he became aware of a foul alien stench. Scrambling shakily to his feet, he saw that many of the Roman soldiers had broken through the corpse-line and were now fleeing downhill in terror; others were being dragged down shrieking by their undead foes. Upon the hilltop he beheld the white form of Elissa struggling madly upon the altar before the glowing shapes of the Ark and the Eidolon, while before her stood Maxentius, the blue disc glowing upon his brow; he was still surrounded by his luminous shield of force yet staring southward with an expression of horror on his face. Then Simon felt the ground faintly tremble as if to the tread of a monstrous invisible being—saw a swath of grass and shrubbery inexorably advancing toward the altar....

Gripping his sword determinedly, the Samaritan forced himself up the slope, only to find that much of his strength had fled. The effects of the *krax* were rapidly wearing off and a great fatigue was descending upon him, making his limbs seem heavy as lead and his uphill progress like that of a man running in a pool of water. He cursed through gritted teeth, knowing that he could never get to Elissa in time nor be able to pierce his enemy's force shield if he did, let alone stave off the monstrous invisible Thing that was bearing down on them both....

Suddenly he saw a dark, circular object dart across the livid sky and recognized it as the wizard Taggart's supernatural craft. He saw the silhouettes of two men within in—the slender form of Taggart himself, hunched over the controls, and the squat body and pointed ears of the venerable Daramos. The latter held a bowl in his stubby paws. As the craft sped directly over the altar, Daramos tilted the bowl and poured forth a trail of white dust that slowly drifted earthward, expanding and thinning as it did so. And then, as the dust settled like a pale mist over and about the area of the altar, Simon saw a *shape* slowly and dimly becoming visible within it.

"IÄ! ABBA YOG-SOTHONI!"

Simon screamed and again fell to his knees as he beheld the Thing that was uttering those monstrous thunder-croakings. He had sensed that it was huge, but now he saw that it was vast beyond belief, greater in bulk than even the mansion of Annas. Its aspect was unutterably hideous—a churning oblate mass resembling the tentacles of octopi and the articulated legs of spiders. Dozens of great dark eyes leered and glowered on stubby stalks protruding from its sides, and its monstrous bulk was borne along upon dozens of thick, caterpillar-like legs as it bore down on the altar. But worst of all, and the thing that almost shook Simon's sanity to its foundations, was the sight of the partial *face* atop the mountainous abomination—the half-human, half-goatish features that adorned its limpet-cone of a head and writhed in an expression of hate and fury.

Then, mercifully, the dust cloud dissipated and the vision was gone. Yet Maxentius, Simon noted, continued to stand as if frozen in terror, eyes bulging and glaring in the Thing's direction *as if he could yet see it.*

The wizard craft curved back and swept down in a graceful arc nearly to the ground, pausing directly beside the altar. Simon saw Daramos deftly grip Elissa in his short but powerful arms and lift her onboard, and immediately the sky craft was again underway; he saw a blue-white glare of power lance from Taggart's death-wand, glimpsed great writhing tentacles and groping spider-appendages briefly outlined in fire—and then the craft was arcing above him and wheeling up into the sky, hurtling away in the direction of Annas' villa.

Maxentius screamed in mad terror. Simon turned, saw the slimy swath of the invisible monstrosity surge over the Roman—and then the man's screams ceased as if abruptly smothered. The tribune, his features still working in soundless terror, rose slowly just above the hilltop inside his blue shield of energy, like a bubble trapped in viscous fluid, and in that moment Simon realized that his hated enemy had been *swallowed,* force-shield and all, by the gargantuan invisible abomination from Tartarus!

Lightnings flashed. Thunder growled from the skies, and the titanic being that had engulfed Maxentius bellowed thunderously in answer. Simon leaped up, turned and fled in terror down the slope, saw as he did so that the surviving legionaries were far ahead of him and dashing frantically toward Jerusalem. The walking corpses that had not been hacked to bits were continuing their shambling advance up the hillside, some with mere stumps of limbs or great abdominal gashes from which guts trailed, but none of them paid Simon any heed. Then more lightnings flashed and he saw that the bolts were lancing down into the city, dozens of them—no, scores! The sound of thunder was nearly continuous now, a horrendous deafening din, and upon glancing upward Simon saw that the lightnings were crackling forth in waves from the heart of the expanding and swirling sky disc. From atop the Mount of Offense he could hear, even above the cataract of thunders, the voice of the invisible monstrosity bellowing:

"Eh-ya-ya-yahaah—e'yayayaaaa . . . ngh'aaaa . . . ngh'aaa . . . ABBA! ABBA! YOG-SOTHONI!"

Then a single great lightning bolt shot forth from the sky disc, down the throbbing pillar of light to the Altar of Solomon, shaking the very earth as it struck the Greater Son. Simon was swept from his feet, then half deafened by the cataclysmic peal of thunder that immediately followed. Staggering up, he was again bowled over by a shock wave of humid, foul air that rolled down upon him like an invisible tidal wave. For a few moments he writhed on the ground, choking and gasping while he clutched and clung to bushes for dear life. . . .

Then the foul wave passed and Simon stood up shakily. The air still thundered steadily as dozens of lightning bolts continued to crash down into Jerusalem from the sky disc, while toward that monstrous Gate there now poured upward from the summit of the Mount of Offense a gigantic, skyward-dwindling cloud of churning vapors. As it roiled majestically heavenward like an invert tornado Simon thought he could glimpse a tiny bubble of bluish light caught high up within it—a bubble containing a diminutive and diminishing human figure—and for an instant he even seemed to hear a vanishing scream of terror as the tiny blue sphere receded from sight. Then he turned away, unable to bear any longer the glare of those churning blue-white globes of light beyond the tornado's apex, fearful that at any moment they might burst forth from the Gate with the scorching, destroying radiance of a thousand suns. And in that instant there came to him a memory—or, was it a Voice from the sky, half-audible amid the thunders?—the words of a passage concerning the Great Goddess from the ancient Persian text of Ostanes:

I am become Kali, Mistress of Doom, the destroyer of worlds. . . .

Then, to his great relief, the sky disc began to very slowly dim and fade as the upward-spiraling pillar of thundering cloud thinned and finally vanished into it. The lightnings dwindled; the thunders waned and eventually ceased. Simon saw a few of the living dead lurching away down the slope, fleeing awkwardly southwestward toward the Valley of Hinnom; the rest lay hacked, burned and blasted among the carcases of the Roman legionaries.

Simon staggered back up the slope a few paces, retrieved the sword of Cratos and sheathed it, then began to walk wearily and painfully northward toward the villa of Annas.

"It is done, friend Taggart," said Daramos, looking back at the rapidly vanishing pillar of whirling cloud. "See, already the Gate is beginning to dim and dwindle in the sky. The world has been spared a great devastation. But now, we must return to the clearing in the grove behind the mansion of Annas." He turned to Elissa who, eyeing the dwarf and the black-clad wizard with obvious fear, was cringing away from them as far as her bound limbs would allow. "My Lady, you are now safe and your persecutor has perished most terribly. I shall now release you—"

"Be careful, Daramos," said Taggart as he manipulated the controls of his sky craft. "I'm sure she's scared out of her wits. Don't let her jump over the side."

But Elissa, looking into the dwarf's large almond eyes, felt her fear subsiding. Despite her uncanny situation and the strangeness of the two beings in whose power she now found herself, she somehow knew that she was indeed safe, as the dwarf had said. There was something about his face, grotesquely flattened and alien though it was, that made it impossible for her to distrust him—a strangely commingled humor and sadness that yet suggested a deep inner calm and vast wisdom. She felt him working at the cords that bound her, and so supple and sure were his stubby fingers that in seconds she found herself free.

Trembling, she sat up, then weakly rose to her knees and peered over the rim of the craft. The sight of treetops fleeting past just *below* her brought back a surge of fear.

"Don't worry," said Taggart in Latin. "We'll be on the ground in a few seconds more. . . . There."

The craft quickly dropped down within a large clearing surrounded by trees on three sides and bordered to the north by the pillared portico of a mansion, which Elissa recognized as that of Annas. As it came to rest just above the ground the dwarf suddenly leaped over the side.

"Daramos!" Taggart called out. "Where are you going?"

Without replying the dwarf hurried off toward a small stone cube of a hut that stood within the clearing. In the stark light of the dwindling Gate which still illumined all the landscape Elissa could see a large white dove standing just in front of the hut. It appeared to be thrusting its beak underneath the stout wood door. In the next moment it withdrew and flapped upward into the nearest tree—and then from the hut came the sound like a whistle being blown, high, thin and eerie.

Daramos halted, turned and ran back to the craft as fast as his short legs would carry him. "Too late, friend Taggart," he said as he clambered in. "The imprisoned wizard has summoned the *Byakhim!*"

Elissa, wondering what new dangers might be impending, suddenly heard a cracked, high-pitched voice shouting wildly behind the door of the hut. It seemed to be intoning a strange, alien-tongued chant:

"Iä! Iä! Assatur! Assatur cf'ayak 'vulgtmm, vugtlagln, vulgtmm! Ai! Ai! Assatur!"

Then from the direction of the dwindling sky Gate there came a sound as of great wings beating the air. These sounds rapidly grew louder, as though great invisible beings were winging down from the skies, and presently gusts of wind began to agitate the trees and cause the grasses to stir. Taggart looked up tensely, then touched a glowing square on the panel before him. Instantly the transparent blue force shield sprang into being about the craft.

The gusts grew ever more intense, kicking up swirling billows of dust from the clearing, and Elissa gasped as she realized that they came in rhythm with those monstrous wingbeats. Invisible demons of great size were evidently hovering over the clearing, descending into it. . . .

The stone hut began to tremble, to crack along its base—and then, incredibly, it was slowly lifted off its base and into the air. For a few moments it drifted off southward, accompanied by the diminishing sound of the monstrous wingbeats, and vanished beyond the black silhouettes of the treetops. After another moment came a sound of splintering branches and a thunderous crash that caused the ground to tremble slightly. Evidently the hut had been released by the winged demons to drop into the grove!

A tall, dark-robed man stepped over the foundation of the hut that had been his prison and advanced toward the sky craft. His hair and long beard were white under the stark glare from the Gate, which had now dwindled again to the size of a great blazing star, and Elissa recognized with amazement the tall form of old Yosef of Aphairema. Yet there was something different about him now—a fierceness of expression, a glare almost of madness in his eyes. In his right hand he held the slim golden chalice, in his left a small bronze tube..

"He has drunk of the Golden Nectar," said Daramos softly. "Look at his eyes—they see things that ours cannot."

"Watch him." Taggart fingered the bulky weapon holstered on his right hip. "If he tries to send the *Byakhim* against us, I'll. . . ."

But the old sorcerer, thrusting the chalice and the demon-whistle into a pocket within his robes, strode forward a few paces, scowling fiercely, then halted and pointed one lean, bony finger accusingly toward Taggart.

"A curse upon you, Adversary of Mankind!" he intoned in a loud voice that trembled with anger. "O faithless one who did once serve our great cause, but who has now turned traitor, a curse be upon you! For you have saved your own life at the cost of untold future sufferings. My Master would have rid this world of all pain and fear, but because of you it will now know untold centuries; perhaps even countless millennia, of future tortures and terrors. Think well on this, O accursed Adversary, as you journey forth from this world to range the star-ways and the aeons, for you know well that what I say is true. Because of you mankind shall continue to wax in pain and fear upon this world, swelling in numbers, increasing in greed, festering like a plague down the generations, waging ever greater wars, dealing to one another endless sufferings and dreadful dooms!"

"Yosef—" Elissa thought she detected a contrite note in Taggart's voice. "Yosef, I chose *life*. Is that so—?"

"Enough, serpent! Speak no more to me. I go now, to aid in preserving the Master's seed upon this world, that when the stars again come right many generations from now the Gate may again be opened. *"Iä! Iä! Assatur fhtagn . . .!"*

The sound of great wingbeats again grew louder and billows of dust blew up from the ground. Taggart watched the old sorcerer closely, again fingering his holster. Old Yosef turned his back to the craft, strode away a few paces into the billowing dust, then suddenly sprang up a foot or two off the ground—and, amazingly, did not fall back. Elissa gasped to see the venerable sorcerer scrambling grotesquely in mid-air, as if struggling to mount an invisible steed!

Daramos raised his glyph-inscribed bowl, whose bottom was lined with a thin residue of white powder, and blew into it in the direction of the scrambling sorcerer. A cloud of fine white dust puffed forth to hang briefly in the air—and Elissa screamed aloud. For in the brief time before that haze of powder settled she saw that old Yosef was mounting one of four enormous, black, bat-winged monstrosities whose mighty churning pinions were the cause of all the whipping winds. In another moment the sorcerer bestrode the thing's back and it was carrying him into the sky, followed by the other three and the frantically flapping white dove. Then the powder dissipated and settled, and Elissa could see only the dark-robed form of old Yosef receding swiftly away into the northern sky. For a moment she heard him calling out loudly, madly:

"Iä! Iä! Assatur!"

—And then he was gone.

"You did not blast him to ashes, friend Taggart," observed Daramos blandly after a long silence.

"I could not." The black-clad wizard frowned in somber thought. "He was right, you know. Everything he said to me was true. Perhaps I have acted wrongly in my selfishness."

Daramos smiled wisely; the crinkles at the outer corners of his almond eyes deepened. "Right or wrong, we are all here talking to one another because of your actions. Because of you, friend Taggart, all upon this world have a future to face, a new chance to play this game of life, which the Goddess has devised, and perhaps discover those roles which most please Her."

Elissa, only half comprehending this strange dialogue, suddenly glimpsed movement at the south end of the clearing. A man had just emerged from the grove—a tall, dark-haired man with a great sword hanging sheathed at his hip. He staggered in his step, his dark tunic hung half in rags and his flesh was mottled with bruises and spotted with small, dark wounds.

"Simon!"

"So it is!" Taggart punched a glowing square and the force shield vanished from about the craft. "He's evidently been through quite an ordeal."

Elissa leaped over the rim and ran across the clearing, threw herself into the man's arms and clung to him. "Simon! Simon!"

"Thank the gods you're safe, Elissa!" he gasped, weakly returning her embrace. "I thought we were both doomed. . . . Lord of Gerizim! Such a chain of mad perils we've been through this night—or is it day . . .? And just now, as I was coming through this grove, something nearly dropped a house on me—"

Abruptly his eyes closed and he went limp in her arms.

"Simon!" She eased his dead weight to the grass as gently as she could. "Simon, please don't die!"

She sensed Taggart and Daramos at her side, bending over the man. The dwarf laid a hand on one of Simon's arms, then nodded confidently. "He will live, but he is completely exhausted."

Taggart carefully lifted one of the man's eyelids. "It looks like it's partly due to a krax reaction. Menander must have given him the entire pill. I can fix him up fairly quickly, but he'll certainly need a long rest."

"There are many bedchambers in the upper story of the mansion," said Daramos, "and the place is quite deserted."

Taggart nodded. "Good. Here, help me get him into the craft, then we'll take him up to the roof and carry him down inside. . . ."

Menander woke from a light doze and, seeing the first pale gleam of day silhouetting the battlements of the distant city, rose to his feet. Shivering slightly in the cool air, he pulled his white Levite's robe more closely about him, then crept forth from the clump of boulders amid which had been hiding and began to stride eastward toward the grove of tombs.

He had left that grove the night before, afraid to stay there after Taggart's departure. From his hiding place he had seen the unnatural star expand to a whirling radiant disc, had heard the sounds of alien drums and flutes increasing menacingly, had then heard monstrous intonations thundering from the Mount of Offense beyond the city, and subsequently had witnessed the titanic barrage of lightning bolts emerging from the disc to blast the city itself. Immediately afterward he had seen the hellish tornado-cone spiraling upward into the heavens, the shrinking of the sky disc and, after all these appalling events, the slow fading of the star as it westered in the constellation of the Great Dragon. After that, night had returned and he had endured several hours of darkness and dread. Now, as he hurried toward the tombs in the gray dawnlight, Menander anxiously wondered if that titanic cataract of lightnings had left anyone alive in Jerusalem.

He entered the grove and passed through it cautiously, eyeing every tomb and tree-trunk with apprehension, but no sign did he see of any of those hideous living dead he had encountered the day before . . . or was it two days? Surely it seemed that long or longer—for, had not the night been divided by an eerie and terrifying day, and the previous day by an equally unnatural night . . .?

Then he came to the tomb of the rabbi Yeshua and found, to his surprise, that the great stone disc that had sealed it was now lying flat on the ground. Evidently the tremor of the previous star-illumined "day" had caused it to fall away. Menander ran forward and, peering into the blackness of the tomb, called out softly:

"Carbo! Are you there?"

There was, of course, no answer, and immediately Menander felt foolish. *How can he reply without the use of a tongue or throat?* The lad crept inside and, when his eyes had adjusted to the dim gray light, began to search the small chamber. He was rather surprised, despite what Taggart and Daramos had told him concerning the physical dissolution of an Outside One after death, that there was no trace of the original Rabbi Yeshua save the crumpled grave-cloths and a thin whitish crust of dried residue upon the slab and floor.

In a few moments he realized that there was no trace of Carbo either. Sighing, he sat down upon the stone ledge and mused wearily with elbows on knees, chin cupped in his hands. Taggart must have been right—Carbo had gotten out through the tiny crack behind the stone disc. But where could he have gone? Could he had lived long on this world, so alien to him, without finding some other host to dwell within? Had he entered into some animal or bird, or perhaps even another human being? Or had he perished during that mad midnight cataclysm of lightning and thunder?

Menander felt a deep sadness settle over him. He muttered to himself, chokingly, "Carbo, Carbo! Oh, how can I find you? How can I let you know that I am here, searching for you? How --?"

"That is very easy," said a strange yet familiar voice within his right ear.

"Carbo!" Menander sat bolt upright. "You . . . you're *here?"*

"Exactly as 'here' as you are."

"But how . . . when . . .?"

"I spent the night within the inner bark of that big terebinth tree just outside," said Carbo. "At first light I put forth a few eyelets—anyone would have thought they were mere dewdrops—and before long I saw you coming. While you sat here I emerged from the tree and again availed myself of your hospitality."

"You certainly are subtle about it, Carbo! I didn't feel a thing. Oh, I'm so glad to have you back! I was so worried—when I heard the whine of the old sorcerer Yosef's magic device, I knew you'd been expelled from the rabbi's body. I'd hug you, old friend, if you were outside me rather than within. I have so much to tell you—"

"Wait!" cautioned the voice. "I hear something outside."

The hearing in Menander's right ear grew more acute and then he, too, heard it—footsteps approaching on the path. There followed expressions of surprise from the throats of at least two women. Many hurrying footfalls then sounded, and in the next moment the lad saw that a beautiful dark-haired woman was peering in at the tomb's entrance, her face pale in the dawn's gray light. It was the Lady Miriam, a deep sadness in her eyes, and in that moment Menander's heart went out to her.

"Oh, look!" she cried. "Look Mother—Nicodemus! There is someone sitting inside the tomb—"

Several more persons, most of them women, crowded up close behind her to peer within. Among them Menander recognized the old albino woman, the dumpy innkeeper Martha, the graybeard Nicodemus and Yosef's young apprentice Zethos. He stood up and said to them:

"Don't be surprised. You came here to pay last respects to your teacher Yeshua the Nazarene, I am sure, but you will not find him here among the dead, for he is alive."

"Impossible!" exclaimed Zethos. "In this very spot I saw—" Abruptly he ceased speaking and looked uneasy, as if feeling that he had said too much.

Miriam's face brightened as if with new hope. "Zethos told me it would be futile for me to come here to pay my last respects. Tell me, young man: Was my Lord and Master, the rabbi Yeshua, laid in this tomb or not?"

"He was, My Lady," said Menander, "but as you can see, he is not here now. I saw him alive not long ago in this very grove. He said that he was setting out on the road to Galilee."

The woman's voice became radiant with joy. "You saw him! You spoke with him! Oh, young man, how wonderful you are!" She turned to those with her, her dark eyes tearful yet alight with excitement and happiness. "Did you hear, O Mother? Did you hear, Zethos? Out Master is alive!"

"It's . . . not possible," muttered Zethos.

"Yet it's true—I know it! Come, we must hurry on toward Aphairema and overtake our Master on the road." She turned and walked away from the tomb, calling out to two of her servants, "Joel—Reuben—go find as many of the Master's followers as you can. Tell them that he lives and that they are to follow us on the road to Aphairema and Galilee. Hurry!"

In a few moments more the group, save for the two servants who had been sent on their errand, had left the grove and were proceeding northward toward the road to Aphairema. Menander stood at the edge of the cemetery and watched them go, hoping for a last glance or gesture from the Lady Miriam—but only Zethos and the dumpy Martha turned to cast back at him brief scowls of suspicion and disapproval.

"No doubt those two recognized me from last night, Carbo," muttered the youth as the group vanished away in the distance. "Well, it doesn't matter. Let's go on now to Bethany and see if we can rejoin Dositheus and the Thirty there."

As he set out he felt glad in his heart that he had been able to bring joy to the beautiful Lady Miriam, who reminded him so strangely of Lotis. Then a sadness again settled upon him as he recalled Taggart's warning that the rabbi Yeshua, her beloved Lord and Master, could live but a few more brief weeks at most before his second doom overtook him.

Proceeding northeast, he came upon the Bethany road and followed it eastward. Here he noticed that crowds were streaming forth from every gate in the city's north wall, cramming the roads as they fled with their animals laden with possessions. All during the dark hours they had huddled within Jerusalem's walls, trembling in terror that the lightnings might begin again. Now, with the dawn, they were deserting the accursed city for the safety of the villages and the hills.

Once past the northern wall, Menander found that he no longer had to fight the press, for all the mob on that part of the road was streaming eastward. To his right he could see all down the length of the now-deserted Kidron Valley, whose expanse was thickly dotted with hundreds of sagging and collapsed tents, whose owners had fled during the night. There were not even the usual looters among all those abandoned possessions. Menander saw terror in the faces of all those about him. He heard occasional shouted prayers and curses, but for the most part the people fled in silence. Forgotten were all thoughts of the Passover festival, for the memories of the pilgrims were seared with the vision of an Eye of Doom blazing in the sky and sending forth lightning-blasts of destruction.

At the crossroad that led south to Gethsemene Menander spied a group that had turned aside to rest a short distance away—a unique contrast to the hurrying and fearful crowds that streamed eastward. Suddenly he recognized the tall, slightly bent form of old Dositheus. Shouting with joy, he turned aside and ran to join the group which he now recognized as the Thirty. His joy increased as he saw the slender form of Lotis among them.

"Oh, Lotis!" he exclaimed breathlessly as they embraced. "I saw the lightnings come crashing down into the city, and I was so afraid for you—"

"We were frightened, too, Menander. But now, it appears that the rabbi Samezer's synagogue may have been the only one in Jerusalem that was not blasted down to ruin last night."

"It is true," said the little rabbi, "and surely it is because we alone were performing the rites of Yhtill, the White Goddess. In all other synagogues the Feast of the Slain Lamb was in progress, and for this dire affront to Her Consort the Goddess has smitten them all with her vengeful lightnings."

"Perhaps so," said Menander. "But tell me: Why do all of you linger here?"

"We were watching the road in hopes of seeing you or Simon in the crowd," said the gray-bearded Isagoras.

"Also," added Dositheus, "Lotis feels that her mistress Elissa has been again captured and taken to the mansion of Annas." His eyes sparked grimly as he tightly gripped his long oak staff. "I have been advocating that we go there now with all haste, for Elissa of Sychar is too fine a woman to perish at the hands of that vulture-priest Annas or that jackal-tribune Maxentius."

Isagoras glanced at Dositheus sharply. "Yes, she's indeed a lady to be admired. Very well, let us go there immediately. Parmenion, you and two others of your choice shall stay here and continue to watch for Simon."

The group proceeded southward on the Gethsemene road, presently passing the east wall of the Garden on their right. Beyond this point the ridge making up the Mount of Olives sloped off a bit more steeply on either hand. Menander marveled at how utterly deserted was this road while, far behind them, the teeming crowds of fleeing pilgrims continued to choke the road to Bethany and Jericho.

It was not yet midmorning when they came in sight of the northernmost wall surrounding the grounds of Annas' estate. Isagoras called the group to a halt and said uneasily, "Friends, we should go on from here with extreme caution, for we are not equipped to openly fight Roman legionaries or Temple guards."

"Or demons," added Samezer. "Who can say what sorceries Annas may have performed in order to protect this place?"

"Go cautiously among the trees, then," said Dositheus. "Menander and I shall scout ahead, for we have been trained in the arts of stealth by the great mage Daramos himself."

The plan was adopted, and soon the young Samaritan and his old mentor were stealing rapidly through the shrubbery toward the wall, keeping just far enough from the road to escape detection by watching eyes. Upon nearing the main gate, however, they were surprised to find that it stood wide open and that there were no guards anywhere in sight.

Then they were doubly surprised to find that Lotis was accompanying them. Despite Dositheus' boast concerning their stealth, she had evidently followed them through the trees and shrubbery unseen.

"Menander," she whispered, a touch of reproof in her voice, "you have fled from me into danger too many times, leaving me to wonder and worry about you. This time I am coming along." She glanced toward the open archway in the wall. "Do you see any Romans or priests?"

"No. But, Lotis, you shouldn't have—"

"Silence!" hissed Dositheus tensely. "Keep down. Someone is coming out—a man in black, and. . . ."

Menander gripped Lotis' arm, pulled her down with him. For a long minute they lay still, hearts beating, listening to footsteps that drew closer and closer to their hiding place. Then the footsteps stopped and a deep, familiar voice said:

"You may come out of hiding, my friends. There is no danger here."

"Daramos!" Menander stood up. "Look, Lotis, it's my mentor Daramos, the wise old mage I told you of—and there's the wizard Taggart with him! Come —don't be afraid."

He took her hand and led her out of the thicket onto the road. Dositheus followed them closely.

"Greeting, O Mentor," said the old Samaritan, bowing slightly to the brown-robed dwarf, "—and to you also, Taggart the Wizard. It is good to find friends here rather than the foes we anticipated."

Taggart nodded in acknowledgment, then turned to Daramos. "You were right, old friend. Here they are. But how in the galaxy did you know it?"

"I can often sense the approach of friends or enemies. Come, Dositheus—enter. There are no foes here. Menander, I see that this young woman is she whose True Spirit complements your own."

"Her name is Lotis," said Dositheus hastily, "and she is very concerned about her mistress, Elissa of Sychar, whom she believes to have been brought here by Roman captors. Is the woman indeed in this house?"

Daramos beamed so widely that his eyes became mere crinkle-cornered slits and his head seemed even flatter than usual. "She is, friend Dositheus, and you do well to be concerned for her, for she is a True Spirit indeed—though as yet she does not know it in full consciousness."

"Oh, thank the Lord of Gerizim!" said Lotis. Then, hesitantly, "But what of Simon, O venerable Daramos—?"

It was Taggart who answered. "He's here, too, Lotis. Both he and your mistress have been through quite an ordeal, but they are going to be all right."

Lotis caught the meaning of the wizard's carefully-enunciated Latin in spite of her lack of familiarity with the language, sensed that it had something to do with the blue-glowing disc upon his forehead. "Oh, thank all the gods!" she cried, then turned to Menander and held him close, sobbing with relief.

EPILOGUE

The Thirty—all fifteen or so of them—spent the rest of the day in the spacious and sumptuous mansion of Annas, gratefully assuaging their hunger from its plenteous food stores and resting from their recent exertions and anxieties.

The Kidron Valley and the Mount of Olives remained utterly deserted all day long. Not a soul emerged from any of Jerusalem's eastern gates, though distant multitudes could be continually seen streaming away from the city toward the north and the west. Once a large gang of armed bandits came up the slope from the arid eastward ravines, hoping to plunder the mansion in the confusion; but the pilotless sky craft of Taggart, set to patrol the periphery of the villa's grounds, detected them by means of its unhuman intelligence and blasted the majority of them to ashes. The survivors, fleeing in terror, spread such tales among the multitudes that for many days no man dared to approach the demon-warded mansion and the nearby Mount of Offense.

Dositheus, especially, found himself in what he considered a veritable treasure-store, spending long hours in Annas' magic-room, perusing many of the ancient scrolls the old sorcerer had collected. The *El-Halal* of the olden Canaanite priest Mattan he considered an especially valuable find. In the end he gathered together several of the rarest scrolls and bundled them into a saddlebag, together with vials and jars of various fluids and powders, including those necessary to concoct the powder of Ben Ghazi by means of which invisible beings might be seen. Daramos watched him with calm amusement.

"Have a care how you use those things, friend Dositheus," cautioned the dwarfish mage. "Have I not often instructed you that thievery adversely affects the psyche, and that the state of the psyche may in turn affect the outcome of the rites one performs?"

"Thievery?" said Dositheus indignantly. "You mistake my intent, venerable Daramos. I take these things in order to benefit humankind. Better that I should be burdened with the possession of them than that they should remain in the hands of such an evil sorcerer as Annas."

So saying, he turned and left the chamber, somewhat irritated by the dwarfish mage's wide grin, yet not neglecting to take with him his packsack full of arcane loot.

In one of the corridors he was pleased to encounter his stately countrywoman Elissa of Sychar, now garbed most becomingly in a demure blue-dyed gown and a maroon robe trimmed with saffron, both taken from one of Annas' lavish wardrobes. Yet he also immediately noticed that her large dark eyes were wet with tears.

"Is anything the matter, My Lady?" he asked respectfully.

"No. . . ." she said hesitantly. Then, seeing the genuine concern in his eyes, she blurted out, "Oh, venerable Dositheus! It's Simon—"

Dositheus felt a chill. "Is he well? I saw him not long ago—he seemed to be sleeping peacefully."

"He is well. He awoke half an hour ago, and we talked. I told him that my home in Sychar would henceforth be his if he wished; moreover, that I would purchase the house of his parents and restore it to him because of all the evil Maxentius did to him and his family. But he . . . he said. . . ."

"He refused your offer," said Dositheus quietly.

"Yes." Elissa choked back a sob. "Oh, Venerable One!—he told me that he can never more live at ease in houses—that he must henceforth roam the world, fighting the Romans until their evil empire no longer plagues all the nations. He is mad, Dositheus, and I fear he will perish in his madness."

The old Samaritan nodded somberly. "I have known Simon for many years, Elissa, and he has always spoken so. All his enemies here in Judea and Samaria have now perished—his chief enemy, Maxentius, perhaps more horribly than any human ever perished before, judging from what Daramos has told me—yet Simon's wounds run very deep. He must pursue his own destiny if he is ever to find peace one day. You will only harm yourself if you do not let him go."

"I feel that you speak truth, Venerable One. And yet—"

"Please, call me 'Venerable One' no more, My Lady. My name is Dositheus, and I would be your friend. If rumor is to be believed, all of your five former husbands were almost as mature as I, though obviously not as hale and hearty. Did you address each of them as 'Venerable One'?"

Elissa frowned and stepped back a pace; but then, seeing the twinkle in Dositheus' eyes, here indignation dissolved and she laughed aloud.

"You are indeed a friend, Dositheus," she exclaimed, "for you have broken through my sorrow and scattered it with one blow!" Then, more thoughtfully, "I know that you are right, friend and comforter. Simon is not for me, no matter how much I feel drawn to him, for always he has seemed drawn to the memory of a woman who is now dead. More, I sensed that he saw something of this dead woman in the woman Miriam, wife of the rabbi Yeshua. . . ."

"He sensed the Goddess in her, even as he sensed it in his lost Helen," said Dositheus. "Yet the Goddess takes many forms, and had Simon attained to my level of perception he would have seen in you an even greater manifestation of Her. You have not yet come to a full awareness of your inmost Being, My Lady, and yet you have heretofore displayed a sure and sound instinct in that you have always selected mature husbands rather than callow ones. True, your choice of Maxentius for a lover was a great lapse in judgment, but I am sure that these recent dire perils have cured you of such lapses forever. To insure that, however, I pledge to be to you a friend, always ready and available to give counsel; for I am now the leader of the mystical order of the Thirty, dedicated to serving the Goddess, and our holy gathering place in Aenon is not all that far from Sychar, you know."

Elissa laughed heartily. "You are a great rogue, Dositheus, yet I think I like you all the more for that, for you have scattered my sorrow as surely as the morning breeze scatters the mists. Even the Goddess must value a friendship such as you offer, and who am I to refuse to humor a . . . a mature man who fancies me to be one of Her incarnations?"

Dositheus bowed slightly, lifted her hand and kissed it, then gazed up into her eyes with an unsettling expression of mingled humor and reverence.

Simon, emerging onto the roof of the mansion, saw that it was now late afternoon. Daramos and Taggart were standing beside the wizard's sky craft, while near them clustered a small group that included Menander, Lotis, Isagoras and several other members of the Thirty. Upon the wizard's brow glowed one of the bluish thought-discs. Simon strode forward and joined the gathering.

"How are you, friend, Simon?" said Daramos.

"Tired, but otherwise I feel a new man. You have great medical skills, O Mentor. I see that even my worst wounds are almost completely healed."

"Give friend Taggart the credit for that," said Daramos.

"No, Daramos," said Taggart. "The credit, Simon, goes to our friend Balaam. I let him give you a thorough internal cleansing and healing while you slept. After all, one good turn deserves another."

"What!" Simon involuntarily felt of his chest with both hands. "You mean, he's inside—?"

"No, no." Taggart smiled slightly. "He's back with me. I have promised him that when I leave this planet with the Galactics he will be returned to his own world of the Six Suns." The wizard turned to Menander. "Your friend Carbo is welcome to come, too, if he wishes."

Simon saw the lad stiffen, a worried look on his face. Then, he seemed to be pondering or . . . listening? Finally he smiled, apparently relieved, and answered, "Carbo has heard all, O Wizard. He thanks you but says he prefers to stay here with me. But must you really leave this world?"

"Yes. But first, I must return Daramos to Persepolis. Also there is the problem of what to do about *those.*"

Simon looked southward toward where the wizard was pointing, saw the altar atop the distant Mount of Offense. Upon it, gleaming in the light of the westering sun, stood two objects—the Ark and the Eidolon. Incredibly, neither the great lightning-blast that had destroyed the monstrous being that had engulfed Maxentius, nor the vortex that swallowed him, had disturbed those two sinister objects at all. Whether the rescue of Elissa by Daramos, or the interruption of the ritual by Taggart, or the ineptness of Maxentius in completing the ritual, was the cause of the lightning bolt that struck the Greater Son, Simon could not say

"They must again be hidden away from mankind," Taggart went on, "for any tampering with them could initiate any number of disasters."

"Shouldn't they be destroyed, then?" said Simon.

The wizard shook his head. "The beings who designed the things took care to prevent that. Any attempt to destroy them, or even remove them from this planet, would automatically induce . . . defensive measures . . . on their part. They were made to aid in the opening of the Gate at the auspicious times, and those who anciently sealed them up within the earth were dealing with them in the only way they could."

Isagoras spoke up, "I know a priest in Egypt who has charge of all the ancient tombs and temples near Avaris. Take me there, O Taggart, and I will see to it that the Ark and the Eidolon are hidden away in secret underground chambers where no man will ever again find them."

Taggart nodded. "Good, Isagoras. Come—we'll go immediately."

"I ask to go with you also, dark wizard," said Simon, "for my task here is accomplished and I would wander. My enemies have all perished, some by dooms even more terrible than those I had hoped for them, yet my heart is a void and my ache for vengeance remains. The evil empire of Rome abides still, daily crucifying multitudes of men like the defiant Gestas and the good and pious Dysmas—yet how can I hope to slay all Romans who deserve slaying? Perhaps, Isagoras, your priest friend can direct me to a quiet temple in Egypt where I may withdraw from the world and study as an acolyte, learning to calm my soul rather than acquiring further skills to aid me in vengeance. At any rate, I wish to leave these accursed lands of Judea and Samaria, so full of dark memories for me, and where Karakossan demons still lurk and wait amid the tombs."

Menander and Lotis both rushed up to him, tears in their eyes. "We will go with you, Simon," Menander cried.

"No, good friends. I must go alone, and you must go with Dositheus and the Thirty and the Lady Elissa. That is the best way."

Both of them felt the finality of Simon's announcement and embraced him sadly.

"And where will *you* go, then, O Taggart?" said Menander. "And when will you return?"

The man in black gazed eastward, out over the brown ridges and ravines. "First back to the Galactic sky craft," he said, "then out to the stars and beyond. When or whether I shall ever return to this planet, or even to this particular time-stream, I do not know."

Daramos blinked slowly, meditatively, then smiled. "Friend Taggart, you leave this world and this time-stream secure in their existence, thereby ensuring the foundation of your own existence as well. Yet you must know,

O star-wanderer, that above time itself there is a greater Time still, and that in its fullness all worlds and beings must dissolve back into Her who is without beginning or end."

"You are remarkable, old comrade," said Taggart, his eyes troubled. "Perhaps I have done the wrong thing out of fear of my own extinction. Perhaps Taaran and the rabbi Yeshua and old Yosef were right in feeling that the existence of this world does not justify the suffering it engenders."

"Yet now," said Daramos, "we of this world may each continue to decide this thing individually. Because of you, friend Taggart, all of us True Spirits who dwell upon this planet may continue to seek to serve the Goddess and thereby know Life."

"And yet," said Simon grimly, "the old sorcerer Yosef implied that someday the Goat-man would return to Earth in a new guise. Is there no way to protect future generations from his impending evil?"

"Evil?" Daramos again smiled, a trifle sadly it seemed. "Speak not so rashly, Simon, concerning things you do not yet understand."

"Still," said Lotis, "was he not, in a way, an enemy of the Goddess, the source of all life?"

"Aye, and of all mankind?" added Menandeer. "He had vast powers and mant to use them to destroy all of us. His father was not human, but an unearthly being from beyond the skies. Was not the Roman centurion right when he cried out that the man was surely the son of a god?"

"No." Again Taggart gazed thoughtfully eastward across the desolate ridges and ravines. "No. It is true that the rabbi was not entirely human, that there was in his heritage something monstrous and trans-stellar. Yet in another way he was more human and more humane than anyone else on this planet. Though he was the spawn of beings beyond all human understanding, yet he was born and grew up as a human upon this world, experiencing and knowing all human fears and sufferings. He possessed more-than-human powers, yet never did he use those powers to kill or injure any living thing, but only to comfort and heal. And though he plotted to obliterate all life on this planet, even that was out of kindness; and, to accomplish it, he allowed himself to undergo more suffering than any human is capable of experiencing."

Taggart shook his head somberly. "No, Menander. Whatever his origins, the rabbi Yeshua was more than a god or the son of a god. He was a good man."

LaVergne, TN USA
19 August 2009
155112LV00002B/1/P